William Wilkie Collins (8 January 1824 – 23 September 1889) was an English novelist, playwright, and short story writer, best known for The Woman in White (1859), No Name (1862), Armadale (1866) and The Moonstone (1868). The last has been called the first modern English detective novel. Born to the family of painter William Collins in London, he grew up in Italy and France, learning French and Italian. He began work as a clerk for a tea merchant. After his first novel, Antonina, appeared in 1850, he met Charles Dickens, who became a close friend and mentor. Some of Collins's works appeared first in Dickens's journals All the Year Round and Household Words and they collaborated on drama and fiction. Collins published his best known works in the 1860s, achieving financial stability and an international following. However, he began suffering from gout. Taking opium for the pain developed into an addiction. In the 1870s and 1880s the quality of his writing declined along with his health. Collins was critical of the institution of marriage: he split his time between Caroline Graves, except for a two-year separation, and his common-law wife Martha Rudd, with whom he had three children. (Source: Wikipedia)

Literary works:
Basil (1852)
Hide and Seek (1854)
The Dead Secret (1856)
The Frozen Deep (1857)
"A House to Let" (1858)
"The Haunted House"
The Woman in White (1860)
No Name (1862)
Armadale (1866)
No Thoroughfare (1867)
The Moonstone (1868)
Man and Wife (1870)
Poor Miss Finch (1872)
The Law and the Lady (1875)
The Fallen Leaves (1879)

THRONE CLASSICS

The New Magdalen
&
The Two Destinies
wilkie collins

First Printing: 2020

ISBN 978-93-90171-54-5 (paperback)

ISBN 978-93-90171-55-2 (Hardcover)

Published by Throne Classics

www.throneclassics.com

Contents

The New Magdalen
&
The Two Destinies

THE NEW MAGDALEN

FIRST SCENE.—The Cottage on the Frontier.

PREAMBLE.

THE place is France.

The time is autumn, in the year eighteen hundred and seventy—the year of the war between France and Germany.

The persons are, Captain Arnault, of the French army; Surgeon Surville, of the French ambulance; Surgeon Wetzel, of the German army; Mercy Merrick, attached as nurse to the French ambulance; and Grace Roseberry, a traveling lady on her way to England.

CHAPTER I. THE TWO WOMEN.

IT was a dark night. The rain was pouring in torrents.

Late in the evening a skirmishing party of the French and a skirmishing party of the Germans had met, by accident, near the little village of Lagrange, close to the German frontier. In the struggle that followed, the French had (for once) got the better of the enemy. For the time, at least, a few hundreds out of the host of the invaders had been forced back over the frontier. It was a trifling affair, occurring not long after the great German victory of Weissenbourg, and the newspapers took little or no notice of it.

Captain Arnault, commanding on the French side, sat alone in one of the cottages of the village, inhabited by the miller of the district. The Captain was reading, by the light of a solitary tallow-candle, some intercepted dispatches taken from the Germans. He had suffered the wood fire, scattered over the large open grate, to burn low; the red embers only faintly illuminated a part of the room. On the floor behind him lay some of the miller's empty sacks. In a corner opposite to him was the miller's solid walnut-wood bed. On the walls all around him were the miller's colored prints, representing a happy mixture of devotional and domestic subjects. A door of communication leading into the kitchen of the cottage had been torn from its hinges, and used to carry the men wounded in the skirmish from the field. They were now comfortably laid at rest in the kitchen, under the care of the French surgeon and the English nurse attached to the ambulance. A piece of coarse canvas screened the opening between the two rooms in place of the door. A second door, leading from the bed-chamber into the yard, was locked; and the wooden shutter protecting the one window of the room was carefully barred. Sentinels, doubled in number, were placed at all the outposts. The French commander had neglected no precaution which could reasonably insure for himself and for his men a quiet and comfortable night.

Still absorbed in his perusal of the dispatches, and now and then making notes of what he read by the help of writing materials placed at his side,

Captain Arnault was interrupted by the appearance of an intruder in the room. Surgeon Surville, entering from the kitchen, drew aside the canvas screen, and approached the little round table at which his superior officer was sitting.

"What is it?" said the captain, sharply.

"A question to ask," replied the surgeon. "Are we safe for the night?"

"Why do you want to know?" inquired the captain, suspiciously.

The surgeon pointed to the kitchen, now the hospital devoted to the wounded men.

"The poor fellows are anxious about the next few hours," he replied. "They dread a surprise, and they ask me if there is any reasonable hope of their having one night's rest. What do you think of the chances?"

The captain shrugged his shoulders. The surgeon persisted.

"Surely you ought to know?" he said.

"I know that we are in possession of the village for the present," retorted Captain Arnault, "and I know no more. Here are the papers of the enemy." He held them up and shook them impatiently as he spoke. "They give me no information that I can rely on. For all I can tell to the contrary, the main body of the Germans, outnumbering us ten to one, may be nearer this cottage than the main body of the French. Draw your own conclusions. I have nothing more to say."

Having answered in those discouraging terms, Captain Arnault got on his feet, drew the hood of his great-coat over his head, and lit a cigar at the candle.

"Where are you going?" asked the surgeon.

"To visit the outposts."

"Do you want this room for a little while?"

"Not for some hours to come. Are you thinking of moving any of your wounded men in here?"

"I was thinking of the English lady," answered the surgeon. "The kitchen is not quite the place for her. She would be more comfortable here; and the English nurse might keep her company."

Captain Arnault smiled, not very pleasantly. "They are two fine women," he said, "and Surgeon Surville is a ladies' man. Let them come in, if they are rash enough to trust themselves here with you." He checked himself on the point of going out, and looked back distrustfully at the lighted candle. "Caution the women," he said, "to limit the exercise of their curiosity to the inside of this room."

"What do you mean?"

The captain's forefinger pointed significantly to the closed window-shutter.

"Did you ever know a woman who could resist looking out of window?" he asked. "Dark as it is, sooner or later these ladies of yours will feel tempted to open that shutter. Tell them I don't want the light of the candle to betray my headquarters to the German scouts. How is the weather? Still raining?"

"Pouring."

"So much the better. The Germans won't see us." With that consolatory remark he unlocked the door leading into the yard, and walked out.

The surgeon lifted the canvas screen and called into the kitchen:

"Miss Merrick, have you time to take a little rest?"

"Plenty of time," answered a soft voice with an underlying melancholy in it, plainly distinguishable though it had only spoken three words.

"Come in, then," continued the surgeon, "and bring the English lady with you. Here is a quiet room all to yourselves."

He held back the canvas, and the two women appeared.

The nurse led the way—tall, lithe, graceful—attired in her uniform dress of neat black stuff, with plain linen collar and cuffs, and with the scarlet cross of the Geneva Convention embroidered on her left shoulder. Pale and sad, her expression and manner both eloquently suggestive of suppressed suffering and sorrow, there was an innate nobility in the carriage of this woman's head, an innate grandeur in the gaze of her large gray eyes and in the lines of her finely proportioned face, which made her irresistibly striking and beautiful, seen under any circumstances and clad in any dress. Her companion, darker in complexion and smaller in stature, possessed attractions which were quite marked enough to account for the surgeon's polite anxiety to shelter her in the captain's room. The common consent of mankind would have declared her to be an unusually pretty woman. She wore the large gray cloak that covered her from head to foot with a grace that lent its own attractions to a plain and even a shabby article of dress. The languor in her movements, and the uncertainty of tone in her voice as she thanked the surgeon suggested that she was suffering from fatigue. Her dark eyes searched the dimly-lighted room timidly, and she held fast by the nurse's arm with the air of a woman whose nerves had been severely shaken by some recent alarm.

"You have one thing to remember, ladies," said the surgeon. "Beware of opening the shutter, for fear of the light being seen through the window. For the rest, we are free to make ourselves as comfortable here as we can. Compose yourself, dear madam, and rely on the protection of a Frenchman who is devoted to you!" He gallantly emphasized his last words by raising the hand of the English lady to his lips. At the moment when he kissed it the canvas screen was again drawn aside. A person in the service of the ambulance appeared, announcing that a bandage had slipped, and that one of the wounded men was to all appearance bleeding to death. The surgeon, submitting to destiny with the worst possible grace, dropped the charming Englishwoman's hand, and returned to his duties in the kitchen. The two ladies were left together in the room.

"Will you take a chair, madam?" asked the nurse.

"Don't call me 'madam,'" returned the young lady, cordially. "My name is Grace Roseberry. What is your name?"

The nurse hesitated. "Not a pretty name, like yours," she said, and

15

hesitated again. "Call me 'Mercy Merrick,'" she added, after a moment's consideration.

Had she given an assumed name? Was there some unhappy celebrity attached to her own name? Miss Roseberry did not wait to ask herself these questions. "How can I thank you," she exclaimed, gratefully, "for your sisterly kindness to a stranger like me?"

"I have only done my duty," said Mercy Merrick, a little coldly. "Don't speak of it."

"I must speak of it. What a situation you found me in when the French soldiers had driven the Germans away! My traveling-carriage stopped; the horses seized; I myself in a strange country at nightfall, robbed of my money and my luggage, and drenched to the skin by the pouring rain! I am indebted to you for shelter in this place—I am wearing your clothes—I should have died of the fright and the exposure but for you. What return can I make for such services as these?"

Mercy placed a chair for her guest near the captain's table, and seated herself, at some little distance, on an old chest in a corner of the room. "May I ask you a question?" she said, abruptly.

"A hundred questions," cried Grace, "if you like." She looked at the expiring fire, and at the dimly visible figure of her companion seated in the obscurest corner of the room. "That wretched candle hardly gives any light," she said, impatiently. "It won't last much longer. Can't we make the place more cheerful? Come out of your corner. Call for more wood and more lights."

Mercy remained in her corner and shook her head. "Candles and wood are scarce things here," she answered. "We must be patient, even if we are left in the dark. Tell me," she went on, raising her quiet voice a little, "how came you to risk crossing the frontier in wartime?"

Grace's voice dropped when she answered the question. Grace's momentary gayety of manner suddenly left her.

"I had urgent reasons," she said, "for returning to England."

16

"Alone?" rejoined the other. "Without any one to protect you?"

Grace's head sank on her bosom. "I have left my only protector—my father—in the English burial-ground at Rome," she answered simply. "My mother died, years since, in Canada."

The shadowy figure of the nurse suddenly changed its position on the chest. She had started as the last word passed Miss Roseberry's lips.

"Do you know Canada?" asked Grace.

"Well," was the brief answer—reluctantly given, short as it was.

"Were you ever near Port Logan?"

"I once lived within a few miles of Port Logan."

"When?"

"Some time since." With those words Mercy Merrick shrank back into her corner and changed the subject. "Your relatives in England must be very anxious about you," she said.

Grace sighed. "I have no relatives in England. You can hardly imagine a person more friendless than I am. We went away from Canada, when my father's health failed, to try the climate of Italy, by the doctor's advice. His death has left me not only friendless but poor." She paused, and took a leather letter-case from the pocket of the large gray cloak which the nurse had lent to her. "My prospects in life," she resumed, "are all contained in this little case. Here is the one treasure I contrived to conceal when I was robbed of my other things."

Mercy could just see the letter-case as Grace held it up in the deepening obscurity of the room. "Have you got money in it?" she asked.

"No; only a few family papers, and a letter from my father, introducing me to an elderly lady in England—a connection of his by marriage, whom I have never seen. The lady has consented to receive me as her companion and reader. If I don't return to England soon, some other person may get the place."

"Have you no other resource?"

"None. My education has been neglected—we led a wild life in the far West. I am quite unfit to go out as a governess. I am absolutely dependent on this stranger, who receives me for my father's sake." She put the letter-case back in the pocket of her cloak, and ended her little narrative as unaffectedly as she had begun it. "Mine is a sad story, is it not?" she said.

The voice of the nurse answered her suddenly and bitterly in these strange words:

"There are sadder stories than yours. There are thousands of miserable women who would ask for no greater blessing than to change places with you."

Grace started. "What can there possibly be to envy in such a lot as mine?"

"Your unblemished character, and your prospect of being established honorably in a respectable house."

Grace turned in her chair, and looked wonderingly into the dim corner of the room.

"How strangely you say that!" she exclaimed. There was no answer; the shadowy figure on the chest never moved. Grace rose impulsively, and drawing her chair after her, approached the nurse. "Is there some romance in your life?" she asked. "Why have you sacrificed yourself to the terrible duties which I find you performing here? You interest me indescribably. Give me your hand."

Mercy shrank back, and refused the offered hand.

"Are we not friends?" Grace asked, in astonishment.

"We can never be friends."

"Why not?"

The nurse was dumb. Grace called to mind the hesitation that she had shown when she had mentioned her name, and drew a new conclusion from it. "Should I be guessing right," she asked, eagerly, "if I guessed you to be some great lady in disguise?"

Mercy laughed to herself—low and bitterly. "I a great lady!" she said, contemptuously. "For Heaven's sake, let us talk of something else!"

Grace's curiosity was thoroughly roused. She persisted. "Once more," she whispered, persuasively, "let us be friends." She gently laid her hand as she spoke on Mercy's shoulder. Mercy roughly shook it off. There was a rudeness in the action which would have offended the most patient woman living. Grace drew back indignantly. "Ah!" she cried, "you are cruel."

"I am kind," answered the nurse, speaking more sternly than ever.

"Is it kind to keep me at a distance? I have told you my story."

The nurse's voice rose excitedly. "Don't tempt me to speak out," she said; "you will regret it."

Grace declined to accept the warning. "I have placed confidence in you," she went on. "It is ungenerous to lay me under an obligation, and then to shut me out of your confidence in return."

"You will have it?" said Mercy Merrick. "You shall have it! Sit down again." Grace's heart began to quicken its beat in expectation of the disclosure that was to come. She drew her chair closer to the chest on which the nurse was sitting. With a firm hand Mercy put the chair back to a distance from her. "Not so near me!" she said, harshly.

"Why not?"

"Not so near," repeated the sternly resolute voice. "Wait till you have heard what I have to say."

Grace obeyed without a word more. There was a momentary silence. A faint flash of light leaped up from the expiring candle, and showed Mercy crouching on the chest, with her elbows on her knees, and her face hidden in her hands. The next instant the room was buried in obscurity. As the darkness fell on the two women the nurse spoke.

CHAPTER II. MAGDALEN—IN MODERN TIMES.

"WHEN your mother was alive were you ever out with her after nightfall in the streets of a great city?"

In those extraordinary terms Mercy Merrick opened the confidential interview which Grace Roseberry had forced on her. Grace answered, simply, "I don't understand you."

"I will put it in another way," said the nurse. Its unnatural hardness and sternness of tone passed away from her voice, and its native gentleness and sadness returned, as she made that reply. "You read the newspapers like the rest of the world," she went on; "have you ever read of your unhappy fellow-creatures (the starving outcasts of the population) whom Want has driven into Sin?"

Still wondering, Grace answered that she had read of such things often, in newspapers and in books.

"Have you heard—when those starving and sinning fellow-creatures happened to be women—of Refuges established to protect and reclaim them?"

The wonder in Grace's mind passed away, and a vague suspicion of something painful to come took its place. "These are extraordinary questions," she said, nervously. "What do you mean?"

"Answer me," the nurse insisted. "Have you heard of the Refuges? Have you heard of the Women?"

"Yes."

"Move your chair a little further away from me." She paused. Her voice, without losing its steadiness, fell to its lowest tones. "I was once of those women," she said, quietly.

Grace sprang to her feet with a faint cry. She stood petrified— incapable of uttering a word.

"I have been in a Refuge," pursued the sweet, sad voice of the other woman. "I have been in a Prison. Do you still wish to be my friend? Do you still insist on sitting close by me and taking my hand?" She waited for a reply, and no reply came. "You see you were wrong," she went on, gently, "when you called me cruel—and I was right when I told you I was kind."

At that appeal Grace composed herself, and spoke. "I don't wish to offend you—" she began, confusedly.

Mercy Merrick stopped her there.

"You don't offend me," she said, without the faintest note of displeasure in her tone. "I am accustomed to stand in the pillory of my own past life. I sometimes ask myself if it was all my fault. I sometimes wonder if Society had no duties toward me when I was a child selling matches in the street—when I was a hard-working girl fainting at my needle for want of food." Her voice faltered a little for the first time as it pronounced those words; she waited a moment, and recovered herself. "It's too late to dwell on these things now," she said, resignedly. "Society can subscribe to reclaim me; but Society can't take me back. You see me here in a place of trust—patiently, humbly, doing all the good I can. It doesn't matter! Here, or elsewhere, what I am can never alter what I was. For three years past all that a sincerely penitent woman can do I have done. It doesn't matter! Once let my past story be known, and the shadow of it covers me; the kindest people shrink."

She waited again. Would a word of sympathy come to comfort her from the other woman's lips? No! Miss Roseberry was shocked; Miss Roseberry was confused. "I am very sorry for you," was all that Miss Roseberry could say.

"Everybody is sorry for me," answered the nurse, as patiently as ever; "everybody is kind to me. But the lost place is not to be regained. I can't get back! I can't get back?" she cried, with a passionate outburst of despair— checked instantly the moment it had escaped her. "Shall I tell you what my experience has been?" she resumed. "Will you hear the story of Magdalen— in modern times?"

Grace drew back a step; Mercy instantly understood her.

"I am going to tell you nothing that you need shrink from hearing," she said. "A lady in your position would not understand the trials and the struggles that I have passed through. My story shall begin at the Refuge. The matron sent me out to service with the character that I had honestly earned—the character of a reclaimed woman. I justified the confidence placed in me; I was a faithful servant. One day my mistress sent for me—a kind mistress, if ever there was one yet. 'Mercy, I am sorry for you; it has come out that I took you from a Refuge; I shall lose every servant in the house; you must go.' I went back to the matron—another kind woman. She received me like a mother. 'We will try again, Mercy; don't be cast down.' I told you I had been in Canada?"

Grace began to feel interested in spite of herself. She answered with something like warmth in her tone. She returned to her chair—placed at its safe and significant distance from the chest.

The nurse went on:

"My next place was in Canada, with an officer's wife: gentlefolks who had emigrated. More kindness; and, this time, a pleasant, peaceful life for me. I said to myself, 'Is the lost place regained? Have I got back?' My mistress died. New people came into our neighborhood. There was a young lady among them—my master began to think of another wife. I have the misfortune (in my situation) to be what is called a handsome woman; I rouse the curiosity of strangers. The new people asked questions about me; my master's answers did not satisfy them. In a word, they found me out. The old story again! 'Mercy, I am very sorry; scandal is busy with you and with me; we are innocent, but there is no help for it—we must part.' I left the place; having gained one advantage during my stay in Canada, which I find of use to me here."

"What is it?"

"Our nearest neighbors were French-Canadians. I learned to speak the French language."

"Did you return to London?"

"Where else could I go, without a character?" said Mercy, sadly. "I went back again to the matron. Sickness had broken out in the Refuge; I made myself useful as a nurse. One of the doctors was struck with me—'fell in love' with me, as the phrase is. He would have married me. The nurse, as an honest woman, was bound to tell him the truth. He never appeared again. The old story! I began to be weary of saying to myself, 'I can't get back! I can't get back!' Despair got hold of me, the despair that hardens the heart. I might have committed suicide; I might even have drifted back into my old life—but for one man."

At those last words her voice—quiet and even through the earlier part of her sad story—began to falter once more. She stopped, following silently the memories and associations roused in her by what she had just said. Had she forgotten the presence of another person in the room? Grace's curiosity left Grace no resource but to say a word on her side.

"Who was the man?" she asked. "How did he befriend you?"

"Befriend me? He doesn't even know that such a person as I am is in existence."

That strange answer, naturally enough, only strengthened the anxiety of Grace to hear more. "You said just now—" she began.

"I said just now that he saved me. He did save me; you shall hear how. One Sunday our regular clergyman at the Refuge was not able to officiate. His place was taken by a stranger, quite a young man. The matron told us the stranger's name was Julian Gray. I sat in the back row of seats, under the shadow of the gallery, where I could see him without his seeing me. His text was from the words, 'Joy shall be in heaven over one sinner that repenteth, more than over ninety and nine just persons, which need no repentance.' What happier women might have thought of his sermon I cannot say; there was not a dry eye among us at the Refuge. As for me, he touched my heart as no man has touched it before or since. The hard despair melted in me at the sound of his voice; the weary round of my life showed its nobler side again while he spoke. From that time I have accepted my hard lot, I have been a patient woman. I might have been something more, I might have been a happy woman, if I could have prevailed on myself to speak to Julian Gray."

"What hindered you from speaking to him?"

"I was afraid."

"Afraid of what?"

"Afraid of making my hard life harder still."

A woman who could have sympathized with her would perhaps have guessed what those words meant. Grace was simply embarrassed by her; and Grace failed to guess.

"I don't understand you," she said.

There was no alternative for Mercy but to own the truth in plain words. She sighed, and said the words. "I was afraid I might interest him in my sorrows, and might set my heart on him in return." The utter absence of any fellow-feeling with her on Grace's side expressed itself unconsciously in the plainest terms.

"You!" she exclaimed, in a tone of blank astonishment.

The nurse rose slowly to her feet. Grace's expression of surprise told her plainly—almost brutally—that her confession had gone far enough.

"I astonish you?" she said. "Ah, my young lady, you don't know what rough usage a woman's heart can bear, and still beat truly! Before I saw Julian Gray I only knew men as objects of horror to me. Let us drop the subject. The preacher at the Refuge is nothing but a remembrance now—the one welcome remembrance of my life! I have nothing more to tell you. You insisted on hearing my story—you have heard it."

"I have not heard how you found employment here," said Grace, continuing the conversation with uneasy politeness, as she best might.

Mercy crossed the room, and slowly raked together the last living embers of the fire.

"The matron has friends in France," she answered, "who are connected with the military hospitals. It was not difficult to get me the place, under those circumstances. Society can find a use for me here. My hand is as light, my words of comfort are as welcome, among those suffering wretches" (she pointed to the room in which the wounded men were lying) "as if I was the most reputable woman breathing. And if a stray shot comes my way before the war is over—well! Society will be rid of me on easy terms."

She stood looking thoughtfully into the wreck of the fire—as if she saw in it the wreck of her own life. Common humanity made it an act of necessity to say something to her. Grace considered—advanced a step toward her—stopped—and took refuge in the most trivial of all the common phrases which one human being can address to another.

"If there is anything I can do for you—" she began. The sentence, halting there, was never finished. Miss Roseberry was just merciful enough toward the lost woman who had rescued and sheltered her to feel that it was needless to say more.

The nurse lifted her noble head and advanced slowly toward the canvas screen to return to her duties. "Miss Roseberry might have taken my hand!" she thought to herself, bitterly. No! Miss Roseberry stood there at a distance, at a loss what to say next. "What can you do for me?" Mercy asked, stung by the cold courtesy of her companion into a momentary outbreak of contempt. "Can you change my identity? Can you give me the name and the place of an innocent woman? If I only had your chance! If I only had your reputation and your prospects!" She laid one hand over her bosom, and controlled herself. "Stay here," she resumed, "while I go back to my work. I will see that your clothes are dried. You shall wear my clothes as short a time as possible."

With those melancholy words—touchingly, not bitterly spoken—she moved to pass into the kitchen, when she noticed that the pattering sound of the rain against the window was audible no more. Dropping the canvas for the moment, she retraced her steps, and, unfastening the wooden shutter, looked out.

The moon was rising dimly in the watery sky; the rain had ceased; the friendly darkness which had hidden the French position from the German scouts was lessening every moment. In a few hours more (if nothing happened) the English lady might resume her journey. In a few hours more the morning would dawn.

Mercy lifted her hand to close the shutter. Before she could fasten it the report of a rifle-shot reached the cottage from one of the distant posts. It was followed almost instantly by a second report, nearer and louder than the first. Mercy paused, with the shutter in her hand, and listened intently for the next sound.

CHAPTER III. THE GERMAN SHELL.

A THIRD rifle-shot rang through the night air, close to the cottage. Grace started and approached the window in alarm.

"What does that firing mean?" she asked.

"Signals from the outposts," the nurse quietly replied.

"Is there any danger? Have the Germans come back?"

Surgeon Surville answered the question. He lifted the canvas screen, and looked into the room as Miss Roseberry spoke.

"The Germans are advancing on us," he said. "Their vanguard is in sight."

Grace sank on the chair near her, trembling from head to foot. Mercy advanced to the surgeon, and put the decisive question to him.

"Do we defend the position?" she inquired.

Surgeon Surville ominously shook his head.

"Impossible! We are outnumbered as usual—ten to one."

The shrill roll of the French drums was heard outside.

"There is the retreat sounded!" said the surgeon. "The captain is not a man to think twice about what he does. We are left to take care of ourselves. In five minutes we must be out of this place."

A volley of rifle-shots rang out as he spoke. The German vanguard was attacking the French at the outposts. Grace caught the surgeon entreatingly by the arm. "Take me with you," she cried. "Oh, sir, I have suffered from the Germans already! Don't forsake me, if they come back!" The surgeon was equal to the occasion; he placed the hand of the pretty Englishwoman on his breast. "Fear nothing, madam," he said, looking as if he could have annihilated the whole German force with his own invincible arm. "A Frenchman's heart beats under your hand. A Frenchman's devotion protects you." Grace's head sank on his shoulder. Monsieur Surville felt that he had asserted himself; he looked round invitingly at Mercy. She, too, was an attractive woman. The Frenchman had another shoulder at her service. Unhappily the room was dark—the look was lost on Mercy. She was thinking of the helpless men in the inner chamber, and she quietly recalled the surgeon to a sense of his professional duties.

"What is to become of the sick and wounded?" she asked.

Monsieur Surville shrugged one shoulder—the shoulder that was free.

"The strongest among them we can take away with us," he said. "The others must be left here. Fear nothing for yourself, dear lady. There will be a place for you in the baggage-wagon."

"And for me, too?" Grace pleaded, eagerly.

The surgeon's invincible arm stole round the young lady's waist, and answered mutely with a squeeze.

"Take her with you," said Mercy. "My place is with the men whom you leave behind."

Grace listened in amazement. "Think what you risk," she said "if you stop here."

Mercy pointed to her left shoulder.

"Don't alarm yourself on my account," she answered; "the red cross will protect me."

Another roll of the drum warned the susceptible surgeon to take his place as director-general of the ambulance without any further delay. He conducted Grace to a chair, and placed both her hands on his heart this time, to reconcile her to the misfortune of his absence. "Wait here till I return for you," he whispered. "Fear nothing, my charming friend. Say to yourself, 'Surville is the soul of honor! Surville is devoted to me!'" He struck his breast; he again forgot the obscurity in the room, and cast one look of unutterable homage at his charming friend. "A bientot!" he cried, and kissed his hand and disappeared.

As the canvas screen fell over him the sharp report of the rifle-firing was suddenly and grandly dominated by the roar of cannon. The instant after a shell exploded in the garden outside, within a few yards of the window.

Grace sank on her knees with a shriek of terror. Mercy, without losing her self-possession, advanced to the window and looked out.

"The moon has risen," she said. "The Germans are shelling the village."

Grace rose, and ran to her for protection.

"Take me away!" she cried. "We shall be killed if we stay here." She stopped, looking in astonishment at the tall black figure of the nurse, standing immovably by the window. "Are you made of iron?" she exclaimed. "Will nothing frighten you?"

Mercy smiled sadly. "Why should I be afraid of losing my life?" she answered. "I have nothing worth living for!"

The roar of the cannon shook the cottage for the second time. A second shell exploded in the courtyard, on the opposite side of the building.

Bewildered by the noise, panic-stricken as the danger from the shells threatened the cottage more and more nearly, Grace threw her arms round the nurse, and clung, in the abject familiarity of terror, to the woman whose hand she had shrunk from touching not five minutes since. "Where is it safest?" she cried. "Where can I hide myself?"

"How can I tell where the next shell will fall?" Mercy answered, quietly.

The steady composure of the one woman seemed to madden the other. Releasing the nurse, Grace looked wildly round for a way of escape from the cottage. Making first for the kitchen, she was driven back by the clamor and confusion attending the removal of those among the wounded who were strong enough to be placed in the wagon. A second look round showed her the door leading into the yard. She rushed to it with a cry of relief. She had just laid her hand on the lock when the third report of cannon burst over the place.

Starting back a step, Grace lifted her hands mechanically to her ears. At the same moment the third shell burst through the roof of the cottage, and exploded in the room, just inside the door. Mercy sprang forward, unhurt, from her place at the window. The burning fragments of the shell were already firing the dry wooden floor, and in the midst of them, dimly seen through the smoke, lay the insensible body of her companion in the room. Even at that dreadful moment the nurse's presence of mind did not fail her. Hurrying back to the place that she had just left, near which she had already noticed the miller's empty sacks lying in a heap, she seized two of them, and, throwing them on the smoldering floor, trampled out the fire. That done, she knelt by the senseless woman, and lifted her head.

Was she wounded? or dead?

Mercy raised one helpless hand, and laid her fingers on the wrist. While she was still vainly trying to feel for the beating of the pulse, Surgeon Surville (alarmed for the ladies) hurried in to inquire if any harm had been done.

Mercy called to him to approach. "I am afraid the shell has struck her," she said, yielding her place to him. "See if she is badly hurt."

The surgeon's anxiety for his charming patient expressed itself briefly in an oath, with a prodigious emphasis laid on one of the letters in it—the letter R. "Take off her cloak," he cried, raising his hand to her neck. "Poor angel! She has turned in falling; the string is twisted round her throat."

Mercy removed the cloak. It dropped on the floor as the surgeon lifted Grace in his arms. "Get a candle," he said, impatiently; "they will give you one in the kitchen." He tried to feel the pulse: his hand trembled, the noise and confusion in the kitchen bewildered him. "Just Heaven!" he exclaimed. "My emotions overpower me!" Mercy approached him with the candle. The light disclosed the frightful injury which a fragment of the shell had inflicted on the Englishwoman's head. Surgeon Surville's manner altered on the instant. The expression of anxiety left his face; its professional composure covered it suddenly like a mask. What was the object of his admiration now? An inert burden in his arms—nothing more.

The change in his face was not lost on Mercy. Her large gray eyes watched him attentively. "Is the lady seriously wounded?" she asked.

"Don't trouble yourself to hold the light any longer," was the cool reply. "It's all over—I can do nothing for her."

"Dead?"

Surgeon Surville nodded and shook his fist in the direction of the outposts. "Accursed Germans!" he cried, and looked down at the dead face on his arm, and shrugged his shoulders resignedly. "The fortune of war!" he said as he lifted the body and placed it on the bed in one corner of the room. "Next time, nurse, it may be you or me. Who knows? Bah! the problem of human destiny disgusts me." He turned from the bed, and illustrated his disgust by spitting on the fragments of the exploded shell. "We must leave her there," he resumed. "She was once a charming person—she is nothing now. Come away, Miss Mercy, before it is too late."

He offered his arm to the nurse; the creaking of the baggage-wagon, starting on its journey, was heard outside, and the shrill roll of the drums was renewed in the distance. The retreat had begun.

Mercy drew aside the canvas, and saw the badly wounded men, left helpless at the mercy of the enemy, on their straw beds. She refused the offer of Monsieur Surville's arm.

"I have already told you that I shall stay here," she answered.

Monsieur Surville lifted his hands in polite remonstrance. Mercy held back the curtain, and pointed to the cottage door.

"Go," she said. "My mind is made up."

Even at that final moment the Frenchman asserted himself. He made his exit with unimpaired grace and dignity. "Madam," he said, "you are sublime!" With that parting compliment the man of gallantry—true to the last to his admiration of the sex—bowed, with his hand on his heart, and left the cottage.

Mercy dropped the canvas over the doorway. She was alone with the dead woman.

The last tramp of footsteps, the last rumbling of the wagon wheels, died away in the distance. No renewal of firing from the position occupied by the enemy disturbed the silence that followed. The Germans knew that the French were in retreat. A few minutes more and they would take possession of the abandoned village: the tumult of their approach should become audible at the cottage. In the meantime the stillness was terrible. Even the wounded wretches who were left in the kitchen waited their fate in silence.

Alone in the room, Mercy's first look was directed to the bed.

The two women had met in the confusion of the first skirmish at the close of twilight. Separated, on their arrival at the cottage, by the duties required of the nurse, they had only met again in the captain's room. The acquaintance between them had been a short one; and it had given no promise of ripening into friendship. But the fatal accident had roused Mercy's interest in the stranger. She took the candle, and approached the corpse of the woman who had been literally killed at her side.

She stood by the bed, looking down in the silence of the night at the stillness of the dead face.

It was a striking face—once seen (in life or in death) not to be forgotten afterward. The forehead was unusually low and broad; the eyes unusually far apart; the mouth and chin remarkably small. With tender hands Mercy smoothed the disheveled hair and arranged the crumpled dress. "Not five minutes since," she thought to herself, "I was longing to change places with you!" She turned from the bed with a sigh. "I wish I could change places now!"

The silence began to oppress her. She walked slowly to the other end of the room.

The cloak on the floor—her own cloak, which she had lent to Miss

Roseberry—attracted her attention as she passed it. She picked it up and brushed the dust from it, and laid it across a chair. This done, she put the light back on the table, and going to the window, listened for the first sounds of the German advance. The faint passage of the wind through some trees near at hand was the only sound that caught her ears. She turned from the window, and seated herself at the table, thinking. Was there any duty still left undone that Christian charity owed to the dead? Was there any further service that pressed for performance in the interval before the Germans appeared?

Mercy recalled the conversation that had passed between her ill-fated companion and herself. Miss Roseberry had spoken of her object in returning to England. She had mentioned a lady—a connection by marriage, to whom she was personally a stranger—who was waiting to receive her. Some one capable of stating how the poor creature had met with her death ought to write to her only friend. Who was to do it? There was nobody to do it but the one witness of the catastrophe now left in the cottage—Mercy herself.

She lifted the cloak from the chair on which she had placed it, and took from the pocket the leather letter-case which Grace had shown to her. The only way of discovering the address to write to in England was to open the case and examine the papers inside. Mercy opened the case—and stopped, feeling a strange reluctance to carry the investigation any farther.

A moment's consideration satisfied her that her scruples were misplaced. If she respected the case as inviolable, the Germans would certainly not hesitate to examine it, and the Germans would hardly trouble themselves to write to England. Which were the fittest eyes to inspect the papers of the deceased lady—the eyes of men and foreigners, or the eyes of her own countrywoman? Mercy's hesitation left her. She emptied the contents of the case on the table.

That trifling action decided the whole future course of her life.

CHAPTER IV. THE TEMPTATION.

Some letters, tied together with a ribbon, attracted Mercy's attention first. The ink in which the addresses were written had faded with age. The letters, directed alternately to Colonel Roseberry and to the Honorable Mrs. Roseberry, contained a correspondence between the husband and wife at a time when the Colonel's military duties had obliged him to be absent from home. Mercy tied the letters up again, and passed on to the papers that lay next in order under her hand.

These consisted of a few leaves pinned together, and headed (in a woman's handwriting) "My Journal at Rome." A brief examination showed that the journal had been written by Miss Roseberry, and that it was mainly devoted to a record of the last days of her father's life.

After replacing the journal and the correspondence in the case, the one paper left on the table was a letter. The envelope, which was unclosed, bore this address: "Lady Janet Roy, Mablethorpe House, Kensington, London." Mercy took the inclosure from the open envelope. The first lines she read informed her that she had found the Colonel's letter of introduction, presenting his daughter to her protectress on her arrival in England.

Mercy read the letter through. It was described by the writer as the last efforts of a dying man. Colonel Roseberry wrote affectionately of his daughter's merits, and regretfully of her neglected education—ascribing the latter to the pecuniary losses which had forced him to emigrate to Canada in the character of a poor man. Fervent expressions of gratitude followed, addressed to Lady Janet. "I owe it to you," the letter concluded, "that I am dying with my mind at ease about the future of my darling girl. To your generous protection I commit the one treasure I have left to me on earth. Through your long lifetime you have nobly used your high rank and your great fortune as a means of doing good. I believe it will not be counted among the least of your virtues hereafter that you comforted the last hours of an old soldier by opening your heart and your home to his friendless child."

So the letter ended. Mercy laid it down with a heavy heart. What a chance the poor girl had lost! A woman of rank and fortune waiting to receive her—a woman so merciful and so generous that the father's mind had been easy about the daughter on his deathbed—and there the daughter lay, beyond the reach of Lady Janet's kindness, beyond the need of Lady Janet's help!

The French captain's writing-materials were left on the table. Mercy turned the letter over so that she might write the news of Miss Roseberry's death on the blank page at the end. She was still considering what expressions she should use, when the sound of complaining voices from the next room caught her ear. The wounded men left behind were moaning for help—the deserted soldiers were losing their fortitude at last.

She entered the kitchen. A cry of delight welcomed her appearance—the mere sight of her composed the men. From one straw bed to another she passed with comforting words that gave them hope, with skilled and tender hands that soothed their pain. They kissed the hem of her black dress, they called her their guardian angel, as the beautiful creature moved among them, and bent over their hard pillows her gentle, compassionate face. "I will be with you when the Germans come," she said, as she left them to return to her unwritten letter. "Courage, my poor fellows! you are not deserted by your nurse."

"Courage, madam!" the men replied; "and God bless you!"

If the firing had been resumed at that moment—if a shell had struck her dead in the act of succoring the afflicted, what Christian judgment would have hesitated to declare that there was a place for this woman in heaven? But if the war ended and left her still living, where was the place for her on earth? Where were her prospects? Where was her home?

She returned to the letter. Instead, however, of seating herself to write, she stood by the table, absently looking down at the morsel of paper.

A strange fancy had sprung to life in her mind on re-entering the room; she herself smiled faintly at the extravagance of it. What if she were to ask Lady Janet Roy to let her supply Miss Roseberry's place? She had met with

35

Miss Roseberry under critical circumstances, and she had done for her all that one woman could do to help another. There was in this circumstance some little claim to notice, perhaps, if Lady Janet had no other companion and reader in view. Suppose she ventured to plead her own cause—what would the noble and merciful lady do? She would write back, and say, "Send me references to your character, and I will see what can be done." Her character! Her references! Mercy laughed bitterly, and sat down to write in the fewest words all that was needed from her—a plain statement of the facts.

No! Not a line could she put on the paper. That fancy of hers was not to be dismissed at will. Her mind was perversely busy now with an imaginative picture of the beauty of Mablethorpe House and the comfort and elegance of the life that was led there. Once more she thought of the chance which Miss Roseberry had lost. Unhappy creature! what a home would have been open to her if the shell had only fallen on the side of the window, instead of on the side of the yard!

Mercy pushed the letter away from her, and walked impatiently to and fro in the room.

The perversity in her thoughts was not to be mastered in that way. Her mind only abandoned one useless train of reflection to occupy itself with another. She was now looking by anticipation at her own future. What were her prospects (if she lived through it) when the war was over? The experience of the past delineated with pitiless fidelity the dreary scene. Go where she might, do what she might, it would always end in the same way. Curiosity and admiration excited by her beauty; inquiries made about her; the story of the past discovered; Society charitably sorry for her; Society generously subscribing for her; and still, through all the years of her life, the same result in the end—the shadow of the old disgrace surrounding her as with a pestilence, isolating her among other women, branding her, even when she had earned her pardon in the sight of God, with the mark of an indelible disgrace in the sight of man: there was the prospect! And she was only five-and-twenty last birthday; she was in the prime of her health and her strength; she might live, in the course of nature, fifty years more!

She stopped again at the bedside; she looked again at the face of the corpse.

To what end had the shell struck the woman who had some hope in her life, and spared the woman who had none? The words she had herself spoken to Grace Roseberry came back to her as she thought of it. "If I only had your chance! If I only had your reputation and your prospects!" And there was the chance wasted! there were the enviable prospects thrown away! It was almost maddening to contemplate that result, feeling her own position as she felt it. In the bitter mockery of despair she bent over the lifeless figure, and spoke to it as if it had ears to hear her. "Oh!" she said, longingly, "if you could be Mercy Merrick, and if I could be Grace Roseberry, now!"

The instant the words passed her lips she started into an erect position. She stood by the bed with her eyes staring wildly into empty space; with her brain in a flame; with her heart beating as if it would stifle her. "If you could be Mercy Merrick, and if I could be Grace Roseberry, now!" In one breathless moment the thought assumed a new development in her mind. In one breathless moment the conviction struck her like an electric shock. She might be Grace Roseberry if she dared! There was absolutely nothing to stop her from presenting herself to Lady Janet Roy under Grace's name and in Grace's place!

What were the risks? Where was the weak point in the scheme?

Grace had said it herself in so many words—she and Lady Janet had never seen each other. Her friends were in Canada; her relations in England were dead. Mercy knew the place in which she had lived—the place called Port Logan—as well as she had known it herself. Mercy had only to read the manuscript journal to be able to answer any questions relating to the visit to Rome and to Colonel Roseberry's death. She had no accomplished lady to personate: Grace had spoken herself—her father's letter spoke also in the plainest terms—of her neglected education. Everything, literally everything, was in the lost woman's favor. The people with whom she had been connected in the ambulance had gone, to return no more. Her own clothes were on Miss Roseberry at that moment—marked with her own name. Miss Roseberry's clothes, marked with her name, were drying, at Mercy's disposal, in the next room. The way of escape from the unendurable humiliation of her present life lay open before her at last. What a prospect it was! A new identity, which she might own anywhere! a new name, which was beyond reproach! a new past life, into which all the world might search, and be welcome! Her color rose, her eyes sparkled; she had never been so irresistibly beautiful as she looked at the moment when the new future disclosed itself, radiant with new hope.

She waited a minute, until she could look at her own daring project from another point of view. Where was the harm of it? what did her conscience say?

As to Grace, in the first place. What injury was she doing to a woman who was dead? The question answered itself. No injury to the woman. No injury to her relations. Her relations were dead also.

As to Lady Janet, in the second place. If she served her new mistress faithfully, if she filled her new sphere honorably, if she was diligent under instruction and grateful for kindness—if, in one word, she was all that she might be and would be in the heavenly peace and security of that new life— what injury was she doing to Lady Janet? Once more the question answered itself. She might, and would, give Lady Janet cause to bless the day when she first entered the house.

She snatched up Colonel Roseberry's letter, and put it into the case with the other papers. The opportunity was before her; the chances were all in her favor; her conscience said nothing against trying the daring scheme. She decided then and there—"I'll do it!"

Something jarred on her finer sense, something offended her better nature, as she put the case into the pocket of her dress. She had decided, and yet she was not at ease; she was not quite sure of having fairly questioned her conscience yet. What if she laid the letter-case on the table again, and waited until her excitement had all cooled down, and then put the contemplated project soberly on its trial before her own sense of right and wrong?

She thought once—and hesitated. Before she could think twice, the distant tramp of marching footsteps and the distant clatter of horses' hoofs were wafted to her on the night air. The Germans were entering the village! In a few minutes more they would appear in the cottage; they would summon her to give an account of herself. There was no time for waiting until she was composed again. Which should it be—the new life, as Grace Roseberry? or the old life, as Mercy Merrick?

She looked for the last time at the bed. Grace's course was run; Grace's future was at her disposal. Her resolute nature, forced to a choice on the instant, held by the daring alternative. She persisted in the determination to take Grace's place.

The tramping footsteps of the Germans came nearer and nearer. The voices of the officers were audible, giving the words of command.

She seated herself at the table, waiting steadily for what was to come.

The ineradicable instinct of the sex directed her eyes to her dress, before the Germans appeared. Looking it over to see that it was in perfect order, her eyes fell upon the red cross on her left shoulder. In a moment it struck her that her nurse's costume might involve her in a needless risk. It associated her with a public position; it might lead to inquiries at a later time, and those inquiries might betray her.

She looked round. The gray cloak which she had lent to Grace attracted her attention. She took it up, and covered herself with it from head to foot.

The cloak was just arranged round her when she heard the outer door thrust open, and voices speaking in a strange tongue, and arms grounded in the room behind her. Should she wait to be discovered? or should she show herself of her own accord? It was less trying to such a nature as hers to show herself than to wait. She advanced to enter the kitchen. The canvas curtain, as she stretched out her hand to it, was suddenly drawn back from the other side, and three men confronted her in the open doorway.

CHAPTER V. THE GERMAN SURGEON.

THE youngest of the three strangers—judging by features, complexion, and manner—was apparently an Englishman. He wore a military cap and military boots, but was otherwise dressed as a civilian. Next to him stood an officer in Prussian uniform, and next to the officer was the third and the oldest of the party. He also was dressed in uniform, but his appearance was far from being suggestive of the appearance of a military man. He halted on one foot, he stooped at the shoulders, and instead of a sword at his side he carried a stick in his hand. After looking sharply through a large pair of tortoise-shell spectacles, first at Mercy, then at the bed, then all round the room, he turned with a cynical composure of manner to the Prussian officer, and broke the silence in these words:

"A woman ill on the bed; another woman in attendance on her, and no one else in the room. Any necessity, major, for setting a guard here?"

"No necessity," answered the major. He wheeled round on his heel and returned to the kitchen. The German surgeon advanced a little, led by his professional instinct, in the direction of the bedside. The young Englishman, whose eyes had remained riveted in admiration on Mercy, drew the canvas screen over the doorway and respectfully addressed her in the French language.

"May I ask if I am speaking to a French lady?" he said.

"I am an Englishwoman," Mercy replied.

The surgeon heard the answer. Stopping short on his way to the bed, he pointed to the recumbent figure on it, and said to Mercy, in good English, spoken with a strong German accent.

"Can I be of any use there?"

His manner was ironically courteous, his harsh voice was pitched in one sardonic monotony of tone. Mercy took an instantaneous dislike to this hobbling, ugly old man, staring at her rudely through his great tortoiseshell spectacles.

"You can be of no use, sir," she said, shortly. "The lady was killed when your troops shelled this cottage."

The Englishman started, and looked compassionately toward the bed. The German refreshed himself with a pinch of snuff, and put another question.

"Has the body been examined by a medical man?" he asked.

Mercy ungraciously limited her reply to the one necessary word "Yes."

The present surgeon was not a man to be daunted by a lady's disapproval of him. He went on with his questions.

"Who has examined the body?" he inquired next.

Mercy answered, "The doctor attached to the French ambulance."

The German grunted in contemptuous disapproval of all Frenchmen, and all French institutions. The Englishman seized his first opportunity of addressing himself to Mercy once more.

"Is the lady a countrywoman of ours?" he asked, gently.

Mercy considered before she answered him. With the object she had in view, there might be serious reasons for speaking with extreme caution when she spoke of Grace.

"I believe so," she said. "We met here by accident. I know nothing of her."

"Not even her name?" inquired the German surgeon.

Mercy's resolution was hardly equal yet to giving her own name openly as the name of Grace. She took refuge in flat denial.

"Not even her name," she repeated obstinately.

The old man stared at her more rudely than ever, considered with himself, and took the candle from the table. He hobbled back to the bed and examined the figure laid on it in silence. The Englishman continued the conversation, no longer concealing the interest that he felt in the beautiful woman who stood before him.

"Pardon me," he said, "you are very young to be alone in war-time in such a place as this."

The sudden outbreak of a disturbance in the kitchen relieved Mercy from any immediate necessity for answering him. She heard the voices of the wounded men raised in feeble remonstrance, and the harsh command of the foreign officers bidding them be silent. The generous instincts of the woman instantly prevailed over every personal consideration imposed on her by the position which she had assumed. Reckless whether she betrayed herself or not as nurse in the French ambulance, she instantly drew aside the canvas to enter the kitchen. A German sentinel barred the way to her, and announced, in his own language, that no strangers were admitted. The Englishman politely interposing, asked if she had any special object in wishing to enter the room.

"The poor Frenchmen!" she said, earnestly, her heart upbraiding her for having forgotten them. "The poor wounded Frenchmen!"

The German surgeon advanced from the bedside, and took the matter up before the Englishman could say a word more.

"You have nothing to do with the wounded Frenchmen," he croaked, in the harshest notes of his voice. "The wounded Frenchmen are my business, and not yours. They are our prisoners, and they are being moved to our ambulance. I am Ingatius Wetzel, chief of the medical staff—and I tell you this. Hold your tongue." He turned to the sentinel and added in German, "Draw the curtain again; and if the woman persists, put her back into this room with your own hand."

Mercy attempted to remonstrate. The Englishman respectfully took her arm, and drew her out of the sentinel's reach.

"It is useless to resist," he said. "The German discipline never gives way. There is not the least need to be uneasy about the Frenchmen. The ambulance under Surgeon Wetzel is admirably administered. I answer for it, the men will be well treated." He saw the tears in her eyes as he spoke; his admiration for her rose higher and higher. "Kind as well as beautiful," he thought. "What a charming creature!"

"Well!" said Ignatius Wetzel, eying Mercy sternly through his spectacles. "Are you satisfied? And will you hold your tongue?"

She yielded: it was plainly useless to resist. But for the surgeon's resistance, her devotion to the wounded men might have stopped her on the downward way that she was going. If she could only have been absorbed again, mind and body, in her good work as a nurse, the temptation might even yet have found her strong enough to resist it. The fatal severity of the German discipline had snapped asunder the last tie that bound her to her better self. Her face hardened as she walked away proudly from Surgeon Wetzel, and took a chair.

The Englishman followed her, and reverted to the question of her present situation in the cottage.

"Don't suppose that I want to alarm you," he said. "There is, I repeat, no need to be anxious about the Frenchmen, but there is serious reason for anxiety on your own account. The action will be renewed round this village by daylight; you ought really to be in a place of safety. I am an officer in the English army—my name is Horace Holmcroft. I shall be delighted to be of use to you, and I can be of use, if you will let me. May I ask if you are traveling?"

Mercy gathered the cloak which concealed her nurse's dress more closely round her, and committed herself silently to her first overt act of deception. She bowed her head in the affirmative.

"Are you on your way to England?"

"Yes."

"In that case I can pass you through the German lines, and forward you at once on your journey."

Mercy looked at him in unconcealed surprise. His strongly-felt interest in her was restrained within the strictest limits of good-breeding: he was unmistakably a gentleman. Did he really mean what he had just said?

"You can pass me through the German lines?" she repeated. "You must possess extraordinary influence, sir, to be able to do that."

Mr. Horace Holmcroft smiled.

"I possess the influence that no one can resist," he answered—"the influence of the Press. I am serving here as war correspondent of one of our great English newspapers. If I ask him, the commanding officer will grant you a pass. He is close to this cottage. What do you say?"

She summoned her resolution—not without difficulty, even now—and took him at his word.

"I gratefully accept your offer, sir."

He advanced a step toward the kitchen, and stopped.

"It may be well to make the application as privately as possible," he said. "I shall be questioned if I pass through that room. Is there no other way out of the cottage?"

Mercy showed him the door leading into the yard. He bowed—and left her.

She looked furtively toward the German surgeon. Ignatius Wetzel was still at the bed, bending over the body, and apparently absorbed in examining the wound which had been inflicted by the shell. Mercy's instinctive aversion to the old man increased tenfold, now that she was left alone with him. She withdrew uneasily to the window, and looked out at the moonlight.

Had she committed herself to the fraud? Hardly, yet. She had committed herself to returning to England—nothing more. There was no necessity, thus far, which forced her to present herself at Mablethorpe House, in Grace's place. There was still time to reconsider her resolution—still time to write the account of the accident, as she had proposed, and to send it with the letter-case to Lady Janet Roy. Suppose she finally decided on taking this course, what was to become of her when she found herself in England again? There was no alternative open but to apply once more to her friend the matron. There was nothing for her to do but to return to the Refuge!

The Refuge! The matron! What past association with these two was now presenting itself uninvited, and taking the foremost place in her mind? Of whom was she now thinking, in that strange place, and at that crisis in her life? Of the man whose words had found their way to her heart, whose influence had strengthened and comforted her, in the chapel of the Refuge. One of the finest passages in his sermon had been especially devoted by Julian Gray to warning the congregation whom he addressed against the degrading influences of falsehood and deceit. The terms in which he had appealed to the miserable women round him—terms of sympathy and encouragement never addressed to them before—came back to Mercy Merrick as if she had heard them an hour since. She turned deadly pale as they now pleaded with her once more. "Oh!" she whispered to herself, as she thought of what she had proposed and planned, "what have I done? what have I done?"

She turned from the window with some vague idea in her mind of following Mr. Holmcroft and calling him back. As she faced the bed again she also confronted Ignatius Wetzel. He was just stepping forward to speak to her, with a white handkerchief—the handkerchief which she had lent to Grace—held up in his hand.

"I have found this in her pocket," he said. "Here is her name written on it. She must be a countrywoman of yours." He read the letters marked on the handkerchief with some difficulty. "Her name is—Mercy Merrick."

His lips had said it—not hers! He had given her the name.

"'Mercy Merrick' is an English name?" pursued Ignatius Wetzel, with his eyes steadily fixed on her. "Is it not so?"

The hold on her mind of the past association with Julian Gray began to relax. One present and pressing question now possessed itself of the foremost place in her thoughts. Should she correct the error into which the German had fallen? The time had come—to speak, and assert her own identity; or to be silent, and commit herself to the fraud.

45

Horace Holmcroft entered the room again at the moment when Surgeon Wetzel's staring eyes were still fastened on her, waiting for her reply.

"I have not overrated my interest," he said, pointing to a little slip of paper in his hand. "Here is the pass. Have you got pen and ink? I must fill up the form."

Mercy pointed to the writing materials on the table. Horace seated himself, and dipped the pen in the ink.

"Pray don't think that I wish to intrude myself into your affairs," he said. "I am obliged to ask you one or two plain questions. What is your name?"

A sudden trembling seized her. She supported herself against the foot of the bed. Her whole future existence depended on her answer. She was incapable of uttering a word.

Ignatius Wetzel stood her friend for once. His croaking voice filled the empty gap of silence exactly at the right time. He doggedly held the handkerchief under her eyes. He obstinately repeated: "Mercy Merrick is an English name. Is it not so?"

Horace Holmcroft looked up from the table. "Mercy Merrick?" he said. "Who is Mercy Merrick?"

Surgeon Wetzel pointed to the corpse on the bed.

"I have found the name on the handkerchief," he said. "This lady, it seems, had not curiosity enough to look for the name of her own countrywoman." He made that mocking allusion to Mercy with a tone which was almost a tone of suspicion, and a look which was almost a look of contempt. Her quick temper instantly resented the discourtesy of which she had been made the object. The irritation of the moment—so often do the most trifling motives determine the most serious human actions—decided her on the course that she should pursue. She turned her back scornfully on the rude old man, and left him in the delusion that he had discovered the dead woman's name.

Horace returned to the business of filling up the form. "Pardon me for pressing the question," he said. "You know what German discipline is by this time. What is your name?"

She answered him recklessly, defiantly, without fairly realizing what she was doing until it was done.

"Grace Roseberry," she said.

The words were hardly out of her mouth before she would have given everything she possessed in the world to recall them.

"Miss?" asked Horace, smiling.

She could only answer him by bowing her head.

He wrote: "Miss Grace Roseberry"—reflected for a moment—and then added, interrogatively, "Returning to her friends in England?" Her friends in England? Mercy's heart swelled: she silently replied by another sign. He wrote the words after the name, and shook the sandbox over the wet ink. "That will be enough," he said, rising and presenting the pass to Mercy; "I will see you through the lines myself, and arrange for your being sent on by the railway. Where is your luggage?"

Mercy pointed toward the front door of the building. "In a shed outside the cottage," she answered. "It is not much; I can do everything for myself if the sentinel will let me pass through the kitchen."

Horace pointed to the paper in her hand. "You can go where you like now," he said. "Shall I wait for you here or outside?"

Mercy glanced distrustfully at Ignatius Wetzel. He was again absorbed in his endless examination of the body on the bed. If she left him alone with Mr. Holmcroft, there was no knowing what the hateful old man might not say of her. She answered:

"Wait for me outside, if you please."

The sentinel drew back with a military salute at the sight of the pass. All the French prisoners had been removed; there were not more than half-a-dozen Germans in the kitchen, and the greater part of them were asleep. Mercy took Grace Roseberry's clothes from the corner in which they had been left to dry, and made for the shed—a rough structure of wood, built out from the cottage wall. At the front door she encountered a second sentinel, and showed her pass for the second time. She spoke to this man, asking him if he understood French. He answered that he understood a little. Mercy gave him a piece of money, and said: "I am going to pack up my luggage in the shed. Be kind enough to see that nobody disturbs me." The sentinel saluted, in token that he understood. Mercy disappeared in the dark interior of the shed.

Left alone with Surgeon Wetzel, Horace noticed the strange old man still bending intently over the English lady who had been killed by the shell.

"Anything remarkable," he asked, "in the manner of that poor creature's death?"

"Nothing to put in a newspaper," retorted the cynic, pursuing his investigations as attentively as ever.

"Interesting to a doctor—eh?" said Horace.

"Yes. Interesting to a doctor," was the gruff reply.

Horace good-humoredly accepted the hint implied in those words. He quitted the room by the door leading into the yard, and waited for the charming Englishwoman, as he had been instructed, outside the cottage.

Left by himself, Ignatius Wetzel, after a first cautious look all round him, opened the upper part of Grace's dress, and laid his left hand on her heart. Taking a little steel instrument from his waistcoat pocket with the other hand, he applied it carefully to the wound, raised a morsel of the broken and depressed bone of the skull, and waited for the result. "Aha!" he cried, addressing with a terrible gayety the senseless creature under his hands. "The Frenchman says you are dead, my dear—does he? The Frenchman is a Quack! The Frenchman is an Ass!" He lifted his head, and called into the kitchen. "Max!" A sleepy young German, covered with a dresser's apron from his chin to his feet, drew the curtain, and waited for his instructions. "Bring me my black bag," said Ignatius Wetzel. Having given that order, he rubbed his hands cheerfully, and shook himself like a dog. "Now I am quite happy," croaked the terrible old man, with his fierce eyes leering sidelong at the bed. "My dear, dead Englishwoman, I would not have missed this meeting with you for all the money I have in the world. Ha! you infernal French Quack, you call it death, do you? I call it suspended animation from pressure on the brain!"

Max appeared with the black bag.

Ignatius Wetzel selected two fearful instruments, bright and new, and hugged them to his bosom. "My little boys," he said, tenderly, as if they were his children; "my blessed little boys, come to work!" He turned to the assistant. "Do you remember the battle of Solferino, Max—and the Austrian soldier I operated on for a wound on the head?"

The assistant's sleepy eyes opened wide; he was evidently interested. "I remember," he said. "I held the candle."

The master led the way to the bed.

"I am not satisfied with the result of that operation at Solferino," he said; "I have wanted to try again ever since. It's true that I saved the man's life, but I failed to give him back his reason along with it. It might have been something wrong in the operation, or it might have been something wrong in the man. Whichever it was, he will live and die mad. Now look here, my little Max, at this dear young lady on the bed. She gives me just what I wanted; here is the case at Solferino once more. You shall hold the candle again, my good boy; stand there, and look with all your eyes. I am going to try if I can save the life and the reason too this time."

He tucked up the cuffs of his coat and began the operation. As his fearful instruments touched Grace's head, the voice of the sentinel at the nearest outpost was heard, giving the word in German which permitted Mercy to take the first step on her journey to England:

"Pass the English lady!"

The operation proceeded. The voice of the sentinel at the next post was heard more faintly, in its turn: "Pass the English lady!"

The operation ended. Ignatius Wetzel held up his hand for silence and put his ear close to the patient's mouth.

The first trembling breath of returning life fluttered over Grace Roseberry's lips and touched the old man's wrinkled cheek. "Aha!" he cried. "Good girl! you breathe—you live!" As he spoke, the voice of the sentinel at the final limit of the German lines (barely audible in the distance) gave the word for the last time:

"Pass the English lady!"

SECOND SCENE.—Mablethorpe House.

PREAMBLE.

THE place is England.

The time is winter, in the year eighteen hundred and seventy.

The persons are, Julian Gray, Horace Holmcroft, Lady Janet Roy, Grace Roseberry, and Mercy Merrick.

CHAPTER VI. LADY JANET'S COMPANION.

IT is a glorious winter's day. The sky is clear, the frost is hard, the ice bears for skating.

The dining-room of the ancient mansion called Mablethorpe House, situated in the London suburb of Kensington, is famous among artists and other persons of taste for the carved wood-work, of Italian origin, which covers the walls on three sides. On the fourth side the march of modern improvement has broken in, and has varied and brightened the scene by means of a conservatory, forming an entrance to the room through a winter-garden of rare plants and flowers. On your right hand, as you stand fronting the conservatory, the monotony of the paneled wall is relieved by a quaintly patterned door of old inlaid wood, leading into the library, and thence, across the great hall, to the other reception-rooms of the house. A corresponding door on the left hand gives access to the billiard-room, to the smoking-room next to it, and to a smaller hall commanding one of the secondary entrances to the building. On the left side also is the ample fireplace, surmounted by its marble mantelpiece, carved in the profusely and confusedly ornate style of eighty years since. To the educated eye the dining-room, with its modern furniture and conservatory, its ancient walls and doors, and its lofty mantelpiece (neither very old nor very new), presents a startling, almost a revolutionary, mixture of the decorative workmanship of widely differing schools. To the ignorant eye the one result produced is an impression of perfect luxury and comfort, united in the friendliest combination, and developed on the largest scale.

The clock has just struck two. The table is spread for luncheon.

The persons seated at the table are three in number. First, Lady Janet Roy. Second, a young lady who is her reader and companion. Third, a guest staying in the house, who has already appeared in these pages under the name of Horace Holmcroft—attached to the German army as war correspondent of an English newspaper.

Lady Janet Roy needs but little introduction. Everybody with the slightest pretension to experience in London society knows Lady Janet Roy.

Who has not heard of her old lace and her priceless rubies? Who has not admired her commanding figure, her beautifully dressed white hair, her wonderful black eyes, which still preserve their youthful brightness, after first opening on the world seventy years since? Who has not felt the charm of her frank, easily flowing talk, her inexhaustible spirits, her good-humored, gracious sociability of manner? Where is the modern hermit who is not familiarly acquainted, by hearsay at least, with the fantastic novelty and humor of her opinions; with her generous encouragement of rising merit of any sort, in all ranks, high or low; with her charities, which know no distinction between abroad and at home; with her large indulgence, which no ingratitude can discourage, and no servility pervert? Everybody has heard of the popular old lady—the childless widow of a long-forgotten lord. Everybody knows Lady Janet Roy.

But who knows the handsome young woman sitting on her right hand, playing with her luncheon instead of eating it? Nobody really knows her.

She is prettily dressed in gray poplin, trimmed with gray velvet, and set off by a ribbon of deep red tied in a bow at the throat. She is nearly as tall as Lady Janet herself, and possesses a grace and beauty of figure not always seen in women who rise above the medium height. Judging by a certain innate grandeur in the carriage of her head and in the expression of her large melancholy gray eyes, believers in blood and breeding will be apt to guess that this is another noble lady. Alas! she is nothing but Lady Janet's companion and reader. Her head, crowned with its lovely light brown hair, bends with a gentle respect when Lady Janet speaks. Her fine firm hand is easily and incessantly watchful to supply Lady Janet's slightest wants. The old lady—affectionately familiar with her—speaks to her as she might speak to an adopted child. But the gratitude of the beautiful companion has always the same restraint in its acknowledgment of kindness; the smile of the beautiful companion has always the same underlying sadness when it responds to Lady Janet's hearty laugh. Is there something wrong here, under the surface? Is she suffering in mind, or suffering in body? What is the matter with her?

The matter with her is secret remorse. This delicate and beautiful creature pines under the slow torment of constant self-reproach.

To the mistress of the house, and to all who inhabit it or enter it, she is known as Grace Roseberry, the orphan relative by marriage of Lady Janet Roy. To herself alone she is known as the outcast of the London streets; the inmate of the London Refuge; the lost woman who has stolen her way back—after vainly trying to fight her way back—to Home and Name. There she sits in the grim shadow of her own terrible secret, disguised in another person's identity, and established in another person's place. Mercy Merrick had only to dare, and to become Grace Roseberry if she pleased. She has dared, and she has been Grace Roseberry for nearly four months past.

At this moment, while Lady Janet is talking to Horace Holmcroft, something that has passed between them has set her thinking of the day when she took the first fatal step which committed her to the fraud.

How marvelously easy of accomplishment the act of personation had been! At first sight Lady Janet had yielded to the fascination of the noble and interesting face. No need to present the stolen letter; no need to repeat the ready-made story. The old lady had put the letter aside unopened, and had stopped the story at the first words. "Your face is your introduction, my dear; your father can say nothing for you which you have not already said for yourself." There was the welcome which established her firmly in her false identity at the outset. Thanks to her own experience, and thanks to the "Journal" of events at Rome, questions about her life in Canada and questions about Colonel Roseberry's illness found her ready with answers which (even if suspicion had existed) would have disarmed suspicion on the spot. While the true Grace was slowly and painfully winning her way back to life on her bed in a German hospital, the false Grace was presented to Lady Janet's friends as the relative by marriage of the Mistress of Mablethorpe House. From that time forward nothing had happened to rouse in her the faintest suspicion that Grace Roseberry was other than a dead-and-buried woman. So far as she now knew—so far as any one now knew—she might live out her life in perfect security (if her conscience would let her), respected, distinguished, and beloved, in the position which she had usurped.

She rose abruptly from the table. The effort of her life was to shake herself free of the remembrances which haunted her perpetually as they were haunting her now. Her memory was her worst enemy; her one refuge from it was in change of occupation and change of scene.

"May I go into the conservatory, Lady Janet?" she asked.

"Certainly, my dear."

She bent her head to her protectress, looked for a moment with a steady, compassionate attention at Horace Holmcroft, and, slowly crossing the room, entered the winter-garden. The eyes of Horace followed her, as long as she was in view, with a curious contradictory expression of admiration and disapproval. When she had passed out of sight the admiration vanished, but the disapproval remained. The face of the young man contracted into a frown: he sat silent, with his fork in his hand, playing absently with the fragments on his plate.

"Take some French pie, Horace," said Lady Janet.

"No, thank you."

"Some more chicken, then?"

"No more chicken."

"Will nothing tempt you?"

"I will take some more wine, if you will allow me."

He filled his glass (for the fifth or sixth time) with claret, and emptied it sullenly at a draught. Lady Janet's bright eyes watched him with sardonic attention; Lady Janet's ready tongue spoke out as freely as usual what was passing in her mind at the time.

"The air of Kensington doesn't seem to suit you, my young friend," she said. "The longer you have been my guest, the oftener you fill your glass and empty your cigar-case. Those are bad signs in a young man. When you first came here you arrived invalided by a wound. In your place, I should not have exposed myself to be shot, with no other object in view than describing a battle in a newspaper. I suppose tastes differ. Are you ill? Does your wound still plague you?"

"Not in the least."

"Are you out of spirits?"

Horace Holmcroft dropped his fork, rested his elbows on the table, and answered:

"Awfully."

Even Lady Janet's large toleration had its limits. It embraced every human offense except a breach of good manners. She snatched up the nearest weapon of correction at hand—a tablespoon—and rapped her young friend smartly with it on the arm that was nearest to her.

"My table is not the club table," said the old lady. "Hold up your head. Don't look at your fork—look at me. I allow nobody to be out of spirits in My house. I consider it to be a reflection on Me. If our quiet life here doesn't suit you, say so plainly, and find something else to do. There is employment to be had, I suppose—if you choose to apply for it? You needn't smile. I don't want to see your teeth—I want an answer."

Horace admitted, with all needful gravity, that there was employment to be had. The war between France and Germany, he remarked, was still going on: the newspaper had offered to employ him again in the capacity of correspondent.

"Don't speak of the newspapers and the war!" cried Lady Janet, with a sudden explosion of anger, which was genuine anger this time. "I detest the newspapers! I won't allow the newspapers to enter this house. I lay the whole blame of the blood shed between France and Germany at their door."

Horace's eyes opened wide in amazement. The old lady was evidently in earnest. "What can you possibly mean?" he asked. "Are the newspapers responsible for the war?"

"Entirely responsible," answered Lady Janet. "Why, you don't understand the age you live in! Does anybody do anything nowadays (fighting included) without wishing to see it in the newspapers? I subscribe to a charity; thou art presented with a testimonial; he preaches a sermon; we suffer a grievance; you make a discovery; they go to church and get married. And I, thou, he; we, you, they, all want one and the same thing—we want to see it in the papers. Are kings, soldiers, and diplomatists exceptions to the general rule of humanity? Not they! I tell you seriously, if the newspapers of Europe had one and all decided not to take the smallest notice in print of the war between France and Germany, it is my firm conviction the war would have come to an end for want of encouragement long since. Let the pen cease to advertise the sword, and I, for one, can see the result. No report—no fighting."

"Your views have the merit of perfect novelty, ma'am," said Horace. "Would you object to see them in the newspapers?"

Lady Janet worsted her young friend with his own weapons.

"Don't I live in the latter part of the nineteenth century?" she asked. "In the newspapers, did you say? In large type, Horace, if you love me!"

Horace changed the subject.

"You blame me for being out of spirits," he said; "and you seem to think it is because I am tired of my pleasant life at Mablethorpe House. I am not in the least tired, Lady Janet." He looked toward the conservatory: the frown showed itself on his face once more. "The truth is," he resumed, "I am not satisfied with Grace Roseberry."

"What has Grace done?"

"She persists in prolonging our engagement. Nothing will persuade her to fix the day for our marriage."

It was true! Mercy had been mad enough to listen to him, and to love him. But Mercy was not vile enough to marry him under her false character, and in her false name. Between three and four months had elapsed since Horace had been sent home from the war, wounded, and had found the beautiful Englishwoman whom he had befriended in France established at

Mablethorpe House. Invited to become Lady Janet's guest (he had passed his holidays as a school-boy under Lady Janet's roof)—free to spend the idle time of his convalescence from morning to night in Mercy's society—the impression originally produced on him in a French cottage soon strengthened into love. Before the month was out Horace had declared himself, and had discovered that he spoke to willing ears. From that moment it was only a question of persisting long enough in the resolution to gain his point. The marriage engagement was ratified—most reluctantly on the lady's side—and there the further progress of Horace Holmcroft's suit came to an end. Try as he might, he failed to persuade his betrothed wife to fix the day for the marriage. There were no obstacles in her way. She had no near relations of her own to consult. As a connection of Lady Janet's by marriage, Horace's mother and sisters were ready to receive her with all the honors due to a new member of the family. No pecuniary considerations made it necessary, in this case, to wait for a favorable time. Horace was an only son; and he had succeeded to his father's estate with an ample income to support it. On both sides alike there was absolutely nothing to prevent the two young people from being married as soon as the settlements could be drawn. And yet, to all appearance, here was a long engagement in prospect, with no better reason than the lady's incomprehensible perversity to explain the delay. "Can you account for Grace's conduct?" asked Lady Janet. Her manner changed as she put the question. She looked and spoke like a person who was perplexed and annoyed.

"I hardly like to own it," Horace answered, "but I am afraid she has some motive for deferring our marriage which she cannot confide either to you or to me."

Lady Janet started.

"What makes you think that?" she asked.

"I have once or twice caught her in tears. Every now and then— sometimes when she is talking quite gayly—she suddenly changes color and becomes silent and depressed. Just now, when she left the table (didn't you notice it?), she looked at me in the strangest way—almost as if she was sorry for me. What do these things mean?"

Horace's reply, instead of increasing Lady Janet's anxiety, seemed to relieve it. He had observed nothing which she had not noticed herself. "You foolish boy!" she said, "the meaning is plain enough. Grace has been out of health for some time past. The doctor recommends change of air. I shall take her away with me."

"It would be more to the purpose," Horace rejoined, "if I took her away with me. She might consent, if you would only use your influence. Is it asking too much to ask you to persuade her? My mother and my sisters have written to her, and have produced no effect. Do me the greatest of all kindnesses— speak to her to-day!" He paused, and possessing himself of Lady Janet's hand, pressed it entreatingly. "You have always been so good to me," he said, softly, and pressed it again.

The old lady looked at him. It was impossible to dispute that there were attractions in Horace Holmcroft's face which made it well worth looking at. Many a woman might have envied him his clear complexion, his bright blue eyes, and the warm amber tint in his light Saxon hair. Men—especially men skilled in observing physiognomy—might have noticed in the shape of his forehead and in the line of his upper lip the signs indicative of a moral nature deficient in largeness and breadth—of a mind easily accessible to strong prejudices, and obstinate in maintaining those prejudices in the face of conviction itself.

To the observation of women these remote defects were too far below the surface to be visible. He charmed the sex in general by his rare personal advantages, and by the graceful deference of his manner. To Lady Janet he was endeared, not by his own merits only, but by old associations that were connected with him. His father had been one of her many admirers in her young days. Circumstances had parted them. Her marriage to another man had been a childless marriage. In past times, when the boy Horace had come to her from school, she had cherished a secret fancy (too absurd to be communicated to any living creature) that he ought to have been her son, and might have been her son, if she had married his father! She smiled charmingly, old as she was—she yielded as his mother might have yielded—when the young man took her hand and entreated her to interest herself in his marriage. "Must I really speak to Grace?" she asked, with a gentleness of tone and manner far from characteristic, on ordinary occasions, of the lady of Mablethorpe House. Horace saw that he had gained his point. He sprang to his feet; his eyes turned eagerly in the direction of the conservatory; his handsome face was radiant with hope. Lady Janet (with her mind full of his father) stole a last look at him, sighed as she thought of the vanished days, and recovered herself.

"Go to the smoking-room," she said, giving him a push toward the door. "Away with you, and cultivate the favorite vice of the nineteenth century." Horace attempted to express his gratitude. "Go and smoke!" was all she said, pushing him out. "Go and smoke!"

Left by herself, Lady Janet took a turn in the room, and considered a little.

Horace's discontent was not unreasonable. There was really no excuse for the delay of which he complained. Whether the young lady had a special motive for hanging back, or whether she was merely fretting because she did not know her own mind, it was, in either case, necessary to come to a distinct understanding, sooner or later, on the serious question of the marriage. The difficulty was, how to approach the subject without giving offense. "I don't understand the young women of the present generation," thought Lady Janet. "In my time, when we were fond of a man, we were ready to marry him at a moment's notice. And this is an age of progress! They ought to be readier still."

Arriving, by her own process of induction, at this inevitable conclusion, she decided to try what her influence could accomplish, and to trust to the inspiration of the moment for exerting it in the right way. "Grace!" she called out, approaching the conservatory door. The tall, lithe figure in its gray dress glided into view, and stood relieved against the green background of the winter-garden.

"Did your ladyship call me?"

"Yes; I want to speak to you. Come and sit down by me."

With those words Lady Janet led the way to a sofa, and placed her companion by her side.

CHAPTER VII. THE MAN IS COMING.

"You look very pale this morning, my child."

Mercy sighed wearily. "I am not well," she answered. "The slightest noises startle me. I feel tired if I only walk across the room."

Lady Janet patted her kindly on the shoulder. "We must try what a change will do for you. Which shall it be? the Continent or the sea-side?"

"Your ladyship is too kind to me."

"It is impossible to be too kind to you."

Mercy started. The color flowed charmingly over her pale face. "Oh!" she exclaimed, impulsively. "Say that again!"

"Say it again?" repeated Lady Janet, with a look of surprise.

"Yes! Don't think me presuming; only think me vain. I can't hear you say too often that you have learned to like me. Is it really a pleasure to you to have me in the house? Have I always behaved well since I have been with you?"

(The one excuse for the act of personation—if excuse there could be—lay in the affirmative answer to those questions. It would be something, surely, to say of the false Grace that the true Grace could not have been worthier of her welcome, if the true Grace had been received at Mablethorpe House!)

Lady Janet was partly touched, partly amused, by the extraordinary earnestness of the appeal that had been made to her.

"Have you behaved well?" she repeated. "My dear, you talk as if you were a child!" She laid her hand caressingly on Mercy's arm, and continued, in a graver tone: "It is hardly too much to say, Grace, that I bless the day when you first came to me. I do believe I could be hardly fonder of you if you were my own daughter."

Mercy suddenly turned her head aside, so as to hide her face. Lady Janet, still touching her arm, felt it tremble. "What is the matter with you?" she asked, in her abrupt, downright manner.

"I am only very grateful to your ladyship—that is all." The words were spoken faintly, in broken tones. The face was still averted from Lady Janet's view. "What have I said to provoke this?" wondered the old lady. "Is she in the melting mood to-day? If she is, now is the time to say a word for Horace!" Keeping that excellent object in view, Lady Janet approached the delicate topic with all needful caution at starting.

"We have got on so well together," she resumed, "that it will not be easy for either of us to feel reconciled to a change in our lives. At my age, it will fall hardest on me. What shall I do, Grace, when the day comes for parting with my adopted daughter?"

Mercy started, and showed her face again. The traces of tears were in her eyes. "Why should I leave you?" she asked, in a tone of alarm.

"Surely you know!" exclaimed Lady Janet.

"Indeed I don't. Tell me why."

"Ask Horace to tell you."

The last allusion was too plain to be misunderstood. Mercy's head drooped. She began to tremble again. Lady Janet looked at her in blank amazement.

"Is there anything wrong between Horace and you?" she asked.

"No."

"You know your own heart, my dear child? You have surely not encouraged Horace without loving him?"

"Oh no!"

"And yet—"

For the first time in their experience of each other Mercy ventured to interrupt her benefactress. "Dear Lady Janet," she interposed, gently, "I am in

63

no hurry to be married. There will be plenty of time in the future to talk of that. You had something you wished to say to me. What is it?"

It was no easy matter to disconcert Lady Janet Roy. But that last question fairly reduced her to silence. After all that had passed, there sat her young companion, innocent of the faintest suspicion of the subject that was to be discussed between them! "What are the young women of the present time made of?" thought the old lady, utterly at a loss to know what to say next. Mercy waited, on her side, with an impenetrable patience which only aggravated the difficulties of the position. The silence was fast threatening to bring the interview to a sudden and untimely end, when the door from the library opened, and a man-servant, bearing a little silver salver, entered the room.

Lady Janet's rising sense of annoyance instantly seized on the servant as a victim. "What do you want?" she asked, sharply. "I never rang for you."

"A letter, my lady. The messenger waits for an answer."

The man presented his salver with the letter on it, and withdrew.

Lady Janet recognized the handwriting on the address with a look of surprise. "Excuse me, my dear," she said, pausing, with her old-fashioned courtesy, before she opened the envelope. Mercy made the necessary acknowledgment, and moved away to the other end of the room, little thinking that the arrival of the letter marked a crisis in her life. Lady Janet put on her spectacles. "Odd that he should have come back already!" she said to herself, as she threw the empty envelope on the table.

The letter contained these lines, the writer of them being no other than the man who had preached in the chapel of the Refuge:

"DEAR AUNT—I am back again in London before my time. My friend the rector has shortened his holiday, and has resumed his duties in the country. I am afraid you will blame me when you hear of the reasons which have hastened his return. The sooner I make my confession, the easier I shall feel. Besides, I have a special object in wishing to see you as soon as possible. May I follow my letter to Mablethorpe House? And may I present a lady to you—a perfect stranger—in whom I am interested? Pray say Yes, by the bearer, and oblige your affectionate nephew,

"JULIAN GRAY."

Lady Janet referred again suspiciously to the sentence in the letter which alluded to the "lady."

Julian Gray was her only surviving nephew, the son of a favorite sister whom she had lost. He would have held no very exalted position in the estimation of his aunt—who regarded his views in politics and religion with the strongest aversion—but for his marked resemblance to his mother. This pleaded for him with the old lady, aided as it was by the pride that she secretly felt in the early celebrity which the young clergyman had achieved as a writer and a preacher. Thanks to these mitigating circumstances, and to Julian's inexhaustible good-humor, the aunt and the nephew generally met on friendly terms. Apart from what she called "his detestable opinions," Lady Janet was sufficiently interested in Julian to feel some curiosity about the mysterious "lady" mentioned in the letter. Had he determined to settle in life? Was his choice already made? And if so, would it prove to be a choice acceptable to the family? Lady Janet's bright face showed signs of doubt as she asked herself that last question. Julian's liberal views were capable of leading him to dangerous extremes. His aunt shook her head ominously as she rose from the sofa and advanced to the library door.

"Grace," she said, pausing and turning round, "I have a note to write to my nephew. I shall be back directly."

Mercy approached her, from the opposite extremity of the room, with an exclamation of surprise.

"Your nephew?" she repeated. "Your ladyship never told me you had a nephew."

Lady Janet laughed. "I must have had it on the tip of my tongue to tell you, over and over again," she said. "But we have had so many things to talk about—and, to own the truth, my nephew is not one of my favorite subjects of conversation. I don't mean that I dislike him; I detest his principles, my dear, that's all. However, you shall form your own opinion of him; he is coming to see me to-day. Wait here till I return; I have something more to say about Horace."

Mercy opened the library door for her, closed it again, and walked slowly to and fro alone in the room, thinking.

Was her mind running on Lady Janet's nephew? No. Lady Janet's brief allusion to her relative had not led her into alluding to him by his name. Mercy was still as ignorant as ever that the preacher at the Refuge and the nephew of her benefactress were one and the same man. Her memory was busy now with the tribute which Lady Janet had paid to her at the outset of the interview between them: "It is hardly too much to say, Grace, that I bless the day when you first came to me." For the moment there was balm for her wounded spirit in the remembrance of those words. Grace Roseberry herself could surely have earned no sweeter praise than the praise that she had won. The next instant she was seized with a sudden horror of her own successful fraud. The sense of her degradation had never been so bitterly present to her as at that moment. If she could only confess the truth—if she could innocently enjoy her harmless life at Mablethorpe House—what a grateful, happy woman she might be! Was it possible (if she made the confession) to trust to her own good conduct to plead her excuse? No! Her calmer sense warned her that it was hopeless. The place she had won—honestly won—in Lady Janet's estimation had been obtained by a trick. Nothing could alter, nothing could excuse, that. She took out her handkerchief and dashed away the useless tears that had gathered in her eyes, and tried to turn her thoughts some other way. What was it Lady Janet had said on going into the library? She had said she was coming back to speak about Horace. Mercy guessed what the object was; she knew but too well what Horace wanted of her. How was she to meet the emergency? In the name of Heaven, what was to be done? Could she let the man who loved her—the man whom she loved—drift blindfold into marriage with such a woman as she had been? No! it was her duty to warn him. How? Could she break his heart, could she lay his life waste by speaking the cruel words which might part them forever? "I can't tell him! I won't tell him!" she burst out, passionately. "The disgrace of it would kill me!" Her varying mood changed as the words escaped her. A reckless defiance of her own better nature—that saddest of all the forms in which a woman's misery can express itself—filled her heart with its poisoning bitterness. She sat down again on the sofa with eyes that glittered and cheeks suffused with an angry red. "I am no worse than another woman!" she thought. "Another woman might have married him for his money." The next moment the miserable insufficiency of her own excuse for deceiving him showed its hollowness, self-exposed. She covered her face with her hands, and found refuge—where she had often found refuge before—in the helpless resignation of despair. "Oh, that I had died before I entered this house! Oh, that I could die and have done with it at this moment!" So the struggle had ended with her hundreds of times already. So it ended now.

The door leading into the billiard-room opened softly. Horace Holmcroft had waited to hear the result of Lady Janet's interference in his favor until he could wait no longer.

He looked in cautiously, ready to withdraw again unnoticed if the two were still talking together. The absence of Lady Janet suggested that the interview had come to an end. Was his betrothed wife waiting alone to speak to him on his return to the room? He advanced a few steps. She never moved; she sat heedless, absorbed in her thoughts. Were they thoughts of him? He advanced a little nearer, and called to her.

"Grace!"

She sprang to her feet, with a faint cry. "I wish you wouldn't startle me," she said, irritably, sinking back on the sofa. "Any sudden alarm sets my heart beating as if it would choke me."

Horace pleaded for pardon with a lover's humility. In her present state of nervous irritation she was not to be appeased. She looked away from him in silence. Entirely ignorant of the paroxysm of mental suffering through which she had just passed, he seated himself by her side, and asked her gently if she had seen Lady Janet. She made an affirmative answer with an unreasonable impatience of tone and manner which would have warned an older and more experienced man to give her time before he spoke again. Horace was young, and weary of the suspense that he had endured in the other room. He unwisely pressed her with another question.

"Has Lady Janet said anything to you—"

She turned on him angrily before he could finish the sentence. "You have tried to make her hurry me into marrying you," she burst out. "I see it in your face!"

Plain as the warning was this time, Horace still failed to interpret it in the right way. "Don't be angry!" he said, good-humoredly. "Is it so very inexcusable to ask Lady Janet to intercede for me? I have tried to persuade you in vain. My mother and my sisters have pleaded for me, and you turn a deaf ear—"

She could endure it no longer. She stamped her foot on the door with hysterical vehemence. "I am weary of hearing of your mother and your sisters!" she broke in violently. "You talk of nothing else."

It was just possible to make one more mistake in dealing with her—and Horace made it. He took offense, on his side, and rose from the sofa. His mother and sisters were high authorities in his estimation; they variously represented his ideal of perfection in women. He withdrew to the opposite extremity of the room, and administered the severest reproof that he could think of on the spur of the moment.

"It would be well, Grace, if you followed the example set you by my mother and my sisters," he said. "They are not in the habit of speaking cruelly to those who love them."

To all appearance the rebuke failed to produce the slightest effect. She seemed to be as indifferent to it as if it had not reached her ears. There was a spirit in her—a miserable spirit, born of her own bitter experience—which rose in revolt against Horace's habitual glorification of the ladies of his family. "It sickens me," she thought to herself, "to hear of the virtues of women who have never been tempted! Where is the merit of living reputably, when your life is one course of prosperity and enjoyment? Has his mother known starvation? Have his sisters been left forsaken in the street?" It hardened her heart—it almost reconciled her to deceiving him—when he set his relatives up as patterns for her. Would he never understand that women detested having other women exhibited as examples to them? She looked round at him with a sense of impatient wonder. He was sitting at the luncheon-table, with his back turned on her, and his head resting on his hand. If he had attempted to rejoin her, she would have repelled him; if he had spoken, she would have met him with a sharp reply. He sat apart from her, without uttering a word. In a man's hands silence is the most terrible of all protests to the woman who loves him. Violence she can endure. Words she is always ready to meet by words on her side. Silence conquers her. After a moment's hesitation, Mercy left the sofa and advanced submissively toward the table. She had offended him—and she alone was in fault. How should he know it, poor fellow, when he innocently mortified her? Step by step she drew closer and closer. He never looked round; he never moved. She laid her hand timidly on his shoulder. "Forgive me, Horace," she whispered in his ear. "I am suffering this morning; I am not myself. I didn't mean what I said. Pray forgive me." There was no resisting the caressing tenderness of voice and manner which accompanied those words. He looked up; he took her hand. She bent over him, and touched his forehead with her lips. "Am I forgiven?" she asked.

"Oh, my darling," he said, "if you only knew how I loved you!"

"I do know it," she answered, gently, twining his hair round her finger, and arranging it over his forehead where his hand had ruffled it.

They were completely absorbed in each other, or they must, at that moment, have heard the library door open at the other end of the room.

Lady Janet had written the necessary reply to her nephew, and had returned, faithful to her engagement, to plead the cause of Horace. The first object that met her view was her client pleading, with conspicuous success, for himself! "I am not wanted, evidently," thought the old lady. She noiselessly closed the door again and left the lovers by themselves.

Horace returned, with unwise persistency, to the question of the deferred marriage. At the first words that he spoke she drew back directly—sadly, not angrily.

"Don't press me to-day," she said; "I am not well to-day."

He rose and looked at her anxiously. "May I speak about it to-morrow?"

"Yes, to-morrow." She returned to the sofa, and changed the subject. "What a time Lady Janet is away!" she said. "What can be keeping her so long?"

Horace did his best to appear interested in the question of Lady Janet's prolonged absence. "What made her leave you?" he asked, standing at the back of the sofa and leaning over her.

"She went into the library to write a note to her nephew. By-the-by, who is her nephew?"

"Is it possible you don't know?"

"Indeed, I don't."

"You have heard of him, no doubt," said Horace. "Lady Janet's nephew is a celebrated man." He paused, and stooping nearer to her, lifted a love-lock that lay over her shoulder and pressed it to his lips. "Lady Janet's nephew," he resumed, "is Julian Gray."

She started off her seat, and looked round at him in blank, bewildered terror, as if she doubted the evidence of her own senses.

Horace was completely taken by surprise. "My dear Grace!" he exclaimed; "what have I said or done to startle you this time?"

She held up her hand for silence. "Lady Janet's nephew is Julian Gray," she repeated; "and I only know it now!"

Horace's perplexity increased. "My darling, now you do know it, what is there to alarm you?" he asked.

(There was enough to alarm the boldest woman living—in such a position, and with such a temperament as hers. To her mind the personation of Grace Roseberry had suddenly assumed a new aspect: the aspect of a fatality. It had led her blindfold to the house in which she and the preacher at the Refuge were to meet. He was coming—the man who had reached her inmost heart, who had influenced her whole life! Was the day of reckoning coming with him?)

"Don't notice me," she said, faintly. "I have been ill all the morning. You saw it yourself when you came in here; even the sound of your voice alarmed me. I shall be better directly. I am afraid I startled you?"

"My dear Grace, it almost looked as if you were terrified at the sound of Julian's name! He is a public celebrity, I know; and I have seen ladies start and stare at him when he entered a room. But you looked perfectly panic-stricken."

She rallied her courage by a desperate effort; she laughed—a harsh, uneasy laugh—and stopped him by putting her hand over his mouth. "Absurd!" she said, lightly. "As if Mr. Julian Gray had anything to do with my looks! I am better already. See for yourself!" She looked round at him again with a ghastly gayety; and returned, with a desperate assumption of indifference, to the subject of Lady Janet's nephew. "Of course I have heard of him," she said. "Do you know that he is expected here to-day? Don't stand there behind me—it's so hard to talk to you. Come and sit down."

He obeyed—but she had not quite satisfied him yet. His face had not lost its expression of anxiety and surprise. She persisted in playing her part, determined to set at rest in him any possible suspicion that she had reasons of her own for being afraid of Julian Gray. "Tell me about this famous man of yours," she said, putting her arm familiarly through his arm. "What is he like?"

The caressing action and the easy tone had their effect on Horace. His face began to clear; he answered her lightly on his side.

"Prepare yourself to meet the most unclerical of clergymen," he said. "Julian is a lost sheep among the parsons, and a thorn in the side of his bishop. Preaches, if they ask him, in Dissenters' chapels. Declines to set up any pretensions to priestly authority and priestly power. Goes about doing good on a plan of his own. Is quite resigned never to rise to the high places in his profession. Says it's rising high enough for him to be the Archdeacon of the afflicted, the Dean of the hungry, and the Bishop of the poor. With all his oddities, as good a fellow as ever lived. Immensely popular with the women. They all go to him for advice. I wish you would go, too."

Mercy changed color. "What do you mean?" she asked, sharply.

"Julian is famous for his powers of persuasion," said Horace, smiling. "If he spoke to you, Grace, he would prevail on you to fix the day. Suppose I ask Julian to plead for me?"

He made the proposal in jest. Mercy's unquiet mind accepted it as addressed to her in earnest. "He will do it," she thought, with a sense of indescribable terror, "if I don't stop him!" There is but one chance for her. The only certain way to prevent Horace from appealing to his friend was to grant what Horace wished for before his friend entered the house. She laid her hand on his shoulder; she hid the terrible anxieties that were devouring her under an assumption of coquetry painful and pitiable to see.

"Don't talk nonsense!" she said, gayly. "What were we saying just now—before we began to speak of Mr. Julian Gray?"

"We were wondering what had become of Lady Janet," Horace replied.

She tapped him impatiently on the shoulder. "No! no! It was something you said before that."

Her eyes completed what her words had left unsaid. Horace's arm stole round her waist.

"I was saying that I loved you," he answered, in a whisper.

"Only that?"

"Are you tired of hearing it?"

She smiled charmingly. "Are you so very much in earnest about—about—" She stopped, and looked away from him.

"About our marriage?"

"Yes."

"It is the one dearest wish of my life."

"Really?"

"Really."

There was a pause. Mercy's fingers toyed nervously with the trinkets at her watch-chain. "When would you like it to be?" she said, very softly, with her whole attention fixed on the watch-chain.

She had never spoken, she had never looked, as she spoke and looked now. Horace was afraid to believe in his own good fortune. "Oh, Grace!" he exclaimed, "you are not trifling with me?"

"What makes you think I am trifling with you?"

Horace was innocent enough to answer her seriously. "You would not even let me speak of our marriage just now," he said.

"Never mind what I did just now," she retorted, petulantly. "They say women are changeable. It is one of the defects of the sex."

"Heaven be praised for the defects of the sex!" cried Horace, with devout sincerity. "Do you really leave me to decide?"

"If you insist on it."

Horace considered for a moment—the subject being the law of marriage. "We may be married by license in a fortnight," he said. "I fix this day fortnight."

She held up her hands in protest.

"Why not? My lawyer is ready. There are no preparations to make. You said when you accepted me that it was to be a private marriage."

Mercy was obliged to own that she had certainly said that.

"We might be married at once—if the law would only let us. This day fortnight! Say—Yes!" He drew her closer to him. There was a pause. The mask of coquetry—badly worn from the first—dropped from her. Her sad gray eyes rested compassionately on his eager face. "Don't look so serious!" he said. "Only one little word, Grace! Only Yes."

She sighed, and said it. He kissed her passionately. It was only by a resolute effort that she released herself.

"Leave me!" she said, faintly. "Pray leave me by myself!"

She was in earnest—strangely in earnest. She was trembling from head to foot. Horace rose to leave her. "I will find Lady Janet," he said; "I long to show the dear old lady that I have recovered my spirits, and to tell her why." He turned round at the library door. "You won't go away? You will let me see you again when you are more composed?"

"I will wait here," said Mercy.

Satisfied with that reply, he left the room.

Her hands dropped on her lap; her head sank back wearily on the cushions at the head of the sofa. There was a dazed sensation in her: her mind felt stunned. She wondered vacantly whether she was awake or dreaming. Had she really said the word which pledged her to marry Horace Holmcroft in a fortnight? A fortnight! Something might happen in that time to prevent it: she might find her way in a fortnight out of the terrible position in which she stood. Anyway, come what might of it, she had chosen the preferable alternative to a private interview with Julian Gray. She raised herself from her recumbent position with a start, as the idea of the interview—dismissed for the last few minutes—possessed itself again of her mind. Her excited imagination figured Julian Gray as present in the room at that moment, speaking to her as Horace had proposed. She saw him seated close at her side—this man who had shaken her to the soul when he was in the pulpit, and when she was listening to him (unseen) at the other end of the chapel—she saw him close by her, looking her searchingly in the face; seeing her shameful secret in her eyes; hearing it in her voice; feeling it in her trembling hands; forcing it out of her word by word, till she fell prostrate at his feet with the confession of the fraud. Her head dropped again on the cushions; she hid her face in horror of the scene which her excited fancy had conjured up. Even now, when she had made that dreaded interview needless, could she feel sure (meeting him only on the most distant terms) of not betraying herself? She could not feel sure. Something in her shuddered and shrank at the bare idea of finding herself in the same room with him. She felt it, she knew it: her guilty conscience owned and feared its master in Julian Gray!

The minutes passed. The violence of her agitation began to tell physically on her weakened frame.

She found herself crying silently without knowing why. A weight was on her head, a weariness was in all her limbs. She sank lower on the cushions— her eyes closed—the monotonous ticking of the clock on the mantelpiece grew drowsily fainter and fainter on her ear. Little by little she dropped into slumber—slumber so light that she started when a morsel of coal fell into the grate, or when the birds chirped and twittered in their aviary in the winter-garden.

Lady Janet and Horace came in. She was faintly conscious of persons in the room. After an interval she opened her eyes, and half rose to speak to them. The room was empty again. They had stolen out softly and left her to repose. Her eyes closed once more. She dropped back into slumber, and from slumber, in the favoring warmth and quiet of the place, into deep and dreamless sleep.

CHAPTER VIII. THE MAN APPEARS.

After an interval of rest Mercy was aroused by the shutting of a glass door at the far end of the conservatory. This door, leading into the garden, was used only by the inmates of the house, or by old friends privileged to enter the reception-rooms by that way. Assuming that either Horace or Lady Janet was returning to the dining-room, Mercy raised herself a little on the' sofa and listened.

The voice of one of the men-servants caught her ear. It was answered by another voice, which instantly set her trembling in every limb.

She started up, and listened again in speechless terror. Yes! there was no mistaking it. The voice that was answering the servant was the unforgotten voice which she had heard at the Refuge. The visitor who had come in by the glass door was—Julian Gray!

His rapid footsteps advanced nearer and nearer to the dining-room. She recovered herself sufficiently to hurry to the library door. Her hand shook so that she failed at first to open it. She had just succeeded when she heard him again—speaking to her.

"Pray don't run away! I am nothing very formidable. Only Lady Janet's nephew—Julian Gray."

She turned slowly, spell-bound by his voice, and confronted him in silence.

He was standing, hat in hand, at the entrance to the conservatory, dressed in black, and wearing a white cravat, but with a studious avoidance of anything specially clerical in the make and form of his clothes. Young as he was, there were marks of care already on his face, and the hair was prematurely thin and scanty over his forehead. His slight, active figure was of no more than the middle height. His complexion was pale. The lower part of his face, without beard or whiskers, was in no way remarkable. An average observer would have passed him by without notice but for his eyes. These alone made a marked man of him. The unusual size of the orbits in which they were set was enough of itself to attract attention; it gave a grandeur to his head, which the head, broad and firm as it was, did not possess. As to the eyes themselves, the soft, lustrous brightness of them defied analysis No two people could agree about their color; divided opinion declaring alternately that they were dark gray or black. Painters had tried to reproduce them, and had given up the effort, in despair of seizing any one expression in the bewildering variety of expressions which they presented to view. They were eyes that could charm at one moment and terrify at another; eyes that could set people laughing or crying almost at will. In action and in repose they were irresistible alike. When they first descried Mercy running to the door, they brightened gayly with the merriment of a child. When she turned and faced him, they changed instantly, softening and glowing as they mutely owned the interest and the admiration which the first sight of her had roused in him. His tone and manner altered at the same time. He addressed her with the deepest respect when he spoke his next words.

"Let me entreat you to favor me by resuming your seat," he said. "And let me ask your pardon if I have thoughtlessly intruded on you."

He paused, waiting for her reply before he advanced into the room. Still spell-bound by his voice, she recovered self-control enough to bow to him and to resume her place on the sofa. It was impossible to leave him now. After looking at her for a moment, he entered the room without speaking to her again. She was beginning to perplex as well as to interest him. "No common sorrow," he thought, "has set its mark on that woman's face; no common heart beats in that woman's breast. Who can she be?"

Mercy rallied her courage, and forced herself to speak to him.

"Lady Janet is in the library, I believe," she said, timidly. "Shall I tell her you are here?"

"Don't disturb Lady Janet, and don't disturb yourself." With that answer he approached the luncheon-table, delicately giving her time to feel more at her ease. He took up what Horace had left of the bottle of claret, and poured it into a glass. "My aunt's claret shall represent my aunt for the present," he said, smiling, as he turned toward her once more. "I have had a long walk, and I may venture to help myself in this house without invitation. Is it useless to offer you anything?"

Mercy made the necessary reply. She was beginning already, after her remarkable experience of him, to wonder at his easy manners and his light way of talking.

He emptied his glass with the air of a man who thoroughly understood and enjoyed good wine. "My aunt's claret is worthy of my aunt," he said, with comic gravity, as he set down the glass. "Both are the genuine products of Nature." He seated himself at the table and looked critically at the different dishes left on it. One dish especially attracted his attention. "What is this?" he went on. "A French pie! It seems grossly unfair to taste French wine and to pass over French pie without notice." He took up a knife and fork, and enjoyed the pie as critically as he had enjoyed the wine. "Worthy of the Great Nation!" he exclaimed, with enthusiasm. "Vive la France!"

Mercy listened and looked, in inexpressible astonishment. He was utterly unlike the picture which her fancy had drawn of him in everyday life. Take off his white cravat, and nobody would have discovered that this famous preacher was a clergyman!

He helped himself to another plateful of the pie, and spoke more directly to Mercy, alternately eating and talking as composedly and pleasantly as if they had known each other for years.

"I came here by way of Kensington Gardens," he said. "For some time past I have been living in a flat, ugly, barren, agricultural district. You can't think how pleasant I found the picture presented by the Gardens, as a contrast. The ladies in their rich winter dresses, the smart nursery maids, the lovely children, the ever moving crowd skating on the ice of the Round Pond; it was all so exhilarating after what I have been used to, that I actually caught myself whistling as I walked through the brilliant scene! (In my time boys used always to whistle when they were in good spirits, and I have not got over the habit yet.) Who do you think I met when I was in full song?"

As well as her amazement would let her, Mercy excused herself from guessing. She had never in all her life before spoken to any living being so confusedly and so unintelligently as she now spoke to Julian Gray!

He went on more gayly than ever, without appearing to notice the effect that he had produced on her.

"Whom did I meet," he repeated, "when I was in full song? My bishop! If I had been whistling a sacred melody, his lordship might perhaps have excused my vulgarity out of consideration for my music. Unfortunately, the composition I was executing at the moment (I am one of the loudest of living whistlers) was by Verdi—"La Donna e Mobile"—familiar, no doubt, to his lordship on the street organs. He recognized the tune, poor man, and when I took off my hat to him he looked the other way. Strange, in a world that is bursting with sin and sorrow, to treat such a trifle seriously as a cheerful clergyman whistling a tune!" He pushed away his plate as he said the last words, and went on simply and earnestly in an altered tone. "I have never been able," he said, "to see why we should assert ourselves among other men as belonging to a particular caste, and as being forbidden, in any harmless thing, to do as other people do. The disciples of old set us no such example; they were wiser and better than we are. I venture to say that one of the worst obstacles in the way of our doing good among our fellow-creatures is raised by the mere assumption of the clerical manner and the clerical voice. For my part, I set up no claim to be more sacred and more reverend than any other Christian man who does what good he can." He glanced brightly at Mercy, looking at him in helpless perplexity. The spirit of fun took possession of him again. "Are you a Radical?" he asked, with a humorous twinkle in his large lustrous eyes. "I am!"

Mercy tried hard to understand him, and tried in vain. Could this be the preacher whose words had charmed, purified, ennobled her? Was this the man whose sermon had drawn tears from women about her whom she knew to be shameless and hardened in crime? Yes! The eyes that now rested on her humorously were the beautiful eyes which had once looked into her soul. The voice that had just addressed a jesting question to her was the deep and mellow voice which had once thrilled her to the heart. In the pulpit he was an angel of mercy; out of the pulpit he was a boy let loose from school.

"Don't let me startle you," he said, good-naturedly, noticing her confusion. "Public opinion has called me by harder names than the name of 'Radical.' I have been spending my time lately—as I told you just now—in an agricultural district. My business there was to perform the duty for the rector of the place, who wanted a holiday. How do you think the experiment has ended? The Squire of the parish calls me a Communist; the farmers denounce me as an Incendiary; my friend the rector has been recalled in a hurry, and I have now the honor of speaking to you in the character of a banished man who has made a respectable neighborhood too hot to hold him."

With that frank avowal he left the luncheon table, and took a chair near Mercy.

"You will naturally be anxious," he went on, "to know what my offense was. Do you understand Political Economy and the Laws of Supply and Demand?"

Mercy owned that she did not understand them.

"No more do I—in a Christian country," he said. "That was my offense. You shall hear my confession (just as my aunt will hear it) in two words." He paused for a little while; his variable manner changed again. Mercy, shyly looking at him, saw a new expression in his eyes—an expression which recalled her first remembrance of him as nothing had recalled it yet. "I had no idea," he resumed, "of what the life of a farm-laborer really was, in some parts of England, until I undertook the rector's duties. Never before had I seen such dire wretchedness as I saw in the cottages. Never before had I met with such noble patience under suffering as I found among the people. The martyrs of old could endure, and die. I asked myself if they could endure, and live, like the martyrs whom I saw round me?—live, week after week, month after month, year after year, on the brink of starvation; live, and see their pining children growing up round them, to work and want in their turn; live, with the poor man's parish prison to look to as the end, when hunger and labor have done their worst! Was God's beautiful earth made to hold such misery as this? I can hardly think of it, I can hardly speak of it, even now, with dry eyes!"

His head sank on his breast. He waited—mastering his emotion before he spoke again. Now, at last, she knew him once more. Now he was the man, indeed, whom she had expected to see. Unconsciously she sat listening, with her eyes fixed on his face, with his heart hanging on his words, in the very attitude of the by-gone day when she had heard him for the first time!

"I did all I could to plead for the helpless ones," he resumed. "I went round among the holders of the land to say a word for the tillers of the land. 'These patient people don't want much' (I said); 'in the name of Christ, give them enough to live on!' Political Economy shrieked at the horrid proposal; the Laws of Supply and Demand veiled their majestic faces in dismay. Starvation wages were the right wages, I was told. And why? Because the laborer was obliged to accept them! I determined, so far as one man could do it, that the laborer should not be obliged to accept them. I collected my own resources—I wrote to my friends—and I removed some of the poor fellows to parts of England where their work was better paid. Such was the conduct which made the neighborhood too hot to hold me. So let it be! I mean to go on. I am known in London; I can raise subscriptions. The vile Laws of Supply and Demand shall find labor scarce in that agricultural district; and pitiless Political Economy shall spend a few extra shillings on the poor, as certainly as I am that Radical, Communist, and Incendiary—Julian Gray!"

He rose—making a little gesture of apology for the warmth with which he had spoken—and took a turn in the room. Fired by his enthusiasm, Mercy followed him. Her purse was in her hand, when he turned and faced her.

"Pray let me offer my little tribute—such as it is!" she said, eagerly.

A momentary flush spread over his pale cheeks as he looked at the beautiful compassionate face pleading with him.

"No! no!" he said, smiling; "though I am a parson, I don't carry the begging-box everywhere." Mercy attempted to press the purse on him. The quaint humor began to twinkle again in his eyes as he abruptly drew back from it. "Don't tempt me!" he said. "The frailest of all human creatures is a clergyman tempted by a subscription." Mercy persisted, and conquered; she made him prove the truth of his own profound observation of clerical human nature by taking a piece of money from the purse. "If I must take it—I must!" he remarked. "Thank you for setting the good example! thank you for giving the timely help! What name shall I put down on my list?"

Mercy's eyes looked confusedly away from him. "No name," she said, in a low voice. "My subscription is anonymous."

As she replied, the library door opened. To her infinite relief—to Julian's secret disappointment—Lady Janet Roy and Horace Holmcroft entered the room together.

"Julian!" exclaimed Lady Janet, holding up her hands in astonishment.

He kissed his aunt on the cheek. "Your ladyship is looking charmingly." He gave his hand to Horace. Horace took it, and passed on to Mercy. They walked away together slowly to the other end of the room. Julian seized on the chance which left him free to speak privately to his aunt.

"I came in through the conservatory," he said. "And I found that young lady in the room. Who is she?"

"Are you very much interested in her?" asked Lady Janet, in her gravely ironical way.

Julian answered in one expressive word. "Indescribably!"

Lady Janet called to Mercy to join her.

"My dear," she said, "let me formally present my nephew to you. Julian, this is Miss Grace Roseberry—" She suddenly checked herself. The instant she pronounced the name, Julian started as if it was a surprise to him. "What is it?" she asked, sharply.

"Nothing," he answered, bowing to Mercy, with a marked absence of his former ease of manner. She returned the courtesy a little restrainedly on her side. She, too, had seen him start when Lady Janet mentioned the name by which she was known. The start meant something. What could it be? Why did he turn aside, after bowing to her, and address himself to Horace, with an absent look in his face, as if his thoughts were far away from his words? A complete change had come over him; and it dated from the moment when his aunt had pronounced the name that was not her name—-the name that she had stolen!

Lady Janet claimed Julian's attention, and left Horace free to return to Mercy. "Your room is ready for you," she said. "You will stay here, of course?" Julian accepted the invitation—-still with the air of a man whose mind was preoccupied. Instead of looking at his aunt when he made his reply, he looked round at Mercy with a troubled curiosity in his face, very strange to see. Lady Janet tapped him impatiently on the shoulder. "I expect people to look at me when people speak to me," she said. "What are you staring at my adopted daughter for?"

"Your adopted daughter?" Julian repeated—looking at his aunt this time, and looking very earnestly.

"Certainly! As Colonel Roseberry's daughter, she is connected with me by marriage already. Did you think I had picked up a foundling?"

Julian's face cleared; he looked relieved. "I had forgotten the Colonel," he answered. "Of course the young lady is related to us, as you say."

"Charmed, I am sure, to have satisfied you that Grace is not an impostor," said Lady Janet, with satirical humility. She took Julian's arm and drew him out of hearing of Horace and Mercy. "About that letter of yours?" she proceeded. "There is one line in it that rouses my curiosity. Who is the mysterious 'lady' whom you wish to present to me?"

Julian started, and changed color.

"I can't tell you now," he said, in a whisper.

"Why not?"

To Lady Janet's unutterable astonishment, instead of replying, Julian looked round at her adopted daughter once more.

"What has she got to do with it?" asked the old lady, out of all patience with him.

"It is impossible for me to tell you," he answered, gravely, "while Miss Roseberry is in the room."

CHAPTER IX. NEWS FROM MANNHEIM.

LADY JANET'S curiosity was by this time thoroughly aroused. Summoned to explain who the nameless lady mentioned in his letter could possibly be, Julian had looked at her adopted daughter. Asked next to explain what her adopted daughter had got to do with it, he had declared that he could not answer while Miss Roseberry was in the room.

What did he mean? Lady Janet determined to find out.

"I hate all mysteries," she said to Julian. "And as for secrets, I consider them to be one of the forms of ill-breeding. People in our rank of life ought to be above whispering in corners. If you must have your mystery, I can offer you a corner in the library. Come with me."

Julian followed his aunt very reluctantly. Whatever the mystery might be, he was plainly embarrassed by being called upon to reveal it at a moment's notice. Lady Janet settled herself in her chair, prepared to question and cross-question her nephew, when an obstacle appeared at the other end of the library, in the shape of a man-servant with a message. One of Lady Janet's neighbors had called by appointment to take her to the meeting of a certain committee which assembled that day. The servant announced that the neighbor—an elderly lady—was then waiting in her carriage at the door.

Lady Janet's ready invention set the obstacle aside without a moment's delay. She directed the servant to show her visitor into the drawing-room, and to say that she was unexpectedly engaged, but that Miss Roseberry would see the lady immediately. She then turned to Julian, and said, with her most satirical emphasis of tone and manner: "Would it be an additional convenience if Miss Roseberry was not only out of the room before you disclose your secret, but out of the house?"

Julian gravely answered: "It may possibly be quite as well if Miss Roseberry is out of the house."

Lady Janet led the way back to the dining-room.

"My dear Grace," she said, "you looked flushed and feverish when I saw you asleep on the sofa a little while since. It will do you no harm to have a drive in the fresh air. Our friend has called to take me to the committee meeting. I have sent to tell her that I am engaged—and I shall be much obliged if you will go in my place."

Mercy looked a little alarmed. "Does your ladyship mean the committee meeting of the Samaritan Convalescent Home? The members, as I understand it, are to decide to-day which of the plans for the new building they are to adopt. I cannot surely presume to vote in your place?"

"You can vote, my dear child, just as well as I can," replied the old lady. "Architecture is one of the lost arts. You know nothing about it; I know nothing about it; the architects themselves know nothing about it. One plan is, no doubt, just as bad as the other. Vote, as I should vote, with the majority. Or as poor dear Dr. Johnson said, 'Shout with the loudest mob.' Away with you—and don't keep the committee waiting."

Horace hastened to open the door for Mercy.

"How long shall you be away?" he whispered, confidentially. "I had a thousand things to say to you, and they have interrupted us."

"I shall be back in an hour."

"We shall have the room to ourselves by that time. Come here when you return. You will find me waiting for you."

Mercy pressed his hand significantly and went out. Lady Janet turned to Julian, who had thus far remained in the background, still, to all appearance, as unwilling as ever to enlighten his aunt.

"Well?" she said. "What is tying your tongue now? Grace is out of the room; why won't you begin? Is Horace in the way?"

"Not in the least. I am only a little uneasy—"

"Uneasy about what?"

"I am afraid you have put that charming creature to some inconvenience in sending her away just at this time."

Horace looked up suddenly, with a flush on his face.

"When you say 'that charming creature,'" he asked, sharply, "I suppose you mean Miss Roseberry?"

"Certainly," answered Julian. "Why not?"

Lady Janet interposed. "Gently, Julian," she said. "Grace has only been introduced to you hitherto in the character of my adopted daughter—"

"And it seems to be high time," Horace added, haughtily, "that I should present her next in the character of my engaged wife."

Julian looked at Horace as if he could hardly credit the evidence of his own ears. "Your wife!" he exclaimed, with an irrepressible outburst of disappointment and surprise.

"Yes. My wife," returned Horace. "We are to be married in a fortnight. May I ask," he added, with angry humility, "if you disapprove of the marriage?"

Lady Janet interposed once more. "Nonsense, Horace," she said. "Julian congratulates you, of course."

Julian coldly and absently echoed the words. "Oh, yes! I congratulate you, of course."

Lady Janet returned to the main object of the interview.

"Now we thoroughly understand one another," she said, "let us speak of a lady who has dropped out of the conversation for the last minute or two. I mean, Julian, the mysterious lady of your letter. We are alone, as you desired. Lift the veil, my reverend nephew, which hides her from mortal eyes! Blush, if you like—and can. Is she the future Mrs. Julian Gray?"

"She is a perfect stranger to me," Julian answered, quietly.

"A perfect stranger! You wrote me word you were interested in her."

"I am interested in her. And, what is more, you are interested in her, too."

Lady Janet's fingers drummed impatiently on the table. "Have I not warned you, Julian, that I hate mysteries? Will you, or will you not, explain yourself?"

Before it was possible to answer, Horace rose from his chair. "Perhaps I am in the way?" he said.

Julian signed to him to sit down again.

"I have already told Lady Janet that you are not in the way," he answered. "I now tell you—as Miss Roseberry's future husband—that you, too, have an interest in hearing what I have to say."

Horace resumed his seat with an air of suspicious surprise. Julian addressed himself to Lady Janet.

"You have often heard me speak," he began, "of my old friend and school-fellow, John Cressingham?"

"Yes. The English consul at Mannheim?"

"The same. When I returned from the country I found among my other letters a long letter from the consul. I have brought it with me, and I propose to read certain passages from it, which tell a very strange story more plainly and more credibly than I can tell it in my own words."

"Will it be very long?" inquired Lady Janet, looking with some alarm at the closely written sheets of paper which her nephew spread open before him.

Horace followed with a question on his side.

"You are sure I am interested in it?" he asked. "The consul at Mannheim is a total stranger to me."

"I answer for it," replied Julian, gravely, "neither my aunt's patience nor yours, Horace, will be thrown away if you will favor me by listening attentively to what I am about to read."

With those words he began his first extract from the consul's letter.

* * * "'My memory is a bad one for dates. But full three months must have passed since information was sent to me of an English patient, received at the hospital here, whose case I, as English consul, might feel an interest in investigating.

"'I went the same day to the hospital, and was taken to the bedside.

"'The patient was a woman—young, and (when in health), I should think, very pretty. When I first saw her she looked, to my uninstructed eye, like a dead woman. I noticed that her head had a bandage over it, and I asked what was the nature of the injury that she had received. The answer informed me that the poor creature had been present, nobody knew why or wherefore, at a skirmish or night attack between the Germans and the French, and that the injury to her head had been inflicted by a fragment of a German shell.'"

Horace—thus far leaning back carelessly in his chair—suddenly raised himself and exclaimed, "Good heavens! can this be the woman I saw laid out for dead in the French cottage?"

"It is impossible for me to say," replied Julian. "Listen to the rest of it. The consul's letter may answer your question."

He went on with his reading:

"'The wounded woman had been reported dead, and had been left by the French in their retreat, at the time when the German forces took possession of the enemy's position. She was found on a bed in a cottage by the director of the German ambulance—'"

"Ignatius Wetzel?" cried Horace.

"Ignatius Wetzel," repeated Julian, looking at the letter.

"It is the same!" said Horace. "Lady Janet, we are really interested in this. You remember my telling you how I first met with Grace? And you have heard more about it since, no doubt, from Grace herself?"

"She has a horror of referring to that part of her journey home," replied Lady Janet. "She mentioned her having been stopped on the frontier, and her finding herself accidentally in the company of another Englishwoman, a perfect stranger to her. I naturally asked questions on my side, and was shocked to hear that she had seen the woman killed by a German shell almost close at her side. Neither she nor I have had any relish for returning to the subject since. You were quite right, Julian, to avoid speaking of it while she was in the room. I understand it all now. Grace, I suppose, mentioned my name to her fellow-traveler. The woman is, no doubt, in want of assistance, and she applies to me through you. I will help her; but she must not come here until I have prepared Grace for seeing her again, a living woman. For the present there is no reason why they should meet."

"I am not sure about that," said Julian, in low tones, without looking up at his aunt.

"What do you mean? Is the mystery not at an end yet?"

"The mystery has not even begun yet. Let my friend the consul proceed."

Julian returned for the second time to his extract from the letter:

"'After a careful examination of the supposed corpse, the German surgeon arrived at the conclusion that a case of suspended animation had (in the hurry of the French retreat) been mistaken for a case of death. Feeling a professional interest in the subject, he decided on putting his opinion to the test. He operated on the patient with complete success. After performing the operation he kept her for some days under his own care, and then transferred her to the nearest hospital—the hospital at Mannheim. He was obliged to return to his duties as army surgeon, and he left his patient in the condition in which I saw her, insensible on the bed. Neither he nor the hospital authorities knew anything whatever about the woman. No papers were found on her. All the doctors could do, when I asked them for information with a view to communicating with her friends, was to show me her linen marked with her, name. I left the hospital after taking down the name in my pocket-book. It was "Mercy Merrick."'"

Lady Janet produced her pocket-book. "Let me take the name down too," she said. "I never heard it before, and I might otherwise forget it. Go on, Julian."

Julian advanced to his second extract from the consul's letter:

"'Under these circumstances, I could only wait to hear from the hospital when the patient was sufficiently recovered to be able to speak to me. Some weeks passed without my receiving any communication from the doctors. On calling to make inquiries I was informed that fever had set in, and that the poor creature's condition now alternated between exhaustion and delirium. In her delirious moments the name of your aunt, Lady Janet Roy, frequently escaped her. Otherwise her wanderings were for the most part quite unintelligible to the people at her bedside. I thought once or twice of writing to you, and of begging you to speak to Lady Janet. But as the doctors informed me that the chances of life or death were at this time almost equally balanced, I decided to wait until time should determine whether it was necessary to trouble you or not.'"

"You know best, Julian," said Lady Janet. "But I own I don't quite see in what way I am interested in this part of the story."

"Just what I was going to say," added Horace. "It is very sad, no doubt. But what have we to do with it?"

"Let me read my third extract," Julian answered, "and you will see."

He turned to the third extract, and read as follows:

"'At last I received a message from the hospital informing me that Mercy Merrick was out of danger, and that she was capable (though still very weak) of answering any questions which I might think it desirable to put to her. On reaching the hospital, I was requested, rather to my surprise, to pay my first visit to the head physician in his private room. "I think it right," said this gentleman, "to warn you, before you see the patient, to be very careful how you speak to her, and not to irritate her by showing any surprise or expressing any doubts if she talks to you in an extravagant manner. We differ in opinion about her here. Some of us (myself among the number) doubt whether the recovery of her mind has accompanied the recovery of her bodily powers. Without pronouncing her to be mad—she is perfectly gentle and harmless—

we are nevertheless of opinion that she is suffering under a species of insane delusion. Bear in mind the caution which I have given you—and now go and judge for yourself." I obeyed, in some little perplexity and surprise. The sufferer, when I approached her bed, looked sadly weak and worn; but, so far as I could judge, seemed to be in full possession of herself. Her tone and manner were unquestionably the tone and manner of a lady. After briefly introducing myself, I assured her that I should be glad, both officially and personally, if I could be of any assistance to her. In saying these trifling words I happened to address her by the name I had seen marked on her clothes. The instant the words "Miss Merrick" passed my lips a wild, vindictive expression appeared in her eyes. She exclaimed angrily, "Don't call me by that hateful name! It's not my name. All the people here persecute me by calling me Mercy Merrick. And when I am angry with them they show me the clothes. Say what I may, they persist in believing they are my clothes. Don't you do the same, if you want to be friends with me." Remembering what the physician had said to me, I made the necessary excuses and succeeded in soothing her. Without reverting to the irritating topic of the name, I merely inquired what her plans were, and assured her that she might command my services if she required them. "Why do you want to know what my plans are?" she asked, suspiciously. I reminded her in reply that I held the position of English consul, and that my object was, if possible, to be of some assistance to her. "You can be of the greatest assistance to me," she said, eagerly. "Find Mercy Merrick!" I saw the vindictive look come back into her eyes, and an angry flush rising on her white cheeks. Abstaining from showing any surprise, I asked her who Mercy Merrick was. "A vile woman, by her own confession," was the quick reply. "How am I to find her?" I inquired next. "Look for a woman in a black dress, with the Red Geneva Cross on her shoulder; she is a nurse in the French ambulance." "What has she done?" "I have lost my papers; I have lost my own clothes; Mercy Merrick has taken them." "How do you know that Mercy Merrick has taken them?" "Nobody else could have taken them—that's how I know it. Do you believe me or not?" She as beginning to excite herself again; I assured her that I would at once send to make inquiries after Mercy Merrick. She turned round contented on the pillow. "There's a good man!" she said. "Come back and tell me when you have caught her." Such was my first interview with the English patient at the hospital at Mannheim. It is needless to say that I doubted the existence of the absent person described as a nurse. However, it was possible to make inquiries by applying to the surgeon, Ignatius Wetzel, whose whereabouts was known to his friends in Mannheim. I wrote to him, and received his answer in due time. After the night attack of the Germans had made them masters of the French position, he had entered the cottage occupied by the French ambulance. He had found the wounded Frenchmen left behind, but had seen no such person in attendance on them as the nurse in the black dress with the red cross on her shoulder. The only living woman in the place was a young English lady, in a gray traveling cloak, who had been stopped on the frontier, and who was forwarded on her way home by the war correspondent of an English journal.'"

"That was Grace," said Lady Janet.

"And I was the war correspondent," added Horace.

"A few words more," said Julian, "and you will understand my object in claiming your attention."

He returned to the letter for the last time, and concluded his extracts from it as follows:

"'Instead of attending at the hospital myself, I communicated by letter the failure of my attempt to discover the missing nurse. For some little time afterward I heard no more of the sick woman, whom I shall still call Mercy Merrick. It was only yesterday that I received another summons to visit the patient. She had by this time sufficiently recovered to claim her discharge, and she had announced her intention of returning forthwith to England. The head physician, feeling a sense of responsibility, had sent for me. It was impossible to detain her on the ground that she was not fit to be trusted by herself at large, in consequence of the difference of opinion among the doctors on the case. All that could be done was to give me due notice, and to leave the matter in my hands. On seeing her for the second time, I found her sullen and reserved. She openly attributed my inability to find the nurse to want of zeal for her interests on my part. I had, on my side, no authority whatever to detain her. I could only inquire whether she had money enough to pay her traveling expenses. Her reply informed me that the chaplain of the hospital had mentioned her forlorn situation in the town, and that the English residents had subscribed a small sum of money to enable her to return to her own country. Satisfied on this head, I asked next if she had friends to go to in England. "I have one friend," she answered, "who is a host in herself—Lady Janet Roy." You may imagine my surprise when I heard this. I found it quite useless to make any further inquiries as to how she came to know your aunt, whether your aunt expected her, and so on. My questions evidently offended her; they were received in sulky silence. Under these circumstances, well knowing that I can trust implicitly to your humane sympathy for misfortune, I have decided (after careful reflection) to insure the poor creature's safety when she arrives in London by giving her a letter to you. You will hear what she says, and you will be better able to discover than I am whether she really has any claim on Lady Janet Roy. One last word of information, which it may be necessary to add, and I shall close this inordinately long letter. At my first interview with her I abstained, as I have already told you, from irritating her by any inquiries on the subject of her name. On this second occasion, however, I decided on putting the question.'"

As he read those last words, Julian became aware of a sudden movement on the part of his aunt. Lady Janet had risen softly from her chair and had passed behind him with the purpose of reading the consul's letter for herself over her nephew's shoulder. Julian detected the action just in time to frustrate Lady Janet's intention by placing his hand over the last two lines of the letter.

"What do you do that for?" inquired his aunt, sharply.

"You are welcome, Lady Janet, to read the close of the letter for yourself," Julian replied. "But before you do so I am anxious to prepare you for a very great surprise. Compose yourself and let me read on slowly, with your eye on me, until I uncover the last two words which close my friend's letter."

He read the end of the letter, as he had proposed, in these terms:

"'I looked the woman straight in the face, and I said to her, "You have denied that the name marked on the clothes which you wore when you came here was your name. If you are not Mercy Merrick, who are you?" She

93

answered, instantly, "My name is ———""

Julian removed his hand from the page. Lady Janet looked at the next two words, and started back with a loud cry of astonishment, which brought Horace instantly to his feet.

"Tell me, one of you!" he cried. "What name did she give?"

Julian told him.

"GRACE ROSEBERRY."

CHAPTER X. A COUNCIL OF THREE.

FOR a moment Horace stood thunderstruck, looking in blank astonishment at Lady Janet. His first words, as soon as he had recovered himself, were addressed to Julian. "Is this a joke?" he asked, sternly. "If it is, I for one don't see the humor of it."

Julian pointed to the closely written pages of the consul's letter. "A man writes in earnest," he said, "when he writes at such length as this. The woman seriously gave the name of Grace Roseberry, and when she left Mannheim she traveled to England for the express purpose of presenting herself to Lady Janet Roy." He turned to his aunt. "You saw me start," he went on, "when you first mentioned Miss Roseberry's name in my hearing. Now you know why." He addressed himself once more to Horace. "You heard me say that you, as Miss Roseberry's future husband, had an interest in being present at my interview with Lady Janet. Now you know why."

"The woman is plainly mad," said Lady Janet. "But it is certainly a startling form of madness when one first hears of it. Of course we must keep the matter, for the present at least, a secret from Grace."

"There can be no doubt," Horace agreed, "that Grace must be kept in the dark, in her present state of health. The servants had better be warned beforehand, in case of this adventuress or madwoman, whichever she may be, attempting to make her way into the house."

"It shall be done immediately," said Lady Janet. "What surprises me Julian (ring the bell, if you please), is that you should describe yourself in your letter as feeling an interest in this person."

Julian answered—without ringing the bell.

"I am more interested than ever," he said, "now I find that Miss Roseberry herself is your guest at Mablethorpe House."

"You were always perverse, Julian, as a child, in your likings and dislikings," Lady Janet rejoined. "Why don't you ring the bell?"

"For one good reason, my dear aunt. I don't wish to hear you tell your servants to close the door on this friendless creature."

Lady Janet cast a look at her nephew which plainly expressed that she thought he had taken a liberty with her.

"You don't expect me to see the woman?" she asked, in a tone of cold surprise.

"I hope you will not refuse to see her," Julian answered, quietly. "I was out when she called. I must hear what she has to say—and I should infinitely prefer hearing it in your presence. When I got your reply to my letter, permitting me to present her to you, I wrote to her immediately, appointing a meeting here."

Lady Janet lifted her bright black eyes in mute expostulation to the carved Cupids and wreaths on the dining-room ceiling.

"When am I to have the honor of the lady's visit?" she inquired, with ironical resignation.

"To-day," answered her nephew, with impenetrable patience.

"At what hour?"

Julian composedly consulted his watch. "She is ten minutes after her time," he said, and put his watch back in his pocket again.

At the same moment the servant appeared, and advanced to Julian, carrying a visiting card on his little silver tray.

"A lady to see you, sir."

Julian took the card, and, bowing, handed it to his aunt.

"Here she is," he said, just as quietly as ever.

Lady Janet looked at the card, and tossed it indignantly back to her nephew. "Miss Roseberry!" she exclaimed. "Printed—actually printed on her card! Julian, even MY patience has its limits. I refuse to see her!"

The servant was still waiting—not like a human being who took an interest in the proceedings, but (as became a perfectly bred footman) like an article of furniture artfully constructed to come and go at the word of command. Julian gave the word of command, addressing the admirably constructed automaton by the name of "James."

"Where is the lady now?" he asked.

"In the breakfast-room, sir."

"Leave her there, if you please, and wait outside within hearing of the bell."

The legs of the furniture-footman acted, and took him noiselessly out of the room. Julian turned to his aunt.

"Forgive me," he said, "for venturing to give the man his orders in your presence. I am very anxious that you should not decide hastily. Surely we ought to hear what this lady has to say?"

Horace dissented widely from his friend's opinion. "It's an insult to Grace," he broke out, warmly, "to hear what she has to say!"

Lady Janet nodded her head in high approval. "I think so, too," said her ladyship, crossing her handsome old hands resolutely on her lap.

Julian applied himself to answering Horace first.

"Pardon me," he said. "I have no intention of presuming to reflect on Miss Roseberry, or of bringing her into the matter at all.—The consul's letter," he went on, speaking to his aunt, "mentions, if you remember, that the medical authorities of Mannheim were divided in opinion on their patient's case. Some of them—the physician-in-chief being among the number—believe that the recovery of her mind has not accompanied the recovery of her body."

"In other words," Lady Janet remarked, "a madwoman is in my house, and I am expected to receive her!"

"Don't let us exaggerate," said Julian, gently. "It can serve no good interest, in this serious matter, to exaggerate anything. The consul assures us, on the authority of the doctor, that she is perfectly gentle and harmless. If she is really the victim of a mental delusion, the poor creature is surely an object of compassion, and she ought to be placed under proper care. Ask your own kind heart, my dear aunt, if it would not be downright cruelty to turn this forlorn woman adrift in the world without making some inquiry first."

Lady Janet's inbred sense of justice admitted not over willingly—the reasonableness as well as the humanity of the view expressed in those words. "There is some truth in that, Julian," she said, shifting her position uneasily in her chair, and looking at Horace. "Don't you think so, too?" she added.

"I can't say I do," answered Horace, in the positive tone of a man whose obstinacy is proof against every form of appeal that can be addressed to him.

The patience of Julian was firm enough to be a match for the obstinacy of Horace. "At any rate," he resumed, with undiminished good temper, "we are all three equally interested in setting this matter at rest. I put it to you, Lady Janet, if we are not favored, at this lucky moment, with the very opportunity that we want? Miss Roseberry is not only out of the room, but out of the house. If we let this chance slip, who can say what awkward accident may not happen in the course of the next few days?"

"Let the woman come in," cried Lady Janet, deciding headlong, with her customary impatience of all delay. "At once, Julian—before Grace can come back. Will you ring the bell this time?"

This time Julian rang it. "May I give the man his orders?" he respectfully inquired of his aunt.

"Give him anything you like, and have done with it!" retorted the irritable old lady, getting briskly on her feet, and taking a turn in the room to compose herself.

The servant withdrew, with orders to show the visitor in.

Horace crossed the room at the same time—apparently with the intention of leaving it by the door at the opposite end.

"You are not going away?" exclaimed Lady Janet.

"I see no use in my remaining here," replied Horace, not very graciously.

"In that case," retorted Lady Janet, "remain here because I wish it."

"Certainly—if you wish it. Only remember," he added, more obstinately than ever, "that I differ entirely from Julian's view. In my opinion the woman has no claim on us."

A passing movement of irritation escaped Julian for the first time. "Don't be hard, Horace," he said, sharply. "All women have a claim on us."

They had unconsciously gathered together, in the heat of the little debate, turning their backs on the library door. At the last words of the reproof administered by Julian to Horace, their attention was recalled to passing events by the slight noise produced by the opening and closing of the door. With one accord the three turned and looked in the direction from which the sounds had come.

CHAPTER XI. THE DEAD ALIVE.

JUST inside the door there appeared the figure of a small woman dressed in plain and poor black garments. She silently lifted her black net veil and disclosed a dull, pale, worn, weary face. The forehead was low and broad; the eyes were unusually far apart; the lower features were remarkably small and delicate. In health (as the consul at Mannheim had remarked) this woman must have possessed, if not absolute beauty, at least rare attractions peculiarly her own. As it was now, suffering—sullen, silent, self-contained suffering—had marred its beauty. Attention and even curiosity it might still rouse. Admiration or interest it could excite no longer.

The small, thin, black figure stood immovably inside the door. The dull, worn, white face looked silently at the three persons in the room.

The three persons in the room, on their side, stood for a moment without moving, and looked silently at the stranger on the threshold. There was something either in the woman herself, or in the sudden and stealthy manner of her appearance in the room, which froze, as if with the touch of an invisible cold hand, the sympathies of all three. Accustomed to the world, habitually at their ease in every social emergency, they were now silenced for the first time in their lives by the first serious sense of embarrassment which they had felt since they were children in the presence of a stranger.

Had the appearance of the true Grace Roseberry aroused in their minds a suspicion of the woman who had stolen her name, and taken her place in the house?

Not so much as the shadow of a suspicion of Mercy was at the bottom of the strange sense of uneasiness which had now deprived them alike of their habitual courtesy and their habitual presence of mind. It was as practically impossible for any one of the three to doubt the identity of the adopted daughter of the house as it would be for you who read these lines to doubt the identity of the nearest and dearest relative you have in the world. Circumstances had fortified Mercy behind the strongest of all natural rights—the right of first possession. Circumstances had armed her with the most irresistible of all natural forces—the force of previous association and previous habit. Not by so much as a hair-breadth was the position of the false Grace Roseberry shaken by the first appearance of the true Grace Roseberry within the doors of Mablethorpe House. Lady Janet felt suddenly repelled, without knowing why. Julian and Horace felt suddenly repelled, without knowing why. Asked to describe their own sensations at the moment, they would have shaken their heads in despair, and would have answered in those words. The vague presentiment of some misfortune to come had entered the room with the entrance of the woman in black. But it moved invisibly; and it spoke as all presentiments speak, in the Unknown Tongue.

A moment passed. The crackling of the fire and the ticking of the clock were the only sounds audible in the room.

The voice of the visitor—hard, clear, and quiet—was the first voice that broke the silence.

"Mr. Julian Gray?" she said, looking interrogatively from one of the two gentlemen to the other.

Julian advanced a few steps, instantly recovering his self-possession. "I am sorry I was not at home," he said, "when you called with your letter from the consul. Pray take a chair."

By way of setting the example, Lady Janet seated herself at some little distance, with Horace in attendance standing near. She bowed to the stranger with studious politeness, but without uttering a word, before she settled herself in her chair. "I am obliged to listen to this person," thought the old lady. "But I am not obliged to speak to her. That is Julian's business—not mine. Don't stand, Horace! You fidget me. Sit down." Armed beforehand in her policy of silence, Lady Janet folded her handsome hands as usual, and waited for the proceedings to begin, like a judge on the bench.

"Will you take a chair?" Julian repeated, observing that the visitor appeared neither to heed nor to hear his first words of welcome to her.

At this second appeal she spoke to him. "Is that Lady Janet Roy?" she asked, with her eyes fixed on the mistress of the house.

Julian answered, and drew back to watch the result.

The woman in the poor black garments changed her position for the first time. She moved slowly across the room to the place at which Lady Janet was sitting, and addressed her respectfully with perfect self-possession of manner. Her whole demeanor, from the moment when she had appeared at the door, had expressed—at once plainly and becomingly—confidence in the reception that awaited her.

"Almost the last words my father said to me on his death-bed," she began, "were words, madam, which told me to expect protection and kindness from you."

It was not Lady Janet's business to speak. She listened with the blandest attention. She waited with the most exasperating silence to hear more.

Grace Roseberry drew back a step—not intimidated—only mortified and surprised. "Was my father wrong?" she asked, with a simple dignity of tone and manner which forced Lady Janet to abandon her policy of silence, in spite of herself.

"Who was your father?" she asked, coldly.

Grace Roseberry answered the question in a tone of stern surprise.

"Has the servant not given you my card?" she said. "Don't you know my name?"

"Which of your names?" rejoined Lady Janet.

"I don't understand your ladyship."

"I will make myself understood. You asked me if I knew your name. I ask you, in return, which name it is? The name on your card is 'Miss Roseberry.' The name marked on your clothes, when you were in the hospital, was 'Mercy Merrick.'"

The self-possession which Grace had maintained from the moment when she had entered the dining-room, seemed now, for the first time, to be on the point of failing her. She turned, and looked appealingly at Julian, who had thus far kept his place apart, listening attentively.

"Surely," she said, "your friend, the consul, has told you in his letter about the mark on the clothes?"

Something of the girlish hesitation and timidity which had marked her demeanor at her interview with Mercy in the French cottage re-appeared in her tone and manner as she spoke those words. The changes—mostly changes for the worse—wrought in her by the suffering through which she had passed since that time were now (for the moment) effaced. All that was left of the better and simpler side of her character asserted itself in her brief appeal to Julian. She had hitherto repelled him. He began to feel a certain compassionate interest in her now.

"The consul has informed me of what you said to him," he answered, kindly. "But, if you will take my advice, I recommend you to tell your story to Lady Janet in your own words."

Grace again addressed herself with submissive reluctance to Lady Janet.

"The clothes your ladyship speaks of," she said, "were the clothes of another woman. The rain was pouring when the soldiers detained me on the frontier. I had been exposed for hours to the weather—I was wet to the skin. The clothes marked 'Mercy Merrick' were the clothes lent to me by Mercy Merrick herself while my own things were drying. I was struck by the shell in those clothes. I was carried away insensible in those clothes after the operation had been performed on me."

Lady Janet listened to perfection—and did no more. She turned confidentially to Horace, and said to him, in her gracefully ironical way: "She is ready with her explanation."

Horace answered in the same tone: "A great deal too ready."

Grace looked from one of them to the other. A faint flush of color showed itself in her face for the first time.

"Am I to understand," she asked, with proud composure, "that you don't believe me?"

Lady Janet maintained her policy of silence. She waved one hand courteously toward Julian, as if to say, "Address your inquiries to the gentleman who introduces you." Julian, noticing the gesture, and observing the rising color in Grace's cheeks, interfered directly in the interests of peace

"Lady Janet asked you a question just now," he said; "Lady Janet inquired who your father was."

"My father was the late Colonel Roseberry."

Lady Janet made another confidential remark to Horace. "Her assurance amazes me!" she exclaimed.

Julian interposed before his aunt could add a word more. "Pray let us hear her," he said, in a tone of entreaty which had something of the imperative in it this time. He turned to Grace. "Have you any proof to produce," he added, in his gentler voice, "which will satisfy us that you are Colonel Roseberry's daughter?"

Grace looked at him indignantly. "Proof!" she repeated. "Is my word not enough?"

Julian kept his temper perfectly. "Pardon me," he rejoined, "you forget that you and Lady Janet meet now for the first time. Try to put yourself in my aunt's place. How is she to know that you are the late Colonel Roseberry's daughter?"

Grace's head sunk on her breast; she dropped into the nearest chair. The expression of her face changed instantly from anger to discouragement. "Ah," she exclaimed, bitterly, "if I only had the letters that have been stolen from me!"

"Letters," asked Julian, "introducing you to Lady Janet?"

"Yes." She turned suddenly to Lady Janet. "Let me tell you how I lost them," she said, in the first tones of entreaty which had escaped her yet.

Lady Janet hesitated. It was not in her generous nature to resist the appeal that had just been made to her. The sympathies of Horace were far less easily reached. He lightly launched a new shaft of satire—intended for the private amusement of Lady Janet. "Another explanation!" he exclaimed, with a look of comic resignation.

Julian overheard the words. His large lustrous eyes fixed themselves on Horace with a look of unmeasured contempt.

"The least you can do," he said, sternly, "is not to irritate her. It is so easy to irritate her!" He addressed himself again to Grace, endeavoring to help her through her difficulty in a new way. "Never mind explaining yourself for the moment," he said. "In the absence of your letters, have you any one in London who can speak to your identity?"

Grace shook her head sadly. "I have no friends in London," she answered.

It was impossible for Lady Janet—who had never in her life heard of anybody without friends in London—to pass this over without notice. "No friends in London!" she repeated, turning to Horace.

Horace shot another shaft of light satire. "Of course not!" he rejoined.

Grace saw them comparing notes. "My friends are in Canada," she broke out, impetuously. "Plenty of friends who could speak for me, if I could only bring them here."

As a place of reference—mentioned in the capital city of England—Canada, there is no denying it, is open to objection on the ground of distance. Horace was ready with another shot. "Far enough off, certainly," he said.

"Far enough off, as you say," Lady Janet agreed.

Once more Julian's inexhaustible kindness strove to obtain a hearing for the stranger who had been confided to his care. "A little patience, Lady Janet," he pleaded. "A little consideration, Horace, for a friendless woman."

"Thank you, sir," said Grace. "It is very kind of you to try and help me, but it is useless. They won't even listen to me." She attempted to rise from her chair as she pronounced the last words. Julian gently laid his hand on her shoulder and obliged her to resume her seat.

"I will listen to you," he said. "You referred me just now to the consul's letter. The consul tells me you suspected some one of taking your papers and your clothes."

"I don't suspect," was the quick reply; "I am certain! I tell you positively Mercy Merrick was the thief. She was alone with me when I was struck down by the shell. She was the only person who knew that I had letters of introduction about me. She confessed to my face that she had been a bad woman—she had been in a prison—she had come out of a refuge—"

Julian stopped her there with one plain question, which threw a doubt on the whole story.

"The consul tells me you asked him to search for Mercy Merrick," he said. "Is it not true that he caused inquiries to be made, and that no trace of any such person was to be heard of?"

"The consul took no pains to find her," Grace answered, angrily. "He was, like everybody else, in a conspiracy to neglect and misjudge me."

Lady Janet and Horace exchanged looks. This time it was impossible for Julian to blame them. The further the stranger's narrative advanced, the less worthy of serious attention he felt it to be. The longer she spoke, the more disadvantageously she challenged comparison with the absent woman, whose name she so obstinately and so audaciously persisted in assuming as her own.

"Granting all that you have said," Julian resumed, with a last effort of patience, "what use could Mercy Merrick make of your letters and your clothes?"

"What use?" repeated Grace, amazed at his not seeing the position as she saw it. "My clothes were marked with my name. One of my papers was a letter from my father, introducing me to Lady Janet. A woman out of a refuge would be quite capable of presenting herself here in my place."

Spoken entirely at random, spoken without so much as a fragment of evidence to support them, those last words still had their effect. They cast a reflection on Lady Janet's adopted daughter which was too outrageous to be borne. Lady Janet rose instantly. "Give me your arm, Horace," she said, turning to leave the room. "I have heard enough."

Horace respectfully offered his arm. "Your ladyship is quite right," he answered. "A more monstrous story never was invented."

He spoke, in the warmth of his indignation, loud enough for Grace to hear him. "What is there monstrous in it?" she asked, advancing a step toward him, defiantly.

Julian checked her. He too—though he had only once seen Mercy—felt an angry sense of the insult offered to the beautiful creature who had interested him at his first sight of her. "Silence!" he said, speaking sternly to Grace for the first time. "You are offending—justly offending—Lady Janet. You are talking worse than absurdly—you are talking offensively—when you speak of another woman presenting herself here in your place."

Grace's blood was up. Stung by Julian's reproof, she turned on him a look which was almost a look of fury.

"Are you a clergyman? Are you an educated man?" she asked. "Have you never read of cases of false personation, in newspapers and books? I blindly confided in Mercy Merrick before I found out what her character really was. She left the cottage—I know it, from the surgeon who brought me to life again—firmly persuaded that the shell had killed me. My papers and my clothes disappeared at the same time. Is there nothing suspicious in these circumstances? There were people at the Hospital who thought them highly suspicious—people who warned me that I might find an impostor in my place." She suddenly paused. The rustling sound of a silk dress had caught her ear. Lady Janet was leaving the room, with Horace, by way of the conservatory. With a last desperate effort of resolution, Grace sprung forward and placed herself in front of them.

"One word, Lady Janet, before you turn your back on me," she said, firmly. "One word, and I will be content. Has Colonel Roseberry's letter found its way to this house or not? If it has, did a woman bring it to you?"

Lady Janet looked—as only a great lady can look, when a person of inferior rank has presumed to fail in respect toward her.

"You are surely not aware," she said, with icy composure, "that these questions are an insult to Me?"

"And worse than an insult," Horace added, warmly, "to Grace!"

The little resolute black figure (still barring the way to the conservatory) was suddenly shaken from head to foot. The woman's eyes traveled backward and forward between Lady Janet and Horace with the light of a new suspicion in them.

"Grace!" she exclaimed. "What Grace? That's my name. Lady Janet, you have got the letter! The woman is here!"

Lady Janet dropped Horace's arm, and retraced her steps to the place at which her nephew was standing.

"Julian," she said. "You force me, for the first time in my life, to remind you of the respect that is due to me in my own house. Send that woman away."

Without waiting to be answered, she turned back again, and once more took Horace's arm.

"Stand back, if you please," she said, quietly, to Grace.

Grace held her ground.

"The woman is here!" she repeated. "Confront me with her—and then send me away, if you like."

Julian advanced, and firmly took her by the arm. "You forget what is due to Lady Janet," he said, drawing her aside. "You forget what is due to yourself."

With a desperate effort, Grace broke away from him, and stopped Lady Janet on the threshold of the conservatory door.

"Justice!" she cried, shaking her clinched hand with hysterical frenzy in the air. "I claim my right to meet that woman face to face! Where is she? Confront me with her! Confront me with her!"

While those wild words were pouring from her lips, the rumbling of carriage wheels became audible on the drive in front of the house. In the all-absorbing agitation of the moment, the sound of the wheels (followed by the opening of the house door) passed unnoticed by the persons in the dining-room. Horace's voice was still raised in angry protest against the insult offered to Lady Janet; Lady Janet herself (leaving him for the second time) was vehemently ringing the bell to summon the servants; Julian had once more taken the infuriated woman by the arms and was trying vainly to compose her—when the library door was opened quietly by a young lady wearing a mantle and a bonnet. Mercy Merrick (true to the appointment which she had made with Horace) entered the room.

The first eyes that discovered her presence on the scene were the eyes of Grace Roseberry. Starting violently in Julian's grasp, she pointed toward the library door. "Ah!" she cried, with a shriek of vindictive delight. "There she is!"

Mercy turned as the sound of the scream rang through the room, and met—resting on her in savage triumph—the living gaze of the woman whose identity she had stolen, whose body she had left laid out for dead. On the instant of that terrible discovery—with her eyes fixed helplessly on the fierce eyes that had found her—she dropped senseless on the floor.

CHAPTER XII. EXIT JULIAN.

JULIAN happened to be standing nearest to Mercy. He was the first at her side when she fell.

In the cry of alarm which burst from him, as he raised her for a moment in his arms, in the expression of his eyes when he looked at her death-like face, there escaped the plain—too plain—confession of the interest which he felt in her, of the admiration which she had aroused in him. Horace detected it. There was the quick suspicion of jealousy in the movement by which he joined Julian; there was the ready resentment of jealousy in the tone in which he pronounced the words, "Leave her to me." Julian resigned her in silence. A faint flush appeared on his pale face as he drew back while Horace carried her to the sofa. His eyes sunk to the ground; he seemed to be meditating self-reproachfully on the tone in which his friend had spoken to him. After having been the first to take an active part in meeting the calamity that had happened, he was now, to all appearance, insensible to everything that was passing in the room.

A touch on his shoulder roused him.

He turned and looked round. The woman who had done the mischief—the stranger in the poor black garments—was standing behind him. She pointed to the prostrate figure on the sofa, with a merciless smile.

"You wanted a proof just now," she said. "There it is!"

Horace heard her. He suddenly left the sofa and joined Julian. His face, naturally ruddy, was pale with suppressed fury.

"Take that wretch away!" he said. "Instantly! or I won't answer for what I may do."

Those words recalled Julian to himself. He looked round the room. Lady Janet and the housekeeper were together, in attendance on the swooning woman. The startled servants were congregated in the library doorway. One of them offered to run to the nearest doctor; another asked if he should fetch the police. Julian silenced them by a gesture, and turned to Horace. "Compose yourself," he said. "Leave me to remove her quietly from the house." He took Grace by the hand as he spoke. She hesitated, and tried to release herself. Julian pointed to the group at the sofa, and to the servants looking on. "You have made an enemy of every one in this room," he said, "and you have not a friend in London. Do you wish to make an enemy of me? Her head drooped; she made no reply; she waited, dumbly obedient to the firmer will than her own. Julian ordered the servants crowding together in the doorway to withdraw. He followed them into the library, leading Grace after him by the hand. Before closing the door he paused, and looked back into the dining-room.

"Is she recovering?" he asked, after a moment's hesitation.

Lady Janet's voice answered him. "Not yet."

"Shall I send for the nearest doctor?"

Horace interposed. He declined to let Julian associate himself, even in that indirect manner, with Mercy's recovery.

"If the doctor is wanted," he said, "I will go for him myself."

Julian closed the library door. He absently released Grace; he mechanically pointed to a chair. She sat down in silent surprise, following him with her eyes as he walked slowly to and fro in the room.

For the moment his mind was far away from her, and from all that had happened since her appearance in the house. It was impossible that a man of his fineness of perception could mistake the meaning of Horace's conduct toward him. He was questioning his own heart, on the subject of Mercy, sternly and unreservedly as it was his habit to do. "After only once seeing her," he thought, "has she produced such an impression on me that Horace can discover it, before I have even suspected it myself? Can the time have come already when I owe it to my friend to see her no more?" He stopped irritably in his walk. As a man devoted to a serious calling in life, there was something that wounded his self-respect in the bare suspicion that he could be guilty of the purely sentimental extravagance called "love at first sight."

He had paused exactly opposite to the chair in which Grace was seated. Weary of the silence, she seized the opportunity of speaking to him.

"I have come here with you as you wished," she said. "Are you going to help me? Am I to count on you as my friend?"

He looked at her vacantly. It cost him an effort before he could give her the attention that she had claimed.

"You have been hard on me," Grace went on. "But you showed me some kindness at first; you tried to make them give me a fair hearing. I ask you, as a just man, do you doubt now that the woman on the sofa in the next room is an impostor who has taken my place? Can there be any plainer confession that she is Mercy Merrick than the confession she has made? You saw it; they saw it. She fainted at the sight of me."

Julian crossed the room—still without answering her—and rang the bell. When the servant appeared, he told the man to fetch a cab.

Grace rose from her chair. "What is the cab for?" she asked, sharply.

"For you and for me," Julian replied. "I am going to take you back to your lodgings."

"I refuse to go. My place is in this house. Neither Lady Janet nor you can get over the plain facts. All I asked was to be confronted with her. And what did she do when she came into the room? She fainted at the sight of me."

Reiterating her one triumphant assertion, she fixed her eyes on Julian with a look which said plainly: Answer that if you can. In mercy to her, Julian answered it on the spot.

"As far as I understand," he said, "you appear to take it for granted that no innocent woman would have fainted on first seeing you. I have something to tell you which will alter your opinion. On her arrival in England this lady informed my aunt that she had met with you accidentally on the French frontier, and that she had seen you (so far as she knew) struck dead at her side by a shell. Remember that, and recall what happened just now. Without a word to warn her of your restoration to life, she finds herself suddenly face to face with you, a living woman—and this at a time when it is easy for any one who looks at her to see that she is in delicate health. What is there wonderful, what is there unaccountable, in her fainting under such circumstances as these?"

The question was plainly put. Where was the answer to it?

There was no answer to it. Mercy's wisely candid statement of the manner in which she had first met with Grace, and of the accident which had followed had served Mercy's purpose but too well. It was simply impossible for persons acquainted with that statement to attach a guilty meaning to the swoon. The false Grace Roseberry was still as far beyond the reach of suspicion as ever, and the true Grace was quick enough to see it. She sank into the chair from which she had risen; her hands fell in hopeless despair on her lap.

"Everything is against me," she said. "The truth itself turns liar, and takes her side." She paused, and rallied her sinking courage. "No!" she cried, resolutely, "I won't submit to have my name and my place taken from me by a vile adventuress! Say what you like, I insist on exposing her; I won't leave the house!"

The servant entered the room, and announced that the cab was at the door.

Grace turned to Julian with a defiant wave of her hand. "Don't let me detain you," she said. "I see I have neither advice nor help to expect from Mr. Julian Gray."

Julian beckoned to the servant to follow him into a corner of the room.

"Do you know if the doctor has been sent for?" he asked.

"I believe not, sir. It is said in the servants' hall that the doctor is not wanted."

Julian was too anxious to be satisfied with a report from the servants' hall. He hastily wrote on a slip of paper: "Has she recovered?" and gave the note to the man, with directions to take it to Lady Janet.

"Did you hear what I said?" Grace inquired, while the messenger was absent in the dining room.

"I will answer you directly," said Julian.

The servant appeared again as he spoke, with some lines in pencil written by Lady Janet on the back of Julian's note. "Thank God, we have revived her. In a few minutes we hope to be able to take her to her room."

The nearest way to Mercy's room was through the library. Grace's immediate removal had now become a necessity which was not to be trifled with. Julian addressed himself to meeting the difficulty the instant he was left alone with Grace.

"Listen to me," he said. "The cab is waiting, and I have my last words to say to you. You are now (thanks to the consul's recommendation) in my care. Decide at once whether you will remain under my charge, or whether you will transfer yourself to the charge of the police."

Grace started. "What do you mean?" she asked, angrily.

"If you wish to remain under my charge," Julian proceeded, "you will accompany me at once to the cab. In that case I will undertake to give you an opportunity of telling your story to my own lawyer. He will be a fitter person to advise you than I am. Nothing will induce we to believe that the lady whom you have accused has committed, or is capable of committing, such a fraud as you charge her with. You will hear what the lawyer thinks, if you come with me. If you refuse, I shall have no choice but to send into the next room, and tell them that you are still here. The result will be that you will find yourself in charge of the police. Take which course you like: I will give you a minute to decide in. And remember this—if I appear to express myself harshly, it is your conduct which forces me to speak out. I mean kindly toward you; I am advising you honestly for your good."

He took out his watch to count the minute.

Grace stole one furtive glance at his steady, resolute face. She was perfectly unmoved by the manly consideration for her which Julian's last words had expressed. All she understood was that he was not a man to be trifled with. Future opportunities would offer themselves of returning secretly to the house. She determined to yield—and deceive him.

"I am ready to go," she said, rising with dogged submission. "Your turn now," she muttered to herself, as she turned to the looking-glass to arrange her shawl. "My turn will come."

Julian advanced toward her, as if to offer her his arm, and checked himself. Firmly persuaded as he was that her mind was deranged—readily as he admitted that she claimed, in virtue of her affliction, every indulgence that he could extend to her—there was something repellent to him at that moment in the bare idea of touching her. The image of the beautiful creature who was the object of her monstrous accusation—the image of Mercy as she lay helpless for a moment in his arms—was vivid in his mind while he opened the door that led into the hall, and drew back to let Grace pass out before him. He left the servant to help her into the cab. The man respectfully addressed him as he took his seat opposite to Grace.

"I am ordered to say that your room is ready, sir, and that her ladyship expects you to dinner."

Absorbed in the events which had followed his aunt's invitation, Julian had forgotten his engagement to stay at Mablethorpe House. Could he return, knowing his own heart as he now knew it? Could he honorably remain, perhaps for weeks together, in Mercy's society, conscious as he now was of the impression which she had produced on him? No. The one honorable course that he could take was to find an excuse for withdrawing from his engagement. "Beg her ladyship not to wait dinner for me," he said. "I will write and make my apologies." The cab drove off. The wondering servant waited on the doorstep, looking after it. "I wouldn't stand in Mr. Julian's shoes for something," he thought, with his mind running on the difficulties of the young clergyman's position. "There she is along with him in the cab. What is he going to do with her after that?"

Julian himself, if it had been put to him at the moment, could not have answered the question.

Lady Janet's anxiety was far from being relieved when Mercy had been restored to her senses and conducted to her own room.

Mercy's mind remained in a condition of unreasoning alarm, which it was impossible to remove. Over and over again she was told that the woman who had terrified her had left the house, and would never be permitted to enter it more; over and over again she was assured that the stranger's frantic assertions were regarded by everybody about her as unworthy of a moment's serious attention. She persisted in doubting whether they were telling her the truth. A shocking distrust of her friends seemed to possess her. She shrunk when Lady Janet approached the bedside. She shuddered when Lady Janet kissed her. She flatly refused to let Horace see her. She asked the strangest questions about Julian Gray, and shook her head suspiciously when they told her that he was absent from the house. At intervals she hid her face in the bedclothes and murmured to herself piteously, "Oh, what shall I do? What shall I do?" At other times her one petition was to be left alone. "I want nobody in my room"—that was her sullen cry—"nobody in my room."

The evening advanced, and brought with it no change for the better. Lady Janet, by the advice of Horace, sent for her own medical adviser.

The doctor shook his head. The symptoms, he said, indicated a serious shock to the nervous system. He wrote a sedative prescription; and he gave (with a happy choice of language) some sound and safe advice. It amounted briefly to this: "Take her away, and try the sea-side." Lady Janet's customary energy acted on the advice, without a moment's needless delay. She gave the necessary directions for packing the trunks overnight, and decided on leaving Mablethorpe House with Mercy the next morning.

Shortly after the doctor had taken his departure a letter from Julian, addressed to Lady Janet, was delivered by private messenger.

Beginning with the necessary apologies for the writer's absence, the letter proceeded in these terms:

"Before I permitted my companion to see the lawyer, I felt the necessity of consulting him as to my present position toward her first.

"I told him—what I think it only right to repeat to you—that I do not feel justified in acting on my own opinion that her mind is deranged. In the case of this friendless woman I want medical authority, and, more even than that, I want some positive proof, to satisfy my conscience as well as to confirm my view.

"Finding me obstinate on this point, the lawyer undertook to consult a physician accustomed to the treatment of the insane, on my behalf.

"After sending a message and receiving the answer, he said, 'Bring the lady here—in half an hour; she shall tell her story to the doctor instead of telling it to me.' The proposal rather staggered me; I asked how it was possible to induce her to do that. He laughed, and answered, 'I shall present the doctor as my senior partner; my senior partner will be the very man to advise her.' You know that I hate all deception, even where the end in view appears to justify it. On this occasion, however, there was no other alternative than to let the lawyer take his own course, or to run the risk of a delay which might be followed by serious results.

"I waited in a room by myself (feeling very uneasy, I own) until the doctor joined me, after the interview was over.

"His opinion is, briefly, this:

"After careful examination of the unfortunate creature, he thinks that there are unmistakably symptoms of mental aberration. But how far the mischief has gone, and whether her case is, or is not, sufficiently grave to render actual restraint necessary, he cannot positively say, in our present state of ignorance as to facts.

"'Thus far,' he observed, 'we know nothing of that part of her delusion which relates to Mercy Merrick. The solution of the difficulty, in this case, is to be found there. I entirely agree with the lady that the inquiries of the consul at Mannheim are far from being conclusive. Furnish me with satisfactory evidence either that there is, or is not, such a person really in existence as Mercy Merrick, and I will give you a positive opinion on the case whenever you choose to ask for it.'

"Those words have decided me on starting for the Continent and renewing the search for Mercy Merrick.

"My friend the lawyer wonders jocosely whether I am in my right senses. His advice is that I should apply to the nearest magistrate, and relieve you and myself of all further trouble in that way.

"Perhaps you agree with him? My dear aunt (as you have often said), I do nothing like other people. I am interested in this case. I cannot abandon a forlorn woman who has been confided to me to the tender mercies of strangers, so long as there is any hope of my making discoveries which may be instrumental in restoring her to herself—perhaps, also, in restoring her to her friends.

"I start by the mail-train of to-night. My plan is to go first to Mannheim and consult with the consul and the hospital doctors; then to find my way to the German surgeon and to question him; and, that done, to make the last and hardest effort of all—the effort to trace the French ambulance and to penetrate the mystery of Mercy Merrick.

"Immediately on my return I will wait on you, and tell you what I have accomplished, or how I have failed.

"In the meanwhile, pray be under no alarm about the reappearance of this unhappy woman at your house. She is fully occupied in writing (at my suggestion) to her friends in Canada; and she is under the care of the landlady at her lodgings—an experienced and trustworthy person, who has satisfied the doctor as well as myself of her fitness for the charge that she has undertaken.

"Pray mention this to Miss Roseberry (whenever you think it desirable), with the respectful expression of my sympathy, and of my best wishes for her speedy restoration to health. And once more forgive me for failing, under stress of necessity, to enjoy the hospitality of Mablethorpe House."

Lady Janet closed Julian's letter, feeling far from satisfied with it. She sat for a while, pondering over what her nephew had written to her.

"One of two things," thought the quick-witted old lady. "Either the lawyer is right, and Julian is a fit companion for the madwoman whom he has taken under his charge, or he has some second motive for this absurd journey of his which he has carefully abstained from mentioning in his letter. What can the motive be?"

At intervals during the night that question recurred to her ladyship again and again. The utmost exercise of her ingenuity failing to answer it, her one resource left was to wait patiently for Julian's return, and, in her own favorite phrase, to "have it out of him" then.

The next morning Lady Janet and her adopted daughter left Mablethorpe House for Brighton; Horace (who had begged to be allowed to accompany them) being sentenced to remain in London by Mercy's express desire. Why—nobody could guess; and Mercy refused to say.

CHAPTER XIII. ENTER JULIAN.

A WEEK has passed. The scene opens again in the dining-room at Mablethorpe House.

The hospitable table bears once more its burden of good things for lunch. But on this occasion Lady Janet sits alone. Her attention is divided between reading her newspaper and feeding her cat. The cat is a sleek and splendid creature. He carries an erect tail. He rolls luxuriously on the soft carpet. He approaches his mistress in a series of coquettish curves. He smells with dainty hesitation at the choicest morsels that can be offered to him. The musical monotony of his purring falls soothingly on her ladyship's ear. She stops in the middle of a leading article and looks with a careworn face at the happy cat. "Upon my honor," cries Lady Janet, thinking, in her inveterately ironical manner, of the cares that trouble her, "all things considered, Tom, I wish I was You!"

The cat starts—not at his mistress's complimentary apostrophe, but at a knock at the door, which follows close upon it. Lady Janet says, carelessly enough, "Come in;" looks round listlessly to see who it is; and starts, like the cat, when the door opens and discloses—Julian Gray!

"You—or your ghost?" she exclaims.

She has noticed already that Julian is paler than usual, and that there is something in his manner at once uneasy and subdued—highly uncharacteristic of him at other times. He takes a seat by her side, and kisses her hand. But—for the first time in his aunt's experience of him—he refuses the good things on the luncheon table, and he has nothing to say to the cat! That neglected animal takes refuge on Lady Janet's lap. Lady Janet, with her eyes fixed expectantly on her nephew (determining to "have it out of him" at the first opportunity), waits to hear what he has to say for himself. Julian has no alternative but to break the silence, and tell his story as he best may.

"I got back from the Continent last night," he began. "And I come here, as I promised, to report myself on my return. How does your ladyship do? How is Miss Roseberry?"

Lady Janet laid an indicative finger on the lace pelerine which ornamented the upper part of her dress. "Here is the old lady, well," she answered—and pointed next to the room above them. "And there," she added, "is the young lady, ill. Is anything the matter with you, Julian?"

"Perhaps I am a little tired after my journey. Never mind me. Is Miss Roseberry still suffering from the shock?"

"What else should she be suffering from? I will never forgive you, Julian, for bringing that crazy impostor into my house."

"My dear aunt, when I was the innocent means of bringing her here I had no idea that such a person as Miss Roseberry was in existence. Nobody laments what has happened more sincerely than I do. Have you had medical advice?"

"I took her to the sea-side a week since by medical advice."

"Has the change of air don e her no good?"

"None whatever. If anything, the change of air has made her worse. Sometimes she sits for hours together, as pale as death, without looking at anything, and without uttering a word. Sometimes she brightens up, and seems as if she was eager to say something; and then Heaven only knows why, checks herself suddenly as if she was afraid to speak. I could support that. But what cuts me to the heart, Julian, is, that she does not appear to trust me and to love me as she did. She seems to be doubtful of me; she seems to be frightened of me. If I did not know that it was simply impossible that such a thing could be, I should really think she suspected me of believing what that wretch said of her. In one word (and between ourselves), I begin to fear she will never get over the fright which caused that fainting-fit. There is serious mischief somewhere; and, try as I may to discover it, it is mischief beyond my finding."

"Can the doctor do nothing?"

Lady Janet's bright black eyes answered before she replied in words, with a look of supreme contempt.

"The doctor!" she repeated, disdainfully. "I brought Grace back last night in sheer despair, and I sent for the doctor this morning. He is at the head of his profession; he is said to be making ten thousand a year; and he knows no more about it than I do. I am quite serious. The great physician has just gone away with two guineas in his pocket. One guinea, for advising me to keep her quiet; another guinea for telling me to trust to time. Do you wonder how he gets on at this rate? My dear boy, they all get on in the same way. The medical profession thrives on two incurable diseases in these modern days—a He-disease and a She-disease. She-disease—nervous depression; He-disease—suppressed gout. Remedies, one guinea, if you go to the doctor; two guineas if the doctor goes to you. I might have bought a new bonnet," cried her ladyship, indignantly, "with the money I have given to that man! Let us change the subject. I lose my temper when I think of it. Besides, I want to know something. Why did you go abroad?"

At that plain question Julian looked unaffectedly surprised. "I wrote to explain," he said. "Have you not received my letter?"

"Oh, I got your letter. It was long enough, in all conscience; and, long as it was, it didn't tell me the one thing I wanted to know."

"What is the 'one thing'?"

Lady Janet's reply pointed—not too palpably at first—at that second motive for Julian's journey which she had suspected Julian of concealing from her.

"I want to know," she said, "why you troubled yourself to make your inquiries on the Continent in person? You know where my old courier is to be found. You have yourself pronounced him to be the most intelligent and trustworthy of men. Answer me honestly—could you not have sent him in your place?"

"I might have sent him," Julian admitted, a little reluctantly.

"You might have sent the courier—and you were under an engagement to stay here as my guest. Answer me honestly once more. Why did you go away?"

Julian hesitated. Lady Janet paused for his reply, with the air of a women who was prepared to wait (if necessary) for the rest of the afternoon.

"I had a reason of my own for going," Julian said at last.

"Yes?" rejoined Lady Janet, prepared to wait (if necessary) till the next morning.

"A reason," Julian resumed, "which I would rather not mention."

"Oh!" said Lady Janet. "Another mystery—eh? And another woman at the bottom of it, no doubt. Thank you—that will do—I am sufficiently answered. No wonder, as a clergyman, that you look a little confused. There is, perhaps, a certain grace, under the circumstances, in looking confused. We will change the subject again. You stay here, of course, now you have come back?"

Once more the famous pulpit orator seemed to find himself in the inconceivable predicament of not knowing what to say. Once more Lady Janet looked resigned to wait (if necessary) until the middle of next week.

Julian took refuge in an answer worthy of the most commonplace man on the face of the civilized earth.

"I beg your ladyship to accept my thanks and my excuses," he said.

Lady Janet's many-ringed fingers, mechanically stroking the cat in her lap, began to stroke him the wrong way.

Lady Janet's inexhaustible patience showed signs of failing her at last.

"Mighty civil, I am sure," she said. "Make it complete. Say, Mr. Julian Gray presents his compliments to Lady Janet Roy, and regrets that a previous engagement—Julian!" exclaimed the old lady, suddenly pushing the cat off her lap, and flinging her last pretense of good temper to the winds—"Julian, I am not to be trifled with! There is but one explanation of your conduct— you are evidently avoiding my house. Is there somebody you dislike in it? Is it me?"

Julian intimated by a gesture that his aunt's last question was absurd. (The much-injured cat elevated his back, waved his tail slowly, walked to the fireplace, and honored the rug by taking a seat on it.)

Lady Janet persisted. "Is it Grace Roseberry?" she asked next.

Even Julian's patience began to show signs of yielding. His manner assumed a sudden decision, his voice rose a tone louder.

"You insist on knowing?" he said. "It is Miss Roseberry."

"You don't like her?" cried Lady Janet, with a sudden burst of angry surprise.

Julian broke out, on his side: "If I see any more of her," he answered, the rare color mounting passionately in his cheeks, "I shall be the unhappiest man living. If I see any more of her, I shall be false to my old friend, who is to marry her. Keep us apart. If you have any regard for my peace of mind, keep us apart."

Unutterable amazement expressed itself in his aunt's lifted hands. Ungovernable curiosity uttered itself in his aunt's next words.

"You don't mean to tell me you are in love with Grace?"

Julian sprung restlessly to his feet, and disturbed the cat at the fireplace. (The cat left the room.)

"I don't know what to tell you," he said; "I can't realize it to myself. No other woman has ever roused the feeling in me which this woman seems to have called to life in an instant. In the hope of forgetting her I broke my engagement here; I purposely seized the opportunity of making those inquiries abroad. Quite useless. I think of her, morning, noon, and night. I see her and hear her, at this moment, as plainly as I see and hear you. She has made herself a part of myself. I don't understand my life without her. My power of will seems to be gone. I said to myself this morning, 'I will write to my aunt; I won't go back to Mablethorpe House.' Here I am in Mablethorpe

House, with a mean subterfuge to justify me to my own conscience. 'I owe it to my aunt to call on my aunt.' That is what I said to myself on the way here; and I was secretly hoping every step of the way that she would come into the room when I got here. I am hoping it now. And she is engaged to Horace Holmcroft—to my oldest friend, to my best friend! Am I an infernal rascal? or am I a weak fool? God knows—I don't. Keep my secret, aunt. I am heartily ashamed of myself; I used to think I was made of better stuff than this. Don't say a word to Horace. I must, and will, conquer it. Let me go."

He snatched up his hat. Lady Janet, rising with the activity of a young woman, pursued him across the room, and stopped him at the door.

"No," answered the resolute old lady, "I won't let you go. Come back with me."

As she said those words she noticed with a certain fond pride the brilliant color mounting in his cheeks—the flashing brightness which lent an added luster to his eyes. He had never, to her mind, looked so handsome before. She took his arm, and led him to the chairs which they had just left. It was shocking, it was wrong (she mentally admitted) to look on Mercy, under the circumstances, with any other eye than the eye of a brother or a friend. In a clergyman (perhaps) doubly shocking, doubly wrong. But, with all her respect for the vested interests of Horace, Lady Janet could not blame Julian. Worse still, she was privately conscious that he had, somehow or other, risen, rather than fallen, in her estimation within the last minute or two. Who could deny that her adopted daughter was a charming creature? Who could wonder if a man of refined tastes admired her? Upon the whole, her ladyship humanely decided that her nephew was rather to be pitied than blamed. What daughter of Eve (no matter whether she was seventeen or seventy) could have honestly arrived at any other conclusion? Do what a man may—let him commit anything he likes, from an error to a crime—so long as there is a woman at the bottom of it, there is an inexhaustible fund of pardon for him in every other woman's heart. "Sit down," said Lady Janet, smiling in spite of herself; "and don't talk in that horrible way again. A man, Julian—especially a famous man like you—ought to know how to control himself."

Julian burst out laughing bitterly.

"Send upstairs for my self-control," he said. "It's in her possession—not in mine. Good morning, aunt."

He rose from his chair. Lady Janet instantly pushed him back into it.

"I insist on your staying here," she said, "if it is only for a few minutes longer. I have something to say to you."

"Does it refer to Miss Roseberry?"

"It refers to the hateful woman who frightened Miss Roseberry. Now are you satisfied?"

Julian bowed, and settled himself in his chair.

"I don't much like to acknowledge it," his aunt went on. "But I want you to understand that I have something really serious to speak about, for once in a way. Julian! that wretch not only frightens Grace—she actually frightens me."

"Frightens you? She is quite harmless, poor thing."

"'Poor thing'!" repeated Lady Janet. "Did you say 'poor thing'?"

"Yes."

"Is it possible that you pity her?"

"From the bottom of my heart."

The old lady's temper gave way again at that reply. "I hate a man who can't hate anybody!" she burst out. "If you had been an ancient Roman, Julian, I believe you would have pitied Nero himself."

Julian cordially agreed with her. "I believe I should," he said, quietly. "All sinners, my dear aunt, are more or less miserable sinners. Nero must have been one of the wretchedest of mankind."

"Wretched!" exclaimed Lady Janet. "Nero wretched! A man who committed robbery, arson and murder to his own violin accompaniment—only wretched! What next, I wonder? When modern philanthropy begins to

126

apologize for Nero, modern philanthropy has arrived at a pretty pass indeed! We shall hear next that Bloody Queen Mary was as playful as a kitten; and if poor dear Henry the Eighth carried anything to an extreme, it was the practice of the domestic virtues. Ah, how I hate cant! What were we talking about just now? You wander from the subject, Julian; you are what I call bird-witted. I protest I forget what I wanted to say to you. No, I won't be reminded of it. I may be an old woman, but I am not in my dotage yet! Why do you sit there staring? Have you nothing to say for yourself? Of all the people in the world, have you lost the use of your tongue?"

Julian's excellent temper and accurate knowledge of his aunt's character exactly fitted him to calm the rising storm. He contrived to lead Lady Janet insensibly back to the lost subject by dexterous reference to a narrative which he had thus far left untold—the narrative of his adventures on the Continent.

"I have a great deal to say, aunt," he replied. "I have not yet told you of my discoveries abroad."

Lady Janet instantly took the bait.

"I knew there was something forgotten," she said. "You have been all this time in the house, and you have told me nothing. Begin directly."

Patient Julian began.

CHAPTER XIV. COMING EVENTS CAST THEIR SHADOWS BEFORE.

"I WENT first to Mannheim, Lady Janet, as I told you I should in my letter, and I heard all that the consul and the hospital doctors could tell me. No new fact of the slightest importance turned up. I got my directions for finding the German surgeon, and I set forth to try what I could make next of the man who performed the operation. On the question of his patient's identity he had (as a perfect stranger to her) nothing to tell me. On the question of her mental condition, however, he made a very important statement. He owned to me that he had operated on another person injured by a shell-wound on the head at the battle of Solferino, and that the patient (recovering also in this case) recovered—mad. That is a remarkable admission; don't you think so?"

Lady Janet's temper had hardly been allowed time enough to subside to its customary level.

"Very remarkable, I dare say," she answered, "to people who feel any doubt of this pitiable lady of yours being mad. I feel no doubt—and, thus far, I find your account of yourself, Julian, tiresome in the extreme. Go on to the end. Did you lay your hand on Mercy Merrick?"

"No."

"Did you hear anything of her?"

"Nothing. Difficulties beset me on every side. The French ambulance had shared in the disasters of France—it was broken up. The wounded Frenchmen were prisoners somewhere in Germany, nobody knew where. The French surgeon had been killed in action. His assistants were scattered—most likely in hiding. I began to despair of making any discovery, when accident threw in my way two Prussian soldiers who had been in the French cottage. They confirmed what the German surgeon told the consul, and what Horace himself told me—namely, that no nurse in a black dress was to be seen in the place. If there had been such a person, she would certainly (the Prussians inform me) have been found in attendance on the injured Frenchmen. The cross of the Geneva Convention would have been amply sufficient to protect her: no woman wearing that badge of honor would have disgraced herself by abandoning the wounded men before the Germans entered the place."

"In short," interposed Lady Janet, "there is no such person as Mercy Merrick."

"I can draw no other conclusion," said Julian, "unless the English doctor's idea is the right one. After hearing what I have just told you, he thinks the woman herself is Mercy Merrick."

Lady Janet held up her hand as a sign that she had an objection to make here.

"You and the doctor seem to have settled everything to your entire satisfaction on both sides," she said. "But there is one difficulty that you have neither of you accounted for yet."

"What is it, aunt?"

"You talk glibly enough, Julian, about this woman's mad assertion that Grace is the missing nurse, and that she is Grace. But you have not explained yet how the idea first got into her head; and, more than that, how it is that she is acquainted with my name and address, and perfectly familiar with Grace's papers and Grace's affairs. These things are a puzzle to a person of my average intelligence. Can your clever friend, the doctor, account for them?"

"Shall I tell you what he said when I saw him this morning?"

"Will it take long?"

"It will take about a minute."

"You agreeably surprise me. Go on."

"You want to know how she gained her knowledge of your name and of Miss Roseberry's affairs," Julian resumed. "The doctor says in one of two ways. Either Miss Roseberry must have spoken of you and of her own affairs while she and the stranger were together in the French cottage, or the stranger must have obtained access privately to Miss Roseberry's papers. Do you agree so far?"

Lady Janet began to feel interested for the first time.

"Perfectly," she said. "I have no doubt Grace rashly talked of matters which an older and wiser person would have kept to herself."

"Very good. Do you also agree that the last idea in the woman's mind when she was struck by the shell might have been (quite probably) the idea of Miss Roseberry's identity and Miss Roseberry's affairs? You think it likely enough? Well, what happens after that? The wounded woman is brought to life by an operation, and she becomes delirious in the hospital at Mannheim. During her delirium the idea of Miss Roseberry's identity ferments in her brain, and assumes its present perverted form. In that form it still remains. As a necessary consequence, she persists in reversing the two identities. She says she is Miss Roseberry, and declares Miss Roseberry to be Mercy Merrick. There is the doctor 's explanation. What do you think of it?"

"Very ingenious, I dare say. The doctor doesn't quite satisfy me, however, for all that. I think—"

What Lady Janet thought was not destined to be expressed. She suddenly checked herself, and held up her hand for the second time.

"Another objection?" inquired Julian.

"Hold your tongue!" cried the old lady. "If you say a word more I shall lose it again."

"Lose what, aunt?"

"What I wanted to say to you ages ago. I have got it back again—it begins with a question. (No more of the doctor—I have had enough of him!) Where is she—your pitiable lady, my crazy wretch—where is she now? Still in London?"

"Yes."

"And still at large?"

"Still with the landlady, at her lodgings."

"Very well. Now answer me this! What is to prevent her from making another attempt to force her way (or steal her way) into my house? How am I to protect Grace, how am I to protect myself, if she comes here again?"

"Is that really what you wished to speak to me about?"

"That, and nothing else."

They were both too deeply interested in the subject of their conversation to look toward the conservatory, and to notice the appearance at that moment of a distant gentleman among the plants and flowers, who had made his way in from the garden outside. Advancing noiselessly on the soft Indian matting, the gentleman ere long revealed himself under the form and features of Horace Holmcroft. Before entering the dining-room he paused, fixing his eyes inquisitively on the back of Lady Janet's visitor—the back being all that he could see in the position he then occupied. After a pause of an instant the visitor spoke, and further uncertainty was at once at an end. Horace, nevertheless, made no movement to enter the room. He had his own jealous distrust of what Julian might be tempted to say at a private interview with his aunt; and he waited a little longer on the chance that his doubts might be verified.

"Neither you nor Miss Roseberry need any protection from the poor deluded creature," Julian went on. "I have gained great influence over her—and I have satisfied her that it is useless to present herself here again."

"I beg your pardon," interposed Horace, speaking from the conservatory door. "You have done nothing of the sort."

(He had heard enough to satisfy him that the talk was not taking the direction which his Suspicions had anticipated. And, as an additional incentive to show himself, a happy chance had now offered him the opportunity of putting Julian in the wrong.)

"Good heavens, Horace!" exclaimed Lady Janet. "Where did you come from? And what do you mean?"

"I heard at the lodge that your ladyship and Grace had returned last night. And I came in at once without troubling the servants, by the shortest way." He turned to Julian next. "The woman you were speaking of just now," he proceeded, "has been here again already—in Lady Janet's absence."

Lady Janet immediately looked at her nephew. Julian reassured her by a gesture.

"Impossible," he said. "There must be some mistake."

"There is no mistake," Horace rejoined. "I am repeating what I have just heard from the lodge-keeper himself. He hesitated to mention it to Lady Janet for fear of alarming her. Only three days since this person had the audacity to ask him for her ladyship's address at the sea-side. Of course he refused to give it."

"You hear that, Julian?" said Lady Janet.

No signs of anger or mortification escaped Julian. The expression in his face at that moment was an expression of sincere distress.

"Pray don't alarm yourself," he said to his aunt, in his quietest tones. "If she attempts to annoy you or Miss Roseberry again, I have it in my power to stop her instantly."

"How?" asked Lady Janet.

"How, indeed!" echoed Horace. "If we give her in charge to the police, we shall become the subject of a public scandal."

"I have managed to avoid all danger of scandal," Julian answered; the expression of distress in his face becoming more and more marked while he spoke. "Before I called here to-day I had a private consultation with the magistrate of the district, and I have made certain arrangements at the police station close by. On receipt of my card, an experienced man, in plain clothes, will present himself at any address that I indicate, and will take her quietly away. The magistrate will hear the charge in his private room, and will examine the evidence which I can produce, showing that she is not accountable for her actions. The proper medical officer will report officially on the case, and the law will place her under the necessary restraint."

Lady Janet and Horace looked at each other in amazement. Julian was, in their opinion, the last man on earth to take the course—at once sensible and severe—which Julian had actually adopted. Lady Janet insisted on an explanation.

"Why do I hear of this now for the first time?" she asked. "Why did you not tell me you had taken these precautions before?"

Julian answered frankly and sadly.

"Because I hoped, aunt, that there would be no necessity for proceeding to extremities. You now force me to acknowledge that the lawyer and the doctor (both of whom I have seen this morning) think, as you do, that she is not to be trusted. It was at their suggestion entirely that I went to the magistrate. They put it to me whether the result of my inquiries abroad—unsatisfactory as it may have been in other respects—did not strengthen the conclusion that the poor woman's mind is deranged. I felt compelled in common honesty to admit that it was so. Having owned this, I was bound to take such precautions as the lawyer and the doctor thought necessary. I have done my duty—sorely against my own will. It is weak of me, I dare say; but I can not bear the thought of treating this afflicted creature harshly. Her delusion is so hopeless! her situation is such a pitiable one!"

His voice faltered. He turned away abruptly and took up his hat. Lady Janet followed him, and spoke to him at the door. Horace smiled satirically, and went to warm himself at the fire.

"Are you going away, Julian?"

"I am only going to the lodge-keeper. I want to give him a word of warning in case of his seeing her again."

"You will come back here?" (Lady Janet lowered her voice to a whisper.) "There is really a reason, Julian, for your not leaving the house now."

"I promise not to go away, aunt, until I have provided for your security. If you, or your adopted daughter, are alarmed by another intrusion, I give you my word of honor my card shall go to the police station, however painfully

I may feel it myself." (He, too, lowered his voice at the next words) "In the meantime, remember what I confessed to you while we were alone. For my sake, let me see as little of Miss Roseberry as possible. Shall I find you in this room when I come back?"

"Yes."

"Alone?"

He laid a strong emphasis, of look as well as of tone, on that one word. Lady Janet understood what the emphasis meant.

"Are you really," she whispered, "as much in love with Grace as that?"

Julian laid one hand on his aunt's arm, and pointed with the other to Horace—standing with his back to them, warming his feet on the fender.

"Well?" said Lady Janet.

"Well," said Julian, with a smile on his lip and a tear in his eye, "I never envied any man as I envy him!"

With those words he left the room.

134

CHAPTER XV. A WOMAN'S REMORSE.

HAVING warmed his feet to his own entire satisfaction, Horace turned round from the fireplace, and discovered that he and Lady Janet were alone.

"Can I see Grace?" he asked.

The easy tone in which he put the question—a tone, as it were, of proprietorship in "Grace"—jarred on Lady Janet at the moment. For the first time in her life she found herself comparing Horace with Julian—to Horace's disadvantage. He was rich; he was a gentleman of ancient lineage; he bore an unblemished character. But who had the strong brain? who had the great heart? Which was the Man of the two?

"Nobody can see her," answered Lady Janet. "Not even you!"

The tone of the reply was sharp, with a dash of irony in it. But where is the modern young man, possessed of health and an independent income, who is capable of understanding that irony can be presumptuous enough to address itself to him? Horace (with perfect politeness) declined to consider himself answered.

"Does your ladyship mean that Miss Roseberry is in bed?" he asked.

"I mean that Miss Roseberry is in her room. I mean that I have twice tried to persuade Miss Roseberry to dress and come downstairs, and tried in vain. I mean that what Miss Roseberry refuses to do for Me, she is not likely to do for You—"

How many more meanings of her own Lady Janet might have gone on enumerating, it is not easy to calculate. At her third sentence a sound in the library caught her ear through the incompletely closed door and suspended the next words on her lips. Horace heard it also. It was the rustling sound (traveling nearer and nearer over the library carpet) of a silken dress.

(In the interval while a coming event remains in a state of uncertainty, what is it the inevitable tendency of every Englishman under thirty to do? His inevitable tendency is to ask somebody to bet on the event. He can no more resist it than he can resist lifting his stick or his umbrella, in the absence of a gun, and pretending to shoot if a bird flies by him while he is out for a walk.)

"What will your ladyship bet that this is not Grace?" cried Horace.

Her ladyship took no notice of the proposal; her attention remained fixed on the library door. The rustling sound stopped for a moment. The door was softly pushed open. The false Grace Roseberry entered the room.

Horace advanced to meet her, opened his lips to speak, and stopped—struck dumb by the change in his affianced wife since he had seen her last. Some terrible oppression seemed to have crushed her. It was as if she had actually shrunk in height as well as in substance. She walked more slowly than usual; she spoke more rarely than usual, and in a lower tone. To those who had seen her before the fatal visit of the stranger from Mannheim, it was the wreck of the woman that now appeared instead of the woman herself. And yet there was the old charm still surviving through it all; the grandeur of the head and eyes, the delicate symmetry of the features, the unsought grace of every movement—in a word, the unconquerable beauty which suffering cannot destroy, and which time itself is powerless to wear out. Lady Janet advanced, and took her with hearty kindness by both hands.

"My dear child, welcome among us again! You have come down stairs to please me?"

She bent her head in silent acknowledgment that it was so. Lady Janet pointed to Horace: "Here is somebody who has been longing to see you, Grace."

She never looked up; she stood submissive, her eyes fixed on a little basket of colored wools which hung on her arm. "Thank you, Lady Janet," she said, faintly. "Thank you, Horace."

Horace placed her arm in his, and led her to the sofa. She shivered as she took her seat, and looked round her. It was the first time she had seen the dining-room since the day when she had found herself face to face with the dead-alive.

"Why do you come here, my love?" asked Lady Janet. "The drawing-room would have been a warmer and a pleasanter place for you."

"I saw a carriage at the front door. I was afraid of meeting with visitors in the drawing-room."

As she made that reply, the servant came in, and announced the visitors' names. Lady Janet sighed wearily. "I must go and get rid of them," she said, resigning herself to circumstances. "What will you do, Grace?"

"I will stay here, if you please."

"I will keep her company," added Horace.

Lady Janet hesitated. She had promised to see her nephew in the dining-room on his return to the house—and to see him alone. Would there be time enough to get rid of the visitors and to establish her adopted daughter in the empty drawing-room before Julian appeared? It was ten minutes' walk to the lodge, and he had to make the gate-keeper understand his instructions. Lady Janet decided that she had time enough at her disposal. She nodded kindly to Mercy, and left her alone with her lover.

Horace seated himself in the vacant place on the sofa. So far as it was in his nature to devote himself to any one he was devoted to Mercy. "I am grieved to see how you have suffered," he said, with honest distress in his face as he looked at her. "Try to forget what has happened."

"I am trying to forget. Do you think of it much?"

"My darling, it is too contemptible to be thought of."

She placed her work-basket on her lap. Her wasted fingers began absently sorting the wools inside.

"Have you seen Mr. Julian Gray?" she asked, suddenly.

"Yes."

"What does he say about it?" She looked at Horace for the first time, steadily scrutinizing his face. Horace took refuge in prevarication.

"I really haven't asked for Julian's opinion," he said.

She looked down again, with a sigh, at the basket on her lap—considered a little—and tried him once more.

"Why has Mr. Julian Gray not been here for a whole week?" she went on. "The servants say he has been abroad. Is that true?"

It was useless to deny it. Horace admitted that the servants were right.

Her fingers, suddenly stopped at their restless work among the wools; her breath quickened perceptibly. What had Julian Gray been doing abroad? Had he been making inquiries? Did he alone, of all the people who saw that terrible meeting, suspect her? Yes! His was the finer intelligence; his was a clergyman's (a London clergyman's) experience of frauds and deceptions, and of the women who were guilty of them. Not a doubt of it now! Julian suspected her.

"When does he come back?" she asked, in tones so low that Horace could barely hear her.

"He has come back already. He returned last night."

A faint shade of color stole slowly over the pallor of her face. She suddenly put her basket away, and clasped her hands together to quiet the trembling of them, before she asked her next question.

"Where is—" She paused to steady her voice. "Where is the person," she resumed, "who came here and frightened me?"

Horace hastened to re-assure her. "The person will not come again," he said. "Don't talk of her! Don't think of her!"

She shook her head. "There is something I want to know," she persisted. "How did Mr. Julian Gray become acquainted with her?"

This was easily answered. Horace mentioned the consul at Mannheim, and the letter of introduction. She listened eagerly, and said her next words in a louder, firmer tone.

"She was quite a stranger, then, to Mr. Julian Gray—before that?"

"Quite a stranger," Horace replied. "No more questions—not another word about her, Grace! I forbid the subject. Come, my own love!" he said, taking her hand and bending over her tenderly, "rally your spirits! We are young—we love each other—now is our time to be happy!"

Her hand turned suddenly cold, and trembled in his. Her head sank with a helpless weariness on her breast. Horace rose in alarm.

"You are cold—you are faint," he said. "Let me get you a glass of wine!—let me mend the fire!"

The decanters were still on the luncheon-table. Horace insisted on her drinking some port-wine. She barely took half the contents of the wine-glass. Even that little told on her sensitive organization; it roused her sinking energies of body and mind. After watching her anxiously, without attracting her notice, Horace left her again to attend to the fire at the other end of the room. Her eyes followed him slowly with a hard and tearless despair. "Rally your spirits," she repeated to herself in a whisper. "My spirits! O God!" She looked round her at the luxury and beauty of the room, as those look who take their leave of familiar scenes. The moment after, her eyes sank, and rested on the rich dress that she wore a gift from Lady Janet. She thought of the past; she thought of the future. Was the time near when she would be back again in the Refuge, or back again in the streets?—she who had been Lady Janet's adopted daughter, and Horace Holmcroft's betrothed wife! A sudden frenzy of recklessness seized on her as she thought of the coming end. Horace was right! Why not rally her spirits? Why not make the most of her time? The last hours of her life in that house were at hand. Why not enjoy her stolen position while she could? "Adventuress!" whispered the mocking spirit within her, "be true to your character. Away with your remorse! Remorse is the luxury of an honest woman." She caught up her basket of wools, inspired by a new idea. "Ring the bell!" she cried out to Horace at the fire-place.

He looked round in wonder. The sound of her voice was so completely altered that he almost fancied there must have been another woman in the room.

"Ring the bell!" she repeated. "I have left my work upstairs. If you want

139

me to be in good spirits, I must have my work."

Still looking at her, Horace put his hand mechanically to the bell and rang. One of the men-servants came in.

"Go upstairs and ask my maid for my work," she said, sharply. Even the man was taken by surprise: it was her habit to speak to the servants with a gentleness and consideration which had long since won all their hearts. "Do you hear me?" she asked, impatiently. The servant bowed, and went out on his errand. She turned to Horace with flashing eyes and fevered cheeks.

"What a comfort it is," she said, "to belong to the upper classes! A poor woman has no maid to dress her, and no footman to send upstairs. Is life worth having, Horace, on less than five thousand a year?"

The servant returned with a strip of embroidery. She took it with an insolent grace, and told him to bring her a footstool. The man obeyed. She tossed the embroidery away from her on the sofa. "On second thoughts, I don't care about my work," she said. "Take it upstairs again." The perfectly trained servant, marveling privately, obeyed once more. Horace, in silent astonishment, advanced to the sofa to observe her more nearly. "How grave you look!" she exclaimed, with an air of flippant unconcern. "You don't approve of my sitting idle, perhaps? Anything to please you! I haven't got to go up and downstairs. Ring the bell again."

"My dear Grace," Horace remonstrated, gravely, "you are quite mistaken. I never even thought of your work."

"Never mind; it's inconsistent to send for my work, and then send it away again. Ring the bell."

Horace looked at her without moving. "Grace," he said, "what has come to you?"

"How should I know?" she retorted, carelessly. "Didn't you tell me to rally my spirits? Will you ring the bell, or must I?"

Horace submitted. He frowned as he walked back to the bell. He was one of the many people who instinctively resent anything that is new to them.

140

This strange outbreak was quite new to him. For the first time in his life he felt sympathy for a servant, when the much-enduring man appeared once more.

"Bring my work back; I have changed my mind." With that brief explanation she reclined luxuriously on the soft sofa-cushions, swinging one of her balls of wool to and fro above her head, and looking at it lazily as she lay back. "I have a remark to make, Horace," she went on, when the door had closed on her messenger. "It is only people in our rank of life who get good servants. Did you notice? Nothing upsets that man's temper. A servant in a poor family should have been impudent; a maid-of-all-work would have wondered when I was going to know my own mind." The man returned with the embroidery. This time she received him graciously; she dismissed him with her thanks. "Have you seen your mother lately, Horace?" she asked, suddenly sitting up and busying herself with her work.

"I saw her yesterday," Horace answered.

"She understands, I hope, that I am not well enough to call on her? She is not offended with me?"

Horace recovered his serenity. The deference to his mother implied in Mercy's questions gently flattered his self-esteem. He resumed his place on the sofa.

"Offended with you!" he answered, smiling. "My dear Grace, she sends you her love. And, more than that, she has a wedding present for you."

Mercy became absorbed in her work; she stooped close over the embroidery—so close that Horace could not see her face. "Do you know what the present is?" she asked, in lowered tones, speaking absently.

"No. I only know it is waiting for you. Shall I go and get it to-day?"

She neither accepted nor refused the proposal—she went on with her work more industriously than ever.

"There is plenty of time," Horace persisted. "I can go before dinner."

Still she took no notice: still she never looked up. "Your mother is very

141

kind to me," she said, abruptly. "I was afraid, at one time, that she would think me hardly good enough to be your wife."

Horace laughed indulgently: his self-esteem was more gently flattered than ever.

"Absurd!" he exclaimed. "My darling, you are connected with Lady Janet Roy. Your family is almost as good as ours."

"Almost?" she repeated. "Only almost?"

The momentary levity of expression vanished from Horace's face. The family question was far too serious a question to be lightly treated A becoming shadow of solemnity stole over his manner. He looked as if it was Sunday, and he was just stepping into church.

"In OUR family," he said, "we trace back—by my father, to the Saxons; by my mother, to the Normans. Lady Janet's family is an old family—on her side only."

Mercy dropped her embroidery, and looked Horace full in the face. She, too, attached no common importance to what she had next to say.

"If I had not been connected with Lady Janet," she began, "would you ever have thought of marrying me?"

"My love! what is the use of asking? You are connected with Lady Janet."

She refused to let him escape answering her in that way.

"Suppose I had not been connected with Lady Janet?" she persisted. "Suppose I had only been a good girl, with nothing but my own merits to speak for me. What would your mother have said then?"

Horace still parried the question—only to find the point of it pressed home on him once more.

"Why do you ask?" he said.

"I ask to be answered," she rejoined. "Would your mother have liked you to marry a poor girl, of no family—with nothing but her own virtues to speak for her?"

Horace was fairly pressed back to the wall.

"If you must know," he replied, "my mother would have refused to sanction such a marriage as that."

"No matter how good the girl might have been?"

There was something defiant—almost threatening—in her tone. Horace was annoyed—and he showed it when he spoke.

"My mother would have respected the girl, without ceasing to respect herself," he said. "My mother would have remembered what was due to the family name."

"And she would have said, No?"

"She would have said, No."

"Ah!"

There was an undertone of angry contempt in the exclamation which made Horace start. "What is the matter?" he asked.

"Nothing," she answered, and took up her embroidery again. There he sat at her side, anxiously looking at her—his hope in the future centered in his marriage! In a week more, if she chose, she might enter that ancient family of which he had spoken so proudly, as his wife. "Oh!" she thought, "if I didn't love him! if I had only his merciless mother to think of!"

Uneasily conscious of some estrangement between them, Horace spoke again. "Surely I have not offended you?" he said.

She turned toward him once more. The work dropped unheeded on her lap. Her grand eyes softened into tenderness. A smile trembled sadly on her delicate lips. She laid one hand caressingly on his shoulder. All the beauty of her voice lent its charm to the next words that she said to him. The woman's heart hungered in its misery for the comfort that could only come from his lips.

143

"You would have loved me, Horace—without stopping to think of the family name?"

The family name again! How strangely she persisted in coming back to that! Horace looked at her without answering, trying vainly to fathom what was passing in her mind.

She took his hand, and wrung it hard—as if she would wring the answer out of him in that way.

"You would have loved me?" she repeated.

The double spell of her voice and her touch was on him. He answered, warmly, "Under any circumstances! under any name!"

She put one arm round his neck, and fixed her eyes on his. "Is that true?" she asked.

"True as t he heaven above us!"

She drank in those few commonplace words with a greedy delight. She forced him to repeat them in a new form.

"No matter who I might have been? For myself alone?"

"For yourself alone."

She threw both arms round him, and laid her head passionately on his breast. "I love you! I love you!! I love you!!!" Her voice rose with hysterical vehemence at each repetition of the words—then suddenly sank to a low hoarse cry of rage and despair. The sense of her true position toward him revealed itself in all its horror as the confession of her love escaped her lips. Her arms dropped from him; she flung herself back on the sofa-cushions, hiding her face in her hands. "Oh, leave me!" she moaned, faintly. "Go! go!"

Horace tried to wind his arm round her, and raise her. She started to her feet, and waved him back from her with a wild action of her hands, as if she was frightened of him. "The wedding present!" she cried, seizing the first pretext that occurred to her. "You offered to bring me your mother's present. I am dying to see what it is. Go and get it!"

Horace tried to compose her. He might as well have tried to compose the winds and the sea.

"Go!" she repeated, pressing one clinched hand on her bosom. "I am not well. Talking excites me—I am hysterical; I shall be better alone. Get me the present. Go!"

"Shall I send Lady Janet? Shall I ring for your maid?"

"Send for nobody! ring for nobody! If you love me—leave me here by myself! leave me instantly!"

"I shall see you when I come back?"

"Yes! yes!"

There was no alternative but to obey her. Unwillingly and forebodingly, Horace left the room.

She drew a deep breath of relief, and dropped into the nearest chair. If Horace had stayed a moment longer—she felt it, she knew it—her head would have given way; she would have burst out before him with the terrible truth. "Oh!" she thought, pressing her cold hands on her burning eyes, "if I could only cry, now there is nobody to see me!"

The room was empty: she had every reason for concluding that she was alone. And yet at that very moment there were ears that listened—there were eyes waiting to see her.

Little by little the door behind her which faced the library and led into the billiard-room was opened noiselessly from without, by an inch at a time. As the opening was enlarged a hand in a black glove, an arm in a black sleeve, appeared, guiding the movement of the door. An interval of a moment passed, and the worn white face of Grace Roseberry showed itself stealthily, looking into the dining-room.

Her eyes brightened with vindictive pleasure as they discovered Mercy sitting alone at the further end of the room. Inch by inch she opened the door more widely, took one step forward, and checked herself. A sound, just

145

audible at the far end of the conservatory, had caught her ear.

She listened—satisfied herself that she was not mistaken—and drawing back with a frown of displeasure, softly closed the door again, so as to hide herself from view. The sound that had disturbed her was the distant murmur of men's voices (apparently two in number) talking together in lowered tones, at the garden entrance to the conservatory.

Who were the men? and what would they do next? They might do one of two things: they might enter the drawing-room, or they might withdraw again by way of the garden. Kneeling behind the door, with her ear at the key-hole, Grace Roseberry waited the event.

CHAPTER XVI. THEY MEET AGAIN.

ABSORBED in herself, Mercy failed to notice the opening door or to hear the murmur of voices in the conservatory.

The one terrible necessity which had been present to her mind at intervals for a week past was confronting her at that moment. She owed to Grace Roseberry the tardy justice of owning the truth. The longer her confession was delayed, the more cruelly she was injuring the woman whom she had robbed of her identity—the friendless woman who had neither witnesses nor papers to produce, who was powerless to right her own wrong. Keenly as she felt this, Mercy failed, nevertheless, to conquer the horror that shook her when she thought of the impending avowal. Day followed day, and still she shrank from the unendurable ordeal of confession—as she was shrinking from it now!

Was it fear for herself that closed her lips?

She trembled—as any human being in her place must have trembled— at the bare idea of finding herself thrown back again on the world, which had no place in it and no hope in it for her. But she could have overcome that terror—she could have resigned herself to that doom.

No! it was not the fear of the confession itself, or the fear of the consequences which must follow it, that still held her silent. The horror that daunted her was the horror of owning to Horace and to Lady Janet that she had cheated them out of their love.

Every day Lady Janet was kinder and kinder. Every day Horace was fonder and fonder of her. How could she confess to Lady Janet? how could she own to Horace that she had imposed upon him? "I can't do it. They are so good to me—I can't do it!" In that hopeless way it had ended during the seven days that had gone by. In that hopeless way it ended again now.

The murmur of the two voices at the further end of the conservatory ceased. The billiard-room door opened again slowly, by an inch at a time.

Mercy still kept her place, unconscious of the events that were passing round her. Sinking under the hard stress laid on it, her mind had drifted little by little into a new train of thought. For the first time she found the courage to question the future in a new way. Supposing her confession to have been made, or supposing the woman whom she had personated to have discovered the means of exposing the fraud, what advantage, she now asked herself, would Miss Roseberry derive from Mercy Merrick's disgrace?

Could Lady Janet transfer to the woman who was really her relative by marriage the affection which she had given to the woman who had pretended to be her relative? No! All the right in the world would not put the true Grace into the false Grace's vacant place. The qualities by which Mercy had won Lady Janet's love were the qualities which were Mercy's won. Lady Janet could do rigid justice—but hers was not the heart to give itself to a stranger (and to give itself unreservedly) a second time. Grace Roseberry would be formally acknowledged—and there it would end.

Was there hope in this new view?

Yes! There was the false hope of making the inevitable atonement by some other means than by the confession of the fraud.

What had Grace Roseberry actually lost by the wrong done to her? She had lost the salary of Lady Janet's "companion and reader." Say that she wanted money, Mercy had her savings from the generous allowance made to her by Lady Janet; Mercy could offer money. Or say that she wanted employment, Mercy's interest with Lady Janet could offer employment, could offer anything Grace might ask for, if she would only come to terms.

Invigorated by the new hope, Mercy rose excitedly, weary of inaction in the empty room. She, who but a few minutes since had shuddered at the thought of their meeting again, was now eager to devise a means of finding her way privately to an interview with Grace. It should be done without loss of time—on that very day, if possible; by the next day at latest. She looked round her mechanically, pondering how to reach the end in view. Her eyes rested by chance on the door of the billiard-room.

Was it fancy? or did she really see the door first open a little, then suddenly and softly close again?

Was it fancy? or did she really hear, at the same moment, a sound behind her as of persons speaking in the conservatory?

She paused; and, looking back in that direction, listened intently. The sound—if she had really heard it—was no longer audible. She advanced toward the billiard-room to set her first doubt at rest. She stretched out her hand to open the door, when the voices (recognizable now as the voices of two men) caught her ear once more.

This time she was able to distinguish the words that were spoken.

"Any further orders, sir?" inquired one of the men.

"Nothing more," replied the other.

Mercy started, and faintly flushed, as the second voice answered the first. She stood irresolute close to the billiard-room, hesitating what to do next.

After an interval the second voice made itself heard again, advancing nearer to the dining-room: "Are you there, aunt?" it asked cautiously. There was a moment's pause. Then the voice spoke for the third time, sounding louder and nearer. "Are you there?" it reiterated; "I have something to tell you." Mercy summoned her resolution and answered: "Lady Janet is not here." She turned as she spoke toward the conservatory door, and confronted on the threshold Julian Gray.

They looked at one another without exchanging a word on either side. The situation—for widely different reasons—was equally embarrassing to both of them.

There—as Julian saw her—was the woman forbidden to him, the woman whom he loved.

There—as Mercy saw him—was the man whom she dreaded, the man whose actions (as she interpreted them) proved that he suspected her.

On the surface of it, the incidents which had marked their first meeting were now exactly repeated, with the one difference that the impulse to

149

withdraw this time appeared to be on the man's side and not on the woman's. It was Mercy who spoke first.

"Did you expect to find Lady Janet here?" she asked, constrainedly. He answered, on his part, more constrainedly still.

"It doesn't matter," he said. "Another time will do."

He drew back as he made the reply. She advanced desperately, with the deliberate intention of detaining him by speaking again.

The attempt which he had made to withdraw, the constraint in his manner when he had answered, had instantly confirmed her in the false conviction that he, and he alone, had guessed the truth! If she was right—if he had secretly made discoveries abroad which placed her entirely at his mercy—the attempt to induce Grace to consent to a compromise with her would be manifestly useless. Her first and foremost interest now was to find out how she really stood in the estimation of Julian Gray. In a terror of suspense, that turned her cold from head to foot, she stopped him on his way out, and spoke to him with the piteous counterfeit of a smile.

"Lady Janet is receiving some visitors," she said. "If you will wait here, she will be back directly."

The effort of hiding her agitation from him had brought a passing color into her cheeks. Worn and wasted as she was, the spell of her beauty was strong enough to hold him against his own will. All he had to tell Lady Janet was that he had met one of the gardeners in the conservatory, and had cautioned him as well as the lodge-keeper. It would have been easy to write this, and to send the note to his aunt on quitting the house. For the sake of his own peace of mind, for the sake of his duty to Horace, he was doubly bound to make the first polite excuse that occurred to him, and to leave her as he had found her, alone in the room. He made the attempt, and hesitated. Despising himself for doing it, he allowed himself to look at her. Their eyes met. Julian stepped into the dining-room.

"If I am not in the way," he said, confusedly, "I will wait, as you kindly propose."

She noticed his embarrassment; she saw that he was strongly restraining himself from looking at her again. Her own eyes dropped to the ground as she made the discovery. Her speech failed her; her heart throbbed faster and faster.

"If I look at him again" (was the thought in her mind) "I shall fall at his feet and tell him all that I have done!"

"If I look at her again" (was the thought in his mind) "I shall fall at her feet and own that I am in love with her!"

With downcast eyes he placed a chair for her. With downcast eyes she bowed to him and took it. A dead silence followed. Never was any human misunderstanding more intricately complete than the misunderstanding which had now established itself between those two.

Mercy's work-basket was near her. She took it, and gained time for composing herself by pretending to arrange the colored wools. He stood behind her chair, looking at the graceful turn of her head, looking at the rich masses of her hair. He reviled himself as the weakest of men, as the falsest of friends, for still remaining near her—and yet he remained.

The silence continued. The billiard-room door opened again noiselessly. The face of the listening woman appeared stealthily behind it.

At the same moment Mercy roused herself and spoke: "Won't you sit down?" she said, softly, still not looking round at him, still busy with her basket of wools.

He turned to get a chair—turned so quickly that he saw the billiard-room door move, as Grace Roseberry closed it again.

"Is there any one in that room?" he asked, addressing Mercy.

"I don't know," she answered. "I thought I saw the door open and shut again a little while ago."

He advanced at once to look into the room. As he did so Mercy dropped one of her balls of wool. He stopped to pick it up for her—then threw open the door and looked into the billiard-room. It was empty.

Had some person been listening, and had that person retreated in time to escape discovery? The open door of the smoking-room showed that room also to be empty. A third door was open—the door of the side hall, leading into the grounds. Julian closed and locked it, and returned to the dining-room.

"I can only suppose," he said to Mercy, "that the billiard-room door was not properly shut, and that the draught of air from the hall must have moved it."

She accepted the explanation in silence. He was, to all appearance, not quite satisfied with it himself. For a moment or two he looked about him uneasily. Then the old fascination fastened its hold on him again. Once more he looked at the graceful turn of her head, at the rich masses of her hair. The courage to put the critical question to him, now that she had lured him into remaining in the room, was still a courage that failed her. She remained as busy as ever with her work—too busy to look at him; too busy to speak to him. The silence became unendurable. He broke it by making a commonplace inquiry after her health. "I am well enough to be ashamed of the anxiety I have caused and the trouble I have given," she answered. "To-day I have got downstairs for the first time. I am trying to do a little work." She looked into the basket. The various specimens of wool in it were partly in balls and partly in loose skeins. The skeins were mixed and tangled. "Here is sad confusion!" she exclaimed, timidly, with a faint smile. "How am I to set it right again?"

"Let me help you," said Julian.

"You!"

"Why not?" he asked, with a momentary return of the quaint humor which she remembered so well. "You forget that I am a curate. Curates are privileged to make themselves useful to young ladies. Let me try."

He took a stool at her feet, and set himself to unravel one of the tangled skeins. In a minute the wool was stretched on his hands, and the loose end was ready for Mercy to wind. There was something in the trivial action, and in the homely attention that it implied, which in some degree quieted her fear of him. She began to roll the wool off his hands into a ball. Thus occupied, she said the daring words which were to lead him little by little into betraying his suspicions, if he did indeed suspect the truth.

CHAPTER XVII. THE GUARDIAN ANGEL.

"You were here when I fainted, were you not?" Mercy began. "You must think me a sad coward, even for a woman."

He shook his head. "I am far from thinking that," he replied. "No courage could have sustained the shock which fell on you. I don't wonder that you fainted. I don't wonder that you have been ill."

She paused in rolling up the ball of wool. What did those words of unexpected sympathy mean? Was he laying a trap for her? Urged by that serious doubt, she questioned him more boldly.

"Horace tells me you have been abroad," she said. "Did you enjoy your holiday?"

"It was no holiday. I went abroad because I thought it right to make certain inquiries—" He stopped there, unwilling to return to a subject that was painful to her.

Her voice sank, her fingers trembled round the ball of wool; but she managed to go on.

"Did you arrive at any results?" she asked.

"At no results worth mentioning."

The caution of that reply renewed her worst suspicions of him. In sheer despair, she spoke out plainly.

"I want to know your opinion—" she began.

"Gently!" said Julian. "You are entangling the wool again."

"I want to know your opinion of the person who so terribly frightened me. Do you think her—"

"Do I think her—what?"

"Do you think her an adventuress?"

(As she said those words the branches of a shrub in the conservatory were noiselessly parted by a hand in a black glove. The face of Grace Roseberry appeared dimly behind the leaves. Undiscovered, she had escaped from the billiard-room, and had stolen her way into the conservatory as the safer hiding-place of the two. Behind the shrub she could see as well as listen. Behind the shrub she waited as patiently as ever.)

"I take a more merciful view," Julian answered. "I believe she is acting under a delusion. I don't blame her: I pity her."

"You pity her?" As Mercy repeated the words, she tore off Julian's hands the last few lengths of wool left, and threw the imperfectly wound skein back into the basket. "Does that mean," she resumed, abruptly, "that you believe her?"

Julian rose from his seat, and looked at Mercy in astonishment.

"Good heavens, Miss Roseberry! what put such an idea as that into your head?"

"I am little better than a stranger to you," she rejoined, with an effort to assume a jesting tone. "You met that person before you met with me. It is not so very far from pitying her to believing her. How could I feel sure that you might not suspect me?"

"Suspect you!" he exclaimed. "You don't know how you distress, how you shock me. Suspect you! The bare idea of it never entered my mind. The man doesn't live who trusts you more implicitly, who believes in you more devotedly, than I do."

His eyes, his voice, his manner, all told her that those words came from the heart. She contrasted his generous confidence in her (the confidence of which she was unworthy) with her ungracious distrust of him. Not only had she wronged Grace Roseberry—she had wronged Julian Gray. Could she deceive him as she had deceived the others? Could she meanly accept that implicit trust, that devoted belief? Never had she felt the base submissions which her own imposture condemned her to undergo with a loathing of them so overwhelming as the loathing that she felt now. In horror of herself, she turned her head aside in silence and shrank from meeting his eye. He noticed the movement, placing his own interpretation on it. Advancing closer, he asked anxiously if he had offended her.

"You don't know how your confidence touches me," she said, without looking up. "You little think how keenly I feel your kindness."

She checked herself abruptly. Her fine tact warned her that she was speaking too warmly—that the expression of her gratitude might strike him as being strangely exaggerated. She handed him her work-basket before he could speak again.

"Will you put it away for me?" she asked, in her quieter tones. "I don't feel able to work just now."

His back was turned on her for a moment, while he placed the basket on a side-table. In that moment her mind advanced at a bound from present to future. Accident might one day put the true Grace in possession of the proofs that she needed, and might reveal the false Grace to him in the identity that was her own. What would he think of her then? Could she make him tell her without betraying herself? She determined to try.

"Children are notoriously insatiable if you once answer their questions, and women are nearly as bad," she said, when Julian returned to her. "Will your patience hold out if I go back for the third time to the person whom we have been speaking of?"

"Try me," he answered, with a smile.

"Suppose you had not taken your merciful view of her?"

"Yes?"

"Suppose you believed that she was wickedly bent on deceiving others for a purpose of her own—would you not shrink from such a woman in horror and disgust?"

"God forbid that I should shrink from any human creature!" he answered, earnestly. "Who among us has a right to do that?"

156

She hardly dared trust herself to believe him. "You would still pity her?" she persisted, "and still feel for her?"

"With all my heart."

"Oh, how good you are!"

He held up his hand in warning. The tones of his voice deepened, the luster of his eyes brightened. She had stirred in the depths of that great heart the faith in which the man lived—the steady principle which guided his modest and noble life.

"No!" he cried. "Don't say that! Say that I try to love my neighbor as myself. Who but a Pharisee can believe that he is better than another? The best among us to-day may, but for the mercy of God, be the worst among us tomorrow. The true Christian virtue is the virtue which never despairs of a fellow-creature. The true Christian faith believes in Man as well as in God. Frail and fallen as we are, we can rise on the wings of repentance from earth to heaven. Humanity is sacred. Humanity has its immortal destiny. Who shall dare say to man or woman, 'There is no hope in you?' Who shall dare say the work is all vile, when that work bears on it the stamp of the Creator's hand?"

He turned away for a moment, struggling with the emotion which she had roused in him.

Her eyes, as they followed him, lighted with a momentary enthusiasm—then sank wearily in the vain regret which comes too late. Ah! if he could have been her friend and her adviser on the fatal day when she first turned her steps toward Mablethorpe House! She sighed bitterly as the hopeless aspiration wrung her heart. He heard the sigh; and, turning again, looked at her with a new interest in his face.

"Miss Roseberry," he said.

She was still absorbed in the bitter memories of the past: she failed to hear him.

"Miss Roseberry," he repeated, approaching her.

She looked up at him with a start.

"May I venture to ask you something?" he said, gently.

She shrank at the question.

"Don't suppose I am speaking out of mere curiosity," he went on. "And pray don't answer me unless you can answer without betraying any confidence which may have been placed in you."

"Confidence!" she repeated. "What confidence do you mean?"

"It has just struck me that you might have felt more than a common interest in the questions which you put to me a moment since," he answered. "Were you by any chance speaking of some unhappy woman—not the person who frightened you, of course—but of some other woman whom you know?"

Her head sank slowly on her bosom. He had plainly no suspicion that she had been speaking of herself: his tone and manner both answered for it that his belief in her was as strong as ever. Still those last words made her tremble; she could not trust herself to reply to them.

He accepted the bending of her head as a reply.

"Are you interested in her?" he asked next.

She faintly answered this time. "Yes."

"Have you encouraged her?"

"I have not dared to encourage her."

His face lighted up suddenly with enthusiasm. "Go to her," he said, "and let me go with you and help you!"

The answer came faintly and mournfully. "She has sunk too low for that!"

He interrupted her with a gesture of impatience.

"What has she done?" he asked.

"She has deceived—basely deceived—innocent people who trusted her. She has wronged—cruelly wronged—another woman."

For the first time Julian seated himself at her side. The interest that was now roused in him was an interest above reproach. He could speak to Mercy without restraint; he could look at Mercy with a pure heart.

"You judge her very harshly," he said. "Do you know how she may have been tried and tempted?"

There was no answer.

"Tell me," he went on, "is the person whom she has injured still living?"

"Yes."

"If the person is still living, she may atone for the wrong. The time may come when this sinner, too, may win our pardon and deserve our respect."

"Could you respect her?" Mercy asked, sadly. "Can such a mind as yours understand what she has gone through?"

A smile, kind and momentary, brightened his attentive face.

"You forget my melancholy experience," he answered. "Young as I am, I have seen more than most men of women who have sinned and suffered. Even after the little that you have told me, I think I can put myself in her place. I can well understand, for instance, that she may have been tempted beyond human resistance. Am I right?"

"You are right."

"She may have had nobody near at the time to advise her, to warn her, to save her. Is that true?"

"It is true."

"Tempted and friendless, self-abandoned to the evil impulse of the moment, this woman may have committed herself headlong to the act which she now vainly repents. She may long to make atonement, and may not know how to begin. All her energies may be crushed under the despair and horror of herself, out of which the truest repentance grows. Is such a woman as this all wicked, all vile? I deny it! She may have a noble nature; and she may show

159

it nobly yet. Give her the opportunity she needs, and our poor fallen fellow-creature may take her place again among the best of us—honored, blameless, happy, once more!"

Mercy's eyes, resting eagerly on him while he was speaking, dropped again despondingly when he had done.

"There is no such future as that," she answered, "for the woman whom I am thinking of. She has lost her opportunity. She has done with hope."

Julian gravely considered with himself for a moment.

"Let us understand each other," he said. "She has committed an act of deception to the injury of another woman. Was that what you told me?"

"Yes."

"And she has gained something to her own advantage by the act."

"Yes."

"Is she threatened with discovery?"

"She is safe from discovery—for the present, at least."

"Safe as long as she closes her lips?"

"As long as she closes her lips."

"There is her opportunity!" cried Julian. "Her future is before her. She has not done with hope!"

With clasped hands, in breathless suspense, Mercy looked at that inspiriting face, and listened to those golden words.

"Explain yourself," she said. "Tell her, through me, what she must do."

"Let her own the truth," answered Julian, "without the base fear of discovery to drive her to it. Let her do justice to the woman whom she has wronged, while that woman is still powerless to expose her. Let her sacrifice everything that she has gained by the fraud to the sacred duty of atonement. If she can do that—for conscience' sake, and for pity's sake—to her own prejudice, to her own shame, to her own loss—then her repentance has nobly revealed the noble nature that is in her; then she is a woman to be trusted, respected, beloved! If I saw the Pharisees and fanatics of this lower earth passing her by in contempt, I would hold out my hand to her before them all. I would say to her in her solitude and her affliction, 'Rise, poor wounded heart! Beautiful, purified soul, God's angels rejoice over you! Take your place among the noblest of God's creatures!'"

In those last sentences he unconsciously repeated the language in which he had spoken, years since, to his congregation in the chapel of the Refuge. With tenfold power and tenfold persuasion they now found their way again to Mercy's heart. Softly, suddenly, mysteriously, a change passed over her. Her troubled face grew beautifully still. The shifting light of terror and suspense vanished from her grand gray eyes, and left in them the steady inner glow of a high and pure resolve.

There was a moment of silence between them. They both had need of silence. Julian was the first to speak again.

"Have I satisfied you that her opportunity is still before her?" he asked. "Do you feel, as I feel, that she has not done with hope?"

"You have satisfied me that the world holds no truer friend to her than you," Mercy answered, gently and gratefully. "She shall prove herself worthy of your generous confidence in her. She shall show you yet that you have not spoken in vain."

Still inevitably failing to understand her, he led the way to the door.

"Don't waste the precious time," he said. "Don't leave her cruelly to herself. If you can't go to her, let me go as your messenger, in your place."

She stopped him by a gesture. He took a step back into the room, and paused, observing with surprise that she made no attempt to move from the chair that she occupied.

"Stay here," she said to him, in suddenly altered tones.

"Pardon me," he rejoined, "I don't understand you."

"You will understand me directly. Give me a little time."

He still lingered near the door, with his eyes fixed inquiringly on her. A man of a lower nature than his, or a man believing in Mercy less devotedly than he believed, would now have felt his first suspicion of her. Julian was as far as ever from suspecting her, even yet. "Do you wish to be alone?" he asked, considerately. "Shall I leave you for a while and return again?"

She looked up with a start of terror. "Leave me?" she repeated, and suddenly checked herself on the point of saying more. Nearly half the length of the room divided them from each other. The words which she was longing to say were words that would never pass her lips unless she could see some encouragement in his face. "No!" she cried out to him, on a sudden, in her sore need, "don't leave me! Come back to me!"

He obeyed her in silence. In silence, on her side, she pointed to the chair near her. He took it. She looked at him, and checked herself again; resolute to make her terrible confession, yet still hesitating how to begin. Her woman's instinct whispered to her, "Find courage in his touch!" She said to him, simply and artlessly said to him, "Give me encouragement. Give me strength. Let me take your hand." He neither answered nor moved. His mind seemed to have become suddenly preoccupied; his eyes rested on her vacantly. He was on the brink of discovering her secret; in another instant he would have found his way to the truth. In that instant, innocently as his sister might have taken it, she took his hand. The soft clasp of her fingers, clinging round his, roused his senses, fired his passion for her, swept out of his mind the pure aspirations which had filled it but the moment before, paralyzed his perception when it was just penetrating the mystery of her disturbed manner and her strange words. All the man in him trembled under the rapture of her touch. But the thought of Horace was still present to him: his hand lay passive in hers; his eyes looked uneasily away from her.

She innocently strengthened her clasp of his hand. She innocently said to him, "Don't look away from me. Your eyes give me courage."

His hand returned the pressure of hers. He tasted to the full the delicious joy of looking at her. She had broken down his last reserves of self-control.

162

The thought of Horace, the sense of honor, became obscured in him. In a moment more he might have said the words which he would have deplored for the rest of his life, if she had not stopped him by speaking first. "I have more to say to you," she resumed abruptly, feeling the animating resolution to lay her heart bare before him at last; "more, far more, than I have said yet. Generous, merciful friend, let me say it here!"

She attempted to throw herself on her knees at his feet. He sprung from his seat and checked her, holding her with both his hands, raising her as he rose himself. In the words which had just escaped her, in the startling action which had accompanied them, the truth burst on him. The guilty woman she had spoken of was herself!

While she was almost in his arms, while her bosom was just touching his, before a word more had passed his lips or hers, the library door opened.

Lady Janet Roy entered the room.

CHAPTER XVIII. THE SEARCH IN THE GROUNDS.

GRACE ROSEBERRY, still listening in the conservatory, saw the door open, and recognized the mistress of the house. She softly drew back, and placed herself in safer hiding, beyond the range of view from the dining-room.

Lady Janet advanced no further than the threshold. She stood there and looked at her nephew and her adopted daughter in stern silence.

Mercy dropped into the chair at her side. Julian kept his place by her. His mind was still stunned by the discovery that had burst on it; his eyes still rested on her in mute terror of inquiry. He was as completely absorbed in the one act of looking at her as if they had been still alone together in the room.

Lady Janet was the first of the three who spoke. She addressed herself to her nephew.

"You were right, Mr. Julian Gray," she said, with her bitterest emphasis of tone and manner. "You ought to have found nobody in this room on your return but me. I detain you no longer. You are free to leave my house."

Julian looked round at his aunt. She was pointing to the door. In the excited state of his sensibilities at that moment the action stung him to the quick. He answered without his customary consideration for his aunt's age and his aunt's position toward him.

"You apparently forget, Lady Janet, that you are not speaking to one of your footmen," he said. "There are serious reasons (of which you know nothing) for my remaining in your house a little longer. You may rely upon my trespassing on your hospitality as short a time as possible."

He turned again to Mercy as he said those words, and surprised her timidly looking up at him. In the instant when their eyes met, the tumult of emotions struggling in him became suddenly stilled. Sorrow for her—compassionating sorrow—rose in the new calm and filled his heart. Now, and now only, he could read in the wasted and noble face how she had suffered. The pity which he had felt for the unnamed woman grew to a tenfold pity for her. The faith which he professed—honestly professed—in the better nature of the unnamed woman strengthened into a tenfold faith in her. He addressed himself again to his aunt, in a gentler tone. "This lady," he resumed, "has something to say to me in private which she has not said yet. That is my reason and my apology for not immediately leaving the house."

Still under the impression of what she had seen on entering the room, Lady Janet looked at him in angry amazement. Was Julian actually ignoring Horace Holmcroft's claims, in the presence of Horace Holmcroft's betrothed wife? She appealed to her adopted daughter. "Grace!" she exclaimed, "have you heard him? Have you nothing to say? Must I remind you—"

She stopped. For the first time in Lady Janet's experience of her young companion, she found herself speaking to ears that were deaf to her. Mercy was incapable of listening. Julian's eyes had told her that Julian understood her at last!

Lady Janet turned to her nephew once more, and addressed him in the hardest words that she had ever spoken to her sister's son.

"If you have any sense of decency," she said—"I say nothing of a sense of honor—you will leave this house, and your acquaintance with that lady will end here. Spare me your protests and excuses; I can place but one interpretation on what I saw when I opened that door."

"You entirely misunderstand what you saw when you opened that door," Julian answered, quietly.

"Perhaps I misunderstand the confession which you made to me not an hour ago?" retorted Lady Janet.

Julian cast a look of alarm at Mercy. "Don't speak of it!" he said, in a whisper. "She might hear you."

"Do you mean to say she doesn't know you are in love with her?"

"Thank God, she has not the faintest suspicion of it!"

There was no mistaking the earnestness with which he made that reply. It proved his innocence as nothing else could have proved it. Lady Janet drew back a step—utterly bewildered; completely at a loss what to say or what to do next.

The silence that followed was broken by a knock at the library door. The man-servant—with news, and bad news, legibly written in his disturbed face and manner—entered the room. In the nervous irritability of the moment, Lady Janet resented the servant's appearance as a positive offense on the part of the harmless man. "Who sent for you?" she asked, sharply. "What do you mean by interrupting us?"

The servant made his excuses in an oddly bewildered manner.

"I beg your ladyship's pardon. I wished to take the liberty—I wanted to speak to Mr. Julian Gray."

"What is it?" asked Julian.

The man looked uneasily at Lady Janet, hesitated, and glanced at the door, as if he wished himself well out of the room again.

"I hardly know if I can tell you, sir, before her ladyship," he answered.

Lady Janet instantly penetrated the secret of her servant's hesitation.

"I know what has happened," she said; "that abominable woman has found her way here again. Am I right?"

The man's eyes helplessly consulted Julian.

"Yes, or no?" cried Lady Janet, imperatively.

"Yes, my lady."

Julian at once assumed the duty of asking the necessary questions.

"Where is she?" he began.

"Somewhere in the grounds, as we suppose, sir."

"Did you see her?"

"No, sir."

"Who saw her?"

"The lodge-keeper's wife."

This looked serious. The lodge-keeper's wife had been present while Julian had given his instructions to her husband. She was not likely to have mistaken the identity of the person whom she had discovered.

"How long since?" Julian asked next.

"Not very long, sir."

"Be more particular. How long?"

"I didn't hear, sir."

"Did the lodge-keeper's wife speak to the person when she saw her?"

"No, sir: she didn't get the chance, as I understand it. She is a stout woman, if you remember. The other was too quick for her—discovered her, sir, and (as the saying is) gave her the slip."

"In what part of the grounds did this happen?"

The servant pointed in the direction of the side hall. "In that part, sir. Either in the Dutch garden or the shrubbery. I am not sure which."

It was plain, by this time, that the man's information was too imperfect to be practically of any use. Julian asked if the lodge-keeper's wife was in the house.

"No, sir. Her husband has gone out to search the grounds in her place, and she is minding the gate. They sent their boy with the message. From what I can make out from the lad, they would be thankful if they could get a word more of advice from you, sir."

Julian reflected for a moment.

So far as he could estimate them, the probabilities were that the stranger from Mannheim had already made her way into the house; that she had been listening in the billiard-room; that she had found time enough to escape him on his approaching to open the door; and that she was now (in the servant's phrase) "somewhere in the grounds," after eluding the pursuit of the lodgekeeper's wife.

The matter was serious. Any mistake in dealing with it might lead to very painful results.

If Julian had correctly anticipated the nature of the confession which Mercy had been on the point of addressing to him, the person whom he had been the means of introducing into the house was—what she had vainly asserted herself to be—no other than the true Grace Roseberry.

Taking this for granted, it was of the utmost importance that he should speak to Grace privately, before she committed herself to any rashly renewed assertion of her claims, and before she could gain access to Lady Janet's adopted daughter. The landlady at her lodgings had already warned him that the object which she held steadily in view was to find her way to "Miss Roseberry" when Lady Janet was not present to take her part, and when no gentleman were at hand to protect her. "Only let me meet her face to face" (she had said), "and I will make her confess herself the impostor that she is!" As matters now stood, it was impossible to estimate too seriously the mischief which might ensue from such a meeting as this. Everything now depended on Julian's skillful management of an exasperated woman; and nobody, at that moment, knew where the woman was.

In this position of affairs, as Julian understood it, there seemed to be no other alternative than to make his inquiries instantly at the lodge and then to direct the search in person.

He looked toward Mercy's chair as he arrived at this resolution. It was at a cruel sacrifice of his own anxieties and his own wishes that he deferred continuing the conversation with her from the critical point at which Lady Janet's appearance had interrupted it.

Mercy had risen while he had been questioning the servant. The attention which she had failed to accord to what had passed between his aunt and himself she had given to the imperfect statement which he had extracted from the man. Her face plainly showed that she had listened as eagerly as Lady Janet had listened; with this remarkable difference between there, that Lady Janet looked frightened, and that Lady Janet's companion showed no signs of alarm. She appeared to be interested; perhaps anxious—nothing more.

Julian spoke a parting word to his aunt.

"Pray compose yourself," he said "I have little doubt, when I can learn the particulars, that we shall easily find this person in the grounds. There is no reason to be uneasy. I am going to superintend the search myself. I will return to you as soon as possible."

Lady Janet listened absently. There was a certain expression in her eyes which suggested to Julian that her mind was busy with some project of its own. He stopped as he passed Mercy, on his way out by the billiard-room door. It cost him a hard effort to control the contending emotions which the mere act of looking at her now awakened in him. His heart beat fast, his voice sank low, as he spoke to her.

"You shall see me again," he said. "I never was more in earnest in promising you my truest help and sympathy than I am now."

She understood him. Her bosom heaved painfully; her eyes fell to the ground—she made no reply. The tears rose in Julian's eyes as he looked at her. He hurriedly left the room.

When he turned to close the billiard-room door, he heard Lady Janet say, "I will be with you again in a moment, Grace; don't go away."

Interpreting these words as meaning that his aunt had some business of her own to attend to in the library, he shut the door. He had just advanced into the smoking-room beyond, when he thought he heard the door open again. He turned round. Lady Janet had followed him.

"Do you wish to speak to me?" he asked.

"I want something of you," Lady Janet answered, "before you go."

"What is it?"

"Your card."

"My card?"

"You have just told me not to be uneasy," said the old lady. "I am uneasy, for all that. I don't feel as sure as you do that this woman really is in the grounds. She may be lurking somewhere in the house, and she may appear when your back in turned. Remember what you told me."

Julian understood the allusion. He made no reply.

"The people at the police station close by," pursued Lady Janet, "have instructions to send an experienced man, in plain clothes, to any address indicated on your card the moment they receive it. That is what you told me. For Grace's protection, I want your card before you leave us."

It was impossible for Julian to mention the reasons which now forbade him to make use of his own precautions—in the very face of the emergency which they had been especially intended to meet. How could he declare the true Grace Roseberry to be mad? How could he give the true Grace Roseberry into custody? On the other hand, he had personally pledged himself (when the circumstances appeared to require it) to place the means of legal protection from insult and annoyance at his aunt's disposal. And now, there stood Lady Janet, unaccustomed to have her wishes disregarded by anybody, with her band extended, waiting for the card!

What was to be done? The one way out of the difficulty appeared to be to submit for the moment. If he succeeded in discovering the missing woman, he could easily take care that she should be subjected to no needless indignity. If she contrived to slip into the house in his absence, he could provide against that contingency by sending a second card privately to the police station, forbidding the officer to stir in the affair until he had received further orders. Julian made one stipulation only before he handed his card to his aunt.

"You will not use this, I am sure, without positive and pressing necessity," he said. "But I must make one condition. Promise me to keep my plan for communicating with the police a strict secret—"

"A strict secret from Grace?" interposed Lady Janet. (Julian bowed.) "Do you suppose I want to frighten her? Do you think I have not had anxiety enough about her already? Of course I shall keep it a secret from Grace!"

Re-assured on this point, Julian hastened out into the grounds. As soon as his back was turned Lady Janet lifted the gold pencil-case which hung at her watch-chain, and wrote on her nephew's card (for the information of the officer in plain clothes), "You are wanted at Mablethorpe House." This done, she put the card into the old-fashioned pocket of her dress, and returned to the dining-room.

Grace was waiting, in obedience to the instructions which she had received.

For the first moment or two not a word was spoken on either side. Now that she was alone with her adopted daughter, a certain coldness and hardness began to show itself in Lady Janet's manner. The discovery that she had made on opening the drawing-room door still hung on her mind. Julian had certainly convinced her that she had misinterpreted what she had seen; but he had convinced her against her will. She had found Mercy deeply agitated; suspiciously silent. Julian might be innocent, she admitted—there was no accounting for the vagaries of men. But the case of Mercy was altogether different. Women did not find themselves in the arms of men without knowing what they were about. Acquitting Julian, Lady Janet declined to acquit Mercy. "There is some secret understanding between them," thought the old lady, "and she's to blame; the women always are!"

Mercy still waited to be spoken to; pale and quiet, silent and submissive. Lady Janet—in a highly uncertain state of temper—was obliged to begin.

"My dear!" she called out, sharply.

"Yes, Lady Janet."

"How much longer are you going to sit there with your mouth shut up and your eyes on the carpet? Have you no opinion to offer on this alarming state of things? You heard what the man said to Julian—I saw you listening. Are you horribly frightened?"

"No, Lady Janet."

"Not even nervous?"

"No, Lady Janet."

"Ha! I should hardly have given you credit for so much courage after my experience of you a week ago. I congratulate you on your recovery."

"Thank you, Lady Janet."

"I am not so composed as you are. We were an excitable set in my youth—and I haven't got the better of it yet. I feel nervous. Do you hear? I feel nervous."

"I am sorry, Lady Janet."

"You are very good. Do you know what I am going to do?"

"No, Lady Janet."

"I am going to summon the household. When I say the household, I mean the men; the women are no use. I am afraid I fail to attract your attention?"

"You have my best attention, Lady Janet."

"You are very good again. I said the women were of no use."

"Yes, Lady Janet."

"I mean to place a man-servant on guard at every entrance to the house. I am going to do it at once. Will you come with me?"

"Can I be of any use if I go with your ladyship?"

"You can't be of the slightest use. I give the orders in this house—not you. I had quite another motive in asking you to come with me. I am more considerate of you than you seem to think—I don't like leaving you here by yourself. Do you understand?

"I am much obliged to your ladyship. I don't mind being left here by myself."

"You don't mind? I never heard of such heroism in my life—out of a novel! Suppose that crazy wretch should find her way in here?"

"She would not frighten me this time as she frightened me before."

"Not too fast, my young lady! Suppose—Good heavens! now I think of it, there is the conservatory. Suppose she should be hidden in there? Julian is searching the grounds. Who is to search the conservatory?"

"With your ladyship's permission, I will search the conservatory."

"You!!!"

"With your ladyship's permission."

"I can hardly believe my own ears! Well, 'Live and learn' is an old proverb. I thought I knew your character. This is a change!"

"You forget, Lady Janet (if I may venture to say so), that the circumstances are changed. She took me by surprise on the last occasion; I am prepared for her now."

"Do you really feel as coolly as you speak?"

"Yes, Lady Janet."

"Have your own way, then. I shall do one thing, however, in case of your having overestimated your own courage. I shall place one of the men in the library. You will only have to ring for him if anything happens. He will give the alarm—and I shall act accordingly. I have my plan," said her Ladyship, comfortably conscious of the card in her pocket. "Don't look as if you wanted to know what it is. I have no intention of saying anything about it—except that it will do. Once more, and for the last time—do you stay here? or do you go with me?"

"I stay here."

She respectfully opened the library door for Lady Janet's departure as she made that reply. Throughout the interview she had been carefully and coldly deferential; she had not once lifted her eyes to Lady Janet's face. The conviction in her that a few hours more would, in all probability, see her dismissed from the house, had of necessity fettered every word that she spoke—had morally separated her already from the injured mistress whose love she had won in disguise. Utterly incapable of attributing the change in her young companion to the true motive, Lady Janet left the room to summon her domestic garrison, thoroughly puzzled and (as a necessary consequence of that condition) thoroughly displeased.

Still holding the library door in her hand, Mercy stood watching with a heavy heart the progress of her benefactress down the length of the room on the way to the front hall beyond. She had honestly loved and respected the warm-hearted, quick-tempered old lady. A sharp pang of pain wrung her as she thought of the time when even the chance utterance of her name would become an unpardonable offense in Lady Janet's house.

But there was no shrinking in her now from the ordeal of the confession. She was not only anxious—she was impatient for Julian's return. Before she slept that night Julian's confidence in her should be a confidence that she had deserved.

"Let her own the truth, without the base fear of discovery to drive her to it. Let her do justice to the woman whom she has wronged, while that woman is still powerless to expose her. Let her sacrifice everything that she has gained by the fraud to the sacred duty of atonement. If she can do that, then her repentance has nobly revealed the noble nature that is in her; then she is a woman to be trusted, respected, beloved." Those words were as vividly present to her as if she still heard them falling from his lips. Those other words which had followed them rang as grandly as ever in her ears: "Rise, poor wounded heart! Beautiful, purified soul, God's angels rejoice over you! Take your place among the noblest of God's creatures!" Did the woman live who could hear Julian Gray say that, and who could hesitate, at any sacrifice, at any loss, to justify his belief in her? "Oh!" she thought, longingly while her eyes followed Lady Janet to the end of the library, "if your worst fears could only be realized! If I could only see Grace Roseberry in this room, how fearlessly I could meet her now!"

She closed the library door, while Lady Janet opened the other door which led into the hall.

As she turned and looked back into the dining-room a cry of astonishment escaped her.

There—as if in answer to the aspiration which was still in her mind; there, established in triumph on the chair that she had just left—sat Grace Roseberry, in sinister silence, waiting for her.

CHAPTER XIX. THE EVIL GENIUS.

RECOVERING from the first overpowering sensation of surprise, Mercy rapidly advanced, eager to say her first penitent words. Grace stopped her by a warning gesture of the hand. "No nearer to me," she said, with a look of contemptuous command. "Stay where you are."

Mercy paused. Grace's reception had startled her. She instinctively took the chair nearest to her to support herself. Grace raised a warning hand for the second time, and issued another command: "I forbid you to be seated in my presence. You have no right to be in this house at all. Remember, if you please, who you are, and who I am."

The tone in which those words were spoken was an insult in itself. Mercy suddenly lifted her head; the angry answer was on her lips. She checked it, and submitted in silence. "I will be worthy of Julian Gray's confidence in me," she thought, as she stood patiently by the chair. "I will bear anything from the woman whom I have wronged."

In silence the two faced each other; alone together, for the first time since they had met in the French cottage. The contrast between them was strange to see. Grace Roseberry, seated in her chair, little and lean, with her dull white complexion, with her hard, threatening face, with her shrunken figure clad in its plain and poor black garments, looked like a being of a lower sphere, compared with Mercy Merrick, standing erect in her rich silken dress; her tall, shapely figure towering over the little creature before her; her grand head bent in graceful submission; gentle, patient, beautiful; a woman whom it was a privilege to look at and a distinction to admire. If a stranger had been told that those two had played their parts in a romance of real life—that one of them was really connected by the ties of relationship with Lady Janet Roy, and that the other had successfully attempted to personate her—he would inevitably, if it had been left to him to guess which was which, have picked out Grace as the counterfeit and Mercy as the true woman.

Grace broke the silence. She had waited to open her lips until she had eyed her conquered victim all over, with disdainfully minute attention, from head to foot.

"Stand there. I like to look at you," she said, speaking with a spiteful relish of her own cruel words. "It's no use fainting this time. You have not got Lady Janet Roy to bring you to. There are no gentlemen here to-day to pity you and pick you up. Mercy Merrick, I have got you at last. Thank God, my turn has come! You can't escape me now!"

All the littleness of heart and mind which had first shown itself in Grace at the meeting in the cottage, when Mercy told the sad story of her life, now revealed itself once more. The woman who in those past times had felt no impulse to take a suffering and a penitent fellow-creature by the hand was the same woman who could feel no pity, who could spare no insolence of triumph, now. Mercy's sweet voice answered her patiently, in low, pleading tones.

"I have not avoided you," she said. "I would have gone to you of my own accord if I had known that you were here. It is my heartfelt wish to own that I have sinned against you, and to make all the atonement that I can. I am too anxious to deserve your forgiveness to have any fear of seeing you."

Conciliatory as the reply was, it was spoken with a simple and modest dignity of manner which roused Grace Roseberry to fury.

"How dare you speak to me as if you were any equal?" she burst out. "You stand there and answer me as if you had your right and your place in this house. You audacious woman! I have my right and my place here—and what am I obliged to do? I am obliged to hang about in the grounds, and fly from the sight of the servants, and hide like a thief, and wait like a beggar, and all for what? For the chance of having a word with you. Yes! you, madam! with the air of the Refuge and the dirt of the streets on you!"

Mercy's head sank lower; her hand trembled as it held by the back of the chair.

It was hard to bear the reiterated insults heaped on her, but Julian's influence still made itself felt. She answered as patiently as ever.

"If it is your pleasure to use hard words to me," she said, "I have no right to resent them."

"You have no right to anything!" Grace retorted. "You have no right to the gown on your back. Look at yourself, and look at Me!" Her eyes traveled with a tigerish stare over Mercy's costly silk dress. "Who gave you that dress? who gave you those jewels? I know! Lady Janet gave them to Grace Roseberry. Are you Grace Roseberry? That dress is mine. Take off your bracelets and your brooch. They were meant for me."

"You may soon have them, Miss Roseberry. They will not be in my possession many hours longer."

"What do you mean?"

"However badly you may use me, it is my duty to undo the harm that I have done. I am bound to do you justice—I am determined to confess the truth."

Grace smiled scornfully.

"You confess!" she said. "Do you think I am fool enough to believe that? You are one shameful brazen lie from head to foot! Are you the woman to give up your silks and your jewels, and your position in this house, and to go back to the Refuge of your own accord? Not you—not you!"

A first faint flush of color showed itself, stealing slowly over Mercy's face; but she still held resolutely by the good influence which Julian had left behind him. She could still say to herself, "Anything rather than disappoint Julian Gray." Sustained by the courage which he had called to life in her, she submitted to her martyrdom as bravely as ever. But there was an ominous change in her now: she could only submit in silence; she could no longer trust herself to answer.

The mute endurance in her face additionally exasperated Grace Roseberry.

"You won't confess," she went on. "You have had a week to confess in, and you have not done it yet. No, no! you are of the sort that cheat and lie to the last. I am glad of it; I shall have the joy of exposing you myself before the whole house. I shall be the blessed means of casting you back on the streets. Oh! it will be almost worth all I have gone through to see you with a policeman's hand on your arm, and the mob pointing at you and mocking you on your way to jail!"

This time the sting struck deep; the outrage was beyond endurance. Mercy gave the woman who had again and again deliberately insulted her a first warning.

"Miss Roseberry," she said, "I have borne without a murmur the bitterest words you could say to me. Spare me any more insults. Indeed, indeed, I am eager to restore you to your just rights. With my whole heart I say it to you—I am resolved to confess everything!"

She spoke with trembling earnestness of tone. Grace listened with a hard smile of incredulity and a hard look of contempt.

"You are not far from the bell," she said; "ring it."

Mercy looked at her in speechless surprise.

"You are a perfect picture of repentance—you are dying to own the truth," pursued the other, satirically. "Own it before everybody, and own it at once. Call in Lady Janet—call in Mr. Gray and Mr. Holmcroft—call in the servants. Go down on your knees and acknowledge yourself an impostor before them all. Then I will believe you—not before."

"Don't, don't turn me against you!" cried Mercy, entreatingly.

"What do I care whether you are against me or not?"

"Don't—for your own sake, don't go on provoking me much longer!"

"For my own sake? You insolent creature! Do you mean to threaten me?"

With a last desperate effort, her heart beating faster and faster, the blood burning hotter and hotter in her cheeks, Mercy still controlled herself.

"Have some compassion on me!" she pleaded. "Badly as I have

behaved to you, I am still a woman like yourself. I can't face the shame of acknowledging what I have done before the whole house. Lady Janet treats me like a daughter; Mr. Holmcroft has engaged himself to marry me. I can't tell Lady Janet and Mr. Holmcroft to their faces that I have cheated them out of their love. But they shall know it, for all that. I can, and will, before I rest to-night, tell the whole truth to Mr. Julian Gray."

Grace burst out laughing. "Aha!" she exclaimed, with a cynical outburst of gayety. "Now we have come to it at last!"

"Take care!" said Mercy. "Take care!"

"Mr. Julian Gray! I was behind the billiard-room door—I saw you coax Mr. Julian Gray to come in! confession loses all its horrors, and becomes quite a luxury, with Mr. Julian Gray!"

"No more, Miss Roseberry! no more! For God's sake, don't put me beside myself! You have tortured me enough already."

"You haven't been on the streets for nothing. You are a woman with resources; you know the value of having two strings to your bow. If Mr. Holmcroft fails you, you have got Mr. Julian Gray. Ah! you sicken me. I'll see that Mr. Holmcroft's eyes are opened; he shall know what a woman he might have married but for Me—"

She checked herself; the next refinement of insult remained suspended on her lips.

The woman whom she had outraged suddenly advanced on her. Her eyes, staring helplessly upward, saw Mercy Merrick's face, white with the terrible anger which drives the blood back on the heart, bending threateningly over her.

"'You will see that Mr. Holmcroft's eyes are opened,'" Mercy slowly repeated; "'he shall know what a woman he might have married but for you!'"

She paused, and followed those words by a question which struck a creeping terror through Grace Roseberry, from the hair of her head to the soles of her feet:

"Who are you?"

The suppressed fury of look and tone which accompanied that question told, as no violence could have told it, that the limits of Mercy's endurance had been found at last. In the guardian angel's absence the evil genius had done its evil work. The better nature which Julian Gray had brought to life sank, poisoned by the vile venom of a womanly spiteful tongue. An easy and a terrible means of avenging the outrages heaped on her was within Mercy's reach, if she chose to take it. In the frenzy of her indignation she never hesitated—she took it.

"Who are you?" she asked for the second time.

Grace roused herself and attempted to speak. Mercy stopped her with a scornful gesture of her hand.

"I remember!" she went on, with the same fiercely suppressed rage. "You are the madwoman from the German hospital who came here a week ago. I am not afraid of you this time. Sit down and rest yourself, Mercy Merrick."

Deliberately giving her that name to her face, Mercy turned from her and took the chair which Grace had forbidden her to occupy when the interview began. Grace started to her feet.

"What does this mean?" she asked.

"It means," answered Mercy, contemptuously, "that I recall every word I said to you just now. It means that I am resolved to keep my place in this house."

"Are you out of your senses?"

"You are not far from the bell. Ring it. Do what you asked me to do. Call in the whole household, and ask them which of us is mad—you or I."

"Mercy Merrick! you shall repent this to the last hour of your life!"

Mercy rose again, and fixed her flashing eyes on the woman who still defied her.

"I have had enough of you!" she said. "Leave the house while you can

181

leave it. Stay here, and I will send for Lady Janet Roy."

"You can't send for her! You daren't send for her!"

"I can and I dare. You have not a shadow of a proof against me. I have got the papers; I am in possession of the place; I have established myself in Lady Janet's confidence. I mean to deserve your opinion of me—I will keep my dresses and my jewels and my position in the house. I deny that I have done wrong. Society has used me cruelly; I owe nothing to Society. I have a right to take any advantage of it if I can. I deny that I have injured you. How was I to know that you would come to life again? Have I degraded your name and your character? I have done honor to both. I have won everybody's liking and everybody's respect. Do you think Lady Janet would have loved you as she loves me? Not she! I tell you to your face I have filled the false position more creditably than you could have filled the true one, and I mean to keep it. I won't give up your name; I won't restore your character! Do your worst; I defy you!"

She poured out those reckless words in one headlong flow which defied interruption. There was no answering her until she was too breathless to say more. Grace seized her opportunity the moment it was within her reach.

"You defy me?" she returned, resolutely. "You won't defy me long. I have written to Canada. My friends will speak for me."

"What of it, if they do? Your friends are strangers here. I am Lady Janet's adopted daughter. Do you think she will believe your friends? She will believe me. She will burn their letters if they write. She will forbid the house to them if they come. I shall be Mrs. Horace Holmcroft in a week's time. Who can shake my position? Who can injure Me?"

"Wait a little. You forget the matron at the Refuge."

"Find her, if you can. I never told you her name. I never told you where the Refuge was."

"I will advertise your name, and find the matron in that way."

"Advertise in every newspaper in London. Do you think I gave a stranger like you the name I really bore in the Refuge? I gave you the name I assumed when I left England. No such person as Mercy Merrick is known to the matron. No such person is known to Mr. Holmcroft. He saw me at the French cottage while you were senseless on the bed. I had my gray cloak on; neither he nor any of them saw me in my nurse's dress. Inquiries have been made about me on the Continent—and (I happen to know from the person who made them) with no result. I am safe in your place; I am known by your name. I am Grace Roseberry; and you are Mercy Merrick. Disprove it, if you can!"

Summing up the unassailable security of her false position in those closing words, Mercy pointed significantly to the billiard-room door.

"You were hiding there, by your own confession," she said. "You know your way out by that door. Will you leave the room?"

"I won't stir a step!"

Mercy walked to a side-table, and struck the bell placed on it.

At the same moment the billiard-room door opened. Julian Gray appeared—returning from his unsuccessful search in the grounds.

He had barely crossed the threshold before the library door was thrown open next by the servant posted in the room. The man drew back respectfully, and gave admission to Lady Janet Roy. She was followed by Horace Holmcroft with his mother's wedding present to Mercy in his hand.

CHAPTER XX. THE POLICEMAN IN PLAIN CLOTHES.

JULIAN looked round the room, and stopped at the door which he had just opened.

His eyes rested first on Mercy, next on Grace.

The disturbed faces of both the women told him but too plainly that the disaster which he had dreaded had actually happened. They had met without any third person to interfere between them. To what extremities the hostile interview might have led it was impossible for him to guess. In his aunt's presence he could only wait his opportunity of speaking to Mercy, and be ready to interpose if anything was ignorantly done which might give just cause of offense to Grace.

Lady Janet's course of action on entering the dining-room was in perfect harmony with Lady Janet's character.

Instantly discovering the intruder, she looked sharply at Mercy. "What did I tell you?" she asked. "Are you frightened? No! not in the least frightened! Wonderful!" She turned to the servant. "Wait in the library; I may want you again." She looked at Julian. "Leave it all to me; I can manage it." She made a sign to Horace. "Stay where you are, and hold your tongue." Having now said all that was necessary to every one else, she advanced to the part of the room in which Grace was standing, with lowering brows and firmly shut lips, defiant of everybody.

"I have no desire to offend you, or to act harshly toward you," her ladyship began, very quietly. "I only suggest that your visits to my house cannot possibly lead to any satisfactory result. I hope you will not oblige me to say any harder words than these—I hope you will understand that I wish you to withdraw."

The order of dismissal could hardly have been issued with more humane consideration for the supposed mental infirmity of the person to whom it was addressed. Grace instantly resisted it in the plainest possible terms.

"In justice to my father's memory and in justice to myself," she answered, "I insist on a hearing. I refuse to withdraw." She deliberately took a chair and seated herself in the presence of the mistress of the house.

Lady Janet waited a moment—steadily controlling her temper. In the interval of silence Julian seized the opportunity of remonstrating with Grace.

"Is this what you promised me?" he asked, gently. "You gave me your word that you would not return to Mablethorpe House."

Before he could say more Lady Janet had got her temper under command. She began her answer to Grace by pointing with a peremptory forefinger to the library door.

"If you have not made up your mind to take my advice by the time I have walked back to that door," she said, "I will put it out of your power to set me at defiance. I am used to be obeyed, and I will be obeyed. You force me to use hard words. I warn you before it is too late. Go!"

She returned slowly toward the library. Julian attempted to interfere with another word of remonstrance. His aunt stopped him by a gesture which said, plainly, "I insist on acting for myself." He looked next at Mercy. Would she remain passive? Yes. She never lifted her head; she never moved from the place in which she was standing apart from the rest. Horace himself tried to attract her attention, and tried in vain.

Arrived at the library door, Lady Janet looked over her shoulder at the little immovable black figure in the chair.

"Will you go?" she asked, for the last time.

Grace started up angrily from her seat, and fixed her viperish eyes on Mercy.

"I won't be turned out of your ladyship's house in the presence of that impostor," she said. "I may yield to force, but I will yield to nothing else. I insist on my right to the place that she has stolen from me. It's no use scolding me," she added, turning doggedly to Julian. "As long as that woman is here under my name I can't and won't keep away from the house. I warn her, in your presence, that I have written to my friends in Canada! I dare her before you all to deny that she is the outcast and adventuress, Mercy Merrick!"

The challenge forced Mercy to take part in the proceedings in her own defense. She had pledged herself to meet and defy Grace Roseberry on her own ground. She attempted to speak—Horace stopped her.

"You degrade yourself if you answer her," he said. "Take my arm, and let us leave the room."

"Yes! Take her out!" cried Grace. "She may well be ashamed to face an honest woman. It's her place to leave the room—not mine!"

Mercy drew her hand out of Horace's arm. "I decline to leave the room," she said, quietly.

Horace still tried to persuade her to withdraw. "I can't bear to hear you insulted," he rejoined. "The woman offends me, though I know she is not responsible for what she says."

"Nobody's endurance will be tried much longer," said Lady Janet. She glanced at Julian, and taking from her pocket the card which he had given to her, opened the library door.

"Go to the police station," she said to the servant in an undertone, "and give that card to the inspector on duty. Tell him there is not a moment to lose."

"Stop!" said Julian, before his aunt could close the door again.

"Stop?" repeated Lady Janet, sharply. "I have given the man his orders. What do you mean?"

"Before you send the card I wish to say a word in private to this lady," replied Julian, indicating Grace. "When that is done," he continued, approaching Mercy, and pointedly addressing himself to her, "I shall have a request to make—I shall ask you to give me an opportunity of speaking to you without interruption."

His tone pointed the allusion. Mercy shrank from looking at him. The signs of painful agitation began to show themselves in her shifting color and her uneasy silence. Roused by Julian's significantly distant reference to what had passed between them, her better impulses were struggling already to recover their influence over her. She might, at that critical moment, have yielded to the promptings of her own nobler nature—she might have risen superior to the galling remembrance of the insults that had been heaped upon her—if Grace's malice had not seen in her hesitation a means of referring offensively once again to her interview with Julian Gray.

"Pray don't think twice about trusting him alone with me," she said, with a sardonic affectation of politeness. "I am not interested in making a conquest of Mr. Julian Gray."

The jealous distrust in Horace (already awakened by Julian's request) now attempted to assert itself openly. Before he could speak, Mercy's indignation had dictated Mercy's answer.

"I am much obliged to you, Mr. Gray," she said, addressing Julian (but still not raising her eyes to his). "I have nothing more to say. There is no need for me to trouble you again."

In those rash words she recalled the confession to which she stood pledged. In those rash words she committed herself to keeping the position that she had usurped, in the face of the woman whom she had deprived of it!

Horace was silenced, but not satisfied. He saw Julian's eyes fixed in sad and searching attention on Mercy's face while she was speaking. He heard Julian sigh to himself when she had done. He observed Julian—after a moment's serious consideration, and a moment's glance backward at the stranger in the poor black clothes—lift his head with the air of a man who had taken a sudden resolution.

"Bring me that card directly," he said to the servant. His tone announced that he was not to be trifled with. The man obeyed.

Without answering Lady Janet—who still peremptorily insisted on her right to act for herself—Julian took the pencil from his pocketbook and added his signature to the writing already inscribed on the card. When he had handed it back to the servant he made his apologies to his aunt.

"Pardon me for venturing to interfere," he said "There is a serious reason for what I have done, which I will explain to you at a fitter time. In the meanwhile I offer no further obstruction to the course which you propose taking. On the contrary, I have just assisted you in gaining the end that you have in view."

As he said that he held up the pencil with which he had signed his name.

Lady Janet, naturally perplexed, and (with some reason, perhaps) offended as well, made no answer. She waved her hand to the servant, and sent him away with the card.

There was silence in the room. The eyes of all the persons present turned more or less anxiously on Julian. Mercy was vaguely surprised and alarmed. Horace, like Lady Janet, felt offended, without clearly knowing why. Even Grace Roseberry herself was subdued by her own presentiment of some coming interference for which she was completely unprepared. Julian's words and actions, from the moment when he had written on the card, were involved in a mystery to which not one of the persons round him held the clew.

The motive which had animated his conduct may, nevertheless, be described in two words: Julian still held to his faith in the inbred nobility of Mercy's nature.

He had inferred, with little difficulty, from the language which Grace had used toward Mercy in his presence, that the injured woman must have taken pitiless advantage of her position at the interview which he had interrupted. Instead of appealing to Mercy's sympathies and Mercy's sense of right—instead of accepting the expression of her sincere contrition, and encouraging her to make the completest and the speediest atonement—Grace had evidently outraged and insulted her. As a necessary result, her endurance had given way—under her own sense of intolerable severity and intolerable wrong.

The remedy for the mischief thus done was, as Julian had first seen it, to speak privately with Grace, to soothe her by owning that his opinion of the justice of her claims had undergone a change in her favor, and then to persuade her, in her own interests, to let him carry to Mercy such expressions of apology and regret as might lead to a friendly understanding between them.

With those motives, he had made his request to be permitted to speak separately to the one and the other. The scene that had followed, the new insult offered by Grace, and the answer which it had wrung from Mercy, had convinced him that no such interference as he had contemplated would have the slightest prospect of success.

The only remedy now left to try was the desperate remedy of letting things take their course, and trusting implicitly to Mercy's better nature for the result.

Let her see the police officer in plain clothes enter the room. Let her understand clearly what the result of his interference would be. Let her confront the alternative of consigning Grace Roseberry to a mad-house or of confessing the truth—and what would happen? If Julian's confidence in her was a confidence soundly placed, she would nobly pardon the outrages that had been heaped upon her, and she would do justice to the woman whom she had wronged.

If, on the other hand, his belief in her was nothing better than the blind belief of an infatuated man—if she faced the alternative and persisted in asserting her assumed identity—what then?

Julian's faith in Mercy refused to let that darker side of the question find a place in his thoughts. It rested entirely with him to bring the officer into the house. He had prevented Lady Janet from making any mischievous use of his card by sending to the police station and warning them to attend to no message which they might receive unless the card produced bore his signature. Knowing the responsibility that he was taking on himself—knowing that Mercy had made no confession to him to which it was possible to appeal—he had signed his name without an instant's hesitation: and there he stood now, looking at the woman whose better nature he was determined to vindicate, the only calm person in the room.

Horace's jealousy saw something suspiciously suggestive of a private understanding in Julian's earnest attention and in Mercy's downcast face. Having no excuse for open interference, he made an effort to part them.

"You spoke just now," he said to Julian, "of wishing to say a word in private to that person." (He pointed to Grace.) "Shall we retire, or will you take her into the library?"

"I refuse to have anything to say to him," Grace burst out, before Julian could answer. "I happen to know that he is the last person to do me justice. He has been effectually hoodwinked. If I speak to anybody privately, it ought to be to you. You have the greatest interest of any of them in finding out the truth."

"What do you mean?"

"Do you want to marry an outcast from the streets?"

Horace took one step forward toward her. There was a look in his face which plainly betrayed that he was capable of turning her out of the house with his own hands. Lady Janet stopped him.

"You were right in suggesting just now that Grace had better leave the room," she said. "Let us all three go. Julian will remain here and give the man his directions when he arrives. Come."

No. By a strange contradiction it was Horace himself who now interfered to prevent Mercy from leaving the room. In the heat of his indignation he lost all sense of his own dignity; he descended to the level of a woman whose intellect he believed to be deranged. To the surprise of every one present, he stepped back and took from the table a jewel-case which he had placed there when he came into the room. It was the wedding present from his mother which he had brought to his betrothed wife. His outraged self-esteem seized the opportunity of vindicating Mercy by a public bestowal of the gift.

"Wait!" he called out, sternly. "That wretch shall have her answer. She has sense enough to see and sense enough to hear. Let her see and hear!"

He opened the jewel-case, and took from it a magnificent pearl necklace in an antique setting.

"Grace," he said, with his highest distinction of manner, "my mother sends you her love and her congratulations on our approaching marriage. She begs you to accept, as part of your bridal dress, these pearls. She was married in them herself. They have been in our family for centuries. As one of the family, honored and beloved, my mother offers them to my wife."

He lifted the necklace to clasp it round Mercy's neck.

Julian watched her in breathless suspense. Would she sustain the ordeal through which Horace had innocently condemned her to pass?

Yes! In the insolent presence of Grace Roseberry, what was there now that she could not sustain? Her pride was in arms. Her lovely eyes lighted up as only a woman's eyes can light up when they see jewelry. Her grand head bent gracefully to receive the necklace. Her face warmed into color; her beauty rallied its charms. Her triumph over Grace Roseberry was complete! Julian's head sank. For one sad moment he secretly asked himself the question: "Have I been mistaken in her?"

Horace arrayed her in the pearls.

"Your husband puts these pearls on your neck, love," he said, proudly, and paused to look at her. "Now," he added, with a contemptuous backward glance at Grace, "we may go into the library. She has seen, and she has heard."

He believed that he had silenced her. He had simply furnished her sharp tongue with a new sting.

"You will hear, and you will see, when my proofs come from Canada," she retorted. "You will hear that your wife has stolen my name and my character! You will see your wife dismissed from this house!"

Mercy turned on her with an uncontrollable outburst of passion.

"You are mad!" she cried.

Lady Janet caught the electric infection of anger in the air of the room. She, too, turned on Grace. She, too, said it:

"You are mad!"

Horace followed Lady Janet. He was beside himself. He fixed his pitiless eyes on Grace, and echoed the contagious words:

"You are mad!"

She was silenced, she was daunted at last. The treble accusation revealed to her, for the first time, the frightful suspicion to which she had exposed herself. She shrank back with a low cry of horror, and struck against a chair. She would have fallen if Julian had not sprung forward and caught her.

Lady Janet led the way into the library. She opened the door—started—and suddenly stepped aside, so as to leave the entrance free.

A man appeared in the open doorway.

He was not a gentleman; he was not a workman; he was not a servant. He was vilely dressed, in glossy black broadcloth. His frockcoat hung on him instead of fitting him. His waistcoat was too short and too tight over the chest. His trousers were a pair of shapeless black bags. His gloves were too large for him. His highly-polished boots creaked detestably whenever he moved. He had odiously watchful eyes—eyes that looked skilled in peeping through key-holes. His large ears, set forward like the ears of a monkey, pleaded guilty to meanly listening behind other people's doors. His manner was quietly confidential when he spoke, impenetrably self-possessed when he was silent. A lurking air of secret service enveloped the fellow, like an atmosphere of his own, from head to foot. He looked all round the magnificent room without betraying either surprise or admiration. He closely investigated every person in it with one glance of his cunningly watchful eyes. Making his bow to Lady Janet, he silently showed her, as his introduction, the card that had summoned him. And then he stood at ease, self-revealed in his own sinister identity—a police officer in plain clothes.

Nobody spoke to him. Everybody shrank inwardly as if a reptile had crawled into the room.

He looked backward and forward, perfectly unembarrassed, between

Julian and Horace.

"Is Mr. Julian Gray here?" he asked.

Julian led Grace to a seat. Her eyes were fixed on the man. She trembled—she whispered, "Who is he?" Julian spoke to the police officer without answering her.

"Wait there," he said, pointing to a chair in the most distant corner of the room. "I will speak to you directly."

The man advanced to the chair, marching to the discord of his creaking boots. He privately valued the carpet at so much a yard as he walked over it. He privately valued the chair at so much the dozen as he sat down on it. He was quite at his ease: it was no matter to him whether he waited and did nothing, or whether he pried into the private character of every one in the room, as long as he was paid for it.

Even Lady Janet's resolution to act for herself was not proof against the appearance of the policeman in plain clothes. She left it to her nephew to take the lead. Julian glanced at Mercy before he stirred further in the matter. He alone knew that the end rested now not with him but with her.

She felt his eye on her while her own eyes were looking at the man. She turned her head—hesitated—and suddenly approached Julian. Like Grace Roseberry, she was trembling. Like Grace Roseberry, she whispered, "Who is he?"

Julian told her plainly who he was.

"Why is he here?"

"Can't you guess?"

"No!"

Horace left Lady Janet, and joined Mercy and Julian—impatient of the private colloquy between them.

"Am I in the way?" he inquired.

193

Julian drew back a little, understanding Horace perfectly. He looked round at Grace. Nearly the whole length of the spacious room divided them from the place in which she was sitting. She had never moved since he had placed her in a chair. The direst of all terrors was in possession of her—terror of the unknown. There was no fear of her interfering, and no fear of her hearing what they said so long as they were careful to speak in guarded tones. Julian set the example by lowering his voice.

"Ask Horace why the police officer is here?" he said to Mercy.

She put the question directly. "Why is he here?"

Horace looked across the room at Grace, and answered, "He is here to relieve us of that woman."

"Do you mean that he will take her away?"

"Yes."

"Where will he take her to?"

"To the police station."

Mercy started, and looked at Julian. He was still watching the slightest changes in her face. She looked back again at Horace.

"To the police station!" she repeated. "What for?"

"How can you ask the question?" said Horace, irritably. "To be placed under restraint, of course."

"Do you mean prison?"

"I mean an asylum."

Again Mercy turned to Julian. There was horror now, as well as surprise, in her face. "Oh!" she said to him, "Horace is surely wrong? It can't be?"

Julian left it to Horace to answer. Every facility in him seemed to be still absorbed in watching Mercy's face. She was compelled to address herself to Horace once more.

"What sort of asylum?" she asked. "You don't surely mean a madhouse?"

"I do," he rejoined. "The workhouse first, perhaps—and then the madhouse. What is there to surprise you in that? You yourself told her to her face she was mad. Good Heavens! how pale you are! What is the matter?"

She turned to Julian for the third time. The terrible alternative that was offered to her had showed itself at last, without reserve or disguise. Restore the identity that you have stolen, or shut her up in a madhouse—it rests with you to choose! In that form the situation shaped itself in her mind. She chose on the instant. Before she opened her lips the higher nature in her spoke to Julian, in her eyes. The steady inner light that he had seen in them once already shone in them again, brighter and purer than before. The conscience that he had fortified, the soul that he had saved, looked at him and said, Doubt us no more!

"Send that man out of the house."

Those were her first words. She spoke (pointing to the police officer) in clear, ringing, resolute tones, audible in the remotest corner of the room.

Julian's hand stole unobserved to hers, and told her, in its momentary pressure, to count on his brotherly sympathy and help. All the other persons in the room looked at her in speechless surprise. Grace rose from her chair. Even the man in plain clothes started to his feet. Lady Janet (hurriedly joining Horace, and fully sharing his perplexity and alarm) took Mercy impulsively by the arm, and shook it, as if to rouse her to a sense of what she was doing. Mercy held firm; Mercy resolutely repeated what she had said: "Send that man out of the house."

Lady Janet lost all her patience with her. "What has come to you?" she asked, sternly. "Do you know what you are saying? The man is here in your interest, as well as in mine; the man is here to spare you, as well as me, further annoyance and insult. And you insist—insist, in my presence—on his being sent away! What does it mean?"

"You shall know what it means, Lady Janet, in half an hour. I don't insist—I only reiterate my entreaty. Let the man be sent away."

Julian stepped aside (with his aunt's eyes angrily following him) and spoke to the police officer. "Go back to the station," he said, "and wait there till you hear from me."

The meanly vigilant eyes of the man in plain clothes traveled sidelong from Julian to Mercy, and valued her beauty as they had valued the carpet and the chairs. "The old story," he thought. "The nice-looking woman is always at the bottom of it; and, sooner or later, the nice-looking woman has her way." He marched back across the room, to the discord of his own creaking boots, bowed, with a villainous smile which put the worst construction on everything, and vanished through the library door.

Lady Janet's high breeding restrained her from saying anything until the police officer was out of hearing. Then, and not till then, she appealed to Julian.

"I presume you are in the secret of this?" she said. "I suppose you have some reason for setting my authority at defiance in my own house?"

"I have never yet failed to respect your ladyship," Julian answered. "Before long you will know that I am not failing in respect toward you now."

Lady Janet looked across the room. Grace was listening eagerly, conscious that events had taken some mysterious turn in her favor within the last minute.

"Is it part of your new arrangement of my affairs," her ladyship continued, "that this person is to remain in the house?"

The terror that had daunted Grace had not lost all hold of her yet. She left it to Julian to reply. Before he could speak Mercy crossed the room and whispered to her, "Give me time to confess it in writing. I can't own it before them—with this round my neck." She pointed to the necklace. Grace cast a threatening glance at her, and suddenly looked away again in silence.

Mercy answered Lady Janet's question. "I beg your ladyship to permit her to remain until the half hour is over," she said. "My request will have explained itself by that time."

Lady Janet raised no further obstacles. For something in Mercy's face, or in Mercy's tone, seemed to have silenced her, as it had silenced Grace. Horace was the next who spoke. In tones of suppressed rage and suspicion he addressed himself to Mercy, standing fronting him by Julian's side.

"Am I included," he asked, "in the arrangement which engages you to explain your extraordinary conduct in half an hour?"

His hand had placed his mother's wedding present round Mercy's neck. A sharp pang wrung her as she looked at Horace, and saw how deeply she had already distressed and offended him. The tears rose in her eyes; she humbly and faintly answered him.

"If you please," was all she could say, before the cruel swelling at her heart rose and silenced her.

Horace's sense of injury refused to be soothed by such simple submission as this.

"I dislike mysteries and innuendoes," he went on, harshly. "In my family circle we are accustomed to meet each other frankly. Why am I to wait half an hour for an explanation which might be given now? What am I to wait for?"

Lady Janet recovered herself as Horace spoke.

"I entirely agree with you," she said. "I ask, too, what are we to wait for?"

Even Julian's self-possession failed him when his aunt repeated that cruelly plain question. How would Mercy answer it? Would her courage still hold out?

"You have asked me what you are to wait for," she said to Horace, quietly and firmly. "Wait to hear something more of Mercy Merrick."

Lady Janet listened with a look of weary disgust.

"Don't return to that!" she said. "We know enough about Mercy Merrick already."

"Pardon me—your ladyship does not know. I am the only person who can inform you."

"You?"

She bent her head respectfully.

"I have begged you, Lady Janet, to give me half an hour," she went on. "In half an hour I solemnly engage myself to produce Mercy Merrick in this room. Lady Janet Roy, Mr. Horace Holmcroft, you are to wait for that."

Steadily pledging herself in those terms to make her confession, she unclasped the pearls from her neck, put them away in their cases and placed it in Horace's hand. "Keep it," she said, with a momentary faltering in her voice, "until we meet again."

Horace took the case in silence; he looked and acted like a man whose mind was paralyzed by surprise. His hand moved mechanically. His eyes followed Mercy with a vacant, questioning look. Lady Janet seemed, in her different way, to share the strange oppression that had fallen on him. A vague sense of dread and distress hung like a cloud over her mind. At that memorable moment she felt her age, she looked her age, as she had never felt it or looked it yet.

"Have I your ladyship's leave," said Mercy, respectfully, "to go to my room?"

Lady Janet mutely granted the request. Mercy's last look, before she went out, was a look at Grace. "Are you satisfied now?" the grand gray eyes seemed to say, mournfully. Grace turned her head aside, with a quick, petulant action. Even her narrow nature opened for a moment unwillingly, and let pity in a little way, in spite of itself.

Mercy's parting words recommended Grace to Julian's care:

"You will see that she is allowed a room to wait in? You will warn her yourself when the half hour has expired?"

Julian opened the library door for her.

"Well done! Nobly done!" he whispered. "All my sympathy is with you—all my help is yours."

Her eyes looked at him, and thanked him, through her gathering tears. His own eyes were dimmed. She passed quietly down the room, and was lost to him before he had shut the door again.

CHAPTER XXI. THE FOOTSTEP IN THE CORRIDOR.

MERCY was alone.

She had secured one half hour of retirement in her own room, designing to devote that interval to the writing of her confession, in the form of a letter addressed to Julian Gray.

No recent change in her position had, as yet, mitigated her horror of acknowledging to Horace and to Lady Janet that she had won her way to their hearts in disguise. Through Julian only could she say the words which were to establish Grace Roseberry in her right position in the house.

How was her confession to be addressed to him? In writing? or by word of mouth?

After all that had happened, from the time when Lady Janet's appearance had interrupted them, she would have felt relief rather than embarrassment in personally opening her heart to the man who had so delicately understood her, who had so faithfully befriended her in her sorest need. But the repeated betrayals of Horace's jealous suspicion of Julian warned her that she would only be surrounding herself with new difficulties, and be placing Julian in a position of painful embarrassment, if she admitted him to a private interview while Horace was in the house.

The one course left to take was the course that she had adopted. Determining to address the narrative of the Fraud to Julian in the form of a letter, she arranged to add, at the close, certain instructions, pointing out to him the line of conduct which she wished him to pursue.

These instructions contemplated the communication of her letter to Lady Janet and to Horace in the library, while Mercy—self-confessed as the missing woman whom she had pledged herself to produce—awaited in the adjoining room whatever sentence it pleased them to pronounce on her. Her resolution not to screen herself behind Julian from any consequences which might follow the confession had taken root in her mind from the moment when Horace had harshly asked her (and when Lady Janet had joined him in asking) why she delayed her explanation, and what she was keeping them waiting for. Out of the very pain which those questions inflicted, the idea of waiting her sentence in her own person in one room, while her letter to Julian was speaking for her in another, had sprung to life. "Let them break my heart if they like," she had thought to herself, in the self-abasement of that bitter moment; "it will be no more than I have deserved."

She locked her door and opened her writing-desk. Knowing what she had to do, she tried to collect herself and do it.

The effort was in vain. Those persons who study writing as an art are probably the only persons who can measure the vast distance which separates a conception as it exists in the mind from the reduction of that conception to form and shape in words. The heavy stress of agitation that had been laid on Mercy for hours together had utterly unfitted her for the delicate and difficult process of arranging the events of a narrative in their due sequence and their due proportion toward each other. Again and again she tried to begin her letter, and again and again she was baffled by the same hopeless confusion of ideas. She gave up the struggle in despair.

A sense of sinking at her heart, a weight of hysterical oppression on her bosom, warned her not to leave herself unoccupied, a prey to morbid self-investigation and imaginary alarms.

She turned instinctively, for a temporary employment of some kind, to the consideration of her own future. Here there were no intricacies or entanglements. The prospect began and ended with her return to the Refuge, if the matron would receive her. She did no injustice to Julian Gray; that great heart would feel for her, that kind hand would be held out to her, she knew. But what would happen if she thoughtlessly accepted all that his sympathy might offer? Scandal would point to her beauty and to his youth, and would place its own vile interpretation on the purest friendship that could exist between them. And he would be the sufferer, for he had a character—a clergyman's character—to lose. No. For his sake, out of gratitude to him, the farewell to Mablethorpe House must be also the farewell to Julian Gray.

The precious minutes were passing. She resolved to write to the matron and ask if she might hope to be forgiven and employed at the Refuge again. Occupation over the letter that was easy to write might have its fortifying effect on her mind, and might pave the way for resuming the letter that was hard to write. She waited a moment at the window, thinking of the past life to which she was soon to return, before she took up the pen again.

Her window looked eastward. The dusky glare of lighted London met her as her eyes rested on the sky. It seemed to beckon her back to the horror of the cruel streets—to point her way mockingly to the bridges over the black river—to lure her to the top of the parapet, and the dreadful leap into God's arms, or into annihilation—who knew which?

She turned, shuddering, from the window. "Will it end in that way," she asked herself, "if the matron says No?"

She began her letter.

"DEAR MADAM—So long a time has passed since you heard from me that I almost shrink from writing to you. I am afraid you have already given me up in your own mind as a hard-hearted, ungrateful woman.

"I have been leading a false life; I have not been fit to write to you before to-day. Now, when I am doing what I can to atone to those whom I have injured—now, when I repent with my whole heart—may I ask leave to return to the friend who has borne with me and helped me through many miserable years? Oh, madam, do not cast me off! I have no one to turn to but you.

"Will you let me own everything to you? Will you forgive me when you know what I have done? Will you take me back into the Refuge, if you have any employment for me by which I may earn my shelter and my bread?

"Before the night comes I must leave the house from which I am now writing. I have nowhere to go to. The little money, the few valuable possessions I have, must be left behind me: they have been obtained under false pretenses; they are not mine. No more forlorn creature than I am lives at this moment. You are a Christian woman. Not for my sake—for Christ's sake—pity me and take me back.

"I am a good nurse, as you know, and I am a quick worker with my needle. In one way or the other can you not find occupation for me?

"I could also teach, in a very unpretending way. But that is useless. Who would trust their children to a woman without a character? There is no hope for me in this direction. And yet I am so fond of children! I think I could be, not happy again, perhaps, but content with my lot, if I could be associated with them in some way. Are there not charitable societies which are trying to help and protect destitute children wandering about the streets? I think of my own wretched childhood—and oh! I should so like to be employed in saving other children from ending as I have ended. I could work, for such an object as that, from morning to night, and never feel weary. All my heart would be in it; and I should have this advantage over happy and prosperous women—I should have nothing else to think of. Surely they might trust me with the poor little starving wanderers of the streets—if you said a word for me? If I am asking too much, please forgive me. I am so wretched, madam—so lonely and so weary of my life.

"There is only one thing more. My time here is very short. Will you please reply to this letter (to say yes or no) by telegram?

"The name by which you know me is not the name by which I have been known here. I must beg you to address the telegram to 'The Reverend Julian Gray, Mablethorpe House, Kensington.' He is here, and he will show it to me. No words of mine can describe what I owe to him. He has never despaired of me—he has saved me from myself. God bless and reward the kindest, truest, best man I have ever known!

"I have no more to say, except to ask you to excuse this long letter, and to believe me your grateful servant, ——."

She signed and inclosed the letter, and wrote the address. Then, for the first time, an obstacle which she ought to have seen before showed itself, standing straight in her way.

There was no time to forward her letter in the ordinary manner by post. It must be taken to its destination by a private messenger. Lady Janet's servants had hitherto been, one and all, at her disposal. Could she presume to employ them on her own affairs, when she might be dismissed from the house, a disgraced woman, in half an hour's time? Of the two alternatives it seemed better to take her chance, and present herself at the Refuge without asking leave first.

While she was still considering the question she was startled by a knock at her door. On opening it she admitted Lady Janet's maid, with a morsel of folded note-paper in her hand.

"From my lady, miss," said the woman, giving her the note. "There is no answer."

Mercy stopped her as she was about to leave the room. The appearance of the maid suggested an inquiry to her. She asked if any of the servants were likely to be going into town that afternoon.

"Yes, miss. One of the grooms is going on horseback, with a message to her ladyship's coach-maker."

The Refuge was close by the coach-maker's place of business. Under the circumstances, Mercy was emboldened to make use of the man. It was a pardonable liberty to employ his services now.

"Will you kindly give the groom that letter for me?" she said. "It will not take him out of his way. He has only to deliver it—nothing more."

The woman willingly complied with the request. Left once more by herself, Mercy looked at the little note which had been placed in her hands.

It was the first time that her benefactress had employed this formal method of communicating with her when they were both in the house. What did such a departure from established habits mean? Had she received her notice of dismissal? Had Lady Janet's quick intelligence found its way already to a suspicion of the truth? Mercy's nerves were unstrung. She trembled pitiably as she opened the folded note.

It began without a form of address, and it ended without a signature. Thus it ran:

"I must request you to delay for a little while the explanation which you have promised me. At my age, painful surprises are very trying things. I must have time to compose myself, before I can hear what you have to say. You shall not be kept waiting longer than I can help. In the meanwhile everything will go on as usual. My nephew Julian, and Horace Holmcroft, and the lady whom I found in the dining-room, will, by my desire, remain in the house until I am able to meet them, and to meet you, again."

There the note ended. To what conclusion did it point?

Had Lady Janet really guessed the truth? or had she only surmised that her adopted daughter was connected in some discreditable manner with the mystery of "Mercy Merrick"? The line in which she referred to the intruder in the dining-room as "the lady" showed very remarkably that her opinions had undergone a change in that quarter. But was the phrase enough of itself to justify the inference that she had actually anticipated the nature of Mercy's confession? It was not easy to decide that doubt at the moment—and it proved to be equally difficult to throw any light on it at an aftertime. To the end of her life Lady Janet resolutely refused to communicate to any one the conclusions which she might have privately formed, the griefs which she might have secretly stifled, on that memorable day.

Amid much, however, which was beset with uncertainty, one thing at least was clear. The time at Mercy's disposal in her own room had been indefinitely prolonged by Mercy's benefactress. Hours might pass before the disclosure to which she stood committed would be expected from her. In those hours she might surely compose her mind sufficiently to be able to write her letter of confession to Julian Gray.

Once more she placed the sheet of paper before her. Resting her head on her hand as she sat at the table, she tried to trace her way through the labyrinth of the past, beginning with the day when she had met Grace Roseberry in the French cottage, and ending with the day which had brought them face to face, for the second time, in the dining-room at Mablethorpe House.

The chain of events began to unroll itself in her mind clearly, link by link.

She remarked, as she pursued the retrospect, how strangely Chance, or Fate, had paved the way for the act of personation, in the first place.

If they had met under ordinary circumstances, neither Mercy nor Grace would have trusted each other with the confidences which had been exchanged between them. As the event had happened, they had come together, under those extraordinary circumstances of common trial and common peril, in a strange country, which would especially predispose two women of the same nation to open their hearts to each other. In no other way could Mercy have obtained at a first interview that fatal knowledge of Grace's position and Grace's affairs which had placed temptation before her as the necessary consequence that followed the bursting of the German shell.

Advancing from this point through the succeeding series of events which had so naturally and yet so strangely favored the perpetration of the fraud, Mercy reached the later period when Grace had followed her to England. Here again she remarked, in the second place, how Chance, or Fate, had once more paved the way for that second meeting which had confronted them with one another at Mablethorpe House.

She had, as she well remembered, attended at a certain assembly (convened by a charitable society) in the character of Lady Janet's representative, at Lady Janet's own request. For that reason she had been absent from the house when Grace had entered it. If her return had been delayed by a few minutes only, Julian would have had time to take Grace out of the room, and the terrible meeting which had stretched Mercy senseless on the floor would never have taken place. As the event had happened, the period of her absence had been fatally shortened by what appeared at the time to be, the commonest possible occurrence. The persons assembled at the society's rooms had disagreed so seriously on the business which had brought them together as to render it necessary to take the ordinary course of adjourning the proceedings to a future day. And Chance, or Fate, had so timed that adjournment as to bring Mercy back into the dining-room exactly at the moment when Grace Roseberry insisted on being confronted with the woman who had taken her place.

She had never yet seen the circumstances in this sinister light. She was alone in her room, at a crisis in her life. She was worn and weakened by emotions which had shaken her to the soul.

Little by little she felt the enervating influences let loose on her, in her lonely position, by her new train of thought. Little by little her heart began to sink under the stealthy chill of superstitious dread. Vaguely horrible presentiments throbbed in her with her pulses, flowed through her with her blood. Mystic oppressions of hidden disaster hovered over her in the atmosphere of the room. The cheerful candle-light turned traitor to her and grew dim. Supernatural murmurs trembled round the house in the moaning of the winter wind. She was afraid to look behind her. On a sudden she felt her own cold hands covering her face, without knowing when she had lifted them to it, or why.

Still helpless, under the horror that held her, she suddenly heard footsteps—a man's footsteps—in the corridor outside. At other times the sound would have startled her: now it broke the spell. The footsteps suggested life, companionship, human interposition—no matter of what sort. She mechanically took up her pen; she found herself beginning to remember her letter to Julian Gray.

At the same moment the footsteps stopped outside her door. The man knocked.

She still felt shaken. She was hardly mistress of herself yet. A faint cry of alarm escaped her at the sound of the knock. Before it could be repeated she had rallied her courage, and had opened the door.

The man in the corridor was Horace Holmcroft.

His ruddy complexion had turned pale. His hair (of which he was especially careful at other times) was in disorder. The superficial polish of his manner was gone; the undisguised man, sullen, distrustful, irritated to the last degree of endurance, showed through. He looked at her with a watchfully suspicious eye; he spoke to her, without preface or apology, in a coldly angry voice.

"Are you aware," he asked, "of what is going on downstairs?"

"I have not left my room," she answered. "I know that Lady Janet has deferred the explanation which I had promised to give her, and I know no more."

"Has nobody told you what Lady Janet did after you left us? Has nobody told you that she politely placed her own boudoir at the disposal of the very woman whom she had ordered half an hour before to leave the house? Do you really not know that Mr. Julian Gray has himself conducted this suddenly-honored guest to her place of retirement? and that I am left alone in the midst of these changes, contradictions, and mysteries—the only person who is kept out in the dark?"

"It is surely needless to ask me these questions," said Mercy, gently. "Who could possibly have told me what was going on below stairs before you knocked at my door?"

He looked at her with an ironical affectation of surprise.

"You are strangely forgetful to-day," he said. "Surely your friend Mr. Julian Gray might have told you? I am astonished to hear that he has not had his private interview yet."

"I don't understand you, Horace."

"I don't want you to understand me," he retorted, irritably. "The proper person to understand me is Julian Gray. I look to him to account to me for the confidential relations which seem to have been established between you behind my back. He has avoided me thus far, but I shall find my way to him yet."

His manner threatened more than his words expressed. In Mercy's nervous condition at the moment, it suggested to her that he might attempt to fasten a quarrel on Julian Gray.

"You are entirely mistaken," she said, warmly. "You are ungratefully doubting your best and truest friend. I say nothing of myself. You will soon discover why I patiently submit to suspicions which other women would resent as an insult."

"Let me discover it at once. Now! Without wasting a moment more!"

There had hitherto been some little distance between them. Mercy had listened, waiting on the threshold of her door; Horace had spoken, standing against the opposite wall of the corridor. When he said his last words he suddenly stepped forward, and (with something imperative in the gesture) laid his hand on her arm. The strong grasp of it almost hurt her. She struggled to release herself.

"Let me go!" she said. "What do you mean?"

He dropped her arm as suddenly as he had taken it.

"You shall know what I mean," he replied. "A woman who has grossly outraged and insulted you—whose only excuse is that she is mad—is detained in the house at your desire, I might almost say at your command, when the police officer is waiting to take her away. I have a right to know what this means. I am engaged to marry you. If you won't trust other people, you are bound to explain yourself to Me. I refuse to wait for Lady Janet's convenience. I insist (if you force me to say so)—I insist on knowing the real nature of your connection with this affair. You have obliged me to follow you here; it is my only opportunity of speaking to you. You avoid me; you shut yourself up from me in your own room. I am not your husband yet—I have no right to follow you in. But there are other rooms open to us. The library is at our disposal, and I will take care that we are not interrupted. I am now going there, and I have a last question to ask. You are to be my wife in a week's time: will you take me into your confidence or not?"

To hesitate was, in this case, literally to be lost. Mercy's sense of justice told her that Horace had claimed no more than his due. She answered instantly:

"I will follow you to the library, Horace, in five minutes."

Her prompt and frank compliance with his wishes surprised and touched him. He took her hand.

She had endured all that his angry sense of injury could say. His gratitude wounded her to the quick. The bitterest moment she had felt yet was the moment in which he raised her hand to his lips, and murmured tenderly, "My own true Grace!" She could only sign to him to leave her, and hurry back into her own room.

Her first feeling, when she found herself alone again, was wonder—wonder that it should never have occurred to her, until he had himself suggested it, that her betrothed husband had the foremost right to her confession. Her horror at owning to either of them that she had cheated them out of their love had hitherto placed Horace and Lady Janet on the same level. She now saw for the first time that there was no comparison between the claims which they respectively had on her. She owned an allegiance to Horace to which Lady Janet could assert no right. Cost her what it might to avow the truth to him with her own lips, the cruel sacrifice must be made.

Without a moment's hesitation she put away her writing materials. It amazed her that she should ever have thought of using Julian Gray as an interpreter between the man to whom she was betrothed and herself. Julian's sympathy (she thought) must have made a strong impression on her indeed to blind her to a duty which was beyond all compromise, which admitted of no dispute!

She had asked for five minutes of delay before she followed Horace. It was too long a time.

Her one chance of finding courage to crush him with the dreadful revelation of who she really was, of what she had really done, was to plunge headlong into the disclosure without giving herself time to think. The shame of it would overpower her if she gave herself time to think.

She turned to the door to follow him at once.

Even at that terrible moment the most ineradicable of all a woman's instincts—the instinct of personal self-respect—brought her to a pause. She had passed through more than one terrible trial since she had dressed to go downstairs. Remembering this, she stopped mechanically, retraced her steps, and looked at herself in the glass.

There was no motive of vanity in what she now did. The action was as unconscious as if she had buttoned an unfastened glove, or shaken out a crumpled dress. Not the faintest idea crossed her mind of looking to see if her beauty might still plead for her, and of trying to set it off at its best.

A momentary smile, the most weary, the most hopeless, that ever saddened a woman's face, appeared in the reflection which her mirror gave her back. "Haggard, ghastly, old before my time!" she said to herself. "Well! better so. He will feel it less—he will not regret me."

With that thought she went downstairs to meet him in the library.

CHAPTER XXII. THE MAN IN THE DINING-ROOM.

IN the great emergencies of life we feel, or we act, as our dispositions incline us. But we never think. Mercy's mind was a blank as she descended the stairs. On her way down she was conscious of nothing but the one headlong impulse to get to the library in the shortest possible space of time. Arrived at the door, the impulse capriciously left her. She stopped on the mat, wondering why she had hurried herself, with time to spare. Her heart sank; the fever of her excitement changed suddenly to a chill as she faced the closed door, and asked herself the question, Dare I go in?

Her own hand answered her. She lifted it to turn the handle of the lock. It dropped again helplessly at her side.

The sense of her own irresolution wrung from her a low exclamation of despair. Faint as it was, it had apparently not passed unheard. The door was opened from within—and Horace stood before her.

He drew aside to let her pass into the room. But he never followed her in. He stood in the doorway, and spoke to her, keeping the door open with his hand.

"Do you mind waiting here for me?" he asked.

She looked at him, in vacant surprise, doubting whether she had heard him aright.

"It will not be for long," he went on. "I am far too anxious to hear what you have to tell me to submit to any needless delays. The truth is, I have had a message from Lady Janet."

(From Lady Janet! What could Lady Janet want with him, at a time when she was bent on composing herself in the retirement of her own room?)

"I ought to have said two messages," Horace proceeded. "The first was given to me on my way downstairs. Lady Janet wished to see me immediately. I sent an excuse. A second message followed. Lady Janet would accept no excuse. If I refused to go to her I should be merely obliging her to come to me. It is impossible to risk being interrupted in that way; my only alternative is to get the thing over as soon as possible. Do you mind waiting?"

"Certainly not. Have you any idea of what Lady Janet wants with you?"

"No. Whatever it is, she shall not keep me long away from you. You will be quite alone here; I have warned the servants not to show any one in." With those words he left her.

Mercy's first sensation was a sensation of relief—soon lost in a feeling of shame at the weakness which could welcome any temporary relief in such a position as hers. The emotion thus roused merged, in its turn, into a sense of impatient regret. "But for Lady Janet's message," she thought to herself, "I might have known my fate by this time!"

The slow minutes followed each other drearily. She paced to and fro in the library, faster and faster, under the intolerable irritation, the maddening uncertainty, of her own suspense. Ere long, even the spacious room seemed to be too small for her. The sober monotony of the long book-lined shelves oppressed and offended her. She threw open the door which led into the dining-room, and dashed in, eager for a change of objects, athirst for more space and more air.

At the first step she checked herself; rooted to the spot, under a sudden revulsion of feeling which quieted her in an instant.

The room was only illuminated by the waning fire-light. A man was obscurely visible, seated on the sofa, with his elbows on his knees and his head resting on his hands. He looked up as the open door let in the light from the library lamps. The mellow glow reached his face and revealed Julian Gray.

Mercy was standing with her back to the light; her face being necessarily hidden in deep shadow. He recognized her by her figure, and by the attitude into which it unconsciously fell. That unsought grace, that lithe long beauty of line, belonged to but one woman in the house. He rose, and approached her.

"I have been wishing to see you," he said, "and hoping that accident

213

might bring about some such meeting as this."

He offered her a chair. Mercy hesitated before she took her seat. This was their first meeting alone since Lady Janet had interrupted her at the moment when she was about to confide to Julian the melancholy story of the past. Was he anxious to seize the opportunity of returning to her confession? The terms in which he had addressed her seemed to imply it. She put the question to him in plain words,

"I feel the deepest interest in hearing all that you have still to confide to me," he answered. "But anxious as I may be, I will not hurry you. I will wait, if you wish it."

"I am afraid I must own that I do wish it," Mercy rejoined. "Not on my account—but because my time is at the disposal of Horace Holmcroft. I expect to see him in a few minutes."

"Could you give me those few minutes?" Julian asked. "I have something on my side to say to you which I think you ought to know before you see any one—Horace himself included."

He spoke with a certain depression of tone which was not associated with her previous experience of him. His face looked prematurely old and careworn in the red light of the fire. Something had plainly happened to sadden and to disappoint him since they had last met.

"I willingly offer you all the time that I have at my own command," Mercy replied. "Does what you have to tell me relate to Lady Janet?"

He gave her no direct reply. "What I have to tell you of Lady Janet," he said, gravely, "is soon told. So far as she is concerned you have nothing more to dread. Lady Janet knows all."

Even the heavy weight of oppression caused by the impending interview with Horace failed to hold its place in Mercy's mind when Julian answered her in those words.

"Come into the lighted room," she said, faintly. "It is too terrible to hear you say that in the dark."

Julian followed her into the library. Her limbs trembled under her. She dropped into a chair, and shrank under his great bright eyes, as he stood by her side looking sadly down on her.

"Lady Janet knows all!" she repeated, with her head on her breast, and the tears falling slowly over her cheeks. "Have you told her?"

"I have said nothing to Lady Janet or to any one. Your confidence is a sacred confidence to me, until you have spoken first."

"Has Lady Janet said anything to you?"

"Not a word. She has looked at you with the vigilant eyes of love; she has listened to you with the quick hearing of love—and she has found her own way to the truth. She will not speak of it to me—she will not speak of it to any living creature. I only know now how dearly she loved you. In spite of herself she clings to you still. Her life, poor soul, has been a barren one; unworthy, miserably unworthy, of such a nature as hers. Her marriage was loveless and childless. She has had admirers, but never, in the higher sense of the word, a friend. All the best years of her life have been wasted in the unsatisfied longing for something to love. At the end of her life You have filled the void. Her heart has found its youth again, through You. At her age—at any age—is such a tie as this to be rudely broken at the mere bidding of circumstances? No! She will suffer anything, risk anything, forgive anything, rather than own, even to herself, that she has been deceived in you. There is more than her happiness at stake; there is pride, a noble pride, in such love as hers, which will ignore the plainest discovery and deny the most unanswerable truth. I am firmly convinced—from my own knowledge of her character, and from what I have observed in her to-day—that she will find some excuse for refusing to hear your confession. And more than that, I believe (if the exertion of her influence can do it) that she will leave no means untried of preventing you from acknowledging your true position here to any living creature. I take a serious responsibility on myself in telling you this— and I don't shrink from it. You ought to know, and you shall know, what trials and what temptations may yet lie before you."

He paused—leaving Mercy time to compose herself, if she wished to speak to him.

She felt that there was a necessity for her speaking to him. He was plainly not aware that Lady Janet had already written to her to defer her promised explanation. This circumstance was in itself a confirmation of the opinion which he had expressed. She ought to mention it to him; she tried to mention it to him. But she was not equal to the effort. The few simple words in which he had touched on the tie that bound Lady Janet to her had wrung her heart. Her tears choked her. She could only sign to him to go on.

"You may wonder at my speaking so positively," he continued, "with nothing better than my own conviction to justify me. I can only say that I have watched Lady Janet too closely to feel any doubt. I saw the moment in which the truth flashed on her, as plainly as I now see you. It did not disclose itself gradually—it burst on her, as it burst on me. She suspected nothing—she was frankly indignant at your sudden interference and your strange language—until the time came in which you pledged yourself to produce Mercy Merrick. Then (and then only) the truth broke on her mind, trebly revealed to her in your words, your voice, and your look. Then (and then only) I saw a marked change come over her, and remain in her while she remained in the room. I dread to think of what she may do in the first reckless despair of the discovery that she has made. I distrust—though God knows I am not naturally a suspicious man—the most apparently trifling events that are now taking place about us. You have held nobly to your resolution to own the truth. Prepare yourself, before the evening is over, to be tried and tempted again."

Mercy lifted her head. Fear took the place of grief in her eyes, as they rested in startled inquiry on Julian's face.

"How is it possible that temptation can come to me now?" she asked.

"I will leave it to events to answer that question," he said. "You will not have long to wait. In the meantime I have put you on your guard." He stooped, and spoke his next words earnestly, close at her ear. "Hold fast by the admirable courage which you have shown thus far," he went on. "Suffer anything rather than suffer the degradation of yourself. Be the woman whom

I once spoke of—the woman I still have in my mind—who can nobly reveal the noble nature that is in her. And never forget this—my faith in you is as firm as ever!"

She looked at him proudly and gratefully.

"I am pledged to justify your faith in me," she said. "I have put it out of my own power to yield. Horace has my promise that I will explain everything to him, in this room."

Julian started.

"Has Horace himself asked it of you?" he inquired. "He, at least, has no suspicion of the truth."

"Horace has appealed to my duty to him as his betrothed wife," she answered. "He has the first claim to my confidence—he resents my silence, and he has a right to resent it. Terrible as it will be to open his eyes to the truth, I must do it if he asks me."

She was looking at Julian while she spoke. The old longing to associate with the hard trial of the confession the one man who had felt for her, and believed in her, revived under another form. If she could only know, while she was saying the fatal words to Horace, that Julian was listening too, she would be encouraged to meet the worst that could happen! As the idea crossed her mind, she observed that Julian was looking toward the door through which they had lately passed. In an instant she saw the means to her end. Hardly waiting to hear the few kind expressions of sympathy and approval which he addressed to her, she hinted timidly at the proposal which she had now to make to him.

"Are you going back into the next room?" she asked.

"Not if you object to it," he replied.

"I don't object. I want you to be there."

"After Horace has joined you?"

"Yes. After Horace has joined me."

"Do you wish to see me when it is over?"

She summoned her resolution, and told him frankly what she had in her mind.

"I want you to be near me while I am speaking to Horace," she said. "It will give me courage if I can feel that I am speaking to you as well as to him. I can count on your sympathy—and sympathy is so precious to me now! Am I asking too much, if I ask you to leave the door unclosed when you go back to the dining-room? Think of the dreadful trial—to him as well as to me! I am only a woman; I am afraid I may sink under it, if I have no friend near me. And I have no friend but you."

In those simple words she tried her powers of persuasion on him for the first time.

Between perplexity and distress Julian was, for the moment, at a loss how to answer her. The love for Mercy which he dared not acknowledge was as vital a feeling in him as the faith in her which he had been free to avow. To refuse anything that she asked of him in her sore need—and, more even than that, to refuse to hear the confession which it had been her first impulse to make to him—these were cruel sacrifices to his sense of what was due to Horace and of what was due to himself. But shrink as he might, even from the appearance of deserting her, it was impossible for him (except under a reserve which was almost equivalent to a denial) to grant her request.

"All that I can do I will do," he said. "The doors shall be left unclosed, and I will remain in the next room, on this condition, that Horace knows of it as well as you. I should be unworthy of your confidence in me if I consented to be a listener on any other terms. You understand that, I am sure, as well as I do."

She had never thought of her proposal to him in this light. Woman-like, she had thought of nothing but the comfort of having him near her. She understood him now. A faint flush of shame rose on her pale cheeks as she thanked him. He delicately relieved her from her embarrassment by putting a question which naturally occurred under the circumstances.

"Where is Horace all this time?" he asked. "Why is he not here?"

"He has been called away," she answered, "by a message from Lady Janet."

The reply more than astonished Julian; it seemed almost to alarm him. He returned to Mercy's chair; he said to her, eagerly, "Are you sure?"

"Horace himself told me that Lady Janet had insisted on seeing him."

"When?"

"Not long ago. He asked me to wait for him here while he went upstairs."

Julian's face darkened ominously.

"This confirms my worst fears," he said. "Have you had any communication with Lady Janet?"

Mercy replied by showing him his aunt's note. He read it carefully through.

"Did I not tell you," he said, "that she would find some excuse for refusing to hear your confession? She begins by delaying it, simply to gain time for something else which she has it in her mind to do. When did you receive this note? Soon after you went upstairs?"

"About a quarter of an hour after, as well as I can guess."

"Do you know what happened down here after you left us?"

"Horace told me that Lady Janet had offered Miss Roseberry the use of her boudoir."

"Any more?"

"He said that you had shown her the way to the room."

"Did he tell you what happened after that?"

"No."

"Then I must tell you. If I can do nothing more in this serious state of things, I can at least prevent your being taken by surprise. In the first place, it is right you should know that I had a motive for accompanying Miss Roseberry to the boudoir. I was anxious (for your sake) to make some appeal to her better self—if she had any better self to address. I own I had doubts of my success—judging by what I had already seen of her. My doubts were confirmed. In the ordinary intercourse of life I should merely have thought her a commonplace, uninteresting woman. Seeing her as I saw her while we were alone—in other words, penetrating below the surface—I have never, in all my sad experience, met with such a hopelessly narrow, mean, and low nature as hers. Understanding, as she could not fail to do, what the sudden change in Lady Janet's behavior toward her really meant, her one idea was to take the cruelest possible advantage of it. So far from feeling any consideration for you, she was only additionally imbittered toward you. She protested against your being permitted to claim the merit of placing her in her right position here by your own voluntary avowal of the truth. She insisted on publicly denouncing you, and on forcing Lady Janet to dismiss you, unheard, before the whole household! 'Now I can have my revenge! At last Lady Janet is afraid of me!' Those were her own words—I am almost ashamed to repeat them—those, on my honor, were her own words! Every possible humiliation to be heaped on you; no consideration to be shown for Lady Janet's age and Lady Janet's position; nothing, absolutely nothing, to be allowed to interfere with Miss Roseberry's vengeance and Miss Roseberry's triumph! There is this woman's shameless view of what is due to her, as stated by herself in the plainest terms. I kept my temper; I did all I could to bring her to a better frame of mind. I might as well have pleaded—I won't say with a savage; savages are sometimes accessible to remonstrance, if you know how to reach them—I might as well have pleaded with a hungry animal to abstain from eating while food was within its reach. I had just given up the hopeless effort in disgust, when Lady Janet's maid appeared with a message for Miss Roseberry from her mistress: 'My lady's compliments, ma'am, and she will be glad to see you at your earliest convenience, in her room.'"

Another surprise! Grace Roseberry invited to an interview with Lady Janet! It would have been impossible to believe it, if Julian had not heard the invitation given with his own ears.

"She instantly rose," Julian proceeded. "'I won't keep her ladyship waiting a moment,' she said; 'show me the way.' She signed to the maid to go out of the room first, and then turned round and spoke to me from the door. I despair of describing the insolent exultation of her manner. I can only repeat her words: 'This is exactly what I wanted! I had intended to insist on seeing Lady Janet: she saves me the trouble. I am infinitely obliged to her.' With that she nodded to me, and closed the door. I have not seen her, I have not heard of her, since. For all I know, she may be still with my aunt, and Horace may have found her there when he entered the room."

"What can Lady Janet have to say to her?" Mercy asked, eagerly.

"It is impossible even to guess. When you found me in the dining-room I was considering that very question. I cannot imagine that any neutral ground can exist on which it is possible for Lady Janet and this woman to meet. In her present frame of mind she will in all probability insult Lady Janet before she has been five minutes in the room. I own I am completely puzzled. The one conclusion I can arrive at is that the note which my aunt sent to you, the private interview with Miss Roseberry which has followed, and the summons to Horace which has succeeded in its turn, are all links in the same chain of events, and are all tending to that renewed temptation against which I have already warned you."

Mercy held up her hand for silence. She looked toward the door that opened on the hall; had she heard a footstep outside? No. All was still. Not a sign yet of Horace's return.

"Oh!" she exclaimed, "what would I not give to know what is going on upstairs!"

"You will soon know it now," said Julian. "It is impossible that our present uncertainty can last much longer."

He turned away, intending to go back to the room in which she had found him. Looking at her situation from a man's point of view, he naturally assumed that the best service he could now render to Mercy would be to leave her to prepare herself for the interview with Horace. Before he had taken three steps away from her she showed him the difference between the woman's point of view and the man's. The idea of considering beforehand what she should say never entered her mind. In her horror of being left by herself at that critical moment, she forgot every other consideration. Even the warning remembrance of Horace's jealous distrust of Julian passed away from her, for the moment, as completely as if it never had a place in her memory. "Don't leave me!" she cried. "I can't wait here alone. Come back—come back!"

She rose impulsively while she spoke, as if to follow him into the dining-room, if he persisted in leaving her.

A momentary expression of doubt crossed Julian's face as he retraced his steps and signed to her to be seated again. Could she be depended on (he asked himself) to sustain the coming test of her resolution, when she had not courage enough to wait for events in a room by herself? Julian had yet to learn that a woman's courage rises with the greatness of the emergency. Ask her to accompany you through a field in which some harmless cattle happen to be grazing, and it is doubtful, in nine cases out of ten, if she will do it. Ask her, as one of the passengers in a ship on fire, to help in setting an example of composure to the rest, and it is certain, in nine cases out of ten, that she will do it. As soon as Julian had taken a chair near her, Mercy was calm again.

"Are you sure of your resolution?" he asked.

"I am certain of it," she answered, "as long as you don't leave me by myself."

The talk between them dropped there. They sat together in silence, with their eyes fixed on the door, waiting for Horace to come in.

After the lapse of a few minutes their attention was attracted by a sound outside in the grounds. A carriage of some sort was plainly audible approaching the house.

The carriage stopped; the bell rang; the front door was opened. Had a visitor arrived? No voice could be heard making inquiries. No footsteps but the servant's footsteps crossed the hall. Along pause followed, the carriage remaining at the door. Instead of bringing some one to the house, it had apparently arrived to take some one away.

The next event was the return of the servant to the front door. They listened again. Again no second footstep was audible. The door was closed; the servant recrossed the hall; the carriage was driven away. Judging by sounds alone, no one had arrived at the house, and no one had left the house.

Julian looked at Mercy. "Do you understand this?" he asked.

She silently shook her head.

"If any person has gone away in the carriage," Julian went on, "that person can hardly have been a man, or we must have heard him in the hall."

The conclusion which her companion had just drawn from the noiseless departure of the supposed visitor raised a sudden doubt in Mercy's mind.

"Go and inquire!" she said, eagerly.

Julian left the room, and returned again, after a brief absence, with signs of grave anxiety in his face and manner.

"I told you I dreaded the most trifling events that were passing about us," he said. "An event, which is far from being trifling, has just happened. The carriage which we heard approaching along the drive turns out to have been a cab sent for from the house. The person who has gone away in it—"

"Is a woman, as you supposed?"

"Yes."

Mercy rose excitedly from her chair.

"It can't be Grace Roseberry?" she exclaimed.

"It is Grace Roseberry."

"Has she gone away alone?"

"Alone—after an interview with Lady Janet."

"Did she go willingly?"

"She herself sent the servant for the cab."

"What does it mean?"

"It is useless to inquire. We shall soon know."

They resumed their seats, waiting, as they had waited already, with their eyes on the library door.

CHAPTER XXIII. LADY JANET AT BAY.

THE narrative leaves Julian and Mercy for a while, and, ascending to the upper regions of the house, follows the march of events in Lady Janet's room.

The maid had delivered her mistress's note to Mercy, and had gone away again on her second errand to Grace Roseberry in her boudoir. Lady Janet was seated at her writing-table, waiting for the appearance of the woman whom she had summoned to her presence. A single lamp diffused its mild light over the books, pictures, and busts round her, leaving the further end of the room, in which the bed was placed, almost lost in obscurity. The works of art were all portraits; the books were all presentation copies from the authors. It was Lady Janet's fancy to associate her bedroom with memorials of the various persons whom she had known in the long course of her life—all of them more or less distinguished, most of them, by this time, gathered with the dead.

She sat near her writing-table, lying back in her easy-chair—the living realization of the picture which Julian's description had drawn. Her eyes were fixed on a photographic likeness of Mercy, which was so raised upon a little gilt easel as to enable her to contemplate it under the full light of the lamp. The bright, mobile old face was strangely and sadly changed. The brow was fixed; the mouth was rigid; the whole face would have been like a mask, molded in the hardest forms of passive resistance and suppressed rage, but for the light and life still thrown over it by the eyes. There was something unutterably touching in the keen hungering tenderness of the look which they fixed on the portrait, intensified by an underlying expression of fond and patient reproach. The danger which Julian so wisely dreaded was in the rest of the face; the love which he had so truly described was in the eyes alone. They still spoke of the cruelly profaned affection which had been the one immeasurable joy, the one inexhaustible hope of Lady Janet's closing life. The brow expressed nothing but her obstinate determination to stand by the wreck of that joy, to rekindle the dead ashes of that hope. The lips were only eloquent of her unflinching resolution to ignore the hateful present and to save the sacred past. "My idol may be shattered, but none of you shall know it. I stop the march of discovery; I extinguish the light of truth. I am deaf to your words; am blind to your proofs. At seventy years old, my idol is my life. It shall be my idol still."

The silence in the bedroom was broken by a murmuring of women's voices outside the door.

Lady Janet instantly raised herself in the chair and snatched the photograph off the easel. She laid the portrait face downward, among some papers on the table, then abruptly changed her mind, and hid it among the thick folds of lace which clothed her neck and bosom. There was a world of love in the action itself, and in the sudden softening of the eyes which accompanied it. The next moment Lady Janet's mask was on. Any superficial observer who had seen her now would have said, "This is a hard woman!"

The door was opened by the maid. Grace Roseberry entered the room.

She advanced rapidly, with a defiant assurance in her manner, and a lofty carriage of her head. She sat down in the chair, to which Lady Janet silently pointed, with a thump; she returned Lady Janet's grave bow with a nod and a smile. Every movement and every look of the little, worn, white-faced, shabbily dressed woman expressed insolent triumph, and said, as if in words, "My turn has come!"

"I am glad to wait on your ladyship," she began, without giving Lady Janet an opportunity of speaking first. "Indeed, I should have felt it my duty to request an interview, if you had not sent your maid to invite me up here."

"You would have felt it your duty to request an interview?" Lady Janet repeated, very quietly. "Why?"

The tone in which that one last word was spoken embarrassed Grace at the outset. It established as great a distance between Lady Janet and herself as if she had been lifted in her chair and conveyed bodily to the other end of the room.

"I am surprised that your ladyship should not understand me," she said, struggling to conceal her confusion. "Especially after your kind offer of your own boudoir."

Lady Janet remained perfectly unmoved. "I do not understand you," she answered, just as quietly as ever.

Grace's temper came to her assistance. She recovered the assurance which had marked her first appearance on the scene.

"In that case," she resumed, "I must enter into particulars, in justice to myself. I can place but one interpretation on the extraordinary change in your ladyship's behavior to me downstairs. The conduct of that abominable woman has at last opened your eyes to the deception that has been practiced on you. For some reason of your own, however, you have not yet chosen to recognize me openly. In this painful position something is due to my own self-respect. I cannot, and will not, permit Mercy Merrick to claim the merit of restoring me to my proper place in this house. After what I have suffered it is quite impossible for me to endure that. I should have requested an interview (if you had not sent for me) for the express purpose of claiming this person's immediate expulsion from the house. I claim it now as a proper concession to Me. Whatever you or Mr. Julian Gray may do, I will not tamely permit her to exhibit herself as an interesting penitent. It is really a little too much to hear this brazen adventuress appoint her own time for explaining herself. It is too deliberately insulting to see her sail out of the room—with a clergyman of the Church of England opening the door for her—as if she was laying me under an obligation! I can forgive much, Lady Janet—including the terms in which you thought it decent to order me out of your house. I am quite willing to accept the offer of your boudoir, as the expression on your part of a better frame of mind. But even Christian Charity has its limits. The continued presence of that wretch under your roof is, you will permit me to remark, not only a monument of your own weakness, but a perfectly insufferable insult to Me."

There she stopped abruptly—not for want of words, but for want of a listener.

227

Lady Janet was not even pretending to attend to her. Lady Janet, with a deliberate rudeness entirely foreign to her usual habits, was composedly busying herself in arranging the various papers scattered about the table. Some she tied together with little morsels of string; some she placed under paper-weights; some she deposited in the fantastic pigeon-holes of a little Japanese cabinet—working with a placid enjoyment of her own orderly occupation, and perfectly unaware, to all outward appearance, that any second person was in the room. She looked up, with her papers in both hands, when Grace stopped, and said, quietly,

"Have you done?"

"Is your ladyship's purpose in sending for me to treat me with studied rudeness?" Grace retorted, angrily.

"My purpose in sending for you is to say something as soon as you will allow me the opportunity."

The impenetrable composure of that reply took Grace completely by surprise. She had no retort ready. In sheer astonishment she waited silently with her eyes riveted on the mistress of the house.

Lady Janet put down her papers, and settled herself comfortably in the easy-chair, preparatory to opening the interview on her side.

"The little that I have to say to you," she began, "may be said in a question. Am I right in supposing that you have no present employment, and that a little advance in money (delicately offered) would be very acceptable to you?"

"Do you mean to insult me, Lady Janet?"

"Certainly not. I mean to ask you a question."

"Your question is an insult."

"My question is a kindness, if you will only understand it as it is intended. I don't complain of your not understanding it. I don't even hold you responsible for any one of the many breaches of good manners which you have committed since you have been in this room. I was honestly anxious to be of some service to you, and you have repelled my advances. I am sorry. Let us drop the subject."

Expressing herself in the most perfect temper in those terms, Lady Janet resumed the arrangement of her papers, and became unconscious once more of the presence of any second person in the room.

Grace opened her lips to reply with the utmost intemperance of an angry woman, and thinking better of it, controlled herself. It was plainly useless to take the violent way with Lady Janet Roy. Her age and her social position were enough of themselves to repel any violence. She evidently knew that, and trusted to it. Grace resolved to meet the enemy on the neutral ground of politeness, as the most promising ground that she could occupy under present circumstances.

"If I have said anything hasty, I beg to apologize to your ladyship," she began. "May I ask if your only object in sending for me was to inquire into my pecuniary affairs, with a view to assisting me?"

"That," said Lady Janet, "was my only object."

"You had nothing to say to me on the subject of Mercy Merrick?"

"Nothing whatever. I am weary of hearing of Mercy Merrick. Have you any more questions to ask me?"

"I have one more."

"Yes?"

"I wish to ask your ladyship whether you propose to recognize me in the presence of your household as the late Colonel Roseberry's daughter?"

"I have already recognized you as a lady in embarrassed circumstances, who has peculiar claims on my consideration and forbearance. If you wish me to repeat those words in the presence of the servants (absurd as it is), I am ready to comply with your request."

Grace's temper began to get the better of her prudent resolutions.

"Lady Janet!" she said; "this won't do. I must request you to express yourself plainly. You talk of my peculiar claims on your forbearance. What claims do you mean?"

"It will be painful to both of us if we enter into details," replied Lady Janet. "Pray don't let us enter into details."

"I insist on it, madam."

"Pray don't insist on it."

Grace was deaf to remonstrance.

"I ask you in plain words," she went on, "do you acknowledge that you have been deceived by an adventuress who has personated me? Do you mean to restore me to my proper place in this house?"

Lady Janet returned to the arrangement of her papers.

"Does your ladyship refuse to listen to me?"

Lady Janet looked up from her papers as blandly as ever.

"If you persist in returning to your delusion," she said, "you will oblige me to persist in returning to my papers."

"What is my delusion, if you please?"

"Your delusion is expressed in the questions you have just put to me. Your delusion constitutes your peculiar claim on my forbearance. Nothing you can say or do will shake my forbearance. When I first found you in the dining-room, I acted most improperly; I lost my temper. I did worse; I was foolish enough and imprudent enough to send for a police officer. I owe you every possible atonement (afflicted as you are) for treating you in that cruel manner. I offered you the use of my boudoir, as part of my atonement. I sent for you, in the hope that you would allow me to assist you, as part of my atonement. You may behave rudely to me, you may speak in the most abusive terms of my adopted daughter; I will submit to anything, as part of my atonement. So long as you abstain from speaking on one painful subject, I will listen to you with the greatest pleasure. Whenever you return to that subject I shall return to my papers."

Grace looked at Lady Janet with an evil smile.

"I begin to understand your ladyship," she said. "You are ashamed to acknowledge that you have been grossly imposed upon. Your only alternative, of course, is to ignore everything that has happened. Pray count on my forbearance. I am not at all offended—I am merely amused. It is not every day that a lady of high rank exhibits herself in such a position as yours to an obscure woman like me. Your humane consideration for me dates, I presume, from the time when your adopted daughter set you the example, by ordering the police officer out of the room?"

Lady Janet's composure was proof even against this assault on it. She gravely accepted Grace's inquiry as a question addressed to her in perfect good faith.

"I am not at all surprised," she replied, "to find that my adopted daughter's interference has exposed her to misrepresentation. She ought to have remonstrated with me privately before she interfered. But she has one fault—she is too impulsive. I have never, in all my experience, met with such a warm-hearted person as she is. Always too considerate of others; always too forgetful of herself! The mere appearance of the police officer placed you in a situation to appeal to her compassion, and her impulses carried her away as usual. My fault! All my fault!"

Grace changed her tone once more. She was quick enough to discern that Lady Janet was a match for her with her own weapons.

"We have had enough of this," she said. "It is time to be serious. Your adopted daughter (as you call her) is Mercy Merrick, and you know it."

Lady Janet returned to her papers.

"I am Grace Roseberry, whose name she has stolen, and you know that."

Lady Janet went on with her papers.

Grace got up from her chair.

"I accept your silence, Lady Janet," she said, "as an acknowledgment of your deliberate resolution to suppress the truth. You are evidently determined to receive the adventuress as the true woman; and you don't scruple to face the consequences of that proceeding, by pretending to my face to believe that I am mad. I will not allow myself to be impudently cheated out of my rights in this way. You will hear from me again madam, when the Canadian mail arrives in England."

She walked toward the door. This time Lady Janet answered, as readily and as explicitly as it was possible to desire.

"I shall refuse to receive your letters," she said.

Grace returned a few steps, threateningly.

"My letters shall be followed by my witnesses," she proceeded.

"I shall refuse to receive your witnesses."

"Refuse at your peril. I will appeal to the law."

Lady Janet smiled.

"I don't pretend to much knowledge of the subject," she said; "but I should be surprised indeed if I discovered that you had any claim on me which the law could enforce. However, let us suppose that you can set the law in action. You know as well as I do that the only motive power which can do that is—money. I am rich; fees, costs, and all the rest of it are matters of no sort of consequence to me. May I ask if you are in the same position?"

The question silenced Grace. So far as money was concerned, she was literally at the end of her resources. Her only friends were friends in Canada. After what she had said to him in the boudoir, it would be quite useless to appeal to the sympathies of Julian Gray. In the pecuniary sense, and in one word, she was absolutely incapable of gratifying her own vindictive longings. And there sat the mistress of Mablethorpe House, perfectly well aware of it.

Lady Janet pointed to the empty chair.

"Suppose you sit down again?" she suggested. "The course of our interview seems to have brought us back to the question that I asked you when you came into my room. Instead of threatening me with the law, suppose you consider the propriety of permitting me to be of some use to you. I am in the habit of assisting ladies in embarrassed circumstances, and nobody knows of it but my steward—who keeps the accounts—and myself. Once more, let me inquire if a little advance of the pecuniary sort (delicately offered) would be acceptable to you?"

Grace returned slowly to the chair that she had left. She stood by it, with one hand grasping the top rail, and with her eyes fixed in mocking scrutiny on Lady Janet's face.

"At last your ladyship shows your hand," she said. "Hush-money!"

"You will send me back to my papers," rejoined Lady Janet. "How obstinate you are!"

Grace's hand closed tighter and tighter round the rail of the chair. Without witnesses, without means, without so much as a refuge—thanks to her own coarse cruelties of language and conduct—in the sympathies of others, the sense of her isolation and her helplessness was almost maddening at that final moment. A woman of finer sensibilities would have instantly left the room. Grace's impenetrably hard and narrow mind impelled her to meet the emergency in a very different way. A last base vengeance, to which Lady Janet had voluntarily exposed herself, was still within her reach. "For the present," she thought, "there is but one way of being even with your ladyship. I can cost you as much as possible."

"Pray make some allowances for me," she said. "I am not obstinate—I am only a little awkward at matching the audacity of a lady of high rank. I shall improve with practice. My own language is, as I am painfully aware, only plain English. Permit me to withdraw it, and to substitute yours. What advance is your ladyship (delicately) prepared to offer me?"

Lady Janet opened a drawer, and took out her check-book.

The moment of relief had come at last! The only question now left to discuss was evidently the question of amount. Lady Janet considered a little. The question of amount was (to her mind) in some sort a question of conscience as well. Her love for Mercy and her loathing for Grace, her horror of seeing her darling degraded and her affection profaned by a public exposure, had hurried her—there was no disputing it—into treating an injured woman harshly. Hateful as Grace Roseberry might be, her father had left her, in his last moments, with Lady Janet's full concurrence, to Lady Janet's care. But for Mercy she would have been received at Mablethorpe House as Lady Janet's companion, with a salary of one hundred pounds a year. On the other hand, how long (with such a temper as she had revealed) would Grace have remained in the service of her protectress? She would probably have been dismissed in a few weeks, with a year's salary to compensate her, and with a recommendation to some suitable employment. What would be a fair compensation now? Lady Janet decided that five years' salary immediately given, and future assistance rendered if necessary, would represent a fit remembrance of the late Colonel Roseberry's claims, and a liberal pecuniary acknowledgment of any harshness of treatment which Grace might have sustained at her hands. At the same time, and for the further satisfying of her own conscience, she determined to discover the sum which Grace herself would consider sufficient by the simple process of making Grace herself propose the terms.

"It is impossible for me to make you an offer," she said, "for this reason—your need of money will depend greatly on your future plans. I am quite ignorant of your future plans."

"Perhaps your ladyship will kindly advise me?" said Grace, satirically.

"I cannot altogether undertake to advise you," Lady Janet replied. "I can only suppose that you will scarcely remain in England, where you have no friends. Whether you go to law with me or not, you will surely feel the necessity of communicating personally with your friends in Canada. Am I right?"

Grace was quite quick enough to understand this as it was meant. Properly interpreted, the answer signified—"If you take your compensation in money, it is understood, as part of the bargain that you don't remain in England to annoy me."

234

"Your ladyship is quite right," she said. "I shall certainly not remain in England. I shall consult my friends—and," she added, mentally, "go to law with you afterward, if I possibly can, with your own money!"

"You will return to Canada," Lady Janet proceeded; "and your prospects there will be, probably, a little uncertain at first. Taking this into consideration, at what amount do you estimate, in your own mind, the pecuniary assistance which you will require?"

"May I count on your ladyship's, kindness to correct me if my own ignorant calculations turn out to be wrong?" Grace asked, innocently.

Here again the words, properly interpreted, had a special signification of their own: "It is stipulated, on my part, that I put myself up to auction, and that my estimate shall be regulated by your ladyship's highest bid." Thoroughly understanding the stipulation, Lady Janet bowed, and waited gravely.

Gravely, on her side, Grace began.

"I am afraid I should want more than a hundred pounds," she said.

Lady Janet made her first bid. "I think so too."

"More, perhaps, than two hundred?"

Lady Janet made her second bid. "Probably."

"More than three hundred? Four hundred? Five hundred?"

Lady Janet made her highest bid. "Five hundred pounds will do," she said.

In spite of herself, Grace's rising color betrayed her ungovernable excitement. From her earliest childhood she had been accustomed to see shillings and sixpences carefully considered before they were parted with. She had never known her father to possess so much as five golden sovereigns at his own disposal (unencumbered by debt) in all her experience of him. The atmosphere in which she had lived and breathed was the all-stifling one of genteel poverty. There was something horrible in the greedy eagerness of her eyes as they watched Lady Janet, to see if she was really sufficiently in earnest to give away five hundred pounds sterling with a stroke of her pen.

Lady Janet wrote the check in a few seconds, and pushed it across the table.

Grace's hungry eyes devoured the golden line, "Pay to myself or bearer five hundred pounds," and verified the signature beneath, "Janet Roy." Once sure of the money whenever she chose to take it, the native meanness of her nature instantly asserted itself. She tossed her head, and let the check lie on the table, with an overacted appearance of caring very little whether she took it or not.

"Your ladyship is not to suppose that I snap at your check," she said.

Lady Janet leaned back in her chair and closed her eyes. The very sight of Grace Roseberry sickened her. Her mind filled suddenly with the image of Mercy. She longed to feast her eyes again on that grand beauty, to fill her ears again with the melody of that gentle voice.

"I require time to consider—in justice to my own self-respect," Grace went on.

Lady Janet wearily made a sign, granting time to consider.

"Your ladyship's boudoir is, I presume, still at my disposal?"

Lady Janet silently granted the boudoir.

"And your ladyship's servants are at my orders, if I have occasion to employ them?"

Lady Janet suddenly opened her eyes. "The whole household is at your orders," she cried, furiously. "Leave me!"

Grace was far from being offended. If anything, she was gratified—there was a certain triumph in having stung Lady Janet into an open outbreak of temper. She insisted forthwith on another condition.

"In the event of my deciding to receive the check," she said, "I cannot, consistently with my own self-respect, permit it to be delivered to me otherwise than inclosed. Your ladyship will (if necessary) be so kind as to inclose it. Good-evening."

She sauntered to the door, looking from side to side, with an air of supreme disparagement, at the priceless treasures of art which adorned the walls. Her eyes dropped superciliously on the carpet (the design of a famous French painter), as if her feet condescended in walking over it. The audacity with which she had entered the room had been marked enough; it shrank to nothing before the infinitely superior proportions of the insolence with which she left it.

The instant the door was closed Lady Janet rose from her chair. Reckless of the wintry chill in the outer air, she threw open one of the windows. "Pah!" she exclaimed, with a shudder of disgust, "the very air of the room is tainted by her!"

She returned to her chair. Her mood changed as she sat down again—her heart was with Mercy once more. "Oh, my love!" she murmured "how low I have stooped, how miserably I have degraded myself—and all for You!" The bitterness of the retrospect was unendurable. The inbred force of the woman's nature took refuge from it in an outburst of defiance and despair. "Whatever she has done, that wretch deserves it! Not a living creature in this house shall say she has deceived me. She has not deceived me—she loves me! What do I care whether she has given me her true name or not! She has given me her true heart. What right had Julian to play upon her feelings and pry into her secrets? My poor, tempted, tortured child! I won't hear her confession. Not another word shall she say to any living creature. I am mistress—I will forbid it at once!" She snatched a sheet of notepaper from the case; hesitated, and threw it from her on the table. "Why not send for my darling?" she thought. "Why write?" She hesitated once more, and resigned the idea. "No! I can't trust myself! I daren't see her yet!"

She took up the sheet of paper again, and wrote her second message to Mercy. This time the note began fondly with a familiar form of address.

"MY DEAR CHILD—I have had time to think and compose myself a little, since I last wrote, requesting you to defer the explanation which you had promised me. I already understand (and appreciate) the motives which led you to interfere as you did downstairs, and I now ask you to entirely abandon the explanation. It will, I am sure, be painful to you (for reasons of your own into which I have no wish to inquire) to produce the person of whom you spoke, and as you know already, I myself am weary of hearing of her. Besides, there is really no need now for you to explain anything. The stranger whose visits here have caused us so much pain and anxiety will trouble us no more. She leaves England of her own free will, after a conversation with me which has perfectly succeeded in composing and satisfying her. Not a word more, my dear, to me, or to my nephew, or to any other human creature, of what has happened in the dining-room to-day. When we next meet, let it be understood between us that the past is henceforth and forever buried to oblivion. This is not only the earnest request—it is, if necessary, the positive command, of your mother and friend,

"JANET ROY.

"P.S.—I shall find opportunities (before you leave your room) of speaking separately to my nephew and to Horace Holmcroft. You need dread no embarrassment, when you next meet them. I will not ask you to answer my note in writing. Say yes to the maid who will bring it to you, and I shall know we understand each other."

After sealing the envelope which inclosed these lines, Lady Janet addressed it, as usual, to "Miss Grace Roseberry." She was just rising to ring the bell, when the maid appeared with a message from the boudoir. The woman's tones and looks showed plainly that she had been made the object of Grace's insolent self-assertion as well as her mistress.

"If you please, my lady, the person downstairs wishes—"

Lady Janet, frowning contemptuously, interrupted the message at the outset. "I know what the person downstairs wishes. She has sent you for a letter from me?"

"Yes, my lady."

"Anything more?"

"She has sent one of the men-servants, my lady, for a cab. If your ladyship had only heard how she spoke to him!"

Lady Janet intimated by a sign that she would rather not hear. She at once inclosed the check in an undirected envelope.

"Take that to her," she said, "and then come back to me."

Dismissing Grace Roseberry from all further consideration, Lady Janet sat, with her letter to Mercy in her hand, reflecting on her position, and on the efforts which it might still demand from her. Pursuing this train of thought, it now occurred to her that accident might bring Horace and Mercy together at any moment, and that, in Horace's present frame of mind, he would certainly insist on the very explanation which it was the foremost interest of her life to suppress. The dread of this disaster was in full possession of her when the maid returned.

"Where is Mr. Holmcroft?" she asked, the moment the woman entered the room.

"I saw him open the library door, my lady, just now, on my way upstairs."

"Was he alone?"

"Yes, my lady."

"Go to him, and say I want to see him here immediately."

The maid withdrew on her second errand. Lady Janet rose restlessly, and closed the open window. Her impatient desire to make sure of Horace so completely mastered her that she left her room, and met the woman in the corridor on her return. Receiving Horace's message of excuse, she instantly sent back the peremptory rejoinder, "Say that he will oblige me to go to him, if he persists in refusing to come to me. And, stay!" she added, remembering the undelivered letter. "Send Miss Roseberry's maid here; I want her."

Left alone again, Lady Janet paced once or twice up and down the corridor—then grew suddenly weary of the sight of it, and went back to her room. The two maids returned together. One of them, having announced

Horace's submission, was dismissed. The other was sent to Mercy's room with Lady Janet's letter. In a minute or two the messenger appeared again, with the news that she had found the room empty.

"Have you any idea where Miss Roseberry is?"

"No, my lady."

Lady Janet reflected for a moment. If Horace presented himself without any needless delay, the plain inference would he that she had succeeded in separating him from Mercy. If his appearance was suspiciously deferred, she decided on personally searching for Mercy in the reception rooms on the lower floor of the house.

"What have you done with the letter?" she asked.

"I left it on Miss Roseberry's table, my lady."

"Very well. Keep within hearing of the bell, in case I want you again."

Another minute brought Lady Janet's suspense to an end. She heard the welcome sound of a knock at her door from a man's hand. Horace hurriedly entered the room.

"What is it you want with me, Lady Janet?" he inquired, not very graciously.

"Sit down, Horace, and you shall hear."

Horace did not accept the invitation. "Excuse me," he said, "if I mention that I am rather in a hurry."

"Why are you in a hurry?"

"I have reasons for wishing to see Grace as soon as possible."

"And I have reasons," Lady Janet rejoined, "for wishing to speak to you about Grace before you see her; serious reasons. Sit down."

Horace started. "Serious reasons?" he repeated. "You surprise me."

"I shall surprise you still more before I have done."

Their eyes met as Lady Janet answered in those terms. Horace observed signs of agitation in her, which he now noticed for the first time. His face darkened with an expression of sullen distrust—and he took the chair in silence.

CHAPTER XXIV. LADY JANET'S LETTER.

THE narrative leaves Lady Janet and Horace Holmcroft together, and returns to Julian and Mercy in the library.

An interval passed—a long interval, measured by the impatient reckoning of suspense—after the cab which had taken Grace Roseberry away had left the house. The minutes followed each other; and still the warning sound of Horace's footsteps was not heard on the marble pavement of the hall. By common (though unexpressed) consent, Julian and Mercy avoided touching upon the one subject on which they were now both interested alike. With their thoughts fixed secretly in vain speculation on the nature of the interview which was then taking place in Lady Janet's room, they tried to speak on topics indifferent to both of them—tried, and failed, and tried again. In a last and longest pause of silence between them, the next event happened. The door from the hall was softly and suddenly opened.

Was it Horace? No—not even yet. The person who had opened the door was only Mercy's maid.

"My lady's love, miss; and will you please to read this directly?"

Giving her message in those terms, the woman produced from the pocket of her apron Lady Janet's second letter to Mercy, with a strip of paper oddly pinned round the envelope. Mercy detached the paper, and found on the inner side some lines in pencil, hurriedly written in Lady Janet's hand. They ran thus.

"Don't lose a moment in reading my letter. And mind this, when H. returns to you—meet him firmly: say nothing."

Enlightened by the warning words which Julian had spoken to her, Mercy was at no loss to place the right interpretation on those strange lines. Instead of immediately opening the letter, she stopped the maid at the library door. Julian's suspicion of the most trifling events that were taking place in the house had found its way from his mind to hers. "Wait!" she said. "I don't understand what is going on upstairs; I want to ask you something."

The woman came back—not very willingly.

"How did you know I was here?" Mercy inquired.

"If you please, miss, her ladyship ordered me to take the letter to you some little time since. You were not in your room, and I left it on your table."

"I understand that. But how came you to bring the letter here?"

"My lady rang for me, miss. Before I could knock at her door she came out into the corridor with that morsel of paper in her hand—"

"So as to keep you from entering her room?"

"Yes, miss. Her ladyship wrote on the paper in a great hurry, and told me to pin it round the letter that I had left in your room. I was to take them both together to you, and to let nobody see me. 'You will find Miss Roseberry in the library' (her ladyship says), 'and run, run, run! there isn't a moment to lose!' Those were her own words, miss."

"Did you hear anything in the room before Lady Janet came out and met you?"

The woman hesitated, and looked at Julian.

"I hardly know whether I ought to tell you, miss."

Julian turned away to leave the library. Mercy stopped him by a motion of her hand.

"You know that I shall not get you into any trouble," she said to the maid. "And you may speak quite safely before Mr. Julian Gray."

Thus re-assured, the maid spoke.

"To own the truth, miss, I heard Mr. Holmcroft in my lady's room. His voice sounded as if he was angry. I may say they were both angry—Mr. Holmcroft and my lady." (She turned to Julian.) "And just before her ladyship came out, sir, I heard your name, as if it was you they were having words about. I can't say exactly what it was; I hadn't time to hear. And I didn't listen, miss; the door was ajar; and the voices were so loud nobody could help hearing them."

It was useless to detain the woman any longer. Having given her leave to withdraw, Mercy turned to Julian.

"Why were they quarreling about you?" she asked.

Julian pointed to the unopened letter in her hand.

"The answer to your question may be there," he said. "Read the letter while you have the chance. And if I can advise you, say so at once."

With a strange reluctance she opened the envelope. With a sinking heart she read the lines in which Lady Janet, as "mother and friend," commanded her absolutely to suppress the confession which she had pledged herself to make in the sacred interests of justice and truth. A low cry of despair escaped her, as the cruel complication in her position revealed itself in all its unmerited hardship. "Oh, Lady Janet, Lady Janet!" she thought, "there was but one trial more left in my hard lot—and it comes to me from you!"

She handed the letter to Julian. He took it from her in silence. His pale complexion turned paler still as he read it. His eyes rested on her compassionately as he handed it back.

"To my mind," he said, "Lady Janet herself sets all further doubt at rest. Her letter tells me what she wanted when she sent for Horace, and why my name was mentioned between them."

"Tell me!" cried Mercy, eagerly.

He did not immediately answer her. He sat down again in the chair by her side, and pointed to the letter.

"Has Lady Janet shaken your resolution?" he asked.

"She has strengthened my resolution," Mercy answered. "She has added a new bitterness to my remorse."

She did not mean it harshly, but the reply sounded harshly in Julian's

244

ears. It stirred the generous impulses, which were the strongest impulses in his nature. He who had once pleaded with Mercy for compassionate consideration for herself now pleaded with her for compassionate consideration for Lady Janet. With persuasive gentleness he drew a little nearer, and laid his hand on her arm.

"Don't judge her harshly," he said. "She is wrong, miserably wrong. She has recklessly degraded herself; she has recklessly tempted you. Still, is it generous—is it even just—to hold her responsible for deliberate sin? She is at the close of her days; she can feel no new affection; she can never replace you. View her position in that light, and you will see (as I see) that it is no base motive which has led her astray. Think of her wounded heart and her wasted life—and say to yourself forgivingly, She loves me!"

Mercy's eyes filled with tears.

"I do say it!" she answered. "Not forgivingly—it is I who have need of forgiveness. I say it gratefully when I think of her—I say it with shame and sorrow when I think of myself."

He took her hand for the first time. He looked, guiltlessly looked, at her downcast face. He spoke as he had spoken at the memorable interview between them which had made a new woman of her.

"I can imagine no crueler trial," he said, "than the trial that is now before you. The benefactress to whom you owe everything asks nothing from you but your silence. The person whom you have wronged is no longer present to stimulate your resolution to speak. Horace himself (unless I am entirely mistaken) will not hold you to the explanation that you have promised. The temptation to keep your false position in this house is, I do not scruple to say, all but irresistible. Sister and friend! can you still justify my faith in you? Will you still own the truth, without the base fear of discovery to drive you to it?"

She lifted her head, with the steady light of resolution shining again in her grand, gray eyes. Her low, sweet voice answered him, without a faltering note in it,

"I will!"

"You will do justice to the woman whom you have wronged—unworthy as she is; powerless as she is to expose you?"

"I will!"

"You will sacrifice everything you have gained by the fraud to the sacred duty of atonement? You will suffer anything—even though you offend the second mother who has loved you and sinned for you—rather than suffer the degradation of yourself?"

Her hand closed firmly on his. Again, and for the last time, she answered,

"I will!"

His voice had not trembled yet. It failed him now. His next words were spoken in faint whispering tones—to himself; not to her.

"Thank God for this day!" he said. "I have been of some service to one of the noblest of God's creatures!"

Some subtle influence, as he spoke, passed from his hand to hers. It trembled through her nerves; it entwined itself mysteriously with the finest sensibilities in her nature; it softly opened her heart to a first vague surmising of the devotion that she had inspired in him. A faint glow of color, lovely in its faintness, stole over her face and neck. Her breathing quickened tremblingly. She drew her hand away from him, and sighed when she had released it.

He rose suddenly to his feet and left her, without a word or a look, walking slowly down the length of the room. When he turned and came back to her, his face was composed; he was master of himself again.

Mercy was the first to speak. She turned the conversation from herself by reverting to the proceedings in Lady Janet's room.

"You spoke of Horace just now," she said, "in terms which surprised me. You appeared to think that he would not hold me to my explanation. Is that one of the conclusions which you draw from Lady Janet's letter?"

"Most assuredly," Julian answered. "You will see the conclusion as I see it if we return for a moment to Grace Roseberry's departure from the house."

Mercy interrupted him there. "Can you guess," she asked, "how Lady Janet prevailed upon her to go?"

"I hardly like to own it," said Julian. "There is an expression in the letter which suggests to me that Lady Janet has offered her money, and that she has taken the bribe."

"Oh, I can't think that!"

"Let us return to Horace. Miss Roseberry once out of the house, but one serious obstacle is left in Lady Janet's way. That obstacle is Horace Holmcroft."

"How is Horace an obstacle?"

"He is an obstacle in this sense. He is under an engagement to marry you in a week's time; and Lady Janet is determined to keep him (as she is determined to keep every one else) in ignorance of the truth. She will do that without scruple. But the inbred sense of honor in her is not utterly silenced yet. She cannot, she dare not, let Horace make you his wife under the false impression that you are Colonel Roseberry's daughter. You see the situation? On the one hand, she won't enlighten him. On the other hand, she cannot allow him to marry you blindfold. In this emergency what is she to do? There is but one alternative that I can discover. She must persuade Horace (or she must irritate Horace) into acting for himself, and breaking off the engagement on his own responsibility."

Mercy stopped him. "Impossible!" she cried, warmly. "Impossible!"

"Look again at her letter," Julian rejoined. "It tells, you plainly that you need fear no embarrassment when you next meet Horace. If words mean anything, those words mean that he will not claim from you the confidence which you have promised to repose in him. On what condition is it possible for him to abstain from doing that? On the one condition that you have ceased to represent the first and foremost interest of his life."

Mercy still held firm. "You are wronging Lady Janet," she said.

Julian smiled sadly.

"Try to look at it," he answered, "from Lady Janet's point of view. Do you suppose she sees anything derogatory to her in attempting to break off the marriage? I will answer for it, she believes she is doing you a kindness. In one sense it would be a kindness to spare you the shame of a humiliating confession, and to save you (possibly) from being rejected to your face by the man you love. In my opinion, the thing is done already. I have reasons of my own for believing that my aunt will succeed far more easily than she could anticipate. Horace's temper will help her."

Mercy's mind began to yield to him, in spite of herself.

"What do you mean by Horace's temper?" she inquired.

"Must you ask me that?" he said, drawing back a little from her.

"I must."

"I mean by Horace's temper, Horace's unworthy distrust of the interest that I feel in you."

She instantly understood him. And more than that, she secretly admired him for the scrupulous delicacy with which he had expressed himself. Another man would not have thought of sparing her in that way. Another man would have said, plainly, "Horace is jealous of me."

Julian did not wait for her to answer him. He considerately went on.

"For the reason that I have just mentioned," he said, "Horace will be easily irritated into taking a course which, in his calmer moments, nothing would induce him to adopt. Until I heard what your maid said to you I had thought (for your sake) of retiring before he joined you here. Now I know that my name has been introduced, and has made mischief upstairs, I feel the necessity (for your sake again) of meeting Horace and his temper face to face before you see him. Let me, if I can, prepare him to hear you without any angry feeling in his mind toward you. Do you object to retire to the next room for a few minutes in the event of his coming back to the library?"

Mercy's courage instantly rose with the emergency. She refused to leave the two men together.

"Don't think me insensible to your kindness," she said. "If I leave you with Horace I may expose you to insult. I refuse to do that. What makes you doubt his coming back?"

"His prolonged absence makes me doubt it," Julian replied. "In my belief, the marriage is broken off. He may go as Grace Roseberry has gone. You may never see him again."

The instant the opinion was uttered, it was practically contradicted by the man himself. Horace opened the library door.

CHAPTER XXV. THE CONFESSION

HE stopped just inside the door. His first look was for Mercy; his is second look was for Julian.

"I knew it!" he said, with an assumption of sardonic composure. "If I could only have persuaded Lady Janet to bet, I should have won a hundred pounds." He advanced to Julian, with a sudden change from irony to anger. "Would you like to hear what the bet was?" he asked.

"I should prefer seeing you able to control yourself in the presence of this lady," Julian answered, quietly.

"I offered to lay Lady Janet two hundred pounds to one," Horace proceeded, "that I should find you here, making love to Miss Roseberry behind my back."

Mercy interfered before Julian could reply.

"If you cannot speak without insulting one of us," she said, "permit me to request that you will not address yourself to Mr. Julian Gray."

Horace bowed to her with a mockery of respect.

"Pray don't alarm yourself—I am pledged to be scrupulously civil to both of you," he said. "Lady Janet only allowed me to leave her on condition of my promising to behave with perfect politeness. What else can I do? I have two privileged people to deal with—a parson and a woman. The parson's profession protects him, and the woman's sex protects her. You have got me at a disadvantage, and you both of you know it. I beg to apologize if I have forgotten the clergyman's profession and the lady's sex."

"You have forgotten more than that," said Julian. "You have forgotten that you were born a gentleman and bred a man of honor. So far as I am concerned, I don't ask you to remember that I am a clergyman—I obtrude my profession on nobody—I only ask you to remember your birth and your breeding. It is quite bad enough to cruelly and unjustly suspect an old friend who has never forgotten what he owes to you and to himself. But it is still more unworthy of you to acknowledge those suspicions in the hearing of a woman whom your own choice has doubly bound you to respect."

He stopped. The two eyed each other for a moment in silence.

It was impossible for Mercy to look at them, as she was looking now, without drawing the inevitable comparison between the manly force and dignity of Julian and the womanish malice and irritability of Horace. A last faithful impulse of loyalty toward the man to whom she had been betrothed impelled her to part them, before Horace had hopelessly degraded himself in her estimation by contrast with Julian.

"You had better wait to speak to me," she said to him, "until we are alone."

"Certainly," Horace answered with a sneer, "if Mr. Julian Gray will permit it."

Mercy turned to Julian, with a look which said plainly, "Pity us both, and leave us!"

"Do you wish me to go?" he asked.

"Add to all your other kindnesses to me," she answered. "Wait for me in that room."

She pointed to the door that led into the dining-room. Julian hesitated.

"You promise to let me know it if I can be of the smallest service to you?" he said.

"Yes, yes!" She followed him as he withdrew, and added, rapidly, in a whisper, "Leave the door ajar!"

He made no answer. As she returned to Horace he entered the dining-room. The one concession he could make to her he did make. He closed the door so noiselessly that not even her quick hearing could detect that he had shut it.

Mercy spoke to Horace, without waiting to let him speak first.

"I have promised you an explanation of my conduct," she said, in accents that trembled a little in spite of herself. "I am ready to perform my promise."

"I have a question to ask you before you do that," he rejoined. "Can you speak the truth?"

"I am waiting to speak the truth."

"I will give you an opportunity. Are you or are you not in love with Julian Gray?"

"You ought to be ashamed to ask the question!"

"Is that your only answer?"

"I have never been unfaithful to you, Horace, even in thought. If I had not been true to you, should I feel my position as you see I feel it now?"

He smiled bitterly. "I have my own opinion of your fidelity and of his honor," he said. "You couldn't even send him into the next room without whispering to him first. Never mind that now. At least you know that Julian Gray is in love with you."

"Mr. Julian Gray has never breathed a word of it to me."

"A man can show a woman that he loves her, without saying it in words."

Mercy's power of endurance began to fail her. Not even Grace Roseberry had spoken more insultingly to her of Julian than Horace was speaking now. "Whoever says that of Mr. Julian Gray, lies!" she answered, warmly.

"Then Lady Janet lies," Horace retorted.

"Lady Janet never said it! Lady Janet is incapable of saying it!"

"She may not have said it in so many words; but she never denied it when I said it. I reminded her of the time when Julian Gray first heard from me that I was going to marry you: he was so overwhelmed that he was barely capable of being civil to me. Lady Janet was present, and could not deny it. I asked her if she had observed, since then, signs of a confidential understanding between you two. She could not deny the signs. I asked if she had ever found you two together. She could not deny that she had found you together, this very day, under circumstances which justified suspicion. Yes! yes! Look as angry as you like! you don't know what has been going on upstairs. Lady Janet is bent on breaking off our engagement—and Julian Gray is at the bottom of it."

As to Julian, Horace was utterly wrong. But as to Lady Janet, he echoed the warning words which Julian himself had spoken to Mercy. She was staggered, but she still held to her own opinion. "I don't believe it," she said, firmly.

He advanced a step, and fixed his angry eyes on her searchingly.

"Do you know why Lady Janet sent for me?" he asked.

"No."

"Then I will tell you. Lady Janet is a stanch friend of yours, there is no denying that. She wished to inform me that she had altered her mind about your promised explanation of your conduct. She said, 'Reflection has convinced me that no explanation is required; I have laid my positive commands on my adopted daughter that no explanation shall take place.' Has she done that?"

"Yes."

"Now observe! I waited till she had finished, and then I said, 'What have I to do with this?' Lady Janet has one merit—she speaks out. 'You are to do as I do,' she answered. 'You are to consider that no explanation is required, and you are to consign the whole matter to oblivion from this time forth.' 'Are you serious?' I asked. 'Quite serious.' 'In that case I have to inform your ladyship that you insist on more than you may suppose: you insist on my breaking my engagement to Miss Roseberry. Either I am to have the explanation that she has promised me, or I refuse to marry her.' How do you think Lady Janet took that? She shut up her lips, and she spread out her hands, and she looked at me as much as to say, 'Just as you please! Refuse if you like; it's nothing to me!'"

He paused for a moment. Mercy remained silent, on her side: she

253

foresaw what was coming. Mistaken in supposing that Horace had left the house, Julian had, beyond all doubt, been equally in error in concluding that he had been entrapped into breaking off the engagement upstairs.

"Do you understand me so far?" Horace asked.

"I understand you perfectly."

"I will not trouble you much longer," he resumed. "I said to Lady Janet, 'Be so good as to answer me in plain words. Do you still insist on closing Miss Roseberry's lips?' 'I still insist,' she answered. 'No explanation is required. If you are base enough to suspect your betrothed wife, I am just enough to believe in my adopted daughter.' I replied—and I beg you will give your best attention to what I am now going to say—I replied to that, 'It is not fair to charge me with suspecting her. I don't understand her confidential relations with Julian Gray, and I don't understand her language and conduct in the presence of the police officer. I claim it as my right to be satisfied on both those points—in the character of the man who is to marry her.' There was my answer. I spare you all that followed. I only repeat what I said to Lady Janet. She has commanded you to be silent. If you obey her commands, I owe it to myself and I owe it to my family to release you from your engagement. Choose between your duty to Lady Janet and your duty to Me."

He had mastered his temper at last: he spoke with dignity, and he spoke to the point. His position was unassailable; he claimed nothing but his right.

"My choice was made," Mercy answered, "when I gave you my promise upstairs."

She waited a little, struggling to control herself on the brink of the terrible revelation that was coming. Her eyes dropped before his; her heart beat faster and faster; but she struggled bravely. With a desperate courage she faced the position. "If you are ready to listen," she went on, "I am ready to tell you why I insisted on having the police officer sent out of the house."

Horace held up his hand warningly.

"Stop!" he said; "that is not all."

His infatuated jealousy of Julian (fatally misinterpreting her agitation) distrusted her at the very outset. She had limited herself to clearing up the one question of her interference with the officer of justice. The other question of her relations with Julian she had deliberately passed over. Horace instantly drew his own ungenerous conclusion.

"Let us not misunderstand one another," he said. "The explanation of your conduct in the other room is only one of the explanations which you owe me. You have something else to account for. Let us begin with that, if you please."

She looked at him in unaffected surprise.

"What else have I to account for?" she asked.

He again repeated his reply to Lady Janet.

"I have told you already," he said. "I don't understand your confidential relations with Julian Gray."

Mercy's color rose; Mercy's eyes began to brighten.

"Don't return to that!" she cried, with an irrepressible outbreak of disgust. "Don't, for God's sake, make me despise you at such a moment as this!"

His obstinacy only gathered fresh encouragement from that appeal to his better sense.

"I insist on returning to it."

She had resolved to bear anything from him—as her fit punishment for the deception of which she had been guilty. But it was not in womanhood (at the moment when the first words of her confession were trembling on her lips) to endure Horace's unworthy suspicion of her. She rose from her seat and met his eye firmly.

"I refuse to degrade myself, and to degrade Mr. Julian Gray, by answering you," she said.

"Consider what you are doing," he rejoined. "Change your mind, before it is too late!"

"You have had my reply."

Those resolute words, that steady resistance, seemed to infuriate him. He caught her roughly by the arm.

"You are as false as hell!" he cried. "It's all over between you and me!"

The loud threatening tone in which he had spoken penetrated through the closed door of the dining-room. The door instantly opened. Julian returned to the library.

He had just set foot in the room, when there was a knock at the other door—the door that opened on the hall. One of the men-servants appeared, with a telegraphic message in his hand. Mercy was the first to see it. It was the Matron's answer to the letter which she had sent to the Refuge.

"For Mr. Julian Gray?" she asked.

"Yes, miss."

"Give it to me."

She signed to the man to withdraw, and herself gave the telegram to Julian. "It is addressed to you, at my request," she said. "You will recognize the name of the person who sends it, and you will find a message in it for me."

Horace interfered before Julian could open the telegram.

"Another private understanding between you!" he said. "Give me that telegram."

Julian looked at him with quiet contempt.

"It is directed to Me," he answered—and opened the envelope.

The message inside was expressed in these terms: "I am as deeply interested in her as you are. Say that I have received her letter, and that I welcome her back to the Refuge with all my heart. I have business this evening in the neighborhood. I will call for her myself at Mablethorpe House."

The message explained itself. Of her own free-will she had made the expiation complete! Of her own free-will she was going back to the martyrdom of her old life! Bound as he knew himself to be to let no compromising word or action escape him in the presence of Horace, the irrepressible expression of Julian's admiration glowed in his eyes as they rested on Mercy. Horace detected the look. He sprang forward and tried to snatch the telegram out of Julian's hand.

"Give it to me!" he said. "I will have it!"

Julian silently put him back at arms-length.

Maddened with rage, he lifted his hand threateningly. "Give it to me!" he repeated between his set teeth, "or it will be the worse for you!"

"Give it to me!" said Mercy, suddenly placing herself between them.

Julian gave it. She turned, and offered it to Horace, looking at him with a steady eye, holding it out to him with a steady hand.

"Read it," she said.

Julian's generous nature pitied the man who had insulted him. Julian's great heart only remembered the friend of former times.

"Spare him!" he said to Mercy. "Remember he is unprepared."

She neither answered nor moved. Nothing stirred the horrible torpor of her resignation to her fate. She knew that the time had come.

Julian appealed to Horace.

"Don't read it!" he cried. "Hear what she has to say to you first!"

Horace's hand answered him with a contemptuous gesture. Horace's eyes devoured, word by word, the Matron's message.

He looked up when he had read it through. There was a ghastly change in his face as he turned it on Mercy.

She stood between the two men like a statue. The life in her seemed to have died out, except in her eyes. Her eyes rested on Horace with a steady, glittering calmness.

The silence was only broken by the low murmuring of Julian's voice. His face was hidden in his hands—he was praying for them.

Horace spoke, laying his finger on the telegram. His voice had changed with the change in his face. The tone was low and trembling: no one would have recognized it as the tone of Horace's voice.

"What does this mean?" he said to Mercy. "It can't be for you?"

"It is for me."

"What have You to do with a Refuge?"

Without a change in her face, without a movement in her limbs, she spoke the fatal words:

"I have come from a Refuge, and I am going back to a Refuge. Mr. Horace Holmcroft, I am Mercy Merrick."

CHAPTER XXVI. GREAT HEART AND LITTLE HEART.

THERE was a pause.

The moments passed—and not one of the three moved. The moments passed—and not one of the three spoke. Insensibly the words of supplication died away on Julian's lips. Even his energy failed to sustain him, tried as it now was by the crushing oppression of suspense. The first trifling movement which suggested the idea of change, and which so brought with it the first vague sense of relief, came from Mercy. Incapable of sustaining the prolonged effort of standing, she drew back a little and took a chair. No outward manifestation of emotion escaped her. There she sat—with the death-like torpor of resignation in her face—waiting her sentence in silence from the man at whom she had hurled the whole terrible confession of the truth in one sentence!

Julian lifted his head as she moved. He looked at Horace, and advancing a few steps, looked again. There was fear in his face, as he suddenly turned it toward Mercy.

"Speak to him!" he said, in a whisper. "Rouse him, before it's too late!"

She moved mechanically in her chair; she looked mechanically at Julian.

"What more have I to say to him?" she asked, in faint, weary tones. "Did I not tell him everything when I told him my name?"

The natural sound of her voice might have failed to affect Horace. The altered sound of it roused him. He approached Mercy's chair, with a dull surprise in his face, and put his hand, in a weak, wavering way, on her shoulder. In that position he stood for a while, looking down at her in silence.

The one idea in him that found its way outward to expression was the idea of Julian. Without moving his hand, without looking up from Mercy, he spoke for the first time since the shock had fallen on him.

"Where is Julian?" he asked, very quietly.

"I am here, Horace—close by you."

"Will you do me a service?"

"Certainly. How can I help you?"

He considered a little before he replied. His hand left Mercy's shoulder, and went up to his head—then dropped at his side. His next words were spoken in a sadly helpless, bewildered way.

"I have an idea, Julian, that I have been somehow to blame. I said some hard words to you. It was a little while since. I don't clearly remember what it was all about. My temper has been a good deal tried in this house; I have never been used to the sort of thing that goes on here—secrets and mysteries, and hateful low-lived quarrels. We have no secrets and mysteries at home. And as for quarrels—ridiculous! My mother and my sisters are highly bred women (you know them); gentlewomen, in the best sense of the word. When I am with them I have no anxieties. I am not harassed at home by doubts of who people are, and confusion about names, and so on. I suspect the contrast weighs a little on my mind and upsets it. They make me over-suspicious among them here, and it ends in my feeling doubts and fears that I can't get over: doubts about you and fears about myself. I have got a fear about myself now. I want you to help me. Shall I make an apology first?"

"Don't say a word. Tell me what I can do."

He turned his face toward Julian for the first time.

"Just look at me," he said. "Does it strike you that I am at all wrong in my mind? Tell me the truth, old fellow."

"Your nerves are a little shaken, Horace. Nothing more."

He considered again after that reply, his eyes remaining anxiously fixed on Julian's face.

"My nerves are a little shaken," he repeated. "That is true; I feel they are shaken. I should like, if you don't mind, to make sure that it's no worse. Will you help me to try if my memory is all right?"

"I will do anything you like."

"Ah! you are a good fellow, Julian—and a clear-headed fellow too, which is very important just now. Look here! I say it's about a week since the troubles began in this house. Do you say so too?"

"Yes."

"The troubles came in with the coming of a woman from Germany, a stranger to us, who behaved very violently in the dining-room there. Am I right, so far?"

"Quite right."

"The woman carried matters with a high hand. She claimed Colonel Roseberry—I wish to be strictly accurate—she claimed the late Colonel Roseberry as her father. She told a tiresome story about her having been robbed of her papers and her name by an impostor who had personated her. She said the name of the impostor was Mercy Merrick. And she afterward put the climax to it all: she pointed to the lady who is engaged to be my wife, and declared that she was Mercy Merrick. Tell me again, is that right or wrong?"

Julian answered him as before. He went on, speaking more confidently and more excitedly than he had spoken yet.

"Now attend to this, Julian. I am going to pass from my memory of what happened a week ago to my memory of what happened five minutes since. You were present; I want to know if you heard it too." He paused, and, without taking his eyes off Julian, pointed backward to Mercy. "There is the lady who is engaged to marry me," he resumed. "Did I, or did I not, hear her say that she had come out of a Refuge, and that she was going back to a Refuge? Did I, or did I not, hear her own to my face that her name was Mercy Merrick? Answer me, Julian. My good friend, answer me, for the sake of old times."

His voice faltered as he spoke those imploring words. Under the dull blank of his face there appeared the first signs of emotion slowly forcing its way outward. The stunned mind was reviving faintly. Julian saw his opportunity of aiding the recovery, and seized it. He took Horace gently by the arm, and pointed to Mercy.

"There is your answer!" he said. "Look!—and pity her."

She had not once interrupted them while they had been speaking: she had changed her position again, and that was all. There was a writing-table at the side of her chair; her outstretched arms rested on it. Her head had dropped on her arms, and her face was hidden. Julian's judgment had not misled him; the utter self-abandonment of her attitude answered Horace as no human language could have answered him. He looked at her. A quick spasm of pain passed across his face. He turned once more to the faithful friend who had forgiven him. His head fell on Julian's shoulder, and he burst into tears.

Mercy started wildly to her feet, and looked at the two men.

"O God" she cried, "what have I done!"

Julian quieted her by a motion of his hand.

"You have helped me to save him," he said. "Let his tears have their way. Wait."

He put one arm round Horace to support him. The manly tenderness of the action, the complete and noble pardon of past injuries which it implied, touched Mercy to the heart. She went back to her chair. Again shame and sorrow overpowered her, and again she hid her face from view.

Julian led Horace to a seat, and silently waited by him until he had recovered his self-control. He gratefully took the kind hand that had sustained him: he said, simply, almost boyishly, "Thank you, Julian. I am better now."

"Are you composed enough to listen to what is said to you?" Julian asked.

"Yes. Do you wish to speak to me?"

Julian left him without immediately replying, and returned to Mercy.

"The time has come," he said. "Tell him all—truly, unreservedly, as you would tell it to me."

She shuddered as he spoke. "Have I not told him enough?" she asked. "Do you want me to break his heart? Look at him! Look what I have done already!"

Horace shrank from the ordeal as Mercy shrank from it.

"No, no! I can't listen to it! I daren't listen to it!" he cried, and rose to leave the room.

Julian had taken the good work in hand: he never faltered over it for an instant. Horace had loved her—how dearly Julian now knew for the first time. The bare possibility that she might earn her pardon if she was allowed to plead her own cause was a possibility still left. To let her win on Horace to forgive her, was death to the love that still filled his heart in secret. But he never hesitated. With a resolution which the weaker man was powerless to resist, he took him by the arm and led him back to his place.

"For her sake, and for your sake, you shall not condemn her unheard," he said to Horace, firmly. "One temptation to deceive you after another has tried her, and she has resisted them all. With no discovery to fear, with a letter from the benefactress who loves her commanding her to be silent, with everything that a woman values in this world to lose, if she owns what she has done—this woman, for the truth's sake, has spoken the truth. Does she deserve nothing at your hands in return for that? Respect her, Horace—and hear her."

Horace yielded. Julian turned to Mercy.

"You have allowed me to guide you so far," he said. "Will you allow me to guide you still?"

Her eyes sank before his; her bosom rose and fell rapidly. His influence over her maintained its sway. She bowed her head in speechless submission.

"Tell him," Julian proceeded, in accents of entreaty, not of command— "tell him what your life has been. Tell him how you were tried and tempted, with no friend near to speak the words which might have saved you. And then," he added, raising her from the chair, "let him judge you—if he can!"

He attempted to lead her across the room to the place which Horace occupied. But her submission had its limits. Half-way to the place she stopped, and refused to go further. Julian offered her a chair. She declined to take it. Standing with one hand on the back of the chair, she waited for the word from Horace which would permit her to speak. She was resigned to the ordeal. Her face was calm; her mind was clear. The hardest of all humiliations to endure—the humiliation of acknowledging her name—she had passed through. Nothing remained but to show her gratitude to Julian by acceding to his wishes, and to ask pardon of Horace before they parted forever. In a little while the Matron would arrive at the house—and then it would be over.

Unwillingly Horace looked at her. Their eyes met. He broke out suddenly with something of his former violence.

"I can't realize it even now!" he cried. "Is it true that you are not Grace Roseberry? Don't look at me! Say in one word—Yes or No!"

She answered him, humbly and sadly, "Yes."

"You have done what that woman accused you of doing? Am I to believe that?"

"You are to believe it, sir."

All the weakness of Horace's character disclosed itself when she made that reply.

"Infamous!" he exclaimed. "What excuse can you make for the cruel deception you have practiced on me? Too bad! too bad! There can be no excuse for you!"

She accepted his reproaches with unshaken resignation. "I have deserved it!" was all she said to herself, "I have deserved it!"

Julian interposed once more in Mercy's defense.

"Wait till you are sure there is no excuse for her, Horace," he said, quietly. "Grant her justice, if you can grant no more. I leave you together."

264

He advanced toward the door of the dining-room. Horace's weakness disclosed itself once more.

"Don't leave me alone with her!" he burst out. "The misery of it is more than I can bear!"

Julian looked at Mercy. Her face brightened faintly. That momentary expression of relief told him how truly he would be befriending her if he consented to remain in the room. A position of retirement was offered to him by a recess formed by the central bay-window of the library. If he occupied this place, they could see or not see that he was present, as their own inclinations might decide them.

"I will stay with you, Horace, as long as you wish me to be here." Having answered in those terms, he stopped as he passed Mercy, on his way to the window. His quick and kindly insight told him that he might still be of some service to her. A hint from him might show her the shortest and the easiest way of making her confession. Delicately and briefly he gave her the hint. "The first time I met you," he said, "I saw that your life had had its troubles. Let us hear how those troubles began."

He withdrew to his place in the recess. For the first time, since the fatal evening when she and Grace Roseberry had met in the French cottage, Mercy Merrick looked back into the purgatory on earth of her past life, and told her sad story simply and truly in these words.

CHAPTER XXVII. MAGDALEN'S APPRENTICESHIP.

"MR. JULIAN GRAY has asked me to tell him, and to tell you, Mr. Holmcroft, how my troubles began. They began before my recollection. They began with my birth.

"My mother (as I have heard her say) ruined her prospects, when she was quite a young girl, by a marriage with one of her father's servants—the groom who rode out with her. She suffered, poor creature, the usual penalty of such conduct as hers. After a short time she and her husband were separated—on the condition of her sacrificing to the man whom she had married the whole of the little fortune that she possessed in her right.

"Gaining her freedom, my mother had to gain her daily bread next. Her family refused to take her back. She attached herself to a company of strolling players.

"She was earning a bare living in this way, when my father accidentally met with her. He was a man of high rank, proud of his position, and well known in the society of that time for his many accomplishments and his refined tastes. My mother's beauty fascinated him. He took her from the strolling players, and surrounded her with every luxury that a woman could desire in a house of her own.

"I don't know how long they lived together. I only know that my father, at the time of my first recollections, had abandoned her. She had excited his suspicions of her fidelity—suspicions which cruelly wronged her, as she declared to her dying day. I believed her, because she was my mother. But I cannot expect others to do as I did—I can only repeat what she said. My father left her absolutely penniless. He never saw her again; and he refused to go to her when she sent to him in her last moments on earth.

"She was back again among the strolling players when I first remember her. It was not an unhappy time for me. I was the favorite pet and plaything of the poor actors. They taught me to sing and to dance at an age when other children are just beginning to learn to read. At five years old I was in what is called 'the profession,' and had made my poor little reputation in booths at country fairs. As early as that, Mr. Holmcroft, I had begun to live under an assumed name—the prettiest name they could invent for me 'to look well in the bills.' It was sometimes a hard struggle for us, in bad seasons, to keep body and soul together. Learning to sing and dance in public often meant learning to bear hunger and cold in private, when I was apprenticed to the stage. And yet I have lived to look back on my days with the strolling players as the happiest days of my life!

"I was ten years old when the first serious misfortune that I can remember fell upon me. My mother died, worn out in the prime of her life. And not long afterward the strolling company, brought to the end of its resources by a succession of bad seasons, was broken up.

"I was left on the world, a nameless, penniless outcast, with one fatal inheritance—God knows, I can speak of it without vanity, after what I have gone through!—the inheritance of my mother's beauty.

"My only friends were the poor starved-out players. Two of them (husband and wife) obtained engagements in another company, and I was included in the bargain The new manager by whom I was employed was a drunkard and a brute. One night I made a trifling mistake in the course of the performances—and I was savagely beaten for it. Perhaps I had inherited some of my father's spirit—without, I hope, also inheriting my father's pitiless nature. However that may be, I resolved (no matter what became of me) never again to serve the man who had beaten me. I unlocked the door of our miserable lodging at daybreak the next morning; and, at ten years old, with my little bundle in my hand, I faced the world alone.

"My mother had confided to me, in her last moments, my father's name and the address of his house in London. 'He may feel some compassion for you' (she said), 'though he feels none for me: try him.' I had a few shillings, the last pitiful remains of my wages, in my pocket; and I was not far from London. But I never went near my father: child as I was, I would have starved and died rather than go to him. I had loved my mother dearly; and I hated the man who had turned his back on her when she lay on her deathbed. It made no difference to Me that he happened to be my father.

"Does this confession revolt you? You look at me, Mr. Holmcroft, as if it did.

"Think a little, sir. Does what I have just said condemn me as a heartless creature, even in my earliest years? What is a father to a child—when the child has never sat on his knee, and never had a kiss or a present from him? If we had met in the street, we should not have known each other. Perhaps in after-days, when I was starving in London, I may have begged of my father without knowing it; and he may have thrown his daughter a penny to get rid of her, without knowing it either! What is there sacred in the relations between father and child, when they are such relations as these? Even the flowers of the field cannot grow without light and air to help them! How is a child's love to grow, with nothing to help it?

"My small savings would have been soon exhausted, even if I had been old enough and strong enough to protect them myself. As things were, my few shillings were taken from me by gypsies. I had no reason to complain. They gave me food and the shelter of their tents, and they made me of use to them in various ways. After a while hard times came to the gypsies, as they had come to the strolling players. Some of them were imprisoned; the rest were dispersed. It was the season for hop-gathering at the time. I got employment among the hop-pickers next; and that done, I went to London with my new friends.

"I have no wish to weary and pain you by dwelling on this part of my childhood in detail. It will be enough if I tell you that I sank lower and lower until I ended in selling matches in the street. My mother's legacy got me many a sixpence which my matches would never have charmed out of the pockets of strangers if I had been an ugly child. My face. which was destined to be my greatest misfortune in after-years, was my best friend in those days.

"Is there anything, Mr. Holmcroft, in the life I am now trying to describe which reminds you of a day when we were out walking together not long since?

"I surprised and offended you, I remember; and it was not possible for me to explain my conduct at the time. Do you recollect the little wandering girl, with the miserable faded nosegay in her hand, who ran after us, and begged for a half-penny? I shocked you by bursting out crying when the child asked us to buy her a bit of bread. Now you know why I was so sorry for her. Now you know why I offended you the next day by breaking an engagement with your mother and sisters, and going to see that child in her wretched home. After what I have confessed, you will admit that my poor little sister in adversity had the first claim on me.

"Let me go on. I am sorry if I have distressed you. Let me go on.

"The forlorn wanderers of the streets have (as I found it) one way always open to them of presenting their sufferings to the notice of their rich and charitable fellow-creatures. They have only to break the law—and they make a public appearance in a court of justice. If the circumstances connected with their offense are of an interesting kind, they gain a second advantage: they are advertised all over England by a report in the newspapers.

"Yes! even I have my knowledge of the law. I know that it completely overlooked me as long as I respected it. But on two different occasions it became my best friend when I set it at defiance! My first fortunate offense was committed when I was just twelve years old.

"It was evening time. I was half dead with starvation; the rain was falling; the night was coming on. I begged—openly, loudly, as only a hungry child can beg. An old lady in a carriage at a shop door complained of my importunity. The policeman did his duty. The law gave me a supper and shelter at the station-house that night. I appeared at the police court, and, questioned by the magistrate, I told my story truly. It was the every-day story of thousands of children like me; but it had one element of interest in it. I confessed to having had a father (he was then dead) who had been a man of rank; and I owned (just as openly as I owned everything else) that I had never applied to him for help, in resentment of his treatment of my mother. This incident was new, I suppose; it led to the appearance of my 'case' in the newspapers. The reporters further served my interests by describing me as 'pretty and interesting.' Subscriptions were sent to the court. A benevolent married couple, in a respectable sphere of life, visited the workhouse to see me. I produced a favorable impression on them—especially on the wife. I was literally friendless; I had no unwelcome relatives to follow me and claim me. The wife was childless; the husband was a good-natured man. It ended in their taking me away with them to try me in service.

"I have always felt the aspiration, no matter how low I may have fallen, to struggle upward to a position above me; to rise, in spite of fortune, superior to my lot in life. Perhaps some of my father's pride may be at the root of this restless feeling in me. It seems to be a part of my nature. It brought me into this house—and it will go with me out of this house. Is it my curse or my blessing? I am not able to decide.

"On the first night when I slept in my new home I said to myself, 'They have taken me to be their servant: I will be something more than that—they shall end in taking me for their child.' Before I had been a week in the house I was the wife's favorite companion in the absence of her husband at his place of business. She was a highly accomplished woman, greatly her husband's superior in cultivation, and, unfortunately for herself, also his superior in years. The love was all on her side. Excepting certain occasions on which he roused her jealousy, they lived together on sufficiently friendly terms. She was one of the many wives who resign themselves to be disappointed in their husbands—and he was one of the many husbands who never know what their wives really think of them. Her one great happiness was in teaching me. I was eager to learn; I made rapid progress. At my pliant age I soon acquired the refinements of language and manner which characterized my mistress. It is only the truth to say that the cultivation which has made me capable of personating a lady was her work.

"For three happy years I lived under that friendly roof. I was between fifteen and sixteen years of age, when the fatal inheritance from my mother cast its first shadow on my life. One miserable day the wife's motherly love for me changed in an instant to the jealous hatred that never forgives. Can you guess the reason? The husband fell in love with me.

"I was innocent; I was blameless. He owned it himself to the clergyman who was with him at his death. By that time years had passed. It was too late to justify me.

"He was at an age (when I was under his care) when men are usually supposed to regard women with tranquillity, if not with indifference. It had been the habit of years with me to look on him as my second father. In my innocent ignorance of the feeling which really inspired him, I permitted him to indulge in little paternal familiarities with me, which inflamed his guilty passion. His wife discovered him—not I. No words can describe my astonishment and my horror when the first outbreak of her indignation forced on me the knowledge of the truth. On my knees I declared myself guiltless. On my knees I implored her to do justice to my purity and my youth. At other times the sweetest and the most considerate of women, jealousy had now transformed her to a perfect fury. She accused me of deliberately encouraging him; she declared she would turn me out of the house with her own hands. Like other easy-tempered men, her husband had reserves of anger in him which it was dangerous to provoke. When his wife lifted her hand against me, he lost all self-control, on his side. He openly told her that life was worth nothing to him without me. He openly avowed his resolution to go with me when I left the house. The maddened woman seized him by the arm—I saw that, and saw no more. I ran out into the street, panic-stricken. A cab was passing. I got into it before he could open the house door, and drove to the only place of refuge I could think of—a small shop, kept by the widowed sister of one of our servants. Here I obtained shelter for the night. The next day he discovered me. He made his vile proposals; he offered me the whole of his fortune; he declared his resolution, say what I might, to return the next day. That night, by help of the good woman who had taken care of me—under cover of the darkness, as if I had been to blame!—I was secretly removed to the East End of London, and placed under the charge of a trustworthy person who lived, in a very humble way, by letting lodgings.

"Here, in a little back garret at the top of the house, I was thrown again on the world—an age when it was doubly perilous for me to be left to my own resources to earn the bread I ate and the roof that covered me.

"I claim no credit to myself—young as I was, placed as I was between the easy life of Vice and the hard life of Virtue—for acting as I did. The man simply horrified me: my natural impulse was to escape from him. But let it be remembered, before I approach the saddest part of my sad story, that I was an innocent girl, and that I was at least not to blame.

"Forgive me for dwelling as I have done on my early years. I shrink from speaking of the events that are still to come.

"In losing the esteem of my first benefactress, I had, in my friendless position, lost all hold on an honest life—except the one frail hold of needle-work. The only reference of which I could now dispose was the recommendation of me by my landlady to a place of business which largely employed expert needle-women. It is needless for me to tell you how miserably work of that sort is remunerated: you have read about it in the newspapers. As long as my health lasted I contrived to live and to keep out of debt. Few girls could have resisted as long as I did the slowly-poisoning influences of crowded work-room, insufficient nourishment, and almost total privation of exercise. My life as a child had been a life in the open air: it had helped to strengthen a constitution naturally hardy, naturally free from all taint of hereditary disease. But my time came at last. Under the cruel stress laid on it my health gave way. I was struck down by low fever, and sentence was pronounced on me by my fellow-lodgers: 'Ah, poor thing, her troubles will soon be at an end!'

"The prediction might have proved true—I might never have committed the errors and endured the sufferings of after years—if I had fallen ill in another house.

"But it was my good, or my evil, fortune—I dare not say which—to have interested in myself and my sorrows an actress at a suburban theatre, who occupied the room under mine. Except when her stage duties took her away for two or three hours in the evening, this noble creature never left my bedside. Ill as she could afford it, her purse paid my inevitable expenses while I lay helpless. The landlady, moved by her example, accepted half the weekly rent of my room. The doctor, with the Christian kindness of his profession, would take no fees. All that the tenderest care could accomplish was lavished on me; my youth and my constitution did the rest. I struggled back to life—

and then I took up my needle again.

"It may surprise you that I should have failed (having an actress for my dearest friend) to use the means of introduction thus offered to me to try the stage—especially as my childish training had given me, in some small degree, a familiarity with the Art.

"I had only one motive for shrinking from an appearance at the theatre—but it was strong enough to induce me to submit to any alternative that remained, no matter how hopeless it might be. If I showed myself on the public stage, my discovery by the man from whom I had escaped would be only a question of time. I knew him to be habitually a play-goer and a subscriber to a theatrical newspaper. I had even heard him speak of the theatre to which my friend was attached, and compare it advantageously with places of amusement of far higher pretensions. Sooner or later, if I joined the company he would be certain to go and see 'the new actress.' The bare thought of it reconciled me to returning to my needle. Before I was strong enough to endure the atmosphere of the crowded workroom I obtained permission, as a favor, to resume my occupation at home.

"Surely my choice was the choice of a virtuous girl? And yet the day when I returned to my needle was the fatal day of my life.

"I had now not only to provide for the wants of the passing hour—I had my debts to pay. It was only to be done by toiling harder than ever, and by living more poorly than ever. I soon paid the penalty, in my weakened state, of leading such a life as this. One evening my head turned suddenly giddy; my heart throbbed frightfully. I managed to open the window, and to let the fresh air into the room, and I felt better. But I was not sufficiently recovered to be able to thread my needle. I thought to myself, 'If I go out for half an hour, a little exercise may put me right again.' I had not, as I suppose, been out more than ten minutes when the attack from which I had suffered in my room was renewed. There was no shop near in which I could take refuge. I tried to ring the bell of the nearest house door. Before I could reach it I fainted in the street.

"How long hunger and weakness left me at the mercy of the first stranger who might pass by, it is impossible for me to say.

"When I partially recovered my senses I was conscious of being under shelter somewhere, and of having a wine-glass containing some cordial drink held to my lips by a man. I managed to swallow—I don't know how little, or how much. The stimulant had a very strange effect on me. Reviving me at first, it ended in stupefying me. I lost my senses once more.

"When I next recovered myself, the day was breaking. I was in a bed in a strange room. A nameless terror seized me. I called out. Three or four women came in, whose faces betrayed, even to my inexperienced eyes, the shameless infamy of their lives. I started up in the bed. I implored them to tell me where I was, and what had happened—

"Spare me! I can say no more. Not long since you heard Miss Roseberry call me an outcast from the streets. Now you know—as God is my judge I am speaking the truth!—now you know what made me an outcast, and in what measure I deserved my disgrace."

Her voice faltered, her resolution failed her, for the first time.

"Give me a few minutes," she said, in low, pleading tones. "If I try to go on now, I am afraid I shall cry."

She took the chair which Julian had placed for her, turning her face aside so that neither of the men could see it. One of her hands was pressed over her bosom, the other hung listlessly at her side.

Julian rose from the place that he had occupied. Horace neither moved nor spoke. His head was on his breast: the traces of tears on his cheeks owned mutely that she had touched his heart. Would he forgive her? Julian passed on, and approached Mercy's chair.

In silence he took the hand which hung at her side. In silence he lifted it to his lips and kissed it, as her brother might have kissed it. She started, but she never looked up. Some strange fear of discovery seemed to possess her. "Horace?" she whispered, timidly. Julian made no reply. He went back to his place, and allowed her to think it was Horace.

The sacrifice was immense enough—feeling toward her as he felt—to be worthy of the man who made it.

A few minutes had been all she asked for. In a few minutes she turned toward them again. Her sweet voice was steady once more; her eyes rested softly on Horace as she went on.

"What was it possible for a friendless girl in my position to do, when the full knowledge of the outrage had been revealed to me?

"If I had possessed near and dear relatives to protect and advise me, the wretches into whose hands I had fallen might have felt the penalty of the law. I knew no more of the formalities which set the law in motion than a child. But I had another alternative (you will say). Charitable societies would have received me and helped me, if I had stated my case to them. I knew no more of the charitable societies than I knew of the law. At least, then, I might have gone back to the honest people among whom I had lived? When I received my freedom, after the interval of some days, I was ashamed to go back to the honest people. Helplessly and hopelessly, without sin or choice of mine, I drifted, as thousands of other women have drifted, into the life which set a mark on me for the rest of my days.

"Are you surprised at the ignorance which this confession reveals?

"You, who have your solicitors to inform you of legal remedies and your newspapers, circulars, and active friends to sound the praises of charitable institutions continually in your ears—you, who possess these advantages, have no idea of the outer world of ignorance in which your lost fellow-creatures live. They know nothing (unless they are rogues accustomed to prey on society) of your benevolent schemes to help them. The purpose of public charities, and the way to discover and apply to them, ought to be posted at the corner of every street. What do we know of public dinners and eloquent sermons and neatly printed circulars? Every now and then the ease of some forlorn creature (generally of a woman) who has committed suicide, within five minutes' walk, perhaps, of an institution which would have opened its doors to her, appears in the newspapers, shocks you dreadfully, and is then forgotten again. Take as much pains to make charities and asylums known among the people without money as are taken to make a new play, a new journal, or a new medicine known among the people with money and you will save many a lost creature who is perishing now.

"You will forgive and understand me if I say no more of this period of my life. Let me pass to the new incident in my career which brought me for the second time before the public notice in a court of law.

"Sad as my experience has been, it has not taught me to think ill of human nature. I had found kind hearts to feel for me in my former troubles; and I had friends—faithful, self-denying, generous friends—among my sisters in adversity now. One of these poor women (she has gone, I am glad to think, from the world that used her so hardly) especially attracted my sympathies. She was the gentlest, the most unselfish creature I have ever met with. We lived together like sisters. More than once in the dark hours when the thought of self-destruction comes to a desperate woman, the image of my poor devoted friend, left to suffer alone, rose in my mind and restrained me. You will hardly understand it, but even we had our happy days. When she or I had a few shillings to spare, we used to offer one another little presents, and enjoy our simple pleasure in giving and receiving as keenly as if we had been the most reputable women living.

"One day I took my friend into a shop to buy her a ribbon—only a bow for her dress. She was to choose it, and I was to pay for it, and it was to be the prettiest ribbon that money could buy.

"The shop was full; we had to wait a little before we could be served.

"Next to me, as I stood at the counter with my companion, was a gaudily-dressed woman, looking at some handkerchiefs. The handkerchiefs were finely embroidered, but the smart lady was hard to please. She tumbled them up disdainfully in a heap, and asked for other specimens from the stock in the shop. The man, in clearing the handkerchiefs out of the way, suddenly missed one. He was quite sure of it, from a peculiarity in the embroidery which made the handkerchief especially noticeable. I was poorly dressed, and I was close to the handkerchiefs. After one look at me he shouted to the superintendent: 'Shut the door! There is a thief in the shop!'

"The door was closed; the lost handkerchief was vainly sought for on the counter and on the floor. A robbery had been committed; and I was accused of being the thief.

"I will say nothing of what I felt—I will only tell you what happened.

"I was searched, and the handkerchief was discovered on me. The woman who had stood next to me, on finding herself threatened with discovery, had no doubt contrived to slip the stolen handkerchief into my pocket. Only an accomplished thief could have escaped detection in that way without my knowledge. It was useless, in the face of the facts, to declare my innocence. I had no character to appeal to. My friend tried to speak for me; but what was she? Only a lost woman like myself. My landlady's evidence in favor of my honesty produced no effect; it was against her that she let lodgings to people in my position. I was prosecuted, and found guilty. The tale of my disgrace is now complete, Mr. Holmcroft. No matter whether I was innocent or not, the shame of it remains—I have been imprisoned for theft.

"The matron of the prison was the next person who took an interest in me. She reported favorably of my behavior to the authorities and when I had served my time (as the phrase was among us) she gave me a letter to the kind friend and guardian of my later years—to the lady who is coming here to take me back with her to the Refuge.

"From this time the story of my life is little more than the story of a woman's vain efforts to recover her lost place in the world.

"The matron, on receiving me into the Refuge, frankly acknowledged that there were terrible obstacles in my way. But she saw that I was sincere, and she felt a good woman's sympathy and compassion for me. On my side, I did not shrink from beginning the slow and weary journey back again to a reputable life from the humblest starting-point—from domestic service. After first earning my new character in the Refuge, I obtained a trial in a respectable house. I worked hard, and worked uncomplainingly; but my mother's fatal legacy was against me from the first. My personal appearance excited remark; my manners and habits were not the manners and habits of the women among whom my lot was cast. I tried one place after another—always with the same results. Suspicion and jealousy I could endure; but I was defenseless when curiosity assailed me in its turn. Sooner or later inquiry led to discovery. Sometimes the servants threatened to give warning in a body—and I was obliged to go. Sometimes, where there was a young man in the family, scandal pointed at me and at him—and again I was obliged to go. If you care to know it, Miss Roseberry can tell you the story of those sad days. I confided it to her on the memorable night when we met in the French cottage; I have no heart repeat it now. After a while I wearied of the hopeless struggle. Despair laid its hold on me—I lost all hope in the mercy of God. More than once I walked to one or other of the bridges, and looked over the parapet at the river, and said to myself 'Other women have done it: why shouldn't I?'

"You saved me at that time, Mr. Gray—as you have saved me since. I was one of your congregation when you preached in the chapel of the Refuge You reconciled others besides me to our hard pilgrimage. In their name and in mine, sir, I thank you.

"I forget how long it was after the bright day when you comforted and sustained us that the war broke out between France and Germany. But I can never forget the evening when the matron sent for me into her own room and said, 'My dear, your life here is a wasted life. If you have courage enough left to try it, I can give you another chance.'

"I passed through a month of probation in a London hospital. A week after that I wore the red cross of the Geneva Convention—I was appointed nurse in a French ambulance. When you first saw me, Mr. Holmcroft, I still had my nurse's dress on, hidden from you and from everybody under a gray cloak.

"You know what the next event was; you know how I entered this house.

"I have not tried to make the worst of my trials and troubles in telling you what my life has been. I have honestly described it for what it was when I met with Miss Roseberry—a life without hope. May you never know the temptation that tried me when the shell struck its victim in the French cottage! There she lay—dead! Her name was untainted. Her future promised me the reward which had been denied to the honest efforts of a penitent woman. My

278

lost place in the world was offered back to me on the one condition that I stooped to win it by a fraud. I had no prospect to look forward to; I had no friend near to advise me and to save me; the fairest years of my womanhood had been wasted in the vain struggle to recover my good name. Such was my position when the possibility of personating Miss Roseberry first forced itself on my mind. Impulsively, recklessly—wickedly, if you like—I seized the opportunity, and let you pass me through the German lines under Miss Roseberry's name. Arrived in England, having had time to reflect, I made my first and last effort to draw back before it was too late. I went to the Refuge, and stopped on the opposite side of the street, looking at it. The old hopeless life of irretrievable disgrace confronted me as I fixed my eyes on the familiar door; the horror of returning to that life was more than I could force myself to endure. An empty cab passed me at the moment. The driver held up his hand. In sheer despair I stopped him, and when he said 'Where to?' in sheer despair again I answered, 'Mablethorpe House.'

"Of what I have suffered in secret since my own successful deception established me under Lady Janet's care I shall say nothing. Many things which must have surprised you in my conduct are made plain to you by this time. You must have noticed long since that I was not a happy woman. Now you know why.

"My confession is made; my conscience has spoken at last. You are released from your promise to me—you are free. Thank Mr. Julian Gray if I stand here self-accused of the offense, that I have committed, before the man whom I have wronged."

CHAPTER XXVIII. SENTENCE IS PRONOUNCED ON HER.

IT was done. The last tones of her voice died away in silence.

Her eyes still rested on Horace. After hearing what he had heard could he resist that gentle, pleading look? Would he forgive her? A while since Julian had seen tears on his cheeks, and had believed that he felt for her. Why was he now silent? Was it possible that he only felt for himself?

For the last time—at the crisis of her life—Julian spoke for her. He had never loved her as he loved her at that moment; it tried even his generous nature to plead her cause with Horace against himself. But he had promised her, without reserve, all the help that her truest friend could offer. Faithfully and manfully he redeemed his promise.

"Horace!" he said.

Horace slowly looked up. Julian rose and approached him.

"She has told you to thank me, if her conscience has spoken. Thank the noble nature which answered when I called upon it! Own the priceless value of a woman who can speak the truth. Her heartfelt repentance is a joy in heaven. Shall it not plead for her on earth? Honor her, if you are a Christian! Feel for her, if you are a man!"

He waited. Horace never answered him.

Mercy's eyes turned tearfully on Julian. His heart was the heart that felt for her! His words were the words which comforted and pardoned her! When she looked back again at Horace, it was with an effort. His last hold on her was lost. In her inmost mind a thought rose unbidden—a thought which was not to be repressed. "Can I ever have loved this man?"

She advanced a step toward him; it was not possible, even yet, to completely forgot the past. She held out her hand.

He rose on his side—without looking at her.

"Before we part forever," she said to him, "will you take my hand as a token that you forgive me?"

He hesitated. He half lifted his hand. The next moment the generous impulse died away in him. In its place came the mean fear of what might happen if he trusted himself to the dangerous fascination of her touch. His hand dropped again at his side; he turned away quickly.

"I can't forgive her!" he said.

With that horrible confession—without even a last look at her—he left the room.

At the moment when he opened the door Julian's contempt for him burst its way through all restraints.

"Horace," he said, "I pity you!"

As the words escaped him he looked back at Mercy. She had turned aside from both of them—she had retired to a distant part of the library The first bitter foretaste of what was in store for her when she faced the world again had come to her from Horace! The energy which had sustained her thus far quailed before the dreadful prospect—doubly dreadful to a woman—of obloquy and contempt. She sank on her knees before a little couch in the darkest corner of the room. "O Christ, have mercy on me!" That was her prayer—no more.

Julian followed her. He waited a little. Then his kind hand touched her; his friendly voice fell consolingly on her ear.

"Rise, poor wounded heart! Beautiful, purified soul, God's angels rejoice over you! Take your place among the noblest of God's creatures!"

He raised her as he spoke. All her heart went out to him. She caught his hand—she pressed it to her bosom; she pressed it to her lips—then dropped it suddenly, and stood before him trembling like a frightened child.

"Forgive me!" was all she could say. "I was so lost and lonely—and you are so good to me!"

She tried to leave him. It was useless—her strength was gone; she caught at the head of the couch to support herself. He looked at her. The confession of his love was just rising to his lips—he looked again, and checked it. No, not at that moment; not when she was helpless and ashamed; not when her weakness might make her yield, only to regret it at a later time. The great heart which had spared her and felt for her from the first spared her and felt for her now.

He, too, left her—but not without a word at parting.

"Don't think of your future life just yet," he said, gently. "I have something to propose when rest and quiet have restored you." He opened the nearest door—the door of the dining-room—and went out.

The servants engaged in completing the decoration of the dinner-table noticed, when "Mr. Julian" entered the room, that his eyes were "brighter than ever." He looked (they remarked) like a man who "expected good news." They were inclined to suspect—though he was certainly rather young for it—that her ladyship's nephew was in a fair way of preferment in the Church.

Mercy seated herself on the couch.

There are limits, in the physical organization of man, to the action of pain. When suffering has reached a given point of intensity the nervous sensibility becomes incapable of feeling more. The rule of Nature, in this respect, applies not only to sufferers in the body, but to sufferers in the mind as well. Grief, rage, terror, have also their appointed limits. The moral sensibility, like the nervous sensibility, reaches its period of absolute exhaustion, and feels no more.

The capacity for suffering in Mercy had attained its term. Alone in the library, she could feel the physical relief of repose; she could vaguely recall Julian's parting words to her, and sadly wonder what they meant—she could do no more.

An interval passed; a brief interval of perfect rest.

She recovered herself sufficiently to be able to look at her watch and to estimate the lapse of time that might yet pass before Julian returned to her as he had promised. While her mind was still languidly following this train of thought she was disturbed by the ringing of a bell in the hall, used to summon the servant whose duties were connected with that part of the house. In leaving the library, Horace had gone out by the door which led into the hall, and had failed to close it. She plainly heard the bell—and a moment later (more plainly still) she heard Lady Janet's voice!

She started to her feet. Lady Janet's letter was still in the pocket of her apron—the letter which imperatively commanded her to abstain from making the very confession that had just passed her lips! It was near the dinner hour, and the library was the favorite place in which the mistress of the house and her guests assembled at that time. It was no matter of doubt; it was an absolute certainty that Lady Janet had only stopped in the hall on her way into the room.

The alternative for Mercy lay between instantly leaving the library by the dining-room door—or remaining where she was, at the risk of being sooner or later compelled to own that she had deliberately disobeyed her benefactress. Exhausted by what she had already suffered, she stood trembling and irresolute, incapable of deciding which alternative she should choose.

Lady Janet's voice, clear and resolute, penetrated into the room. She was reprimanding the servant who had answered the bell.

"Is it your duty in my house to look after the lamps?"

"Yes, my lady."

"And is it my duty to pay you your wages?"

"If you please, my lady."

"Why do I find the light in the hall dim, and the wick of that lamp smoking? I have not failed in my duty to You. Don't let me find you failing again in your duty to Me."

(Never had Lady Janet's voice sounded so sternly in Mercy's ear as it sounded now. If she spoke with that tone of severity to a servant who had neglected a lamp, what had her adopted daughter to expect when she discovered that her entreaties and her commands had been alike set at defiance?)

Having administered her reprimand, Lady Janet had not done with the servant yet. She had a question to put to him next.

"Where is Miss Roseberry?"

"In the library, my lady."

Mercy returned to the couch. She could stand no longer; she had not even resolution enough left to lift her eyes to the door.

Lady Janet came in more rapidly than usual. She advanced to the couch, and tapped Mercy playfully on the cheek with two of her fingers.

"You lazy child! Not dressed for dinner? Oh, fie, fie!"

Her tone was as playfully affectionate as the action which had accompanied her words. In speechless astonishment Mercy looked up at her.

Always remarkable for the taste and splendor of her dress, Lady Janet had on this occasion surpassed herself. There she stood revealed in her grandest velvet, her richest jewelry, her finest lace—with no one to entertain at the dinner-table but the ordinary members of the circle at Mablethorpe House. Noticing this as strange to begin with, Mercy further observed, for the first time in her experience, that Lady Janet's eyes avoided meeting hers. The old lady took her place companionably on the couch; she ridiculed her "lazy child's" plain dress, without an ornament of any sort on it, with her best grace; she affectionately put her arm round Mercy's waist, and rearranged with her own hand the disordered locks of Mercy's hair—but the instant Mercy herself looked at her, Lady Janet's eyes discovered something supremely interesting in the familiar objects that surrounded her on the library walls.

How were these changes to be interpreted? To what possible conclusion did they point?

Julian's profounder knowledge of human nature, if Julian had been present, might have found a clew to the mystery. He might have surmised (incredible as it was) that Mercy's timidity before Lady Janet was fully reciprocated by Lady Janet's timidity before Mercy. It was even so. The woman whose immovable composure had conquered Grace Roseberry's utmost insolence in the hour of her triumph—the woman who, without once flinching, had faced every other consequence of her resolution to ignore Mercy's true position in the house—quailed for the first time when she found herself face to face with the very person for whom she had suffered and sacrificed so much. She had shrunk from the meeting with Mercy, as Mercy had shrunk from the meeting with her. The splendor of her dress meant simply that, when other excuses for delaying the meeting downstairs had all been exhausted, the excuse of a long, and elaborate toilet had been tried next. Even the moments occupied in reprimanding the servant had been moments seized on as the pretext for another delay. The hasty entrance into the room, the nervous assumption of playfulness in language and manner, the evasive and wandering eyes, were all referable to the same cause. In the presence of others, Lady Janet had successfully silenced the protest of her own inbred delicacy and inbred sense of honor. In the presence of Mercy, whom she loved with a mother's love—in the presence of Mercy, for whom she had stooped to deliberate concealment of the truth—all that was high and noble in the woman's nature rose in her and rebuked her. What will the daughter of my adoption, the child of my first and last experience of maternal love, think of me, now that I have made myself an accomplice in the fraud of which she is ashamed? How can I look her in the face, when I have not hesitated, out of selfish consideration for my own tranquillity, to forbid that frank avowal of the truth which her finer sense of duty had spontaneously bound her to make? Those were the torturing questions in Lady Janet's mind, while her arm was wound affectionately round Mercy's waist, while her fingers were busying themselves familiarly with the arrangement of Mercy's hair. Thence, and thence only, sprang the impulse which set her talking, with an uneasy affectation of frivolity, of any topic within the range of conversation, so long as it related to the future, and completely ignored the present and the past.

"The winter here is unendurable," Lady Janet began. "I have been thinking, Grace, about what we had better do next."

Mercy started. Lady Janet had called her "Grace." Lady Janet was still deliberately assuming to be innocent of the faintest suspicion of the truth.

"No," resumed her ladyship, affecting to misunderstand Mercy's movement, "you are not to go up now and dress. There is no time, and I am quite ready to excuse you. You are a foil to me, my dear. You have reached the perfection of shabbiness. Ah! I remember when I had my whims and fancies too, and when I looked well in anything I wore, just as you do. No more of that. As I was saying, I have been thinking and planning what we are to do. We really can't stay here. Cold one day, and hot the next—what a climate! As for society, what do we lose if we go away? There is no such thing as society now. Assemblies of well-dressed mobs meet at each other's houses, tear each other's clothes, tread on each other's toes. If you are particularly lucky, you sit on the staircase, you get a tepid ice, and you hear vapid talk in slang phrases all round you. There is modern society. If we had a good opera, it would be something to stay in London for. Look at the programme for the season on that table—promising as much as possible on paper, and performing as little as possible on the stage. The same works, sung by the same singers year after year, to the same stupid people—in short the dullest musical evenings in Europe. No! the more I think of it, the more plainly I perceive that there is but one sensible choice before us: we must go abroad. Set that pretty head to work; choose north or south, east or west; it's all the same to me. Where shall we go?"

Mercy looked at her quickly as she put the question.

Lady Janet, more quickly yet, looked away at the programme of the opera-house. Still the same melancholy false pretenses! still the same useless and cruel delay! Incapable of enduring the position now forced upon her, Mercy put her hand into the pocket of her apron, and drew from it Lady Janet's letter.

"Will your ladyship forgive me," she began, in faint, faltering tones, "if I venture on a painful subject? I hardly dare acknowledge—" In spite of her resolution to speak out plainly, the memory of past love and past kindness prevailed with her; the next words died away on her lips. She could only hold up the letter.

Lady Janet declined to see the letter. Lady Janet suddenly became absorbed in the arrangement of her bracelets.

"I know what you daren't acknowledge, you foolish child!" she exclaimed. "You daren't acknowledge that you are tired of this dull house. My dear! I am entirely of your opinion—I am weary of my own magnificence; I long to be living in one snug little room, with one servant to wait on me. I'll tell you what we will do. We will go to Paris, in the first place. My excellent Migliore, prince of couriers, shall be the only person in attendance. He shall take a lodging for us in one of the unfashionable quarters of Paris. We will rough it, Grace (to use the slang phrase), merely for a change. We will lead what they call a 'Bohemian life.' I know plenty of writers and painters and actors in Paris—the liveliest society in the world, my dear, until one gets tired of them. We will dine at the restaurant, and go to the play, and drive about in shabby little hired carriages. And when it begins to get monotonous (which it is only too sure to do!) we will spread our wings and fly to Italy, and cheat the winter in that way. There is a plan for you! Migliore is in town. I will send to him this evening, and we will start to-morrow."

Mercy made another effort.

"I entreat your ladyship to pardon me," she resumed. "I have something serious to say. I am afraid—"

"I understand. You are afraid of crossing the Channel, and you don't like to acknowledge it. Pooh! The passage barely lasts two hours; we will shut ourselves up in a private cabin. I will send at once—the courier may be engaged. Ring the bell."

"Lady Janet, I must submit to my hard lot. I cannot hope to associate myself again with any future plans of yours—"

"What! you are afraid of our 'Bohemian life' in Paris? Observe this, Grace! If there is one thing I hate more than another, it is 'an old head on young shoulders.' I say no more. Ring the bell."

"This cannot go on, Lady Janet! No words can say how unworthy I feel of your kindness, how ashamed I am—"

"Upon my honor, my dear, I agree with you. You ought to be ashamed, at your age, of making me get up to ring the bell."

Her obstinacy was immovable; she attempted to rise from the couch. But one choice was left to Mercy. She anticipated Lady Janet, and rang the bell.

The man-servant came in. He had his little letter-tray in his hand, with a card on it, and a sheet of paper beside the card, which looked like an open letter.

"You know where my courier lives when he is in London?' asked Lady Janet.

"Yes, my lady."

"Send one of the grooms to him on horseback; I am in a hurry. The courier is to come here without fail to-morrow morning—in time for the tidal train to Paris. You understand?"

"Yes, my lady."

"What have you got there? Anything for me?"

"For Miss Roseberry, my lady."

As he answered, the man handed the card and the open letter to Mercy.

"The lady is waiting in the morning-room, miss. She wished me to say she has time to spare, and she will wait for you if you are not ready yet."

Having delivered his message in those terms, he withdrew.

Mercy read the name on the card. The matron had arrived! She looked at the letter next. It appeared to be a printed circular, with some lines in pencil added on the empty page. Printed lines and written lines swam before her eyes. She felt, rather than saw, Lady Janet's attention steadily and suspiciously fixed on her. With the matron's arrival the foredoomed end of the flimsy false pretenses and the cruel delays had come.

"A friend of yours, my dear?"

"Yes, Lady Janet."

"Am I acquainted with her?"

"I think not, Lady Janet."

"You appear to be agitated. Does your visitor bring bad news? Is there anything that I can do for you?"

"You can add—immeasurably add, madam—to all your past kindness, if you will only bear with me and forgive me."

"Bear with you and forgive you? I don't understand."

"I will try to explain. Whatever else you may think of me, Lady Janet, for God's sake don't think me ungrateful!"

Lady Janet held up her hand for silence.

"I dislike explanations," she said, sharply. "Nobody ought to know that better than you. Perhaps the lady's letter will explain for you. Why have you not looked at it yet?"

"I am in great trouble, madam, as you noticed just now—"

"Have you any objection to my knowing who your visitor is?"

"No, Lady Janet."

"Let me look at her card, then."

Mercy gave the matron's card to Lady Janet, as she had given the matron's telegram to Horace.

Lady Janet read the name on the card—considered—decided that it was a name quite unknown to her—and looked next at the address: "Western District Refuge, Milburn Road."

"A lady connected with a Refuge?" she said, speaking to herself; "and calling here by appointment—if I remember the servant's message? A strange time to choose, if she has come for a subscription!"

She paused. Her brow contracted; her face hardened. A word from her would now have brought the interview to its inevitable end, and she refused to speak the word. To the last moment she persisted in ignoring the truth! Placing the card on the couch at her side, she pointed with her long yellow-white forefinger to the printed letter lying side by side with her own letter on Mercy's lap.

"Do you mean to read it, or not?" she asked.

Mercy lifted her eyes, fast filling with tears, to Lady Janet's face.

"May I beg that your ladyship will read it for me?" she said—and placed the matron's letter in Lady Janet's hand.

It was a printed circular announcing a new development in the charitable work of the Refuge. Subscribers were informed that it had been decided to extend the shelter and the training of the institution (thus far devoted to fallen women alone) so as to include destitute and helpless children found wandering in the streets. The question of the number of children to be thus rescued and protected was left dependent, as a matter of course, on the bounty of the friends of the Refuge, the cost of the maintenance of each child being stated at the lowest possible rate. A list of influential persons who had increased their subscriptions so as to cover the cost, and a brief statement of the progress already made with the new work, completed the appeal, and brought the circular to its end.

The lines traced in pencil (in the matron's handwriting) followed on the blank page.

"Your letter tells me, my dear, that you would like—remembering your own childhood—to be employed when you return among us in saving other poor children left helpless on the world. Our circular will inform you that I am able to meet your wishes. My first errand this evening in your neighborhood was to take charge of a poor child—a little girl—who stands sadly in need of our care. I have ventured to bring her with me, thinking she might help to reconcile you to the coming change in your life. You will find us both waiting to go back with you to the old home. I write this instead of saying it, hearing from the servant that you are not alone, and being unwilling to intrude myself, as a stranger, on the lady of the house."

Lady Janet read the penciled lines, as she had read the printed sentences, aloud. Without a word of comment she laid the letter where she had laid the card; and, rising from her seat, stood for a moment in stern silence, looking at Mercy. The sudden change in her which the letter had produced—quietly as it had taken place—was terrible to see. On the frowning brow, in the flashing eyes, on the hardened lips, outraged love and outraged pride looked down on the lost woman, and said, as if in words, You have roused us at last.

"If that letter means anything," she said, "it means you are about to leave my house. There can be but one reason for your taking such a step as that."

"It is the only atonement I can make, madam."

"I see another letter on your lap. Is it my letter?"

"Yes."

"Have you read it?"

"I have read it."

"Have you seen Horace Holmcroft?"

"Yes."

"Have you told Horace Holmcroft—"

"Oh, Lady Janet—"

"Don't interrupt me. Have you told Horace Holmcroft what my letter positively forbade you to communicate, either to him or to any living creature? I want no protestations and excuses. Answer me instantly, and answer in one word—Yes, or No."

Not even that haughty language, not even those pitiless tones, could extinguish in Mercy's heart the sacred memories of past kindness and past love. She fell on her knees—her outstretched hands touched Lady Janet's

291

dress. Lady Janet sharply drew her dress away, and sternly repeated her last words.

"Yes? or No?"

"Yes."

She had owned it at last! To this end Lady Janet had submitted to Grace Roseberry; had offended Horace Holmcroft; had stooped, for the first time in her life, to concealments and compromises that degraded her. After all that she had sacrificed and suffered, there Mercy knelt at her feet, self-convicted of violating her commands, trampling on her feelings, deserting her house! And who was the woman who had done this? The same woman who had perpetrated the fraud, and who had persisted in the fraud until her benefactress had descended to become her accomplice. Then, and then only, she had suddenly discovered that it was her sacred duty to tell the truth!

In proud silence the great lady met the blow that had fallen on her. In proud silence she turned her back on her adopted daughter and walked to the door.

Mercy made her last appeal to the kind friend whom she had offended— to the second mother whom she had loved.

"Lady Janet! Lady Janet! Don't leave me without a word. Oh, madam, try to feel for me a little! I am returning to a life of humiliation—the shadow of my old disgrace is falling on me once more. We shall never meet again. Even though I have not deserved it, let my repentance plead with you! Say you forgive me!"

Lady Janet turned round on the threshold of the door.

"I never forgive ingratitude," she said. "Go back to the Refuge."

The door opened and closed on her. Mercy was alone again in the room.

Unforgiven by Horace, unforgiven by Lady Janet! She put her hands to her burning head and tried to think. Oh, for the cool air of the night! Oh, for the friendly shelter of the Refuge! She could feel those sad longings in her: it was impossible to think.

She rang the bell—and shrank back the instant she had done it. Had she any right to take that liberty? She ought to have thought of it before she rang. Habit—all habit. How many hundreds of times she had rung the bell at Mablethorpe House!

The servant came in. She amazed the man—she spoke to him so timidly: she even apologized for troubling him!

"I am sorry to disturb you. Will you be so kind as to say to the lady that I am ready for her?"

"Wait to give that message," said a voice behind them, "until you hear the bell rung again."

Mercy looked round in amazement. Julian had returned to the library by the dining-room door.

CHAPTER XXIX. THE LAST TRIAL.

THE servant left them together. Mercy spoke first.

"Mr. Gray!" she exclaimed, "why have you delayed my message? If you knew all, you would know that it is far from being a kindness to me to keep me in this house."

He advanced closer to her—surprised by her words, alarmed by her looks.

"Has any one been here in my absence?" he asked.

"Lady Janet has been here in your absence. I can't speak of it—my heart feels crushed—I can bear no more. Let me go!"

Briefly as she had replied, she had said enough. Julian's knowledge of Lady Janet's character told him what had happened. His face showed plainly that he was disappointed as well as distressed.

"I had hoped to have been with you when you and my aunt met, and to have prevented this," he said. "Believe me, she will atone for all that she may have harshly and hastily done when she has had time to think. Try not to regret it, if she has made your hard sacrifice harder still. She has only raised you the higher—she has additionally ennobled you and endeared you in my estimation. Forgive me if I own this in plain words. I cannot control myself—I feel too strongly."

At other times Mercy might have heard the coming avowal in his tones, might have discovered it in his eyes. As it was, her delicate insight was dulled, her fine perception was blunted. She held out her hand to him, feeling a vague conviction that he was kinder to her than ever—and feeling no more.

"I must thank you for the last time," she said. "As long as life is left, my gratitude will be a part of my life. Let me go. While I can still control myself, let me go!"

She tried to leave him, and ring the bell. He held her hand firmly, and drew her closer to him.

"To the Refuge?" he asked.

"Yes," she said. "Home again!"

"Don't say that!" he exclaimed. "I can't bear to hear it. Don't call the Refuge your home!"

"What else is it? Where else can I go?"

"I have come here to tell you. I said, if you remember, I had something to propose."

She felt the fervent pressure of his hand; she saw the mounting enthusiasm flashing in his eyes. Her weary mind roused itself a little. She began to tremble under the electric influence of his touch.

"Something to propose?" she repeated, "What is there to propose?"

"Let me ask you a question on my side. What have you done to-day?"

"You know what I have done: it is your work," she answered, humbly. "Why return to it now?"

"I return to it for the last time; I return to it with a purpose which you will soon understand. You have abandoned your marriage engagement; you have forfeited Lady Janet's love; you have ruined all your worldly prospects; you are now returning, self-devoted, to a life which you have yourself described as a life without hope. And all this you have done of your own free-will—at a time when you are absolutely secure of your position in the house—for the sake of speaking the truth. Now tell me, is a woman who can make that sacrifice a woman who will prove unworthy of the trust if a man places in her keeping his honor and his name?"

She understood him at last. She broke away from him with a cry. She stood with her hands clasped, trembling and looking at him.

He gave her no time to think. The words poured from his lips without conscious will or conscious effort of his own.

"Mercy, from the first moment when I saw you I loved you! You are free; I may own it; I may ask you to be my wife!"

She drew back from him further and further, with a wild imploring gesture of her hand.

"No! no!" she cried. "Think of what you are saying! think of what you would sacrifice! It cannot, must not be."

His face darkened with a sudden dread. His head fell on his breast. His voice sank so low that she could barely hear it.

"I had forgotten something," he said. "You've reminded me of it."

She ventured back a little nearer to him. "Have I offended you?"

He smiled sadly. "You have enlightened me. I had forgotten that it doesn't follow, because I love you, that you should love me in return. Say that it is so, Mercy, and I leave you."

A faint tinge of color rose on her face—then left it again paler than ever. Her eyes looked downward timidly under the eager gaze that he fastened on her.

"How can I say so?" she answered, simply. "Where is the woman in my place whose heart could resist you?"

He eagerly advanced; he held out his arms to her in breathless, speechless joy. She drew back from him once more with a look that horrified him—a look of blank despair.

"Am I fit to be your wife?" she asked. "Must I remind you of what you owe to your high position, your spotless integrity, your famous name? Think of all that you have done for me, and then think of the black ingratitude of it if I ruin you for life by consenting to our marriage—if I selfishly, cruelly, wickedly, drag you down to the level of a woman like me!"

"I raise you to my level when I make you my wife," he answered. "For

296

Heaven's sake do me justice! Don't refer me to the world and its opinions. It rests with you, and you alone, to make the misery or the happiness of my life. The world! Good God! what can the world give me in exchange for You?"

She clasped her hands imploringly; the tears flowed fast over her cheeks.

"Oh, have pity on my weakness!" she cried. "Kindest, best of men, help me to do my hard duty toward you! It is so hard, after all that I have suffered—when my heart is yearning for peace and happiness and love!" She checked herself, shuddering at the words that had escaped her. "Remember how Mr. Holmcroft has used me! Remember how Lady Janet has left me! Remember what I have told you of my life! The scorn of every creature you know would strike at you through me. No! no! no! Not a word more. Spare me! pity me! leave me!"

Her voice failed her; sobs choked her utterance. He sprang to her and took her in his arms. She was incapable of resisting him; but there was no yielding in her. Her head lay on his bosom, passive—horribly passive, like the head of a corpse.

"Mercy! My darling! We will go away—we will leave England—we will take refuge among new people in a new world—I will change my name—I will break with relatives, friends, everybody. Anything, anything, rather than lose you!"

She lifted her head slowly and looked at him.

He suddenly released her; he reeled back like a man staggered by a blow, and dropped into a chair. Before she had uttered a word he saw the terrible resolution in her face—Death, rather than yield to her own weakness and disgrace him.

She stood with her hands lightly clasped in front of her. Her grand head was raised; her soft gray eyes shone again undimmed by tears. The storm of emotion had swept over her and had passed away A sad tranquillity was in her face; a gentle resignation was in her voice. The calm of a martyr was the calm that confronted him as she spoke her last words.

"A woman who has lived my life, a woman who has suffered what I have suffered, may love you—as I love you—but she must not be your wife. That place is too high above her. Any other place is too far below her and below you." She paused, and advancing to the bell, gave the signal for her departure. That done, she slowly retraced her steps until she stood at Julian's side.

Tenderly she lifted his head and laid it for a moment on her bosom. Silently she stooped and touched his forehead with her lips. All the gratitude that filled her heart and all the sacrifice that rent it were in those two actions—so modestly, so tenderly performed! As the last lingering pressure of her fingers left him, Julian burst into tears.

The servant answered the bell. At the moment he opened the door a woman's voice was audible in the hall speaking to him.

"Let the child go in," the voice said. "I will wait here."

The child appeared—the same forlorn little creature who had reminded Mercy of her own early years on the day when she and Horace Holmcroft had been out for their walk.

There was no beauty in this child; no halo of romance brightened the commonplace horror of her story. She came cringing into the room, staring stupidly at the magnificence all round her—the daughter of the London streets! the pet creation of the laws of political economy! the savage and terrible product of a worn-out system of government and of a civilization rotten to its core! Cleaned for the first time in her life, fed sufficiently for the first time in her life, dressed in clothes instead of rags for the first time in her life, Mercy's sister in adversity crept fearfully over the beautiful carpet, and stopped wonder-struck before the marbles of an inlaid table—a blot of mud on the splendor of the room.

Mercy turned from Julian to meet the child. The woman's heart, hungering in its horrible isolation for something that it might harmlessly love, welcomed the rescued waif of the streets as a consolation sent from God. She caught the stupefied little creature up in her arms. "Kiss me!" she whispered, in the reckless agony of the moment. "Call me sister!" The child stared, vacantly. Sister meant nothing to her mind but an older girl who was strong enough to beat her.

She put the child down again, and turned for a last look at the man whose happiness she had wrecked—in pity to him.

He had never moved. His head was down; his face was hidden. She went back to him a few steps.

"The others have gone from me without one kind word. Can you forgive me?"

He held out his hand to her without looking up. Sorely as she had wounded him, his generous nature understood her. True to her from the first, he was true to her still.

"God bless and comfort you," he said, in broken tones. "The earth holds no nobler woman than you."

She knelt and kissed the kind hand that pressed hers for the last time. "It doesn't end with this world," she whispered: "there is a better world to come!" Then she rose, and went back to the child. Hand in hand the two citizens of the Government of God—outcasts of the government of Man—passed slowly down the length of the room. Then out into the hall. Then out into the night. The heavy clang of the closing door tolled the knell of their departure. They were gone.

But the orderly routine of the house—inexorable as death—pursued its appointed course. As the clock struck the hour the dinner-bell rang. An interval of a minute passed, and marked the limit of delay. The butler appeared at the dining-room door.

"Dinner is served, sir."

Julian looked up. The empty room met his eyes. Something white lay on the carpet close by him. It was her handkerchief—wet with her tears. He took it up and pressed it to his lips. Was that to be the last of her? Had she left him forever?

The native energy of the man, arming itself with all the might of his love, kindled in him again. No! While life was in him, while time was before him, there was the hope of winning her yet!

He turned to the servant, reckless of what his face might betray.

"Where is Lady Janet?"

"In the dining-room, sir."

He reflected for a moment. His own influence had failed. Through what other influence could he now hope to reach her? As the question crossed his mind the light broke on him. He saw the way back to her—through the influence of Lady Janet.

"Her ladyship is waiting, sir."

Julian entered the dining-room.

EPILOGUE:

CONTAINING SELECTIONS FROM THE CORRESPONDENCE OF MISS GRACE ROSEBERRY AND MR. HORACE HOLMCROFT; TO WHICH ARE ADDED EXTRACTS FROM THE DIARY OF THE REVEREND JULIAN GRAY.

I.

From MR. HORACE HOLMCROFT to MISS GRACE ROSEBERRY.

"I HASTEN to thank you, dear Miss Roseberry, for your last kind letter, received by yesterday's mail from Canada. Believe me, I appreciate your generous readiness to pardon and forget what I so rudely said to you at a time when the arts of an adventuress had blinded me to the truth. In the grace which has forgiven me I recognize the inbred sense of justice of a true lady. Birth and breeding can never fail to assert themselves: I believe in them, thank God, more firmly than ever.

"You ask me to keep you informed of the progress of Julian Gray's infatuation, and of the course of conduct pursued toward him by Mercy Merrick.

"If you had not favored me by explaining your object, I might have felt some surprise at receiving from a lady in your position such a request as this. But the motives by which you describe yourself as being actuated are beyond dispute. The existence of Society, as you truly say, is threatened by the present lamentable prevalence of Liberal ideas throughout the length and breadth of the land. We can only hope to protect ourselves against impostors interested in gaining a position among persons of our rank by becoming in some sort (unpleasant as it may be) familiar with the arts by which imposture too frequently succeeds. If we wish to know to what daring lengths cunning can go, to what pitiable self-delusion credulity can consent, we must watch the proceedings—even while we shrink from them—of a Mercy Merrick and a Julian Gray.

"In taking up my narrative again where my last letter left off, I must venture to set you right on one point.

"Certain expressions which have escaped your pen suggest to me that you blame Julian Gray as the cause of Lady Janet's regrettable visit to the Refuge the day after Mercy Merrick had left her house. This is not quite correct. Julian, as you will presently see, has enough to answer for without being held responsible for errors of judgment in which he has had no share. Lady Janet (as she herself told me) went to the Refuge of her own free-will to ask Mercy Merrick's pardon for the language which she had used on the previous day. 'I passed a night of such misery as no words can describe'—this, I assure you, is what her ladyship really said to me—'thinking over what my vile pride and selfishness and obstinacy had made me say and do. I would have gone down on my knees to beg her pardon if she would have let me. My first happy moment was when I won her consent to come and visit me sometimes at Mablethorpe House.'

"You will, I am sure, agree with me that such extravagance as this is to be pitied rather than blamed. How sad to see the decay of the faculties with advancing age! It is a matter of grave anxiety to consider how much longer poor Lady Janet can be trusted to manage her own affairs. I shall take an opportunity of touching on the matter delicately when I next see her lawyer.

"I am straying from my subject. And—is it not strange?—I am writing to you as confidentially as if we were old friends.

"To return to Julian Gray. Innocent of instigating his aunt's first visit to the Refuge, he is guilty of having induced her to go there for the second time the day after I had dispatched my last letter to you. Lady Janet's object on this occasion was neither more nor less than to plead her nephew's cause as humble suitor for the hand of Mercy Merrick. Imagine the descent of one of the oldest families in England inviting an adventuress in a Refuge to honor a clergyman of the Church of England by becoming his wife! In what times do we live! My dear mother shed tears of shame when she heard of it. How you would love and admire my mother!

"I dined at Mablethorpe House, by previous appointment, on the day when Lady Janet returned from her degrading errand.

"'Well?' I said, waiting, of course, until the servant was out of the room.

"'Well,' Lady Janet answered, 'Julian was quite right.'

"'Quite right in what?'

"'In saying that the earth holds no nobler woman than Mercy Merrick.'

"'Has she refused him again?'

"'She has refused him again.'

"'Thank God!' I felt it fervently, and I said it fervently. Lady Janet laid down her knife and fork, and fixed one of her fierce looks on me.

"'It may not be your fault, Horace,' she said, 'if your nature is incapable of comprehending what is great and generous in other natures higher than yours. But the least you can do is to distrust your own capacity of appreciation. For the future keep your opinions (on questions which you don't understand) modestly to yourself. I have a tenderness for you for your father's sake; and I take the most favorable view of your conduct toward Mercy Merrick. I humanely consider it the conduct of a fool.' (Her own words, Miss Roseberry. I assure you once more, her own words.) 'But don't trespass too far on my indulgence—don't insinuate again that a woman who is good enough (if she died this night) to go to heaven, is not good enough to be my nephew's wife.'

"I expressed to you my conviction a little way back that it was doubtful whether poor Lady Janet would be much longer competent to manage her own affairs. Perhaps you thought me hasty then? What do you think now?

"It was, of course, useless to reply seriously to the extraordinary reprimand that I had received. Besides, I was really shocked by a decay of principle which proceeded but too plainly from decay of the mental powers. I made a soothing and respectful reply, and I was favored in return with some account of what had really happened at the Refuge. My mother and my sisters were disgusted when I repeated the particulars to them. You will be disgusted too.

"The interesting penitent (expecting Lady Janet's visit) was, of course, discovered in a touching domestic position! She had a foundling baby asleep on her lap; and she was teaching the alphabet to an ugly little vagabond girl whose acquaintance she had first made in the street. Just the sort of artful tableau vivant to impose on an old lady—was it not?

"You will understand what followed, when Lady Janet opened her matrimonial negotiation. Having perfected herself in her part, Mercy Merrick, to do her justice, was not the woman to play it badly. The most magnanimous sentiments flowed from her lips. She declared that her future life was devoted to acts of charity, typified, of course, by the foundling infant and the ugly little girl. However she might personally suffer, whatever might be the sacrifice of her own feelings—observe how artfully this was put, to insinuate that she was herself in love with him!—she could not accept from Mr. Julian Gray an honor of which she was unworthy. Her gratitude to him and her interest in him alike forbade her to compromise his brilliant future by consenting to a marriage which would degrade him in the estimation of all his friends. She thanked him (with tears); she thanked Lady Janet (with more tears); but she dare not, in the interests of his honor and his happiness, accept the hand that he offered to her. God bless and comfort him; and God help her to bear with her hard lot!

"The object of this contemptible comedy is plain enough to my mind. She is simply holding off (Julian, as you know, is a poor man) until the influence of Lady Janet's persuasion is backed by the opening of Lady Janet's purse. In one word—Settlements! But for the profanity of the woman's language, and the really lamentable credulity of the poor old lady, the whole thing would make a fit subject for a burlesque.

"But the saddest part of the story is still to come.

"In due course of time the lady's decision was communicated to Julian Gray. He took leave of his senses on the spot. Can you believe it?—he has resigned his curacy! At a time when the church is thronged every Sunday to hear him preach, this madman shuts the door and walks out of the pulpit. Even Lady Janet was not far enough gone in folly to abet him in this. She remonstrated, like the rest of his friends. Perfectly useless! He had but one answer to everything they could say: 'My career is closed.' What stuff!

"You will ask, naturally enough, what this perverse man is going to do next. I don't scruple to say that he is bent on committing suicide. Pray do not be alarmed! There is no fear of the pistol, the rope, or the river. Julian is simply courting death—within the limits of the law.

"This is strong language, I know. You shall hear what the facts are, and judge for yourself.

"Having resigned his curacy, his next proceeding was to offer his services, as volunteer, to a new missionary enterprise on the West Coast of Africa. The persons at the head of the mission proved, most fortunately, to have a proper sense of their duty. Expressing their conviction of the value of Julian's assistance in the most handsome terms, they made it nevertheless a condition of entertaining his proposal that he should submit to examination by a competent medical man. After some hesitation he consented to this. The doctor's report was conclusive. In Julian's present state of health the climate of West Africa would in all probability kill him in three months' time.

"Foiled in his first attempt, he addressed himself next to a London Mission. Here it was impossible to raise the question of climate, and here, I grieve to say, he has succeeded.

"He is now working—in other words, he is now deliberately risking his life—in the Mission to Green Anchor Fields. The district known by this name is situated in a remote part of London, near the Thames. It is notoriously infested by the most desperate and degraded set of wretches in the whole metropolitan population, and it is so thickly inhabited that it is hardly ever completely free from epidemic disease. In this horrible place, and among these dangerous people, Julian is now employing himself from morning to night. None of his old friends ever see him. Since he joined the Mission he has not even called on Lady Janet Roy.

"My pledge is redeemed—the facts are before you. Am I wrong in taking my gloomy view of the prospect? I cannot forget that this unhappy man was once my friend, and I really see no hope for him in the future. Deliberately self-exposed to the violence of ruffians and the outbreak of disease, who is to extricate him from his shocking position? The one person who can do it is the person whose association with him would be his ruin—Mercy Merrick. Heaven only knows what disasters it may be my painful duty to communicate to you in my next letter!

"You are so kind as to ask me to tell you something about myself and my plans.

"I have very little to say on either head. After what I have suffered—my feelings trampled on, my confidence betrayed—I am as yet hardly capable of deciding what I shall do. Returning to my old profession—to the army—is out of the question, in these leveling days, when any obscure person who can pass an examination may call himself my brother officer, and may one day, perhaps, command me as my superior in rank. If I think of any career, it is the career of diplomacy. Birth and breeding have not quite disappeared as essential qualifications in that branch of the public service. But I have decided nothing as yet.

"My mother and sisters, in the event of your returning to England, desire me to say that it will afford them the greatest pleasure to make your acquaintance. Sympathizing with me, they do not forget what you too have suffered. A warm welcome awaits you when you pay your first visit at our house. Most truly yours,

"HORACE HOLMCROFT."

II.

From MISS GRACE ROSEBERRY to MR. HORACE HOLMCROFT.

"DEAR MR. HOLMCROFT—I snatch a few moments from my other avocations to thank you for your most interesting and delightful letter. How well you describe, how accurately you judge! If Literature stood a little higher as a profession, I should almost advise you—but no! if you entered Literature, how could you associate with the people whom you would be likely to meet?

"Between ourselves, I always thought Mr. Julian Gray an overrated man.

I will not say he has justified my opinion. I will only say I pity him. But, dear Mr. Holmcroft, how can you, with your sound judgment, place the sad alternatives now before him on the same level? To die in Green Anchor Fields, or to fall into the clutches of that vile wretch—is there any comparison between the two? Better a thousand times die at the post of duty than marry Mercy Merrick.

"As I have written the creature's name, I may add—so as to have all the sooner done with the subject—that I shall look with anxiety for your next letter. Do not suppose that I feel the smallest curiosity about this degraded and designing woman. My interest in her is purely religious. To persons of my devout turn of mind she is an awful warning. When I feel Satan near me—it will be such a means of grace to think of Mercy Merrick!

"Poor Lady Janet! I noticed those signs of mental decay to which you so feelingly allude at the last interview I had with her in Mablethorpe House. If you can find an opportunity, will you say that I wish her well, here and hereafter? and will you please add that I do not omit to remember her in my prayers?

"There is just a chance of my visiting England toward the close of the autumn. My fortunes have changed since I wrote last. I have been received as reader and companion by a lady who is the wife of one of our high judicial functionaries in this part of the world. I do not take much interest in him; he is what they call a 'self-made man.' His wife is charming. Besides being a person of highly intellectual tastes, she is greatly her husband's superior—as you will understand when I tell you that she is related to the Gommerys of Pommery; not the Pommerys of Gommery, who (as your knowledge of our old families will inform you) only claim kindred with the younger branch of that ancient race.

"In the elegant and improving companionship which I now enjoy I should feel quite happy but for one drawback. The climate of Canada is not favorable to my kind patroness, and her medical advisers recommend her to winter in London. In this event, I am to have the privilege of accompanying her. Is it necessary to add that my first visit will be paid at your house? I feel already united by sympathy to your mother and your sisters. There is a sort of freemasonry among gentlewomen, is there not? With best thanks and remembrances, and many delightful anticipations of your next letter, believe me, dear Mr. Holmcroft,

"Truly yours,

"GRACE ROSEBERRY."

III.

From MR. HORACE HOLMCROFT to MISS GRACE ROSEBERRY.

"MY DEAR MISS ROSEBERRY—Pray excuse my long silence. I have waited for mail after mail, in the hope of being able to send you some good news at last. It is useless to wait longer. My worst forebodings have been realized: my painful duty compels me to write a letter which will surprise and shock you.

"Let me describe events in their order as they happened. In this way I may hope to gradually prepare your mind for what is to come.

"About three weeks after I wrote to you last, Julian Gray paid the penalty of his headlong rashness. I do not mean that he suffered any actual violence at the hands of the people among whom he had cast his lot. On the contrary, he succeeded, incredible as it may appear, in producing a favorable impression on the ruffians about him. As I understand it, they began by respecting his courage in venturing among them alone; and they ended in discovering that he was really interested in promoting their welfare. It is to the other peril, indicated in my last letter, that he has fallen a victim—the peril of disease. Not long after he began his labors in the district fever broke out. We only heard that Julian had been struck down by the epidemic when it was too late to remove him from the lodging that he occupied in the neighborhood. I made inquiries personally the moment the news reached us. The doctor in attendance refused to answer for his life.

"In this alarming state of things poor Lady Janet, impulsive and unreasonable as usual, insisted on leaving Mablethorpe House and taking up her residence near her nephew.

"Finding it impossible to persuade her of the folly of removing from home and its comforts at her age, I felt it my duty to accompany her. We found accommodation (such as it was) in a river-side inn, used by ship-captains and commercial travelers. I took it on myself to provide the best medical assistance, Lady Janet's insane prejudices against doctors impelling her to leave this important part of the arrangements entirely in my hands.

"It is needless to weary you by entering into details on the subject of Julian's illness.

"The fever pursued the ordinary course, and was characterized by the usual intervals of delirium and exhaustion succeeding each other. Subsequent events, which it is, unfortunately, necessary to relate to you, leave me no choice but to dwell (as briefly as possible) on the painful subject of the delirium. In other cases the wanderings of fever-stricken people present, I am told, a certain variety of range. In Julian's case they were limited to one topic. He talked incessantly of Mercy Merrick. His invariable petition to his medical attendants entreated them to send for her to nurse him. Day and night that one idea was in his mind, and that one name on his lips.

"The doctors naturally made inquiries as to this absent person. I was obliged (in confidence) to state the circumstances to them plainly.

"The eminent physician whom I had called in to superintend the treatment behaved admirably. Though he has risen from the lower order of the people, he has, strange to say, the instincts of a gentleman. He thoroughly understood our trying position, and felt all the importance of preventing such a person as Mercy Merrick from seizing the opportunity of intruding herself at the bedside. A soothing prescription (I have his own authority for saying it) was all that was required to meet the patient's case. The local doctor, on the other hand, a young man (and evidently a red-hot radical), proved to be obstinate, and, considering his position, insolent as well. 'I have nothing to do with the lady's character, and with your opinion of it,' he said to me. 'I have only, to the best of my judgment, to point out to you the likeliest means of saving the patient's life. Our art is at the end of its resources. Send for

Mercy Merrick, no matter who she is or what she is. There is just a chance—especially if she proves to be a sensible person and a good nurse—that he may astonish you all by recognizing her. In that case only, his recovery is probable. If you persist in disregarding his entreaties, if you let the delirium go on for four-and-twenty hours more, he is a dead man.'

"Lady Janet was, most unluckily, present when this impudent opinion was delivered at the bedside.

"Need I tell you the sequel? Called upon to choose between the course indicated by a physician who is making his five thousand a year, and who is certain of the next medical baronetcy, and the advice volunteered by an obscure general practitioner at the East End of London, who is not making his five hundred a year—need I stop to inform you of her ladyship's decision? You know her; and you will only too well understand that her next proceeding was to pay a third visit to the Refuge.

"Two hours later—I give you my word of honor I am not exaggerating—Mercy Merrick was established at Julian's bedside.

"The excuse, of course, was that it was her duty not to let any private scruples of her own stand in the way, when a medical authority had declared that she might save the patient's life. You will not be surprised to hear that I withdrew from the scene. The physician followed my example—after having written his soothing prescription, and having been grossly insulted by the local practitioner's refusing to make use of it. I went back in the doctor's carriage. He spoke most feelingly and properly. Without giving any positive opinion, I could see that he had abandoned all hope of Julian's recovery. 'We are in the hands of Providence, Mr. Holmcroft;' those were his last words as he set me down at my mother's door.

"I have hardly the heart to go on. If I studied my own wishes, I should feel inclined to stop here.

"Let me, at least, hasten to the end. In two or three days' time I received my first intelligence of the patient and his nurse. Lady Janet informed me that he had recognized her. When I heard this I felt prepared for what was to come. The next report announced that he was gaining strength, and the next that he was out of danger. Upon this Lady Janet returned to Mablethorpe House. I called there a week ago—and heard that he had been removed to the sea-side. I called yesterday—and received the latest information from her ladyship's own lips. My pen almost refuses to write it. Mercy Merrick has consented to marry him!

"An outrage on Society—that is how my mother and my sisters view it; that is how you will view it too. My mother has herself struck Julian's name off her invitation-list. The servants have their orders, if he presumes to call: 'Not at home.'

"I am unhappily only too certain that I am correct in writing to you of this disgraceful marriage as of a settled thing. Lady Janet went the length of showing me the letters—one from Julian, the other from the woman herself. Fancy Mercy Merrick in correspondence with Lady Janet Roy! addressing her as 'My dear Lady Janet,' and signing, 'Yours affectionately!'

"I had not the patience to read either of the letters through. Julian's tone is the tone of a Socialist; in my opinion his bishop ought to be informed of it. As for her she plays her part just as cleverly with her pen as she played it with her tongue. 'I cannot disguise from myself that I am wrong in yielding.... Sad forebodings fill my mind when I think of the future.... I feel as if the first contemptuous look that is cast at my husband will destroy my happiness, though it may not disturb him.... As long as I was parted from him I could control my own weakness, I could accept my hard lot. But how can I resist him after having watched for weeks at his bedside; after having seen his first smile, and heard his first grateful words to me while I was slowly helping him back to life?'

"There is the tone which she takes through four closely written pages of nauseous humility and clap-trap sentiment! It is enough to make one despise women. Thank God, there is the contrast at hand to remind me of what is due to the better few among the sex. I feel that my mother and my sisters are doubly precious to me now. May I add, on the side of consolation, that I prize with hardly inferior gratitude the privilege of corresponding with you?

"Farewell for the present. I am too rudely shaken in my most cherished convictions, I am too depressed and disheartened, to write more. All good wishes go with you, dear Miss Roseberry, until we meet.

"Most truly yours,

"HORACE HOLMCROFT."

IV.

Extracts from the DIARY of THE REVEREND JULIAN GRAY.

FIRST EXTRACT.

...."A month to-day since we were married! I have only one thing to say: I would cheerfully go through all that I have suffered to live this one month over again. I never knew what happiness was until now. And better still, I have persuaded Mercy that it is all her doing. I have scattered her misgivings to the winds; she is obliged to submit to evidence, and to own that she can make the happiness of my life.

"We go back to London to-morrow. She regrets leaving the tranquil retirement of this remote sea-side place—she dreads change. I care nothing for it. It is all one to me where I go, so long as my wife is with me."

SECOND EXTRACT.

"The first cloud has risen. I entered the room unexpectedly just now, and found her in tears.

"With considerable difficulty I persuaded her to tell me what had happened. Are there any limits to the mischief that can be done by the tongue of a foolish woman? The landlady at my lodgings is the woman, in this case. Having no decided plans for the future as yet, we returned (most unfortunately, as the event has proved) to the rooms in London which I inhabited in my bachelor days. They are still mine for six weeks to come, and Mercy was unwilling to let me incur the expense of taking her to a hotel. At breakfast this morning I rashly congratulated myself (in my wife's hearing) on finding that a much smaller collection than usual of letters and cards had accumulated in my absence. Breakfast over, I was obliged to go out. Painfully sensitive, poor thing, to any change in my experience of the little world around me which it is possible to connect with the event of my marriage, Mercy questioned the landlady, in my absence, about the diminished number of my visitors and my correspondents. The woman seized the opportunity of gossiping about me and my affairs, and my wife's quick perception drew the right conclusion unerringly. My marriage has decided certain wise heads of families on discontinuing their social relations with me. The facts, unfortunately, speak for themselves. People who in former years habitually called upon me and invited me—or who, in the event of my absence, habitually wrote to me at this season—have abstained with a remarkable unanimity from calling, inviting, or writing now.

"It would have been sheer waste of time—to say nothing of its also implying a want of confidence in my wife—if I had attempted to set things right by disputing Mercy's conclusion. I could only satisfy her that not so much as the shadow of disappointment or mortification rested on my mind. In this way I have, to some extent, succeeded in composing my poor darling. But the wound has been inflicted, and the wound is felt. There is no disguising that result. I must face it boldly.

"Trifling as this incident is in my estimation, it has decided me on one point already. In shaping my future course I am now resolved to act on my own convictions—in preference to taking the well-meant advice of such friends as are still left to me.

"All my little success in life has been gained in the pulpit. I am what is termed a popular preacher—but I have never, in my secret self, felt any exultation in my own notoriety, or any extraordinary respect for the means by which it has been won. In the first place, I have a very low idea of the importance of oratory as an intellectual accomplishment. There is no other art in which the conditions of success are so easy of attainment; there is no other art in the practice of which so much that is purely superficial passes itself off habitually for something that claims to be profound. Then, again, how poor it is in the results which it achieves! Take my own case. How often (for example) have I thundered with all my heart and soul against the wicked extravagance of dress among women—against their filthy false hair and their nauseous powders and paints! How often (to take another example) have I denounced the mercenary and material spirit of the age—the habitual corruptions and dishonesties of commerce, in high places and in low! What good have I done? I have delighted the very people whom it was my object to rebuke. 'What a charming sermon!' 'More eloquent than ever!' 'I used to dread the sermon at the other church—do you know, I quite look forward to it now.' That is the effect I produce on Sunday. On Monday the women are off to the milliners to spend more money than ever; the city men are off to business to make more money than ever—while my grocer, loud in my praises in his Sunday coat, turns up his week-day sleeves and adulterates his favorite preacher's sugar as cheerfully as usual!

"I have often, in past years, felt the objections to pursuing my career which are here indicated. They were bitterly present to my mind when I resigned my curacy, and they strongly influence me now.

"I am weary of my cheaply won success in the pulpit. I am weary of society as I find it in my time. I felt some respect for myself, and some heart and hope in my works among the miserable wretches in Green Anchor Fields. But I can not, and must not, return among them: I have no right, now, to trifle with my health and my life. I must go back to my preaching, or I must leave England. Among a primitive people, away from the cities—in the far and fertile West of the great American continent—I might live happily with my wife, and do good among my neighbors, secure of providing for our wants out of the modest little income which is almost useless to me here. In the life which I thus picture to myself I see love, peace, health, and duties and occupations that are worthy of a Christian man. What prospect is before me if I take the advice of my friends and stay here? Work of which I am weary, because I have long since ceased to respect it; petty malice that strikes at me through my wife, and mortifies and humiliates her, turn where she may. If I had only myself to think of, I might defy the worst that malice can do. But I have Mercy to think of—Mercy, whom I love better than my own life! Women live, poor things, in the opinions of others. I have had one warning already of what my wife is likely to suffer at the hands of my 'friends'—

Heaven forgive me for misusing the word! Shall I deliberately expose her to fresh mortifications?—and this for the sake of returning to a career the rewards of which I no longer prize? No! We will both be happy—we will both be free! God is merciful, Nature is kind, Love is true, in the New World as well as the Old. To the New World we will go!"

THIRD EXTRACT.

"I hardly know whether I have done right or wrong. I mentioned yesterday to Lady Janet the cold reception of me on my return to London, and the painful sense of it felt by my wife.

"My aunt looks at the matter from her own peculiar point of view, and makes light of it accordingly. 'You never did, and never will, understand Society, Julian,' said her ladyship. 'These poor stupid people simply don't know what to do. They are waiting to be told by a person of distinction whether they are, or are not, to recognize your marriage. In plain English, they are waiting to be led by Me. Consider it done. I will lead them.'

"I thought my aunt was joking. The event of to-day has shown me that she is terribly in earnest. Lady Janet has issued invitations for one of her grand balls at Mablethorpe House; and she has caused the report to be circulated everywhere that the object of the festival is 'to celebrate the marriage of Mr. and Mrs. Julian Gray!'

"I at first refused to be present. To my amazement, however, Mercy sides with my aunt. She reminds me of all that we both owe to Lady Janet; and she has persuaded me to alter my mind. We are to go to the ball—at my wife express request!

"The meaning of this, as I interpret it, is that my poor love is still pursued in secret by the dread that my marriage has injured me in the general estimation. She will suffer anything, risk anything, believe anything, to be freed from that one haunting doubt. Lady Janet predicts a social triumph; and my wife's despair—not my wife's conviction—accepts the prophecy. As for me, I am prepared for the result. It will end in our going to the New World, and trying Society in its infancy, among the forests and the plains. I shall quietly prepare for our departure, and own what I have done at the right time—that is to say, when the ball is over."

FOURTH EXTRACT.

"I have met with the man for my purpose—an old college friend of mine, now partner in a firm of ship-owners, largely concerned in emigration.

"One of their vessels sails for America, from the port of London, in a fortnight, touching at Plymouth. By a fortunate coincidence, Lady Janet's ball takes place in a fortnight. I see my way.

"Helped by the kindness of my friend, I have arranged to have a cabin kept in reserve, on payment of a small deposit. If the ball ends (as I believe it will) in new mortifications for Mercy—do what they may, I defy them to mortify me—I have only to say the word by telegraph, and we shall catch the ship at Plymouth.

"I know the effect it will have when I break the news to her, but I am prepared with my remedy. The pages of my diary, written in past years, will show plainly enough that it is not she who is driving me away from England. She will see the longing in me for other work and other scenes expressing itself over and over again long before the time when we first met."

FIFTH EXTRACT.

"Mercy's ball dress—a present from kind Lady Janet—is finished. I was allowed to see the first trial, or preliminary rehearsal, of this work of art. I don't in the least understand the merits of silk and lace; but one thing I know—my wife will be the most beautiful woman at the ball.

"The same day I called on Lady Janet to thank her, and encountered a new revelation of the wayward and original character of my dear old aunt.

"She was on the point of tearing up a letter when I went into her room. Seeing me, she suspended her purpose and handed me the letter. It was in Mercy's handwriting. Lady Janet pointed to a passage on the last page. 'Tell your wife, with my love,' she said, 'that I am the most obstinate woman of the two. I positively refuse to read her, as I positively refuse to listen to her, whenever she attempts to return to that one subject. Now give me the letter back.' I gave it back, and saw it torn up before my face. The 'one subject' prohibited to Mercy as sternly as ever is still the subject of the personation of Grace Roseberry! Nothing could have been more naturally introduced, or more delicately managed, than my wife's brief reference to the subject. No matter. The reading of the first line was enough. Lady Janet shut her eyes and destroyed the letter—Lady Janet is determined to live and die absolutely ignorant of the true story of 'Mercy Merrick.' What unanswerable riddles we are! Is it wonderful if we perpetually fail to understand one another?"

SIXTH EXTRACT.

"The morning after the ball.

"It is done and over. Society has beaten Lady Janet. I have neither patience nor time to write at length of it. We leave for Plymouth by the afternoon express.

"We were rather late in arriving at the ball. The magnificent rooms were filling fast. Walking through them with my wife, she drew my attention to a circumstance which I had not noticed at the time. 'Julian,' she said, 'look round among the lades, and tell me if you see anything strange.' As I looked round the band began playing a waltz. I observed that a few people only passed by us to the dancing-room. I noticed next that of those few fewer still were young. At last it burst upon me. With certain exceptions (so rare as to prove the rule), there were no young girls at Lady Janet's ball. I took Mercy at once back to the reception-room. Lady Janet's face showed that she, too, was aware of what had happened. The guests were still arriving. We received the men and their wives, the men and their mothers, the men and their grandmothers—but, in place of their unmarried daughters, elaborate excuses, offered with a shameless politeness wonderful to see. Yes! This was how the matrons in high life had got over the difficulty of meeting Mrs. Julian Gray at Lady Janet's house.

"Let me do strict justice to every one. The ladies who were present showed the needful respect for their hostess. They did their duty—no, overdid it, is perhaps the better phrase.

"I really had no adequate idea of the coarseness and rudeness which have filtered their way through society in these later times until I saw the reception accorded to my wife. The days of prudery and prejudice are days gone by. Excessive amiability and excessive liberality are the two favorite assumptions of the modern generation. To see the women expressing their liberal forgetfulness of my wifely misfortunes, and the men their amiable anxiety to encourage her husband; to hear the same set phrases repeated in every room—'So charmed to make your acquaintance, Mrs. Gray; so much obliged to dear Lady Janet for giving us this opportunity!—Julian, old man, what a beautiful creature! I envy you; upon my honor, I envy you!'—to receive this sort of welcome, emphasized by obtrusive hand-shakings, sometimes actually by downright kissings of my wife, and then to look round and see that not one in thirty of these very people had brought their unmarried daughters to the ball, was, I honestly believe, to see civilized human nature in its basest conceivable aspect. The New World may have its disappointments in store for us, but it cannot possibly show us any spectacle so abject as the spectacle which we witnessed last night at my aunt's ball.

"Lady Janet marked her sense of the proceeding adopted by her guests by leaving them to themselves. Her guests remained and supped heartily notwithstanding. They all knew by experience that there were no stale dishes and no cheap wines at Mablethorpe House. They drank to the end of the bottle, and they ate to the last truffle in the dish.

"Mercy and I had an interview with my aunt upstairs before we left. I felt it necessary to state plainly my resolution to leave England. The scene that followed was so painful that I cannot prevail on myself to return to it in these pages. My wife is reconciled to our departure; and Lady Janet accompanies us as far as Plymouth—these are the results. No words can express my sense of relief, now that it is all settled. The one sorrow I shall carry away with me from the shores of England will be the sorrow of parting with dear, warm-hearted Lady Janet. At her age it is a parting for life.

"So closes my connection with my own country. While I have Mercy by my side I face the unknown future, certain of carrying my happiness with me, go where I may. We shall find five hundred adventurers like ourselves when we join the emigrant ship, for whom their native land has no occupation and no home. Gentlemen of the Statistical Department, add two more to the number of social failures produced by England in the year of our Lord eighteen hundred and seventy-one—Julian Gray and Mercy Merrick."

THE TWO DESTINIES

The Prelude.

THE GUEST WRITES AND TELLS THE STORY OF THE DINNER PARTY.

MANY years have passed since my wife and I left the United States to pay our first visit to England.

We were provided with letters of introduction, as a matter of course. Among them there was a letter which had been written for us by my wife's brother. It presented us to an English gentleman who held a high rank on the list of his old and valued friends.

"You will become acquainted with Mr. George Germaine," my brother-in-law said, when we took leave of him, "at a very interesting period of his life. My last news of him tells me that he is just married. I know nothing of the lady, or of the circumstances under which my friend first met with her. But of this I am certain: married or single, George Germaine will give you and your wife a hearty welcome to England, for my sake."

The day after our arrival in London, we left our letter of introduction at the house of Mr. Germaine.

The next morning we went to see a favorite object of American interest, in the metropolis of England—the Tower of London. The citizens of the United States find this relic of the good old times of great use in raising their national estimate of the value of republican institutions. On getting back to the hotel, the cards of Mr. and Mrs. Germaine told us that they had already returned our visit. The same evening we received an invitation to dine with the newly married couple. It was inclosed in a little note from Mrs. Germaine to my wife, warning us that we were not to expect to meet a large party.

"It is the first dinner we give, on our return from our wedding tour" (the lady wrote); "and you will only be introduced to a few of my husband's old friends."

In America, and (as I hear) on the continent of Europe also, when your host invites you to dine at a given hour, you pay him the compliment of arriving punctually at his house. In England alone, the incomprehensible and discourteous custom prevails of keeping the host and the dinner waiting for half an hour or more—without any assignable reason and without any better excuse than the purely formal apology that is implied in the words, "Sorry to be late."

Arriving at the appointed time at the house of Mr. and Mrs. Germaine, we had every reason to congratulate ourselves on the ignorant punctuality which had brought us into the drawing-room half an hour in advance of the other guests.

In the first place, there was so much heartiness, and so little ceremony, in the welcome accorded to us, that we almost fancied ourselves back in our own country. In the second place, both husband and wife interested us the moment we set eyes on them. The lady, especially, although she was not, strictly speaking, a beautiful woman, quite fascinated us. There was an artless charm in her face and manner, a simple grace in all her movements, a low, delicious melody in her voice, which we Americans felt to be simply irresistible. And then, it was so plain (and so pleasant) to see that here at least was a happy marriage! Here were two people who had all their dearest hopes, wishes, and sympathies in common—who looked, if I may risk the expression, born to be man and wife. By the time when the fashionable delay of the half hour had expired, we were talking together as familiarly and as confidentially as if we had been all four of us old friends.

Eight o'clock struck, and the first of the English guests appeared.

Having forgotten this gentleman's name, I must beg leave to distinguish him by means of a letter of the alphabet. Let me call him Mr. A. When he entered the room alone, our host and hostess both started, and both looked surprised. Apparently they expected him to be accompanied by some other person. Mr. Germaine put a curious question to his friend.

"Where is your wife?" he asked.

Mr. A answered for the absent lady by a neat little apology, expressed in these words:

"She has got a bad cold. She is very sorry. She begs me to make her excuses."

He had just time to deliver his message, before another unaccompanied gentleman appeared. Reverting to the letters of the alphabet, let me call him Mr. B. Once more, I noticed that our host and hostess started when they saw him enter the room alone. And, rather to my surprise, I heard Mr. Germaine put his curious question again to the new guest:

"Where is your wife?"

The answer—with slight variations—was Mr. A's neat little apology, repeated by Mr. B.

"I am very sorry. Mrs. B has got a bad headache. She is subject to bad headaches. She begs me to make her excuses."

Mr. and Mrs. Germaine glanced at one another. The husband's face plainly expressed the suspicion which this second apology had roused in his mind. The wife was steady and calm. An interval passed—a silent interval. Mr. A and Mr. B retired together guiltily into a corner. My wife and I looked at the pictures.

Mrs. Germaine was the first to relieve us from our own intolerable silence. Two more guests, it appeared, were still wanting to complete the party. "Shall we have dinner at once, George?" she said to her husband. "Or shall we wait for Mr. and Mrs. C?"

"We will wait five minutes," he answered, shortly—with his eye on Mr. A and Mr. B, guiltily secluded in their corner.

The drawing-room door opened. We all knew that a third married lady was expected; we all looked toward the door in unutterable anticipation.

Our unexpressed hopes rested silently on the possible appearance of Mrs. C. Would that admirable, but unknown, woman, at once charm and relieve us by her presence? I shudder as I write it. Mr. C walked into the room—and walked in, alone.

Mr. Germaine suddenly varied his formal inquiry in receiving the new guest.

"Is your wife ill?" he asked.

Mr. C was an elderly man; Mr. C had lived (judging by appearances) in the days when the old-fashioned laws of politeness were still in force. He discovered his two married brethren in their corner, unaccompanied by their wives; and he delivered his apology for his wife with the air of a man who felt unaffectedly ashamed of it:

"Mrs. C is so sorry. She has got such a bad cold. She does so regret not being able to accompany me."

At this third apology, Mr. Germaine's indignation forced its way outward into expression in words.

"Two bad colds and one bad headache," he said, with ironical politeness. "I don't know how your wives agree, gentlemen, when they are well. But when they are ill, their unanimity is wonderful!"

The dinner was announced as that sharp saying passed his lips.

I had the honor of taking Mrs. Germaine to the dining-room. Her sense of the implied insult offered to her by the wives of her husband's friends only showed itself in a trembling, a very slight trembling, of the hand that rested on my arm. My interest in her increased tenfold. Only a woman who had been accustomed to suffer, who had been broken and disciplined to self-restraint, could have endured the moral martyrdom inflicted on her as this woman endured it, from the beginning of the evening to the end.

Am I using the language of exaggeration when I write of my hostess in these terms? Look at the circumstances as they struck two strangers like my wife and myself.

Here was the first dinner party which Mr. and Mrs. Germaine had given since their marriage. Three of Mr. Germaine's friends, all married men, had been invited with their wives to meet Mr. Germaine's wife, and had (evidently) accepted the invitation without reserve. What discoveries had taken place between the giving of the invitation and the giving of the dinner it was impossible to say. The one thing plainly discernible was, that in the interval the three wives had agreed in the resolution to leave their husbands to represent them at Mrs. Germaine's table; and, more amazing still, the husbands had so far approved of the grossly discourteous conduct of the wives as to consent to make the most insultingly trivial excuses for their absence. Could any crueler slur than this have been cast on a woman at the outset of her married life, before the face of her husband, and in the presence of two strangers from another country? Is "martyrdom" too big a word to use in describing what a sensitive person must have suffered, subjected to such treatment as this? Well, I think not.

We took our places at the dinner-table. Don't ask me to describe that most miserable of mortal meetings, that weariest and dreariest of human festivals! It is quite bad enough to remember that evening—it is indeed.

My wife and I did our best to keep the conversation moving as easily and as harmlessly as might be. I may say that we really worked hard. Nevertheless, our success was not very encouraging. Try as we might to overlook them, there were the three empty places of the three absent women, speaking in their own dismal language for themselves. Try as we might to resist it, we all felt the one sad conclusion which those empty places persisted in forcing on our minds. It was surely too plain that some terrible report, affecting the character of the unhappy woman at the head of the table, had unexpectedly come to light, and had at one blow destroyed her position in the estimation of her husband's friends. In the face of the excuses in the drawing-room, in the face of the empty places at the dinner-table, what could the friendliest guests do, to any good purpose, to help the husband and wife in their sore and sudden need? They could say good-night at the earliest possible opportunity, and mercifully leave the married pair to themselves.

Let it at least be recorded to the credit of the three gentlemen, designated in these pages as A, B, and C, that they were sufficiently ashamed of themselves and their wives to be the first members of the dinner party who left the house. In a few minutes more we rose to follow their example. Mrs. Germaine earnestly requested that we would delay our departure.

"Wait a few minutes," she whispered, with a glance at her husband. "I have something to say to you before you go."

She left us, and, taking Mr. Germaine by the arm, led him away to the opposite side of the room. The two held a little colloquy together in low voices. The husband closed the consultation by lifting the wife's hand to his lips.

"Do as you please, my love," he said to her. "I leave it entirely to you."

He sat down sorrowfully, lost in his thoughts. Mrs. Germaine unlocked a cabinet at the further end of the room, and returned to us, alone, carrying a small portfolio in her hand.

"No words of mine can tell you how gratefully I feel your kindness," she said, with perfect simplicity, and with perfect dignity at the same time. "Under very trying circumstances, you have treated me with the tenderness and the sympathy which you might have shown to an old friend. The one return I can make for all that I owe to you is to admit you to my fullest confidence, and to leave you to judge for yourselves whether I deserve the treatment which I have received to-night."

Her eyes filled with tears. She paused to control herself. We both begged her to say no more. Her husband, joining us, added his entreaties to ours. She thanked us, but she persisted. Like most sensitively organized persons, she could be resolute when she believed that the occasion called for it.

"I have a few words more to say," she resumed, addressing my wife. "You are the only married woman who has come to our little dinner party. The marked absence of the other wives explains itself. It is not for me to say whether they are right or wrong in refusing to sit at our table. My dear husband—who knows my whole life as well as I know it myself—expressed the wish that we should invite these ladies. He wrongly supposed that his

326

estimate of me would be the estimate accepted by his friends; and neither he nor I anticipated that the misfortunes of my past life would be revealed by some person acquainted with them, whose treachery we have yet to discover. The least I can do, by way of acknowledging your kindness, is to place you in the same position toward me which the other ladies now occupy. The circumstances under which I have become the wife of Mr. Germaine are, in some respects, very remarkable. They are related, without suppression or reserve, in a little narrative which my husband wrote, at the time of our marriage, for the satisfaction of one of his absent relatives, whose good opinion he was unwilling to forfeit. The manuscript is in this portfolio. After what has happened, I ask you both to read it, as a personal favor to me. It is for you to decide, when you know all, whether I am a fit person for an honest woman to associate with or not."

She held out her hand, with a sweet, sad smile, and bid us good night. My wife, in her impulsive way, forgot the formalities proper to the occasion, and kissed her at parting. At that one little act of sisterly sympathy, the fortitude which the poor creature had preserved all through the evening gave way in an instant. She burst into tears.

I felt as fond of her and as sorry for her as my wife. But (unfortunately) I could not take my wife's privilege of kissing her. On our way downstairs, I found the opportunity of saying a cheering word to her husband as he accompanied us to the door.

"Before I open this," I remarked, pointing to the portfolio under my arm, "my mind is made up, sir, about one thing. If I wasn't married already, I tell you this—I should envy you your wife."

He pointed to the portfolio in his turn.

"Read what I have written there," he said; "and you will understand what those false friends of mine have made me suffer to-night."

The next morning my wife and I opened the portfolio, and read the strange story of George Germaine's marriage.

The Narrative.

GEORGE GERMAINE WRITES,

AND TELLS HIS OWN LOVE STORY.

CHAPTER I. GREENWATER BROAD

LOOK back, my memory, through the dim labyrinth of the past, through the mingling joys and sorrows of twenty years. Rise again, my boyhood's days, by the winding green shores of the little lake. Come to me once more, my child-love, in the innocent beauty of your first ten years of life. Let us live again, my angel, as we lived in our first paradise, before sin and sorrow lifted their flaming swords and drove us out into the world.

The month was March. The last wild fowl of the season were floating on the waters of the lake which, in our Suffolk tongue, we called Greenwater Broad.

Wind where it might, the grassy banks and the overhanging trees tinged the lake with the soft green reflections from which it took its name. In a creek at the south end, the boats were kept—my own pretty sailing boat having a tiny natural harbor all to itself. In a creek at the north end stood the great trap (called a "decoy"), used for snaring the wild fowl which flocked every winter, by thousands and thousands, to Greenwater Broad.

My little Mary and I went out together, hand in hand, to see the last birds of the season lured into the decoy.

The outer part of the strange bird-trap rose from the waters of the lake in a series of circular arches, formed of elastic branches bent to the needed shape, and covered with folds of fine network, making the roof. Little by little diminishing in size, the arches and their net-work followed the secret windings of the creek inland to its end. Built back round the arches, on their landward side, ran a wooden paling, high enough to hide a man kneeling behind it from the view of the birds on the lake. At certain intervals a hole was broken in the paling just large enough to allow of the passage through it of a dog of the terrier or the spaniel breed. And there began and ended the simple yet sufficient mechanism of the decoy.

In those days I was thirteen, and Mary was ten years old. Walking on our way to the lake we had Mary's father with us for guide and companion. The good man served as bailiff on my father's estate. He was, besides, a skilled master in the art of decoying ducks. The dog that helped him (we used no tame ducks as decoys in Suffolk) was a little black terrier; a skilled master also, in his way; a creature who possessed, in equal proportions, the enviable advantages of perfect good-humor and perfect common sense.

The dog followed the bailiff, and we followed the dog.

Arrived at the paling which surrounded the decoy, the dog sat down to wait until he was wanted. The bailiff and the children crouched behind the paling, and peeped through the outermost dog-hole, which commanded a full view of the lake. It was a day without wind; not a ripple stirred the surface of the water; the soft gray clouds filled all the sky, and hid the sun from view.

We peeped through the hole in the paling. There were the wild ducks—collected within easy reach of the decoy—placidly dressing their feathers on the placid surface of the lake.

The bailiff looked at the dog, and made a sign. The dog looked at the bailiff; and, stepping forward quietly, passed through the hole, so as to show himself on the narrow strip of ground shelving down from the outer side of the paling to the lake.

First one duck, then another, then half a dozen together, discovered the dog.

A new object showing itself on the solitary scene instantly became an object of all-devouring curiosity to the ducks. The outermost of them began to swim slowly toward the strange four-footed creature, planted motionless on the bank. By twos and threes, the main body of the waterfowl gradually followed the advanced guard. Swimming nearer and nearer to the dog, the wary ducks suddenly came to a halt, and, poised on the water, viewed from a safe distance the phenomenon on the land.

The bailiff, kneeling behind the paling, whispered, "Trim!"

Hearing his name, the terrier turned about, and retiring through the hole, became lost to the view of the ducks. Motionless on the water, the wild fowl wondered and waited. In a minute more, the dog had trotted round, and had shown himself through the next hole in the paling, pierced further inward where the lake ran up into the outermost of the windings of the creek.

The second appearance of the terrier instantly produced a second fit of curiosity among the ducks. With one accord, they swam forward again, to get another and a nearer view of the dog; then, judging their safe distance once more, they stopped for the second time, under the outermost arch of the decoy. Again the dog vanished, and the puzzled ducks waited. An interval passed, and the third appearance of Trim took place, through a third hole in the paling, pierced further inland up the creek. For the third time irresistible curiosity urged the ducks to advance further and further inward, under the fatal arches of the decoy. A fourth and a fifth time the game went on, until the dog had lured the water-fowl from point to point into the inner recesses of the decoy. There a last appearance of Trim took place. A last advance, a last cautious pause, was made by the ducks. The bailiff touched the strings, the weighed net-work fell vertically into the water, and closed the decoy. There, by dozens and dozens, were the ducks, caught by means of their own curiosity—with nothing but a little dog for a bait! In a few hours afterward they were all dead ducks on their way to the London market.

As the last act in the curious comedy of the decoy came to its end, little Mary laid her hand on my shoulder, and, raising herself on tiptoe, whispered in my ear:

"George, come home with me. I have got something to show you that is better worth seeing than the ducks."

"What is it?"

"It's a surprise. I won't tell you."

"Will you give me a kiss?"

The charming little creature put her slim sun-burned arms round my neck, and answered:

"As many kisses as you like, George."

It was innocently said, on her side. It was innocently done, on mine. The good easy bailiff, looking aside at the moment from his ducks, discovered us pursuing our boy-and-girl courtship in each other's arms. He shook his big forefinger at us, with something of a sad and doubting smile.

"Ah, Master George, Master George!" he said. "When your father comes home, do you think he will approve of his son and heir kissing his bailiff's daughter?"

"When my father comes home," I answered, with great dignity, "I shall tell him the truth. I shall say I am going to marry your daughter."

The bailiff burst out laughing, and looked back again at his ducks.

"Well, well!" we heard him say to himself. "They're only children. There's no call, poor things, to part them yet awhile."

Mary and I had a great dislike to be called children. Properly understood, one of us was a lady aged ten, and the other was a gentleman aged thirteen. We left the good bailiff indignantly, and went away together, hand in hand, to the cottage.

CHAPTER II. TWO YOUNG HEARTS.

"HE is growing too fast," said the doctor to my mother; "and he is getting a great deal too clever for a boy at his age. Remove him from school, ma'am, for six months; let him run about in the open air at home; and if you find him with a book in his hand, take it away directly. There is my prescription."

Those words decided my fate in life.

In obedience to the doctor's advice, I was left an idle boy—without brothers, sisters, or companions of my own age—to roam about the grounds of our lonely country-house. The bailiff's daughter, like me, was an only child; and, like me, she had no playfellows. We met in our wanderings on the solitary shores of the lake. Beginning by being inseparable companions, we ripened and developed into true lovers. Our preliminary courtship concluded, we next proposed (before I returned to school) to burst into complete maturity by becoming man and wife.

I am not writing in jest. Absurd as it may appear to "sensible people," we two children were lovers, if ever there were lovers yet.

We had no pleasures apart from the one all-sufficient pleasure which we found in each other's society. We objected to the night, because it parted us. We entreated our parents, on either side, to let us sleep in the same room. I was angry with my mother, and Mary was disappointed in her father, when they laughed at us, and wondered what we should want next. Looking onward, from those days to the days of my manhood, I can vividly recall such hours of happiness as have fallen to my share. But I remember no delights of that later time comparable to the exquisite and enduring pleasure that filled my young being when I walked with Mary in the woods; when I sailed with Mary in my boat on the lake; when I met Mary, after the cruel separation of the night, and flew into her open arms as if we had been parted for months and months together.

What was the attraction that drew us so closely one to the other, at an age when the sexual sympathies lay dormant in her and in me?

We neither knew nor sought to know. We obeyed the impulse to love one another, as a bird obeys the impulse to fly.

Let it not be supposed that we possessed any natural gifts, or advantages which singled us out as differing in a marked way from other children at our time of life. We possessed nothing of the sort. I had been called a clever boy at school; but there were thousands of other boys, at thousands of other schools, who headed their classes and won their prizes, like me. Personally speaking, I was in no way remarkable—except for being, in the ordinary phrase, "tall for my age." On her side, Mary displayed no striking attractions. She was a fragile child, with mild gray eyes and a pale complexion; singularly undemonstrative, singularly shy and silent, except when she was alone with me. Such beauty as she had, in those early days, lay in a certain artless purity and tenderness of expression, and in the charming reddish-brown color of her hair, varying quaintly and prettily in different lights. To all outward appearance two perfectly commonplace children, we were mysteriously united by some kindred association of the spirit in her and the spirit in me, which not only defied discovery by our young selves, but which lay too deep for investigation by far older and far wiser heads than ours.

You will naturally wonder whether anything was done by our elders to check our precocious attachment, while it was still an innocent love union between a boy and a girl.

Nothing was done by my father, for the simple reason that he was away from home.

He was a man of a restless and speculative turn of mind. Inheriting his estate burdened with debt, his grand ambition was to increase his small available income by his own exertions; to set up an establishment in London; and to climb to political distinction by the ladder of Parliament. An old friend, who had emigrated to America, had proposed to him a speculation in agriculture, in one of the Western States, which was to make both their fortunes. My father's eccentric fancy was struck by the idea. For more than a year past he had been away from us in the United States; and all we knew of him (instructed by his letters) was, that he might be shortly expected to return to us in the enviable character of one of the richest men in England.

As for my poor mother—the sweetest and softest-hearted of women—to see me happy was all that she desired.

The quaint little love romance of the two children amused and interested her. She jested with Mary's father about the coming union between the two families, without one serious thought of the future—without even a foreboding of what might happen when my father returned. "Sufficient for the day is the evil (or the good) thereof," had been my mother's motto all her life. She agreed with the easy philosophy of the bailiff, already recorded in these pages: "They're only children. There's no call, poor things, to part them yet a while."

There was one member of the family, however, who took a sensible and serious view of the matter.

My father's brother paid us a visit in our solitude; discovered what was going on between Mary and me; and was, at first, naturally enough, inclined to laugh at us. Closer investigation altered his way of thinking. He became convinced that my mother was acting like a fool; that the bailiff (a faithful servant, if ever there was one yet) was cunningly advancing his own interests by means of his daughter; and that I was a young idiot, who had developed his native reserves of imbecility at an unusually early period of life. Speaking to my mother under the influence of these strong impressions, my uncle offered to take me back with him to London, and keep me there until I had been brought to my senses by association with his own children, and by careful superintendence under his own roof.

My mother hesitated about accepting this proposal; she had the advantage over my uncle of understanding my disposition. While she was still doubting, while my uncle was still impatiently waiting for her decision, I settled the question for my elders by running away.

I left a letter to represent me in my absence; declaring that no mortal power should part me from Mary, and promising to return and ask my mother's pardon as soon as my uncle had left the house. The strictest search was made for me without discovering a trace of my place of refuge. My uncle departed for London, predicting that I should live to be a disgrace to the family, and announcing that he should transmit his opinion of me to my father in America by the next mail.

The secret of the hiding-place in which I contrived to defy discovery is soon told. I was hidden (without the bailiff's knowledge) in the bedroom of the bailiff's mother. And did the bailiff's mother know it? you will ask. To which I answer: the bailiff's mother did it. And, what is more, gloried in doing it—not, observe, as an act of hostility to my relatives, but simply as a duty that lay on her conscience.

What sort of old woman, in the name of all that is wonderful, was this? Let her appear, and speak for herself—the wild and weird grandmother of gentle little Mary; the Sibyl of modern times, known, far and wide, in our part of Suffolk, as Dame Dermody.

I see her again, as I write, sitting in her son's pretty cottage parlor, hard by the window, so that the light fell over her shoulder while she knitted or read. A little, lean, wiry old woman was Dame Dermody—with fierce black eyes, surmounted by bushy white eyebrows, by a high wrinkled forehead, and by thick white hair gathered neatly under her old-fashioned "mob-cap." Report whispered (and whispered truly) that she had been a lady by birth and breeding, and that she had deliberately closed her prospects in life by marrying a man greatly her inferior in social rank. Whatever her family might think of her marriage, she herself never regretted it. In her estimation her husband's memory was a sacred memory; his spirit was a guardian spirit, watching over her, waking or sleeping, morning or night.

Holding this faith, she was in no respect influenced by those grossly material ideas of modern growth which associate the presence of spiritual beings with clumsy conjuring tricks and monkey antics performed on tables and chairs. Dame Dermody's nobler superstition formed an integral part of her religious convictions—convictions which had long since found their chosen resting-place in the mystic doctrines of Emanuel Swedenborg. The only books which she read were the works of the Swedish Seer. She mixed up Swedenborg's teachings on angels and departed spirits, on love to one's neighbor and purity of life, with wild fancies, and kindred beliefs of her own; and preached the visionary religious doctrines thus derived, not only in the bailiff's household, but also on proselytizing expeditions to the households of her humble neighbors, far and near.

Under her son's roof—after the death of his wife—she reigned a supreme power; priding herself alike on her close attention to her domestic duties, and on her privileged communications with angels and spirits. She would hold long colloquys with the spirit of her dead husband before anybody who happened to be present—colloquys which struck the simple spectators mute with terror. To her mystic view, the love union between Mary and me was something too sacred and too beautiful to be tried by the mean and matter-of-fact tests set up by society. She wrote for us little formulas of prayer and praise, which we were to use when we met and when we parted, day by day. She solemnly warned her son to look upon us as two young consecrated creatures, walking unconsciously on a heavenly path of their own, whose beginning was on earth, but whose bright end was among the angels in a better state of being. Imagine my appearing before such a woman as this, and telling her with tears of despair that I was determined to die, rather than let my uncle part me from little Mary, and you will no longer be astonished at the hospitality which threw open to me the sanctuary of Dame Dermody's own room.

When the safe time came for leaving my hiding-place, I committed a serious mistake. In thanking the old woman at parting, I said to her (with a boy's sense of honor), "I won't tell upon you, Dame. My mother shan't know that you hid me in your bedroom."

The Sibyl laid her dry, fleshless hand on my shoulder, and forced me roughly back into the chair from which I had just risen.

"Boy!" she said, looking through and through me with her fierce black eyes. "Do you dare suppose that I ever did anything that I was ashamed of?

Do you think I am ashamed of what I have done now? Wait there. Your mother may mistake me too. I shall write to your mother."

She put on her great round spectacles with tortoise-shell rims and sat down to her letter. Whenever her thoughts flagged, whenever she was at a loss for an expression, she looked over her shoulder, as if some visible creature were stationed behind her, watching what she wrote; consulted the spirit of her husband, exactly as she might have consulted a living man; smiled softly to herself, and went on with her writing.

"There!" she said, handing me the completed letter with an imperial gesture of indulgence. "His mind and my mind are written there. Go, boy. I pardon you. Give my letter to your mother."

So she always spoke, with the same formal and measured dignity of manner and language.

I gave the letter to my mother. We read it, and marveled over it together. Thus, counseled by the ever-present spirit of her husband, Dame Dermody wrote:

"MADAM—I have taken what you may be inclined to think a great liberty. I have assisted your son George in setting his uncle's authority at defiance. I have encouraged your son George in his resolution to be true, in time and in eternity, to my grandchild, Mary Dermody.

"It is due to you and to me that I should tell you with what motive I have acted in doing these things.

"I hold the belief that all love that is true is foreordained and consecrated in heaven. Spirits destined to be united in the better world are divinely commissioned to discover each other and to begin their union in this world. The only happy marriages are those in which the two destined spirits have succeeded in meeting one another in this sphere of life.

"When the kindred spirits have once met, no human power can really part them. Sooner or later, they must, by divine law, find each other again and become united spirits once more. Worldly wisdom may force them into

337

widely different ways of life; worldly wisdom may delude them, or may make them delude themselves, into contracting an earthly and a fallible union. It matters nothing. The time will certainly come when that union will manifest itself as earthly and fallible; and the two disunited spirits, finding each other again, will become united here for the world beyond this—united, I tell you, in defiance of all human laws and of all human notions of right and wrong.

"This is my belief. I have proved it by my own life. Maid, wife, and widow, I have held to it, and I have found it good.

"I was born, madam, in the rank of society to which you belong. I received the mean, material teaching which fulfills the worldly notion of education. Thanks be to God, my kindred spirit met my spirit while I was still young. I knew true love and true union before I was twenty years of age. I married, madam, in the rank from which Christ chose his apostles—I married a laboring-man. No human language can tell my happiness while we lived united here. His death has not parted us. He helps me to write this letter. In my last hours I shall see him standing among the angels, waiting for me on the banks of the shining river.

"You will now understand the view I take of the tie which unites the young spirits of our children at the bright outset of their lives.

"Believe me, the thing which your husband's brother has proposed to you to do is a sacrilege and a profanation. I own to you freely that I look on what I have done toward thwarting your relative in this matter as an act of virtue. You cannot expect me to think it a serious obstacle to a union predestined in heaven, that your son is the squire's heir, and that my grandchild is only the bailiff's daughter. Dismiss from your mind, I implore you, the unworthy and unchristian prejudices of rank. Are we not all equal before God? Are we not all equal (even in this world) before disease and death? Not your son's happiness only, but your own peace of mind, is concerned in taking heed to my words. I warn you, madam, you cannot hinder the destined union of these two child-spirits, in after-years, as man and wife. Part them now— and YOU will be responsible for the sacrifices, degradations and distresses through which your George and my Mary may be condemned to pass on their way back to each other in later life.

"Now my mind is unburdened. Now I have said all.

"If I have spoken too freely, or have in any other way unwittingly offended, I ask your pardon, and remain, madam, your faithful servant and well-wisher, HELEN DERMODY."

So the letter ended.

To me it is something more than a mere curiosity of epistolary composition. I see in it the prophecy—strangely fulfilled in later years—of events in Mary's life, and in mine, which future pages are now to tell.

My mother decided on leaving the letter unanswered. Like many of her poorer neighbors, she was a little afraid of Dame Dermody; and she was, besides, habitually averse to all discussions which turned on the mysteries of spiritual life. I was reproved, admonished, and forgiven; and there was the end of it.

For some happy weeks Mary and I returned, without hinderance or interruption, to our old intimate companionship The end was coming, however, when we least expected it. My mother was startled, one morning, by a letter from my father, which informed her that he had been unexpectedly obliged to sail for England at a moment's notice; that he had arrived in London, and that he was detained there by business which would admit of no delay. We were to wait for him at home, in daily expectation of seeing him the moment he was free.

This news filled my mother's mind with foreboding doubts of the stability of her husband's grand speculation in America. The sudden departure from the United States, and the mysterious delay in London, were ominous, to her eyes, of misfortune to come. I am now writing of those dark days in the past, when the railway and the electric telegraph were still visions in the minds of inventors. Rapid communication with my father (even if he would have consented to take us into his confidence) was impossible. We had no choice but to wait and hope.

The weary days passed; and still my father's brief letters described him as detained by his business. The morning came when Mary and I went out with Dermody, the bailiff, to see the last wild fowl of the season lured into the decoy; and still the welcome home waited for the master, and waited in vain.

CHAPTER III. SWEDENBORG AND THE SIBYL.

MY narrative may move on again from the point at which it paused in the first chapter.

Mary and I (as you may remember) had left the bailiff alone at the decoy, and had set forth on our way together to Dermody's cottage.

As we approached the garden gate, I saw a servant from the house waiting there. He carried a message from my mother—a message for me.

"My mistress wishes you to go home, Master George, as soon as you can. A letter has come by the coach. My master means to take a post-chaise from London, and sends word that we may expect him in the course of the day."

Mary's attentive face saddened when she heard those words.

"Must you really go away, George," she whispered, "before you see what I have got waiting for you at home?"

I remembered Mary's promised "surprise," the secret of which was only to be revealed to me when we got to the cottage. How could I disappoint her? My poor little lady-love looked ready to cry at the bare prospect of it.

I dismissed the servant with a message of the temporizing sort. My love to my mother—and I would be back at the house in half an hour.

We entered the cottage.

Dame Dermody was sitting in the light of the window, as usual, with one of the mystic books of Emanuel Swedenborg open on her lap. She solemnly lifted her hand on our appearance, signing to us to occupy our customary corner without speaking to her. It was an act of domestic high treason to interrupt the Sibyl at her books. We crept quietly into our places. Mary waited until she saw her grandmother's gray head bend down, and her grandmother's bushy eyebrows contract attentively, over her reading. Then, and then only, the discreet child rose on tiptoe, disappeared noiselessly in the direction of her bedchamber, and came back to me carrying something carefully wrapped up in her best cambric handkerchief.

"Is that the surprise?" I whispered.

Mary whispered back: "Guess what it is?"

"Something for me?"

"Yes. Go on guessing. What is it?"

I guessed three times, and each guess was wrong. Mary decided on helping me by a hint.

"Say your letters," she suggested; "and go on till I stop you."

I began: "A, B, C, D, E, F—" There she stopped me.

"It's the name of a Thing," she said; "and it begins with F."

I guessed, "Fern," "Feather," "Fife." And here my resources failed me.

Mary sighed, and shook her head. "You don't take pains," she said. "You are three whole years older than I am. After all the trouble I have taken to please you, you may be too big to care for my present when you see it. Guess again."

"I can't guess."

"You must!"

"I give it up."

Mary refused to let me give it up. She helped me by another hint.

"What did you once say you wished you had in your boat?" she asked.

"Was it long ago?" I inquired, at a loss for an answer.

"Long, long ago! Before the winter. When the autumn leaves were falling, and you took me out one evening for a sail. Ah, George, you have forgotten!"

Too true, of me and of my brethren, old and young alike! It is always his love that forgets, and her love that remembers. We were only two children, and we were types of the man and the woman already.

Mary lost patience with me. Forgetting the terrible presence of her grandmother, she jumped up, and snatched the concealed object out of her handkerchief.

"There!" she cried, briskly, "now do you know what it is?"

I remembered at last. The thing I had wished for in my boat, all those months ago, was a new flag. And here was the flag, made for me in secret by Mary's own hand! The ground was green silk, with a dove embroidered on it in white, carrying in its beak the typical olive-branch, wrought in gold thread. The work was the tremulous, uncertain work of a child's fingers. But how faithfully my little darling had remembered my wish! how patiently she had plied the needle over the traced lines of the pattern! how industriously she had labored through the dreary winter days! and all for my sake! What words could tell my pride, my gratitude, my happiness?

I too forgot the presence of the Sibyl bending over her book. I took the little workwoman in my arms, and kissed her till I was fairly out of breath and could kiss no longer.

"Mary!" I burst out, in the first heat of my enthusiasm, "my father is coming home to-day. I will speak to him to-night. And I will marry you to-morrow!"

"Boy!" said the awful voice at the other end of the room. "Come here."

Dame Dermody's mystic book was closed; Dame Dermody's weird black eyes were watching us in our corner. I approached her; and Mary followed me timidly, by a footstep at a time.

The Sibyl took me by the hand, with a caressing gentleness which was new in my experience of her.

"Do you prize that toy?" she inquired, looking at the flag. "Hide it!" she cried, before I could answer. "Hide it—or it may be taken from you!"

"Why should I hide it?" I asked. "I want to fly it at the mast of my boat."

"You will never fly it at the mast of your boat!" With that answer she took the flag from me and thrust it impatiently into the breast-pocket of my jacket.

"Don't crumple it, grandmother!" said Mary, piteously.

I repeated my question:

"Why shall I never fly it at the mast of my boat?"

Dame Dermody laid her hand on the closed volume of Swedenborg lying in her lap.

"Three times I have opened this book since the morning," she said. "Three times the words of the prophet warn me that there is trouble coming. Children, it is trouble that is coming to You. I look there," she went on, pointing to the place where a ray of sunlight poured slanting into the room, "and I see my husband in the heavenly light. He bows his head in grief, and he points his unerring hand at You. George and Mary, you are consecrated to each other! Be always worthy of your consecration; be always worthy of yourselves." She paused. Her voice faltered. She looked at us with softening eyes, as those look who know sadly that there is a parting at hand. "Kneel!" she said, in low tones of awe and grief. "It may be the last time I bless you—it may be the last time I pray over you, in this house. Kneel!"

We knelt close together at her feet. I could feel Mary's heart throbbing, as she pressed nearer and nearer to my side. I could feel my own heart quickening its beat, with a fear that was a mystery to me.

"God bless and keep George and Mary, here and hereafter! God prosper, in future days, the union which God's wisdom has willed! Amen. So be it. Amen."

As the last words fell from her lips the cottage door was thrust open. My father—followed by the bailiff—entered the room.

Dame Dermody got slowly on her feet, and looked at him with a stern scrutiny.

"It has come," she said to herself. "It looks with the eyes—it will speak with the voice—of that man."

My father broke the silence that followed, addressing himself to the bailiff.

"You see, Dermody," he said, "here is my son in your cottage—when he ought to be in my house." He turned, and looked at me as I stood with my arm round little Mary, patiently waiting for my opportunity to speak. "George," he said, with the hard smile which was peculiar to him, when he was angry and was trying to hide it, "you are making a fool of yourself there. Leave that child, and come to me."

Now, or never, was my time to declare myself. Judging by appearances, I was still a boy. Judging by my own sensations, I had developed into a man at a moment's notice.

"Papa," I said, "I am glad to see you home again. This is Mary Dermody. I am in love with her, and she is in love with me. I wish to marry her as soon as it is convenient to my mother and you."

My father burst out laughing. Before I could speak again, his humor changed. He had observed that Dermody, too, presumed to be amused. He seemed to become mad with anger, all in a moment.

"I have been told of this infernal tomfoolery," he said, "but I didn't believe it till now. Who has turned the boy's weak head? Who has encouraged him to stand there hugging that girl? If it's you, Dermody, it shall be the worst day's work you ever did in your life." He turned to me again, before the bailiff could defend himself. "Do you hear what I say? I tell you to leave Dermody's girl, and come home with me."

"Yes, papa," I answered. "But I must go back to Mary, if you please, after I have been with you."

Angry as he was, my father was positively staggered by my audacity.

"You young idiot, your insolence exceeds belief!" he burst out. "I tell you this: you will never darken these doors again! You have been taught to disobey me here. You have had things put into your head, here, which no boy of your age ought to know—I'll say more, which no decent people would have let you know."

"I beg your pardon, sir," Dermody interposed, very respectfully and very firmly at the same time. "There are many things which a master in a hot temper is privileged to say to the man who serves him. But you have gone beyond your privilege. You have shamed me, sir, in the presence of my mother, in the hearing of my child—"

My father checked him there.

"You may spare the rest of it," he said. "We are master and servant no longer. When my son came hanging about your cottage, and playing at sweethearts with your girl there, your duty was to close the door on him. You have failed in your duty. I trust you no longer. Take a month's notice, Dermody. You leave my service."

The bailiff steadily met my father on his ground. He was no longer the easy, sweet-tempered, modest man who was the man of my remembrance.

"I beg to decline taking your month's notice, sir," he answered. "You shall have no opportunity of repeating what you have just said to me. I will send in my accounts to-night. And I will leave your service to-morrow."

"We agree for once," retorted my father. "The sooner you go, the better."

He stepped across the room and put his hand on my shoulder.

"Listen to me," he said, making a last effort to control himself. "I don't want to quarrel with you before a discarded servant. There must be an end to this nonsense. Leave these people to pack up and go, and come back to the house with me."

His heavy hand, pressing on my shoulder, seemed to press the spirit of resistance out of me. I so far gave way as to try to melt him by entreaties.

"Oh, papa! papa!" I cried. "Don't part me from Mary! See how pretty and good she is! She has made me a flag for my boat. Let me come here and see her sometimes. I can't live without her."

I could say no more. My poor little Mary burst out crying. Her tears and my entreaties were alike wasted on my father.

"Take your choice," he said, "between coming away of your own accord, or obliging me to take you away by force. I mean to part you and Dermody's girl."

"Neither you nor any man can part them," interposed a voice, speaking behind us. "Rid your mind of that notion, master, before it is too late."

My father looked round quickly, and discovered Dame Dermody facing him in the full light of the window. She had stepped back, at the outset of the dispute, into the corner behind the fireplace. There she had remained, biding her time to speak, until my father's last threat brought her out of her place of retirement.

They looked at each other for a moment. My father seemed to think it beneath his dignity to answer her. He went on with what he had to say to me.

"I shall count three slowly," he resumed. "Before I get to the last number, make up your mind to do what I tell you, or submit to the disgrace of being taken away by force."

"Take him where you may," said Dame Dermody, "he will still be on his way to his marriage with my grandchild."

"And where shall I be, if you please?" asked my father, stung into speaking to her this time.

The answer followed instantly in these startling words:

"You will be on your way to your ruin and your death."

My father turned his back on the prophetess with a smile of contempt.

"One!" he said, beginning to count.

I set my teeth, and clasped both arms round Mary as he spoke. I had inherited some of his temper, and he was now to know it.

"Two!" proceeded my father, after waiting a little.

Mary put her trembling lips to my ear, and whispered: "Let me go, George! I can't bear to see it. Oh, look how he frowns! I know he'll hurt you."

My father lifted his forefinger as a preliminary warning before he counted Three.

"Stop!" cried Dame Dermody.

My father looked round at her again with sardonic astonishment.

"I beg your pardon, ma'am—have you anything particular to say to me?" he asked.

"Man!" returned the Sibyl, "you speak lightly. Have I spoken lightly to You? I warn you to bow your wicked will before a Will that is mightier than yours. The spirits of these children are kindred spirits. For time and for eternity they are united one to the other. Put land and sea between them—they will still be together; they will communicate in visions, they will be revealed to each other in dreams. Bind them by worldly ties; wed your son, in the time to come, to another woman, and my grand-daughter to another man. In vain! I tell you, in vain! You may doom them to misery, you may drive them to sin—the day of their union on earth is still a day predestined in heaven. It will come! it will come! Submit, while the time for submission is yours. You are a doomed man. I see the shadow of disaster, I see the seal of death, on your face. Go; and leave these consecrated ones to walk the dark ways of the world together, in the strength of their innocence, in the light of their love. Go—and God forgive you!" In spite of himself, my father was struck by the irresistible strength of conviction which inspired those words. The bailiff's mother had impressed him as a tragic actress might have impressed him on the stage. She had checked the mocking answer on his lips, but she had not shaken his iron will. His face was as hard as ever when he turned my way once more.

"The last chance, George," he said, and counted the last number:

"Three!"

I neither moved nor answered him.

"You will have it?" he said, as he fastened his hold on my arm.

I fastened my hold on Mary; I whispered to her, "I won't leave you!" She seemed not to hear me. She trembled from head to foot in my arms. A faint cry of terror fluttered from her lips. Dermody instantly stepped forward. Before my father could wrench me away from her, he had said in my ear, "You can give her to me, Master George," and had released his child from my embrace. She stretched her little frail hands out yearningly to me, as she lay in Dermody's arms. "Good-by, dear," she said, faintly. I saw her head sink on her father's bosom as I was dragged to the door. In my helpless rage and misery, I struggled against the cruel hands that had got me with all the strength I had left. I cried out to her, "I love you, Mary! I will come back to you, Mary! I will never marry any one but you!" Step by step, I was forced further and further away. The last I saw of her, my darling's head was still resting on Dermody's breast. Her grandmother stood near, and shook her withered hands at my father, and shrieked her terrible prophecy, in the hysteric frenzy that possessed her when she saw the separation accomplished. "Go!—you go to your ruin! you go to your death!" While her voice still rang in my ears, the cottage door was opened and closed again. It was all over. The modest world of my boyish love and my boyish joy disappeared like the vision of a dream. The empty outer wilderness, which was my father's world, opened before me void of love and void of joy. God forgive me—how I hated him at that moment!

CHAPTER IV. THE CURTAIN FALLS.

FOR the rest of the day, and through the night, I was kept a close prisoner in my room, watched by a man on whose fidelity my father could depend.

The next morning I made an effort to escape, and was discovered before I had got free of the house. Confined again to my room, I contrived to write to Mary, and to slip my note into the willing hand of the housemaid who attended on me. Useless! The vigilance of my guardian was not to be evaded. The woman was suspected and followed, and the letter was taken from her. My father tore it up with his own hands.

Later in the day, my mother was permitted to see me.

She was quite unfit, poor soul, to intercede for me, or to serve my interests in any way. My father had completely overwhelmed her by announcing that his wife and his son were to accompany him, when he returned to America.

"Every farthing he has in the world," said my mother, "is to be thrown into that hateful speculation. He has raised money in London; he has let the house to some rich tradesman for seven years; he has sold the plate, and the jewels that came to me from his mother. The land in America swallows it all up. We have no home, George, and no choice but to go with him."

An hour afterward the post-chaise was at the door.

My father himself took me to the carriage. I broke away from him, with a desperation which not even his resolution could resist. I ran, I flew, along the path that led to Dermody's cottage. The door stood open; the parlor was empty. I went into the kitchen; I went into the upper rooms. Solitude everywhere. The bailiff had left the place; and his mother and his daughter had gone with him. No friend or neighbor lingered near with a message; no letter lay waiting for me; no hint was left to tell me in what direction they had taken their departure. After the insulting words which his master had spoken to him, Dermody's pride was concerned in leaving no trace of his whereabouts; my father might consider it as a trace purposely left with the object of reuniting Mary and me. I had no keepsake to speak to me of my lost darling but the flag which she had embroidered with her own hand. The furniture still remained in the cottage. I sat down in our customary corner, by Mary's empty chair, and looked again at the pretty green flag, and burst out crying.

A light touch roused me. My father had so far yielded as to leave to my mother the responsibility of bringing me back to the traveling carriage.

"We shall not find Mary here, George," she said, gently. "And we may hear of her in London. Come with me."

I rose and silently gave her my hand. Something low down on the clean white door-post caught my eye as we passed it. I stooped, and discovered some writing in pencil. I looked closer—it was writing in Mary's hand! The unformed childish characters traced these last words of farewell:

"Good-by, dear. Don't forget Mary."

I knelt down and kissed the writing. It comforted me—it was like a farewell touch from Mary's hand. I followed my mother quietly to the carriage.

Late that night we were in London.

My good mother did all that the most compassionate kindness could do (in her position) to comfort me. She privately wrote to the solicitors employed by her family, inclosing a description of Dermody and his mother and daughter and directing inquiries to be made at the various coach-offices in London. She also referred the lawyers to two of Dermody's relatives, who lived in the city, and who might know something of his movements after he left my father's service. When she had done this, she had done all that lay in her power. We neither of us possessed money enough to advertise in the newspapers.

A week afterward we sailed for the United States. Twice in that interval I communicated with the lawyers; and twice I was informed that the inquiries had led to nothing.

With this the first epoch in my love story comes to an end.

For ten long years afterward I never again met with my little Mary; I never even heard whether she had lived to grow to womanhood or not. I still kept the green flag, with the dove worked on it. For the rest, the waters of oblivion had closed over the old golden days at Greenwater Broad.

CHAPTER V. MY STORY.

WHEN YOU last saw me, I was a boy of thirteen. You now see me a man of twenty-three.

The story of my life, in the interval between these two ages, is a story that can be soon told.

Speaking of my father first, I have to record that the end of his career did indeed come as Dame Dermody had foretold it. Before we had been a year in America, the total collapse of his land speculation was followed by his death. The catastrophe was complete. But for my mother's little income (settled on her at her marriage) we should both have been left helpless at the mercy of the world.

We made some kind friends among the hearty and hospitable people of the United States, whom we were unaffectedly sorry to leave. But there were reasons which inclined us to return to our own country after my father's death; and we did return accordingly.

Besides her brother-in-law (already mentioned in the earlier pages of my narrative), my mother had another relative—a cousin named Germaine—on whose assistance she mainly relied for starting me, when the time came, in a professional career. I remember it as a family rumor, that Mr. Germaine had been an unsuccessful suitor for my mother's hand in the days when they were young people together. He was still a bachelor at the later period when his eldest brother's death without issue placed him in possession of a handsome fortune. The accession of wealth made no difference in his habits of life: he was a lonely old man, estranged from his other relatives, when my mother and I returned to England. If I could only succeed in pleasing Mr. Germaine, I might consider my prospects (in some degree, at least) as being prospects assured.

This was one consideration that influenced us in leaving America. There was another—in which I was especially interested—that drew me back to the lonely shores of Greenwater Broad.

My only hope of recovering a trace of Mary was to make inquiries among the cottagers in the neighborhood of my old home. The good bailiff had been heartily liked and respected in his little sphere. It seemed at least possible that some among his many friends in Suffolk might have discovered traces of him, in the year that had passed since I had left England. In my dreams of Mary—and I dreamed of her constantly—the lake and its woody banks formed a frequent background in the visionary picture of my lost companion. To the lake shores I looked, with a natural superstition, as to my way back to the one life that had its promise of happiness for me—my life with Mary.

On our arrival in London, I started for Suffolk alone—at my mother's request. At her age she naturally shrank from revisiting the home scenes now occupied by the strangers to whom our house had been let.

Ah, how my heart ached (young as I was) when I saw the familiar green waters of the lake once more! It was evening. The first object that caught my eye was the gayly painted boat, once mine, in which Mary and I had so often sailed together. The people in possession of our house were sailing now. The sound of their laughter floated toward me merrily over the still water. Their flag flew at the little mast-head, from which Mary's flag had never fluttered in the pleasant breeze. I turned my eyes from the boat; it hurt me to look at it. A few steps onward brought me to a promontory on the shore, and revealed the brown archways of the decoy on the opposite bank. There was the paling behind which we had knelt to watch the snaring of the ducks; there was the hole through which "Trim," the terrier, had shown himself to rouse the stupid curiosity of the water-fowl; there, seen at intervals through the trees, was the winding woodland path along which Mary and I had traced our way to Dermody's cottage on the day when my father's cruel hand had torn us from each other. How wisely my good mother had shrunk from looking again at the dear old scenes! I turned my back on the lake, to think with calmer thoughts in the shadowy solitude of the woods.

An hour's walk along the winding banks brought me round to the cottage which had once been Mary's home.

The door was opened by a woman who was a stranger to me. She civilly asked me to enter the parlor. I had suffered enough already; I made my inquiries, standing on the doorstep. They were soon at an end. The woman was a stranger in our part of Suffolk; neither she nor her husband had ever heard of Dermody's name.

I pursued my investigations among the peasantry, passing from cottage to cottage. The twilight came; the moon rose; the lights began to vanish from the lattice-windows; and still I continued my weary pilgrimage; and still, go where I might, the answer to my questions was the same. Nobody knew anything of Dermody. Everybody asked if I had not brought news of him myself. It pains me even now to recall the cruelly complete defeat of every effort which I made on that disastrous evening. I passed the night in one of the cottages; and I returned to London the next day, broken by disappointment, careless what I did, or where I went next.

Still, we were not wholly parted. I saw Mary—as Dame Dermody said I should see her—in dreams.

Sometimes she came to me with the green flag in her hand, and repeated her farewell words—"Don't forget Mary!" Sometimes she led me to our well-remembered corner in the cottage parlor, and opened the paper on which her grandmother had written our prayers for us. We prayed together again, and sung hymns together again, as if the old times had come back. Once she appeared to me, with tears in her eyes, and said, "We must wait, dear: our time has not come yet." Twice I saw her looking at me, like one disturbed by anxious thoughts; and twice I heard her say, "Live patiently, live innocently, George, for my sake."

We settled in London, where my education was undertaken by a private tutor. Before we had been long in our new abode, an unexpected change in our prospects took place. To my mother's astonishment she received an offer of marriage (addressed to her in a letter) from Mr. Germaine.

"I entreat you not to be startled by my proposal!" (the old gentleman wrote). "You can hardly have forgotten that I was once fond of you, in the days when we were both young and both poor. No return to the feelings associated with that time is possible now. At my age, all I ask of you is to be the companion of the closing years of my life, and to give me something of a father's interest in promoting the future welfare of your son. Consider this, my dear, and tell me whether you will take the empty chair at an old man's lonely fireside."

My mother (looking almost as confused, poor soul! as if she had become a young girl again) left the whole responsibility of decision on the shoulders of her son! I was not long in making up my mind. If she said Yes, she would accept the hand of a man of worth and honor, who had been throughout his whole life devoted to her; and she would recover the comfort, the luxury, the social prosperity and position of which my father's reckless course of life had deprived her. Add to this, that I liked Mr. Germaine, and that Mr. Germaine liked me. Under these circumstances, why should my mother say No? She could produce no satisfactory answer to that question when I put it. As the necessary consequence, she became, in due course of time, Mrs. Germaine.

I have only to add that, to the end of her life, my good mother congratulated herself (in this case at least) on having taken her son's advice.

The years went on, and still Mary and I were parted, except in my dreams. The years went on, until the perilous time which comes in every man's life came in mine. I reached the age when the strongest of all the passions seizes on the senses, and asserts its mastery over mind and body alike.

I had hitherto passively endured the wreck of my earliest and dearest hopes: I had lived patiently, and lived innocently, for Mary's sake. Now my patience left me; my innocence was numbered among the lost things of the past. My days, it is true, were still devoted to the tasks set me by my tutor; but my nights were given, in secret, to a reckless profligacy, which (in my present frame of mind) I look back on with disgust and dismay. I profaned my remembrances of Mary in the company of women who had reached the lowest depths of degradation. I impiously said to myself: "I have hoped for her long enough; I have waited for her long enough. The one thing now to do is to enjoy my youth and to forget her."

From the moment when I dropped into this degradation, I might sometimes think regretfully of Mary—at the morning time, when penitent thoughts mostly come to us; but I ceased absolutely to see her in my dreams. We were now, in the completest sense of the word, parted. Mary's pure spirit could hold no communion with mine; Mary's pure spirit had left me.

It is needless to say that I failed to keep the secret of my depravity from the knowledge of my mother. The sight of her grief was the first influence that sobered me. In some degree at least I restrained myself: I made the effort to return to purer ways of life. Mr. Germaine, though I had disappointed him, was too just a man to give me up as lost. He advised me, as a means of self-reform, to make my choice of a profession, and to absorb myself in closer studies than any that I had yet pursued.

I made my peace with this good friend and second father, not only by following his advice, but by adopting the profession to which he had been himself attached before he inherited his fortune—the profession of medicine. Mr. Germaine had been a surgeon: I resolved on being a surgeon too.

Having entered, at rather an earlier age than usual, on my new way of life, I may at least say for myself that I worked hard. I won, and kept, the interest of the professors under whom I studied. On the other hand, it cannot be denied that my reformation was, morally speaking, far from being complete. I worked; but what I did was done selfishly, bitterly, with a hard heart. In religion and morals I adopted the views of a materialist companion of my studies—a worn-out man of more than double my age. I believed in nothing but what I could see, or taste, or feel. I lost all faith in humanity. With the one exception of my mother, I had no respect for women. My remembrances of Mary deteriorated until they became little more than a lost link of association with the past. I still preserved the green flag as a matter of habit; but it was no longer kept about me; it was left undisturbed in a drawer of my writing-desk. Now and then a wholesome doubt, whether my life was not utterly unworthy of me, would rise in my mind. But it held no long possession of my thoughts. Despising others, it was in the logical order of things that I should follow my conclusions to their bitter end, and consistently despise myself.

The term of my majority arrived. I was twenty-one years old; and of the illusions of my youth not a vestige remained.

Neither my mother nor Mr. Germaine could make any positive complaint of my conduct. But they were both thoroughly uneasy about me. After anxious consideration, my step-father arrived at a conclusion. He decided that the one chance of restoring me to my better and brighter self was to try the stimulant of a life among new people and new scenes.

At the period of which I am now writing, the home government had decided on sending a special diplomatic mission to one of the native princes ruling over a remote province of our Indian empire. In the disturbed state of the province at that time, the mission, on its arrival in India, was to be accompanied to the prince's court by an escort, including the military as well as the civil servants of the crown. The surgeon appointed to sail with the expedition from England was an old friend of Mr. Germaine's, and was in want of an assistant on whose capacity he could rely. Through my stepfather's interest, the post was offered to me. I accepted it without hesitation. My only pride left was the miserable pride of indifference. So long as I pursued my profession, the place in which I pursued it was a matter of no importance to my mind.

It was long before we could persuade my mother even to contemplate the new prospect now set before me. When she did at length give way, she yielded most unwillingly. I confess I left her with the tears in my eyes—the first I had shed for many a long year past.

The history of our expedition is part of the history of British India. It has no place in this narrative.

Speaking personally, I have to record that I was rendered incapable of performing my professional duties in less than a week from the time when the mission reached its destination. We were encamped outside the city; and an attack was made on us, under cover of darkness, by the fanatical natives. The attempt was defeated with little difficulty, and with only a trifling loss on our side. I was among the wounded, having been struck by a javelin, or spear, while I was passing from one tent to another.

Inflicted by a European weapon, my injury would have been of no serious consequence. But the tip of the Indian spear had been poisoned. I escaped the mortal danger of lockjaw; but, through some peculiarity in the action of the poison on my constitution (which I am quite unable to explain), the wound obstinately refused to heal.

I was invalided and sent to Calcutta, where the best surgical help was at my disposal. To all appearance, the wound healed there—then broke out again. Twice this happened; and the medical men agreed that the best course to take would be to send me home. They calculated on the invigorating effect of the sea voyage, and, failing this, on the salutary influence of my native air. In the Indian climate I was pronounced incurable.

Two days before the ship sailed a letter from my mother brought me startling news. My life to come—if I had a life to come—had been turned into a new channel. Mr. Germaine had died suddenly, of heart-disease. His will, bearing date at the time when I left England, bequeathed an income for life to my mother, and left the bulk of his property to me, on the one condition that I adopted his name. I accepted the condition, of course, and became George Germaine.

Three months later, my mother and I were restored to each other.

Except that I still had some trouble with my wound, behold me now to all appearance one of the most enviable of existing mortals; promoted to the position of a wealthy gentleman; possessor of a house in London and of a country-seat in Perthshire; and, nevertheless, at twenty-three years of age, one of the most miserable men living!

And Mary?

In the ten years that had now passed over, what had become of Mary?

You have heard my story. Read the few pages that follow, and you will hear hers.

CHAPTER VI. HER STORY.

WHAT I have now to tell you of Mary is derived from information obtained at a date in my life later by many years than any date of which I have written yet. Be pleased to remember this.

Dermody, the bailiff, possessed relatives in London, of whom he occasionally spoke, and relatives in Scotland, whom he never mentioned. My father had a strong prejudice against the Scotch nation. Dermody knew his master well enough to be aware that the prejudice might extend to him, if he spoke of his Scotch kindred. He was a discreet man, and he never mentioned them.

On leaving my father's service, he had made his way, partly by land and partly by sea, to Glasgow—in which city his friends resided. With his character and his experience, Dermody was a man in a thousand to any master who was lucky enough to discover him. His friends bestirred themselves. In six weeks' time he was placed in charge of a gentleman's estate on the eastern coast of Scotland, and was comfortably established with his mother and his daughter in a new home.

The insulting language which my father had addressed to him had sunk deep in Dermody's mind. He wrote privately to his relatives in London, telling them that he had found a new situation which suited him, and that he had his reasons for not at present mentioning his address. In this way he baffled the inquiries which my mother's lawyers (failing to discover a trace of him in other directions) addressed to his London friends. Stung by his old master's reproaches, he sacrificed his daughter and he sacrificed me—partly to his own sense of self-respect, partly to his conviction that the difference between us in rank made it his duty to check all further intercourse before it was too late.

Buried in their retirement in a remote part of Scotland, the little household lived, lost to me, and lost to the world.

In dreams, I had seen and heard Mary. In dreams, Mary saw and heard me. The innocent longings and wishes which filled my heart while I was still a boy were revealed to her in the mystery of sleep. Her grandmother, holding firmly to her faith in the predestined union between us, sustained the girl's courage and cheered her heart. She could hear her father say (as my father had said) that we were parted to meet no more, and could privately think of her happy dreams as the sufficient promise of another future than the future which Dermody contemplated. So she still lived with me in the spirit—and lived in hope.

The first affliction that befell the little household was the death of the grandmother, by the exhaustion of extreme old age. In her last conscious moments, she said to Mary, "Never forget that you and George are spirits consecrated to each other. Wait—in the certain knowledge that no human power can hinder your union in the time to come."

While those words were still vividly present to Mary's mind, our visionary union by dreams was abruptly broken on her side, as it had been abruptly broken on mine. In the first days of my self-degradation, I had ceased to see Mary. Exactly at the same period Mary ceased to see me.

The girl's sensitive nature sunk under the shock. She had now no elder woman to comfort and advise her; she lived alone with her father, who invariably changed the subject whenever she spoke of the old times. The secret sorrow that preys on body and mind alike preyed on her. A cold, caught at the inclement season, turned to fever. For weeks she was in danger of death. When she recovered, her head had been stripped of its beautiful hair by the doctor's order. The sacrifice had been necessary to save her life. It proved to be, in one respect, a cruel sacrifice—her hair never grew plentifully again. When it did reappear, it had completely lost its charming mingled hues of deep red and brown; it was now of one monotonous light-brown color throughout. At first sight, Mary's Scotch friends hardly knew her again.

But Nature made amends for what the head had lost by what the face and the figure gained.

In a year from the date of her illness, the frail little child of the old days at Greenwater Broad had ripened, in the bracing Scotch air and the healthy mode of life, into a comely young woman. Her features were still, as in her early years, not regularly beautiful; but the change in her was not the less marked on that account. The wan face had filled out, and the pale complexion had found its color. As to her figure, its remarkable development was perceived even by the rough people about her. Promising nothing when she was a child, it had now sprung into womanly fullness, symmetry, and grace. It was a strikingly beautiful figure, in the strictest sense of the word.

Morally as well as physically, there were moments, at this period of their lives, when even her own father hardly recognized his daughter of former days. She had lost her childish vivacity—her sweet, equable flow of good humor. Silent and self-absorbed, she went through the daily routine of her duties enduringly. The hope of meeting me again had sunk to a dead hope in her by this time. She made no complaint. The bodily strength that she had gained in these later days had its sympathetic influence in steadying her mind. When her father once or twice ventured to ask if she was still thinking of me, she answered quietly that she had brought herself to share his opinions. She could not doubt that I had long since ceased to think of her. Even if I had remained faithful to her, she was old enough now to know that the difference between us in rank made our union by marriage an impossibility. It would be best (she thought) not to refer any more to the past, best to forget me, as I had forgotten her. So she spoke now. So, tried by the test of appearances, Dame Dermody's confident forecast of our destinies had failed to justify itself, and had taken its place among the predictions that are never fulfilled.

The next notable event in the family annals which followed Mary's illness happened when she had attained the age of nineteen years. Even at this distance of time my heart sinks, my courage fails me, at the critical stage in my narrative which I have now reached.

A storm of unusual severity burst over the eastern coast of Scotland. Among the ships that were lost in the tempest was a vessel bound from Holland, which was wrecked on the rocky shore near Dermody's place of abode. Leading the way in all good actions, the bailiff led the way in rescuing the passengers and crew of the lost ship. He had brought one man alive to land, and was on his way back to the vessel, when two heavy seas, following in close succession, dashed him against the rocks. He was rescued, at the risk of their own lives, by his neighbors. The medical examination disclosed a broken bone and severe bruises and lacerations. So far, Dermody's sufferings were easy of relief. But, after a lapse of time, symptoms appeared in the patient which revealed to his medical attendant the presence of serious internal injury. In the doctor's opinion, he could never hope to resume the active habits of his life. He would be an invalid and a crippled man for the rest of his days.

Under these melancholy circumstances, the bailiff's employer did all that could be strictly expected of him, He hired an assistant to undertake the supervision of the farm work, and he permitted Dermody to occupy his cottage for the next three months. This concession gave the poor man time to recover such relics of strength as were still left to him, and to consult his friends in Glasgow on the doubtful question of his life to come.

The prospect was a serious one. Dermody was quite unfit for any sedentary employment; and the little money that he had saved was not enough to support his daughter and himself. The Scotch friends were willing and kind; but they had domestic claims on them, and they had no money to spare.

In this emergency, the passenger in the wrecked vessel (whose life Dermody had saved) came forward with a proposal which took father and daughter alike by surprise. He made Mary an offer of marriage; on the express understanding (if she accepted him) that her home was to be her father's home also to the end of his life.

The person who thus associated himself with the Dermodys in the time of their trouble was a Dutch gentleman, named Ernest Van Brandt. He possessed a share in a fishing establishment on the shores of the Zuyder Zee; and he was on his way to establish a correspondence with the fisheries in the North of Scotland when the vessel was wrecked. Mary had produced a strong impression on him when they first met. He had lingered in the neighborhood, in the hope of gaining her favorable regard, with time to help him. Personally he was a handsome man, in the prime of life; and he was possessed of a sufficient income to marry on. In making his proposal, he produced references to persons of high social position in Holland, who could answer for him, so far as the questions of character and position were concerned.

Mary was long in considering which course it would be best for her helpless father, and best for herself, to adopt.

The hope of a marriage with me had been a hope abandoned by her years since. No woman looks forward willingly to a life of cheerless celibacy. In thinking of her future, Mary naturally thought of herself in the character of a wife. Could she fairly expect in the time to come to receive any more attractive proposal than the proposal now addressed to her? Mr. Van Brandt had every personal advantage that a woman could desire; he was devotedly in love with her; and he felt a grateful affection for her father as the man to whom he owed his life. With no other hope in her heart—with no other prospect in view—what could she do better than marry Mr. Van Brandt?

Influenced by these considerations, she decided on speaking the fatal word. She said, "Yes."

At the same time, she spoke plainly to Mr. Van Brandt, unreservedly acknowledging that she had contemplated another future than the future now set before her. She did not conceal that there had once been an old love in her heart, and that a new love was more than she could command. Esteem, gratitude, and regard she could honestly offer; and, with time, love might come. For the rest, she had long since disassociated herself from the past, and had definitely given up all the hopes and wishes once connected with it. Repose for her father, and tranquil happiness for herself, were the only favors that she asked of fortune now. These she might find under the roof of an honorable man who loved and respected her. She could promise, on her side, to make him a good and faithful wife, if she could promise no more. It rested with Mr. Van Brandt to say whether he really believed that he would be consulting his own happiness in marrying her on these terms.

Mr. Van Brandt accepted the terms without a moment's hesitation.

They would have been married immediately but for an alarming change for the worse in the condition of Dermody's health. Symptoms showed themselves, which the doctor confessed that he had not anticipated when he had given his opinion on the case. He warned Mary that the end might be near. A physician was summoned from Edinburgh, at Mr. Van Brandt's expense. He confirmed the opinion entertained by the country doctor. For some days longer the good bailiff lingered. On the last morning, he put his daughter's hand in Van Brandt's hand. "Make her happy, sir," he said, in his simple way, "and you will be even with me for saving your life." The same day he died quietly in his daughter's arms.

Mary's future was now entirely in her lover's hands. The relatives in Glasgow had daughters of their own to provide for. The relatives in London resented Dermody's neglect of them. Van Brandt waited, delicately and considerately, until the first violence of the girl's grief had worn itself out, and then he pleaded irresistibly for a husband's claim to console her.

The time at which they were married in Scotland was also the time at which I was on my way home from India. Mary had then reached the age of twenty years.

The story of our ten years' separation is now told; the narrative leaves us at the outset of our new lives.

I am with my mother, beginning my career as a country gentleman on the estate in Perthshire which I have inherited from Mr. Germaine. Mary is with her husband, enjoying her new privileges, learning her new duties, as a wife. She, too, is living in Scotland—living, by a strange fatality, not very far distant from my country-house. I have no suspicion that she is so near to me: the name of Mrs. Van Brandt (even if I had heard it) appeals to no familiar association in my mind. Still the kindred spirits are parted. Still there is no idea on her side, and no idea on mine, that we shall ever meet again.

CHAPTER VII. THE WOMAN ON THE BRIDGE.

MY mother looked in at the library door, and disturbed me over my books.

"I have been hanging a little picture in my room," she said. "Come upstairs, my dear, and give me your opinion of it."

I rose and followed her. She pointed to a miniature portrait, hanging above the mantelpiece.

"Do you know whose likeness that is?" she asked, half sadly, half playfully. "George! Do you really not recognize yourself at thirteen years old?"

How should I recognize myself? Worn by sickness and sorrow; browned by the sun on my long homeward voyage; my hair already growing thin over my forehead; my eyes already habituated to their one sad and weary look; what had I in common with the fair, plump, curly-headed, bright-eyed boy who confronted me in the miniature? The mere sight of the portrait produced the most extraordinary effect on my mind. It struck me with an overwhelming melancholy; it filled me with a despair of myself too dreadful to be endured. Making the best excuse I could to my mother, I left the room. In another minute I was out of the house.

I crossed the park, and left my own possessions behind me. Following a by-road, I came to our well-known river; so beautiful in itself, so famous among trout-fishers throughout Scotland. It was not then the fishing season. No human being was in sight as I took my seat on the bank. The old stone bridge which spanned the stream was within a hundred yards of me; the setting sun still tinged the swift-flowing water under the arches with its red and dying light.

Still the boy's face in the miniature pursued me. Still the portrait seemed to reproach me in a merciless language of its own: "Look at what you were once; think of what you are now!"

I hid my face in the soft, fragrant grass. I thought of the wasted years of my life between thirteen and twenty-three.

How was it to end? If I lived to the ordinary life of man, what prospect had I before me?

Love? Marriage? I burst out laughing as the idea crossed my mind. Since the innocently happy days of my boyhood I had known no more of love than the insect that now crept over my hand as it lay on the grass. My money, to be sure, would buy me a wife; but would my money make her dear to me? dear as Mary had once been, in the golden time when my portrait was first painted?

Mary! Was she still living? Was she married? Should I know her again if I saw her? Absurd! I had not seen her since she was ten years old: she was now a woman, as I was a man. Would she know me if we met? The portrait, still pursuing me, answered the question: "Look at what you were once; think of what you are now!"

I rose and walked backward and forward, and tried to turn the current of my thoughts in some new direction.

It was not to be done. After a banishment of years, Mary had got back again into my mind. I sat down once more on the river bank. The sun was sinking fast. Black shadows hovered under the arches of the old stone bridge. The red light had faded from the swift-flowing water, and had left it overspread with one monotonous hue of steely gray. The first stars looked down peacefully from the cloudless sky. The first shiverings of the night breeze were audible among the trees, and visible here and there in the shallow places of the stream. And still, the darker it grew, the more persistently my portrait led me back to the past, the more vividly the long-lost image of the child Mary showed itself to me in my thoughts.

Was this the prelude of her coming back to me in dreams; in her perfected womanhood, in the young prime of her life?

It might be so.

I was no longer unworthy of her, as I had once been. The effect produced on me by the sight of my portrait was in itself due to moral and mental changes in me for the better, which had been steadily proceeding since the time when my wound had laid me helpless among strangers in a strange land. Sickness, which has made itself teacher and friend to many a man, had made itself teacher and friend to me. I looked back with horror at the vices of my youth; at the fruitless after-days when I had impiously doubted all that is most noble, all that is most consoling in human life. Consecrated by sorrow, purified by repentance, was it vain in me to hope that her spirit and my spirit might yet be united again? Who could tell?

I rose once more. It could serve no good purpose to linger until night by the banks of the river. I had left the house, feeling the impulse which drives us, in certain excited conditions of the mind, to take refuge in movement and change. The remedy had failed; my mind was as strangely disturbed as ever. My wisest course would be to go home, and keep my good mother company over her favorite game of piquet.

I turned to take the road back, and stopped, struck by the tranquil beauty of the last faint light in the western sky, shining behind the black line formed by the parapet of the bridge.

In the grand gathering of the night shadows, in the deep stillness of the dying day, I stood alone and watched the sinking light.

As I looked, there came a change over the scene. Suddenly and softly a living figure glided into view on the bridge. It passed behind the black line of the parapet, in the last long rays of the western light. It crossed the bridge. It paused, and crossed back again half-way. Then it stopped. The minutes passed, and there the figure stood, a motionless black object, behind the black parapet of the bridge.

I advanced a little, moving near enough to obtain a closer view of the dress in which the figure was attired. The dress showed me that the solitary stranger was a woman.

She did not notice me in the shadow which the trees cast on the bank. She stood with her arms folded in her cloak, looking down at the darkening river.

Why was she waiting there at the close of evening alone?

As the question occurred to me, I saw her head move. She looked along the bridge, first on one side of her, then on the other. Was she waiting for some person who was to meet her? Or was she suspicious of observation, and anxious to make sure that she was alone?

A sudden doubt of her purpose in seeking that solitary place, a sudden distrust of the lonely bridge and the swift-flowing river, set my heart beating quickly and roused me to instant action. I hurried up the rising ground which led from the river-bank to the bridge, determined on speaking to her while the opportunity was still mine.

She neither saw nor heard me until I was close to her. I approached with an irrepressible feeling of agitation; not knowing how she might receive me when I spoke to her. The moment she turned and faced me, my composure came back. It was as if, expecting to see a stranger, I had unexpectedly encountered a friend.

And yet she was a stranger. I had never before looked on that grave and noble face, on that grand figure whose exquisite grace and symmetry even her long cloak could not wholly hide. She was not, perhaps, a strictly beautiful woman. There were defects in her which were sufficiently marked to show themselves in the fading light. Her hair, for example, seen under the large garden hat that she wore, looked almost as short as the hair of a man; and the color of it was of that dull, lusterless brown hue which is so commonly seen in English women of the ordinary type. Still, in spite of these drawbacks, there was a latent charm in her expression, there was an inbred fascination in her manner, which instantly found its way to my sympathies and its hold on my admiration. She won me in the moment when I first looked at her.

"May I inquire if you have lost your way?" I asked.

Her eyes rested on my face with a strange look of inquiry in them. She did not appear to be surprised or confused at my venturing to address her.

"I know this part of the country well," I went on. "Can I be of any use to you?"

She still looked at me with steady, inquiring eyes. For a moment, stranger as I was, my face seemed to trouble her as if it had been a face that she had seen and forgotten again. If she really had this idea, she at once dismissed it with a little toss of her head, and looked away at the river as if she felt no further interest in me.

"Thank you. I have not lost my way. I am accustomed to walking alone. Good-evening."

She spoke coldly, but courteously. Her voice was delicious; her bow, as she left me, was the perfection of unaffected grace. She left the bridge on the side by which I had first seen her approach it, and walked slowly away along the darkening track of the highroad.

Still I was not quite satisfied. There was something underlying the charming expression and the fascinating manner which my instinct felt to be something wrong. As I walked away toward the opposite end of the bridge, the doubt began to grow on me whether she had spoken the truth. In leaving the neighborhood of the river, was she simply trying to get rid of me?

I at once resolved to put this suspicion of her to the test. Leaving the bridge, I had only to cross the road beyond, and to enter a plantation on the bank of the river. Here, concealed behind the first tree which was large enough to hide me, I could command a view of the bridge, and I could fairly count on detecting her, if she returned to the river, while there was a ray of light to see her by. It was not easy walking in the obscurity of the plantation: I had almost to grope my way to the nearest tree that suited my purpose.

I had just steadied my foothold on the uneven ground behind the tree, when the stillness of the twilight hour was suddenly broken by the distant sound of a voice.

The voice was a woman's. It was not raised to any high pitch; its accent was the accent of prayer, and the words it uttered were these:

"Christ, have mercy on me!"

There was silence again. A nameless fear crept over me, as I looked out on the bridge.

She was standing on the parapet. Before I could move, before I could cry out, before I could even breathe again freely, she leaped into the river.

The current ran my way. I could see her, as she rose to the surface, floating by in the light on the mid-stream. I ran headlong down the bank. She sank again, in the moment when I stopped to throw aside my hat and coat and to kick off my shoes. I was a practiced swimmer. The instant I was in the water my composure came back to me—I felt like myself again.

The current swept me out into the mid-stream, and greatly increased the speed at which I swam. I was close behind her when she rose for the second time—a shadowy thing, just visible a few inches below the surface of the river. One more stroke, and my left arm was round her; I had her face out of the water. She was insensible. I could hold her in the right way to leave me master of all my movements; I could devote myself, without flurry or fatigue, to the exertion of taking her back to the shore.

My first attempt satisfied me that there was no reasonable hope, burdened as I now was, of breasting the strong current running toward the mid-river from either bank. I tried it on one side, and I tried it on the other, and gave it up. The one choice left was to let myself drift with her down the stream. Some fifty yards lower, the river took a turn round a promontory of land, on which stood a little inn much frequented by anglers in the season. As we approached the place, I made another attempt (again an attempt in vain) to reach the shore. Our last chance now was to be heard by the people of the inn. I shouted at the full pitch of my voice as we drifted past. The cry was answered. A man put off in a boat. In five minutes more I had her safe on the bank again; and the man and I were carrying her to the inn by the river-side.

The landlady and her servant-girl were equally willing to be of service, and equally ignorant of what they were to do. Fortunately, my medical education made me competent to direct them. A good fire, warm blankets, hot water in bottles, were all at my disposal. I showed the women myself how to ply the work of revival. They persevered, and I persevered; and still there she lay, in her perfect beauty of form, without a sign of life perceptible; there she lay, to all outward appearance, dead by drowning.

A last hope was left—the hope of restoring her (if I could construct the apparatus in time) by the process called "artificial respiration." I was just endeavoring to tell the landlady what I wanted and was just conscious of a strange difficulty in expressing myself, when the good woman started back, and looked at me with a scream of terror.

"Good God, sir, you're bleeding!" she cried. "What's the matter? Where are you hurt?"

In the moment when she spoke to me I knew what had happened. The old Indian wound (irritated, doubtless, by the violent exertion that I had imposed on myself) had opened again. I struggled against the sudden sense of faintness that seized on me; I tried to tell the people of the inn what to do. It was useless. I dropped to my knees; my head sunk on the bosom of the woman stretched senseless upon the low couch beneath me. The death-in-life that had got her had got me. Lost to the world about us, we lay, with my blood flowing on her, united in our deathly trance.

Where were our spirits at that moment? Were they together and conscious of each other? United by a spiritual bond, undiscovered and unsuspected by us in the flesh, did we two, who had met as strangers on the fatal bridge, know each other again in the trance? You who have loved and lost—you whose one consolation it has been to believe in other worlds than this—can you turn from my questions in contempt? Can you honestly say that they have never been your questions too?

CHAPTER VIII. THE KINDRED SPIRITS

THE morning sunlight shining in at a badly curtained window; a clumsy wooden bed, with big twisted posts that reached to the ceiling; on one side of the bed, my mother's welcome face; on the other side, an elderly gentleman unremembered by me at that moment—such were the objects that presented themselves to my view, when I first consciously returned to the world that we live in.

"Look, doctor, look! He has come to his senses at last."

"Open your mouth, sir, and take a sup of this." My mother was rejoicing over me on one side of the bed; and the unknown gentleman, addressed as "doctor," was offering me a spoonful of whisky-and-water on the other. He called it the "elixir of life"; and he bid me remark (speaking in a strong Scotch accent) that he tasted it himself to show he was in earnest.

The stimulant did its good work. My head felt less giddy, my mind became clearer. I could speak collectedly to my mother; I could vaguely recall the more marked events of the previous evening. A minute or two more, and the image of the person in whom those events had all centered became a living image in my memory. I tried to raise myself in the bed; I asked, impatiently, "Where is she?"

The doctor produced another spoonful of the elixir of life, and gravely repeated his first address to me.

"Open your mouth, sir, and take a sup of this."

I persisted in repeating my question:

"Where is she?"

The doctor persisted in repeating his formula:

"Take a sup of this."

I was too weak to contest the matter; I obeyed. My medical attendant nodded across the bed to my mother, and said, "Now, he'll do." My mother had some compassion on me. She relieved my anxiety in these plain words:

"The lady has quite recovered, George, thanks to the doctor here."

I looked at my professional colleague with a new interest. He was the legitimate fountainhead of the information that I was dying to have poured into my mind.

"How did you revive her?" I asked. "Where is she now?"

The doctor held up his hand, warning me to stop.

"We shall do well, sir, if we proceed systematically," he began, in a very positive manner. "You will understand, that every time you open your mouth, it will be to take a sup of this, and not to speak. I shall tell you, in due course, and the good lady, your mother, will tell you, all that you have any need to know. As I happen to have been first on what you may call the scene of action, it stands in the fit order of things that I should speak first. You will just permit me to mix a little more of the elixir of life, and then, as the poet says, my plain unvarnished tale I shall deliver."

So he spoke, pronouncing in his strong Scotch accent the most carefully selected English I had ever heard. A hard-headed, square-shouldered, pertinaciously self-willed man—it was plainly useless to contend with him. I turned to my mother's gentle face for encouragement; and I let my doctor have his own way.

"My name," he proceeded, "is MacGlue. I had the honor of presenting my respects at your house yonder when you first came to live in this neighborhood. You don't remember me at present, which is natural enough in the unbalanced condition of your mind, consequent, you will understand (as a professional person yourself) on copious loss of blood."

There my patience gave way.

"Never mind me!" I interposed. "Tell me about the lady!"

"You have opened your mouth, sir!" cried Mr. MacGlue, severely.

374

"You know the penalty—take a sup of this. I told you we should proceed systematically," he went on, after he had forced me to submit to the penalty. "Everything in its place, Mr. Germaine—everything in its place. I was speaking of your bodily condition. Well, sir, and how did I discover your bodily condition? Providentially for you I was driving home yesterday evening by the lower road (which is the road by the river bank), and, drawing near to the inn here (they call it a hotel; it's nothing but an inn), I heard the screeching of the landlady half a mile off. A good woman enough, you will understand, as times go; but a poor creature in any emergency. Keep still, I'm coming to it now. Well, I went in to see if the screeching related to anything wanted in the medical way; and there I found you and the stranger lady in a position which I may truthfully describe as standing in some need of improvement on the score of propriety. Tut! tut! I speak jocosely—you were both in a dead swoon. Having heard what the landlady had to tell me, and having, to the best of my ability, separated history from hysterics in the course of the woman's narrative, I found myself, as it were, placed between two laws. The law of gallantry, you see, pointed to the lady as the first object of my professional services, while the law of humanity (seeing that you were still bleeding) pointed no less imperatively to you. I am no longer a young man: I left the lady to wait. My word! it was no light matter, Mr. Germaine, to deal with your case, and get you carried up here out of the way. That old wound of yours, sir, is not to be trifled with. I bid you beware how you open it again. The next time you go out for an evening walk and you see a lady in the water, you will do well for your own health to leave her there. What's that I see? Are you opening your mouth again? Do you want another sup already?"

"He wants to hear more about the lady," said my mother, interpreting my wishes for me.

"Oh, the lady," resumed Mr. MacGlue, with the air of a man who found no great attraction in the subject proposed to him. "There's not much that I know of to be said about the lady. A fine woman, no doubt. If you could strip the flesh off her bones, you would find a splendid skeleton underneath. For, mind this! there's no such thing as a finely made woman without a good bony scaffolding to build her on at starting. I don't think much of this lady—

morally speaking, you will understand. If I may be permitted to say so in your presence, ma'am, there's a man in the background of that dramatic scene of hers on the bridge. However, not being the man myself, I have nothing to do with that. My business with the lady was just to set her vital machinery going again. And, Heaven knows, she proved a heavy handful! It was even a more obstinate case to deal with, sir, than yours. I never, in all my experience, met with two people more unwilling to come back to this world and its troubles than you two were. And when I had done the business at last, when I was wellnigh swooning myself with the work and the worry of it, guess—I give you leave to speak for this once—guess what were the first words the lady said to me when she came to herself again."

I was too much excited to be able to exercise my ingenuity. "I give it up!" I said, impatiently.

"You may well give it up," remarked Mr. MacGlue. "The first words she addressed, sir, to the man who had dragged her out of the very jaws of death were these: 'How dare you meddle with me? why didn't you leave me to die?' Her exact language—I'll take my Bible oath of it. I was so provoked that I gave her the change back (as the saying is) in her own coin. 'There's the river handy, ma'am,' I said; 'do it again. I, for one, won't stir a hand to save you; I promise you that.' She looked up sharply. 'Are you the man who took me out of the river?' she said. 'God forbid!' says I. 'I'm only the doctor who was fool enough to meddle with you afterward.' She turned to the landlady. 'Who took me out of the river?' she asked. The landlady told her, and mentioned your name. 'Germaine?' she said to herself; 'I know nobody named Germaine; I wonder whether it was the man who spoke to me on the bridge?' 'Yes,' says the landlady; 'Mr. Germaine said he met you on the bridge.' Hearing that, she took a little time to think; and then she asked if she could see Mr. Germaine. 'Whoever he is,' she says, 'he has risked his life to save me, and I ought to thank him for doing that.' 'You can't thank him tonight,' I said; 'I've got him upstairs between life and death, and I've sent for his mother: wait till to-morrow.' She turned on me, looking half frightened, half angry. 'I can't wait,' she says; 'you don't know what you have done among you in bringing me back to life. I must leave this neighborhood; I must be out of Perthshire to-morrow: when does the first coach southward pass this way?' Having nothing to do with the first coach southward, I referred her to the people of the inn. My business (now I had done with the lady) was upstairs in this room, to see how you were getting on. You were getting on as well as I could wish, and your mother was at your bedside. I went home to see what sick people might be waiting for me in the regular way. When I came back this morning, there was the foolish landlady with a new tale to tell 'Gone!' says she. 'Who's gone?' says I. 'The lady,' says she, 'by the first coach this morning!'"

"You don't mean to tell me that she has left the house?" I exclaimed.

"Oh, but I do!" said the doctor, as positively as ever. "Ask madam your mother here, and she'll certify it to your heart's content. I've got other sick ones to visit, and I'm away on my rounds. You'll see no more of the lady; and so much the better, I'm thinking. In two hours' time I'll be back again; and if I don't find you the worse in the interim, I'll see about having you transported from this strange place to the snug bed that knows you at home. Don't let him talk, ma'am, don't let him talk."

With those parting words, Mr. MacGlue left us to ourselves.

"Is it really true?" I said to my mother. "Has she left the inn, without waiting to see me?"

"Nobody could stop her, George," my mother answered. "The lady left the inn this morning by the coach for Edinburgh."

I was bitterly disappointed. Yes: "bitterly" is the word—though she was a stranger to me.

"Did you see her yourself?" I asked.

"I saw her for a few minutes, my dear, on my way up to your room."

"What did she say?"

"She begged me to make her excuses to you. She said, 'Tell Mr. Germaine that my situation is dreadful; no human creature can help me. I must go

377

away. My old life is as much at an end as if your son had left me to drown in the river. I must find a new life for myself, in a new place. Ask Mr. Germaine to forgive me for going away without thanking him. I daren't wait! I may be followed and found out. There is a person whom I am determined never to see again—never! never! never! Good-by; and try to forgive me!' She hid her face in her hands, and said no more. I tried to win her confidence; it was not to be done; I was compelled to leave her. There is some dreadful calamity, George, in that wretched woman's life. And such an interesting creature, too! It was impossible not to pity her, whether she deserved it or not. Everything about her is a mystery, my dear. She speaks English without the slightest foreign accent, and yet she has a foreign name."

"Did she give you her name?"

"No, and I was afraid to ask her to give it. But the landlady here is not a very scrupulous person. She told me she looked at the poor creature's linen while it was drying by the fire. The name marked on it was, 'Van Brandt.'"

"Van Brandt?" I repeated. "That sounds like a Dutch name. And yet you say she spoke like an Englishwoman. Perhaps she was born in England."

"Or perhaps she may be married," suggested my mother; "and Van Brandt may be the name of her husband."

The idea of her being a married woman had something in it repellent to me. I wished my mother had not thought of that last suggestion. I refused to receive it. I persisted in my own belief that the stranger was a single woman. In that character, I could indulge myself in the luxury of thinking of her; I could consider the chances of my being able to trace this charming fugitive, who had taken so strong a hold on my interest—whose desperate attempt at suicide had so nearly cost me my own life.

If she had gone as far as Edinburgh (which she would surely do, being bent on avoiding discovery), the prospect of finding her again—in that great city, and in my present weak state of health—looked doubtful indeed. Still, there was an underlying hopefulness in me which kept my spirits from being seriously depressed. I felt a purely imaginary (perhaps I ought to say, a purely superstitious) conviction that we who had nearly died together, we who had been brought to life together, were surely destined to be involved in some future joys or sorrows common to us both. "I fancy I shall see her again," was my last thought before my weakness overpowered me, and I sunk into a peaceful sleep.

That night I was removed from the inn to my own room at home; and that night I saw her again in a dream.

The image of her was as vividly impressed on me as the far different image of the child Mary, when I used to see it in the days of old. The dream-figure of the woman was robed as I had seen it robed on the bridge. She wore the same broad-brimmed garden-hat of straw. She looked at me as she had looked when I approached her in the dim evening light. After a little her face brightened with a divinely beautiful smile; and she whispered in my ear, "Friend, do you know me?"

I knew her, most assuredly; and yet it was with an incomprehensible after-feeling of doubt. Recognizing her in my dream as the stranger who had so warmly interested me, I was, nevertheless, dissatisfied with myself, as if it had not been the right recognition. I awoke with this idea; and I slept no more that night.

In three days' time I was strong enough to go out driving with my mother, in the comfortable, old-fashioned, open carriage which had once belonged to Mr. Germaine.

On the fourth day we arranged to make an excursion to a little waterfall in our neighborhood. My mother had a great admiration of the place, and had often expressed a wish to possess some memorial of it. I resolved to take my sketch-book: with me, on the chance that I might be able to please her by making a drawing of her favorite scene.

Searching for the sketch-book (which I had not used for years), I found it in an old desk of mine that had remained unopened since my departure for India. In the course of my investigation, I opened a drawer in the desk, and discovered a relic of the old times—my poor little Mary's first work in embroidery, the green flag!

The sight of the forgotten keepsake took my mind back to the bailiff's cottage, and reminded me of Dame Dermody, and her confident prediction about Mary and me.

I smiled as I recalled the old woman's assertion that no human power could "hinder the union of the kindred spirits of the children in the time to come." What had become of the prophesied dreams in which we were to communicate with each other through the term of our separation? Years had passed; and, sleeping or waking, I had seen nothing of Mary. Years had passed; and the first vision of a woman that had come to me had been my dream a few nights since of the stranger whom I had saved from drowning. I thought of these chances and changes in my life, but not contemptuously or bitterly. The new love that was now stealing its way into my heart had softened and humanized me. I said to myself, "Ah, poor little Mary!" and I kissed the green flag, in grateful memory of the days that were gone forever.

We drove to the waterfall.

It was a beautiful day; the lonely sylvan scene was at its brightest and best. A wooden summer-house, commanding a prospect of the falling stream, had been built for the accommodation of pleasure parties by the proprietor of the place. My mother suggested that I should try to make a sketch of the view from this point. I did my best to please her, but I was not satisfied with the result; and I abandoned my drawing before it was half finished. Leaving my sketch-book and pencil on the table of the summer-house, I proposed to my mother to cross a little wooden bridge which spanned the stream, below the fall, and to see how the landscape looked from a new point of view.

The prospect of the waterfall, as seen from the opposite bank, presented even greater difficulties, to an amateur artist like me, than the prospect which he had just left. We returned to the summer-house.

I was the first to approach the open door. I stopped, checked in my advance by an unexpected discovery. The summer-house was no longer empty as we had left it. A lady was seated at the table with my pencil in her hand, writing in my sketch-book!

After waiting a moment, I advanced a few steps nearer to the door, and stopped again in breathless amazement. The stranger in the summer-house was now plainly revealed to me as the woman who had attempted to destroy herself from the bridge!

There was no doubt about it. There was the dress; there was the memorable face which I had seen in the evening light, which I had dreamed of only a few nights since! The woman herself—I saw her as plainly as I saw the sun shining on the waterfall—the woman herself, with my pencil in her hand, writing in my book!

My mother was close behind me. She noticed my agitation. "George!" she exclaimed, "what is the matter with you?"

I pointed through the open door of the summer-house.

"Well?" said my mother. "What am I to look at?"

"Don't you see somebody sitting at the table and writing in my sketch-book?"

My mother eyed me quickly. "Is he going to be ill again?" I heard her say to herself.

At the same moment the woman laid down the pencil and rose slowly to her feet.

She looked at me with sorrowful and pleading eyes: she lifted her hand and beckoned me to approach her. I obeyed. Moving without conscious will of my own, drawn nearer and nearer to her by an irresistible power, I ascended the short flight of stairs which led into the summer-house. Within a few paces of her I stopped. She advanced a step toward me, and laid her hand gently on my bosom. Her touch filled me with strangely united sensations of rapture and awe. After a while, she spoke in low melodious tones, which mingled in my ear with the distant murmur of the falling water, until the two sounds became one. I heard in the murmur, I heard in the voice, these words: "Remember me. Come to me." Her hand dropped from my bosom; a momentary obscurity passed like a flying shadow over the bright daylight in the room. I looked for her when the light came back. She was gone.

My consciousness of passing events returned.

I saw the lengthening shadows outside, which told me that the evening was at hand. I saw the carriage approaching the summerhouse to take us away. I felt my mother's hand on my arm, and heard her voice speaking to me anxiously. I was able to reply by a sign entreating her not to be uneasy about me, but I could do no more. I was absorbed, body and soul, in the one desire to look at the sketch-book. As certainly as I had seen the woman, so certainly I had seen her, with my pencil in her hand, writing in my book.

I advanced to the table on which the book was lying open. I looked at the blank space on the lower part of the page, under the foreground lines of my unfinished drawing. My mother, following me, looked at the page too.

There was the writing! The woman had disappeared, but there were her written words left behind her: visible to my mother as well as to me, readable by my mother's eyes as well as by mine!

These were the words we saw, arranged in two lines, as I copy them here:

When the full moon shines

On Saint Anthony's Well.

CHAPTER IX. NATURAL AND SUPERNATURAL.

I POINTED to the writing in the sketch book, and looked at my mother. I was not mistaken. She had seen it, as I had seen it. But she refused to acknowledge that anything had happened to alarm her—plainly as I could detect it in her face.

"Somebody has been playing a trick on you, George," she said.

I made no reply. It was needless to say anything. My poor mother was evidently as far from being satisfied with her own shallow explanation as I was. The carriage waited for us at the door. We set forth in silence on our drive home.

The sketch-book lay open on my knee. My eyes were fastened on it; my mind was absorbed in recalling the moment when the apparition beckoned me into the summer-house and spoke. Putting the words and the writing together, the conclusion was too plain to be mistaken. The woman whom I had saved from drowning had need of me again.

And this was the same woman who, in her own proper person, had not hesitated to seize the first opportunity of leaving the house in which we had been sheltered together—without stopping to say one grateful word to the man who had preserved her from death! Four days only had elapsed since she had left me, never (to all appearance) to see me again. And now the ghostly apparition of her had returned as to a tried and trusted friend; had commanded me to remember her and to go to her; and had provided against all possibility of my memory playing me false, by writing the words which invited me to meet her "when the full moon shone on Saint Anthony's Well."

What had happened in the interval? What did the supernatural manner of her communication with me mean? What ought my next course of action to be?

My mother roused me from my reflections. She stretched out her hand, and suddenly closed the open book on my knee, as if the sight of the writing in it were unendurable to her.

"Why don't you speak to me, George?" she said. "Why do you keep your thoughts to yourself?"

"My mind is lost in confusion," I answered. "I can suggest nothing and explain nothing. My thoughts are all bent on the one question of what I am to do next. On that point I believe I may say that my mind is made up." I touched the sketch-book as I spoke. "Come what may of it," I said, "I mean to keep the appointment."

My mother looked at me as if she doubted the evidence of her own senses.

"He talks as if it were a real thing!" she exclaimed. "George, you don't really believe that you saw somebody in the summer-house? The place was empty. I tell you positively, when you pointed into the summer-house, the place was empty. You have been thinking and thinking of this woman till you persuade yourself that you have actually seen her."

I opened the sketch-book again. "I thought I saw her writing on this page," I answered. "Look at it, and tell me if I was wrong."

My mother refused to look at it. Steadily as she persisted in taking the rational view, nevertheless the writing frightened her.

"It is not a week yet," she went on, "since I saw you lying between life and death in your bed at the inn. How can you talk of keeping the appointment, in your state of health? An appointment with a shadowy Something in your own imagination, which appears and disappears, and leaves substantial writing behind it! It's ridiculous, George; I wonder you can help laughing at yourself."

She tried to set the example of laughing at me—with the tears in her eyes, poor soul! as she made the useless effort. I began to regret having opened my mind so freely to her.

"Don't take the matter too seriously, mother," I said. "Perhaps I may not be able to find the place. I never heard of Saint Anthony's Well; I have not the least idea where it is. Suppose I make the discovery, and suppose the journey turns out to be an easy one, would you like to go with me?"

"God forbid" cried my mother, fervently. "I will have nothing to do with it, George. You are in a state of delusion; I shall speak to the doctor."

"By all means, my dear mother. Mr. MacGlue is a sensible person. We pass his house on our way home, and we will ask him to dinner. In the meantime, let us say no more on the subject till we see the doctor."

I spoke lightly, but I really meant what I said. My mind was sadly disturbed; my nerves were so shaken that the slightest noises on the road startled me. The opinion of a man like Mr. MacGlue, who looked at all mortal matters from the same immovably practical point of view, might really have its use, in my case, as a species of moral remedy.

We waited until the dessert was on the table, and the servants had left the dining-room. Then I told my story to the Scotch doctor as I have told it here; and, that done, I opened the sketch-book to let him see the writing for himself.

Had I turned to the wrong page?

I started to my feet, and held the book close to the light of the lamp that hung over the dining table. No: I had found the right page. There was my half-finished drawing of the waterfall—but where were the two lines of writing beneath?

Gone!

I strained my eyes; I looked and looked. And the blank white paper looked back at me.

I placed the open leaf before my mother. "You saw it as plainly as I did," I said. "Are my own eyes deceiving me? Look at the bottom of the page."

My mother sunk back in her chair with a cry of terror.

"Gone?" I asked.

"Gone!"

I turned to the doctor. He took me completely by surprise. No incredulous smile appeared on his face; no jesting words passed his lips. He was listening to us attentively. He was waiting gravely to hear more.

"I declare to you, on my word of honor," I said to him, "that I saw the apparition writing with my pencil at the bottom of that page. I declare that I took the book in my hand, and saw these words written in it, 'When the full moon shines on Saint Anthony's Well.' Not more than three hours have passed since that time; and, see for yourself, not a vestige of the writing remains."

"Not a vestige of the writing remains," Mr. MacGlue repeated, quietly.

"If you feel the slightest doubt of what I have told you," I went on, "ask my mother; she will bear witness that she saw the writing too."

"I don't doubt that you both saw the writing," answered Mr. MacGlue, with a composure that surprised me.

"Can you account for it?" I asked.

"Well," said the impenetrable doctor, "if I set my wits at work, I believe I might account for it to the satisfaction of some people. For example, I might give you what they call the rational explanation, to begin with. I might say that you are, to my certain knowledge, in a highly excited nervous condition; and that, when you saw the apparition (as you call it), you simply saw nothing but your own strong impression of an absent woman, who (as I greatly fear) has got on the weak or amatory side of you. I mean no offense, Mr. Germaine—"

"I take no offense, doctor. But excuse me for speaking plainly—the rational explanation is thrown away on me."

"I'll readily excuse you," answered Mr. MacGlue; "the rather that I'm entirely of your opinion. I don't believe in the rational explanation myself."

This was surprising, to say the least of it. "What do you believe in?" I inquired.

Mr. MacGlue declined to let me hurry him.

"Wait a little," he said. "There's the irrational explanation to try next. Maybe it will fit itself to the present state of your mind better than the other. We will say this time that you have really seen the ghost (or double) of a living person. Very good. If you can suppose a disembodied spirit to appear in earthly clothing—of silk or merino, as the case may be—it's no great stretch to suppose, next, that this same spirit is capable of holding a mortal pencil, and of writing mortal words in a mortal sketching-book. And if the ghost vanishes (which your ghost did), it seems supernaturally appropriate that the writing should follow the example and vanish too. And the reason of the vanishment may be (if you want a reason), either that the ghost does not like letting a stranger like me into its secrets, or that vanishing is a settled habit of ghosts and of everything associated with them, or that this ghost has changed its mind in the course of three hours (being the ghost of a woman, I am sure that's not wonderful), and doesn't care to see you 'when the full moon shines on Saint Anthony's Well.' There's the irrational explanation for you. And, speaking for myself, I'm bound to add that I don't set a pin's value on that explanation either."

Mr. MacGlue's sublime indifference to both sides of the question began to irritate me.

"In plain words, doctor," I said, "you don't think the circumstances that I have mentioned to you worthy of serious investigation?"

"I don't think serious investigation capable of dealing with the circumstances," answered the doctor. "Put it in that way, and you put it right. Just look round you. Here we three persons are alive and hearty at this snug table. If (which God forbid!) good Mistress Germaine or yourself were to fall down dead in another moment, I, doctor as I am, could no more explain what first principle of life and movement had been suddenly extinguished in you than the dog there sleeping on the hearth-rug. If I am content to sit down ignorant in the face of such an impenetrable mystery as this—presented to me, day after day, every time I see a living creature come into the world or go out of it—why may I not sit down content in the face of your lady in the summer-house, and say she's altogether beyond my fathoming, and there is an end of her?"

At those words my mother joined in the conversation for the first time.

"Ah, sir," she said, "if you could only persuade my son to take your sensible view, how happy I should be! Would you believe it?—he positively means (if he can find the place) to go to Saint Anthony's Well!"

Even this revelation entirely failed to surprise Mr. MacGlue.

"Ay, ay. He means to keep his appointment with the ghost, does he? Well, I can be of some service to him if he sticks to his resolution. I can tell him of another man who kept a written appointment with a ghost, and what came of it."

This was a startling announcement. Did he really mean what he said?

"Are you in jest or in earnest?" I asked.

"I never joke, sir," said Mr. MacGlue. "No sick person really believes in a doctor who jokes. I defy you to show me a man at the head of our profession who has ever been discovered in high spirits (in medical hours) by his nearest and dearest friend. You may have wondered, I dare say, at seeing me take your strange narrative as coolly as I do. It comes naturally, sir. Yours is not the first story of a ghost and a pencil that I have heard."

"Do you mean to tell me," I said, "that you know of another man who has seen what I have seen?"

"That's just what I mean to tell you," rejoined the doctor. "The man was a far-away Scots cousin of my late wife, who bore the honorable name of Bruce, and followed a seafaring life. I'll take another glass of the sherry wine, just to wet my whistle, as the vulgar saying is, before I begin. Well, you must know, Bruce was mate of a bark at the time I'm speaking of, and he was on a voyage from Liverpool to New Brunswick. At noon one day, he and the captain, having taken their observation of the sun, were hard at it below, working out the latitude and longitude on their slates. Bruce, in his cabin, looked across through the open door of the captain's cabin opposite. 'What do you make it, sir?' says Brace. The man in the captain's cabin looked up. And what did Bruce see? The face of the captain? Devil a bit of it—the face of a total stranger! Up jumps Bruce, with his heart going full gallop all in a moment, and searches for the captain on deck, and finds him much as usual, with his calculations done, and his latitude and longitude off his mind for the day. 'There's somebody at your desk, sir,' says Bruce. 'He's writing on your slate; and he's a total stranger to me.' 'A stranger in my cabin?' says the captain. 'Why, Mr. Bruce, the ship has been six weeks out of port. How did he get on board?' Bruce doesn't know how, but he sticks to his story. Away goes the captain, and bursts like a whirlwind into his cabin, and finds nobody there. Bruce himself is obliged to acknowledge that the place is certainly empty. 'If I didn't know you were a sober man,' says the captain, 'I should charge you with drinking. As it is, I'll hold you accountable for nothing worse than dreaming. Don't do it again, Mr. Bruce.' Bruce sticks to his story; Bruce swears he saw the man writing on the captain's slate. The captain takes up the slate and looks at it. 'Lord save us and bless us!' says he; 'here the writing is, sure enough!' Bruce looks at it too, and sees the writing as plainly as can be, in these words: 'Steer to the nor'-west.' That, and no more.—Ah, goodness me, narrating is dry work, Mr. Germaine. With your leave, I'll take another drop of the sherry wine.

"Well (it's fine old wine, that; look at the oily drops running down the glass)—well, steering to the north-west, you will understand, was out of the captain's course. Nevertheless, finding no solution of the mystery on board the ship, and the weather at the time being fine, the captain determined, while the daylight lasted, to alter his course, and see what came of it. Toward three o'clock in the afternoon an iceberg came of it; with a wrecked ship stove in, and frozen fast to the ice; and the passengers and crew nigh to death with cold and exhaustion. Wonderful enough, you will say; but more remains behind. As the mate was helping one of the rescued passengers up the side of the bark, who should he turn out to be but the very man whose ghostly appearance Bruce had seen in the captain's cabin writing on the captain's slate! And more than that—if your capacity for being surprised isn't clean worn out by this time—the passenger recognized the bark as the very vessel which he had seen in a dream at noon that day. He had even spoken of it to one of the officers on board the wrecked ship when he woke. 'We shall be rescued to-day,' he had said; and he had exactly described the rig of the bark hours and hours before the vessel herself hove in view. Now you know, Mr. Germaine, how my wife's far-away cousin kept an appointment with a ghost, and what came of it." *

Concluding his story in these words, the doctor helped himself to another glass of the "sherry wine." I was not satisfied yet; I wanted to know more.

"The writing on the slate," I said. "Did it remain there, or did it vanish like the writing in my book?"

Mr. MacGlue's answer disappointed me. He had never asked, and had never heard, whether the writing had remained or not. He had told me all that he knew, and he had but one thing more to say, and that was in the nature of a remark with a moral attached to it. "There's a marvelous resemblance, Mr. Germaine, between your story and Bruce's story. The main difference, as I see it, is this. The passenger's appointment proved to be the salvation of a whole ship's company. I very much doubt whether the lady's appointment will prove to be the salvation of You."

I silently reconsidered the strange narrative which had just been related to me. Another man had seen what I had seen—had done what I proposed to do! My mother noticed with grave displeasure the strong impression which Mr. MacGlue had produced on my mind.

"I wish you had kept your story to yourself, doctor," she said, sharply.

"May I ask why, madam?"

"You have confirmed my son, sir, in his resolution to go to Saint Anthony's Well."

Mr. MacGlue quietly consulted his pocket almanac before he replied.

"It's the full moon on the ninth of the month," he said. "That gives Mr. Germaine some days of rest, ma'am, before he takes the journey. If he travels in his own comfortable carriage—whatever I may think, morally speaking, of his enterprise—I can't say, medically speaking, that I believe it will do him much harm."

"You know where Saint Anthony's Well is?" I interposed.

"I must be mighty ignorant of Edinburgh not to know that," replied the doctor.

"Is the Well in Edinburgh, then?"

"It's just outside Edinburgh—looks down on it, as you may say. You follow the old street called the Canongate to the end. You turn to your right past the famous Palace of Holyrood; you cross the Park and the Drive, and take your way upward to the ruins of Anthony's Chapel, on the shoulder of the hill—and there you are! There's a high rock behind the chapel, and at the foot of it you will find the spring they call Anthony's Well. It's thought a pretty view by moonlight; and they tell me it's no longer beset at night by bad characters, as it used to be in the old time."

My mother, in graver and graver displeasure, rose to retire to the drawing-room.

"I confess you have disappointed me," she said to Mr. MacGlue. "I should have thought you would have been the last man to encourage my son in an act of imprudence."

"Craving your pardon, madam, your son requires no encouragement. I can see for myself that his mind is made up. Where is the use of a person like me trying to stop him? Dear madam, if he won't profit by your advice, what hope can I have that he will take mine?"

Mr. MacGlue pointed this artful compliment by a bow of the deepest respect, and threw open the door for my mother to pass out.

When we were left together over our wine, I asked the doctor how soon I might safely start on my journey to Edinburgh.

"Take two days to do the journey, and you may start, if you're bent on it, at the beginning of the week. But mind this," added the prudent doctor, "though I own I'm anxious to hear what comes of your expedition—understand at the same time, so far as the lady is concerned, that I wash my hands of the consequences."—

* *The doctor's narrative is not imaginary. It will be found related in full detail, and authenticated by names and dates, in Robert Dale Owen's very interesting work called "Footfalls on the Boundary of Another World." The author gladly takes this opportunity of acknowledging his obligations to Mr. Owen's remarkable book.*

CHAPTER X. SAINT ANTHONY'S WELL.

I STOOD on the rocky eminence in front of the ruins of Saint Anthony's Chapel, and looked on the magnificent view of Edinburgh and of the old Palace of Holyrood, bathed in the light of the full moon.

The Well, as the doctor's instructions had informed me, was behind the chapel. I waited for some minutes in front of the ruin, partly to recover my breath after ascending the hill; partly, I own, to master the nervous agitation which the sense of my position at that moment had aroused in me. The woman, or the apparition of the woman—it might be either—was perhaps within a few yards of the place that I occupied. Not a living creature appeared in front of the chapel. Not a sound caught my ear from any part of the solitary hill. I tried to fix my whole attention on the beauties of the moonlit view. It was not to be done. My mind was far away from the objects on which my eyes rested. My mind was with the woman whom I had seen in the summer-house writing in my book.

I turned to skirt the side of the chapel. A few steps more over the broken ground brought me within view of the Well, and of the high boulder or rock from the foot of which the waters gushed brightly in the light of the moon.

She was there.

I recognized her figure as she stood leaning against the rock, with her hands crossed in front of her, lost in thought. I recognized her face as she looked up quickly, startled by the sound of my footsteps in the deep stillness of the night.

Was it the woman, or the apparition of the woman? I waited, looking at her in silence.

She spoke. The sound of her voice was not the mysterious sound that I had heard in the summer-house. It was the sound I had heard on the bridge when we first met in the dim evening light.

"Who are you? What do you want?"

As those words passed her lips, she recognized me. "You here!" she went on, advancing a step, in uncontrollable surprise. "What does this mean?"

"I am here," I answered, "to meet you, by your own appointment."

She stepped back again, leaning against the rock. The moonlight shone full upon her face. There was terror as well as astonishment in her eyes while they now looked at me.

"I don't understand you," she said. "I have not seen you since you spoke to me on the bridge."

"Pardon me," I replied. "I have seen you—or the appearance of you—since that time. I heard you speak. I saw you write."

She looked at me with the strangest expression of mingled resentment and curiosity. "What did I say?" she asked. "What did I write?"

"You said, 'Remember me. Come to me.' You wrote, 'When the full moon shines on Saint Anthony's Well.'"

"Where?" she cried. "Where did I do that?"

"In a summer-house which stands by a waterfall," I answered. "Do you know the place?"

Her head sunk back against the rock. A low cry of terror burst from her. Her arm, resting on the rock, dropped at her side. I hurriedly approached her, in the fear that she might fall on the stony ground.

She rallied her failing strength. "Don't touch me!" she exclaimed. "Stand back, sir. You frighten me."

I tried to soothe her. "Why do I frighten you? You know who I am. Can you doubt my interest in you, after I have been the means of saving your life?"

Her reserve vanished in an instant. She advanced without hesitation, and took me by the hand.

"I ought to thank you," she said. "And I do. I am not so ungrateful as I seem. I am not a wicked woman, sir—I was mad with misery when I tried to drown myself. Don't distrust me! Don't despise me!" She stopped; I saw the tears on her cheeks. With a sudden contempt for herself, she dashed them away. Her whole tone and manner altered once more. Her reserve returned; she looked at me with a strange flash of suspicion and defiance in her eyes. "Mind this!" she said, loudly and abruptly, "you were dreaming when you thought you saw me writing. You didn't see me; you never heard me speak. How could I say those familiar words to a stranger like you? It's all your fancy—and you try to frighten me by talking of it as if it was a real thing!" She changed again; her eyes softened to the sad and tender look which made them so irresistibly beautiful. She drew her cloak round her with a shudder, as if she felt the chill of the night air. "What is the matter with me?" I heard her say to herself. "Why do I trust this man in my dreams? And why am I ashamed of it when I wake?"

That strange outburst encouraged me. I risked letting her know that I had overheard her last words.

"If you trust me in your dreams, you only do me justice," I said. "Do me justice now; give me your confidence. You are alone—you are in trouble—you want a friend's help. I am waiting to help you."

She hesitated. I tried to take her hand. The strange creature drew it away with a cry of alarm: her one great fear seemed to be the fear of letting me touch her.

"Give me time to think of it," she said. "You don't know what I have got to think of. Give me till to-morrow; and let me write. Are you staying in Edinburgh?"

I thought it wise to be satisfied—in appearance at least—with this concession. Taking out my card, I wrote on it in pencil the address of the hotel at which I was staying. She read the card by the moonlight when I put it into her hand.

"George!" she repeated to herself, stealing another look at me as the name passed her lips. "'George Germaine.' I never heard of 'Germaine.' But

'George' reminds me of old times." She smiled sadly at some passing fancy or remembrance in which I was not permitted to share. "There is nothing very wonderful in your being called 'George,'" she went on, after a while. "The name is common enough: one meets with it everywhere as a man's name And yet—" Her eyes finished the sentence; her eyes said to me, "I am not so much afraid of you, now I know that you are called 'George.'"

So she unconsciously led me to the brink of discovery!

If I had only asked her what associations she connected with my Christian name—if I had only persuaded her to speak in the briefest and most guarded terms of her past life—the barrier between us, which the change in our names and the lapse of ten years had raised, must have been broken down; the recognition must have followed. But I never even thought of it; and for this simple reason—I was in love with her. The purely selfish idea of winning my way to her favorable regard by taking instant advantage of the new interest that I had awakened in her was the one idea which occurred to my mind.

"Don't wait to write to me," I said. "Don't put it off till to-morrow. Who knows what may happen before to-morrow? Surely I deserve some little return for the sympathy that I feel with you? I don't ask for much. Make me happy by making me of some service to you before we part to-night."

I took her hand, this time, before she was aware of me. The whole woman seemed to yield at my touch. Her hand lay unresistingly in mine; her charming figure came by soft gradations nearer and nearer to me; her head almost touched my shoulder. She murmured in faint accents, broken by sighs, "Don't take advantage of me. I am so friendless; I am so completely in your power." Before I could answer, before I could move, her hand closed on mine; her head sunk on my shoulder: she burst into tears.

Any man, not an inbred and inborn villain, would have respected her at that moment. I put her hand on my arm and led her away gently past the ruined chapel, and down the slope of the hill.

"This lonely place is frightening you," I said. "Let us walk a little, and you will soon be yourself again."

She smiled through her tears like a child.

"Yes," she said, eagerly. "But not that way." I had accidentally taken the direction which led away from the city; she begged me to turn toward the houses and the streets. We walked back toward Edinburgh. She eyed me, as we went on in the moonlight, with innocent, wondering looks. "What an unaccountable influence you have over me!" she exclaimed.

"Did you ever see me, did you ever hear my name, before we met that evening at the river?"

"Never."

"And I never heard your name, and never saw you before. Strange! very strange! Ah! I remember somebody—only an old woman, sir—who might once have explained it. Where shall I find the like of her now?"

She sighed bitterly. The lost friend or relative had evidently been dear to her. "A relation of yours?" I inquired—more to keep her talking than because I felt any interest in any member of her family but herself.

We were again on the brink of discovery. And again it was decreed that we were to advance no further.

"Don't ask me about my relations!" she broke out. "I daren't think of the dead and gone, in the trouble that is trying me now. If I speak of the old times at home, I shall only burst out crying again, and distress you. Talk of something else, sir—talk of something else."

The mystery of the apparition in the summer-house was not cleared up yet. I took my opportunity of approaching the subject.

"You spoke a little while since of dreaming of me," I began. "Tell me your dream."

"I hardly know whether it was a dream or whether it was something else," she answered. "I call it a dream for want of a better word."

"Did it happen at night?"

"No. In the daytime—in the afternoon."

"Late in the afternoon?"

"Yes—close on the evening."

My memory reverted to the doctor's story of the shipwrecked passenger, whose ghostly "double" had appeared in the vessel that was to rescue him, and who had himself seen that vessel in a dream.

"Do you remember the day of the month and the hour?" I asked.

She mentioned the day, and she mentioned the hour. It was the day when my mother and I had visited the waterfall. It was the hour when I had seen the apparition in the summer-house writing in my book!

I stopped in irrepressible astonishment. We had walked by this time nearly as far on the way back to the city as the old Palace of Holyrood. My companion, after a glance at me, turned and looked at the rugged old building, mellowed into quiet beauty by the lovely moonlight.

"This is my favorite walk," she said, simply, "since I have been in Edinburgh. I don't mind the loneliness. I like the perfect tranquillity here at night." She glanced at me again. "What is the matter?" she asked. "You say nothing; you only look at me."

"I want to hear more of your dream," I said. "How did you come to be sleeping in the daytime?"

"It is not easy to say what I was doing," she replied, as we walked on again. "I was miserably anxious and ill. I felt my helpless condition keenly on that day. It was dinner-time, I remember, and I had no appetite. I went upstairs (at the inn where I am staying), and lay down, quite worn out, on my bed. I don't know whether I fainted or whether I slept; I lost all consciousness of what was going on about me, and I got some other consciousness in its place. If this was dreaming, I can only say it was the most vivid dream I ever had in my life."

"Did it begin by your seeing me?" I inquired.

"It began by my seeing your drawing-book—lying open on a table in a summer-house."

"Can you describe the summer-house as you saw it?"

She described not only the summer-house, but the view of the waterfall from the door. She knew the size, she knew the binding, of my sketch-book—locked up in my desk, at that moment, at home in Perthshire!

"And you wrote in the book," I went on. "Do you remember what you wrote?"

She looked away from me confusedly, as if she were ashamed to recall this part of her dream.

"You have mentioned it already," she said. "There is no need for me to go over the words again. Tell me one thing—when you were at the summer-house, did you wait a little on the path to the door before you went in?"

I had waited, surprised by my first view of the woman writing in my book. Having answered her to this effect, I asked what she had done or dreamed of doing at the later moment when I entered the summer-house.

"I did the strangest things," she said, in low, wondering tones. "If you had been my brother, I could hardly have treated you more familiarly. I beckoned to you to come to me. I even laid my hand on your bosom. I spoke to you as I might have spoken to my oldest and dearest friend. I said, 'Remember me. Come to me.' Oh, I was so ashamed of myself when I came to my senses again, and recollected it. Was there ever such familiarity—even in a dream—between a woman and a man whom she had only once seen, and then as a perfect stranger?"

"Did you notice how long it was," I asked, "from the time when you lay down on the bed to the time when you found yourself awake again?"

"I think I can tell you," she replied. "It was the dinner-time of the house (as I said just now) when I went upstairs. Not long after I had come to myself I heard a church clock strike the hour. Reckoning from one time to the other, it must have been quite three hours from the time when I first lay down to the time when I got up again."

Was the clew to the mysterious disappearance of the writing to be found here?

Looking back by the light of later discoveries, I am inclined to think that it was. In three hours the lines traced by the apparition of her had vanished. In three hours she had come to herself, and had felt ashamed of the familiar manner in which she had communicated with me in her sleeping state. While she had trusted me in the trance—trusted me because her spirit was then free to recognize my spirit—the writing had remained on the page. When her waking will counteracted the influence of her sleeping will, the writing disappeared. Is this the explanation? If it is not, where is the explanation to be found?

We walked on until we reached that part of the Canongate street in which she lodged. We stopped at the door.

CHAPTER XI. THE LETTER OF INTRODUCTION.

I LOOKED at the house. It was an inn, of no great size, but of respectable appearance. If I was to be of any use to her that night, the time had come to speak of other subjects than the subject of dreams.

"After all that you have told me," I said, "I will not ask you to admit me any further into your confidence until we meet again. Only let me hear how I can relieve your most pressing anxieties. What are your plans? Can I do anything to help them before you go to rest to-night?"

She thanked me warmly, and hesitated, looking up the street and down the street in evident embarrassment what to say next.

"Do you propose staying in Edinburgh?" I asked.

"Oh no! I don't wish to remain in Scotland. I want to go much further away. I think I should do better in London; at some respectable milliner's, if I could be properly recommended. I am quick at my needle, and I understand cutting out. Or I could keep accounts, if—if anybody would trust me."

She stopped, and looked at me doubtingly, as if she felt far from sure, poor soul, of winning my confidence to begin with. I acted on that hint, with the headlong impetuosity of a man who was in love.

"I can give you exactly the recommendation you want," I said, "whenever you like. Now, if you would prefer it."

Her charming features brightened with pleasure. "Oh, you are indeed a friend to me!" she said, impulsively. Her face clouded again—she saw my proposal in a new light. "Have I any right," she asked, sadly, "to accept what you offer me?"

"Let me give you the letter," I answered, "and you can decide for yourself whether you will use it or not."

I put her arm again in mine, and entered the inn.

She shrunk back in alarm. What would the landlady think if she saw her lodger enter the house at night in company with a stranger, and that stranger a gentleman? The landlady appeared as she made the objection. Reckless what I said or what I did, I introduced myself as her relative, and asked to be shown into a quiet room in which I could write a letter. After one sharp glance at me, the landlady appeared to be satisfied that she was dealing with a gentleman. She led the way into a sort of parlor behind the "bar," placed writing materials on the table, looked at my companion as only one woman can look at another under certain circumstances, and left us by ourselves.

It was the first time I had ever been in a room with her alone. The embarrassing sense of her position had heightened her color and brightened her eyes. She stood, leaning one hand on the table, confused and irresolute, her firm and supple figure falling into an attitude of unsought grace which it was literally a luxury to look at. I said nothing; my eyes confessed my admiration; the writing materials lay untouched before me on the table. How long the silence might have lasted I cannot say. She abruptly broke it. Her instinct warned her that silence might have its dangers, in our position. She turned to me with an effort; she said, uneasily, "I don't think you ought to write your letter to-night, sir."

"Why not?"

"You know nothing of me. Surely you ought not to recommend a person who is a stranger to you? And I am worse than a stranger. I am a miserable wretch who has tried to commit a great sin—I have tried to destroy myself. Perhaps the misery I was in might be some excuse for me, if you knew it. You ought to know it. But it's so late to-night, and I am so sadly tired—and there are some things, sir, which it is not easy for a woman to speak of in the presence of a man."

Her head sunk on her bosom; her delicate lips trembled a little; she said no more. The way to reassure and console her lay plainly enough before me, if I chose to take it. Without stopping to think, I took it.

Reminding her that she had herself proposed writing to me when we met that evening, I suggested that she should wait to tell the sad story of her troubles until it was convenient to her to send me the narrative in the form of a letter. "In the mean time," I added, "I have the most perfect confidence in you; and I beg as a favor that you will let me put it to the proof. I can introduce you to a dressmaker in London who is at the head of a large establishment, and I will do it before I leave you to-night."

I dipped my pen in the ink as I said the words. Let me confess frankly the lengths to which my infatuation led me. The dressmaker to whom I had alluded had been my mother's maid in former years, and had been established in business with money lent by my late step-father, Mr. Germaine. I used both their names without scruple; and I wrote my recommendation in terms which the best of living women and the ablest of existing dressmakers could never have hoped to merit. Will anybody find excuses for me? Those rare persons who have been in love, and who have not completely forgotten it yet, may perhaps find excuses for me. It matters little; I don't deserve them.

I handed her the open letter to read.

She blushed delightfully; she cast one tenderly grateful look at me, which I remembered but too well for many and many an after-day. The next moment, to my astonishment, this changeable creature changed again. Some forgotten consideration seemed to have occurred to her. She turned pale; the soft lines of pleasure in her face hardened, little by little; she regarded me with the saddest look of confusion and distress. Putting the letter down before me on the table, she said, timidly:

"Would you mind adding a postscript, sir?"

I suppressed all appearance of surprise as well as I could, and took up the pen again.

"Would you please say," she went on, "that I am only to be taken on trial, at first? I am not to be engaged for more"—her voice sunk lower and lower, so that I could barely hear the next words—"for more than three months, certain."

It was not in human nature—perhaps I ought to say it was not in the nature of a man who was in my situation—to refrain from showing some curiosity, on being asked to supplement a letter of recommendation by such a postscript as this.

"Have you some other employment in prospect?" I asked.

"None," she answered, with her head down, and her eyes avoiding mine.

An unworthy doubt of her—the mean offspring of jealousy—found its way into my mind.

"Have you some absent friend," I went on, "who is likely to prove a better friend than I am, if you only give him time?"

She lifted her noble head. Her grand, guileless gray eyes rested on me with a look of patient reproach.

"I have not got a friend in the world," she said. "For God's sake, ask me no more questions to-night!"

I rose and gave her the letter once more—with the postscript added, in her own words.

We stood together by the table; we looked at each other in a momentary silence.

"How can I thank you?" she murmured, softly. "Oh, sir, I will indeed be worthy of the confidence that you have shown in me!" Her eyes moistened; her variable color came and went; her dress heaved softly over the lovely outline of her bosom. I don't believe the man lives who could have resisted her at that moment. I lost all power of restraint; I caught her in my arms; I whispered, "I love you!" I kissed her passionately. For a moment she lay helpless and trembling on my breast; for a moment her fragrant lips softly returned the kiss. In an instant more it was over. She tore herself away with a shudder that shook her from head to foot, and threw the letter that I had given to her indignantly at my feet.

"How dare you take advantage of me! How dare you touch me!" she said. "Take your letter back, sir; I refuse to receive it; I will never speak to you again. You don't know what you have done. You don't know how deeply you have wounded me. Oh!" she cried, throwing herself in despair on a sofa that stood near her, "shall I ever recover my self-respect? shall I ever forgive myself for what I have done to-night?"

I implored her pardon; I assured her of my repentance and regret in words which did really come from my heart. The violence of her agitation more than distressed me—I was really alarmed by it.

She composed herself after a while. She rose to her feet with modest dignity, and silently held out her hand in token that my repentance was accepted.

"You will give me time for atonement?" I pleaded. "You will not lose all confidence in me? Let me see you again, if it is only to show that I am not quite unworthy of your pardon—at your own time; in the presence of another person, if you like."

"I will write to you," she said.

"To-morrow?"

"To-morrow."

I took up the letter of recommendation from the floor.

"Make your goodness to me complete," I said. "Don't mortify me by refusing to take my letter."

"I will take your letter," she answered, quietly. "Thank you for writing it. Leave me now, please. Good-night."

I left her, pale and sad, with my letter in her hand. I left her, with my mind in a tumult of contending emotions, which gradually resolved themselves into two master-feelings as I walked on: Love, that adored her more fervently than ever; and Hope, that set the prospect before me of seeing her again on the next day.

CHAPTER XII. THE DISASTERS OF MRS. VAN BRANDT.

A MAN who passes his evening as I had passed mine, may go to bed afterward if he has nothing better to do. But he must not rank among the number of his reasonable anticipations the expectation of getting a night's rest. The morning was well advanced, and the hotel was astir, before I at last closed my eyes in slumber. When I awoke, my watch informed me that it was close on noon.

I rang the bell. My servant appeared with a letter in his hand. It had been left for me, three hours since, by a lady who had driven to the hotel door in a carriage, and had then driven away again. The man had found me sleeping when he entered my bed-chamber, and, having received no orders to wake me overnight, had left the letter on the sitting-room table until he heard my bell.

Easily guessing who my correspondent was, I opened the letter. An inclosure fell out of it—to which, for the moment, I paid no attention. I turned eagerly to the first lines. They announced that the writer had escaped me for the second time: early that morning she had left Edinburgh. The paper inclosed proved to be my letter of introduction to the dressmaker returned to me.

I was more than angry with her—I felt her second flight from me as a downright outrage. In five minutes I had hurried on my clothes and was on my way to the inn in the Canongate as fast as a horse could draw me.

The servants could give me no information. Her escape had been effected without their knowledge.

The landlady, to whom I next addressed myself, deliberately declined to assist me in any way whatever.

"I have given the lady my promise," said this obstinate person, "to answer not one word to any question that you may ask me about her. In my belief, she is acting as becomes an honest woman in removing herself from any further communication with you. I saw you through the keyhole last night, sir. I wish you good-morning."

Returning to my hotel, I left no attempt to discover her untried. I traced the coachman who had driven her. He had set her down at a shop, and had then been dismissed. I questioned the shop-keeper. He remembered that he had sold some articles of linen to a lady with her veil down and a traveling-bag in her hand, and he remembered no more. I circulated a description of her in the different coach offices. Three "elegant young ladies, with their veils down, and with traveling-bags in their hands," answered to the description; and which of the three was the fugitive of whom I was in search, it was impossible to discover. In the days of railways and electric telegraphs I might have succeeded in tracing her. In the days of which I am now writing, she set investigation at defiance.

I read and reread her letter, on the chance that some slip of the pen might furnish the clew which I had failed to find in any other way. Here is the narrative that she addressed to me, copied from the original, word for word:

"DEAR SIR—Forgive me for leaving you again as I left you in Perthshire. After what took place last night, I have no other choice (knowing my own weakness, and the influence that you seem to have over me) than to thank you gratefully for your kindness, and to bid you farewell. My sad position must be my excuse for separating myself from you in this rude manner, and for venturing to send you back your letter of introduction. If I use the letter, I only offer you a means of communicating with me. For your sake, as well as for mine, this must not be. I must never give you a second opportunity of saying that you love me; I must go away, leaving no trace behind by which you can possibly discover me.

"But I cannot forget that I owe my poor life to your compassion and your courage. You, who saved me, have a right to know what the provocation was that drove me to drowning myself, and what my situation is, now that I am (thanks to you) still a living woman. You shall hear my sad story, sir; and I will try to tell it as briefly as possible.

"I was married, not very long since, to a Dutch gentleman, whose name is Van Brandt. Please excuse my entering into family particulars. I have endeavored to write and tell you about my dear lost father and my old home. But the tears come into my eyes when I think of my happy past life. I really cannot see the lines as I try to write them.

"Let me, then, only say that Mr. Van Brandt was well recommended to my good father before I married. I have only now discovered that he obtained these recommendations from his friends under a false pretense, which it is needless to trouble you by mentioning in detail. Ignorant of what he had done, I lived with him happily. I cannot truly declare that he was the object of my first love, but he was the one person in the world whom I had to look up to after my father's death. I esteemed him and respected him, and, if I may say so without vanity, I did indeed make him a good wife.

"So the time went on, sir, prosperously enough, until the evening came when you and I met on the bridge.

"I was out alone in our garden, trimming the shrubs, when the maid-servant came and told me there was a foreign lady in a carriage at the door who desired to say a word to Mrs. Van Brandt. I sent the maid on before to show her into the sitting-room, and I followed to receive my visitor as soon as I had made myself tidy. She was a dreadful woman, with a flushed, fiery face and impudent, bright eyes. 'Are you Mrs. Van Brandt?' she said. I answered, 'Yes.' 'Are you really married to him?' she asked me. That question (naturally enough, I think) upset my temper. I said, 'How dare you doubt it?' She laughed in my face. 'Send for Van Brandt,' she said. I went out into the passage and called him down from the room upstairs in which he was writing. 'Ernest,' I said, 'here is a person who has insulted me. Come down directly.' He left his room the moment he heard me. The woman followed me out into the passage to meet him. She made him a low courtesy. He turned deadly pale the moment he set eyes on her. That frightened me. I said to him, 'For God's sake, what does this mean?' He took me by the arm, and he answered: 'You shall know soon. Go back to your gardening, and don't return to the house till I send for you.' His looks were so shocking, he was so unlike himself, that I declare he daunted me. I let him take me as far as the garden door. He squeezed my hand. 'For my sake, darling,' he whispered, 'do what

I ask of you.' I went into the garden and sat me down on the nearest bench, and waited impatiently for what was to come.

"How long a time passed I don't know. My anxiety got to such a pitch at last that I could bear it no longer. I ventured back to the house.

"I listened in the passage, and heard nothing. I went close to the parlor door, and still there was silence. I took courage, and opened the door.

"The room was empty. There was a letter on the table. It was in my husband's handwriting, and it was addressed to me. I opened it and read it. The letter told me that I was deserted, disgraced, ruined. The woman with the fiery face and the impudent eyes was Van Brandt's lawful wife. She had given him his choice of going away with her at once or of being prosecuted for bigamy. He had gone away with her—gone, and left me.

"Remember, sir, that I had lost both father and mother. I had no friends. I was alone in the world, without a creature near to comfort or advise me. And please to bear in mind that I have a temper which feels even the smallest slights and injuries very keenly. Do you wonder at what I had it in my thoughts to do that evening on the bridge?

"Mind this: I believe I should never have attempted to destroy myself if I could only have burst out crying. No tears came to me. A dull, stunned feeling took hold like a vise on my head and on my heart. I walked straight to the river. I said to myself, quite calmly, as I went along, 'There is the end of it, and the sooner the better.'

"What happened after that, you know as well as I do. I may get on to the next morning—the morning when I so ungratefully left you at the inn by the river-side.

"I had but one reason, sir, for going away by the first conveyance that I could find to take me, and this was the fear that Van Brandt might discover me if I remained in Perthshire. The letter that he had left on the table was full of expressions of love and remorse, to say nothing of excuses for his infamous behavior to me. He declared that he had been entrapped into a private marriage with a profligate woman when he was little more than a lad. They had long since separated by common consent. When he first courted me, he had every reason to believe that she was dead. How he had been deceived in this particular, and how she had discovered that he had married me, he had yet to find out. Knowing her furious temper, he had gone away with her, as the one means of preventing an application to the justices and a scandal in the neighborhood. In a day or two he would purchase his release from her by an addition to the allowance which she had already received from him: he would return to me and take me abroad, out of the way of further annoyance. I was his wife in the sight of Heaven; I was the only woman he had ever loved; and so on, and so on.

"Do you now see, sir, the risk that I ran of his discovering me if I remained in your neighborhood? The bare thought of it made my flesh creep. I was determined never again to see the man who had so cruelly deceived me. I am in the same mind still—with this difference, that I might consent to see him, if I could be positively assured first of the death of his wife. That is not likely to happen. Let me get on with my letter, and tell you what I did on my arrival in Edinburgh.

"The coachman recommended me to the house in the Canongate where you found me lodging. I wrote the same day to relatives of my father, living in Glasgow, to tell them where I was, and in what a forlorn position I found myself.

"I was answered by return of post. The head of the family and his wife requested me to refrain from visiting them in Glasgow. They had business then in hand which would take them to Edinburgh, and I might expect to see them both with the least possible delay.

"They arrived, as they had promised, and they expressed themselves civilly enough. Moreover, they did certainly lend me a small sum of money when they found how poorly my purse was furnished. But I don't think either husband or wife felt much for me. They recommended me, at parting, to apply to my father's other relatives, living in England. I may be doing them an injustice, but I fancy they were eager to get me (as the common phrase is) off their hands.

"The day when the departure of my relatives left me friendless was also the day, sir, when I had that dream or vision of you which I have already related. I lingered on at the house in the Canongate, partly because the landlady was kind to me, partly because I was so depressed by my position that I really did not know what to do next.

"In this wretched condition you discovered me on that favorite walk of mine from Holyrood to Saint Anthony's Well. Believe me, your kind interest in my fortunes has not been thrown away on an ungrateful woman. I could ask Providence for no greater blessing than to find a brother and a friend in you. You have yourself destroyed that hope by what you said and did when we were together in the parlor. I don't blame you: I am afraid my manner (without my knowing it) might have seemed to give you some encouragement. I am only sorry—very, very sorry—to have no honorable choice left but never to see you again.

"After much thinking, I have made up my mind to speak to those other relatives of my father to whom I have not yet applied. The chance that they may help me to earn an honest living is the one chance that I have left. God bless you, Mr. Germaine! I wish you prosperity and happiness from the bottom of my heart; and remain, your grateful servant,

"*M. VAN BRANDT.*

"P.S.—I sign my own name (or the name which I once thought was mine) as a proof that I have honestly written the truth about myself, from first to last. For the future I must, for safety's sake, live under some other name. I should like to go back to my name when I was a happy girl at home. But Van Brandt knows it; and, besides, I have (no matter how innocently) disgraced it. Good-by again, sir; and thank you again."

So the letter concluded.

I read it in the temper of a thoroughly disappointed and thoroughly unreasonable man. Whatever poor Mrs. Van Brandt had done, she had done wrong. It was wrong of her, in the first place, to have married at all. It was wrong of her to contemplate receiving Mr. Van Brandt again, even if his lawful wife had died in the interval. It was wrong of her to return my letter of introduction, after I had given myself the trouble of altering it to suit her capricious fancy. It was wrong of her to take an absurdly prudish view of a stolen kiss and a tender declaration, and to fly from me as if I were as great a scoundrel as Mr. Van Brandt himself. And last, and more than all, it was wrong of her to sign her Christian name in initial only. Here I was, passionately in love with a woman, and not knowing by what fond name to identify her in my thoughts! "M. Van Brandt!" I might call her Maria, Margaret, Martha, Mabel, Magdalen, Mary—no, not Mary. The old boyish love was dead and gone, but I owed some respect to the memory of it. If the "Mary" of my early days were still living, and if I had met her, would she have treated me as this woman had treated me? Never! It was an injury to "Mary" to think even of that heartless creature by her name. Why think of her at all? Why degrade myself by trying to puzzle out a means of tracing her in her letter? It was sheer folly to attempt to trace a woman who had gone I knew not whither, and who herself informed me that she meant to pass under an assumed name. Had I lost all pride, all self-respect? In the flower of my age, with a handsome fortune, with the world before me, full of interesting female faces and charming female figures, what course did it become me to take? To go back to my country-house, and mope over the loss of a woman who had deliberately deserted me? or to send for a courier and a traveling carriage, and forget her gayly among foreign people and foreign scenes? In the state of my temper at that moment, the idea of a pleasure tour in Europe fired my imagination. I first astonished the people at the hotel by ordering all further inquiries after the missing Mrs. Van Brandt to be stopped; and then I opened my writing desk and wrote to tell my mother frankly and fully of my new plans.

The answer arrived by return of post.

To my surprise and delight, my good mother was not satisfied with only formally approving of my new resolution. With an energy which I had not ventured to expect from her, she had made all her arrangements for leaving home, and had started for Edinburgh to join me as my traveling companion. "You shall not go away alone, George," she wrote, "while I have strength and spirits to keep you company."

In three days from the time when I read those words our preparations were completed, and we were on our way to the Continent.

CHAPTER XIII. NOT CURED YET.

WE visited France, Germany, and Italy; and we were absent from England nearly two years.

Had time and change justified my confidence in them? Was the image of Mrs. Van Brandt an image long since dismissed from my mind?

No! Do what I might, I was still (in the prophetic language of Dame Dermody) taking the way to reunion with my kindred spirit in the time to come. For the first two or three months of our travels I was haunted by dreams of the woman who had so resolutely left me. Seeing her in my sleep, always graceful, always charming, always modestly tender toward me, I waited in the ardent hope of again beholding the apparition of her in my waking hours—of again being summoned to meet her at a given place and time. My anticipations were not fulfilled; no apparition showed itself. The dreams themselves grew less frequent and less vivid and then ceased altogether. Was this a sign that the days of her adversity were at an end? Having no further need of help, had she no further remembrance of the man who had tried to help her? Were we never to meet again?

I said to myself: "I am unworthy of the name of man if I don't forget her now!" She still kept her place in my memory, say what I might.

I saw all the wonders of Nature and Art which foreign countries could show me. I lived in the dazzling light of the best society that Paris, Rome, Vienna could assemble. I passed hours on hours in the company of the most accomplished and most beautiful women whom Europe could produce—and still that solitary figure at Saint Anthony's Well, those grand gray eyes that had rested on me so sadly at parting, held their place in my memory, stamped their image on my heart.

Whether I resisted my infatuation, or whether I submitted to it, I still longed for her. I did all I could to conceal the state of my mind from my mother. But her loving eyes discovered the secret: she saw that I suffered, and suffered with me. More than once she said: "George, the good end is not to be gained by traveling; let us go home." More than once I answered, with the bitter and obstinate resolution of despair: "No. Let us try more new people and more new scenes." It was only when I found her health and strength beginning to fail under the stress of continual traveling that I consented to abandon the hopeless search after oblivion, and to turn homeward at last.

I prevailed on my mother to wait and rest at my house in London before she returned to her favorite abode at the country-seat in Perthshire. It is needless to say that I remained in town with her. My mother now represented the one interest that held me nobly and endearingly to life. Politics, literature, agriculture—the customary pursuits of a man in my position—had none of them the slightest attraction for me.

We had arrived in London at what is called "the height of the season." Among the operatic attractions of that year—I am writing of the days when the ballet was still a popular form of public entertainment—there was a certain dancer whose grace and beauty were the objects of universal admiration. I was asked if I had seen her, wherever I went, until my social position, as the one man who was indifferent to the reigning goddess of the stage, became quite unendurable. On the next occasion when I was invited to take a seat in a friend's box, I accepted the proposal; and (far from willingly) I went the way of the world—in other words, I went to the opera.

The first part of the performance had concluded when we got to the theater, and the ballet had not yet begun. My friends amused themselves with looking for familiar faces in the boxes and stalls. I took a chair in a corner and waited, with my mind far away from the theater, from the dancing that was to come. The lady who sat nearest to me (like ladies in general) disliked the neighborhood of a silent man. She determined to make me talk to her.

"Do tell me, Mr. Germaine," she said. "Did you ever see a theater anywhere so full as this theater is to-night?"

She handed me her opera-glass as she spoke. I moved to the front of the box to look at the audience.

It was certainty a wonderful sight. Every available atom of space (as

414

I gradually raised the glass from the floor to the ceiling of the building) appeared to be occupied. Looking upward and upward, my range of view gradually reached the gallery. Even at that distance, the excellent glass which had been put into my hands brought the faces of the audience close to me. I looked first at the persons who occupied the front row of seats in the gallery stalls.

Moving the opera-glass slowly along the semicircle formed by the seats, I suddenly stopped when I reached the middle.

My heart gave a great leap as if it would bound out of my body. There was no mistaking that face among the commonplace faces near it. I had discovered Mrs. Van Brandt!

She sat in front—but not alone. There was a man in the stall immediately behind her, who bent over her and spoke to her from time to time. She listened to him, so far as I could see, with something of a sad and weary look. Who was the man? I might, or might not, find that out. Under any circumstances, I determined to speak to Mrs. Van Brandt.

The curtain rose for the ballet. I made the best excuse I could to my friends, and instantly left the box.

It was useless to attempt to purchase my admission to the gallery. My money was refused. There was not even standing room left in that part of the theater.

But one alternative remained. I returned to the street, to wait for Mrs. Van Brandt at the gallery door until the performance was over.

Who was the man in attendance on her—the man whom I had seen sitting behind her, and talking familiarly over her shoulder? While I paced backward and forward before the door, that one question held possession of my mind, until the oppression of it grew beyond endurance. I went back to my friends in the box, simply and solely to look at the man again.

What excuses I made to account for my strange conduct I cannot now remember. Armed once more with the lady's opera-glass (I borrowed it and kept it without scruple), I alone, of all that vast audience, turned my back on the stage, and riveted my attention on the gallery stalls.

There he sat, in his place behind her, to all appearance spell-bound by the fascinations of the graceful dancer. Mrs. Van Brandt, on the contrary, seemed to find but little attraction in the spectacle presented by the stage. She looked at the dancing (so far as I could see) in an absent, weary manner. When the applause broke out in a perfect frenzy of cries and clapping of hands, she sat perfectly unmoved by the enthusiasm which pervaded the theater. The man behind her (annoyed, as I supposed, by the marked indifference which she showed to the performance) tapped her impatiently on the shoulder, as if he thought that she was quite capable of falling asleep in her stall. The familiarity of the action—confirming the suspicion in my mind which had already identified him with Van Brandt—so enraged me that I said or did something which obliged one of the gentlemen in the box to interfere. "If you can't control yourself," he whispered, "you had better leave us." He spoke with the authority of an old friend. I had sense enough left to take his advice, and return to my post at the gallery door.

A little before midnight the performance ended. The audience began to pour out of the theater.

I drew back into a corner behind the door, facing the gallery stairs, and watched for her. After an interval which seemed to be endless, she and her companion appeared, slowly descending the stairs. She wore a long dark cloak; her head was protected by a quaintly shaped hood, which looked (on her) the most becoming head-dress that a woman could wear. As the two passed me, I heard the man speak to her in a tone of sulky annoyance.

"It's wasting money," he said, "to go to the expense of taking you to the opera."

"I am not well," she answered with her head down and her eyes on the ground. "I am out of spirits to-night."

"Will you ride home or walk?"

"I will walk, if you please."

I followed them unperceived, waiting to present myself to her until the crowd about them had dispersed. In a few minutes they turned into a quiet by-street. I quickened my pace until I was close at her side, and then I took off my hat and spoke to her.

She recognized me with a cry of astonishment. For an instant her face brightened radiantly with the loveliest expression of delight that I ever saw on any human countenance. The moment after, all was changed. The charming features saddened and hardened. She stood before me like a woman overwhelmed by shame—without uttering a word, without taking my offered hand.

Her companion broke the silence.

"Who is this gentleman?" he asked, speaking in a foreign accent, with an under-bred insolence of tone and manner.

She controlled herself the moment he addressed her. "This is Mr. Germaine," she answered: "a gentleman who was very kind to me in Scotland." She raised her eyes for a moment to mine, and took refuge, poor soul, in a conventionally polite inquiry after my health. "I hope you are quite well, Mr. Germaine," said the soft, sweet voice, trembling piteously.

I made the customary reply, and explained that I had seen her at the opera. "Are you staying in London?" I asked. "May I have the honor of calling on you?"

Her companion answered for her before she could speak.

"My wife thanks you, sir, for the compliment you pay her. She doesn't receive visitors. We both wish you good-night."

Saying those words, he took off his hat with a sardonic assumption of respect; and, holding her arm in his, forced her to walk on abruptly with him. Feeling certainly assured by this time that the man was no other than Van Brandt, I was on the point of answering him sharply, when Mrs. Van Brandt checked the rash words as they rose to my lips.

"For my sake!" she whispered, over her shoulder, with an imploring look

417

that instantly silenced me. After all, she was free (if she liked) to go back to the man who had so vilely deceived and deserted her. I bowed and left them, feeling with no common bitterness the humiliation of entering into rivalry with Mr. Van Brandt.

I crossed to the other side of the street. Before I had taken three steps away from her, the old infatuation fastened its hold on me again. I submitted, without a struggle against myself, to the degradation of turning spy and following them home. Keeping well behind, on the opposite side of the way, I tracked them to their own door, and entered in my pocket-book the name of the street and the number of the house.

The hardest critic who reads these lines cannot feel more contemptuously toward me than I felt toward myself. Could I still love a woman after she had deliberately preferred to me a scoundrel who had married her while he was the husband of another wife? Yes! Knowing what I now knew, I felt that I loved her just as dearly as ever. It was incredible, it was shocking; but it was true. For the first time in my life, I tried to take refuge from my sense of my own degradation in drink. I went to my club, and joined a convivial party at a supper table, and poured glass after glass of champagne down my throat, without feeling the slightest sense of exhilaration, without losing for an instant the consciousness of my own contemptible conduct. I went to my bed in despair; and through the wakeful night I weakly cursed the fatal evening at the river-side when I had met her for the first time. But revile her as I might, despise myself as I might, I loved her—I loved her still!

Among the letters laid on my table the next morning there were two which must find their place in this narrative.

The first letter was in a handwriting which I had seen once before, at the hotel in Edinburgh. The writer was Mrs. Van Brandt.

"For your own sake" (the letter ran) "make no attempt to see me, and take no notice of an invitation which I fear you will receive with this note. I am living a degraded life. I have sunk beneath your notice. You owe it to yourself, sir, to forget the miserable woman who now writes to you for the last time, and bids you gratefully a last farewell."

Those sad lines were signed in initials only. It is needless to say that they merely strengthened my resolution to see her at all hazards. I kissed the paper on which her hand had rested, and then I turned to the second letter. It contained the "invitation" to which my correspondent had alluded, and it was expressed in these terms:

"Mr. Van Brandt presents his compliments to Mr. Germaine, and begs to apologize for the somewhat abrupt manner in which he received Mr. Germaine's polite advances. Mr. Van Brandt suffers habitually from nervous irritability, and he felt particularly ill last night. He trusts Mr. Germaine will receive this candid explanation in the spirit in which it is offered; and he begs to add that Mrs. Van Brandt will be delighted to receive Mr. Germaine whenever he may find it convenient to favor her with a visit."

That Mr. Van Brandt had some sordid interest of his own to serve in writing this grotesquely impudent composition, and that the unhappy woman who bore his name was heartily ashamed of the proceeding on which he had ventured, were conclusions easily drawn after reading the two letters. The suspicion of the man and of his motives which I naturally felt produced no hesitation in my mind as to the course which I had determined to pursue. On the contrary, I rejoiced that my way to an interview with Mrs. Van Brandt was smoothed, no matter with what motives, by Mr. Van Brandt himself.

I waited at home until noon, and then I could wait no longer. Leaving a message of excuse for my mother (I had just sense of shame enough left to shrink from facing her), I hastened away to profit by my invitation on the very day when I received it.

CHAPTER XIV. MRS. VAN BRANDT AT HOME.

As I lifted my hand to ring the house bell, the door was opened from within, and no less a person than Mr. Van Brandt himself stood before me. He had his hat on. We had evidently met just as he was going out.

"My dear sir, how good this is of you! You present the best of all replies to my letter in presenting yourself. Mrs. Van Brandt is at home. Mrs. Van Brandt will be delighted. Pray walk in."

He threw open the door of a room on the ground-floor. His politeness was (if possible) even more offensive than his insolence. "Be seated, Mr. Germaine, I beg of you." He turned to the open door, and called up the stairs, in a loud and confident voice:

"Mary! come down directly."

"Mary"! I knew her Christian name at last, and knew it through Van Brandt. No words can tell how the name jarred on me, spoken by his lips. For the first time for years past my mind went back to Mary Dermody and Greenwater Broad. The next moment I heard the rustling of Mrs. Van Brandt's dress on the stairs. As the sound caught my ear, the old times and the old faces vanished again from my thoughts as completely as if they had never existed. What had she in common with the frail, shy little child, her namesake, of other days? What similarity was perceivable in the sooty London lodging-house to remind me of the bailiff's flower-scented cottage by the shores of the lake?

Van Brandt took off his hat, and bowed to me with sickening servility.

"I have a business appointment," he said, "which it is impossible to put off. Pray excuse me. Mrs. Van Brandt will do the honors. Good morning."

The house door opened and closed again. The rustling of the dress came slowly nearer and nearer. She stood before me.

"Mr. Germaine!" she exclaimed, starting back, as if the bare sight of me repelled her. "Is this honorable? Is this worthy of you? You allow me to be entrapped into receiving you, and you accept as your accomplice Mr. Van Brandt! Oh, sir, I have accustomed myself to look up to you as a high-minded man. How bitterly you have disappointed me!"

Her reproaches passed by me unheeded. They only heightened her color; they only added a new rapture to the luxury of looking at her.

"If you loved me as faithfully as I love you," I said, "you would understand why I am here. No sacrifice is too great if it brings me into your presence again after two years of absence."

She suddenly approached me, and fixed her eyes in eager scrutiny on my face.

"There must be some mistake," she said. "You cannot possibly have received my letter, or you have not read it?"

"I have received it, and I have read it."

"And Van Brandt's letter—you have read that too?"

"Yes."

She sat down by the table, and, leaning her arms on it, covered her face with her hands. My answers seemed not only to have distressed, but to have perplexed her. "Are men all alike?" I heard her say. "I thought I might trust in his sense of what was due to himself and of what was compassionate toward me."

I closed the door and seated myself by her side. She removed her hands from her face when she felt me near her. She looked at me with a cold and steady surprise.

"What are you going to do?" she asked.

"I am going to try if I can recover my place in your estimation," I said. "I am going to ask your pity for a man whose whole heart is yours, whose whole life is bound up in you."

She started to her feet, and looked round her incredulously, as if doubting whether she had rightly heard and rightly interpreted my last words. Before I could speak again, she suddenly faced me, and struck her open hand on the table with a passionate resolution which I now saw in her for the first time.

"Stop!" she cried. "There must be an end to this. And an end there shall be. Do you know who that man is who has just left the house? Answer me, Mr. Germaine! I am speaking in earnest."

There was no choice but to answer her. She was indeed in earnest—vehemently in earnest.

"His letter tells me," I said, "that he is Mr. Van Brandt."

She sat down again, and turned her face away from me.

"Do you know how he came to write to you?" she asked. "Do you know what made him invite you to this house?"

I thought of the suspicion that had crossed my mind when I read Van Brandt's letter. I made no reply.

"You force me to tell you the truth," she went on. "He asked me who you were, last night on our way home. I knew that you were rich, and that he wanted money. I told him I knew nothing of your position in the world. He was too cunning to believe me; he went out to the public-house and looked at a directory. He came back and said, 'Mr. Germaine has a house in Berkeley Square and a country-seat in the Highlands. He is not a man for a poor devil like me to offend; I mean to make a friend of him, and I expect you to make a friend of him too.' He sat down and wrote to you. I am living under that man's protection, Mr. Germaine. His wife is not dead, as you may suppose; she is living, and I know her to be living. I wrote to you that I was beneath your notice, and you have obliged me to tell you why. Am I sufficiently degraded to bring you to your senses?"

I drew closer to her. She tried to get up and leave me. I knew my power over her, and used it (as any man in my place would have used it) without scruple. I took her hand.

"I don't believe you have voluntarily degraded yourself," I said. "You have been forced into your present position: there are circumstances which excuse you, and which you are purposely keeping back from me. Nothing will convince me that you are a base woman. Should I love you as I love you, if you were really unworthy of me?"

She struggled to free her hand; I still held it. She tried to change the subject. "There is one thing you haven't told me yet," she said, with a faint, forced smile. "Have you seen the apparition of me again since I left you?"

"No. Have you ever seen me again, as you saw me in your dream at the inn in Edinburgh?"

"Never. Our visions of each other have left us. Can you tell why?"

If we had continued to speak on this subject, we must surely have recognized each other. But the subject dropped. Instead of answering her question, I drew her nearer to me—I returned to the forbidden subject of my love.

"Look at me," I pleaded, "and tell me the truth. Can you see me, can you hear me, and do you feel no answering sympathy in your own heart? Do you really care nothing for me? Have you never once thought of me in all the time that has passed since we last met?"

I spoke as I felt—fervently, passionately. She made a last effort to repel me, and yielded even as she made it. Her hand closed on mine, a low sigh fluttered on her lips. She answered with a sudden self-abandonment; she recklessly cast herself loose from the restraints which had held her up to this time.

"I think of you perpetually," she said. "I was thinking of you at the opera last night. My heart leaped in me when I heard your voice in the street."

"You love me!" I whispered.

"Love you!" she repeated. "My whole heart goes out to you in spite of myself. Degraded as I am, unworthy as I am—knowing as I do that nothing can ever come of it—I love you! I love you!"

She threw her arms round my neck, and held me to her with all her

423

strength. The moment after, she dropped on her knees. "Oh, don't tempt me!" she murmured. "Be merciful—and leave me."

I was beside myself. I spoke as recklessly to her as she had spoken to me.

"Prove that you love me," I said. "Let me rescue you from the degradation of living with that man. Leave him at once and forever. Leave him, and come with me to a future that is worthy of you—your future as my wife."

"Never!" she answered, crouching low at my feet.

"Why not? What obstacle is there?"

"I can't tell you—I daren't tell you."

"Will you write it?"

"No, I can't even write it—to you. Go, I implore you, before Van Brandt comes back. Go, if you love me and pity me."

She had roused my jealousy. I positively refused to leave her.

"I insist on knowing what binds you to that man," I said. "Let him come back! If you won't answer my question, I will put it to him."

She looked at me wildly, with a cry of terror. She saw my resolution in my face.

"Don't frighten me," she said. "Let me think."

She reflected for a moment. Her eyes brightened, as if some new way out of the difficulty had occurred to her.

"Have you a mother living?" she asked.

"Yes."

"Do you think she would come and see me?"

"I am sure she would if I asked her."

She considered with herself once more. "I will tell your mother what the obstacle is," she said, thoughtfully.

424

"When?"

"To-morrow, at this time."

She raised herself on her knees; the tears suddenly filled her eyes. She drew me to her gently. "Kiss me," she whispered. "You will never come here again. Kiss me for the last time."

My lips had barely touched hers, when she started to her feet and snatched up my hat from the chair on which I had placed it.

"Take your hat," she said. "He has come back."

My duller sense of hearing had discovered nothing. I rose and took my hat to quiet her. At the same moment the door of the room opened suddenly and softly. Mr. Van Brandt came in. I saw in his face that he had some vile motive of his own for trying to take us by surprise, and that the result of the experiment had disappointed him.

"You are not going yet?" he said, speaking to me with his eye on Mrs. Van Brandt. "I have hurried over my business in the hope of prevailing on you to stay and take lunch with us. Put down your hat, Mr. Germaine. No ceremony!"

"You are very good," I answered. "My time is limited to-day. I must beg you and Mrs. Van Brandt to excuse me."

I took leave of her as I spoke. She turned deadly pale when she shook hands with me at parting. Had she any open brutality to dread from Van Brandt as soon as my back was turned? The bare suspicion of it made my blood boil. But I thought of her. In her interests, the wise thing and the merciful thing to do was to conciliate the fellow before I left the house.

"I am sorry not to be able to accept your invitation," I said, as we walked together to the door. "Perhaps you will give me another chance?"

His eyes twinkled cunningly. "What do you say to a quiet little dinner here?" he asked. "A slice of mutton, you know, and a bottle of good wine. Only our three selves, and one old friend of mine to make up four. We will have a rubber of whist in the evening. Mary and you partners—eh? When shall it be? Shall we say the day after to-morrow?"

She had followed us to the door, keeping behind Van Brandt while he was speaking to me. When he mentioned the "old friend" and the "rubber of whist," her face expressed the strongest emotions of shame and disgust. The next moment (when she had heard him fix the date of the dinner for "the day after to-morrow") her features became composed again, as if a sudden sense of relief had come to her. What did the change mean? "To-morrow" was the day she had appointed for seeing my mother. Did she really believe, when I had heard what passed at the interview, that I should never enter the house again, and never attempt to see her more? And was this the secret of her composure when she heard the date of the dinner appointed for "the day after to-morrow"?

Asking myself these questions, I accepted my invitation, and left the house with a heavy heart. That farewell kiss, that sudden composure when the day of the dinner was fixed, weighed on my spirits. I would have given twelve years of my life to have annihilated the next twelve hours.

In this frame of mind I reached home, and presented myself in my mother's sitting-room.

"You have gone out earlier than usual to-day," she said. "Did the fine weather tempt you, my dear?" She paused, and looked at me more closely. "George!" she exclaimed, "what has happened to you? Where have you been?"

I told her the truth as honestly as I have told it here.

The color deepened in my mother's face. She looked at me, and spoke to me with a severity which was rare indeed in my experience of her.

"Must I remind you, for the first time in your life, of what is due to your mother?" she asked. "Is it possible that you expect me to visit a woman, who, by her own confession—"

"I expect you to visit a woman who has only to say the word and to be your daughter-in-law," I interposed. "Surely I am not asking what is unworthy of you, if I ask that?"

My mother looked at me in blank dismay.

"Do you mean, George, that you have offered her marriage?"

"Yes."

"And she has said No?"

"She has said No, because there is some obstacle in her way. I have tried vainly to make her explain herself. She has promised to confide everything to you."

The serious nature of the emergency had its effect. My mother yielded. She handed me the little ivory tablets on which she was accustomed to record her engagements. "Write down the name and address," she said resignedly.

"I will go with you," I answered, "and wait in the carriage at the door. I want to hear what has passed between you and Mrs. Van Brandt the instant you have left her."

"Is it as serious as that, George?"

"Yes, mother, it is as serious as that."

CHAPTER XV. THE OBSTACLE BEATS ME.

HOW long was I left alone in the carriage at the door of Mrs. Van Brandt's lodgings? Judging by my sensations, I waited half a life-time. Judging by my watch, I waited half an hour.

When my mother returned to me, the hope which I had entertained of a happy result from her interview with Mrs. Van Brandt was a hope abandoned before she had opened her lips. I saw, in her face, that an obstacle which was beyond my power of removal did indeed stand between me and the dearest wish of my life.

"Tell me the worst," I said, as we drove away from the house, "and tell it at once."

"I must tell it to you, George," my mother answered, sadly, "as she told it to me. She begged me herself to do that. 'We must disappoint him,' she said, 'but pray let it be done as gently as possible.' Beginning in those words, she confided to me the painful story which you know already—the story of her marriage. From that she passed to her meeting with you at Edinburgh, and to the circumstances which have led her to live as she is living now. This latter part of her narrative she especially requested me to repeat to you. Do you feel composed enough to hear it now? Or would you rather wait?"

"Let me hear it now, mother; and tell it, as nearly as you can, in her own words."

"I will repeat what she said to me, my dear, as faithfully as I can. After speaking of her father's death, she told me that she had only two relatives living. 'I have a married aunt in Glasgow, and a married aunt in London,' she said. 'When I left Edinburgh, I went to my aunt in London. She and my father had not been on good terms together; she considered that my father had neglected her. But his death had softened her toward him and toward me. She received me kindly, and she got me a situation in a shop. I kept my situation for three months, and then I was obliged to leave it.'"

My mother paused. I thought directly of the strange postscript which Mrs. Van Brandt had made me add to the letter that I wrote for her at the Edinburgh inn. In that case also she had only contemplated remaining in her employment for three months' time.

"Why was she obliged to leave her situation?" I asked.

"I put that question to her myself," replied my mother. "She made no direct reply—she changed color, and looked confused. 'I will tell you afterward, madam,' she said. 'Please let me go on now. My aunt was angry with me for leaving my employment—and she was more angry still, when I told her the reason. She said I had failed in duty toward her in not speaking frankly at first. We parted coolly. I had saved a little money from my wages; and I did well enough while my savings lasted. When they came to an end, I tried to get employment again, and I failed. My aunt said, and said truly, that her husband's income was barely enough to support his family: she could do nothing for me, and I could do nothing for myself. I wrote to my aunt at Glasgow, and received no answer. Starvation stared me in the face, when I saw in a newspaper an advertisement addressed to me by Mr. Van Brandt. He implored me to write to him; he declared that his life without me was too desolate to be endured; he solemnly promised that there should be no interruption to my tranquillity if I would return to him. If I had only had myself to think of, I would have begged my bread in the streets rather than return to him—'"

I interrupted the narrative at that point.

"What other person could she have had to think of?" I said.

"Is it possible, George," my mother rejoined, "that you have no suspicion of what she was alluding to when she said those words?"

The question passed by me unheeded: my thoughts were dwelling bitterly on Van Brandt and his advertisement. "She answered the advertisement, of course?" I said.

"And she saw Mr. Van Brandt," my mother went on. "She gave me no detailed account of the interview between them. 'He reminded me,' she said, 'of what I knew to be true—that the woman who had entrapped him into marrying her was an incurable drunkard, and that his ever living with her again was out of the question. Still she was alive, and she had a right to the name at least of his wife. I won't attempt to excuse my returning to him, knowing the circumstances as I did. I will only say that I could see no other choice before me, in my position at the time. It is needless to trouble you with what I have suffered since, or to speak of what I may suffer still. I am a lost woman. Be under no alarm, madam, about your son. I shall remember proudly to the end of my life that he once offered me the honor and the happiness of becoming his wife; but I know what is due to him and to you. I have seen him for the last time. The one thing that remains to be done is to satisfy him that our marriage is impossible. You are a mother; you will understand why I reveal the obstacle which stands between us—not to him, but to you.' She rose saying those words, and opened the folding-doors which led from the parlor into a back room. After an absence of a few moments only, she returned."

At that crowning point in the narrative, my mother stopped. Was she afraid to go on? or did she think it needless to say more?

"Well?" I said.

"Must I really tell it to you in words, George? Can't you guess how it ended, even yet?"

There were two difficulties in the way of my understanding her. I had a man's bluntness of perception, and I was half maddened by suspense. Incredible as it may appear, I was too dull to guess the truth even now.

"When she returned to me," my mother resumed, "she was not alone. She had with her a lovely little girl, just old enough to walk with the help of her mother's hand. She tenderly kissed the child, and then she put it on my lap. 'There is my only comfort,' she said, simply; 'and there is the obstacle to my ever becoming Mr. Germaine's wife.'"

Van Brandt's child! Van Brandt's child!

The postscript which she had made me add to my letter; the

incomprehensible withdrawal from the employment in which she was prospering; the disheartening difficulties which had brought her to the brink of starvation; the degrading return to the man who had cruelly deceived her—all was explained, all was excused now! With an infant at the breast, how could she obtain a new employment? With famine staring her in the face, what else could the friendless woman do but return to the father of her child? What claim had I on her, by comparison with him? What did it matter, now that the poor creature secretly returned the love that I felt for her? There was the child, an obstacle between us—there was his hold on her, now that he had got her back! What was my hold worth? All social proprieties and all social laws answered the question: Nothing!

My head sunk on my breast; I received the blow in silence.

My good mother took my hand. "You understand it now, George?" she said, sorrowfully.

"Yes, mother; I understand it."

"There was one thing she wished me to say to you, my dear, which I have not mentioned yet. She entreats you not to suppose that she had the faintest idea of her situation when she attempted to destroy herself. Her first suspicion that it was possible she might become a mother was conveyed to her at Edinburgh, in a conversation with her aunt. It is impossible, George, not to feel compassionately toward this poor woman. Regrettable as her position is, I cannot see that she is to blame for it. She was the innocent victim of a vile fraud when that man married her; she has suffered undeservedly since; and she has behaved nobly to you and to me. I only do her justice in saying that she is a woman in a thousand—a woman worthy, under happier circumstances, to be my daughter and your wife. I feel for you, and feel with you, my dear—I do, with my whole heart."

So this scene in my life was, to all appearance, a scene closed forever. As it had been with my love, in the days of my boyhood, so it was again now with the love of my riper age!

Later in the day, when I had in some degree recovered my self-possession,

I wrote to Mr. Van Brandt—as she had foreseen I should write!—to apologize for breaking my engagement to dine with him.

Could I trust to a letter also, to say the farewell words for me to the woman whom I had loved and lost? No! It was better for her, and better for me, that I should not write. And yet the idea of leaving her in silence was more than my fortitude could endure. Her last words at parting (as they were repeated to me by my mother) had expressed the hope that I should not think hardly of her in the future. How could I assure her that I should think of her tenderly to the end of my life? My mother's delicate tact and true sympathy showed me the way. "Send a little present, George," she said, "to the child. You bear no malice to the poor little child?" God knows I was not hard on the child! I went out myself and bought her a toy. I brought it home, and before I sent it away, I pinned a slip of paper to it, bearing this inscription: "To your little daughter, from George Germaine." There is nothing very pathetic, I suppose, in those words. And yet I burst out crying when I had written them.

The next morning my mother and I set forth for my country-house in Perthshire. London was now unendurable to me. Traveling abroad I had tried already. Nothing was left but to go back to the Highlands, and to try what I could make of my life, with my mother still left to live for.

CHAPTER XVI. MY MOTHER'S DIARY.

THERE is something repellent to me, even at this distance of time, in looking back at the dreary days, of seclusion which followed each other monotonously in my Highland home. The actions of my life, however trifling they may have been, I can find some interest in recalling: they associate me with my fellow-creatures; they connect me, in some degree, with the vigorous movement of the world. But I have no sympathy with the purely selfish pleasure which some men appear to derive from dwelling on the minute anatomy of their own feelings, under the pressure of adverse fortune. Let the domestic record of our stagnant life in Perthshire (so far as I am concerned in it) be presented in my mother's words, not in mine. A few lines of extract from the daily journal which it was her habit to keep will tell all that need be told before this narrative advances to later dates and to newer scenes.

"20th August.—We have been two months at our home in Scotland, and I see no change in George for the better. He is as far as ever, I fear, from being reconciled to his separation from that unhappy woman. Nothing will induce him to confess it himself. He declares that his quiet life here with me is all that he desires. But I know better! I have been into his bedroom late at night. I have heard him talking of her in his sleep, and I have seen the tears on his eyelids. My poor boy! What thousands of charming women there are who would ask nothing better than to be his wife! And the one woman whom he can never marry is the only woman whom he loves!

"25th.—A long conversation about George with Mr. MacGlue. I have never liked this Scotch doctor since he encouraged my son to keep the fatal appointment at Saint Anthony's Well. But he seems to be a clever man in his profession—and I think, in his way, he means kindly toward George. His advice was given as coarsely as usual, and very positively at the same time. 'Nothing will cure your son, madam, of his amatory passion for that half-drowned lady of his but change—and another lady. Send him away by himself this time; and let him feel the want of some kind creature to look after him. And when he meets with that kind creature (they are as plenty as fish in the sea), never trouble your head about it if there's a flaw in her character. I have got a cracked tea-cup which has served me for twenty years. Marry him, ma'am, to the new one with the utmost speed and impetuosity which the law will permit.' I hate Mr. MacGlue's opinions—so coarse and so hard-hearted!—but I sadly fear that I must part with my son for a little while, for his own sake.

"26th.—Where is George to go? I have been thinking of it all through the night, and I cannot arrive at a conclusion. It is so difficult to reconcile myself to letting him go away alone.

"29th.—I have always believed in special providences; and I am now confirmed in my belief. This morning has brought with it a note from our good friend and neighbor at Belhelvie. Sir James is one of the commissioners for the Northern Lights. He is going in a Government vessel to inspect the lighthouses on the North of Scotland, and on the Orkney and Shetland Islands—and, having noticed how worn and ill my poor boy looks, he most kindly invites George to be his guest on the voyage. They will not be absent for more than two months; and the sea (as Sir James reminds me) did wonders for George's health when he returned from India. I could wish for no better opportunity than this of trying what change of air and scene will do for him. However painfully I may feel the separation myself, I shall put a cheerful face on it; and I shall urge George to accept the invitation.

"30th.—I have said all I could; but he still refuses to leave me. I am a miserable, selfish creature. I felt so glad when he said No.

"31st.—Another wakeful night. George must positively send his answer to Sir James to-day. I am determined to do my duty toward my son—he looks so dreadfully pale and ill this morning! Besides, if something is not done to rouse him, how do I know that he may not end in going back to Mrs. Van Brandt after all? From every point of view, I feel bound to insist on his accepting Sir James's invitation. I have only to be firm, and the thing is done. He has never yet disobeyed me, poor fellow. He will not disobey me now.

"2d September.—He has gone! Entirely to please me—entirely against his own wishes. Oh, how is it that such a good son cannot get a good wife! He would make any woman happy. I wonder whether I have done right in sending him away? The wind is moaning in the fir plantation at the back of the house. Is there a storm at sea? I forgot to ask Sir James how big the vessel was. The 'Guide to Scotland' says the coast is rugged; and there is a wild sea between the north shore and the Orkney Islands. I almost regret having insisted so strongly—how foolish I am! We are all in the hands of God. May God bless and prosper my good son!

"10th.—Very uneasy. No letter from George. Ah, how full of trouble this life is! and how strange that we should cling to it as we do!

"15th.—A letter from George! They have done with the north coast and they have crossed the wild sea to the Orkneys. Wonderful weather has favored them so far; and George is in better health and spirits. Ah! how much happiness there is in life if we only have the patience to wait for it.

"2d October.—Another letter. They are safe in the harbor of Lerwick, the chief port in the Shetland Islands. The weather has not latterly been at all favorable. But the amendment in George's health remains. He writes most gratefully of Sir James's unremitting kindness to him. I am so happy, I declare I could kiss Sir James—though he is a great man, and a Commissioner for Northern Lights! In three weeks more (wind and weather permitting) they hope to get back. Never mind my lonely life here, if I can only see George happy and well again! He tells me they have passed a great deal of their time on shore; but not a word does he say about meeting any ladies. Perhaps they are scarce in those wild regions? I have heard of Shetland shawls and Shetland ponies. Are there any Shetland ladies, I wonder?"

CHAPTER XVII. SHETLAND HOSPITALITY.

"GUIDE! Where are we?"

"I can't say for certain."

"Have you lost your way?"

The guide looks slowly all round him, and then looks at me. That is his answer to my question. And that is enough.

The lost persons are three in number. My traveling companion, myself, and the guide. We are seated on three Shetland ponies—so small in stature, that we two strangers were at first literally ashamed to get on their backs. We are surrounded by dripping white mist so dense that we become invisible to one another at a distance of half a dozen yards. We know that we are somewhere on the mainland of the Shetland Isles. We see under the feet of our ponies a mixture of moorland and bog—here, the strip of firm ground that we are standing on, and there, a few feet off, the strip of watery peat-bog, which is deep enough to suffocate us if we step into it. Thus far, and no further, our knowledge extends. This question of the moment is, What are we to do next?

The guide lights his pipe, and reminds me that he warned us against the weather before we started for our ride. My traveling companion looks at me resignedly, with an expression of mild reproach. I deserve it. My rashness is to blame for the disastrous position in which we now find ourselves.

In writing to my mother, I have been careful to report favorably of my health and spirits. But I have not confessed that I still remember the day when I parted with the one hope and renounced the one love which made life precious to me. My torpid condition of mind, at home, has simply given place to a perpetual restlessness, produced by the excitement of my new life. I must now always be doing something—no matter what, so long as it diverts me from my own thoughts. Inaction is unendurable; solitude has become horrible to me. While the other members of the party which has accompanied

Sir James on his voyage of inspection among the lighthouses are content to wait in the harbor of Lerwick for a favorable change in the weather, I am obstinately bent on leaving the comfortable shelter of the vessel to explore some inland ruin of prehistoric times, of which I never heard, and for which I care nothing. The movement is all I want; the ride will fill the hateful void of time. I go, in defiance of sound advice offered to me on all sides. The youngest member of our party catches the infection of my recklessness (in virtue of his youth) and goes with me. And what has come of it? We are blinded by mist; we are lost on a moor; and the treacherous peat-bogs are round us in every direction!

What is to be done?

"Just leave it to the pownies," the guide says.

"Do you mean leave the ponies to find the way?"

"That's it," says the guide. "Drop the bridle, and leave it to the pownies. See for yourselves. I'm away on my powny."

He drops his bridle on the pommel of his saddle, whistles to his pony, and disappears in the mist; riding with his hands in his pockets, and his pipe in his mouth, as composedly as if he were sitting by his own fireside at home.

We have no choice but to follow his example, or to be left alone on the moor. The intelligent little animals, relieved from our stupid supervision, trot off with their noses to the ground, like hounds on the scent. Where the intersecting tract of bog is wide, they skirt round it. Where it is narrow enough to be leaped over, they cross it by a jump. Trot! trot!—away the hardy little creatures go; never stopping, never hesitating. Our "superior intelligence," perfectly useless in the emergency, wonders how it will end. Our guide, in front of us, answers that it will end in the ponies finding their way certainly to the nearest village or the nearest house. "Let the bridles be," is his one warning to us. "Come what may of it, let the bridles be!"

It is easy for the guide to let his bridle be—he is accustomed to place himself in that helpless position under stress of circumstances, and he knows exactly what his pony can do.

To us, however, the situation is a new one; and it looks dangerous in the extreme. More than once I check myself, not without an effort, in the act of resuming the command of my pony on passing the more dangerous points in the journey. The time goes on; and no sign of an inhabited dwelling looms through the mist. I begin to get fidgety and irritable; I find myself secretly doubting the trustworthiness of the guide. While I am in this unsettled frame of mind, my pony approaches a dim, black, winding line, where the bog must be crossed for the hundredth time at least. The breadth of it (deceptively enlarged in appearance by the mist) looks to my eyes beyond the reach of a leap by any pony that ever was foaled. I lose my presence of mind. At the critical moment before the jump is taken, I am foolish enough to seize the bridle, and suddenly check the pony. He starts, throws up his head, and falls instantly as if he had been shot. My right hand, as we drop on the ground together, gets twisted under me, and I feel that I have sprained my wrist.

If I escape with no worse injury than this, I may consider myself well off. But no such good fortune is reserved for me. In his struggles to rise, before I have completely extricated myself from him, the pony kicks me; and, as my ill-luck will have it, his hoof strikes just where the poisoned spear struck me in the past days of my service in India. The old wound opens again—and there I lie bleeding on the barren Shetland moor!

This time my strength has not been exhausted in attempting to breast the current of a swift-flowing river with a drowning woman to support. I preserve my senses; and I am able to give the necessary directions for bandaging the wound with the best materials which we have at our disposal. To mount my pony again is simply out of the question. I must remain where I am, with my traveling companion to look after me; and the guide must trust his pony to discover the nearest place of shelter to which I can be removed.

Before he abandons us on the moor, the man (at my suggestion) takes our "bearings," as correctly as he can by the help of my pocket-compass. This done, he disappears in the mist, with the bridle hanging loose, and the pony's nose to the ground, as before. I am left, under my young friend's care, with a cloak to lie on, and a saddle for a pillow. Our ponies composedly help themselves to such grass as they can find on the moor; keeping always near us as companionably as if they were a couple of dogs. In this position we wait events, while the dripping mist hangs thicker than ever all round us.

The slow minutes follow each other wearily in the majestic silence of the moor. We neither of us acknowledge it in words, but we both feel that hours may pass before the guide discovers us again. The penetrating damp slowly strengthens its clammy hold on me. My companion's pocket-flask of sherry has about a teaspoonful of wine left in the bottom of it. We look at one another—having nothing else to look at in the present state of the weather— and we try to make the best of it. So the slow minutes follow each other, until our watches tell us that forty minutes have elapsed since the guide and his pony vanished from our view.

My friend suggests that we may as well try what our voices can do toward proclaiming our situation to any living creature who may, by the barest possibility, be within hearing of us. I leave him to try the experiment, having no strength to spare for vocal efforts of any sort. My companion shouts at the highest pitch of his voice. Silence follows his first attempt. He tries again; and, this time, an answering hail reaches us faintly through the white fog. A fellow-creature of some sort, guide or stranger, is near us—help is coming at last!

An interval passes; and voices reach our ears—the voices of two men. Then the shadowy appearance of the two becomes visible in the mist. Then the guide advances near enough to be identified. He is followed by a sturdy fellow in a composite dress, which presents him under the double aspect of a groom and a gardener. The guide speaks a few words of rough sympathy. The composite man stands by impenetrably silent; the sight of a disabled stranger fails entirely either to surprise or to interest the gardener-groom.

After a little private consultation, the two men decide to cross their hands, and thus make a seat for me between them. My arms rest on their shoulders; and so they carry me off. My friend trudges behind them, with the saddle and the cloak. The ponies caper and kick, in unrestrained enjoyment of their freedom; and sometimes follow, sometimes precede us, as the humor of the moment inclines them. I am, fortunately for my bearers, a light weight.

After twice resting, they stop altogether, and set me down on the driest place they can find. I look eagerly through the mist for some signs of a dwelling-house—and I see nothing but a little shelving beach, and a sheet of dark water beyond. Where are we?

The gardener-groom vanishes, and appears again on the water, looming large in a boat. I am laid down in the bottom of the boat, with my saddle-pillow; and we shove off, leaving the ponies to the desolate freedom of the moor. They will pick up plenty to eat (the guide says); and when night comes on they will find their own way to shelter in a village hard by. The last I see of the hardy little creatures they are taking a drink of water, side by side, and biting each other sportively in higher spirits than ever!

Slowly we float over the dark water—not a river, as I had at first supposed, but a lake—until we reach the shores of a little island; a flat, lonely, barren patch of ground. I am carried along a rough pathway made of great flat stones, until we reach the firmer earth, and discover a human dwelling-place at last. It is a long, low house of one story high; forming (as well as I can see) three sides of a square. The door stands hospitably open. The hall within is bare and cold and dreary. The men open an inner door, and we enter a long corridor, comfortably warmed by a peat fire. On one wall I notice the closed oaken doors of rooms; on the other, rows on rows of well-filled book-shelves meet my eye. Advancing to the end of the first passage, we turn at right angles into a second. Here a door is opened at last: I find myself in a spacious room, completely and tastefully furnished, having two beds in it, and a large fire burning in the grate. The change to this warm and cheerful place of shelter from the chilly and misty solitude of the moor is so luxuriously delightful that I am quite content, for the first few minutes, to stretch myself on a bed, in lazy enjoyment of my new position; without caring to inquire into whose house we have intruded; without even wondering at the strange absence of master, mistress, or member of the family to welcome our arrival under their hospitable roof.

After a while, the first sense of relief passes away. My dormant curiosity revives. I begin to look about me.

The gardener-groom has disappeared. I discover my traveling companion

440

at the further end of the room, evidently occupied in questioning the guide. A word from me brings him to my bedside. What discoveries has he made? whose is the house in which we are sheltered; and how is it that no member of the family appears to welcome us?

My friend relates his discoveries. The guide listens as attentively to the second-hand narrative as if it were quite new to him.

The house that shelters us belongs to a gentleman of ancient Northern lineage, whose name is Dunross. He has lived in unbroken retirement on the barren island for twenty years past, with no other companion than a daughter, who is his only child. He is generally believed to be one of the most learned men living. The inhabitants of Shetland know him far and wide, under a name in their dialect which means, being interpreted, "The Master of Books." The one occasion on which he and his daughter have been known to leave their island retreat was at a past time when a terrible epidemic disease broke out among the villages in the neighborhood. Father and daughter labored day and night among their poor and afflicted neighbors, with a courage which no danger could shake, with a tender care which no fatigue could exhaust. The father had escaped infection, and the violence of the epidemic was beginning to wear itself out, when the daughter caught the disease. Her life had been preserved, but she never completely recovered her health. She is now an incurable sufferer from some mysterious nervous disorder which nobody understands, and which has kept her a prisoner on the island, self-withdrawn from all human observation, for years past. Among the poor inhabitants of the district, the father and daughter are worshiped as semi-divine beings. Their names come after the Sacred Name in the prayers which the parents teach to their children.

Such is the household (so far as the guide's story goes) on whose privacy we have intruded ourselves! The narrative has a certain interest of its own, no doubt, but it has one defect—it fails entirely to explain the continued absence of Mr. Dunross. Is it possible that he is not aware of our presence in the house? We apply the guide, and make a few further inquiries of him.

"Are we here," I ask, "by permission of Mr. Dunross?"

The guide stares. If I had spoken to him in Greek or Hebrew, I could hardly have puzzled him more effectually. My friend tries him with a simpler form of words.

"Did you ask leave to bring us here when you found your way to the house?"

The guide stares harder than ever, with every appearance of feeling perfectly scandalized by the question.

"Do you think," he asks, sternly, "'that I am fool enough to disturb the Master over his books for such a little matter as bringing you and your friend into this house?"

"Do you mean that you have brought us here without first asking leave?" I exclaim in amazement.

The guide's face brightens; he has beaten the true state of the case into our stupid heads at last! "That's just what I mean!" he says, with an air of infinite relief.

The door opens before we have recovered the shock inflicted on us by this extraordinary discovery. A little, lean, old gentleman, shrouded in a long black dressing-gown, quietly enters the room. The guide steps forward, and respectfully closes the door for him. We are evidently in the presence of The Master of Books!

CHAPTER XVIII. THE DARKENED ROOM.

THE little gentleman advances to my bedside. His silky white hair flows over his shoulders; he looks at us with faded blue eyes; he bows with a sad and subdued courtesy, and says, in the simplest manner, "I bid you welcome, gentlemen, to my house."

We are not content with merely thanking him; we naturally attempt to apologize for our intrusion. Our host defeats the attempt at the outset by making an apology on his own behalf.

"I happened to send for my servant a minute since," he proceeds, "and I only then heard that you were here. It is a custom of the house that nobody interrupts me over my books. Be pleased, sir, to accept my excuses," he adds, addressing himself to me, "for not having sooner placed myself and my household at your disposal. You have met, as I am sorry to hear, with an accident. Will you permit me to send for medical help? I ask the question a little abruptly, fearing that time may be of importance, and knowing that our nearest doctor lives at some distance from this house."

He speaks with a certain quaintly precise choice of words—more like a man dictating a letter than holding a conversation. The subdued sadness of his manner is reflected in the subdued sadness of his face. He and sorrow have apparently been old acquaintances, and have become used to each other for years past. The shadow of some past grief rests quietly and impenetrably over the whole man; I see it in his faded blue eyes, on his broad forehead, on his delicate lips, on his pale shriveled cheeks. My uneasy sense of committing an intrusion on him steadily increases, in spite of his courteous welcome. I explain to him that I am capable of treating my own case, having been myself in practice as a medical man; and this said, I revert to my interrupted excuses. I assure him that it is only within the last few moments that my traveling companion and I have become aware of the liberty which our guide has taken in introducing us, on his own sole responsibility, to the house. Mr. Dunross looks at me, as if he, like the guide, failed entirely to understand what my scruples and excuses mean. After a while the truth dawns on him. A faint smile flickers over his face; he lays his hand in a gentle, fatherly way on my shoulder.

"We are so used here to our Shetland hospitality," he says, "that we are slow to understand the hesitation which a stranger feels in taking advantage of it. Your guide is in no respect to blame, gentlemen. Every house in these islands which is large enough to contain a spare room has its Guests' Chamber, always kept ready for occupation. When you travel my way, you come here as a matter of course; you stay here as long as you like; and, when you go away, I only do my duty as a good Shetlander in accompanying you on the first stage of your journey to bid you godspeed. The customs of centuries past elsewhere are modern customs here. I beg of you to give my servant all the directions which are necessary to your comfort, just as freely as you could give them in your own house."

He turns aside to ring a hand-bell on the table as he speaks; and notices in the guide's face plain signs that the man has taken offense at my disparaging allusion to him.

"Strangers cannot be expected to understand our ways, Andrew," says The Master of Books. "But you and I understand one another—and that is enough."

The guide's rough face reddens with pleasure. If a crowned king on a throne had spoken condescendingly to him, he could hardly have looked more proud of the honor conferred than he looks now. He makes a clumsy attempt to take the Master's hand and kiss it. Mr. Dunross gently repels the attempt, and gives him a little pat on the head. The guide looks at me and my friend as if he had been honored with the highest distinction that an earthly being can receive. The Master's hand had touched him kindly!

In a moment more, the gardener-groom appears at the door to answer the bell.

"You will move the medicine-chest into this room, Peter," says Mr. Dunross. "And you will wait on this gentleman, who is confined to his bed by

444

an accident, exactly as you would wait on me if I were ill. If we both happen to ring for you together, you will answer his bell before you answer mine. The usual changes of linen are, of course, ready in the wardrobe there? Very good. Go now, and tell the cook to prepare a little dinner; and get a bottle of the old Madeira out of the cellar. You will least, in this room. These two gentlemen will be best pleased to dine together. Return here in five minutes' time, in case you are wanted; and show my guest, Peter, that I am right in believing you to be a good nurse as well as a good servant."

The silent and surly Peter brightens under the expression of the Master's confidence in him, as the guide brightened under the influence of the Master's caressing touch. The two men leave the room together.

We take advantage of the momentary silence that follows to introduce ourselves by name to our host, and to inform him of the circumstances under which we happen to be visiting Shetland. He listens in his subdued, courteous way; but he makes no inquiries about our relatives; he shows no interest in the arrival of the Government yacht and the Commissioner for Northern Lights. All sympathy with the doings of the outer world, all curiosity about persons of social position and notoriety, is evidently at an end in Mr. Dunross. For twenty years the little round of his duties and his occupations has been enough for him. Life has lost its priceless value to this man; and when Death comes to him he will receive the king of terrors as he might receive the last of his guests.

"Is there anything else I can do," he says, speaking more to himself than to us, "before I go back to my books?"

Something else occurs to him, even as he puts the question. He addresses my companion, with his faint, sad smile. "This will be a dull life, I am afraid, sir, for you. If you happen to be fond of angling, I can offer you some little amusement in that way. The lake is well stocked with fish; and I have a boy employed in the garden, who will be glad to attend on you in the boat."

My friend happens to be fond of fishing, and gladly accepts the invitation. The Master says his parting words to me before he goes back to his books.

"You may safely trust my man Peter to wait on you, Mr. Germaine, while you are so unfortunate as to be confined to this room. He has the advantage (in cases of illness) of being a very silent, undemonstrative person. At the same time he is careful and considerate, in his own reserved way. As to what I may term the lighter duties at your bedside such as reading to you, writing your letters for you while your right hand is still disabled, regulating the temperature in the room, and so on—though I cannot speak positively, I think it likely that these little services may be rendered to you by another person whom I have not mentioned yet. We shall see what happens in a few hours' time. In the meanwhile, sir, I ask permission to leave you to your rest."

With those words, he walks out of the room as quietly as he walked into it, and leaves his two guests to meditate gratefully on Shetland hospitality. We both wonder what those last mysterious words of our host mean; and we exchange more or less ingenious guesses on the subject of that nameless "other person" who may possibly attend on me—until the arrival of dinner turns our thoughts into a new course.

The dishes are few in number, but cooked to perfection and admirably served. I am too weary to eat much: a glass of the fine old Madeira revives me. We arrange our future plans while we are engaged over the meal. Our return to the yacht in Lerwick harbor is expected on the next day at the latest. As things are, I can only leave my companion to go back to the vessel, and relieve the minds of our friends of any needless alarm about me. On the day after, I engage to send on board a written report of the state of my health, by a messenger who can bring my portmanteau back with him.

These arrangements decided on, my friend goes away (at my own request) to try his skill as an angler in the lake. Assisted by the silent Peter and the well-stocked medicine-chest, I apply the necessary dressings to my wound, wrap myself in the comfortable morning-gown which is always kept ready in the Guests' Chamber, and lie down again on the bed to try the restorative virtues of sleep.

Before he leaves the room, silent Peter goes to the window, and asks in fewest possible words if he shall draw the curtains. In fewer words still—for I am feeling drowsy already—I answer No. I dislike shutting out the cheering light of day. To my morbid fancy, at that moment, it looks like resigning myself deliberately to the horrors of a long illness. The hand-bell is on my bedside table; and I can always ring for Peter if the light keeps me from sleeping. On this understanding, Peter mutely nods his head, and goes out.

For some minutes I lie in lazy contemplation of the companionable fire. Meanwhile the dressings on my wound and the embrocation on my sprained wrist steadily subdue the pains which I have felt so far. Little by little, the bright fire seems to be fading. Little by little, sleep steals on me, and all my troubles are forgotten.

I wake, after what seems to have been a long repose—I wake, feeling the bewilderment which we all experience on opening our eyes for the first time in a bed and a room that are new to us. Gradually collecting my thoughts, I find my perplexity considerably increased by a trifling but curious circumstance. The curtains which I had forbidden Peter to touch are drawn—closely drawn, so as to plunge the whole room in obscurity. And, more surprising still, a high screen with folding sides stands before the fire, and confines the light which it might otherwise give exclusively to the ceiling. I am literally enveloped in shadows. Has night come?

In lazy wonder, I turn my head on the pillow, and look on the other side of my bed.

Dark as it is, I discover instantly that I am not alone.

A shadowy figure stands by my bedside. The dim outline of the dress tells me that it is the figure of a woman. Straining my eyes, I fancy I can discern a wavy black object covering her head and shoulders which looks like a large veil. Her face is turned toward me, but no distinguishing feature in it is visible. She stands like a statue, with her hands crossed in front of her, faintly relieved against the dark substance of her dress. This I can see—and this is all.

There is a moment of silence. The shadowy being finds its voice, and speaks first.

"I hope you feel better, sir, after your rest?"

The voice is low, with a certain faint sweetness or tone which falls soothingly on my ear. The accent is unmistakably the accent of a refined and cultivated person. After making my acknowledgments to the unknown and half-seen lady, I venture to ask the inevitable question, "To whom have I the honor of speaking?"

The lady answers, "I am Miss Dunross; and I hope, if you have no objection to it, to help Peter in nursing you."

This, then, is the "other person" dimly alluded to by our host! I think directly of the heroic conduct of Miss Dunross among her poor and afflicted neighbors; and I do not forget the melancholy result of her devotion to others which has left her an incurable invalid. My anxiety to see this lady more plainly increases a hundred-fold. I beg her to add to my grateful sense of her kindness by telling me why the room is so dark "Surely," I say, "it cannot be night already?"

"You have not been asleep," she answers, "for more than two hours. The mist has disappeared, and the sun is shining."

I take up the bell, standing on the table at my side.

"May I ring for Peter, Miss Dunross?"

"To open the curtains, Mr. Germaine?"

"Yes—with your permission. I own I should like to see the sunlight."

"I will send Peter to you immediately."

The shadowy figure of my new nurse glides away. In another moment, unless I say something to stop her, the woman whom I am so eager to see will have left the room.

"Pray don't go!" I say. "I cannot think of troubling you to take a trifling message for me. The servant will come in, if I only ring the bell."

She pauses—more shadowy than ever—halfway between the bed and the door, and answers a little sadly:

"Peter will not let in the daylight while I am in the room. He closed the curtains by my order."

The reply puzzles me. Why should Peter keep the room dark while Miss Dunross is in it? Are her eyes weak? No; if her eyes were weak, they would be protected by a shade. Dark as it is, I can see that she does not wear a shade. Why has the room been darkened—if not for me? I cannot venture on asking the question—I can only make my excuses in due form.

"Invalids only think of themselves," I say. "I supposed that you had kindly darkened the room on my account."

She glides back to my bedside before she speaks again. When she does answer, it is in these startling words:

"You were mistaken, Mr. Germaine. Your room has been darkened—not on your account, but on mine."

CHAPTER XIX. THE CATS.

MISS DUNROSS had so completely perplexed me, that I was at a loss what to say next.

To ask her plainly why it was necessary to keep the room in darkness while she remained in it, might prove (for all I knew to the contrary) to be an act of positive rudeness. To venture on any general expression of sympathy with her, knowing absolutely nothing of the circumstances, might place us both in an embarrassing position at the outset of our acquaintance. The one thing I could do was to beg that the present arrangement of the room might not be disturbed, and to leave her to decide as to whether she should admit me to her confidence or exclude me from it, at her own sole discretion.

She perfectly understood what was going on in my mind. Taking a chair at the foot of the bed, she told me simply and unreservedly the sad secret of the darkened room.

"If you wish to see much of me, Mr. Germaine," she began, "you must accustom yourself to the world of shadows in which it is my lot to live. Some time since, a dreadful illness raged among the people in our part of this island; and I was so unfortunate as to catch the infection. When I recovered—no! 'Recovery' is not the right word to use—let me say, when I escaped death, I found myself afflicted by a nervous malady which has defied medical help from that time to this. I am suffering (as the doctors explain it to me) from a morbidly sensitive condition of the nerves near the surface to the action of light. If I were to draw the curtains, and look out of that window, I should feel the acutest pain all over my face. If I covered my face, and drew the curtains with my bare hands, I should feel the same pain in my hands. You can just see, perhaps, that I have a very large and very thick veil on my head. I let it fall over my face and neck and hands, when I have occasion to pass along the corridors or to enter my father's study—and I find it protection enough. Don't be too ready to deplore my sad condition, sir! I have got so used to living in the dark that I can see quite well enough for all the purposes of my poor existence. I can read and write in these shadows—I can see you, and be of use to you in many little ways, if you will let me. There is really nothing to be distressed about. My life will not be a long one—I know and feel that. But I hope to be spared long enough to be my father's companion through the closing years of his life. Beyond that, I have no prospect. In the meanwhile, I have my pleasures; and I mean to add to my scanty little stack the pleasure of attending on you. You are quite an event in my life. I look forward to reading to you and writing for you, as some girls look forward to a new dress, or a first ball. Do you think it very strange of me to tell you so openly just what I have in my mind? I can't help it! I say what I think to my father and to our poor neighbors hereabouts—and I can't alter my ways at a moment's notice. I own it when I like people; and I own it when I don't. I have been looking at you while you were asleep; and I have read your face as I might read a book. There are signs of sorrow on your forehead and your lips which it is strange to see in so young a face as yours. I am afraid I shall trouble you with many questions about yourself when we become better acquainted with each other. Let me begin with a question, in my capacity as nurse. Are your pillows comfortable? I can see they want shaking up. Shall I send for Peter to raise you? I am unhappily not strong enough to be able to help you in that way. No? You are able to raise yourself? Wait a little. There! Now lie back—and tell me if I know how to establish the right sort of sympathy between a tumbled pillow and a weary head."

She had so indescribably touched and interested me, stranger as I was, that the sudden cessation of her faint, sweet tones affected me almost with a sense of pain. In trying (clumsily enough) to help her with the pillows, I accidentally touched her hand. It felt so cold and so thin, that even the momentary contact with it startled me. I tried vainly to see her face, now that it was more within reach of my range of view. The merciless darkness kept it as complete a mystery as ever. Had my curiosity escaped her notice? Nothing escaped her notice. Her next words told me plainly that I had been discovered.

"You have been trying to see me," she said. "Has my hand warned you not to try again? I felt that it startled you when you touched it just now."

451

Such quickness of perception as this was not to be deceived; such fearless candor demanded as a right a similar frankness on my side. I owned the truth, and left it to her indulgence to forgive me.

She returned slowly to her chair at the foot of the bed.

"If we are to be friends," she said, "we must begin by understanding one another. Don't associate any romantic ideas of invisible beauty with me, Mr. Germaine. I had but one beauty to boast of before I fell ill—my complexion—and that has gone forever. There is nothing to see in me now but the poor reflection of my former self; the ruin of what was once a woman. I don't say this to distress you—I say it to reconcile you to the darkness as a perpetual obstacle, so far as your eyes are concerned, between you and me. Make the best instead of the worst of your strange position here. It offers you a new sensation to amuse you while you are ill. You have a nurse who is an impersonal creature—a shadow among shadows; a voice to speak to you, and a hand to help you, and nothing more. Enough of myself!" she exclaimed, rising and changing her tone. "What can I do to amuse you?" She considered a little. "I have some odd tastes," she resumed; "and I think I may entertain you if I make you acquainted with one of them. Are you like most other men, Mr. Germaine? Do you hate cats?"

The question startled me. However, I could honestly answer that, in this respect at least, I was not like other men.

"To my thinking," I added, "the cat is a cruelly misunderstood creature—especially in England. Women, no doubt, generally do justice to the affectionate nature of cats. But the men treat them as if they were the natural enemies of the human race. The men drive a cat out of their presence if it ventures upstairs, and set their dogs at it if it shows itself in the street—and then they turn round and accuse the poor creature (whose genial nature must attach itself to something) of being only fond of the kitchen!"

The expression of these unpopular sentiments appeared to raise me greatly in the estimation of Miss Dunross.

"We have one sympathy in common, at any rate," she said. "Now I can amuse you! Prepare for a surprise."

She drew her veil over her face as she spoke, and, partially opening the door, rang my handbell. Peter appeared, and received his instructions.

"Move the screen," said Miss Dunross. Peter obeyed; the ruddy firelight streamed over the floor. Miss Dunross proceeded with her directions. "Open the door of the cats' room, Peter; and bring me my harp. Don't suppose that you are going to listen to a great player, Mr. Germaine," she went on, when Peter had departed on his singular errand, "or that you are likely to see the sort of harp to which you are accustomed, as a man of the modern time. I can only play some old Scotch airs; and my harp is an ancient instrument (with new strings)—an heirloom in our family, some centuries old. When you see my harp, you will think of pictures of St. Cecilia—and you will be treating my performance kindly if you will remember, at the same time, that I am no saint!"

She drew her chair into the firelight, and sounded a whistle which she took from the pocket of her dress. In another moment the lithe and shadowy figures of the cats appeared noiselessly in the red light, answering their mistress's call. I could just count six of them, as the creatures seated themselves demurely in a circle round the chair. Peter followed with the harp, and closed the door after him as he went out. The streak of daylight being now excluded from the room, Miss Dunross threw back her veil, and took the harp on her knee; seating herself, I observed, with her face turned away from the fire.

"You will have light enough to see the cats by," she said, "without having too much light for me. Firelight does not give me the acute pain which I suffer when daylight falls on my face—I feel a certain inconvenience from it, and nothing more."

She touched the strings of her instrument—the ancient harp, as she had said, of the pictured St. Cecilia; or, rather, as I thought, the ancient harp of the Welsh bards. The sound was at first unpleasantly high in pitch, to my untutored ear. At the opening notes of the melody—a slow, wailing, dirgelike air—the cats rose, and circled round their mistress, marching to the tune. Now they followed each other singly; now, at a change in the melody, they walked two and two; and, now again, they separated into divisions of three each, and circled round the chair in opposite directions. The music quickened, and the cats quickened their pace with it. Faster and faster the notes rang out, and faster and faster in the ruddy firelight, the cats, like living shadows, whirled round the still black figure in the chair, with the ancient harp on its knee. Anything so weird, wild, and ghostlike I never imagined before even in a dream! The music changed, and the whirling cats began to leap. One perched itself at a bound on the pedestal of the harp. Four sprung up together, and assumed their places, two on each of her shoulders. The last and smallest of the cats took the last leap, and lighted on her head! There the six creatures kept their positions, motionless as statues! Nothing moved but the wan, white hands over the harp-strings; no sound but the sound of the music stirred in the room. Once more the melody changed. In an instant the six cats were on the floor again, seated round the chair as I had seen them on their first entrance; the harp was laid aside; and the faint, sweet voice said quietly, "I am soon tired—I must leave my cats to conclude their performances tomorrow."

She rose, and approached the bedside.

"I leave you to see the sunset through your window," she said. "From the coming of the darkness to the coming of breakfast-time, you must not count on my services—I am taking my rest. I have no choice but to remain in bed (sleeping when I can) for twelve hours or more. The long repose seems to keep my life in me. Have I and my cats surprised you very much? Am I a witch; and are they my familiar spirits? Remember how few amusements I have, and you will not wonder why I devote myself to teaching these pretty creatures their tricks, and attaching them to me like dogs! They were slow at first, and they taught me excellent lessons of patience. Now they understand what I want of them, and they learn wonderfully well. How you will amuse your friend, when he comes back from fishing, with the story of the young lady who lives in the dark, and keeps a company of performing cats! I shall expect you to amuse me to-morrow—I want you to tell me all about yourself, and how you came to visit these wild islands of ours. Perhaps, as the days go on, and we get better acquainted, you will take me a little more into your confidence, and tell me the true meaning of that story of sorrow which I read on your face while you were asleep? I have just enough of the woman left in me to be the victim of curiosity, when I meet with a person who interests me. Good-by till to-morrow! I wish you a tranquil night, and a pleasant waking.—Come, my familiar spirits! Come, my cat children! it's time we went back to our own side of the house."

She dropped the veil over her face—and, followed by her train of cats, glided out of the room.

Immediately on her departure, Peter appeared and drew back the curtains. The light of the setting sun streamed in at the window. At the same moment my traveling companion returned in high spirits, eager to tell me about his fishing in the lake. The contrast between what I saw and heard now, and what I had seen and heard only a few minutes since, was so extraordinary and so startling that I almost doubted whether the veiled figure with the harp, and the dance of cats, were not the fantastic creations of a dream. I actually asked my friend whether he had found me awake or asleep when he came into the room!

Evening merged into night. The Master of Books made his appearance, to receive the latest news of my health. He spoke and listened absently as if his mind were still pre-occupied by his studies—except when I referred gratefully to his daughter's kindness to me. At her name his faded blue eyes brightened; his drooping head became erect; his sad, subdued voice strengthened in tone.

"Do not hesitate to let her attend on you," he said. "Whatever interests or amuses her, lengthens her life. In her life is the breath of mine. She is more than my daughter; she is the guardian-angel of the house. Go where she may, she carries the air of heaven with her. When you say your prayers, sir, pray God to leave my daughter here a little longer."

He sighed heavily; his head dropped again on his breast—he left me.

The hour advanced; the evening meal was set by my bedside. Silent Peter, taking his leave for the night, developed into speech. "I sleep next door," he said. "Ring when you want me." My traveling companion, taking the second bed in the room, reposed in the happy sleep of youth. In the house there was dead silence. Out of the house, the low song of the night-wind, rising and falling over the lake and the moor, was the one sound to be heard. So the first day ended in the hospitable Shetland house.

CHAPTER XX. THE GREEN FLAG.

"I CONGRATULATE you, Mr. Germaine, on your power of painting in words. Your description gives me a vivid idea of Mrs. Van Brandt."

"Does the portrait please you, Miss Dunross?"

"May I speak as plainly as usual?"

"Certainly!"

"Well, then, plainly, I don't like your Mrs. Van Brandt."

Ten days had passed; and thus far Miss Dunross had made her way into my confidence already!

By what means had she induced me to trust her with those secret and sacred sorrows of my life which I had hitherto kept for my mother's ear alone? I can easily recall the rapid and subtle manner in which her sympathies twined themselves round mine; but I fail entirely to trace the infinite gradations of approach by which she surprised and conquered my habitual reserve. The strongest influence of all, the influence of the eye, was not hers. When the light was admitted into the room she was shrouded in her veil. At all other times the curtains were drawn, the screen was before the fire—I could see dimly the outline of her face, and I could see no more. The secret of her influence was perhaps partly attributable to the simple and sisterly manner in which she spoke to me, and partly to the indescribable interest which associated itself with her mere presence in the room. Her father had told me that she "carried the air of heaven with her." In my experience, I can only say that she carried something with her which softly and inscrutably possessed itself of my will, and made me as unconsciously obedient to her wishes as if I had been her dog. The love-story of my boyhood, in all its particulars, down even to the gift of the green flag; the mystic predictions of Dame Dermody; the loss of every trace of my little Mary of former days; the rescue of Mrs. Van Brandt from the river; the apparition of her in the summer-house; the after-meetings with her in Edinburgh and in London; the final parting which had left its mark of sorrow on my face—all these events, all these sufferings, I confided to her as unreservedly as I have confided them to these pages. And the result, as she sat by me in the darkened room, was summed up, with a woman's headlong impetuosity of judgment, in the words that I have just written—"I don't like your Mrs. Van Brandt!"

"Why not?" I asked.

She answered instantly, "Because you ought to love nobody but Mary."

"But Mary has been lost to me since I was a boy of thirteen."

"Be patient, and you will find her again. Mary is patient—Mary is waiting for you. When you meet her, you will be ashamed to remember that you ever loved Mrs. Van Brandt—you will look on your separation from that woman as the happiest event of your life. I may not live to hear of it—but you will live to own that I was right."

Her perfectly baseless conviction that time would yet bring about my meeting with Mary, partly irritated, partly amused me.

"You seem to agree with Dame Dermody," I said. "You believe that our two destinies are one. No matter what time may elapse, or what may happen in the time, you believe my marriage with Mary is still a marriage delayed, and nothing more?"

"I firmly believe it."

"Without knowing why—except that you dislike the idea of my marrying Mrs. Van Brandt?"

She knew that this view of her motive was not far from being the right one—and, womanlike, she shifted the discussion to new ground.

"Why do you call her Mrs. Van Brandt?" she asked. "Mrs. Van Brandt is the namesake of your first love. If you are so fond of her, why don't you call her Mary?"

I was ashamed to give the true reason—it seemed so utterly unworthy of a man of any sense or spirit. Noticing my hesitation, she insisted on my answering her; she forced me to make my humiliating confession.

"The man who has parted us," I said, "called her Mary. I hate him with such a jealous hatred that he has even disgusted me with the name! It lost all its charm for me when it passed his lips."

I had anticipated that she would laugh at me. No! She suddenly raised her head as if she were looking at me intently in the dark.

"How fond you must be of that woman!" she said. "Do you dream of her now?"

"I never dream of her now."

"Do you expect to see the apparition of her again?"

"It may be so—if a time comes when she is in sore need of help, and when she has no friend to look to but me."

"Did you ever see the apparition of your little Mary?"

"Never!"

"But you used once to see her—as Dame Dermody predicted—in dreams?"

"Yes—when I was a lad."

"And, in the after-time, it was not Mary, but Mrs. Van Brandt who came to you in dreams—who appeared to you in the spirit, when she was far away from you in the body? Poor old Dame Dermody. She little thought, in her life-time, that her prediction would be fullfilled by the wrong woman!"

To that result her inquiries had inscrutably conducted her! If she had only pressed them a little further—if she had not unconsciously led me astray again by the very next question that fell from her lips—she must have communicated to my mind the idea obscurely germinating in hers—the idea of a possible identity between the Mary of my first love and Mrs. Van Brandt!

"Tell me," she went on. "If you met with your little Mary now, what would she be like? What sort of woman would you expect to see?"

I could hardly help laughing. "How can I tell," I rejoined, "at this distance of time?"

"Try!" she said.

Reasoning my way from the known personality to the unknown, I searched my memory for the image of the frail and delicate child of my remembrance: and I drew the picture of a frail and delicate woman—the most absolute contrast imaginable to Mrs. Van Brandt!

The half-realized idea of identity in the mind of Miss Dunross dropped out of it instantly, expelled by the substantial conclusion which the contrast implied. Alike ignorant of the aftergrowth of health, strength, and beauty which time and circumstances had developed in the Mary of my youthful days, we had alike completely and unconsciously misled one another. Once more, I had missed the discovery of the truth, and missed it by a hair-breadth!

"I infinitely prefer your portrait of Mary," said Miss Dunross, "to your portrait of Mrs. Van Brandt. Mary realizes my idea of what a really attractive woman ought to be. How you can have felt any sorrow for the loss of that other person (I detest buxom women!) passes my understanding. I can't tell you how interested I am in Mary! I want to know more about her. Where is that pretty present of needle-work which the poor little thing embroidered for you so industriously? Do let me see the green flag!"

She evidently supposed that I carried the green flag about me! I felt a little confused as I answered her.

"I am sorry to disappoint you. The green flag is somewhere in my house in Perthshire."

"You have not got it with you?" she exclaimed. "You leave her keepsake lying about anywhere? Oh, Mr. Germaine, you have indeed forgotten Mary! A woman, in your place, would have parted with her life rather than part with the one memorial left of the time when she first loved!"

She spoke with such extraordinary earnestness—with such agitation, I might almost say—that she quite startled me.

"Dear Miss Dunross," I remonstrated, "the flag is not lost."

"I should hope not!" she interposed, quickly. "If you lose the green flag, you lose the last relic of Mary—and more than that, if my belief is right."

"What do you believe?"

"You will laugh at me if I tell you. I am afraid my first reading of your face was wrong—I am afraid you are a hard man."

"Indeed you do me an injustice. I entreat you to answer me as frankly as usual. What do I lose in losing the last relic of Mary?"

"You lose the one hope I have for you," she answered, gravely—"the hope of your meeting and your marriage with Mary in the time to come. I was sleepless last night, and I was thinking of your pretty love story by the banks of the bright English lake. The longer I thought, the more firmly I felt the conviction that the poor child's green flag is destined to have its innocent influence in forming your future life. Your happiness is waiting for you in that artless little keepsake! I can't explain or justify this belief of mine. It is one of my eccentricities, I suppose—like training my cats to perform to the music of my harp. But, if I were your old friend, instead of being only your friend of a few days, I would leave you no peace—I would beg and entreat and persist, as only a woman can persist—until I had made Mary's gift as close a companion of yours, as your mother's portrait in the locket there at your watch-chain. While the flag is with you, Mary's influence is with you; Mary's love is still binding you by the dear old tie; and Mary and you, after years of separation, will meet again!"

The fancy was in itself pretty and poetical; the earnestness which had given expression to it would have had its influence over a man of a far harder nature than mine. I confess she had made me ashamed, if she had done nothing more, of my neglect of the green flag.

"I will look for it the moment I am at home again," I said; "and I will take care that it is carefully preserved for the future."

"I want more than that," she rejoined. "If you can't wear the flag about

461

you, I want it always to be with you—to go wherever you go. When they brought your luggage here from the vessel at Lerwick, you were particularly anxious about the safety of your traveling writing-desk—the desk there on the table. Is there anything very valuable in it?"

"It contains my money, and other things that I prize far more highly—my mother's letters, and some family relics which I should be very sorry to lose. Besides, the desk itself has its own familiar interest as my constant traveling companion of many years past."

Miss Dunross rose, and came close to the chair in which I was sitting.

"Let Mary's flag be your constant traveling companion," she said. "You have spoken far too gratefully of my services here as your nurse. Reward me beyond my deserts. Make allowances, Mr. Germaine, for the superstitious fancies of a lonely, dreamy woman. Promise me that the green flag shall take its place among the other little treasures in your desk!"

It is needless to say that I made the allowances and gave the promise—gave it, resolving seriously to abide by it. For the first time since I had known her, she put her poor, wasted hand in mine, and pressed it for a moment. Acting heedlessly under my first grateful impulse, I lifted her hand to my lips before I released it. She started—trembled—and suddenly and silently passed out of the room.

CHAPTER XXI. SHE COMES BETWEEN US.

WHAT emotion had I thoughtlessly aroused in Miss Dunross? Had I offended or distressed her? Or had I, without meaning it, forced on her inner knowledge some deeply seated feeling which she had thus far resolutely ignored?

I looked back through the days of my sojourn in the house; I questioned my own feelings and impressions, on the chance that they might serve me as a means of solving the mystery of her sudden flight from the room.

What effect had she produced on me?

In plain truth, she had simply taken her place in my mind, to the exclusion of every other person and every other subject. In ten days she had taken a hold on my sympathies of which other women would have failed to possess themselves in so many years. I remembered, to my shame, that my mother had but seldom occupied my thoughts. Even the image of Mrs. Van Brandt—except when the conversation had turned on her—had become a faint image in my mind! As to my friends at Lerwick, from Sir James downward, they had all kindly come to see me—and I had secretly and ungratefully rejoiced when their departure left the scene free for the return of my nurse. In two days more the Government vessel was to sail on the return voyage. My wrist was still painful when I tried to use it; but the far more serious injury presented by the re-opened wound was no longer a subject of anxiety to myself or to any one about me. I was sufficiently restored to be capable of making the journey to Lerwick, if I rested for one night at a farm half-way between the town and Mr. Dunross's house. Knowing this, I had nevertheless left the question of rejoining the vessel undecided to the very latest moment. The motive which I pleaded to my friends was—uncertainty as to the sufficient recovery of my strength. The motive which I now confessed to myself was reluctance to leave Miss Dunross.

What was the secret of her power over me? What emotion, what passion, had she awakened in me? Was it love?

No: not love. The place which Mary had once held in my heart, the place which Mrs. Van Brandt had taken in the after-time, was not the place occupied by Miss Dunross. How could I (in the ordinary sense of the word) be in love with a woman whose face I had never seen? whose beauty had faded, never to bloom again? whose wasted life hung by a thread which the accident of a moment might snap? The senses have their share in all love between the sexes which is worthy of the name. They had no share in the feeling with which I regarded Miss Dunross. What was the feeling, then? I can only answer the question in one way. The feeling lay too deep in me for my sounding.

What impression had I produced on her? What sensitive chord had I ignorantly touched, when my lips touched her hand?

I confess I recoiled from pursuing the inquiry which I had deliberately set myself to make. I thought of her shattered health; of her melancholy existence in shadow and solitude; of the rich treasures of such a heart and such a mind as hers, wasted with her wasting life; and I said to myself, Let her secret be sacred! let me never again, by word or deed, bring the trouble which tells of it to the surface! let her heart be veiled from me in the darkness which veils her face!

In this frame of mind toward her, I waited her return.

I had no doubt of seeing her again, sooner or later, on that day. The post to the south went out on the next day; and the early hour of the morning at which the messenger called for our letters made it a matter of ordinary convenience to write overnight. In the disabled state of my hand, Miss Dunross had been accustomed to write home for me, under my dictation: she knew that I owed a letter to my mother, and that I relied as usual on her help. Her return to me, under these circumstances, was simply a question of time: any duty which she had once undertaken was an imperative duty in her estimation, no matter how trifling it might be.

The hours wore on; the day drew to its end—and still she never appeared.

I left my room to enjoy the last sunny gleam of the daylight in the garden attached to the house; first telling Peter where I might be found, if Miss Dunross wanted me. The garden was a wild place, to my southern notions; but it extended for some distance along the shore of the island, and it offered some pleasant views of the lake and the moorland country beyond. Slowly pursuing my walk, I proposed to myself to occupy my mind to some useful purpose by arranging beforehand the composition of the letter which Miss Dunross was to write.

To my great surprise, I found it simply impossible to fix my mind on the subject. Try as I might, my thoughts persisted in wandering from the letter to my mother, and concentrated themselves instead—on Miss Dunross? No. On the question of my returning, or not returning, to Perthshire by the Government vessel? No. By some capricious revulsion of feeling which it seemed impossible to account for, my whole mind was now absorbed on the one subject which had been hitherto so strangely absent from it—the subject of Mrs. Van Brandt!

My memory went back, in defiance of all exercise of my own will, to my last interview with her. I saw her again; I heard her again. I tasted once more the momentary rapture of our last kiss; I felt once more the pang of sorrow that wrung me when I had parted with her and found myself alone in the street. Tears—of which I was ashamed, though nobody was near to see them—filled my eyes when I thought of the months that had passed since we had last looked on one another, and of all that she might have suffered, must have suffered, in that time. Hundreds on hundreds of miles were between us—and yet she was now as near me as if she were walking in the garden by my side!

This strange condition of my mind was matched by an equally strange condition of my body. A mysterious trembling shuddered over me faintly from head to foot. I walked without feeling the ground as I trod on it; I looked about me with no distinct consciousness of what the objects were on which my eyes rested. My hands were cold—and yet I hardly felt it. My head throbbed hotly—and yet I was not sensible of any pain. It seemed as if I were surrounded and enwrapped in some electric atmosphere which altered all the ordinary conditions of sensation. I looked up at the clear, calm sky, and wondered if a thunderstorm was coming. I stopped, and buttoned my coat round me, and questioned myself if I had caught a cold, or if I was going to have a fever. The sun sank below the moorland horizon; the gray twilight trembled over the dark waters of the lake. I went back to the house; and the vivid memory of Mrs. Van Brandt, still in close companionship, went back with me.

The fire in my room had burned low in my absence. One of the closed curtains had been drawn back a few inches, so as to admit through the window a ray of the dying light. On the boundary limit where the light was crossed by the obscurity which filled the rest of the room, I saw Miss Dunross seated, with her veil drawn and her writing-case on her knee, waiting my return.

I hastened to make my excuses. I assured her that I had been careful to tell the servant where to find me. She gently checked me before I could say more.

"It's not Peter's fault," she said. "I told him not to hurry your return to the house. Have you enjoyed your walk?"

She spoke very quietly. The faint, sad voice was fainter and sadder than ever. She kept her head bent over her writing-case, instead of turning it toward me as usual while we were talking. I still felt the mysterious trembling which had oppressed me in the garden. Drawing a chair near the fire, I stirred the embers together, and tried to warm myself. Our positions in the room left some little distance between us. I could only see her sidewise, as she sat by the window in the sheltering darkness of the curtain which still remained drawn.

"I think I have been too long in the garden," I said. "I feel chilled by the cold evening air."

"Will you have some more wood put on the fire?" she asked. "Can I get you anything?"

"No, thank you. I shall do very well here. I see you are kindly ready to write for me."

"Yes," she said, "at your own convenience. When you are ready, my pen is ready."

The unacknowledged reserve that had come between us since we had last spoken together, was, I believe, as painfully felt by her as by me. We were no doubt longing to break through it on either side—if we had only known how. The writing of the letter would occupy us, at any rate. I made another effort to give my mind to the subject—and once more it was an effort made in vain. Knowing what I wanted to say to my mother, my faculties seemed to be paralyzed when I tried to say it. I sat cowering by the fire—and she sat waiting, with her writing-case on her lap.

CHAPTER XXII. SHE CLAIMS ME AGAIN.

THE moments passed; the silence between us continued. Miss Dunross made an attempt to rouse me.

"Have you decided to go back to Scotland with your friends at Lerwick?" she asked.

"It is no easy matter," I replied, "to decide on leaving my friends in this house."

Her head drooped lower on her bosom; her voice sunk as she answered me.

"Think of your mother," she said. "The first duty you owe is your duty to her. Your long absence is a heavy trial to her—your mother is suffering."

"Suffering?" I repeated. "Her letters say nothing—"

"You forget that you have allowed me to read her letters," Miss Dunross interposed. "I see the unwritten and unconscious confession of anxiety in every line that she writes to you. You know, as well as I do, that there is cause for her anxiety. Make her happy by telling her that you sail for home with your friends. Make her happier still by telling her that you grieve no more over the loss of Mrs. Van Brandt. May I write it, in your name and in those words?"

I felt the strangest reluctance to permit her to write in those terms, or in any terms, of Mrs. Van Brandt. The unhappy love-story of my manhood had never been a forbidden subject between us on former occasions. Why did I feel as if it had become a forbidden subject now? Why did I evade giving her a direct reply?

"We have plenty of time before us," I said. "I want to speak to you about yourself."

She lifted her hand in the obscurity that surrounded her, as if to protest against the topic to which I had returned. I persisted, nevertheless, in returning to it.

"If I must go back," I went on, "I may venture to say to you at parting what I have not said yet. I cannot, and will not, believe that you are an incurable invalid. My education, as I have told you, has been the education of a medical man. I am well acquainted with some of the greatest living physicians, in Edinburgh as well as in London. Will you allow me to describe your malady (as I understand it) to men who are accustomed to treat cases of intricate nervous disorder? And will you let me write and tell you the result?"

I waited for her reply. Neither by word nor sign did she encourage the idea of any future communication with her. I ventured to suggest another motive which might induce her to receive a letter from me.

"In any case, I may find it necessary to write to you," I went on. "You firmly believe that I and my little Mary are destined to meet again. If your anticipations are realized, you will expect me to tell you of it, surely?"

Once more I waited. She spoke—but it was not to reply: it was only to change the subject.

"The time is passing," was all she said. "We have not begun your letter to your mother yet."

It would have been cruel to contend with her any longer. Her voice warned me that she was suffering. The faint gleam of light through the parted curtains was fading fast. It was time, indeed, to write the letter. I could find other opportunities of speaking to her before I left the house.

"I am ready," I answered. "Let us begin."

The first sentence was easily dictated to my patient secretary. I informed my mother that my sprained wrist was nearly restored to use, and that nothing prevented my leaving Shetland when the lighthouse commissioner was ready to return. This was all that it was necessary to say on the subject of my health; the disaster of my re-opened wound having been, for obvious reasons, concealed from my mother's knowledge. Miss Dunross silently wrote the opening lines of the letter, and waited for the words that were to follow.

In my next sentence, I announced the date at which the vessel was to sail on the return voyage; and I mentioned the period at which my mother might expect to see me, weather permitting. Those words, also, Miss Dunross wrote—and waited again. I set myself to consider what I should say next. To my surprise and alarm, I found it impossible to fix my mind on the subject. My thoughts wandered away, in the strangest manner, from my letter to Mrs. Van Brandt. I was ashamed of myself; I was angry with myself—I resolved, no matter what I said, that I would positively finish the letter. No! try as I might, the utmost effort of my will availed me nothing. Mrs. Van Brandt's words at our last interview were murmuring in my ears—not a word of my own would come to me!

Miss Dunross laid down her pen, and slowly turned her head to look at me.

"Surely you have something more to add to your letter?" she said.

"Certainly," I answered. "I don't know what is the matter with me. The effort of dictating seems to be beyond my power this evening."

"Can I help you?" she asked.

I gladly accepted the suggestion. "There are many things," I said, "which my mother would be glad to hear, if I were not too stupid to think of them. I am sure I may trust your sympathy to think of them for me."

That rash answer offered Miss Dunross the opportunity of returning to the subject of Mrs. Van Brandt. She seized the opportunity with a woman's persistent resolution when she has her end in view, and is determined to reach it at all hazards.

"You have not told your mother yet," she said, "that your infatuation for Mrs. Van Brandt is at an end. Will you put it in your own words? Or shall I write it for you, imitating your language as well as I can?"

In the state of my mind at that moment, her perseverance conquered me. I thought to myself indolently, "If I say No, she will only return to the subject again, and she will end (after all I owe to her kindness) in making me say Yes." Before I could answer her she had realized my anticipations. She returned to the subject; and she made me say Yes.

"What does your silence mean?" she said. "Do you ask me to help you, and do you refuse to accept the first suggestion I offer?"

"Take up your pen," I rejoined. "It shall be as you wish."

"Will you dictate the words?"

"I will try."

I tried; and this time I succeeded. With the image of Mrs. Van Brandt vividly present to my mind, I arranged the first words of the sentence which was to tell my mother that my "infatuation" was at an end!

"You will be glad to hear," I began, "that time and change are doing their good work."

Miss Dunross wrote the words, and paused in anticipation of the next sentence. The light faded and faded; the room grew darker and darker. I went on.

"I hope I shall cause you no more anxiety, my dear mother, on the subject of Mrs. Van Brandt."

In the deep silence I could hear the pen of my secretary traveling steadily over the paper while it wrote those words.

"Have you written?" I asked, as the sound of the pen ceased.

"I have written," she answered, in her customary quiet tones.

I went on again with my letter.

"The days pass now, and I seldom or never think of her; I hope I am resigned at last to the loss of Mrs. Van Brandt."

As I reached the end of the sentence, I heard a faint cry from Miss Dunross. Looking instantly toward her, I could just see, in the deepening darkness, that her head had fallen on the back of the chair. My first impulse was, of course, to rise and go to her. I had barely got to my feet, when some indescribable dread paralyzed me on the instant. Supporting myself against the chimney-piece, I stood perfectly incapable of advancing a step. The effort to speak was the one effort that I could make.

"Are you ill?" I asked.

She was hardly able to answer me; speaking in a whisper, without raising her head.

"I am frightened," she said.

"What has frightened you?"

I heard her shudder in the darkness. Instead of answering me, she whispered to herself: "What am I to say to him?"

"Tell me what has frightened you?" I repeated. "You know you may trust me with the truth."

She rallied her sinking strength. She answered in these strange words:

"Something has come between me and the letter that I am writing for you."

"What is it?"

"I can't tell you."

"Can you see it?"

"No."

"Can you feel it?"

"Yes!"

"What is it like?"

"Like a breath of cold air between me and the letter."

"Has the window come open?"

"The window is close shut."

"And the door?"

"The door is shut also—as well as I can see. Make sure of it for yourself. Where are you? What are you doing?"

I was looking toward the window. As she spoke her last words, I was conscious of a change in that part of the room.

In the gap between the parted curtains there was a new light shining; not the dim gray twilight of Nature, but a pure and starry radiance, a pale, unearthly light. While I watched it, the starry radiance quivered as if some breath of air had stirred it. When it was still again, there dawned on me through the unearthly luster the figure of a woman. By fine and slow gradations, it became more and more distinct. I knew the noble figure; I knew the sad and tender smile. For the second time I stood in the presence of the apparition of Mrs. Van Brandt.

She was robed, not as I had last seen her, but in the dress which she had worn on the memorable evening when we met on the bridge—in the dress in which she had first appeared to me, by the waterfall in Scotland. The starry light shone round her like a halo. She looked at me with sorrowful and pleading eyes, as she had looked when I saw the apparition of her in the summer-house. She lifted her hand—not beckoning me to approach her, as before, but gently signing to me to remain where I stood.

I waited—feeling awe, but no fear. My heart was all hers as I looked at her.

She moved; gliding from the window to the chair in which Miss Dunross sat; winding her way slowly round it, until she stood at the back. By the light of the pale halo that encircled the ghostly Presence, and moved with it, I could see the dark figure of the living woman seated immovable in the chair. The writing-case was on her lap, with the letter and the pen lying on it. Her arms hung helpless at her sides; her veiled head was now bent forward. She looked as if she had been struck to stone in the act of trying to rise from her seat.

A moment passed—and I saw the ghostly Presence stoop over the living woman. It lifted the writing-case from her lap. It rested the writing-case on her shoulder. Its white fingers took the pen and wrote on the unfinished letter. It put the writing-case back on the lap of the living woman. Still standing behind the chair, it turned toward me. It looked at me once more. And now it beckoned—beckoned to me to approach.

Moving without conscious will of my own, as I had moved when I first saw her in the summer-house—drawn nearer and nearer by an irresistible power—I approached and stopped within a few paces of her. She advanced and laid her hand on my bosom. Again I felt those strangely mingled sensations of rapture and awe, which had once before filled me when I was conscious, spiritually, of her touch. Again she spoke, in the low, melodious tones which I recalled so well. Again she said the words: "Remember me. Come to me." Her hand dropped from my bosom. The pale light in which she stood quivered, sunk, vanished. I saw the twilight glimmering between the curtains—and I saw no more. She had spoken. She had gone.

I was near Miss Dunross—near enough, when I put out my hand, to touch her.

She started and shuddered, like a woman suddenly awakened from a dreadful dream.

"Speak to me!" she whispered. "Let me know that it is you who touched me."

I spoke a few composing words before I questioned her.

"Have you seen anything in the room?"

She answered. "I have been filled with a deadly fear. I have seen nothing but the writing-case lifted from my lap."

"Did you see the hand that lifted it?"

"No."

"Did you see a starry light, and a figure standing in it?"

"No."

"Did you see the writing-case after it was lifted from your lap?"

"I saw it resting on my shoulder."

"Did you see writing on the letter, which was not your writing?"

"I saw a darker shadow on the paper than the shadow in which I am sitting."

"Did it move?"

"It moved across the paper."

"As a pen moves in writing?"

"Yes. As a pen moves in writing."

"May I take the letter?"

She handed it to me.

"May I light a candle?"

She drew her veil more closely over her face, and bowed in silence.

I lighted the candle on the mantel-piece, and looked for the writing.

There, on the blank space in the letter, as I had seen it before on the blank space in the sketch-book—there were the written words which the ghostly Presence had left behind it; arranged once more in two lines, as I copy them here:

At the month's end, In the shadow of Saint Paul's.

CHAPTER XXIII. THE KISS.

SHE had need of me again. She had claimed me again. I felt all the old love, all the old devotion owning her power once more. Whatever had mortified or angered me at our last interview was forgiven and forgotten now. My whole being still thrilled with the mingled awe and rapture of beholding the Vision of her that had come to me for the second time. The minutes passed—and I stood by the fire like a man entranced; thinking only of her spoken words, "Remember me. Come to me;" looking only at her mystic writing, "At the month's end, In the shadow of Saint Paul's."

The month's end was still far off; the apparition of her had shown itself to me, under some subtle prevision of trouble that was still in the future. Ample time was before me for the pilgrimage to which I was self-dedicated already—my pilgrimage to the shadow of Saint Paul's. Other men, in my position, might have hesitated as to the right understanding of the place to which they were bidden. Other men might have wearied their memories by recalling the churches, the institutions, the streets, the towns in foreign countries, all consecrated to Christian reverence by the great apostle's name, and might have fruitlessly asked themselves in which direction they were first to turn their steps. No such difficulty troubled me. My first conclusion was the one conclusion that was acceptable to my mind. "Saint Paul's" meant the famous Cathedral of London. Where the shadow of the great church fell, there, at the month's end, I should find her, or the trace of her. In London once more, and nowhere else, I was destined to see the woman I loved, in the living body, as certainly as I had just seen her in the ghostly presence.

Who could interpret the mysterious sympathies that still united us, in defiance of distance, in defiance of time? Who could predict to what end our lives were tending in the years that were to come?

Those questions were still present to my thoughts; my eyes were still fixed on the mysterious writing—when I became instinctively aware of the strange silence in the room. Instantly the lost remembrance of Miss Dunross came back to me. Stung by my own sense of self-reproach, I turned with a start, and looked toward her chair by the window.

The chair was empty. I was alone in the room.

Why had she left me secretly, without a word of farewell? Because she was suffering, in mind or body? Or because she resented, naturally resented, my neglect of her?

The bare suspicion that I had given her pain was intolerable to me. I rang my bell, to make inquiries.

The bell was answered, not, as usual, by the silent servant Peter, but by a woman of middle age, very quietly and neatly dressed, whom I had once or twice met on the way to and from my room, and of whose exact position in the house I was still ignorant.

"Do you wish to see Peter?" she asked.

"No. I wish to know where Miss Dunross is."

"Miss Dunross is in her room. She has sent me with this letter."

I took the letter, feeling some surprise and uneasiness. It was the first time Miss Dunross had communicated with me in that formal way. I tried to gain further information by questioning her messenger.

"Are you Miss Dunross's maid?" I asked.

"I have served Miss Dunross for many years," was the answer, spoken very ungraciously.

"Do you think she would receive me if I sent you with a message to her?"

"I can't say, sir. The letter may tell you. You will do well to read the letter."

We looked at each other. The woman's preconceived impression of me was evidently an unfavorable one. Had I indeed pained or offended Miss Dunross? And had the servant—perhaps the faithful servant who loved her—

477

discovered and resented it? The woman frowned as she looked at me. It would be a mere waste of words to persist in questioning her. I let her go.

Left by myself again, I read the letter. It began, without any form of address, in these lines:

"I write, instead of speaking to you, because my self-control has already been severely tried, and I am not strong enough to bear more. For my father's sake—not for my own—I must take all the care I can of the little health that I have left.

"Putting together what you have told me of the visionary creature whom you saw in the summer-house in Scotland, and what you said when you questioned me in your room a little while since, I cannot fail to infer that the same vision has shown itself to you, for the second time. The fear that I felt, the strange things that I saw (or thought I saw), may have been imperfect reflections in my mind of what was passing in yours. I do not stop to inquire whether we are both the victims of a delusion, or whether we are the chosen recipients of a supernatural communication. The result, in either case, is enough for me. You are once more under the influence of Mrs. Van Brandt. I will not trust myself to tell you of the anxieties and forebodings by which I am oppressed: I will only acknowledge that my one hope for you is in your speedy reunion with the worthier object of your constancy and devotion. I still believe, and I am consoled in believing, that you and your first love will meet again.

"Having written so far, I leave the subject—not to return to it, except in my own thoughts.

"The necessary preparations for your departure to-morrow are all made. Nothing remains but to wish you a safe and pleasant journey home. Do not, I entreat you, think me insensible of what I owe to you, if I say my farewell words here.

"The little services which you have allowed me to render you have brightened the closing days of my life. You have left me a treasury of happy memories which I shall hoard, when you are gone, with miserly care. Are you willing to add new claims to my grateful remembrance? I ask it of you, as a last favor—do not attempt to see me again! Do not expect me to take a personal leave of you! The saddest of all words is 'Good-by': I have fortitude enough to write it, and no more. God preserve and prosper you—farewell!

"One more request. I beg that you will not forget what you promised me, when I told you my foolish fancy about the green flag. Wherever you go, let Mary's keepsake go with you. No written answer is necessary—I would rather not receive it. Look up, when you leave the house to-morrow, at the center window over the doorway—that will be answer enough."

To say that these melancholy lines brought the tears into my eyes is only to acknowledge that I had sympathies which could be touched. When I had in some degree recovered my composure, the impulse which urged me to write to Miss Dunross was too strong to be resisted. I did not trouble her with a long letter; I only entreated her to reconsider her decision with all the art of persuasion which I could summon to help me. The answer was brought back by the servant who waited on Miss Dunross, in four resolute words: "It can not be." This time the woman spoke out before she left me. "If you have any regard for my mistress," she said sternly, "don't make her write to you again." She looked at me with a last lowering frown, and left the room.

It is needless to say that the faithful servant's words only increased my anxiety to see Miss Dunross once more before we parted—perhaps forever. My one last hope of success in attaining this object lay in approaching her indirectly through the intercession of her father.

I sent Peter to inquire if I might be permitted to pay my respects to his master that evening. My messenger returned with an answer that was a new disappointment to me. Mr. Dunross begged that I would excuse him, if he deferred the proposed interview until the next morning. The next morning was the morning of my departure. Did the message mean that he had no wish to see me again until the time had come to take leave of him? I inquired of Peter whether his master was particularly occupied that evening. He was unable to tell me. "The Master of Books" was not in his study, as usual. When he sent his message to me, he was sitting by the sofa in his daughter's room.

Having answered in those terms, the man left me by myself until the next morning. I do not wish my bitterest enemy a sadder time in his life than the time I passed during the last night of my residence under Mr. Dunross's roof.

After walking to and fro in the room until I was weary, I thought of trying to divert my mind from the sad thoughts that oppressed it by reading. The one candle which I had lighted failed to sufficiently illuminate the room. Advancing to the mantel-piece to light the second candle which stood there, I noticed the unfinished letter to my mother lying where I had placed it, when Miss Dunross's servant first presented herself before me. Having lighted the second candle, I took up the letter to put it away among my other papers. Doing this (while my thoughts were still dwelling on Miss Dunross), I mechanically looked at the letter again—and instantly discovered a change in it.

The written characters traced by the hand of the apparition had vanished! Below the last lines written by Miss Dunross nothing met my eyes now but the blank white paper!

My first impulse was to look at my watch.

When the ghostly presence had written in my sketch-book, the characters had disappeared after an interval of three hours. On this occasion, as nearly as I could calculate, the writing had vanished in one hour only.

Reverting to the conversation which I had held with Mrs. Van Brandt when we met at Saint Anthony's Well, and to the discoveries which followed at a later period of my life, I can only repeat that she had again been the subject of a trance or dream, when the apparition of her showed itself to me for the second time. As before, she had freely trusted me and freely appealed to me to help her, in the dreaming state, when her spirit was free to recognize my spirit. When she had come to herself, after an interval of an hour, she had again felt ashamed of the familiar manner in which she had communicated with me in the trance—had again unconsciously counteracted by her waking-will the influence of her sleeping-will; and had thus caused the writing once more to disappear, in an hour from the moment when the pen had traced (or seemed to trace) it.

This is still the one explanation that I can offer. At the time when the incident happened, I was far from being fully admitted to the confidence of Mrs. Van Brandt; and I was necessarily incapable of arriving at any solution of the mystery, right or wrong. I could only put away the letter, doubting vaguely whether my own senses had not deceived me. After the distressing thoughts which Miss Dunross's letter had roused in my mind, I was in no humor to employ my ingenuity in finding a clew to the mystery of the vanished writing. My nerves were irritated; I felt a sense of angry discontent with myself and with others. "Go where I may" (I thought impatiently), "the disturbing influence of women seems to be the only influence that I am fated to feel." As I still paced backward and forward in my room—it was useless to think now of fixing my attention on a book—I fancied I understood the motives which made men as young as I was retire to end their lives in a monastery. I drew aside the window curtains, and looked out. The only prospect that met my view was the black gulf of darkness in which the lake lay hidden. I could see nothing; I could do nothing; I could think of nothing. The one alternative before me was that of trying to sleep. My medical knowledge told me plainly that natural sleep was, in my nervous condition, one of the unattainable luxuries of life for that night. The medicine-chest which Mr. Dunross had placed at my disposal remained in the room. I mixed for myself a strong sleeping draught, and sullenly took refuge from my troubles in bed.

It is a peculiarity of most of the soporific drugs that they not only act in a totally different manner on different constitutions, but that they are not even to be depended on to act always in the same manner on the same person. I had taken care to extinguish the candles before I got into my bed. Under ordinary circumstances, after I had lain quietly in the darkness for half an hour, the draught that I had taken would have sent me to sleep. In the present state of my nerves the draught stupefied me, and did no more.

Hour after hour I lay perfectly still, with my eyes closed, in the semi-sleeping, semi-wakeful state which is so curiously characteristic of the ordinary repose of a dog. As the night wore on, such a sense of heaviness oppressed my eyelids that it was literally impossible for me to open them—such a masterful languor possessed all my muscles that I could no more move on my pillow than if I had been a corpse. And yet, in this somnolent condition, my mind was able to pursue lazy trains of pleasant thought. My sense of hearing was so acute that it caught the faintest sounds made by the passage of the night-breeze through the rushes of the lake. Inside my bed-chamber, I was even more keenly sensible of those weird night-noises in the heavy furniture of a room, of those sudden settlements of extinct coals in the grate, so familiar to bad sleepers, so startling to overwrought nerves! It is not a scientifically correct statement, but it exactly describes my condition, that night, to say that one half of me was asleep and the other half awake.

How many hours of the night had passed, when my irritable sense of hearing became aware of a new sound in the room, I cannot tell. I can only relate that I found myself on a sudden listening intently, with fast-closed eyes. The sound that disturbed me was the faintest sound imaginable, as of something soft and light traveling slowly over the surface of the carpet, and brushing it just loud enough to be heard.

Little by little, the sound came nearer and nearer to my bed—and then suddenly stopped just as I fancied it was close by me.

I still lay immovable, with closed eyes; drowsily waiting for the next sound that might reach my ears; drowsily content with the silence, if the silence continued. My thoughts (if thoughts they could be called) were drifting back again into their former course, when I became suddenly conscious of soft breathing just above me. The next moment I felt a touch on my forehead—light, soft, tremulous, like the touch of lips that had kissed me. There was a momentary pause. Then a low sigh trembled through the silence. Then I heard again the still, small sound of something brushing its way over the carpet; traveling this time from my bed, and moving so rapidly that in a moment more it was lost in the silence of the night.

Still stupefied by the drug that I had taken, I could lazily wonder what had happened, and I could do no more. Had living lips really touched me? Was the sound that I had heard really the sound of a sigh? Or was it all delusion, beginning and ending in a dream? The time passed without my deciding, or caring to decide, those questions. Minute by minute, the composing influence of the draught began at last to strengthen its hold on my brain. A cloud seemed to pass softly over my last waking impressions. One after another, the ties broke gently that held me to conscious life. I drifted peacefully into perfect sleep.

Shortly after sunrise, I awoke. When I regained the use of my memory, my first clear recollection was the recollection of the soft breathing which I had felt above me—then of the touch on my forehead, and of the sigh which I had heard after it. Was it possible that some one had entered my room in the night? It was quite possible. I had not locked the door—I had never been in the habit of locking the door during my residence under Mr. Dunross's roof.

After thinking it over a little, I rose to examine my room.

Nothing in the shape of a discovery rewarded me, until I reached the door. Though I had not locked it overnight, I had certainly satisfied myself that it was closed before I went to bed. It was now ajar. Had it opened again, through being imperfectly shut? or had a person, after entering and leaving my room, forgotten to close it?

Accidentally looking downward while I was weighing these probabilities, I noticed a small black object on the carpet, lying just under the key, on the inner side of the door. I picked the thing up, and found that it was a torn morsel of black lace.

The instant I saw the fragment, I was reminded of the long black veil, hanging below her waist, which it was the habit of Miss Dunross to wear. Was it her dress, then, that I had heard softly traveling over the carpet; her kiss that had touched my forehead; her sigh that had trembled through the silence? Had the ill-fated and noble creature taken her last leave of me in the dead of night, trusting the preservation of her secret to the deceitful appearances which persuaded her that I was asleep? I looked again at the fragment of black lace. Her long veil might easily have been caught, and torn, by the projecting key, as she passed rapidly through the door on her way out of my room. Sadly and reverently I laid the morsel of lace among the treasured memorials which I had brought with me from home. To the end of her life, I vowed it, she should be left undisturbed in the belief that her secret was safe in her own breast! Ardently as I still longed to take her hand at parting, I now resolved to make no further effort to see her. I might not be master of my own emotions; something in my face or in my manner might betray me to her quick and delicate perception. Knowing what I now knew, the last sacrifice I could make to her would be to obey her wishes. I made the sacrifice.

In an hour more Peter informed me that the ponies were at the door, and that the Master was waiting for me in the outer hall.

I noticed that Mr. Dunross gave me his hand, without looking at me. His faded blue eyes, during the few minutes while we were together, were not once raised from the ground.

"God speed you on your journey, sir, and guide you safely home," he said. "I beg you to forgive me if I fail to accompany you on the first few miles of your journey. There are reasons which oblige me to remain with my daughter in the house."

He was scrupulously, almost painfully, courteous; but there was something in his manner which, for the first time in my experience, seemed designedly to keep me at a distance from him. Knowing the intimate sympathy, the perfect confidence, which existed between the father and daughter, a doubt crossed my mind whether the secret of the past night was entirely a secret to Mr. Dunross. His next words set that doubt at rest, and showed me the truth.

In thanking him for his good wishes, I attempted also to express to him (and through him to Miss Dunross) my sincere sense of gratitude for the kindness which I had received under his roof. He stopped me, politely and resolutely, speaking with that quaintly precise choice of language which I had remarked as characteristic of him at our first interview.

"It is in your power, sir," he said, "to return any obligation which you may think you have incurred on leaving my house. If you will be pleased to consider your residence here as an unimportant episode in your life, which ends—absolutely ends—with your departure, you will more than repay any kindness that you may have received as my guest. In saying this, I speak under a sense of duty which does entire justice to you as a gentleman and a man of honor. In return, I can only trust to you not to misjudge my motives, if I abstain from explaining myself any further."

A faint color flushed his pale cheeks. He waited, with a certain proud resignation, for my reply. I respected her secret, respected it more resolutely than ever, before her father.

"After all that I owe to you, sir," I answered, "your wishes are my commands." Saying that, and saying no more, I bowed to him with marked respect, and left the house.

Mounting my pony at the door, I looked up at the center window, as she had bidden me. It was open; but dark curtains, jealously closed, kept out the light from the room within. At the sound of the pony's hoofs on the rough island road, as the animal moved, the curtains were parted for a few inches only. Through the gap in the dark draperies a wan white hand appeared; waved tremulously a last farewell; and vanished from my view. The curtains closed again on her dark and solitary life. The dreary wind sounded its long, low dirge over the rippling waters of the lake. The ponies took their places in the ferryboat which was kept for the passage of animals to and from the island. With slow, regular strokes the men rowed us to the mainland and took their leave. I looked back at the distant house. I thought of her in the dark room, waiting patiently for death. Burning tears blinded me. The guide took my bridle in his hand: "You're not well, sir," he said; "I will lead the pony."

When I looked again at the landscape round me, we had descended in the interval from the higher ground to the lower. The house and the lake had disappeared, to be seen no more.

CHAPTER XXIV. IN THE SHADOW OF ST. PAUL'S.

In ten days I was at home again—and my mother's arms were round me.

I had left her for my sea-voyage very unwillingly—seeing that she was in delicate health. On my return, I was grieved to observe a change for the worse, for which her letters had not prepared me. Consulting our medical friend, Mr. MacGlue, I found that he, too, had noticed my mother's failing health, but that he attributed it to an easily removable cause—to the climate of Scotland. My mother's childhood and early life had been passed on the southern shores of England. The change to the raw, keen air of the North had been a trying change to a person at her age. In Mr. MacGlue's opinion, the wise course to take would be to return to the South before the autumn was further advanced, and to make our arrangements for passing the coming winter at Penzance or Torquay.

Resolved as I was to keep the mysterious appointment which summoned me to London at the month's end, Mr. MacGlue's suggestion met with no opposition on my part. It had, to my mind, the great merit of obviating the necessity of a second separation from my mother—assuming that she approved of the doctor's advice. I put the question to her the same day. To my infinite relief, she was not only ready, but eager to take the journey to the South. The season had been unusually wet, even for Scotland; and my mother reluctantly confessed that she "did feel a certain longing" for the mild air and genial sunshine of the Devonshire coast.

We arranged to travel in our own comfortable carriage by post—resting, of course, at inns on the road at night. In the days before railways it was no easy matter for an invalid to travel from Perthshire to London—even with a light carriage and four horses. Calculating our rate of progress from the date of our departure, I found that we had just time, and no more, to reach London on the last day of the month.

I shall say nothing of the secret anxieties which weighed on my mind, under these circumstances. Happily for me, on every account, my mother's strength held out. The easy and (as we then thought) the rapid rate of traveling had its invigorating effect on her nerves. She slept better when we rested for the night than she had slept at home. After twice being delayed on the road, we arrived in London at three o'clock on the afternoon of the last day of the month. Had I reached my destination in time?

As I interpreted the writing of the apparition, I had still some hours at my disposal. The phrase, "at the month's end," meant, as I understood it, at the last hour of the last day in the month. If I took up my position "under the shadow of Saint Paul's," say, at ten that night, I should arrive at the place of meeting with two hours to spare, before the last stroke of the clock marked the beginning of the new month.

At half-past nine, I left my mother to rest after her long journey, and privately quit the house. Before ten, I was at my post. The night was fine and clear; and the huge shadow of the cathedral marked distinctly the limits within which I had been bid to wait, on the watch for events.

The great clock of Saint Paul's struck ten—and nothing happened.

The next hour passed very slowly. I walked up and down; at one time absorbed in my own thoughts; at another, engaged in watching the gradual diminution in the number of foot passengers who passed me as the night advanced. The City (as it is called) is the most populous part of London in the daytime; but at night, when it ceases to be the center of commerce, its busy population melts away, and the empty streets assume the appearance of a remote and deserted quarter of the metropolis. As the half hour after ten struck—then the quarter to eleven—then the hour—the pavement steadily became more and more deserted. I could count the foot passengers now by twos and threes; and I could see the places of public refreshment within my view beginning already to close for the night.

I looked at the clock; it pointed to ten minutes past eleven. At that hour, could I hope to meet Mrs. Van Brandt alone in the public street?

The more I thought of it, the less likely such an event seemed to be.

The more reasonable probability was that I might meet her once more, accompanied by some friend—perhaps under the escort of Van Brandt himself. I wondered whether I should preserve my self-control, in the presence of that man, for the second time.

While my thoughts were still pursuing this direction, my attention was recalled to passing events by a sad little voice, putting a strange little question, close at my side.

"If you please, sir, do you know where I can find a chemist's shop open at this time of night?"

I looked round, and discovered a poorly clad little boy, with a basket over his arm, and a morsel of paper in his hand.

"The chemists' shops are all shut," I said. "If you want any medicine, you must ring the night-bell."

"I dursn't do it, sir," replied the small stranger. "I am such a little boy, I'm afraid of their beating me if I ring them up out of their beds, without somebody to speak for me."

The little creature looked at me under the street lamp with such a forlorn experience of being beaten for trifling offenses in his face, that it was impossible to resist the impulse to help him.

"Is it a serious case of illness?" I asked.

"I don't know, sir."

"Have you got a doctor's prescription?"

He held out his morsel of paper.

"I have got this," he said.

I took the paper from him, and looked at it.

It was an ordinary prescription for a tonic mixture. I looked first at the doctor's signature; it was the name of a perfectly obscure person in the profession. Below it was written the name of the patient for whom the medicine had been prescribed. I started as I read it. The name was "Mrs. Brand."

The idea instantly struck me that this (so far as sound went, at any rate) was the English equivalent of Van Brandt.

"Do you know the lady who sent you for the medicine?" I asked.

"Oh yes, sir! She lodges with mother—and she owes for rent. I have done everything she told me, except getting the physic. I've pawned her ring, and I've bought the bread and butter and eggs, and I've taken care of the change. Mother looks to the change for her rent. It isn't my fault, sir, that I've lost myself. I am but ten years old—and all the chemists' shops are shut up!"

Here my little friend's sense of his unmerited misfortunes overpowered him, and he began to cry.

"Don't cry, my man!" I said; "I'll help you. Tell me something more about the lady first. Is she alone?"

"She's got her little girl with her, sir."

My heart quickened its beat. The boy's answer reminded me of that other little girl whom my mother had once seen.

"Is the lady's husband with her?" I asked next.

"No, sir—not now. He was with her; but he went away—and he hasn't come back yet."

I put a last conclusive question.

"Is her husband an Englishman?" I inquired.

"Mother says he's a foreigner," the boy answered.

I turned away to hide my agitation. Even the child might have noticed it!

Passing under the name of "Mrs. Brand"—poor, so poor that she was obliged to pawn her ring—left, by a man who was a foreigner, alone with her little girl—was I on the trace of her at that moment? Was this lost child destined to be the innocent means of leading me back to the woman I loved, in her direst need of sympathy and help? The more I thought of it, the more strongly the idea of returning with the boy to the house in which his mother's lodger lived fastened itself on my mind. The clock struck the quarter past eleven. If my anticipations ended in misleading me, I had still three-quarters of an hour to spare before the month reached its end.

"Where do you live?" I asked.

The boy mentioned a street, the name of which I then heard for the first time. All he could say, when I asked for further particulars, was that he lived close by the river—in which direction, he was too confused and too frightened to be able to tell me.

While we were still trying to understand each other, a cab passed slowly at some little distance. I hailed the man, and mentioned the name of the street to him. He knew it perfectly well. The street was rather more than a mile away from us, in an easterly direction. He undertook to drive me there and to bring me back again to Saint Paul's (if necessary), in less than twenty minutes. I opened the door of the cab, and told my little friend to get in. The boy hesitated.

"Are we going to the chemist's, if you please, sir?" he asked.

"No. You are going home first, with me."

The boy began to cry again.

"Mother will beat me, sir, if I go back without the medicine."

"I will take care that your mother doesn't beat you. I am a doctor myself; and I want to see the lady before we get the medicine."

The announcement of my profession appeared to inspire the boy with a certain confidence. But he still showed no disposition to accompany me to his mother's house.

"Do you mean to charge the lady anything?" he asked. "The money I've

490

got on the ring isn't much. Mother won't like having it taken out of her rent."

"I won't charge the lady a farthing," I answered.

The boy instantly got into the cab. "All right," he said, "as long as mother gets her money."

Alas for the poor! The child's education in the sordid anxieties of life was completed already at ten years old!

We drove away.

CHAPTER XXV. I KEEP MY APPOINTMENT.

THE poverty-stricken aspect of the street when we entered it, the dirty and dilapidated condition of the house when we drew up at the door, would have warned most men, in my position, to prepare themselves for a distressing discovery when they were admitted to the interior of the dwelling. The first impression which the place produced on my mind suggested, on the contrary, that the boy's answers to my questions had led me astray. It was simply impossible to associate Mrs. Van Brandt (as I remembered her) with the spectacle of such squalid poverty as I now beheld. I rang the door-bell, feeling persuaded beforehand that my inquiries would lead to no useful result.

As I lifted my hand to the bell, my little companion's dread of a beating revived in full force. He hid himself behind me; and when I asked what he was about, he answered, confidentially: "Please stand between us, sir, when mother opens the door!"

A tall and truculent woman answered the bell. No introduction was necessary. Holding a cane in her hand, she stood self-proclaimed as my small friend's mother.

"I thought it was that vagabond of a boy of mine," she explained, as an apology for the exhibition of the cane. "He has been gone on an errand more than two hours. What did you please to want, sir?"

I interceded for the unfortunate boy before I entered on my own business.

"I must beg you to forgive your son this time," I said. "I found him lost in the streets; and I have brought him home."

The woman's astonishment when she heard what I had done, and discovered her son behind me, literally struck her dumb. The language of the eye, superseding on this occasion the language of the tongue, plainly revealed the impression that I had produced on her: "You bring my lost brat home in a cab! Mr. Stranger, you are mad."

"I hear that you have a lady named Brand lodging in the house," I went on. "I dare say I am mistaken in supposing her to be a lady of the same name whom I know. But I should like to make sure whether I am right or wrong. Is it too late to disturb your lodger to-night?"

The woman recovered the use of her tongue.

"My lodger is up and waiting for that little fool, who doesn't know his way about London yet!" She emphasized those words by shaking her brawny fist at her son—who instantly returned to his place of refuge behind the tail of my coat. "Have you got the money?" inquired the terrible person, shouting at her hidden offspring over my shoulder. "Or have you lost that as well as your own stupid little self?"

The boy showed himself again, and put the money into his mother's knotty hand. She counted it, with eyes which satisfied themselves fiercely that each coin was of genuine silver—and then became partially pacified.

"Go along upstairs," she growled, addressing her son; "and don't keep the lady waiting any longer. They're half starved, she and her child," the woman proceeded, turning to me. "The food my boy has got for them in his basket will be the first food the mother has tasted today. She's pawned everything by this time; and what she's to do unless you help her is more than I can say. The doctor does what he can; but he told me today, if she wasn't better nourished, it was no use sending for him. Follow the boy; and see for yourself if it's the lady you know."

I listened to the woman, still feeling persuaded that I had acted under a delusion in going to her house. How was it possible to associate the charming object of my heart's worship with the miserable story of destitution which I had just heard? I stopped the boy on the first landing, and told him to announce me simply as a doctor, who had been informed of Mrs. Brand's illness, and who had called to see her.

We ascended a second flight of stairs, and a third. Arrived now at the top of the house, the boy knocked at the door that was nearest to us on the landing. No audible voice replied. He opened the door without ceremony, and went in. I waited outside to hear what was said. The door was left ajar. If the voice of "Mrs. Brand" was (as I believed it would prove to be) the voice of a stranger, I resolved to offer her delicately such help as lay within my power, and to return forthwith to my post under "the shadow of Saint Paul's."

The first voice that spoke to the boy was the voice of a child.

"I'm so hungry, Jemmy—I'm so hungry!"

"All right, missy—I've got you something to eat."

"Be quick, Jemmy! Be quick!"

There was a momentary pause; and then I heard the boy's voice once more.

"There's a slice of bread-and-butter, missy. You must wait for your egg till I can boil it. Don't you eat too fast, or you'll choke yourself. What's the matter with your mamma? Are you asleep, ma'am?"

I could barely hear the answering voice—it was so faint; and it uttered but one word: "No!"

The boy spoke again.

"Cheer up, missus. There's a doctor outside waiting to see you."

This time there was no audible reply. The boy showed himself to me at the door. "Please to come in, sir. I can't make anything of her."

It would have been misplaced delicacy to have hesitated any longer to enter the room. I went in.

There, at the opposite end of a miserably furnished bed-chamber, lying back feebly in a tattered old arm-chair, was one more among the thousands of forlorn creatures, starving that night in the great city. A white handkerchief was laid over her face as if to screen it from the flame of the fire hard by. She lifted the handkerchief, startled by the sound of my footsteps as I entered the room. I looked at her, and saw in the white, wan, death-like face the face of the woman I loved!

For a moment the horror of the discovery turned me faint and giddy. In another instant I was kneeling by her chair. My arm was round her—her head lay on my shoulder. She was past speaking, past crying out: she trembled silently, and that was all. I said nothing. No words passed my lips, no tears came to my relief. I held her to me; and she let me hold her. The child, devouring its bread-and-butter at a little round table, stared at us. The boy, on his knees before the grate, mending the fire, stared at us. And the slow minutes lagged on; and the buzzing of a fly in a corner was the only sound in the room.

The instincts of the profession to which I had been trained, rather than any active sense of the horror of the situation in which I was placed, roused me at last. She was starving! I saw it in the deadly color of her skin; I felt it in the faint, quick flutter of her pulse. I called the boy to me, and sent him to the nearest public-house for wine and biscuits. "Be quick about it," I said; "and you shall have more money for yourself than ever you had in your life!" The boy looked at me, spit on the coins in his hand, said, "That's for luck!" and ran out of the room as never boy ran yet.

I turned to speak my first words of comfort to the mother. The cry of the child stopped me.

"I'm so hungry! I'm so hungry!"

I set more food before the famished child and kissed her. She looked up at me with wondering eyes.

"Are you a new papa?" the little creature asked. "My other papa never kisses me."

I looked at the mother. Her eyes were closed; the tears flowed slowly over her worn, white cheeks. I took her frail hand in mine. "Happier days are coming," I said; "you are my care now." There was no answer. She still trembled silently, and that was all.

In less than five minutes the boy returned, and earned his promised reward. He sat on the floor by the fire counting his treasure, the one happy creature in the room. I soaked some crumbled morsels of biscuit in the wine, and, little by little, I revived her failing strength by nourishment administered at intervals in that cautious form. After a while she raised her head, and looked at me with wondering eyes that were pitiably like the eyes of her child. A faint, delicate flush began to show itself in her face. She spoke to me, for the first time, in whispering tones that I could just hear as I sat close at her side.

"How did you find me? Who showed you the way to this place?"

She paused; painfully recalling the memory of something that was slow to come back. Her color deepened; she found the lost remembrance, and looked at me with a timid curiosity. "What brought you here?" she asked. "Was it my dream?"

"Wait, dearest, till you are stronger, and I will tell you all."

I lifted her gently, and laid her on the wretched bed. The child followed us, and climbing to the bedstead with my help, nestled at her mother's side. I sent the boy away to tell the mistress of the house that I should remain with my patient, watching her progress toward recovery, through the night. He went out, jingling his money joyfully in his pocket. We three were left together.

As the long hours followed each other, she fell at intervals into a broken sleep; waking with a start, and looking at me wildly as if I had been a stranger at her bedside. Toward morning the nourishment which I still carefully administered wrought its healthful change in her pulse, and composed her to quieter slumbers. When the sun rose she was sleeping as peacefully as the child at her side. I was able to leave her, until my return later in the day, under the care of the woman of the house. The magic of money transformed this termagant and terrible person into a docile and attentive nurse—so eager to follow my instructions exactly that she begged me to commit them to writing before I went away. For a moment I still lingered alone at the bedside of the sleeping woman, and satisfied myself for the hundredth time that her life was safe, before I left her. It was the sweetest of all rewards to feel sure of this—to touch her cool forehead lightly with my lips—to look, and look again, at the poor worn face, always dear, always beautiful, to my eyes. change as it might. I closed the door softly and went out in the bright morning, a happy man again. So close together rise the springs of joy and sorrow in human life! So near in our heart, as in our heaven, is the brightest sunshine to the blackest cloud!

CHAPTER XXVI. CONVERSATION WITH MY MOTHER.

I REACHED my own house in time to snatch two or three hours of repose, before I paid my customary morning visit to my mother in her own room. I observed, in her reception of me on this occasion, certain peculiarities of look and manner which were far from being familiar in my experience of her.

When our eyes first met, she regarded me with a wistful, questioning look, as if she were troubled by some doubt which she shrunk from expressing in words. And when I inquired after her health, as usual, she surprised me by answering as impatiently as if she resented my having mentioned the subject. For a moment, I was inclined to think these changes signified that she had discovered my absence from home during the night, and that she had some suspicion of the true cause of it. But she never alluded, even in the most distant manner, to Mrs. Van Brandt; and not a word dropped from her lips which implied, directly or indirectly, that I had pained or disappointed her. I could only conclude that she had something important to say in relation to herself or to me—and that for reasons of her own she unwillingly abstained from giving expression to it at that time.

Reverting to our ordinary topics of conversation, we touched on the subject (always interesting to my mother) of my visit to Shetland. Speaking of this, we naturally spoke also of Miss Dunross. Here, again, when I least expected it, there was another surprise in store for me.

"You were talking the other day," said my mother, "of the green flag which poor Dermody's daughter worked for you, when you were both children. Have you really kept it all this time?"

"Yes."

"Where have you left it? In Scotland?"

"I have brought it with me to London."

"Why?"

"I promised Miss Dunross to take the green flag with me, wherever I might go."

My mother smiled.

"Is it possible, George, that you think about this as the young lady in Shetland thinks? After all the years that have passed, you believe in the green flag being the means of bringing Mary Dermody and yourself together again?"

"Certainly not! I am only humoring one of the fancies of poor Miss Dunross. Could I refuse to grant her trifling request, after all I owed to her kindness?"

The smile left my mother's face. She looked at me attentively.

"Miss Dunross seems to have produced a very favorable impression on you," she said.

"I own it. I feel deeply interested in her."

"If she had not been an incurable invalid, George, I too might have become interested in Miss Dunross—perhaps in the character of my daughter-in-law?"

"It is useless, mother, to speculate on what might have happened. The sad reality is enough."

My mother paused a little before she put her next question to me.

"Did Miss Dunross always keep her veil drawn in your presence, when there happened to be light in the room?"

"Always."

"She never even let you catch a momentary glance at her face?"

"Never."

"And the only reason she gave you was that the light caused her a painful sensation if it fell on her uncovered skin?"

"You say that, mother, as if you doubt whether Miss Dunross told me the truth."

"No, George. I only doubt whether she told you all the truth."

"What do you mean?"

"Don't be offended, my dear. I believe Miss Dunross has some more serious reason for keeping her face hidden than the reason that she gave you."

I was silent. The suspicion which those words implied had never occurred to my mind. I had read in medical books of cases of morbid nervous sensitiveness exactly similar to the case of Miss Dunross, as described by herself—and that had been enough for me. Now that my mother's idea had found its way from her mind to mine, the impression produced on me was painful in the last degree. Horrible imaginings of deformity possessed my brain, and profaned all that was purest and dearest in my recollections of Miss Dunross. It was useless to change the subject—the evil influence that was on me was too potent to be charmed away by talk. Making the best excuse that I could think of for leaving my mother's room, I hurried away to seek a refuge from myself, where alone I could hope to find it, in the presence of Mrs. Van Brandt.

CHAPTER XXVII. CONVERSATION WITH MRS. VAN BRANDT.

THE landlady was taking the air at her own door when I reached the house. Her reply to my inquiries justified my most hopeful anticipations. The poor lodger looked already "like another woman"; and the child was at that moment posted on the stairs, watching for the return of her "new papa."

"There's one thing I should wish to say to you, sir, before you go upstairs," the woman went on. "Don't trust the lady with more money at a time than the money that is wanted for the day's housekeeping. If she has any to spare, it's as likely as not to be wasted on her good-for-nothing husband."

Absorbed in the higher and dearer interests that filled my mind, I had thus far forgotten the very existence of Mr. Van Brandt.

"Where is he?" I asked.

"Where he ought to be," was the answer. "In prison for debt."

In those days a man imprisoned for debt was not infrequently a man imprisoned for life. There was little fear of my visit being shortened by the appearance on the scene of Mr. Van Brandt.

Ascending the stairs, I found the child waiting for me on the upper landing, with a ragged doll in her arms. I had bought a cake for her on my way to the house. She forthwith turned over the doll to my care, and, trotting before me into the room with her cake in her arms, announced my arrival in these words:

"Mamma, I like this papa better than the other. You like him better, too."

The mother's wasted face reddened for a moment, then turned pale again, as she held out her hand to me. I looked at her anxiously, and discerned the welcome signs of recovery, clearly revealed. Her grand gray eyes rested on me again with a glimmer of their old light. The hand that had lain so cold in mine on the past night had life and warmth in it now.

"Should I have died before the morning if you had not come here?" she asked, softly. "Have you saved my life for the second time? I can well believe it."

Before I was aware of her, she bent her head over my hand, and touched it tenderly with her lips. "I am not an ungrateful woman," she murmured— "and yet I don't know how to thank you."

The child looked up quickly from her cake. "Why don't you kiss him?" the quaint little creature asked, with a broad stare of astonishment.

Her head sunk on her breast. She sighed bitterly.

"No more of Me!" she said, suddenly recovering her composure, and suddenly forcing herself to look at me again. "Tell me what happy chance brought you here last night?"

"The same chance," I answered, "which took me to Saint Anthony's Well."

She raised herself eagerly in the chair.

"You have seen me again—as you saw me in the summer-house by the waterfall!" she exclaimed. "Was it in Scotland once more?"

"No. Further away than Scotland—as far away as Shetland."

"Tell me about it! Pray, pray tell me about it!"

I related what had happened as exactly as I could, consistently with maintaining the strictest reserve on one point. Concealing from her the very existence of Miss Dunross, I left her to suppose that the master of the house was the one person whom I had found to receive me during my sojourn under Mr. Dunross's roof.

"That is strange!" she exclaimed, after she had heard me attentively to the end.

"What is strange?" I asked.

She hesitated, searching my face earnestly with her large grave eyes.

"I hardly like speaking of it," she said. "And yet I ought to have no concealments in such a matter from you. I understand everything that you have told me—with one exception. It seems strange to me that you should only have had one old man for your companion while you were at the house in Shetland."

"What other companion did you expect to hear of?" I inquired.

"I expected," she answered, "to hear of a lady in the house."

I cannot positively say that the reply took me by surprise: it forced me to reflect before I spoke again. I knew, by my past experience, that she must have seen me, in my absence from her, while I was spiritually present to her mind in a trance or dream. Had she also seen the daily companion of my life in Shetland—Miss Dunross?

I put the question in a form which left me free to decide whether I should take her unreservedly into my confidence or not.

"Am I right," I began, "in supposing that you dreamed of me in Shetland, as you once before dreamed of me while I was at my house in Perthshire?"

"Yes," she answered. "It was at the close of evening, this time. I fell asleep, or became insensible—I cannot say which. And I saw you again, in a vision or a dream."

"Where did you see me?"

"I first saw you on the bridge over the Scotch river—just as I met you on the evening when you saved my life. After a while the stream and the landscape about it faded, and you faded with them, into darkness. I waited a little, and the darkness melted away slowly. I stood, as it seemed to me, in a circle of starry lights; fronting a window, with a lake behind me, and before me a darkened room. And I looked into the room, and the starry light showed you to me again."

"When did this happen? Do you remember the date?"

"I remember that it was at the beginning of the month. The misfortunes which have since brought me so low had not then fallen on me; and yet, as I stood looking at you, I had the strangest prevision of calamity that was to come. I felt the same absolute reliance on your power to help me that I felt when I first dreamed of you in Scotland. And I did the same familiar things. I laid my hand on your bosom. I said to you: 'Remember me. Come to me.' I even wrote—"

She stopped, shuddering as if a sudden fear had laid its hold on her. Seeing this, and dreading the effect of any violent agitation, I hastened to suggest that we should say no more, for that day, on the subject of her dream.

"No," she answered, firmly. "There is nothing to be gained by giving me time. My dream has left one horrible remembrance on my mind. As long as I live, I believe I shall tremble when I think of what I saw near you in that darkened room."

She stopped again. Was she approaching the subject of the shrouded figure, with the black veil over its head? Was she about to describe her first discovery, in the dream, of Miss Dunross?

"Tell me one thing first," she resumed. "Have I been right in what I have said to you, so far? Is it true that you were in a darkened room when you saw me?"

"Quite true."

"Was the date the beginning of the month? and was the hour the close of evening?"

"Yes."

"Were you alone in the room? Answer me truly!"

"I was not alone."

"Was the master of the house with you? or had you some other companion?"

It would have been worse than useless (after what I had now heard) to attempt to deceive her.

"I had another companion," I answered. "The person in the room with me was a woman."

Her face showed, as I spoke, that she was again shaken by the terrifying recollection to which she had just alluded. I had, by this time, some difficulty myself in preserving my composure. Still, I was determined not to let a word escape me which could operate as a suggestion on the mind of my companion.

"Have you any other question to ask me?" was all I said.

"One more," she answered. "Was there anything unusual in the dress of your companion?"

"Yes. She wore a long black veil, which hung over her head and face, and dropped to below her waist."

Mrs. Van Brandt leaned back in her chair, and covered her eyes with her hands.

"I understand your motive for concealing from me the presence of that miserable woman in the house," she said. "It is good and kind, like all your motives; but it is useless. While I lay in the trance I saw everything exactly as it was in the reality; and I, too, saw that frightful face!"

Those words literally electrified me.

My conversation of that morning with my mother instantly recurred to my memory. I started to my feet.

"Good God!" I exclaimed, "what do you mean?"

"Don't you understand yet?" she asked in amazement on her side. "Must I speak more plainly still? When you saw the apparition of me, did you see me write?"

"Yes. On a letter that the lady was writing for me. I saw the words afterward; the words that brought me to you last night: 'At the month's end, In the shadow of Saint Paul's.'"

"How did I appear to write on the unfinished letter?"

"You lifted the writing-case, on which the letter and the pen lay, off the lady's lap; and, while you wrote, you rested the case on her shoulder."

"Did you notice if the lifting of the case produced any effect on her?"

"I saw no effect produced," I answered. "She remained immovable in her chair."

"I saw it differently in my dream. She raised her hand—not the hand that was nearest to you, but nearest to me. As I lifted the writing-case, she lifted her hand, and parted the folds of the veil from off her face—I suppose to see more clearly. It was only for a moment; and in that moment I saw what the veil hid. Don't let us speak of it! You must have shuddered at that frightful sight in the reality, as I shuddered at it in the dream. You must have asked yourself, as I did: 'Is there nobody to poison the terrible creature, and hide her mercifully in the grave?'"

At those words, she abruptly checked herself. I could say nothing—my face spoke for me. She saw it, and guessed the truth.

"Good heavens!" she cried, "you have not seen her! She must have kept her face hidden from you behind the veil! Oh, why, why did you cheat me into talking of it! I will never speak of it again. See, we are frightening the child! Come here, darling; there is nothing to be afraid of. Come, and bring your cake with you. You shall be a great lady, giving a grand dinner; and we will be two friends whom you have invited to dine with you; and the doll shall be the little girl who comes in after dinner, and has fruit at dessert!" So she ran on, trying vainly to forget the shock that she had inflicted on me in talking nursery nonsense to the child.

Recovering my composure in some degree, I did my best to second the effort that she had made. My quieter thoughts suggested that she might well be self-deceived in believing the horrible spectacle presented to her in the vision to be an actual reflection of the truth. In common justice toward Miss Dunross I ought surely not to accept the conviction of her deformity on no better evidence than the evidence of a dream? Reasonable as it undoubtedly was, this view left certain doubts still lingering in my mind. The child's instinct soon discovered that her mother and I were playfellows who felt no genuine enjoyment of the game. She dismissed her make-believe guests without ceremony, and went back with her doll to the favorite play-ground on which I had met her—the landing outside the door. No persuasion on her mother's part or on mine succeeded in luring her back to us. We were left together, to face each other as best we might—with the forbidden subject of Miss Dunross between us.

CHAPTER XXVIII. LOVE AND MONEY.

FEELING the embarrassment of the moment most painfully on her side, Mrs. Van Brandt spoke first.

"You have said nothing to me about yourself," she began. "Is your life a happier one than it was when we last met?"

"I cannot honestly say that it is," I answered.

"Is there any prospect of your being married?"

"My prospect of being married still rests with you."

"Don't say that!" she exclaimed, with an entreating look at me. "Don't spoil my pleasure in seeing you again by speaking of what can never be! Have you still to be told how it is that you find me here alone with my child?"

I forced myself to mention Van Brandt's name, rather than hear it pass her lips.

"I have been told that Mr. Van Brandt is in prison for debt," I said. "And I saw for myself last night that he had left you helpless."

"He left me the little money he had with him when he was arrested," she rejoined, sadly. "His cruel creditors are more to blame than he is for the poverty that has fallen on us."

Even this negative defense of Van Brandt stung me to the quick.

"I ought to have spoken more guardedly of him," I said, bitterly. "I ought to have remembered that a woman can forgive almost any wrong that a man can inflict on her—when he is the man whom she loves."

She put her hand on my mouth, and stopped me before I could say any more.

"How can you speak so cruelly to me?" she asked. "You know—to my shame I confessed it to you the last time we met—you know that my heart, in secret, is all yours. What 'wrong' are you talking of? Is it the wrong I suffered when Van Brandt married me, with a wife living at the time (and living still)? Do you think I can ever forget the great misfortune of my life—the misfortune that has made me unworthy of you? It is no fault of mine, God knows; but it is not the less true that I am not married, and that the little darling who is playing out there with her doll is my child. And you talk of my being your wife—knowing that!"

"The child accepts me as her second father," I said. "It would be better and happier for us both if you had as little pride as the child."

"Pride?" she repeated. "In such a position as mine? A helpless woman, with a mock-husband in prison for debt! Say that I have not fallen quite so low yet as to forget what is due to you, and you will pay me a compliment that will be nearer to the truth. Am I to marry you for my food and shelter? Am I to marry you, because there is no lawful tie that binds me to the father of my child? Cruelly as he has behaved, he has still that claim upon me. Bad as he is, he has not forsaken me; he has been forced away. My only friend, is it possible that you think me ungrateful enough to consent to be your wife? The woman (in my situation) must be heartless indeed who could destroy your place in the estimation of the world and the regard of your friends! The wretchedest creature that walks the streets would shrink from treating you in that way. Oh, what are men made of? How can you—how can you speak of it!"

I yielded—and spoke of it no more. Every word she uttered only increased my admiration of the noble creature whom I had loved, and lost. What refuge was now left to me? But one refuge; I could still offer to her the sacrifice of myself. Bitterly as I hated the man who had parted us, I loved her dearly enough to be even capable of helping him for her sake. Hopeless infatuation! I don't deny it; I don't excuse it—hopeless infatuation!

"You have forgiven me," I said. "Let me deserve to be forgiven. It is something to be your only friend. You must have plans for the future; tell me unreservedly how I can help you."

"Complete the good work that you have begun," she answered, gratefully.

"Help me back to health. Make me strong enough to submit to a doctor's estimate of my chances of living for some years yet."

"A doctor's estimate of your chances of living?" I repeated. "What do you mean?"

"I hardly know how to tell you," she said, "without speaking again of Mr. Van Brandt."

"Does speaking of him again mean speaking of his debts?" I asked. "Why need you hesitate? You know that there is nothing I will not do to relieve your anxieties."

She looked at me for a moment, in silent distress.

"Oh! do you think I would let you give your money to Van Brandt?" she asked, as soon as she could speak. "I, who owe everything to your devotion to me? Never! Let me tell you the plain truth. There is a serious necessity for his getting out of prison. He must pay his creditors; and he has found out a way of doing it—with my help."

"Your help?" I exclaimed.

"Yes. This is his position, in two words: A little while since, he obtained an excellent offer of employment abroad, from a rich relative of his, and he had made all his arrangements to accept it. Unhappily, he returned to tell me of his good fortune, and the same day he was arrested for debt. His relative has offered to keep the situation open for a certain time, and the time has not yet expired. If he can pay a dividend to his creditors, they will give him his freedom; and he believes he can raise the money if I consent to insure my life."

To insure her life! The snare that had been set for her was plainly revealed in those four words.

In the eye of the law she was, of course, a single woman: she was of age; she was, to all intents and purposes, her own mistress. What was there to prevent her from insuring her life, if she pleased, and from so disposing of the insurance as to give Van Brandt a direct interest in her death? Knowing what I knew of him—believing him, as I did, to be capable of any atrocity—I trembled at the bare idea of what might have happened if I had failed to find my way back to her until a later date. Thanks to the happy accident of my position, the one certain way of protecting her lay easily within my reach. I could offer to lend the scoundrel the money that he wanted at an hour's notice, and he was the man to accept my proposal quite as easily as I could make it.

"You don't seem to approve of our idea," she said, noticing, in evident perplexity, the effect which she had produced on me. "I am very unfortunate; I seem to have innocently disturbed and annoyed you for the second time."

"You are quite mistaken," I replied. "I am only doubting whether your plan for relieving Mr. Van Brandt of his embarrassments is quite so simple as you suppose. Are you aware of the delays that are likely to take place before it will be possible to borrow money on your policy of insurance?"

"I know nothing about it," she said, sadly.

"Will you let me ask the advice of my lawyers? They are trustworthy and experienced men, and I am sure they can be of use to you."

Cautiously as I had expressed myself, her delicacy took the alarm.

"Promise that you won't ask me to borrow money of you for Mr. Van Brandt," she rejoined, "and I will accept your help gratefully."

I could honestly promise that. My one chance of saving her lay in keeping from her knowledge the course that I had now determined to pursue. I rose to go, while my resolution still sustained me. The sooner I made my inquiries (I reminded her) the more speedily our present doubts and difficulties would be resolved.

She rose, as I rose—with the tears in her eyes, and the blush on her cheeks.

"Kiss me," she whispered, "before you go! And don't mind my crying. I am quite happy now. It is only your goodness that overpowers me."

I pressed her to my heart, with the unacknowledged tenderness of a

511

parting embrace. It was impossible to disguise the position in which I had now placed myself. I had, so to speak, pronounced my own sentence of banishment. When my interference had restored my unworthy rival to his freedom, could I submit to the degrading necessity of seeing her in his presence, of speaking to her under his eyes? That sacrifice of myself was beyond me—and I knew it. "For the last time!" I thought, as I held her to me for a moment longer—"for the last time!"

The child ran to meet me with open arms when I stepped out on the landing. My manhood had sustained me through the parting with the mother. It was only when the child's round, innocent little face laid itself lovingly against mine that my fortitude gave way. I was past speaking; I put her down gently in silence, and waited on the lower flight of stairs until I was fit to face the world outside.

CHAPTER XXIX. OUR DESTINIES PART US.

DESCENDING to the ground-floor of the house, I sent to request a moment's interview with the landlady. I had yet to learn in which of the London prisons Van Brandt was confined; and she was the only person to whom I could venture to address the question.

Having answered my inquiries, the woman put her own sordid construction on my motive for visiting the prisoner.

"Has the money you left upstairs gone into his greedy pockets already?" she asked. "If I was as rich as you are, I should let it go. In your place, I wouldn't touch him with a pair of tongs!"

The woman's coarse warning actually proved useful to me; it started a new idea in my mind! Before she spoke, I had been too dull or too preoccupied to see that it was quite needless to degrade myself by personally communicating with Van Brandt in his prison. It only now occurred to me that my legal advisers were, as a matter of course, the proper persons to represent me in the matter—with this additional advantage, that they could keep my share in the transaction a secret even from Van Brandt himself.

I drove at once to the office of my lawyers. The senior partner—the tried friend and adviser of our family—received me.

My instructions, naturally enough, astonished him. He was immediately to satisfy the prisoner's creditors, on my behalf, without mentioning my name to any one. And he was gravely to accept as security for repayment—Mr. Van Brandt's note of hand!

"I thought I was well acquainted with the various methods by which a gentleman can throw away his money," the senior partner remarked. "I congratulate you, Mr. Germaine, on having discovered an entirely new way of effectually emptying your purse. Founding a newspaper, taking a theater, keeping race-horses, gambling at Monaco, are highly efficient as modes of losing money. But they all yield, sir, to paying the debts of Mr. Van Brandt!"

I left him, and went home.

The servant who opened the door had a message for me from my mother. She wished to see me as soon as I was at leisure to speak to her.

I presented myself at once in my mother's sitting-room.

"Well, George?" she said, without a word to prepare me for what was coming. "How have you left Mrs. Van Brandt?"

I was completely thrown off my guard.

"Who has told you that I have seen Mrs. Van Brandt?" I asked.

"My dear, your face has told me. Don't I know by this time how you look and how you speak when Mrs. Van Brandt is in your mind. Sit down by me. I have something to say to you which I wanted to say this morning; but, I hardly know why, my heart failed me. I am bolder now, and I can say it. My son, you still love Mrs. Van Brandt. You have my permission to marry her."

Those were the words! Hardly an hour had elapsed since Mrs. Van Brandt's own lips had told me that our union was impossible. Not even half an hour had passed since I had given the directions which would restore to liberty the man who was the one obstacle to my marriage. And this was the time that my mother had innocently chosen for consenting to receive as her daughter-in-law Mrs. Van Brandt!

"I see that I surprise you," she resumed. "Let me explain my motive as plainly as I can. I should not be speaking the truth, George, if I told you that I have ceased to feel the serious objections that there are to your marrying this lady. The only difference in my way of thinking is, that I am now willing to set my objections aside, out of regard for your happiness. I am an old woman, my dear. In the course of nature, I cannot hope to be with you much longer. When I am gone, who will be left to care for you and love you, in the place of your mother? No one will be left, unless you marry Mrs. Van Brandt. Your happiness is my first consideration, and the woman you love (sadly as she has been led astray) is a woman worthy of a better fate. Marry her."

I could not trust myself to speak. I could only kneel at my mother's feet, and hide my face on her knees, as if I had been a boy again.

"Think of it, George," she said. "And come back to me when you are composed enough to speak as quietly of the future as I do."

She lifted my head and kissed me. As I rose to leave her, I saw something in the dear old eyes that met mine so tenderly, which struck a sudden fear through me, keen and cutting, like a stroke from a knife.

The moment I had closed the door, I went downstairs to the porter in the hall.

"Has my mother left the house," I asked, "while I have been away?"

"No, sir."

"Have any visitors called?"

"One visitor has called, sir."

"Do you know who it was?"

The porter mentioned the name of a celebrated physician—a man at the head of his profession in those days. I instantly took my hat and went to his house.

He had just returned from his round of visits. My card was taken to him, and was followed at once by my admission to his consulting-room.

"You have seen my mother," I said. "Is she seriously ill? and have you not concealed it from her? For God's sake, tell me the truth; I can bear it."

The great man took me kindly by the hand.

"Your mother stands in no need of any warning; she is herself aware of the critical state of her health," he said. "She sent for me to confirm her own conviction. I could not conceal from her—I must not conceal from you—that the vital energies are sinking. She may live for some months longer in a milder air than the air of London. That is all I can say. At her age, her days are numbered."

He gave me time to steady myself under the blow; and then he placed his vast experience, his matured and consummate knowledge, at my disposal. From his dictation, I committed to writing the necessary instructions for watching over the frail tenure of my mother's life.

"Let me give you one word of warning," he said, as we parted. "Your mother is especially desirous that you should know nothing of the precarious condition of her health. Her one anxiety is to see you happy. If she discovers your visit to me, I will not answer for the consequences. Make the best excuse you can think of for at once taking her away from London, and, whatever you may feel in secret, keep up an appearance of good spirits in her presence."

That evening I made my excuse. It was easily found. I had only to tell my poor mother of Mrs. Van Brandt's refusal to marry me, and there was an intelligible motive assigned for my proposing to leave London. The same night I wrote to inform Mrs. Van Brandt of the sad event which was the cause of my sudden departure, and to warn her that there no longer existed the slightest necessity for insuring her life. "My lawyers" (I wrote) "have undertaken to arrange Mr. Van Brandt's affairs immediately. In a few hours he will be at liberty to accept the situation that has been offered to him." The last lines of the letter assured her of my unalterable love, and entreated her to write to me before she left England.

This done, all was done. I was conscious, strange to say, of no acutely painful suffering at this saddest time of my life. There is a limit, morally as well as physically, to our capacity for endurance. I can only describe my sensations under the calamities that had now fallen on me in one way: I felt like a man whose mind had been stunned.

The next day my mother and I set forth on the first stage of our journey to the south coast of Devonshire.

CHAPTER XXX. THE PROSPECT DARKENS.

THREE days after my mother and I had established ourselves at Torquay, I received Mrs. Van Brandt's answer to my letter. After the opening sentences (informing me that Van Brandt had been set at liberty, under circumstances painfully suggestive to the writer of some unacknowledged sacrifice on my part), the letter proceeded in these terms:

"The new employment which Mr. Van Brandt is to undertake secures to us the comforts, if not the luxuries, of life. For the first time since my troubles began, I have the prospect before me of a peaceful existence, among a foreign people from whom all that is false in my position may be concealed—not for my sake, but for the sake of my child. To more than this, to the happiness which some women enjoy, I must not, I dare not, aspire.

"We leave England for the Continent early tomorrow morning. Shall I tell you in what part of Europe my new residence is to be?

"No! You might write to me again; and I might write back. The one poor return I can make to the good angel of my life is to help him to forget me. What right have I to cling to my usurped place in your regard? The time will come when you will give your heart to a woman who is worthier of it than I am. Let me drop out of your life—except as an occasional remembrance, when you sometimes think of the days that have gone forever.

"I shall not be without some consolation on my side, when I too look back at the past. I have been a better woman since I met with you. Live as long as I may, I shall always remember that.

"Yes! The influence that you have had over me has been from first to last an influence for good. Allowing that I have done wrong (in my position) to love you, and, worse even than that, to own it, still the love has been innocent, and the effort to control it has been an honest effort at least. But, apart from this, my heart tells me that I am the better for the sympathy which has united us. I may confess to you what I have never yet acknowledged—now that we are so widely parted, and so little likely to meet again—whenever I have given myself up unrestrainedly to my own better impulses, they have always seemed to lead me to you. Whenever my mind has been most truly at peace, and I have been able to pray with a pure and a penitent heart, I have felt as if there was some unseen tie that was drawing us nearer and nearer together. And, strange to say, this has always happened (just as my dreams of you have always come to me) when I have been separated from Van Brandt. At such times, thinking or dreaming, it has always appeared to me that I knew you far more familiarly than I know you when we meet face to face. Is there really such a thing, I wonder, as a former state of existence? And were we once constant companions in some other sphere, thousands of years since? These are idle guesses. Let it be enough for me to remember that I have been the better for knowing you—without inquiring how or why.

"Farewell, my beloved benefactor, my only friend! The child sends you a kiss; and the mother signs herself your grateful and affectionate

"M. VAN BRANDT."

When I first read those lines, they once more recalled to my memory—very strangely, as I then thought—the predictions of Dame Dermody in the days of my boyhood. Here were the foretold sympathies which were spiritually to unite me to Mary, realized by a stranger whom I had met by chance in the later years of my life!

Thinking in this direction, did I advance no further? Not a step further! Not a suspicion of the truth presented itself to my mind even yet.

Was my own dullness of apprehension to blame for this? Would another man in my position have discovered what I had failed to see?

I look back along the chain of events which runs through my narrative, and I ask myself, Where are the possibilities to be found (in my case, or in the case of any other man) of identifying the child who was Mary Dermody with the woman who was Mrs. Van Brandt? Was there anything left in our faces, when we met again by the Scotch river, to remind us of our younger selves? We had developed, in the interval, from boy and girl to man and woman:

no outward traces were discernible in us of the George and Mary of other days. Disguised from each other by our faces, we were also disguised by our names. Her mock-marriage had changed her surname. My step-father's will had changed mine. Her Christian name was the commonest of all names of women; and mine was almost as far from being remarkable among the names of men. Turning next to the various occasions on which we had met, had we seen enough of each other to drift into recognition on either side, in the ordinary course of talk? We had met but four times in all; once on the bridge, once again in Edinburgh, twice more in London. On each of these occasions, the absorbing anxieties and interests of the passing moment had filled her mind and mine, had inspired her words and mine. When had the events which had brought us together left us with leisure enough and tranquillity enough to look back idly through our lives, and calmly to compare the recollections of our youth? Never! From first to last, the course of events had borne us further and further away from any results that could have led even to a suspicion of the truth. She could only believe when she wrote to me on leaving England—and I could only believe when I read her letter—that we had first met at the river, and that our divergent destinies had ended in parting us forever.

Reading her farewell letter in later days by the light of my matured experience, I note how remarkably Dame Dermody's faith in the purity of the tie that united us as kindred spirits was justified by the result.

It was only when my unknown Mary was parted from Van Brandt—in other words, it was only when she was a pure spirit—that she felt my influence over her as a refining influence on her life, and that the apparition of her communicated with me in the visible and perfect likeness of herself. On my side, when was it that I dreamed of her (as in Scotland), or felt the mysterious warning of her presence in my waking moments (as in Shetland)? Always at the time when my heart opened most tenderly toward her and toward others—when my mind was most free from the bitter doubts, the self-seeking aspirations, which degrade the divinity within us. Then, and then only, my sympathy with her was the perfect sympathy which holds its fidelity unassailable by the chances and changes, the delusions and temptations, of mortal life.

I am writing prematurely of the time when the light came to me. My narrative must return to the time when I was still walking in darkness.

Absorbed in watching over the closing days of my mother's life, I found in the performance of this sacred duty my only consolation under the overthrow of my last hope of marriage with Mrs. Van Brandt. By slow degrees my mother felt the reviving influences of a quiet life and a soft, pure air. The improvement in her health could, as I but too well knew, be only an improvement for a time. Still, it was a relief to see her free from pain, and innocently happy in the presence of her son. Excepting those hours of the day and night which were dedicated to repose, I was never away from her. To this day I remember, with a tenderness which attaches to no other memories of mine, the books that I read to her, the sunny corner on the seashore where I sat with her, the games of cards that we played together, the little trivial gossip that amused her when she was strong enough for nothing else. These are my imperishable relics; these are the deeds of my life that I shall love best to look back on, when the all-infolding shadows of death are closing round me.

In the hours when I was alone, my thoughts—occupying themselves mostly among the persons and events of the past—wandered back, many and many a time, to Shetland and Miss Dunross.

My haunting doubt as to what the black veil had really hidden from me was no longer accompanied by a feeling of horror when it now recurred to my mind. The more vividly my later remembrances of Miss Dunross were associated with the idea of an unutterable bodily affliction, the higher the noble nature of the woman seemed to rise in my esteem. For the first time since I had left Shetland, the temptation now came to me to disregard the injunction which her father had laid on me at parting. When I thought again of the stolen kiss in the dead of night; when I recalled the appearance of the frail white hand, waving to me through the dark curtains its last farewell; and when there mingled with these memories the later remembrance of what my mother had suspected, and of what Mrs. Van Brandt had seen in her dream—the longing in me to find a means of assuring Miss Dunross that she still held her place apart in my memory and my heart was more than mortal fortitude could resist. I was pledged in honor not to return to Shetland, and not to write. How to communicate with her secretly, in some other way, was the constant question in my mind as the days went on. A hint to enlighten me was all that I wanted; and, as the irony of circumstances ordered it, my mother was the person who gave me the hint.

We still spoke, at intervals, of Mrs. Van Brandt. Watching me on those occasions when we were in the company of friends and acquaintances at Torquay, my mother plainly discerned that no other woman, whatever her attractions might be, could take the place in my heart of the woman whom I had lost. Seeing but one prospect of happiness for me, she steadily refused to abandon the idea of my marriage. When a woman has owned that she loves a man (so my mother used to express her opinion), it is that man's fault, no matter what the obstacles may be, if he fails to make her his wife. Reverting to this view in various ways, she pressed it on my consideration one day in these words:

"There is one drawback, George, to my happiness in being here with you. I am an obstacle in the way of your communicating with Mrs. Van Brandt."

"You forget," I said, "that she has left England without telling me where to find her."

"If you were free from the incumbrance of your mother, my dear, you would easily find her. Even as things are, you might surely write to her. Don't mistake my motives, George. If I had any hope of your forgetting her—if I saw you only moderately attracted by one or other of the charming women whom we know here—I should say, let us never speak again or think again of Mrs. Van Brandt. But, my dear, your heart is closed to every woman but one. Be happy in your own way, and let me see it before I die. The wretch to whom that poor creature is sacrificing her life will, sooner or later, ill-treat her or desert her and then she must turn to you. Don't let her think that you are resigned to the loss of her. The more resolutely you set her scruples at defiance, the more she will love you and admire you in secret. Women are like that. Send her a letter, and follow it with a little present. You talked of taking me to the studio of the young artist here who left his card the other day. I am told that he paints admirable portraits in miniatures. Why not send your portrait to Mrs. Van Brandt?"

Here was the idea of which I had been vainly in search! Quite superfluous as a method of pleading my cause with Mrs. Van Brandt, the portrait offered the best of all means of communicating with Miss Dunross, without absolutely violating the engagement to which her father had pledged me. In this way, without writing a word, without even sending a message, I might tell her how gratefully she was remembered; I might remind her of me tenderly in the bitterest moments of her sad and solitary life.

The same day I went to the artist privately. The sittings were afterward continued during the hours while my mother was resting in her room, until the portrait was completed. I caused it to be inclosed in a plain gold locket, with a chain attached; and I forwarded my gift, in the first instance, to the one person whom I could trust to assist me in arranging for the conveyance of it to its destination. This was the old friend (alluded to in these pages as "Sir James") who had taken me with him to Shetland in the Government yacht.

I had no reason, in writing the necessary explanations, to express myself to Sir James with any reserve. On the voyage back we had more than once spoken together confidentially of Miss Dunross. Sir James had heard her sad story from the resident medical man at Lerwick, who had been an old companion of his in their college days. Requesting him to confide my gift to this gentleman, I did not hesitate to acknowledge the doubt that oppressed me in relation to the mystery of the black veil. It was, of course, impossible to decide whether the doctor would be able to relieve that doubt. I could only venture to suggest that the question might be guardedly put, in making the customary inquiries after the health of Miss Dunross.

In those days of slow communication, I had to wait, not for days, but for weeks, before I could expect to receive Sir James's answer. His letter only reached me after an unusually long delay. For this, or for some other reason that I cannot divine, I felt so strongly the foreboding of bad news that I abstained from breaking the seal in my mother's presence. I waited until I could retire to my own room, and then I opened the letter. My presentiment had not deceived me.

Sir James's reply contained these words only: "The letter inclosed tells its own sad story, without help from me. I cannot grieve for her; but I can feel sorry for you."

The letter thus described was addressed to Sir James by the doctor at Lerwick. I copy it (without comment) in these words:

"The late stormy weather has delayed the vessel by means of which we communicate with the mainland. I have only received your letter to-day. With it, there has arrived a little box, containing a gold locket and chain; being the present which you ask me to convey privately to Miss Dunross, from a friend of yours whose name you are not at liberty to mention.

"In transmitting these instructions, you have innocently placed me in a position of extreme difficulty.

"The poor lady for whom the gift is intended is near the end of her life—a life of such complicated and terrible suffering that death comes, in her case, literally as a mercy and a deliverance. Under these melancholy circumstances, I am, I think, not to blame if I hesitate to give her the locket in secret; not knowing with what associations this keepsake may be connected, or of what serious agitation it may not possibly be the cause.

"In this state of doubt I have ventured on opening the locket, and my hesitation is naturally increased. I am quite ignorant of the remembrances which my unhappy patient may connect with the portrait. I don't know whether it will give her pleasure or pain to receive it, in her last moments on earth. I can only decide to take it with me, when I see her to-morrow, and to let circumstances determine whether I shall risk letting her see it or not. Our post to the South only leaves this place in three days' time. I can keep my letter open, and let you know the result.

"I have seen her; and I have just returned to my own house. My distress of mind is great. But I will do my best to write intelligibly and fully of what has happened.

"Her sinking energies, when I first saw her this morning, had rallied for the moment. The nurse informed me that she had slept during the early hours of the new day. Previously to this, there were symptoms of fever, accompanied by some slight delirium. The words that escaped her in this condition appear to have related mainly to an absent person whom she spoke of by the name of 'George.' Her one anxiety, I am told, was to see 'George' again before she died.

"Hearing this, it struck me as barely possible that the portrait in the locket might be the portrait of the absent person. I sent her nurse out of the room, and took her hand in mine. Trusting partly to her own admirable courage and strength of mind, and partly to the confidence which I knew she placed in me as an old friend and adviser, I adverted to the words which had fallen from her in the feverish state. And then I said, 'You know that any secret of yours is safe in my keeping. Tell me, do you expect to receive any little keepsake or memorial from 'George'?

"It was a risk to run. The black veil which she always wears was over her face. I had nothing to tell me of the effect which I was producing on her, except the changing temperature, or the partial movement, of her hand, as it lay in mine, just under the silk coverlet of the bed.

"She said nothing at first. Her hand turned suddenly from cold to hot, and closed with a quick pressure on mine. Her breathing became oppressed. When she spoke, it was with difficulty. She told me nothing; she only put a question:

"'Is he here?' she asked.

"I said, 'Nobody is here but myself.'

"'Is there a letter?'

"I said 'No.'

"She was silent for a while. Her hand turned cold; the grasp of her fingers loosened. She spoke again: 'Be quick, doctor! Whatever it is, give it to me, before I die.'

"I risked the experiment; I opened the locket, and put it into her hand.

"So far as I could discover, she refrained from looking at it at first. She said, 'Turn me in the bed, with my face to the wall.' I obeyed her. With her back turned toward me she lifted her veil; and then (as I suppose) she looked at the portrait. A long, low cry—not of sorrow or pain: a cry of rapture and delight—burst from her. I heard her kiss the portrait. Accustomed as I am in my profession to piteous sights and sounds, I never remember so completely losing my self-control as I lost it at that moment. I was obliged to turn away to the window.

"Hardly a minute can have passed before I was back again at the bedside. In that brief interval she had changed. Her voice had sunk again; it was so weak that I could only hear what she said by leaning over her and placing my ear close to her lips.

"'Put it round my neck,' she whispered.

"I clasped the chain of the locket round her neck. She tried to lift her hand to it, but her strength failed her.

"'Help me to hide it,' she said.

"I guided her hand. She hid the locket in her bosom, under the white dressing-gown which she wore that day. The oppression in her breathing increased. I raised her on the pillow. The pillow was not high enough. I rested her head on my shoulder, and partially opened her veil. She was able to speak once more, feeling a momentary relief.

"'Promise,' she said, 'that no stranger's hand shall touch me. Promise to bury me as I am now.'

"I gave her my promise.

"Her failing breath quickened. She was just able to articulate the next words:

"'Cover my face again.'

"I drew the veil over her face. She rested a while in silence. Suddenly the sound of her laboring respiration ceased. She started, and raised her head from my shoulder.

"'Are you in pain?' I asked.

"'I am in heaven!' she answered.

"Her head dropped back on my breast as she spoke. In that last outburst of joy her last breath had passed. The moment of her supreme happiness and the moment of her death were one. The mercy of God had found her at last.

"I return to my letter before the post goes out.

"I have taken the necessary measures for the performance of my promise. She will be buried with the portrait hidden in her bosom, and with the black veil over her face. No nobler creature ever breathed the breath of life. Tell the stranger who sent her his portrait that her last moments were joyful moments, through his remembrance of her as expressed by his gift.

"I observe a passage in your letter to which I have not yet replied. You ask me if there was any more serious reason for the persistent hiding of her face under the veil than the reason which she was accustomed to give to the persons about her. It is true that she suffered under a morbid sensitiveness to the action of light. It is also true that this was not the only result, or the worst result, of the malady that afflicted her. She had another reason for keeping her face hidden—a reason known to two persons only: to the doctor who lives in the village near her father's house, and to myself. We are both pledged never to divulge to any living creature what our eyes alone have seen. We have kept our terrible secret even from her father; and we shall carry it with us to our graves. I have no more to say on this melancholy subject to the person in whose interest you write. When he thinks of her now, let him think of the beauty which no bodily affliction can profane—the beauty of the freed spirit, eternally happy in its union with the angels of God.

"I may add, before I close my letter, that the poor old father will not be left in cheerless solitude at the lake house. He will pass the remainder of his days under my roof, with my good wife to take care of him, and my children to remind him of the brighter side of life."

So the letter ended. I put it away, and went out. The solitude of my room forewarned me unendurably of the coming solitude in my own life. My interests in this busy world were now narrowed to one object—to the care of my mother's failing health. Of the two women whose hearts had once beaten in loving sympathy with mine, one lay in her grave and the other was lost to me in a foreign land. On the drive by the sea I met my mother, in her little pony-chaise, moving slowly under the mild wintry sunshine. I dismissed the man who was in attendance on her, and walked by the side of the chaise, with the reins in my hand. We chatted quietly on trivial subjects. I closed my eyes to the dreary future that was before me, and tried, in the intervals of the heart-ache, to live resignedly in the passing hour.

CHAPTER XXXI. THE PHYSICIAN'S OPINION.

SIX months have elapsed. Summer-time has come again.

The last parting is over. Prolonged by my care, the days of my mother's life have come to their end. She has died in my arms: her last words have been spoken to me, her last look on earth has been mine. I am now, in the saddest and plainest meaning of the words, alone in the world.

The affliction which has befallen me has left certain duties to be performed that require my presence in London. My house is let; I am staying at a hotel. My friend, Sir James (also in London on business), has rooms near mine. We breakfast and dine together in my sitting-room. For the moment solitude is dreadful to me, and yet I cannot go into society; I shrink from persons who are mere acquaintances. At Sir James's suggestion, however, one visitor at the hotel has been asked to dine with us, who claims distinction as no ordinary guest. The physician who first warned me of the critical state of my mother's health is anxious to hear what I can tell him of her last moments. His time is too precious to be wasted in the earlier hours of the day, and he joins us at the dinner-table when his patients leave him free to visit his friends.

The dinner is nearly at an end. I have made the effort to preserve my self-control; and in few words have told the simple story of my mother's last peaceful days on earth. The conversation turns next on topics of little interest to me: my mind rests after the effort that it has made; my observation is left free to exert itself as usual.

Little by little, while the talk goes on, I observe something in the conduct of the celebrated physician which first puzzles me, and then arouses my suspicion of some motive for his presence which has not been acknowledged, and in which I am concerned.

Over and over again I discover that his eyes are resting on me with a furtive interest and attention which he seems anxious to conceal. Over and over again I notice that he contrives to divert the conversation from general topics, and to lure me into talking of myself; and, stranger still (unless I am quite mistaken), Sir James understands and encourages him. Under various pretenses I am questioned about what I have suffered in the past, and what plans of life I have formed for the future. Among other subjects of personal interest to me, the subject of supernatural appearances is introduced. I am asked if I believe in occult spiritual sympathies, and in ghostly apparitions of dead or distant persons. I am dexterously led into hinting that my views on this difficult and debatable question are in some degree influenced by experiences of my own. Hints, however, are not enough to satisfy the doctor's innocent curiosity; he tries to induce me to relate in detail what I have myself seen and felt. But by this time I am on my guard; I make excuses; I steadily abstain from taking my friend into my confidence. It is more and more plain to me that I am being made the subject of an experiment, in which Sir James and the physician are equally interested. Outwardly assuming to be guiltless of any suspicion of what is going on, I inwardly determine to discover the true motive for the doctor's presence that evening, and for the part that Sir James has taken in inviting him to be my guest.

Events favor my purpose soon after the dessert has been placed on the table.

The waiter enters the room with a letter for me, and announces that the bearer waits to know if there is any answer. I open the envelope, and find inside a few lines from my lawyers, announcing the completion of some formal matter of business. I at once seize the opportunity that is offered to me. Instead of sending a verbal message downstairs, I make my apologies, and use the letter as a pretext for leaving the room.

Dismissing the messenger who waits below, I return to the corridor in which my rooms are situated, and softly open the door of my bed-chamber. A second door communicates with the sitting-room, and has a ventilator in the upper part of it. I have only to stand under the ventilator, and every word of the conversation between Sir James and the physician reaches my ears.

"Then you think I am right?" are the first words I hear, in Sir James's voice.

"Quite right," the doctor answers.

"I have done my best to make him change his dull way of life," Sir James proceeds. "I have asked him to pay a visit to my house in Scotland; I have proposed traveling with him on the Continent; I have offered to take him with me on my next voyage in the yacht. He has but one answer—he simply says No to everything that I can suggest. You have heard from his own lips that he has no definite plans for the future. What is to become of him? What had we better do?"

"It is not easy to say," I hear the physician reply. "To speak plainly, the man's nervous system is seriously deranged. I noticed something strange in him when he first came to consult me about his mother's health. The mischief has not been caused entirely by the affliction of her death. In my belief, his mind has been—what shall I say?—unhinged, for some time past. He is a very reserved person. I suspect he has been oppressed by anxieties which he has kept secret from every one. At his age, the unacknowledged troubles of life are generally troubles caused by women. It is in his temperament to take the romantic view of love; and some matter-of-fact woman of the present day may have bitterly disappointed him. Whatever may be the cause, the effect is plain—his nerves have broken down, and his brain is necessarily affected by whatever affects his nerves. I have known men in his condition who have ended badly. He may drift into insane delusions, if his present course of life is not altered. Did you hear what he said when we talked about ghosts?"

"Sheer nonsense!" Sir James remarks.

"Sheer delusion would be the more correct form of expression," the doctor rejoins. "And other delusions may grow out of it at any moment."

"What is to be done?" persists Sir James. "I may really say for myself, doctor, that I feel a fatherly interest in the poor fellow. His mother was one of my oldest and dearest friends, and he has inherited many of her engaging and endearing qualities. I hope you don't think the case is bad enough to be a case for restraint?"

"Certainly not—as yet," answers the doctor. "So far there is no positive brain disease; and there is accordingly no sort of reason for placing him under restraint. It is essentially a difficult and a doubtful case. Have him privately looked after by a competent person, and thwart him in nothing, if you can possibly help it. The merest trifle may excite his suspicions; and if that happens, we lose all control over him."

"You don't think he suspects us already, do you, doctor?"

"I hope not. I saw him once or twice look at me very strangely; and he has certainly been a long time out of the room."

Hearing this, I wait to hear no more. I return to the sitting-room (by way of the corridor) and resume my place at the table.

The indignation that I feel—naturally enough, I think, under the circumstances—makes a good actor of me for once in my life. I invent the necessary excuse for my long absence, and take my part in the conversation, keeping the strictest guard on every word that escapes me, without betraying any appearance of restraint in my manner. Early in the evening the doctor leaves us to go to a scientific meeting. For half an hour or more Sir James remains with me. By way (as I suppose) of farther testing the state of my mind, he renews the invitation to his house in Scotland. I pretend to feel flattered by his anxiety to secure me as his guest. I undertake to reconsider my first refusal, and to give him a definite answer when we meet the next morning at breakfast. Sir James is delighted. We shake hands cordially, and wish each other good-night. At last I am left alone.

My resolution as to my next course of proceeding is formed without a moment's hesitation. I determine to leave the hotel privately the next morning before Sir James is out of his bedroom.

To what destination I am to betake myself is naturally the next question that arises, and this also I easily decide. During the last days of my mother's life we spoke together frequently of the happy past days when we were living together on the banks of the Greenwater lake. The longing thus inspired to look once more at the old scenes, to live for a while again among the old associations, has grown on me since my mother's death. I have, happily for myself, not spoken of this feeling to Sir James or to any other person. When I am missed at the hotel, there will be no suspicion of the direction in which I have turned my steps. To the old home in Suffolk I resolve to go the next morning. Wandering among the scenes of my boyhood, I can consider with myself how I may best bear the burden of the life that lies before me.

After what I have heard that evening, I confide in nobody. For all I know to the contrary, my own servant may be employed to-morrow as the spy who watches my actions. When the man makes his appearance to take his orders for the night, I tell him to wake me at six the next morning, and release him from further attendance.

I next employ myself in writing two letters. They will be left on the table, to speak for themselves after my departure.

In the first letter I briefly inform Sir James that I have discovered his true reason for inviting the doctor to dinner. While I thank him for the interest he takes in my welfare, I decline to be made the object of any further medical inquiries as to the state of my mind. In due course of time, when my plans are settled, he will hear from me again. Meanwhile, he need feel no anxiety about my safety. It is one among my other delusions to believe that I am still perfectly capable of taking care of myself. My second letter is addressed to the landlord of the hotel, and simply provides for the disposal of my luggage and the payment of my bill.

I enter my bedroom next, and pack a traveling-bag with the few things that I can carry with me. My money is in my dressing-case. Opening it, I discover my pretty keepsake—the green flag! Can I return to "Greenwater Broad," can I look again at the bailiff's cottage, without the one memorial of little Mary that I possess? Besides, have I not promised Miss Dunross that Mary's gift shall always go with me wherever I go? and is the promise not doubly sacred now that she is dead? For a while I sit idly looking at the device on the flag—the white dove embroidered on the green ground, with the golden olive-branch in its beak. The innocent love-story of my early life returns to my memory, and shows me in horrible contrast the life that I am leading now. I fold up the flag and place it carefully in my traveling-bag. This done, all is done. I may rest till the morning comes.

No! I lie down on my bed, and I discover that there is no rest for me that night.

Now that I have no occupation to keep my energies employed, now that my first sense of triumph in the discomfiture of the friends who have plotted against me has had time to subside, my mind reverts to the conversation that I have overheard, and considers it from a new point of view. For the first time, the terrible question confronts me: The doctor's opinion on my case has been given very positively. How do I know that the doctor is not right?

This famous physician has risen to the head of his profession entirely by his own abilities. He is one of the medical men who succeed by means of an ingratiating manner and the dexterous handling of good opportunities. Even his enemies admit that he stands unrivaled in the art of separating the true conditions from the false in the discovery of disease, and in tracing effects accurately to their distant and hidden cause. Is such a man as this likely to be mistaken about me? Is it not far more probable that I am mistaken in my judgment of myself?

When I look back over the past years, am I quite sure that the strange events which I recall may not, in certain cases, be the visionary product of my own disordered brain—realities to me, and to no one else? What are the dreams of Mrs. Van Brandt? What are the ghostly apparitions of her which I believe myself to have seen? Delusions which have been the stealthy growth of years? delusions which are leading me, by slow degrees, nearer and nearer to madness in the end? Is it insane suspicion which has made me so angry with the good friends who have been trying to save my reason? Is it insane terror which sets me on escaping from the hotel like a criminal escaping from prison?

These are the questions which torment me when I am alone in the dead of night. My bed becomes a place of unendurable torture. I rise and dress myself, and wait for the daylight, looking through my open window into the street.

The summer night is short. The gray light of dawn comes to me like a deliverance; the glow of the glorious sunrise cheers my soul once more. Why should I wait in the room that is still haunted by my horrible doubts of the night? I take up my traveling-bag; I leave my letters on the sitting-room table; and I descend the stairs to the house door. The night-porter at the hotel is slumbering in his chair. He wakes as I pass him; and (God help me!) he too looks as if he thought I was mad.

"Going to leave us already, sir?" he says, looking at the bag in my hand.

Mad or sane, I am ready with my reply. I tell him I am going out for a day in the country, and to make it a long day, I must start early.

The man still stares at me. He asks if he shall find some one to carry my bag. I decline to let anybody be disturbed. He inquires if I have any messages to leave for my friend. I inform him that I have left written messages upstairs for Sir James and the landlord. Upon this he draws the bolts and opens the door. To the last he looks at me as if he thought I was mad.

Was he right or wrong? Who can answer for himself? How can I tell?

CHAPTER XXXII. A LAST LOOK AT GREENWATER BROAD.

MY spirits rose as I walked through the bright empty streets, and breathed the fresh morning air.

Taking my way eastward through the great city, I stopped at the first office that I passed, and secured my place by the early coach to Ipswich. Thence I traveled with post-horses to the market-town which was nearest to Greenwater Broad. A walk of a few miles in the cool evening brought me, through well-remembered by-roads, to our old house. By the last rays of the setting sun I looked at the familiar row of windows in front, and saw that the shutters were all closed. Not a living creature was visible anywhere. Not even a dog barked as I rang the great bell at the door. The place was deserted; the house was shut up.

After a long delay, I heard heavy footsteps in the hall. An old man opened the door.

Changed as he was, I remembered him as one of our tenants in the by-gone time. To his astonishment, I greeted him by his name. On his side, he tried hard to recognize me, and tried in vain. No doubt I was the more sadly changed of the two: I was obliged to introduce myself. The poor fellow's withered face brightened slowly and timidly, as if he were half incapable, half afraid, of indulging in the unaccustomed luxury of a smile. In his confusion he bid me welcome home again, as if the house had been mine.

Taking me into the little back-room which he inhabited, the old man gave me all he had to offer—a supper of bacon and eggs and a glass of home-brewed beer. He was evidently puzzled to understand me when I informed him that the only object of my visit was to look once more at the familiar scenes round my old home. But he willingly placed his services at my disposal; and he engaged to do his best, if I wished it, to make me up a bed for the night.

The house had been closed and the establishment of servants had been dismissed for more than a year past. A passion for horse-racing, developed late in life, had ruined the rich retired tradesman who had purchased the estate at the time of our family troubles. He had gone abroad with his wife to live on the little income that had been saved from the wreck of his fortune; and he had left the house and lands in such a state of neglect that no new purchaser had thus far been found to take them. My old friend, "now past his work," had been put in charge of the place. As for Dermody's cottage, it was empty, like the house. I was at perfect liberty to look over it if I liked. There was the key of the door on the bunch with the others; and here was the old man, with his old hat on his head, ready to accompany me wherever I pleased to go. I declined to trouble him to accompany me or to make up a bed in the lonely house. The night was fine, the moon was rising. I had supped; I had rested. When I had seen what I wanted to see, I could easily walk back to the market-town and sleep at the inn. Taking the key in my hand, I set forth alone on the way through the grounds which led to Dermody's cottage.

Again I followed the woodland paths along which I had once idled so happily with my little Mary. At every step I saw something that reminded me of her. Here was the rustic bench on which we had sat together under the shadow of the old cedar-tree, and vowed to be constant to each other to the end of our lives. There was the bright little water spring, from which we drank when we were weary and thirsty in sultry summer days, still bubbling its way downward to the lake as cheerily as ever. As I listened to the companionable murmur of the stream, I almost expected to see her again, in her simple white frock and straw hat, singing to the music of the rivulet, and freshening her nosegay of wild flowers by dipping it in the cool water. A few steps further on and I reached a clearing in the wood and stood on a little promontory of rising ground which commanded the prettiest view of Greenwater lake. A platform of wood was built out from the bank, to be used for bathing by good swimmers who were not afraid of a plunge into deep water. I stood on the platform and looked round me. The trees that fringed the shore on either hand murmured their sweet sylvan music in the night air; the moonlight trembled softly on the rippling water. Away on my right hand I could just see the old wooden shed that once sheltered my boat in the days when Mary went sailing with me and worked the green flag. On my left was the wooden paling that followed the curves of the winding creek, and beyond it rose the brown arches of the decoy for wild fowl, now falling to ruin for want of use. Guided by the radiant moonlight, I could see the very spot on which Mary and I had stood to watch the snaring of the ducks. Through the hole in the paling before which the decoy-dog had shown himself, at Dermody's signal, a water-rat now passed, like a little black shadow on the bright ground, and was lost in the waters of the lake. Look where I might, the happy by-gone time looked back in mockery, and the voices of the past came to me with their burden of reproach: See what your life was once! Is your life worth living now?

I picked up a stone and threw it into the lake. I watched the circling ripples round the place at which it had sunk. I wondered if a practiced swimmer like myself had ever tried to commit suicide by drowning, and had been so resolute to die that he had resisted the temptation to let his own skill keep him from sinking. Something in the lake itself, or something in connection with the thought that it had put into my mind, revolted me. I turned my back suddenly on the lonely view, and took the path through the wood which led to the bailiff's cottage.

Opening the door with my key, I groped my way into the well-remembered parlor; and, unbarring the window-shutters, I let in the light of the moon.

With a heavy heart I looked round me. The old furniture—renewed, perhaps, in one or two places—asserted its mute claim to my recognition in every part of the room. The tender moonlight streamed slanting into the corner in which Mary and I used to nestle together while Dame Dermody was at the window reading her mystic books. Overshadowed by the obscurity in the opposite corner, I discovered the high-backed arm-chair of carved wood in which the Sibyl of the cottage sat on the memorable day when she warned us of our coming separation, and gave us her blessing for the last time. Looking next round the walls of the room, I recognized old friends wherever my eyes happened to rest—the gaudily colored prints; the framed pictures in fine needle-work, which we thought wonderful efforts of art; the old circular mirror to which I used to lift Mary when she wanted "to see her face in the glass." Whenever the moonlight penetrated there, it showed me some familiar object that recalled my happiest days. Again the by-gone time looked back in mockery. Again the voices of the past came to me with their burden of reproach: See what your life was once! Is your life worth living now?

I sat down at the window, where I could just discover, here and there between the trees, the glimmer of the waters of the lake. I thought to myself: "Thus far my mortal journey has brought me. Why not end it here?"

Who would grieve for me if my death were reported to-morrow? Of all living men, I had perhaps the smallest number of friends, the fewest duties to perform toward others, the least reason to hesitate at leaving a world which had no place in it for my ambition, no creature in it for my love.

Besides, what necessity was there for letting it be known that my death was a death of my own seeking? It could easily be left to represent itself as a death by accident.

On that fine summer night, and after a long day of traveling, might I not naturally take a bath in the cool water before I went to bed? And, practiced as I was in the exercise of swimming, might it not nevertheless be my misfortune to be attacked by cramp? On the lonely shores of Greenwater Broad the cry of a drowning man would bring no help at night. The fatal accident would explain itself. There was literally but one difficulty in the way—the difficulty which had already occurred to my mind. Could I sufficiently master the animal instinct of self-preservation to deliberately let myself sink at the first plunge?

The atmosphere in the room felt close and heavy. I went out, and walked to and fro—now in the shadow, and now in the moonlight—under the trees before the cottage door.

Of the moral objections to suicide, not one had any influence over me now. I, who had once found it impossible to excuse, impossible even to understand, the despair which had driven Mrs. Van Brandt to attempt self-destruction—I now contemplated with composure the very act which had horrified me when I saw it committed by another person. Well may we hesitate to condemn the frailties of our fellow-creatures, for the one unanswerable reason that we can never feel sure how soon similar temptations may not lead us to be guilty of the same frailties ourselves. Looking back at the events of the night, I can recall but one consideration that stayed my feet on the fatal path which led back to the lake. I still doubted whether it would be possible for such a swimmer as I was to drown himself. This was all that troubled my mind. For the rest, my will was made, and I had few other affairs which remained unsettled. No lingering hope was left in me of a reunion in the future with Mrs. Van Brandt. She had never written to me again; I had (forgiven) her for having forgotten me. My thoughts of her and of others were the forbearing thoughts of a man whose mind was withdrawn already from the world, whose views were narrowing fast to the one idea of his own death.

I grew weary of walking up and down. The loneliness of the place began to oppress me. The sense of my own indecision irritated my nerves. After a long look at the lake through the trees, I came to a positive conclusion at last. I determined to try if a good swimmer could drown himself.

CHAPTER XXXIII. A VISION OF THE NIGHT.

RETURNING to the cottage parlor, I took a chair by the window and opened my pocket-book at a blank page. I had certain directions to give to my representatives, which might spare them some trouble and uncertainty in the event of my death. Disguising my last instructions under the commonplace heading of "Memoranda on my return to London," I began to write.

I had filled one page of the pocket-book, and had just turned to the next, when I became conscious of a difficulty in fixing my attention on the subject that was before it. I was at once reminded of the similar difficulty which I felt in Shetland, when I had tried vainly to arrange the composition of the letter to my mother which Miss Dunross was to write. By way of completing the parallel, my thoughts wandered now, as they had wandered then, to my latest remembrance of Mrs. Van Brandt. In a minute or two I began to feel once more the strange physical sensations which I had first experienced in the garden at Mr. Dunross's house. The same mysterious trembling shuddered through me from head to foot. I looked about me again, with no distinct consciousness of what the objects were on which my eyes rested. My nerves trembled, on that lovely summer night, as if there had been an electric disturbance in the atmosphere and a storm coming. I laid my pocket-book and pencil on the table, and rose to go out again under the trees. Even the trifling effort to cross the room was an effort made in vain. I stood rooted to the spot, with my face turned toward the moonlight streaming in at the open door.

An interval passed, and as I still looked out through the door, I became aware of something moving far down among the trees that fringed the shore of the lake. The first impression produced on me was of two gray shadows winding their way slowly toward me between the trunks of the trees. By fine degrees the shadows assumed a more and more marked outline, until they presented themselves in the likeness of two robed figures, one taller than the other. While they glided nearer and nearer, their gray obscurity of hue melted away. They brightened softly with an inner light of their own as they slowly approached the open space before the door. For the third time I stood in the ghostly presence of Mrs. Van Brandt; and with her, holding her hand, I beheld a second apparition never before revealed to me, the apparition of her child.

Hand-in-hand, shining in their unearthly brightness through the bright moonlight itself, the two stood before me. The mother's face looked at me once more with the sorrowful and pleading eyes which I remembered so well. But the face of the child was innocently radiant with an angelic smile. I waited in unutterable expectation for the word that was to be spoken, for the movement that was to come. The movement came first. The child released its hold on the mother's hand, and floating slowly upward, remained poised in midair—a softly glowing presence shining out of the dark background of the trees. The mother glided into the room, and stopped at the table on which I had laid my pocket-book and pencil when I could no longer write. As before, she took the pencil and wrote on the blank page. As before, she beckoned to me to step nearer to her. I approached her outstretched hand, and felt once more the mysterious rapture of her touch on my bosom, and heard once more her low, melodious tones repeating the words: "Remember me. Come to me." Her hand dropped from my bosom. The pale light which revealed her to me quivered, sunk, vanished. She had spoken. She had gone.

I drew to me the open pocket-book. And this time I saw, in the writing of the ghostly hand, these words only:

"Follow the Child."

I looked out again at the lonely night landscape.

There, in mid-air, shining softly out of the dark background of the trees, still hovered the starry apparition of the child.

Advancing without conscious will of my own, I crossed the threshold of the door. The softly glowing vision of the child moved away before me among the trees. I followed, like a man spellbound. The apparition, floating slowly onward, led me out of the wood, and past my old home, back to the lonely by-road along which I had walked from the market-town to the house. From time to time, as we two went on our way, the bright figure of the child paused, hovering low in the cloudless sky. Its radiant face looked down smiling on me; it beckoned with its little hand, and floated on again, leading me as the Star led the Eastern sages in the olden time.

I reached the town. The airy figure of the child paused, hovering over the house at which I had left my traveling-carriage in the evening. I ordered the horses to be harnessed again for another journey. The postilion waited for his further directions. I looked up. The child's hand was pointing southward, along the road that led to London. I gave the man his instructions to return to the place at which I had hired the carriage. At intervals, as we proceeded, I looked out through the window. The bright figure of the child still floated on before me gliding low in the cloudless sky. Changing the horses stage by stage, I went on till the night ended—went on till the sun rose in the eastern heaven. And still, whether it was dark or whether it was light, the figure of the child floated on before me in its changeless and mystic light. Mile after mile, it still led the way southward, till we left the country behind us, and passing through the din and turmoil of the great city, stopped under the shadow of the ancient Tower, within view of the river that runs by it.

The postilion came to the carriage door to ask if I had further need of his services. I had called to him to stop, when I saw the figure of the child pause on its airy course. I looked upward again. The child's hand pointed toward the river. I paid the postilion and left the carriage. Floating on before me, the child led the way to a wharf crowded with travelers and their luggage. A vessel lay along-side of the wharf ready to sail. The child led me on board the vessel and paused again, hovering over me in the smoky air.

I looked up. The child looked back at me with its radiant smile, and pointed eastward down the river toward the distant sea. While my eyes were still fixed on the softly glowing figure, I saw it fade away upward and upward into the higher light, as the lark vanishes upward and upward in the morning sky. I was alone again with my earthly fellow-beings—left with no clew to guide me but the remembrance of the child's hand pointing eastward to the distant sea.

A sailor was near me coiling the loosened mooring-rope on the deck. I asked him to what port the vessel was bound. The man looked at me in surly amazement, and answered:

"To Rotterdam."

CHAPTER XXXIV. BY LAND AND SEA.

IT mattered little to me to what port the vessel was bound. Go where I might, I knew that I was on my way to Mrs. Van Brandt. She had need of me again; she had claimed me again. Where the visionary hand of the child had pointed, thither I was destined to go. Abroad or at home, it mattered nothing: when I next set my foot on the land, I should be further directed on the journey which lay before me. I believed this as firmly as I believed that I had been guided, thus far, by the vision of the child.

For two nights I had not slept—my weariness overpowered me. I descended to the cabin, and found an unoccupied corner in which I could lie down to rest. When I awoke, it was night already, and the vessel was at sea.

I went on deck to breathe the fresh air. Before long the sensation of drowsiness returned; I slept again for hours together. My friend, the physician, would no doubt have attributed this prolonged need of repose to the exhausted condition of my brain, previously excited by delusions which had lasted uninterruptedly for many hours together. Let the cause be what it might, during the greater part of the voyage I was awake at intervals only. The rest of the time I lay like a weary animal, lost in sleep.

When I stepped on shore at Rotterdam, my first proceeding was to ask my way to the English Consulate. I had but a small sum of money with me; and, for all I knew to the contrary, it might be well, before I did anything else, to take the necessary measures for replenishing my purse.

I had my traveling-bag with me. On the journey to Greenwater Broad I had left it at the inn in the market-town, and the waiter had placed it in the carriage when I started on my return to London. The bag contained my checkbook, and certain letters which assisted me in proving my identity to the consul. He kindly gave me the necessary introduction to the correspondents at Rotterdam of my bankers in London.

Having obtained my money, and having purchased certain necessaries of which I stood in need, I walked slowly along the street, knowing nothing of what my next proceeding was to be, and waiting confidently for the event which was to guide me. I had not walked a hundred yards before I noticed the name of "Van Brandt" inscribed on the window-blinds of a house which appeared to be devoted to mercantile purposes.

The street door stood open. A second door, on one side of the passage, led into the office. I entered the room and inquired for Mr. Van Brandt. A clerk who spoke English was sent for to communicate with me. He told me there were three partners of that name in the business, and inquired which of them I wished to see. I remembered Van Brandt's Christian name, and mentioned it. No such person as "Mr. Ernest Van Brandt" was known at the office.

"We are only the branch house of the firm of Van Brandt here," the clerk explained. "The head office is at Amsterdam. They may know where Mr. Ernest Van Brandt is to be found, if you inquire there."

It mattered nothing to me where I went, so long as I was on my way to Mrs. Van Brandt. It was too late to travel that day; I slept at a hotel. The night passed quietly and uneventfully. The next morning I set forth by the public conveyance for Amsterdam.

Repeating my inquiries at the head office on my arrival, I was referred to one of the partners in the firm. He spoke English perfectly; and he received me with an appearance of interest which I was at a loss to account for at first.

"Mr. Ernest Van Brandt is well known to me," he said. "May I ask if you are a relative or friend of the English lady who has been introduced here as his wife?"

I answered in the affirmative; adding, "I am here to give any assistance to the lady of which she may stand in need."

The merchant's next words explained the appearance of interest with which he had received me.

"You are most welcome," he said. "You relieve my partners and myself of a great anxiety. I can only explain what I mean by referring for a moment to the business affairs of my firm. We have a fishing establishment in the ancient city of Enkhuizen, on the shores of the Zuyder Zee. Mr. Ernest Van Brandt had a share in it at one time, which he afterward sold. Of late years our profits from this source have been diminishing; and we think of giving up the fishery, unless our prospects in that quarter improve after a further trial. In the meantime, having a vacant situation in the counting-house at Enkhuizen, we thought of Mr. Ernest Van Brandt, and offered him the opportunity of renewing his connection with us, in the capacity of a clerk. He is related to one of my partners; but I am bound in truth to tell you that he is a very bad man. He has awarded us for our kindness to him by embezzling our money; and he has taken to flight—in what direction we have not yet discovered. The English lady and her child are left deserted at Enkhuizen; and until you came here to-day we were quite at a loss to know what to do with them. I don't know whether you are already aware of it, sir; but the lady's position is made doubly distressing by doubts which we entertain of her being really Mr. Ernest Van Brandt's wife. To our certain knowledge, he was privately married to another woman some years since; and we have no evidence whatever that the first wife is dead. If we can help you in any way to assist your unfortunate country-woman, pray believe that our services are at your disposal."

With what breathless interest I listened to these words it is needless to say. Van Brandt had deserted her! Surely (as my poor mother had once said) "she must turn to me now." The hopes that had abandoned me filled my heart once more; the future which I had so long feared to contemplate showed itself again bright with the promise of coming happiness to my view. I thanked the good merchant with a fervor that surprised him. "Only help me to find my way to Enkhuizen," I said, "and I will answer for the rest."

"The journey will put you to some expense," the merchant replied. "Pardon me if I ask the question bluntly. Have you money?"

"Plenty of money."

"Very good. The rest will be easy enough. I will place you under the care of a countryman of yours, who has been employed in our office for many years. The easiest way for you, as a stranger, will be to go by sea; and the Englishman will show you where to hire a boat."

In a few minutes more the clerk and I were on our way to the harbor.

Difficulties which I had not anticipated occurred in finding the boat and in engaging a crew. This done, it was next necessary to purchase provisions for the voyage. Thanks to the experience of my companion, and to the hearty good-will with which he exerted it, my preparations were completed before night-fall. I was able to set sail for my destination on the next day.

The boat had the double advantage, in navigating the Zuyder Zee, of being large, and of drawing very little water; the captain's cabin was at the stern; and the two or three men who formed his crew were berthed forward, in the bows. The whole middle of the boat, partitioned off on the one side and on the other from the captain and the crew, was assigned to me for my cabin. Under these circumstances, I had no reason to complain of want of space; the vessel measuring between fifty and sixty tons. I had a comfortable bed, a table, and chairs. The kitchen was well away from me, in the forward part of the boat. At my own request, I set forth on the voyage without servant or interpreter. I preferred being alone. The Dutch captain had been employed, at a former period of his life, in the mercantile navy of France; and we could communicate, whenever it was necessary or desirable, in the French language.

We left the spires of Amsterdam behind us, and sailed over the smooth waters of the lake on our way to the Zuyder Zee.

The history of this remarkable sea is a romance in itself. In the days when Rome was mistress of the world, it had no existence. Where the waves now roll, vast tracts of forest surrounded a great inland lake, with but one river to serve it as an outlet to the sea. Swelled by a succession of tempests, the lake overflowed its boundaries: its furious waters, destroying every obstacle in their course, rested only when they reached the furthest limits of the land.

The Northern Ocean beyond burst its way in through the gaps of ruin; and from that time the Zuyder Zee existed as we know it now. The years advanced, the generations of man succeeded each other; and on the shores of the new ocean there rose great and populous cities, rich in commerce, renowned in history. For centuries their prosperity lasted, before the next in this mighty series of changes ripened and revealed itself. Isolated from the rest of the world, vain of themselves and their good fortune, careless of the march of progress in the nations round them, the inhabitants of the Zuyder Zee cities sunk into the fatal torpor of a secluded people. The few members of the population who still preserved the relics of their old energy emigrated, while the mass left behind resignedly witnessed the diminution of their commerce and the decay of their institutions. As the years advanced to the nineteenth century, the population was reckoned by hundreds where it had once been numbered by thousands. Trade disappeared; whole streets were left desolate. Harbors, once filled with shipping, were destroyed by the unresisted accumulation of sand. In our own times the decay of these once flourishing cities is so completely beyond remedy, that the next great change in contemplation is the draining of the now dangerous and useless tract of water, and the profitable cultivation of the reclaimed land by generations that are still to come. Such, briefly told, is the strange story of the Zuyder Zee.

As we advanced on our voyage, and left the river, I noticed the tawny hue of the sea, caused by sand-banks which color the shallow water, and which make the navigation dangerous to inexperienced seamen. We found our moorings for the night at the fishing island of Marken—a low, lost, desolate-looking place, as I saw it under the last gleams of the twilight. Here and there, the gabled cottages, perched on hillocks, rose black against the dim gray sky. Here and there, a human figure appeared at the waterside, standing, fixed in contemplation of the strange boat. And that was all I saw of the island of Marken.

Lying awake in the still night, alone on a strange sea, there were moments when I found myself beginning to doubt the reality of my own position.

Was it all a dream? My thoughts of suicide; my vision of the mother and daughter; my journey back to the metropolis, led by the apparition of the child; my voyage to Holland; my night anchorage in the unknown sea—were these, so to speak, all pieces of the same morbid mental puzzle, all delusions from which I might wake at any moment, and find myself restored to my senses again in the hotel at London? Bewildered by doubts which led me further and further from any definite conclusion, I left my bed and went on deck to change the scene. It was a still and cloudy night. In the black void around me, the island was a blacker shadow yet, and nothing more. The one sound that reached my ears was the heavy breathing of the captain and his crew sleeping on either side of me. I waited, looking round and round the circle of darkness in which I stood. No new vision showed itself. When I returned again to the cabin, and slumbered at last, no dreams came to me. All that was mysterious, all that was marvelous, in the later events of my life seemed to have been left behind me in England. Once in Holland, my course had been influenced by circumstances which were perfectly natural, by commonplace discoveries which might have revealed themselves to any man in my position. What did this mean? Had my gifts as a seer of visions departed from me in the new land and among the strange people? Or had my destiny led me to the place at which the troubles of my mortal pilgrimage were to find their end? Who could say?

Early the next morning we set sail once more.

Our course was nearly northward. On one side of me was the tawny sea, changing under certain conditions of the weather to a dull pearl-gray. On the other side was the flat, winding coast, composed alternately of yellow sand and bright-green meadow-lands; diversified at intervals by towns and villages, whose red-tiled roofs and quaint church-steeples rose gayly against the clear blue sky. The captain suggested to me to visit the famous towns of Edam and Hoorn; but I declined to go on shore. My one desire was to reach the ancient city in which Mrs. Van Brandt had been left deserted. As we altered our course, to make for the promontory on which Enkhuizen is situated, the wind fell, then shifted to another quarter, and blew with a force which greatly increased the difficulties of navigation. I still insisted, as long as it was possible to do so, on holding on our course. After sunset, the strength of the wind abated. The night came without a cloud, and the starry firmament gave us its pale and glittering light. In an hour more the capricious wind shifted back again in our favor. Toward ten o'clock we sailed into the desolate harbor of Enkhuizen.

The captain and crew, fatigued by their exertions, ate their frugal suppers and went to their beds. In a few minutes more, I was the only person left awake in the boat.

I ascended to the deck, and looked about me.

Our boat was moored to a deserted quay. Excepting a few fishing vessels visible near us, the harbor of this once prosperous place was a vast solitude of water, varied here and there by dreary banks of sand. Looking inland, I saw the lonely buildings of the Dead City—black, grim, and dreadful under the mysterious starlight. Not a human creature, not even a stray animal, was to be seen anywhere. The place might have been desolated by a pestilence, so empty and so lifeless did it now appear. Little more than a hundred years ago, the record of its population reached sixty thousand. The inhabitants had dwindled to a tenth of that number when I looked at Enkhuizen now!

I considered with myself what my next course of proceeding was to be.

The chances were certainly against my discovering Mrs. Van Brandt if I ventured alone and unguided into the city at night. On the other hand, now that I had reached the place in which she and her child were living, friendless and deserted, could I patiently wait through the weary interval that must elapse before the morning came and the town was astir? I knew my own self-tormenting disposition too well to accept this latter alternative. Whatever came of it, I determined to walk through Enkhuizen on the bare chance of meeting some one who might inform me of Mrs. Van Brandt's address.

First taking the precaution of locking my cabin door, I stepped from the bulwark of the vessel to the lonely quay, and set forth upon my night wanderings through the Dead City.

CHAPTER XXXV. UNDER THE WINDOW.

I SET the position of the harbor by my pocket-compass, and then followed the course of the first street that lay before me.

On either side, as I advanced, the desolate old houses frowned on me. There were no lights in the windows, no lamps in the streets. For a quarter of an hour at least I penetrated deeper and deeper into the city, without encountering a living creature on my way—with only the starlight to guide me. Turning by chance into a street broader than the rest, I at last saw a moving figure, just visible ahead, under the shadows of the houses. I quickened my pace, and found myself following a man in the dress of a peasant. Hearing my footsteps behind him, he turned and looked at me. Discovering that I was a stranger, he lifted a thick cudgel that he carried with him, shook it threateningly, and called to me in his own language (as I gathered by his actions) to stand back. A stranger in Eukhuizen at that time of night was evidently reckoned as a robber in the estimation of this citizen! I had learned on the voyage, from the captain of the boat, how to ask my way in Dutch, if I happened to be by myself in a strange town; and I now repeated my lesson, asking my way to the fishing office of Messrs. Van Brandt. Either my foreign accent made me unintelligible, or the man's suspicions disinclined him to trust me. Again he shook his cudgel, and again he signed to me to stand back. It was useless to persist. I crossed to the opposite side of the way, and soon afterward lost sight of him under the portico of a house.

Still following the windings of the deserted streets, I reached what I at first supposed to be the end of the town.

Before me, for half a mile or more (as well as I could guess), rose a tract of meadow-land, with sheep dotted over it at intervals reposing for the night. I advanced over the grass, and observed here and there, where the ground rose a little, some moldering fragments of brickwork. Looking onward as I reached the middle of the meadow, I perceived on its further side, towering gaunt and black in the night, a lofty arch or gateway, without walls at its sides, without a neighboring building of any sort, far or near. This (as I afterward learned) was one of the ancient gates of the city. The walls, crumbling to ruin, had been destroyed as useless obstacles that cumbered the ground. On the waste meadow-land round me had once stood the shops of the richest merchants, the palaces of the proudest nobles of North Holland. I was actually standing on what had been formerly the wealthy quarter of Enkhuizen! And what was left of it now? A few mounds of broken bricks, a pasture-land of sweet-smelling grass, and a little flock of sheep sleeping.

The mere desolation of the view (apart altogether from its history) struck me with a feeling of horror. My mind seemed to lose its balance in the dreadful stillness that was round me. I felt unutterable forebodings of calamities to come. For the first time, I repented having left England. My thoughts turned regretfully to the woody shores of Greenwater Broad. If I had only held to my resolution, I might have been at rest now in the deep waters of the lake. For what had I lived and planned and traveled since I left Dermody's cottage? Perhaps only to find that I had lost the woman whom I loved—now that I was in the same town with her!

Regaining the outer rows of houses still left standing, I looked about me, intending to return by the street which was known to me already. Just as I thought I had discovered it, I noticed another living creature in the solitary city. A man was standing at the door of one of the outermost houses on my right hand, looking at me.

At the risk of meeting with another rough reception, I determined to make a last effort to discover Mrs. Van Brandt before I returned to the boat.

Seeing that I was approaching him, the stranger met me midway. His dress and manner showed plainly that I had not encountered this time a person in the lower ranks of life. He answered my question civilly in his own language. Seeing that I was at a loss to understand what he said, he invited me by signs to follow him. After walking for a few minutes in a direction which was quite new to me, we stopped in a gloomy little square, with a plot of neglected garden-ground in the middle of it. Pointing to a lower window in one of the houses, in which a light dimly appeared, my guide said in Dutch:

"Office of Van Brandt, sir," bowed, and left me.

I advanced to the window. It was open, and it was just high enough to be above my head. The light in the room found its way outward through the interstices of closed wooden shutters. Still haunted by misgivings of trouble to come, I hesitated to announce my arrival precipitately by ringing the house-bell. How did I know what new calamity might not confront me when the door was opened? I waited under the window and listened.

Hardly a minute passed before I heard a woman's voice in the room. There was no mistaking the charm of those tones. It was the voice of Mrs. Van Brandt.

"Come, darling," she said. "It is very late—you ought to have been in bed two hours ago."

The child's voice answered, "I am not sleepy, mamma."

"But, my dear, remember you have been ill. You may be ill again if you keep out of bed so late as this. Only lie down, and you will soon fall asleep when I put the candle out."

"You must not put the candle out!" the child returned, with strong emphasis. "My new papa is coming. How is he to find his way to us, if you put out the light?"

The mother answered sharply, as if the child's strange words had irritated her.

"You are talking nonsense," she said; "and you must go to bed. Mr. Germaine knows nothing about us. Mr. Germaine is in England."

I could restrain myself no longer. I called out under the window:

"Mr. Germaine is here!"

CHAPTER XXXVI. LOVE AND PRIDE.

A CRY of terror from the room told me that I had been heard. For a moment more nothing happened. Then the child's voice reached me, wild and shrill: "Open the shutters, mamma! I said he was coming—I want to see him!"

There was still an interval of hesitation before the mother opened the shutters. She did it at last. I saw her darkly at the window, with the light behind her, and the child's head just visible above the lower part of the window-frame. The quaint little face moved rapidly up and down, as if my self-appointed daughter were dancing for joy!

"Can I trust my own senses?" said Mrs. Van Brandt. "Is it really Mr. Germaine?"

"How do you do, new papa?" cried the child. "Push open the big door and come in. I want to kiss you."

There was a world of difference between the coldly doubtful tone of the mother and the joyous greeting of the child. Had I forced myself too suddenly on Mrs. Van Brandt? Like all sensitively organized persons, she possessed that inbred sense of self-respect which is pride under another name. Was her pride wounded at the bare idea of my seeing her, deserted as well as deceived—abandoned contemptuously, a helpless burden on strangers—by the man for whom she had sacrificed and suffered so much? And that man a thief, flying from the employers whom he had cheated! I pushed open the heavy oaken street-door, fearing that this might be the true explanation of the change which I had already remarked in her. My apprehensions were confirmed when she unlocked the inner door, leading from the courtyard to the sitting-room, and let me in.

As I took her by both hands and kissed her, she turned her head, so that my lips touched her cheek only. She flushed deeply; her eyes looked away from me as she spoke her few formal words of welcome. When the child flew into my arms, she cried out, irritably, "Don't trouble Mr. Germaine!" I took a chair, with the little one on my knee. Mrs. Van Brandt seated herself at a distance from me. "It is needless, I suppose, to ask you if you know what has happened," she said, turning pale again as suddenly as she had turned red, and keeping her eyes fixed obstinately on the floor.

Before I could answer, the child burst out with the news of her father's disappearance in these words:

"My other papa has run away! My other papa has stolen money! It's time I had a new one, isn't it?" She put her arms round my neck. "And now I've got him!" she cried, at the shrillest pitch of her voice.

The mother looked at us. For a while, the proud, sensitive woman struggled successfully with herself; but the pang that wrung her was not to be endured in silence. With a low cry of pain, she hid her face in her hands. Overwhelmed by the sense of her own degradation, she was even ashamed to let the man who loved her see that she was in tears.

I took the child off my knee. There was a second door in the sitting-room, which happened to be left open. It showed me a bed-chamber within, and a candle burning on the toilet-table.

"Go in there and play," I said. "I want to talk to your mamma."

The child pouted: my proposal did not appear to tempt her. "Give me something to play with," she said. "I'm tired of my toys. Let me see what you have got in your pockets."

Her busy little hands began to search in my coat-pockets. I let her take what she pleased, and so bribed her to run away into the inner room. As soon as she was out of sight, I approached the poor mother and seated myself by her side.

"Think of it as I do," I said. "Now that he has forsaken you, he has left you free to be mine."

She lifted her head instantly; her eyes flashed through her tears.

"Now that he has forsaken me," she answered, "I am more unworthy of

555

you than ever!"

"Why?" I asked.

"Why!" she repeated, passionately. "Has a woman not reached the lowest depths of degradation when she has lived to be deserted by a thief?"

It was hopeless to attempt to reason with her in her present frame of mind. I tried to attract her attention to a less painful subject by referring to the strange succession of events which had brought me to her for the third time. She stopped me impatiently at the outset.

"It seems useless to say once more what we have said on other occasions," she answered. "I understand what has brought you here. I have appeared to you again in a vision, just as I appeared to you twice before."

"No," I said. "Not as you appeared to me twice before. This time I saw you with the child by your side."

That reply roused her. She started, and looked nervously toward the bed-chamber door.

"Don't speak loud!" she said. "Don't let the child hear us! My dream of you this time has left a painful impression on my mind. The child is mixed up in it—and I don't like that. Then the place in which I saw you is associated—" She paused, leaving the sentence unfinished. "I am nervous and wretched to-night," she resumed; "and I don't want to speak of it. And yet, I should like to know whether my dream has misled me, or whether you really were in that cottage, of all places in the world?"

I was at a loss to understand the embarrassment which she appeared to feel in putting her question. There was nothing very wonderful, to my mind, in the discovery that she had been in Suffolk, and that she was acquainted with Greenwater Broad. The lake was known all over the county as a favorite resort of picnic parties; and Dermody's pretty cottage used to be one of the popular attractions of the scene. What really surprised me was to see, as I now plainly saw, that she had some painful association with my old home. I decided on answering her question in such terms as might encourage her to take me into her confidence. In a moment more I should have told her that my boyhood had been passed at Greenwater Broad—in a moment more, we should have recognized each other—when a trivial interruption suspended the words on my lips. The child ran out of the bed-chamber, with a quaintly shaped key in her hand. It was one of the things she had taken out of my pockets and it belonged to the cabin door on board the boat. A sudden fit of curiosity (the insatiable curiosity of a child) had seized her on the subject of this key. She insisted on knowing what door it locked; and, when I had satisfied her on that point, she implored me to take her immediately to see the boat. This entreaty led naturally to a renewal of the disputed question of going, or not going, to bed. By the time the little creature had left us again, with permission to play for a few minutes longer, the conversation between Mrs. Van Brandt and myself had taken a new direction. Speaking now of the child's health, we were led naturally to the kindred subject of the child's connection with her mother's dream.

"She had been ill with fever," Mrs. Van Brandt began; "and she was just getting better again on the day when I was left deserted in this miserable place. Toward evening, she had another attack that frightened me dreadfully. She became perfectly insensible—her little limbs were stiff and cold. There is one doctor here who has not yet abandoned the town. Of course I sent for him. He thought her insensibility was caused by a sort of cataleptic seizure. At the same time, he comforted me by saying that she was in no immediate danger of death; and he left me certain remedies to be given, if certain symptoms appeared. I took her to bed, and held her to me, with the idea of keeping her warm. Without believing in mesmerism, it has since struck me that we might unconsciously have had some influence over each other, which may explain what followed. Do you think it likely?"

"Quite likely. At the same time, the mesmeric theory (if you could believe in it) would carry the explanation further still. Mesmerism would assert, not only that you and the child influenced each other, but that—in spite of the distance—you both influenced me. And in that way, mesmerism would account for my vision as the necessary result of a highly developed sympathy between us. Tell me, did you fall asleep with the child in your arms?"

"Yes. I was completely worn out; and I fell asleep, in spite of my resolution to watch through the night. In my forlorn situation, forsaken in a strange place, I dreamed of you again, and I appealed to you again as my one protector and friend. The only new thing in the dream was, that I thought I had the child with me when I approached you, and that the child put the words into my mind when I wrote in your book. You saw the words, I suppose? and they vanished, as before, no doubt, when I awoke? I found the child still lying, like a dead creature, in my arms. All through the night there was no change in her. She only recovered her senses at noon the next day. Why do you start? What have I said that surprises you?"

There was good reason for my feeling startled, and showing it. On the day and at the hour when the child had come to herself, I had stood on the deck of the vessel, and had seen the apparition of her disappear from my view.

"Did she say anything," I asked, "when she recovered her senses?"

"Yes. She too had been dreaming—dreaming that she was in company with you. She said: 'He is coming to see us, mamma; and I have been showing him the way.' I asked her where she had seen you. She spoke confusedly of more places than one. She talked of trees, and a cottage, and a lake; then of fields and hedges, and lonely lanes; then of a carriage and horses, and a long white road; then of crowded streets and houses, and a river and a ship. As to these last objects, there is nothing very wonderful in what she said. The houses, the river, and the ship which she saw in her dream, she saw in the reality when we took her from London to Rotterdam, on our way here. But as to the other places, especially the cottage and the lake (as she described them) I can only suppose that her dream was the reflection of mine. I had been dreaming of the cottage and the lake, as I once knew them in years long gone by; and—Heaven only knows why—I had associated you with the scene. Never mind going into that now! I don't know what infatuation it is that makes me trifle in this way with old recollections, which affect me painfully in my present position. We were talking of the child's health; let us go back to that."

It was not easy to return to the topic of her child's health. She had revived my curiosity on the subject of her association with Greenwater Broad. The child was still quietly at play in the bedchamber. My second opportunity was before me. I took it.

"I won't distress you," I began. "I will only ask leave, before we change the subject, to put one question to you about the cottage and the lake."

As the fatality that pursued us willed it, it was her turn now to be innocently an obstacle in the way of our discovering each other.

"I can tell you nothing more to-night," she interposed, rising impatiently. "It is time I put the child to bed—and, besides, I can't talk of things that distress me. You must wait for the time—if it ever comes!—when I am calmer and happier than I am now."

She turned to enter the bed-chamber. Acting headlong on the impulse of the moment, I took her by the hand and stopped her.

"You have only to choose," I said, "and the calmer and happier time is yours from this moment."

"Mine?" she repeated. "What do you mean?"

"Say the word," I replied, "and you and your child have a home and a future before you."

She looked at me half bewildered, half angry.

"Do you offer me your protection?" she asked.

"I offer you a husband's protection," I answered. "I ask you to be my wife."

She advanced a step nearer to me, with her eyes riveted on my face.

"You are evidently ignorant of what has really happened," she said. "And yet, God knows, the child spoke plainly enough!"

"The child only told me," I rejoined, "what I had heard already, on my way here."

"All of it?"

"All of it."

"And you still ask me to be your wife?"

"I can imagine no greater happiness than to make you my wife."

"Knowing what you know now?"

"Knowing what I know now, I ask you confidently to give me your hand. Whatever claim that man may once have had, as the father of your child, he has now forfeited it by his infamous desertion of you. In every sense of the word, my darling, you are a free woman. We have had sorrow enough in our lives. Happiness is at last within our reach. Come to me, and say Yes."

I tried to take her in my arms. She drew back as if I had frightened her.

"Never!" she said, firmly.

I whispered my next words, so that the child in the inner room might not hear us.

"You once said you loved me!"

"I do love you!"

"As dearly as ever?"

"More dearly than ever!"

"Kiss me!"

She yielded mechanically; she kissed me—with cold lips, with big tears in her eyes.

"You don't love me!" I burst out, angrily. "You kiss me as if it were a duty. Your lips are cold—your heart is cold. You don't love me!"

She looked at me sadly, with a patient smile.

"One of us must remember the difference between your position and mine," she said. "You are a man of stainless honor, who holds an undisputed rank in the world. And what am I? I am the deserted mistress of a thief. One of us must remember that. You have generously forgotten it. I must bear it in mind. I dare say I am cold. Suffering has that effect on me; and, I own it, I am suffering now."

I was too passionately in love with her to feel the sympathy on which she evidently counted in saying those words. A man can respect a woman's scruples when they appeal to him mutely in her looks or in her tears; but the formal expression of them in words only irritates or annoys him.

"Whose fault is it that you suffer?" I retorted, coldly. "I ask you to make my life a happy one, and your life a happy one. You are a cruelly wronged woman, but you are not a degraded woman. You are worthy to be my wife, and I am ready to declare it publicly. Come back with me to England. My boat is waiting for you; we can set sail in two hours."

She dropped into a chair; her hands fell helplessly into her lap.

"How cruel!" she murmured, "how cruel to tempt me!" She waited a little, and recovered her fatal firmness. "No!" she said. "If I die in doing it, I can still refuse to disgrace you. Leave me, Mr. Germaine. You can show me that one kindness more. For God's sake, leave me!"

I made a last appeal to her tenderness.

"Do you know what my life is if I live without you?" I asked. "My mother is dead. There is not a living creature left in the world whom I love but you. And you ask me to leave you! Where am I to go to? what am I to do? You talk of cruelty! Is there no cruelty in sacrificing the happiness of my life to a miserable scruple of delicacy, to an unreasoning fear of the opinion of the world? I love you and you love me. There is no other consideration worth a straw. Come back with me to England! come back and be my wife!"

She dropped on her knees, and taking my hand put it silently to my lips. I tried to raise her. It was useless: she steadily resisted me.

"Does this mean No?" I asked.

"It means," she said in faint, broken tones, "that I prize your honor beyond my happiness. If I marry you, your career is destroyed by your wife; and the day will come when you will tell me so. I can suffer—I can die; but I can not face such a prospect as that. Forgive me and forget me. I can say no more!"

She let go of my hand, and sank on the floor. The utter despair of that action told me, far more eloquently than the words which she had just spoken, that her resolution was immovable. She had deliberately separated herself from me; her own act had parted us forever.

CHAPTER XXXVII. THE TWO DESTINIES.

I MADE no movement to leave the room; I let no sign of sorrow escape me. At last, my heart was hardened against the woman who had so obstinately rejected me. I stood looking down at her with a merciless anger, the bare remembrance of which fills me at this day with a horror of myself. There is but one excuse for me. The shock of that last overthrow of the one hope that held me to life was more than my reason could endure. On that dreadful night (whatever I may have been at other times), I myself believe it, I was a maddened man.

I was the first to break the silence.

"Get up," I said coldly.

She lifted her face from the floor, and looked at me as if she doubted whether she had heard aright.

"Put on your hat and cloak," I resumed. "I must ask you to go back with me as far as the boat."

She rose slowly. Her eyes rested on my face with a dull, bewildered look.

"Why am I to go with you to the boat?" she asked.

The child heard her. The child ran up to us with her little hat in one hand, and the key of the cabin in the other.

"I'm ready," she said. "I will open the cabin door."

Her mother signed to her to go back to the bed-chamber. She went back as far as the door which led into the courtyard, and waited there, listening. I turned to Mrs. Van Brandt with immovable composure, and answered the question which she had addressed to me.

"You are left," I said, "without the means of getting away from this place. In two hours more the tide will be in my favor, and I shall sail at once on the return voyage. We part, this time, never to meet again. Before I go I am resolved to leave you properly provided for. My money is in my traveling-bag in the cabin. For that reason, I am obliged to ask you to go with me as far as the boat."

"I thank you gratefully for your kindness," she said. "I don't stand in such serious need of help as you suppose."

"It is useless to attempt to deceive me," I proceeded. "I have spoken with the head partner of the house of Van Brandt at Amsterdam, and I know exactly what your position is. Your pride must bend low enough to take from my hands the means of subsistence for yourself and your child. If I had died in England—"

I stopped. The unexpressed idea in my mind was to tell her that she would inherit a legacy under my will, and that she might quite as becomingly take money from me in my life-time as take it from my executors after my death. In forming this thought into words, the associations which it called naturally into being revived in me the memory of my contemplated suicide in the Greenwater lake. Mingling with the remembrance thus aroused, there rose in me unbidden, a temptation so overpoweringly vile, and yet so irresistible in the state of my mind at the moment, that it shook me to the soul. "You have nothing to live for, now that she has refused to be yours," the fiend in me whispered. "Take your leap into the next world, and make the woman whom you love take it with you!" While I was still looking at her, while my last words to her faltered on my lips, the horrible facilities for the perpetration of the double crime revealed themselves enticingly to my view. My boat was moored in the one part of the decaying harbor in which deep water still lay at the foot of the quay. I had only to induce her to follow me when I stepped on the deck, to seize her in my arms, and to jump overboard with her before she could utter a cry for help. My drowsy sailors, as I knew by experience, were hard to wake, and slow to move even when they were roused at last. We should both be drowned before the youngest and the quickest of them could get up from his bed and make his way to the deck. Yes! We should both be struck together out of the ranks of the living at one and the same moment. And why not? She who had again and again refused to be my wife—did she deserve that I should leave her free to go back, perhaps, for the second time to Van Brandt? On the evening when I had saved her from the waters of the Scotch river, I had made myself master of her fate. She had tried to destroy herself by drowning; she should drown now, in the arms of the man who had once thrown himself between her and death!

Self-abandoned to such atrocious reasoning as this, I stood face to face with her, and returned deliberately to my unfinished sentence.

"If I had died in England, you would have been provided for by my will. What you would have taken from me then, you may take from me now. Come to the boat."

A change passed over her face as I spoke; a vague doubt of me began to show itself in her eyes. She drew back a little, without making any reply.

"Come to the boat," I reiterated.

"It is too late." With that answer, she looked across the room at the child, still waiting by the door. "Come, Elfie," she said, calling the little creature by one of her favorite nicknames. "Come to bed."

I too looked at Elfie. Might she not, I asked myself, be made the innocent means of forcing her mother to leave the house? Trusting to the child's fearless character, and her eagerness to see the boat, I suddenly opened the door. As I had anticipated, she instantly ran out. The second door, leading into the square, I had not closed when I entered the courtyard. In another moment Elfie was out in the square, triumphing in her freedom. The shrill little voice broke the death-like stillness of the place and hour, calling to me again and again to take her to the boat.

I turned to Mrs. Van Brandt. The stratagem had succeeded. Elfie's mother could hardly refuse to follow when Elfie led the way.

"Will you go with us?" I asked. "Or must I send the money back by the child?"

Her eyes rested on me for a moment with a deepening expression of distrust, then looked away again. She began to turn pale. "You are not like yourself to-night," she said. Without a word more, she took her hat and cloak and went out before me into the square. I followed her, closing the doors behind me. She made an attempt to induce the child to approach her. "Come, darling," she said, enticingly—"come and take my hand."

But Elfie was not to be caught: she took to her heels, and answered from a safe distance. "No," said the child; "you will take me back and put me to bed." She retreated a little further, and held up the key: "I shall go first," she cried, "and open the door."

She trotted off a few steps in the direction of the harbor, and waited for what was to happen next. Her mother suddenly turned, and looked close at me under the light of the stars.

"Are the sailors on board the boat?" she asked.

The question startled me. Had she any suspicion of my purpose? Had my face warned her of lurking danger if she went to the boat? It was impossible. The more likely motive for her inquiry was to find a new excuse for not accompanying me to the harbor. If I told her that the men were on board, she might answer, "Why not employ one of your sailors to bring the money to me at the house?" I took care to anticipate the suggestion in making my reply.

"They may be honest men," I said, watching her carefully; "but I don't know them well enough to trust them with money."

To my surprise, she watched me just as carefully on her side, and deliberately repeated her question:

"Are the sailors on board the boat?"

I informed her that the captain and crew slept in the boat, and paused to see what would follow. My reply seemed to rouse her resolution. After a moment's consideration, she turned toward the place at which the child was waiting for us. "Let us go, as you insist on it," she said, quietly. I made no further remark. Side by side, in silence we followed Elfie on our way to the boat.

Not a human creature passed us in the streets; not a light glimmered on us from the grim black houses. Twice the child stopped, and (still keeping slyly out of her mother's reach) ran back to me, wondering at my silence. "Why don't you speak?" she asked. "Have you and mamma quarreled?"

I was incapable of answering her—I could think of nothing but my contemplated crime. Neither fear nor remorse troubled me. Every better instinct, every nobler feeling that I had once possessed, seemed to be dead and gone. Not even a thought of the child's future troubled my mind. I had no power of looking on further than the fatal leap from the boat: beyond that there was an utter blank. For the time being—I can only repeat it, my moral sense was obscured, my mental faculties were thrown completely off their balance. The animal part of me lived and moved as usual; the viler animal instincts in me plotted and planned, and that was all. Nobody, looking at me, would have seen anything but a dull quietude in my face, an immovable composure in my manner. And yet no madman was fitter for restraint, or less responsible morally for his own actions, than I was at that moment.

The night air blew more freshly on our faces. Still led by the child, we had passed through the last street—we were out on the empty open space which was the landward boundary of the harbor. In a minute more we stood on the quay, within a step of the gunwale of the boat. I noticed a change in the appearance of the harbor since I had seen it last. Some fishing-boats had come in during my absence. They moored, some immediately astern and some immediately ahead of my own vessel. I looked anxiously to see if any of the fishermen were on board and stirring. Not a living being appeared anywhere. The men were on shore with their wives and their families.

Elfie held out her arms to be lifted on board my boat. Mrs. Van Brandt stepped between us as I stooped to take her up.

"We will wait here," she said, "while you go into the cabin and get the money."

Those words placed it beyond all doubt that she had her suspicions of me—suspicions, probably, which led her to fear not for her life, but for her freedom. She might dread being kept a prisoner in the boat, and being carried away by me against her will. More than this she could not thus far possibly apprehend. The child saved me the trouble of making any remonstrance. She was determined to go with me. "I must see the cabin," she cried, holding up the key. "I must open the door myself."

She twisted herself out of her mother's hands, and ran round to the other side of me. I lifted her over the gunwale of the boat in an instant. Before I could turn round, her mother had followed her, and was standing on the deck.

The cabin door, in the position which she now occupied, was on her left hand. The child was close behind her. I was on her right. Before us was the open deck, and the low gunwale of the boat overlooking the deep water. In a moment we might step across; in a moment we might take the fatal plunge. The bare thought of it brought the mad wickedness in me to its climax. I became suddenly incapable of restraining myself. I threw my arm round her waist with a loud laugh. "Come," I said, trying to drag her across the deck— "come and look at the water."

She released herself by a sudden effort of strength that astonished me. With a faint cry of horror, she turned to take the child by the hand and get back to the quay. I placed myself between her and the sides of the boat, and cut off her retreat in that way. Still laughing, I asked her what she was frightened about. She drew back, and snatched the key of the cabin door out of the child's hand. The cabin was the one place of refuge now left, to which she could escape from the deck of the boat. In the terror of the moment, she never hesitated. She unlocked the door, and hurried down the two or three steps which led into the cabin, taking the child with her. I followed them, conscious that I had betrayed myself, yet still obstinately, stupidly, madly bent on carrying out my purpose. "I have only to behave quietly," I thought to myself, "and I shall persuade her to go on deck again."

My lamp was burning as I had left it; my traveling-bag was on the table. Still holding the child, she stood, pale as death, waiting for me. Elfie's wondering eyes rested inquiringly on my face as I approached them. She looked half inclined to cry; the suddenness of the mother's action had frightened the child. I did my best to compose Elfie before I spoke to her mother. I pointed out the different objects which were likely to interest her in the cabin. "Go and look at them," I said, "go and amuse yourself."

The child still hesitated. "Are you angry with me?" she asked.

"No, no!"

"Are you angry with mamma?"

"Certainly not." I turned to Mrs. Van Brandt. "Tell Elfie if I am angry with you," I said.

She was perfectly aware, in her critical position, of the necessity of humoring me. Between us, we succeeded in composing the child. She turned away to examine, in high delight, the new and strange objects which surrounded her. Meanwhile her mother and I stood together, looking at each other by the light of the lamp, with an assumed composure which hid our true faces like a mask. In that horrible situation, the grotesque and the terrible, always together in this strange life of ours, came together now. On either side of us, the one sound that broke the sinister and threatening silence was the lumpish snoring of the sleeping captain and crew.

She was the first to speak.

"If you wish to give me the money," she said, trying to propitiate me in that way, "I am ready to take it now."

I unlocked my traveling-bag. As I looked into it for the leather case which held my money, my overpowering desire to get her on deck again, my mad impatience to commit the fatal act, became too strong to be controlled.

"We shall be cooler on deck," I said. "Let us take the bag up there."

She showed wonderful courage. I could almost see the cry for help rising to her lips. She repressed it; she had still presence of mind enough to foresee what might happen before she could rouse the sleeping men.

"We have a light here to count the money by," she answered. "I don't feel at all too warm in the cabin. Let us stay here a little longer. See how Elfie is amusing herself!"

Her eyes rested on me as she spoke. Something in the expression of them quieted me for the time. I was able to pause and think. I might take her on deck by force before the men could interfere. But her cries would rouse them; they would hear the splash in the water, and they might be quick enough to rescue us. It would be wiser, perhaps, to wait a little and trust to my cunning to delude her into leaving the cabin of her own accord. I put the bag back on the table, and began to search for the leather money-case. My hands were strangely clumsy and helpless. I could only find the case after scattering half the contents of the bag on the table. The child was near me at the time, and noticed what I was doing.

"Oh, how awkward you are!" she burst out, in her frankly fearless way. "Let me put your bag tidy. Do, please!"

I granted the request impatiently. Elfie's restless desire to be always doing something, instead of amusing me, as usual, irritated me now. The interest that I had once felt in the charming little creature was all gone. An innocent love was a feeling that was stifled in the poisoned atmosphere of my mind that night.

The money I had with me was mostly composed of notes of the Bank of England. Carefully keeping up appearances, I set aside the sum that would probably be required to take a traveler back to London; and I put all that remained into the hands of Mrs. Van Brandt. Could she suspect me of a design on her life now?

"That will do for the present," I said. "I can communicate with you in the future through Messrs. Van Brandt, of Amsterdam."

She took the money mechanically. Her hand trembled; her eyes met mine with a look of piteous entreaty. She tried to revive my old tenderness for her; she made a last appeal to my forbearance and consideration.

"We may part friends," she said, in low, trembling tones. "And as friends we may meet again, when time has taught you to think forgivingly of what has passed between us, to-night."

She offered me her hand. I looked at her without taking it. I penetrated her motive in appealing to my old regard for her. Still suspecting me, she had tried her last chance of getting safely on shore.

"The less we say of the past, the better," I answered, with ironical politeness. "It is getting late. And you will agree with me that Elfie ought to be in her bed." I looked round at the child. "Be quick, Elfie," I said; "your mamma is going away." I opened the cabin door, and offered my arm to Mrs. Van Brandt. "This boat is my house for the time being," I resumed. "When ladies take leave of me after a visit, I escort them to the dock. Pray take my arm."

She started back. For the second time she was on the point of crying for help, and for the second time she kept that last desperate alternative in reserve.

"I haven't seen your cabin yet," she said, her eyes wild with fear, a forced smile on her lips, as she spoke. "There are several little things here that interest me. Give me another minute or two to look at them."

She turned away to get nearer to the child, under pretense of looking round the cabin. I stood on guard before the open door, watching her. She made a second pretense: she noisily overthrew a chair as if by accident, and then waited to discover whether her trick had succeeded in waking the men.

The heavy snoring went on; not a sound of a person moving was audible on either side of us.

"My men are heavy sleepers," I said, smiling significantly. "Don't be alarmed; you have not disturbed them. Nothing wakes these Dutch sailors when they are once safe in port."

She made no reply. My patience was exhausted. I left the door and advanced toward her. She retreated in speechless terror, passing behind the table to the other end of the cabin. I followed her until she had reached the extremity of the room and could get no further. She met the look I fixed on her; she shrunk into a corner, and called for help. In the deadly terror that possessed her, she lost the use of her voice. A low moaning, hardly louder than a whisper, was all that passed her lips. Already, in imagination, I stood with her on the gunwale, already I felt the cold contact of the water—when I was startled by a cry behind me. I turned round. The cry had come from Elfie. She had apparently just discovered some new object in the bag, and she was holding it up in admiration, high above her head. "Mamma! mamma!" the child cried, excitedly, "look at this pretty thing! Oh, do, do ask him if I may have it!"

Her mother ran to her, eager to seize the poorest excuse for getting away from me. I followed; I stretched out my hands to seize her. She suddenly turned round on me, a woman transformed. A bright flush was on her face, an eager wonder sparkled in her eyes. Snatching Elfie's coveted object out of the child's hand, she held it up before me. I saw it under the lamp-light. It was my little forgotten keepsake—the Green Flag!

"How came you by this?" she asked, in breathless anticipation of my reply. Not the slightest trace was left in her face of the terror that had convulsed it barely a minute since! "How came you by this?" she repeated, seizing me by the arm and shaking me, in the ungovernable impatience that possessed her.

My head turned giddy, my heart beat furiously under the conflict of emotions that she had roused in me. My eyes were riveted on the green flag. The words that I wanted to speak were words that refused to come to me. I answered, mechanically: "I have had it since I was a boy."

She dropped her hold on me, and lifted her hands with a gesture of ecstatic gratitude. A lovely, angelic brightness flowed like light from heaven over her face. For one moment she stood enraptured. The next she clasped me passionately to her bosom, and whispered in my ear: "I am Mary Dermody! I made it for You!"

The shock of discovery, following so closely on all that I had suffered before it, was too much for me. I sank, fainting, in her arms.

When I came to myself I was lying on my bed in the cabin. Elfie was playing with the green flag, and Mary was sitting by me with my hand in hers. One long look of love passed silently from her eyes to mine—from mine to hers. In that look the kindred spirits were united; The Two Destinies were fulfilled.

THE END OF THE STORY.

The Finale.

THE WIFE WRITES, AND CLOSES THE STORY.

THERE was a little introductory narrative prefixed to "The Two Destinies," which you may possibly have forgotten by this time.

The narrative was written by myself—a citizen of the United States, visiting England with his wife. It described a dinner-party at which we were present, given by Mr. and Mrs. Germaine, in celebration of their marriage; and it mentioned the circumstances under which we were intrusted with the story which has just come to an end in these pages. Having read the manuscript, Mr. and Mrs. Germaine left it to us to decide whether we should continue our friendly intercourse with them or not.

At 3 o'clock P.M. we closed the last leaf of the story. Five minutes later I sealed it up in its cover; my wife put her bonnet on, and there we were, bound straight for Mr. Germaine's house, when the servant brought a letter into the room, addressed to my wife.

She opened it, looked at the signature, and discovered that it was "Mary Germaine." Seeing this, we sat down side by side to read the letter before we did anything else.

On reflection, it strikes me that you may do well to read it, too. Mrs. Germaine is surely by this time a person in whom you feel some interest. And she is on that account, as I think, the fittest person to close the story. Here is her letter:

"DEAR MADAM (or may I say—'dear friend'?)—Be prepared, if you please, for a little surprise. When you read these lines we shall have left London for the Continent.

"After you went away last night, my husband decided on taking this journey. Seeing how keenly he felt the insult offered to me by the ladies whom we had asked to our table, I willingly prepared for our sudden departure. When Mr. Germaine is far away from his false friends, my experience of him tells me that he will recover his tranquillity. That is enough for me.

"My little daughter goes with us, of course. Early this morning I drove to the school in the suburbs at which she is being educated, and took her away with me. It is needless to say that she was delighted at the prospect of traveling. She shocked the schoolmistress by waving her hat over her head and crying 'Hooray,' like a boy. The good lady was very careful to inform me that my daughter could not possibly have learned to cry 'Hooray' in her house.

"You have probably by this time read the narrative which I have committed to your care. I hardly dare ask how I stand in your estimation now. Is it possible that I might have seen you and your good husband if we had not left London so suddenly? As things are, I must now tell you in writing what I should infinitely have preferred saying to you with your friendly hand in mine.

"Your knowledge of the world has no doubt already attributed the absence of the ladies at our dinner-table to some report affecting my character. You are quite right. While I was taking Elfie away from her school, my husband called on one of his friends who dined with us (Mr. Waring), and insisted on an explanation. Mr. Waring referred him to the woman who is known to you by this time as Mr. Van Brandt's lawful wife. In her intervals of sobriety she possesses some musical talent; Mrs. Waring had met with her at a concert for a charity, and had been interested in the story of her wrongs, as she called them. My name was, of course, mentioned. I was described as a 'cast-off mistress' of Van Brandt, who had persuaded Mr. Germaine into disgracing himself by marrying her, and becoming the step-father of her child. Mrs. Waring thereupon communicated what she had heard to other ladies who were her friends. The result you saw for yourselves when you dined at our house.

"I inform you of what has happened without making any comment. Mr. Germaine's narrative has already told you that I foresaw the deplorable consequences which might follow our marriage, and that I over and over again (God knows at what cost of misery to myself) refused to be his wife. It was only when my poor little green flag had revealed us to each other that I lost all control over myself. The old time on the banks of the lake came back to me; my heart hungered for its darling of happier days; and I said Yes, when (as you may think) I ought to have still said No. Will you take poor old Dame Dermody's view of it, and believe that the kindred spirits, once reunited, could be parted no more? Or will you take my view, which is simpler still? I do love him so dearly, and he is so fond of me!

"In the meantime, our departure from England seems to be the wisest course that we can adopt. As long as this woman lives she will say again of me what she has said already, whenever she can find the opportunity. My child might hear the reports about her mother, and might be injured by them when she gets older. We propose to take up our abode, for a time at least, in the neighborhood of Naples. Here, or further away yet, we may hope to live without annoyance among a people whose social law is the law of mercy. Whatever may happen, we have always one last consolation to sustain us—we have love.

"You talked of traveling on the Continent when you dined with us. If you should wander our way, the English consul at Naples is a friend of my husband's, and he will have our address. I wonder whether we shall ever meet again? It does seem hard to charge the misfortunes of my life on me, as if they were my faults.

"Speaking of my misfortunes, I may say, before I close this letter, that the man to whom I owe them is never likely to cross my path again. The Van Brandts of Amsterdam have received certain information that he is now on his way to New Zealand. They are determined to prosecute him if he returns. He is little likely to give them the opportunity.

"The traveling-carriage is at the door: I must say good-by. My husband sends to you both his kindest regards and best wishes. His manuscript will be quite safe (when you leave London) if you send it to his bankers, at the address inclosed. Think of me sometimes—and think of me kindly. I appeal confidently to your kindness, for I don't forget that you kissed me at parting. Your grateful friend (if you will let her be your friend),

> *"MARY GERMAINE."*

We are rather impulsive people in the United States, and we decide on long journeys by sea or land without making the slightest fuss about it. My wife and I looked at each other when we had read Mrs. Germaine's letter.

"London is dull," I remarked, and waited to see what came of it.

My wife read my remark the right way directly.

"Suppose we try Naples?" she said.

That is all. Permit us to wish you good-by. We are off to Naples.

About Author

Early life

Collins was born at 11 New Cavendish Street, Marylebone, London, the son of a well-known Royal Academician landscape painter, William Collins and his wife, Harriet Geddes. Named after his father, he swiftly became known by his middle name, which honoured his godfather, David Wilkie. The family moved to Pond Street, Hampstead, in 1826. In 1828 Collins's brother Charles Allston Collins was born. Between 1829 and 1830, the Collins family moved twice, first to Hampstead Square and then to Porchester Terrace, Bayswater. Wilkie and Charles received their early education from their mother at home. The Collins family were deeply religious, and Collins's mother enforced strict church attendance on her sons, which Wilkie disliked.

In 1835, Collins began attending school at the Maida Vale academy. From 1836 to 1838, he lived with his parents in Italy and France, which made a great impression on him. He learned Italian while the family was in Italy and began learning French, in which he would eventually become fluent. From 1838 to 1840, he attended the Reverend Cole's private boarding school in Highbury, where he was bullied by a boy who would force Collins to tell him a story before allowing him to go to sleep. "It was this brute who first awakened in me, his poor little victim, a power of which but for him I might never have been aware.... When I left school I continued story telling for my own pleasure", Collins later said.

In 1840 the family moved to 85 Oxford Terrace, Bayswater. In late 1840, he left school and was apprenticed as a clerk to the firm of tea merchants Antrobus & Co, owned by a friend of Wilkie's father. He disliked his clerical work but remained employed by the company for more than five years. Collins's first story The Last Stage Coachman, was published in the Illuminated Magazine in August 1843. In 1844 he travelled to Paris with Charles Ward. That same year he wrote his first novel, Iolani, or Tahiti as It Was; a Romance, which was submitted to Chapman and Hall but rejected in 1845. The novel remained unpublished during his lifetime. Collins said of it:

"My youthful imagination ran riot among the noble savages, in scenes which caused the respectable British publisher to declare that it was impossible to put his name on the title page of such a novel." It was during the writing of this novel that Collins's father first learned that his assumptions that Wilkie would follow him in becoming a painter were mistaken.

William Collins had intended Wilkie for a clergyman and was disappointed in his son's lack of interest. In 1846 he instead entered Lincoln's Inn to study law, on the initiative of his father, who wanted him to have a steady income. Wilkie showed only a slight interest in law and spent most of his time with friends and on working on a second novel, Antonina, or the Fall of Rome. After his father's death in 1847, Collins produced his first published book, Memoirs of the Life of William Collins, Esq., R. A., published in 1848. The family moved to 38 Blandford Square soon afterwards, where they used their drawing room for amateur theatricals. In 1849, Collins exhibited a painting, "The Smugglers' Retreat", at the Royal Academy summer exhibition. Antonina was published by Richard Bentley in February 1850. Collins went on a walking tour of Cornwall with artist Henry Brandling in July and August 1850. He managed to complete his legal studies and be called to the bar in 1851. Though he never formally practised, he used his legal knowledge in many of his novels.

Early writing career

An instrumental event in his career was an introduction in March 1851 to Charles Dickens by a mutual friend, through the painter Augustus Egg. They became lifelong friends and collaborators. In May of that year, Collins acted with Dickens in Edward Bulwer-Lytton's play Not So Bad As We Seem. Among the audience were Queen Victoria and Prince Albert. Collins's story "A Terribly Strange Bed," his first contribution to Household Words, appeared in April, 1852. In May 1852 he went on tour with Dickens's company of amateur actors, again performing Not So Bad As We Seem, but with a more substantial role. Collins's novel Basil was published by Bentley in November. During the writing of Hide and Seek, in early 1853, Collins suffered what was probably his first attack of gout, which would plague him for the rest of his life. He was ill from April to early July. After that he stayed with Dickens in Boulogne from July to September 1853, then toured Switzerland and Italy with Dickens and Egg from October to December. Collins published Hide and Seek in June 1854.

During this period Collins extended the variety of his writing, publishing articles in George Henry Lewes's paper The Leader, short stories and essays for Bentley's Miscellany, dramatic criticism and the travel book Rambles Beyond Railways. His first play, The Lighthouse, was performed by Dickens's theatrical company at Tavistock House, in 1855. His first collection of short stories, After Dark, was published by Smith, Elder in February 1856. His novel A Rogue's Life was serialised in Household Words in March 1856. Around then, Collins began using laudanum regularly to treat his gout. He became addicted and struggled with that problem later in life.

Collins joined the staff of Household Words in October 1856. In 1856–57 he collaborated closely with Dickens on a play, The Frozen Deep, first performed in Tavistock. Collins's novel The Dead Secret was serialised in Household Words from January to June 1857 and published in volume form by Bradbury and Evans. Collins's play The Lighthouse was performed at the Olympic Theatre in August. The Lazy Tour of Two Idle Apprentices, based on Dickens's and Collins's walking tour in the north of England, was serialised in Household Words in October 1857. In 1858 he collaborated with Dickens and other writers on the story "A House to Let".

1860s

According to biographer Melisa Klimaszewski, "The novels Collins published in the 1860s are the best and most enduring of his career. The Woman in White, No Name, Armadale, and The Moonstone, written in less than a decade, show Collins not just as a master of his craft, but as an innovater and provocateur. These four works, which secured him an international reputation, and sold in large numbers, ensured his financial stability, and allowed him to support many others".

The Woman in White was serialised in All the Year Round from November 1859 to August 1860 and was a great success. The novel was published in book form soon after serial publication ended, and it reached an eighth edition by November 1860. His increased stature as a writer made Collins resign his position with All the Year Round in 1862 to focus on novel writing. During the planning of his next novel, No Name, he continued to suffer from gout, and it now especially affected his eyes. Serial publication of No Name began in early 1862 and finished in 1863. By this time the laudanum he was taking for his continual gout became a serious problem.

At the beginning of 1863, he travelled to German spas and Italy for his health, with Caroline Graves. In 1864, he began work on his novel Armadale, travelling in August to do research for it. It was published serially in The Cornhill Magazine in 1864–66. His play No Thoroughfare, co-written with Dickens, was published as the 1867 Christmas number of All the Year Round and dramatised at the Adelphi Theatre on 26 December. It enjoyed a run of 200 nights before being taken on tour.

Collins's search for background information for Armadale took him to the Norfolk Broads and the small village of Winterton-on-Sea. His novel The Moonstone was serialised in All the Year Round from January to August 1868. His mother, Harriet Collins, died that year.

Later years

In 1870, his novel Man and Wife was published. This year also saw the death of Charles Dickens, which caused him great sadness. He said of their early days together, "We saw each other every day, and were as fond of each other as men could be."

The Woman in White was dramatised and produced at the Olympic Theatre in October 1871.

Collins's novel Poor Miss Finch was serialised in Cassell's Magazine from October to March 1872. His short novel Miss or Mrs? was published in the 1872 Christmas number of the Graphic. His novel The New Magdalen was serialised from October 1872 to July 1873. His younger brother, Charles Allston Collins, died later in 1873. Charles had married Dickens's younger daughter, Kate.

In 1873–74, Collins toured the United States and Canada, giving readings of his work. The American writers he met included Oliver Wendell Holmes, Sr., and Mark Twain, and he began a friendship with the photographer Napoleon Sarony, who took several portraits of him.

His novel The Law and the Lady, serialised in the Graphic from September to March 1875, was followed by a short novel, The Haunted Hotel, which was serialised from June to November 1878. His later novels include Jezebel's Daughter (1880), The Black Robe (1881), Heart and Science (1883) and The Evil Genius (1886). In 1884, Collins was elected Vice-President of the Society of Authors, which had been founded by his friend and fellow novelist Walter Besant.

The inconsistent quality of Collins's dramatic and fictional works in the last decade of his life was accompanied by a general decline in his health, including diminished eyesight. He was often unable to leave home and had difficulty writing. During these last years, he focused on mentoring younger writers, including the novelist Hall Caine, and helped to protect other writers from copyright infringement of their works. His writing became a way for him to fight his illness without allowing it to keep him bedridden. His stepdaughter Harriet also served as an amanuensis for several years. His last novel, Blind Love, was finished posthumously by Walter Besant.

Death

Collins died at 82 Wimpole Street, following a paralytic stroke. He is buried in Kensal Green Cemetery, West London. His headstone describes him as the author of The Woman in White. Caroline Graves died in 1895 and was buried with Collins. Martha Rudd died in 1919.

Personal life

In 1858 Collins began living with Caroline Graves and her daughter Harriet. Caroline came from a humble family, having married young, had a child, and been widowed. Collins lived close to the small shop kept by Caroline, and the two may have met in the neighborhood in the mid–1850s. He treated Harriet, whom he called Carrie, as his own daughter, and helped to provide for her education. Excepting one short separation, they lived together for the rest of Collins's life. Collins disliked the institution of marriage, but remained dedicated to Caroline and Harriet, considering them to be his family. Caroline had wanted to marry Collins. She left him while he wrote The Moonstone and was suffering an attack of acute gout. She then married a younger man named Joseph Clow, but returned to Collins after two years.

In 1868, Collins met Martha Rudd in Winterton-on-Sea in Norfolk, and the two began a liaison. She was 19 years old and from a large, poor family. She moved to London to be closer to him a few years later. Their daughter Marian was born in 1869, their second daughter, Harriet Constance, in 1871 and their son, William Charles, in 1874. When he was with Martha he assumed the name William Dawson, and she and their children used the last name of Dawson themselves.

For the last 20 years of his life Collins divided his time between Caroline, who lived with him at his home in Gloucester Place, and Martha who was nearby.

Like his friend Charles Dickens, Collins was a professing Christian.

Works

Collins's works were classified at the time as "sensation novels", a genre seen nowadays as the precursor to detective and suspense fiction. He also wrote penetratingly on the plight of women and on the social and domestic issues of his time. For example, his 1854 Hide and Seek contained one of the first portrayals of a deaf character in English literature. As did many writers of his time, Collins published most of his novels as serials in magazines such as Dickens's All the Year Round and was known as a master of the form, creating just the right degree of suspense to keep his audience reading from week to week. Sales of All The Year Round increased when The Woman in White followed A Tale of Two Cities.

Collins enjoyed ten years of great success following publication of The Woman in White in 1859. His next novel, No Name combined social commentary – the absurdity of the law as it applied to children of unmarried parents (see Illegitimacy in fiction) – with a densely plotted revenge thriller.

Armadale, the first and only of Collins's major novels of the 1860s to be serialised in a magazine other than All the Year Round, provoked strong criticism, generally centred upon its transgressive villainess Lydia Gwilt, and provoked in part by Collins's typically confrontational preface. The novel was simultaneously a financial coup for its author and a comparative commercial failure: the sum paid by Cornhill for the serialisation rights was exceptional, eclipsing by a substantial margin the prices paid for the vast majority of similar novels, yet the novel failed to recoup its publisher's investment. The Moonstone, published in 1868, and the last novel of what is generally regarded as the most successful decade of its author's career, was, despite a somewhat cool reception from both Dickens and the critics, a significant return to form and reestablished the market value of an author whose success on the competitive Victorian literary market had been gradually waning in the wake of his first perceived masterpiece. Viewed by many to represent the advent of the detective story within the tradition of the English novel, The Moonstone remains one of Collins's most critically acclaimed productions, identified by T. S. Eliot as "the first, the longest, and the best of modern English detective novels... in a genre invented by Collins and not by Poe," and Dorothy L. Sayers referred to it as "probably the very finest detective story ever written".

After The Moonstone, Collins's novels contained fewer thriller elements and more social commentary. The subject matter continued to be sensational, but his popularity declined. The poet Algernon Charles Swinburne commented: "What brought good Wilkie's genius nigh perdition? / Some demon whispered—'Wilkie! have a mission.'"

Factors most often cited have been the death of Dickens in 1870, and with it the loss of his literary mentoring, Collins's increased dependence upon laudanum, and his penchant for using his fiction to rail against social injustices. His novels and novellas of the 1870s and 1880s are generally regarded as inferior to his previous productions and receive comparatively little critical attention today[when?].

The Woman in White and The Moonstone share an unusual narrative structure, somewhat resembling an epistolary novel, in which different portions of the book have different narrators, each with a distinct narrative voice. Armadale has this to a lesser extent through the correspondence between some characters. (Source: Wikipedia)

CPSIA information can be obtained
at www.ICGtesting.com
Printed in the USA
LVHW091553230620
658719LV00002B/234

9 789390 171545